# The Song of Hild

— Vibeke Vasbo —

Translated from the Danish by
Gaye Kynoch

Sacristy
Press

**Sacristy Press**

PO Box 612, Durham, DH1 9HT

www.sacristy.co.uk

Danish edition first published in 1991 by Gyldendal, Denmark
English translation first published in 2018 by Sacristy Press, Durham

Sacristy Limited, registered in England & Wales, number 7565667

**British Library Cataloguing-in-Publication Data**
A catalogue record for the book is available from the British Library

ISBN 978-1-910519-86-8

A full list of people and places
mentioned in this book
can be found at

# www.SONGofHILD.com

**With special thanks to:**
Professor Else Roesdahl, University of Aarhus
The late Professor Christine Fell, University of Nottingham

**We gratefully acknowledge grants from:**
Konsul George Jorck og Hustru Emma Jorck's Fond
**DANISH ARTS FOUNDATION**

A MAP
— showing the —
**PRINCIPAL PLACES**
mentioned in this book

THE PICTS

DALRIADA

✝ Iona

RHEGED

IRISH

Magilros ✝

Coludesburh ✝
Lindisfarena ✝
• Bebbanburh
• Ad Gefrin

BERNICIA

*Tuidi*

*Tina*  THE GREAT WALL  *Wall*

✝ Tinanmude

Hagustaldesea ✝

*Wiur*

Ediscum ✝    ✝ Heruteu

Cetrecht •    *Tese*    *Esca*    ✝ Streonæshalch
                                    • Hræfenclif
Læstingaeu ✝   *Welburn*    ✝ Hacanos
Hrypum ✝

Eoforwik •    DEIRA    • Mædeltun

Loidis •    Burh •    • Godmundingaham

*Rippel*

ELMET

100 miles

*Mærse*    PEOCLOND    *Idle*    LINDSEY    *Humbre*

Ynys Seiriol
Môn •    ✝    Lindcylene •

Aberffraw •    GWYNEDD    • Legaceaster
Clynnog Fawr ✝    • Dolwyddelan

*Treante*

W A L A S

*Safern*

Liccidfeld    ROTAN-
✝            LAND

• Tamoworthig

MIDDLE
ANGLES

EAST
ANGLES

MAGON-
SÆTAN

M E R C I A

Elge •
Beaduricsworth    ✝

• Rendlæsham

DYFED

HWICCE

EAST
SAXONS

Bathum •

Lunden •

Hrofesceaster •    • Cantwaraburh ✝

WEST
SAXONS

SOUTH
SAXONS    KENT

CORNWALUM

# RATHER A LIVE DOG
# THAN A DEAD LION

*– the birth of Hundfrid and Wilbrord –*

Had you been able to look down through the thick woodland covering the uplands north of the Vale of Pickering, and seen into the light alder thicket alongside Hodge Beck, at the spot where it crosses the track between Pickering and Helmsley, then at about ten o'clock on the morning of October the thirteenth in the year 633 you might have seen a party of horsemen drawing to a halt.

It was obvious they had set out in great haste and urgency; there were no carts, just untidy collections of cloth bundles lashed to the saddles. A few heavily-laden packhorses were managing to keep up with the riding mounts.

The sweating, hard-ridden beasts were watered in the beck at the ford; the riders quenched their thirsts and cooled their faces and hands.

Rain fell silently and persistently. Some of the fugitives took refuge in the thicket to answer the call of nature. One of them was a finely-dressed young woman; the many thick layers of clothing couldn't hide the fact that she was heavily pregnant. Having relieved herself, she straightened up quickly—so quickly that everything went dark before her eyes. She tried to grab hold of a tree, but her huge belly got in the way; she slipped in the clayey soil and fell.

By the time she regained consciousness and crawled out of the wet and sticky mire, it was afternoon. Her head was throbbing, but she knew they had to press on immediately; she hurried back to the ford.

She could only see a few of her retinue; they were lying on the ground, but they weren't just taking a nap. First she saw her wetnurse, then her handmaid and young half-cousin; all with their skirts pushed up and their sex laid bare. The young cousin's crotch was a mass of blood, and her fair, almost white hair, which she had worn in a thick plait on the left side of her head, had been hacked off—some of her scalp had been sliced away with it.

A moorhen flapped up and the young woman gave a start. The beck babbled along its course, flowing over the legs of the wetnurse. A chaffinch warbled loudly and relentlessly from an overhanging branch. The stillness between these two prattling wellsprings of sound was overwhelming, and it took quite a time before she dared break it by putting one foot in front of the other and moving away.

She found the men just a short distance from the beck. Her swordbearer with a gaping wound where there should have been a head, his right arm almost severed; not just killed but, like the women, slashed all over. The cupbearer close by, crouching, his back hacked to pieces; she couldn't see his front. The steward and the young groom were missing, also a handmaid and two kitchen maids.

Apart from the slaves, these were the people who had been left behind on the estate: women, the slenderest boys and the men who were either too old or in some way too feeble to be of any use on the battlefield. Their job had been to protect the settlement. All the horses had gone. She wasn't used to walking.

Having seen what there was to see, she retraced her steps, away from the road.

And then she had her first contraction. She instinctively moved away from the dead, walked uphill alongside the beck. When the spasms struck, she had to get down on her knees or on all fours. The rain intensified.

She was lying on her side during a contraction when she spotted an opening higher up the slope. She moved slowly—it looked like the entrance to a cave. She crawled in, and there she lay when her waters broke. She had no idea what was oozing out of her, she just brushed it away with her hand, out to all the other wetness. She stayed there throughout the evening and night, shifting around in the narrow space as the contractions quickened.

The blackbird had just started to sing when she gave birth to her first child. As the sky grew light, the second one arrived. She dealt with the umbilical cord as she had seen the dogs do at home. Both babies screamed. She wrapped one of her underskirts around each of them and put them to her breasts. Something else forced its way out: a large brownish-blue clot, looking like a sheep's liver. It wasn't a baby—not any longer, at least—and she shoved the clot into the corner of the cave.

'Your father is a coward,' she said to the child on the left.

They were both boys. To the one on the right, she said: 'Your father is a king's son and he lives.'

And then she had to laugh. Paulinus had so often said, half in jest when the men's boasting about their feats became too much for him: 'Better to be a live dog than a dead lion.'

'Hundfrid,' she said to the child on the left, his name suddenly apparent. 'Your father is a yellow hound. But he is better off than the king.'

She looked down at the still nameless child on the right. 'Your father is better off than his older brother. Wilbrord!'

Welcome, Hundfrid and Wilbrord.

She had laid the tightly-wrapped babies close together and gone down to the beck. Everything inside her was sore and painful and she walked awkwardly. But there was also an almost floating ease to her body, now relieved of its burden. She gulped water, washed her face and rubbed the blood and slime from her legs and crotch.

She was walking downhill towards the ford when a flock of noisy ravens screamed up into the air. The sound of hoofbeats, distinct hoofbeats; she gathered her skirts and ran back to the cave. The babies were lying quite still; she didn't touch them, but bared her breasts for them to drink and held a large corner of her top skirt ready—to smother them if her breasts weren't enough to keep them quiet.

It felt like an age before the horses came to a standstill at the ford. Even the hungriest raven had to abandon its feast, with rasping protests. Perhaps there were twenty horses, perhaps thirty. Through the rain, she heard the sound of male voices and shouting and the clanking of metal against metal, horses whinnying and slurping. Branches were bent over and flicked back, twigs snapped under men's heavy footsteps; one was on his way up along the beck—he stopped.

She saw him from the side; he was staring at the ground, a man about the same age as her husband, the coward. Twenty-two years old or less, short and stocky, hair shining like fire under a shabby leather riding-cap. He was spattered with wet mud, but also with something else, stiff, not fresh: brownish specks up his sleeves and large rust-coloured blotches on his tunic. The kind of stains that have to be soaked in cold water for a long time before they work loose. An axe in his belt, decorated with what looked like spiral patterns the natives used. Maybe a young wife at home.

He turned in her direction, his gaze tracking her footprints across the sodden earth. They weren't hard to follow. She could even see them herself.

He cleared his nostrils and began to walk slowly towards the entrance to the cave—as if his mind was on something else. She didn't move; there was only the one way out.

The young woman in the cave was just thinking that maybe he had a young wife at home when he turned round, his eyes tracking the footprints in her direction. But it wasn't true. His thoughts were not on the footprints, which he merely noted, purely professionally, but on the milkmaid at his parents' estate in Dolwyddelan, ten or more years ago, before she married and moved away. He used to sneak along behind her in the mornings when she went to the beck to wash herself. From his hiding place in the thick oak coppice his eyes had clung to her big white rounded breasts and her shining domed buttocks—in his mind, he had caressed and kissed those wonders hundreds of times.

She would even strip naked every sun-day morning and douse herself with water. In the summertime she occasionally sat down with a splash and let the beck flow over her body. Oh to be a fish, he had thought, trying to control his breathing for fear it would give him away.

He had never dared approach her, but she wouldn't have made a suitable wife for him anyway. He'd had her, though, many years later, at a wedding party in Beddcelert. When her husband had keeled over with the other drunkards, he'd had her in a dark corner of the hayloft; she had been eager, her legs clasped tight and firm around his loins. For several weeks he had felt dizzy at the thought of her wild passion and her white body in the half-light. But it hadn't matched that early vision by the beck. Her breasts were still ample, almost glowing, but no longer the two thrusting domes that had made him gasp for breath behind the oak thicket. She had borne two children, and he'd heard that one of them was a little red-haired girl. Her husband's hair had been black. He smiled and hitched up his trousers.

These were his thoughts as he approached the cave from the side, automatically pulling out his hand axe, ready for the quarry. The entrance was wider than a man but only half as high, and in all likelihood there was only the one in there. The cave might be so deep that he'd have to smoke him out. There were plenty of wet twigs—probably the simplest method. He was already looking forward to his riches; maybe he'd got his hands on a gold-wearer. Some of the bodies down by the ford had undoubtedly been just that—even though the gold had gone, of course, along with their weapons and everything else.

You always hoped that this time you'd get a gold-wearer. And he'd been lucky a couple of times. He didn't rate glass beads, but he always took them; his mother and his sister were fond of things like that. And fine fabrics. They had made up some of the cloth for him. His best garment, worn for Mass and other special occasions, was a cloak of finely-spun crimson flax he'd picked up from a skirmish with the barbarians in Mercia—before they'd entered an alliance with them.

It wasn't that the foreigners had better ornaments and weapons and clothes, not at all. It was just that their things were different. Something new to take home. Those foreigners certainly knew all about weapons! Of course, a sword wasn't a better sword for having inlaid garnets and multi-coloured glass on the hilt and scabbard. These new people went for showy rather than beauty; that was just their nature, but there was no denying they knew how to use their gaudy weapons. They could swing a sword and throw a spear, and better archers weren't to be found at home in Walas. They were formidable.

It occurred to him that the man inside the cave might already have taken aim, and he momentarily considered calling for assistance. But he wasn't in the mood for sharing—neither the prize nor the prestige. Fortune hadn't been on his side so far this expedition; he'd been positioned too far back. The men from Mercia had insisted on using their own battle plan—one of their conditions for making the alliance—so he couldn't rush forward as he usually did. They all had to wait for a signal from Penda, Mercia's commander—he seemed to know what he was doing. Everything had indeed gone far better than they could have hoped, and they'd all been promised great rewards after the campaign. But that wasn't any reason not to pick up some loot along the way.

He bent over and took a quick glance inside the cave, but he couldn't see anything. He tried again, and this time he glimpsed something white, motionless. He crept over to the other side of the entrance, a good grip on his axe, before taking another look.

He gradually realized what was inside the cave, and he stayed his ground. He shifted the axe into his other hand and moved to the middle of the entrance. Stretching out his right hand, he reached in until the tips of his fingers brushed across an ample, smooth and white female breast. A warm liquid wetted his fingers. Not a sound came from the woman, but a bundle of cloths in front of her gave off little grunting noises.

He withdrew his hand and made do with looking. The woman's silk-embroidered headdress was slightly askew, a lock of hair had escaped, hair as radiantly copper-red as his own. Around her neck she wore a costly holy cross, gold with inlaid garnets, equal-armed and with a circular segment at the centre. Finely crafted. And the chain was made of gold, too.

She sat bolt upright, staring at him without batting an eyelid. Then she looked away and carefully pulled the bundle of cloths towards her. She extricated a very small baby—it seemed no bigger than a puppy to him—and placed it to her left breast. The man reached out and touched her again.

'Hundfrid,' she said, pointing at the baby, which had begun to suck. Without taking him from her breast, she carefully unravelled another child from the bundle.

'Wilbrord,' she said, and he ran his finger across the baby's forehead and implausibly tiny flat nose.

'Willor,' he echoed.

What strange names these people gave their children. He stroked the other one, Hunni, on the back of his head. They both had more hair than his sister's babies when they were born.

There was a shout, and the world crowded in on them with the sound of horses and impatient male voices. The man turned and shouted a word from the Britons' language, which she understood to mean: nothing.

The other child awoke with a little cry, and the woman put him to her breast. The man shouted the word again. Both babies flinched.

He turned to her, pointed at his chest.

'Tancwoystel,' he whispered.

'Hildeburh,' she replied. 'Hild, I am called.'

'Hild,' he said, 'Hunni and Willor.'

He nodded and disappeared, running back to the others. Not long after, she heard them set off.

The hoofbeats gradually faded—leaving just the sound of her breathing, the beck and the tireless chaffinch, which had at no point ceased its song.

She made the sign of the cross over the babies and said the Lord's Prayer. She prayed to her god, asking him to protect her, her infants and her husband—and to reunite them. When this was done, the rain stopped.

She'd have to find a new wetnurse for the babies. They were eager to suck, but it wasn't milk that filled her breasts; it was more like water.

She didn't know what had bewitched her. Perhaps ill fortune had descended upon the whole country and was just pretending to let her and her babies escape. Perhaps fate had filled her breasts with water because it had been decided the infants should die: enter the world and open their eyes, only to discover that their mother's breasts were a deception. So they would starve to death. And then she would too.

She wouldn't let that happen.

First she had to find something to eat. Maybe there were blackberries in the forest, and mushrooms. The dead might be carrying some food. She bundled up the babies and left the cave. The Welshman's footprints were still visible in the earth.

She saw a trout jump in the beck. As a child, she had sometimes been lucky and caught them in her hands, near the little waterfalls above Ad Gefrin, where the beck had been full of trout. She crept over to the bank and made the lightning grab of her childhood, she even had it in her hand, but then it was gone. They had to be whipped up onto dry land in one sweeping movement, and not many had been able to do that. Osfrid, the king's eldest son, had been the best, followed by her sister, Hereswid, until she grew large and clumsy and that was the end of that. And now it was all over for Osfrid too; he had fallen along with King Edwin, apparently just a couple of horse-lengths from him, struck down by a spear—the turning point of the battle.

Hild was familiar enough with the king to know that losing his eldest son was more likely to take the fighting spirit from him than rouse him to take revenge. Perhaps the mutterings of the old people were right; perhaps he should never have let himself be baptized, because after that he had grown even more melancholy. He would rather sit and ruminate than ride out to expand the realm. For the last few years he hadn't even bothered trying, and if anyone warily implied that perhaps a campaign would not come amiss, well, then the king became irate and lectured them about the primary necessity of consolidating the realm internally and securing law and order.

This didn't impress the noblemen, who had always made sure their idea of law and order paid off anyway, plus a little extra. They were more interested in any opportunity to flex their muscles and show their neighbours what was what. Last year, they had finally got their chance; reports of King Edwin's disinclination for battle had reached Walas, so King Cædwalla of Gwynedd had decided he could probably get away with paying Edwin less tax than was actually due—at which point Edwin certainly hadn't shown any reluctance to use the sword. King Cædwalla would long remember how he had been obliged to flee to Ynys Seiriol, the little islet off the eastern tip of the island of Môn, and stay put while his royal estate of Aberffraw and all of fertile Môn, Gwynedd's granary, had been ravaged and razed. His people would have to look elsewhere for winter supplies and for seed grain—and wonder how they would pay next year's tax.

Sitting on the little islet, watching the billowing clouds of smoke, Cædwalla had to listen to the Northumbrians' shouted taunts and ridicule ringing over the narrow strait while they waited for boats to carry them across.

'Have they got their tails between their legs, the Welsh dogs?' bellowed Hild's husband, Eadfrid; and his older brother, Osfrid, had roared: 'I thought lions avoided water!'

This was in reference to King Cædwalla's delight in hearing himself called 'The Lion of Gwynedd' or 'Lion of the Britons'. Cædwalla was famous for paying a gold ring in bardic reward to anyone who turned up with a poem—however clumsy and halting it might be—in which there was some mention of him as lion.

'Where does the lion hone his sharp claws now?' Hild's husband had shouted. He'd been cocky back then. Hild knew every single word that had echoed across the strait, so often had memories been refreshed over the fine mead served in their hall at home in Mædeltun and in Edwin's hall at Ad Gefrin. And the stories hadn't wearied over the years. Just become more wearisome. In her opinion.

Had King Cædwalla's patron saint, the holy Seiriol, not stepped in that day, the world would have been a very different place now. The holy Seiriol had appeared before Edwin and his men as they stood on the beach flinging insults across to his sacred isle. In a white cowl, bathed in bright light, a holy cross held aloft. Summoned from his abode in Heaven by his distressed servant Cædwalla. On the pebbly beach, under the crag, over there on his own isle, he had faced them.

This had crushed Edwin. He couldn't be persuaded to continue, not at any price. When the boats arrived, Edwin had sailed back to mainland Gwynedd. Under no circumstances would he pursue Cædwalla—not after the holy Seiriol had intervened, keeping them apart. The men from Northumbria had to make do with plundering whatever they came across on their homeward journey. There had been plenty of booty, and they had made a good job of destroying the Welsh corn supplies. The elders were nonetheless annoyed that King Cædwalla had been spared; he'd been there for the taking. For them it wasn't enough simply to place such a crushing tax on Cædwalla's realm that his people had to look abroad to get through the winter and salvage the sowing season.

Cædwalla had escaped with his life, which added further fuel to the noblemen's mutterings about King Edwin having lost much of his old warrior instinct by breaking with the gods of his forefathers. They found it increasingly difficult to see how the new god and his son Jesus Christ could be greater kings than Woden and Thunor and Tiw—all of whom had proven their powers from time immemorial.

Many of those who had been baptized along with King Edwin had fallen during the last expedition to Walas, which didn't exactly show any ability on the part of this new master to take care of his servants. And what about Cædwalla, who had always served this foreign god the Lord and his son! Not much to respect there, slinking off to seek shelter on Seiriol's isle!

The noblemen had been whispering these thoughts to one another for the past year; it had been an unsettled time. And now they were all dead—except, that is, Eadfrid, Hild's husband. He had surrendered.

She mustn't entertain the thought, but couldn't stop herself. She wished he had fallen with the others—so her children wouldn't grow up to learn that their father was a coward. Such shame could never be washed off. Not for Eadfrid, not for her and not for her sons. Paulinus could say what he liked, but this was a matter about which he knew nothing; he had forsaken his kin and promised the Lord to serve King Jesus in everything, and now he no longer understood the significance of a man's reputation and the honour of a lineage. But she—Hild—she understood.

She walked alongside the beck. The bodies were no prettier a sight for all the rain splashing mud over them. She would rather go back to the cave, but she had to find something to eat.

She swallowed her distaste, said the Lord's Prayer, made the sign of the cross over the wetnurse and searched through the woman's clothes. She found a lump of wheat loaf and quickly ate half of it, her face turned away. The wetnurse had always carried some kind of food, and often this fine wheat bread, which had given both Hild and her sister much pleasure all through their childhood—as it was doing again now for Hild. She dragged the woman onto the bank, so she wasn't half-submerged in the beck, and pulled her skirts down to cover her legs. It was heavy work, and it made Hild's belly ache. But she owed it to the wetnurse.

The cupbearer would surely have been carrying something too. He would never have set off without personal provisions, no matter how many packhorses they took with them. She struggled when turning him over to get at his pockets, but was rewarded with a good-sized chunk of dried meat and a little knife. Ants had already started on the meat, which she rinsed in the beck—strange, she thought, when there was so much fresh flesh for them here.

She had to search the others, too, and noticed that the fingers of her cousin's left hand had been chopped off.

Hild had swapped rings with her cousin the previous evening: their pledge that the cousin would be at her side during the birth and would take care of the child should Hild not be spared. The cousin had also promised to bury Hild in consecrated ground, no matter what happened.

Her cousin had been nervous when the men set forth, even though she didn't have a husband taking part in the battle. She'd probably had a foreboding of what was going to happen. Hild knew that her cousin didn't always comply with Paulinus' total ban on any kind of pagan practice or magic. If she was really frightened about something, she wasn't above casting lots or, in all secrecy, killing some little animal and taking auguries from its entrails. She might even use a fly or a spider if she couldn't get hold of a mouse or a grass snake.

And now she had received her punishment. Fate had taken her maidenhood, then her life, then all her jewels. She had even had to forfeit her fingers.

The Lord's punishment could be most terrible. As Paulinus had said. Hild made the sign of the cross over her ill-fated half-cousin, and re-arranged the skirts to cover her bloodied crotch—which did little to improve the outrageous and dreadful sight. The ravens had been there too, a big and noisy flock whose hoarse screams could be heard right up in the cave. Her people were practically unrecognizable. She would like to be able to bury them; even though it couldn't be in consecrated ground.

Her swordbearer was still wearing the fine cloak his daughter had woven for his nameday. He'd been so proud of it, especially the sealskin trimming, and he'd worn it on special occasions. Woven in the diamond pattern that had become fashionable. Not every daughter could make such a cloak for her father, as he had said many a time.

He was right—it was a good cloak, far too good to lie here in the mud. The gashes and stab rents could probably be repaired. In any case, it would be perfect for carrying Hundfrid and Wilbrord. It wasn't difficult to remove the cloak—he had no head, after all—and she carried it to the beck and washed the neckline where it was swollen and stiff with congealed blood. It wasn't going to be easy to get it dry as everything was soaked through after the rain. She hung it on a rowan tree just outside the entrance to the cave. The sun had come out, giving off a little warmth. The trees still had a good number of leaves, which made it easier to hide, easier to move on.

Once the babies had fallen asleep again, she went to look for mushrooms, but didn't find many. The dried meat was the best food she'd found, but she had to ration it; she had about a third left.

At her fourth attempt, she managed to catch a fish in the beck. It wasn't of a size you'd usually bother with. She gutted it with the cupbearer's knife and ate it just as it was. It didn't taste good, but then she hadn't expected it to.

This is how Friday the fourteenth of October in the year 633 passed for Hildeburh, daughter of Hereric and Breguswid, wife of Eadfrid, the king's son who had surrendered to Penda, the commander of Mercia.

Next day she caught another fish. While she was eating it, she noticed a robin calling to her from a hazel bush. Her mother had come to see her. She felt warmed all over and could have cried with happiness.

'I have borne two sons,' she whispered. 'I'll be all right.'

She put a small piece of fish on the ground. The robin stared at it for a moment, turned its head to one side, turned it to the other side, looked straight at her, jumped down from its branch, snapped up the piece of fish and flew away.

A very good omen.

Now she was certain she wouldn't be left wanting. She ate the last of the bread and half of the remaining meat. She found quite a few bilberries in a clearing, and some shrivelled blackberries. They tasted good, and she could hold them in her mouth for a long time. She didn't dare wander too far. Her breasts hurt. It was difficult to get Wilbrord to suck. She hoped the robin would come up to the cave and bless them.

She went down to the ford several times to shoo away the ravens; she knew it wasn't much use. Late in the afternoon, she tried to drag all the bodies together under one tree. She had to give up on the cupbearer, he was impossible to shift at all; she managed to pull the others across, and she covered them with branches and fallen leaves. She also placed some branches over the cupbearer, said the Lord's Prayer and made the sign of the cross. That was all the funeral she could give them.

At night the wolves came. First she heard them in the far distance; she grabbed the babies and put them to her breast even though they'd only just suckled. She couldn't risk going out, because then the wolves would pick up traces of her scent, so she reached out and broke off a rowan branch. She started digging up the earth in the cave, using the branch and the little knife, trying to block the entrance. It was slow work, the soil was solid and clayey. Big pieces of bone surfaced, and small shards; she pushed them all towards the entrance. Anything and everything could be used.

She had only managed to build a little mound in the opening by the time she heard the wolves close by; the branch was her best defence. She lay the babies as far back in the cave as she could, the cloak draped loosely over them, even though they didn't scream as much now and not so piercingly.

But she would scream; she wouldn't spare her voice if the wolves found them. She clutched the branch in her hand and looked up at the moon hanging above the trees. A waxing moon. Another good omen.

The wolves stopped at the ford and stayed there until dawn. They fought over the food. It was a large pack. She didn't hear them run off, but at sunrise she heard the ravens return, and then she slept a little.

She was woken by the pressure of her milk. Even though her breasts had been bewitched, she had to let her babies suckle—it was all she could do for them. They seemed to be getting smaller and thinner; they'd surely had a little roundness in their cheeks when they were born. And they were weaker, too. Even Hundfrid no longer snatched out briskly for her nipple as he had at first. She wept over the death of the wetnurse and over her own inability to give her babies what they needed. Now they would all die here in the cave while Eadfrid rotted away in his captivity. And he would never know that his wife had borne him sons.

All morning, in between giving the babies breast, she lay and wept. She knew she had to screen the entrance to the cave; the wolves would return, maybe they wouldn't have had their fill at the ford, and those at the bottom of the pack, the ones not allowed to join in the meal, would seek nourishment elsewhere. She also knew she'd have to go out as early as possible so her scent would have time to fade before nightfall, if at all.

But she didn't have the energy to move a muscle. Her breasts ached, and yet all she could give her sons was water. She wept again, she was thirsty, but she didn't dare leave the cave. Fate had spared her three times, now her luck had run out. She snuggled the babies tightly to her body and lay down to await darkness and the wolves.

There she lay, staring into space, when one of the bones she had dug up during the night caught her attention. It looked odd. Almost like the jawbone of a cat, just much bigger; with a cat's long eye-teeth. She reached out for it, examined it carefully. It must have been a really big cat. And suddenly she laughed, again hearing Paulinus' gravelly voice: 'Better to be a live dog than a dead lion.'

The manic laughter took hold. Here she lay, live dog, with a dead lion and her two cubs, descendants of the coward who had not even attempted to avenge his father and his brother, and who had given himself up to the slayers of his kin. That, at least, was how the story went, and she still hoped it wasn't true. But she was here, and her cubs lived. She sat up and put them to her breast again.

And a miracle occurred—her mother must have made it happen—milk flowed from her breasts, real milk, which would nourish her children so they could grow up and avenge the injustice done to their father's brother and their father's father, given that their father couldn't.

It was mid-afternoon. She carried her babies down to the beck and washed them as best she could. They were so small; they weighed next to nothing and squirmed when the cold water touched their skin. She quenched her thirst and ate the last of the meat. She looked up, and there was the robin, head on one side. When she spoke to it, the bird flew off—westward, and so she knew which direction she should take.

She quickly bound the children on her back, in the swordbearer's cloak, putting in the lion's jawbone as protection. She had to cross the ford; the ravens had returned and settled again. She tried to avert her eyes from the spot where she had gathered her people, but their remains were now everywhere, thanks to the wolves. Even the cupbearer, huge as he'd been—there wasn't much left of him. She pinched her nose and hurried past. She would walk until she came upon the Deira Way, the king's road, and follow it south to Mercia. There she would find her husband.

# Star the Cow and the
# Good-Luck Snakes

*– on Frigyd's farm –*

She walked at a brisk pace, alert to the sound of hoofbeats, but she didn't meet a living soul. She did come across a dead one, though—her handmaid; the men must have taken her with them before they raped her. Strange to let her walk this far first. Perhaps she had tried to escape. She was so swollen, her flesh pecked and hacked by ravens, that Hild only identified the body by its clothes. Had it not been for the flocking birds and that distinctive stench, she wouldn't even have noticed her lying there just inside the forest. At least now she could arrange two branches in the form of a holy cross on her handmaid's chest, and say the Lord's Prayer. Then she had to move on.

She only stopped to pick nuts from the hazel bushes. They were good and fresh, and a pair of squirrels had begun to stock up for winter.

The occasional gap between trees afforded a view of the flat marshland she and her entourage had travelled across earlier. There was nothing else—no people, no animals, just a couple of herons flying along the course of the river. She hurried on.

The sound of a cow lowing made her jump. Continuing with caution, she spotted a farmhouse just off the track, and she hid among the trees to wait, but the building was completely silent, no smoke rising from the vent.

The cow lowed again. The sound came from the house, through an open door in the long side. Hild approached warily. A section of the thatch roof was charred; the fire had obviously been put out by the rain. She would have to go in for the night.

Inside she found seven people: two elderly men and five women, one of whom was very young. She saw two cows standing at the far end of the building, eyes blood-shot and udders distended. Two cows were lying on the floor, dead and swollen. She had to cover her nose and mouth, such was the stench. She managed with some difficulty to force open the door in the other long side.

Hild loosened her cloak and placed the babies on a bench. She found a pail and, before doing anything else, she milked the cows. It was not a job she was used to, but she put all her strength into it and emptied udders so very afflicted by flying venom that they had swollen to twice their normal size. One of the cows lowed, as if in gratitude. She put a large dish of milk on the floor, for the house wights, and drank a little herself. It tasted of misery.

'When the milk is good, the wights shall have a big dishful,' she said out loud, once to the west and once to the east. She went outside and fetched water from the well; the cow that had lowed was given the first drink.

She found eight large loaves, and dried meat hanging from the crossbeam; she cut off a chunk, and didn't forget to put some out for the wights before she ate—outside, on a stone sheltered by the house. It was difficult to breathe inside.

Hild then set to work. The beer barrel had been smashed to pieces, the floor was still wet and sticky. This was a blessing in disguise as the reeking beer almost overpowered the stench from the rotting bodies. One of the corpses proved impossible to drag out, and she had to leave the dead cows too. They were the worst.

She found linen in a wooden chest; she swaddled the babies. They had to be bound tightly so as not to get crooked legs, and this was her first attempt. She really did need a wetnurse.

Otherwise, the farmhouse had everything they needed, all three. As long as she didn't light a fire, no one would know they were there.

While sitting quietly feeding the babies, she noticed a few grass snakes on the floor. One of them slid up to the milk pail and drank from it. Grass snakes in the house were a sign of luck—and if they ate from the kitchen utensils, well, that was the best sign of all. She was certain they had luck on their side; there was now plenty of milk in her breasts, and the babies helped themselves greedily.

Having settled the infants, she lay on the floor with her arms outstretched and thanked the Lord for letting her mother lead them to such a favourable place.

On the second day, Hild began to feel strangely uncomfortable in the house. As if eyes were watching her; she didn't feel safe.

Hardly surprising with all these corpses, she thought, and wondered how she could get the last one out of the house and then bury them all. But first the babies had to be fed. All that good milk of hers would make them healthy. Their cheeks seemed to have started filling out already.

She was breastfeeding the boys when suddenly she knew with absolute certainty that she was being watched. Turning quickly, she caught a glimpse of something small; it vanished. Brown woollen clothing. The house wight.

Hild froze with fear. The children weren't yet baptized, so she couldn't let them out of her sight. But maybe they'd already been swapped with the wight's hideous issue. She unwrapped Hundfrid and inspected him closely. He looked just like he usually did—the little red blotch on his neck, the longish earlobes. Wilbrord also looked like himself—a brown oblong mark in the hollow of his right knee, and those fathomless blue eyes. They both had a dense covering of light down on their backs, and unusually long eyelashes. She was in no doubt that these were her sons, both of them.

She took them with her to the well, hoisted up a pail of water and returned to the house, the babies in one arm, the bucket in the other. There was no godparent, no one who could attest to their baptism.

The lowing cow would have to be the witness. It was a blessed animal. The Lord had chosen a cowshed for his place of birth, and the cow had been elevated to glory when Matthew the evangelist had chosen it as his emblem.

'Lord Jesus, have mercy on this child, Wilbrord, son of Eadfrid and Hildeburh,' she said, arms outstretched.

She took a firm grip on the boy's nose and mouth and dipped him three times in the water bucket, in the name of the Father, the Son and the Holy Spirit.

Wilbrord screamed loudly. A good sign. She dried and wrapped him before baptizing Hundfrid. The cow then let out a long bellow, as if to confirm sponsorship and bless the twins. With both reborn babies in her arms, Hild lay down next to the cow and said the Lord's Prayer aloud on behalf of them all.

The cow was dark golden, long-haired, with sweeping pointed horns. It had a white patch on its forehead. This was Star. Hild patted its dirty back. The cow's milk was good now and the animal warmed the room. It was a living creature, on a more adult and equal footing with her than were the children. Even if it was a dumb animal, its eyes held all the wisdom and patience in the world. You could tell it had borne its young in pain and solitude.

She cleared away the dung under Star and settled down to rub her with straw. This would serve no purpose for the other cow, which was now unable to stand up; with all the blood and flying venom oozing from its udders, it was unlikely to last the night. Then she would have one more corpse. And one less source of warmth. But Star was a lovely cow. Hild sang robustly as the hide became shiny and golden.

Stealthy little footsteps could be heard from the other end of the room. Glancing up quickly, Hild caught a glimpse of the wight as it slipped behind the large wooden chest against the west wall. It couldn't harm her and it couldn't swap the babies for changelings now, but she felt it would be for the best with a Lord's Prayer. The wight could still spoil the milk and foment ill fortune.

As she was saying her prayer, a little head appeared over the lid of the chest. Dark curly hair, large almost black eyes, mouth open. It looked like a child, a real child, and it vanished instantly. She was almost certain it was a child. She started her song again, from the beginning, and when she reached the end she sang it once more.

The head reappeared. She saw it without having to turn, and then a slender torso popped up behind the wooden chest.

Hild was relieved to see it was just a human child. She spoke aloud to the babies, lifted them into the air and cuddled them, told them about their father who had not fallen in battle, but had been taken prisoner—rather a live dog than a dead lion—and lived a long way away.

And while filling the room with sound and movement, she felt the child approach until it was standing right by her side, staring at her.

'Look at his smile,' said Hild without turning, and the child walked up to Hundfrid and looked.

'It's because he's full. He's eaten and eaten, and that's what I need to do too,' said Hild.

She fetched some bread and settled down to eat, babbling on and occasionally handing a little chunk to the child, who automatically took it and ate. Hild stood up, still chattering, and fetched a jug of milk, poured a beaker and drank, then passed the rest to the child. The little girl drank.

'I think you're called Hereswid,' said Hild, 'because that's my sister's name.'

'Frigyd,' she replied. Her eyes were bottomless black pools.

'Frigyd,' repeated Hild, 'that's a good name. And you must be four years old.'

The child shook her head and Hild refilled the beaker with milk, which the little girl gulped down. She looked exhausted, desolate and dejected, as indeed she was.

Frigyd didn't leave Hild's side for the rest of the day. Wherever Hild went, Frigyd clutched her skirt and tagged along. But she didn't say anything. She made do with nodding or shaking her head.

In the evening they lay down together to rest. Hild said evening prayers, Frigyd's big black eyes fixed on her. Even asleep, Frigyd didn't loosen her grasp on Hild's skirt.

The babies were growing, there was no doubt about that, but they weren't the chubby and sturdy infants they had been at first, and this saddened Hild. She thought they were losing a touch of their special character, day by day, beginning to look more ordinary. But she was getting to know them, and they had very different temperaments. Wilbrord was more fiery and impatient than his brother, and he had better lungs. So he was mostly number one.

Hundfrid could lie staring into space and then suddenly flail his arms and legs as if he was seeing grand visions. He was happiest when he could hear his mother's voice. When she began a song he made little noises, as if he wanted to sing along, and then he would lie quite still and listen. Hild was always able to soothe him by singing. At the end of the song he would twitch and jerk and try to say something to make it keep going. She spent nearly all day chatting and singing.

It was different with Wilbrord. He didn't like lying by himself, not even when she sang. He wanted to be picked up and carried, he had to feel the warmth of hands and body, and he loved it when she spun round with him. His big deep-blue eyes stared out on the world, and Hild wondered what he made of the dead man and the dead cows in the house. Perhaps he thought this was just how it was; perhaps he would grow up in the belief that bodies covered in sword gashes were part of the furnishings, and that cows always died of thirst and flying venom. Hild couldn't bear the thought, and covered the huge corpse with a cloak. But this caused Frigyd great distress; she shouted and pulled the cloak away.

'Was he your father?' asked Hild. Although rarely getting an answer, she talked to Frigyd constantly.

The little girl nodded and pulled up a stool to the head of the corpse. She wasn't going to risk her father being covered again. She sat watching over him for the rest of the morning, until Hild finally lured her away with milk.

'Your father's sleeping, he needs a cover.'

Frigyd was instantly on guard. She returned to the stool and resumed her watch.

'Surely he shouldn't lie there and freeze?' asked Hild. Frigyd shifted the stool a little so she was between her father and this lady, her eyes darting between the one and the other.

Hild fetched water and washed her children, humming a song she knew to be one of Frigyd's favourites. From the corner of her eye, while she was changing the babies, she watched Frigyd drag the cover across the floor and arrange it over her father as if he were asleep. His head was left uncovered and had probably never been pretty, but it had become more and more peculiar and unrecognizable. Fortunately there wasn't any blood on it.

Wilbrord would have to make what he could of the world he had entered—some people were fat, fetid and blank-faced, or some people killed one another. Both were true, but she thought it was too early to learn such details. She had enjoyed a secure and happy childhood, under the protection of King Edwin: Edwin's peace. Now that everything was shattered, she thought a lot about those days. Her own children and Frigyd would grow up in a very different world.

Hild had spent most of her childhood at Edwin's royal estate, Ad Gefrin, by the Glene river in Bernicia, with her mother Breguswid and sister Hereswid. Her older brother had lived with them until his abduction. No one had seen him since. He had been six years old when he disappeared. That was the only misfortune to have befallen them.

They had often accompanied King Edwin on his journeys around the realm, when the taxes had to be collected, so Hild was familiar with every part of his far-reaching kingdom and had even travelled all the way down to Lindsey. But Ad Gefrin was the children's favourite place, and a very safe spot when Edwin first imposed peace in the region. There were sentry posts on every hilltop, and the children could roam as they pleased beyond the estate fences.

They used to run up into the hills, along the old track next to the stream. To their left, they had the hill where wild goats grazed, thus the estate was called Ad Gefrin—the Place of the Hill of the Goats—and to the right, a smaller hill that had also been inhabited by giants in olden times. Later the Britons, the native people, had lived up there; now that they had been driven away, the king's sentries used it. They kept a few head of cattle, enclosed by the giants' thick stone walls, and were largely self-sufficient. The sentries moved post every week and knew the area in and out, as did the children.

Having passed the Hill of the Goats and followed the stream, more hilltops appeared on both sides, with new sentry posts, and then the ground sloped steadily down to the waterfalls, where the children played and learnt to catch fish. On one side of the stream there was a farm, with barley growing on the terraced hillside. It was a lovely place to visit, and the children from the royal settlement were always invited in for wheat bread and milk. Hereswid preferred goat milk, the others would rather have cow milk, and when the weather was hot they were given beer. The beer was good up there.

Best of all was a spot just beyond the stream at the foot of the Hill of the Goats. Before you reached the next stream there was a little meadow with the most glorious thick grass and a dome-shaped rock thrusting into the air. It was so big that two of you could sit on it, but true happiness was to have it all to yourself so you could lean right back. Then it was practically like a real grown-up chair, and you could almost stretch out. On a summer's day, when the sun had been shining for a while, it was the most blissful feeling, eyes closed, listening to the beck alongside and the skylarks and curlews above. You could just relax and float away in that chair. And when you opened your eyes again, the four manned hills were still there. Nothing was so delightful, and yet so secure, as reclining on that smooth rock.

In order to share the pleasure equally, Hild and Hereswid would take it in turns to sit in the chair. The boys weren't interested, they just ran on or, if it was that time of year, collected caddis worms in the beck. Hereswid was the elder of the two, so she sat first, and Hild had to wait a little way off, so as not to disturb her. Once Hild had finished reciting the entire poem about Sigurd's fight with the dragon, it was time for her turn, which lasted until Hereswid had recited the same poem. Hild's sit in the chair was a bit shorter than Hereswid's, because Hild took longer to get through the poem. As they grew older and quicker at reciting, the sitting time was extended with the poem about Sigurd's encounter with Brynhild. They never cheated. There were occasions when they weren't quite honest, but never about this.

'Frig's Seat!' said Hereswid.

Hild admired her older sister, she always found the right words. Of course it was Frig's Seat. What could be more delicious for the lovely Frig than to sit here and let the sun shine upon her. And perhaps receive suitors.

When they were on their own they played Courting Frig. It was one of the best games Hild knew. Given that there were sentry posts all around, they couldn't behave exactly as Frig would have done, but they could say what they were going to do and then hint at it through gesture and facial expression. Thus they learnt to play at one thing while, from a distance, looking as if they were doing something else entirely. They gained many an advantage from this skill—later in life, too.

Frig lived in the area. At her convenience she came by and sat down, leant back and received suitors. There was no way of knowing when she would come, and it seemed to be mostly in the spring, but she came quite often. Hild and Hereswid would pick a few flowers and put them around the stone, and if they had brought along food they would leave some for her. It had always gone when they returned. Hild didn't think this proved Frig had been there, as someone else could have eaten it, occasionally at least. But Hereswid was convinced.

It didn't quite tally with Hild's respect for this beautiful and most wondrous of women to picture her being lured and captured by bait, like foxes, bears and wolves. Frig was, after all, greater and finer than a wild animal, and therefore Hild stubbornly persisted in telling her sister that Frig coming by to pick up their gifts was only one possibility.

'When you think about it properly,' she said, 'why should she eat what we put out when she can have all the apples and all the pork and mead she could possibly want?'

'Because it's a gift,' answered Hereswid brusquely. 'And she's not nearly as fancy as you think.'

They saved the best titbits from the table for the beauteous one, and lay in wait to catch a glimpse of her; but they never did.

'Hardly surprising,' said Hild out loud, while attempting to empty Star's udders, 'because Frig simply doesn't exist. If she does, then it's only as an air demon. And you're not allowed to leave gifts for her.'

She had learnt these facts from Paulinus, the monk who had taught them the language of Latin, the art of writing and the true faith. Prior to his arrival on these shores, they had all walked in the darkness of superstition. They hadn't known how pernicious a game they had been playing.

She no longer knew Paulinus' whereabouts, nor even if he was still alive.

He'd certainly had his hands full with the flock of children the queen had assigned him to teach. He wasn't used to such liveliness and the ungodliness had shocked him. Paulinus hadn't looked leniently on their paganism, especially after they'd been baptized.

Frig and Eostre—who put life into women's wombs and vitality into the dead grain—how could you suddenly forget them? Or mighty Hreda, she who ruled under the earth, down with the dead, and who, every year, in her own month, released the little green shoots in her chosen order and quantity corresponding, more or less, to the degree of attention people had paid her during the preceding year. And Erce, mother of the earth, to whom they had made a sacrifice every birthday in order to thank her for calling them forth from the darkness and admitting them to the brief shimmer of life.

Of course they couldn't just forget the goddesses who had meant so much to them while they were growing up. The goddesses they had celebrated at their special times—Hreda in her month, when the new growth began to appear, followed by Eostre in *her* month, when everything multiplied; Erce on their birthdays and Frig when there was a wedding or just talk of a wedding and all its ramifications. The songs they had sung about the bounteous goddesses didn't just vanish from the mind the instant they were told it was all wrong—were told the Lord, the new god, wouldn't stand for it.

One thing really saddened Hild: not being able to sing the whole range of songs she had known since childhood; some she had to hum. They would come over her when a familiar smell suddenly filled her nostrils, or at the sight of a flower or the sound of something someone said—then her mouth ran with old songs and she had a struggle to restrain herself from singing them out loud. Some you couldn't even sing in your head without failing in your fidelity to the Lord. It was difficult to disown them, so the Lord's Prayer came in useful: if you were on the verge of forsaking the faith, you could say a Lord's Prayer instead, and if the song insisted on escaping, you could put the words of the Lord's Prayer to the tune, or sing the Lord's name or some of the other holy words Paulinus had taught them.

Hild remembered with pleasure the day she had been received in baptism by Jesus Christ and pledged her faith to the Lord. King Edwin and nearly all his top people had been baptized in the holy Peter's newly-built church in Eoforwik: the kingdom of Northumbria had commended itself to the service of the Lord. As there were so many of them, their servants and slaves had a long wait. Paulinus had baptized there for days on end, and when they returned to Ad Gefrin he had carried on doing so for weeks, standing in the cold waters of the Glene river.

Hild and Hereswid were of high enough birth to be baptized with the king, on Easter Sunday itself, falling that year on the twelfth day of Eostre's month. They had worn their white baptismal robes for a whole week afterwards. Hereswid wanted to keep hers on, but this was not seemly, said Paulinus, and the handmaid had to undress her.

Eostre's lilies were in full bloom in Eoforwik, but travelling northwards they became fewer and further between, and around Ad Gefrin they were still only in bud. It felt like being transported backwards in time to meet the beginnings of another spring. Hild's first thought as they approached Ad Gefrin was of Frig's Seat, and as soon as they had toured the royal settlement and seen all the new-born babies they ran up to the rock.

Hereswid sat first and dragged out the time by recounting, at length, a dream. Hild had great difficulty awaiting her turn. The stone was still a little chilly when she sat down, and it didn't feel quite the same as usual. Either it had shrunk from all the winter cold or she had grown. The contours against her back and thighs didn't match her memory, and she had to concentrate in order to be quite sure this really was the sensation of Frig's Seat. Then it was lovely, just slightly different and new.

'Time's up!' shouted Hereswid, and it was already over. As Hild began reciting the long poem, the sun came out. Everything glistened with moisture, twinkling at her from the beck and pools of water and the still-wet blades of grass. The skylarks sang high above, a screeching curlew flew past and a frog plopped in the beck. Hild looked for caddis worms—both the kind with little needles on their bellies and the ones with grains of sand. A pair of ravens soared by, their hoarse grunts echoing down the valley. They were Woden's birds; she hurled a stone at them, with no chance of hitting. Woden had to get the message that he was no longer her lord; now she was exclusively loyal to the Lord God.

Paulinus had said they were reborn. In baptism they became new people and now nothing was as it had been. Hild could indeed feel that something had happened to her. Things were growing and tickling and stretching inside; her nipples were beginning to bulge, tender as boils; if she made a hasty movement she would likely as not get in the way of herself; she spilled and dropped things almost as often as Hereswid, the butter-fingers. Their mother said this would pass if they stopped thinking about it. Hild was glad it had started with Hereswid and not her. You could already see Hereswid's swellings through her clothes, and men had begun to look at her in a different way.

Part of Hild hoped she'd soon be getting those kind of glances from the young men; but another part wanted things to stay as they were. Even though a lot had already changed. They hardly ever played with the boys anymore. Eadfrid had gone to the royal estate of Rendlæsham in the kingdom of the East Angles, and Osfrid was getting married soon. He'd travelled to Cetreht after the Easter festival, and would be taking over the royal estate there.

They were going to his wedding; he was marrying a Frankish king's daughter—none of them had ever seen her.

Hild was going to marry Eadfrid; their fathers had made an agreement before Hild had even been born. Hereswid was due to marry one of the king's sons from East Anglia; at least, negotiations were underway between the East Angles and her mother and King Edwin. Then Hereswid would belong to a different lineage, and bear its children. But they could still write to one another—once they were a bit better at writing—and visit.

She pictured herself as the lady of the house. Wearing a large white headdress, she opened her arms to receive the sister dismounting from a horse in the yard. Her husband would be seated, solid and growling, at the centre of the high table in the hall, and she herself would walk around pouring mead for Hereswid and her retinue. Hereswid would always travel with a large retinue, and maybe she would already speak a little strangely, like they spoke down there. When everyone had retired for the night, they would sit and tell one another about their new kinsfolk and about all the places they had seen on their travels through distant regions and the strange people they had come across in the big outside world. Their travels would take them much further afield than Lindsey; they would traverse the whole land, travel all the way up to the Picts.

Being a grown-up couldn't come soon enough; she wished the rebirth had been slightly more substantial. She jumped down across the track and up onto a slope where she had spotted a few flowers: coltsfoot and primroses. She gathered them all, taking care not to lift any soil, and picked out the finest and roundest stones from the beck.

Hereswid seemed to be asleep. For the last few days she had been unusually surly, complaining of stomach ache, but now she looked peaceful and normal.

Hild walked very quietly round her three times, at a distance of three paces. Then she bowed to Frig's Seat and walked three times round the other way. She bowed again and returned, placing stones in a circle as she went, alternating the stones with three flowers. With every stone she said to herself: Ave Frig. That would surely help.

Hereswid woke up the very second Hild had finished. She was irritated by Hild's capers and had reached an age when she no longer knew if she cared to join in the game. She wandered off, squatted in the grass and relieved herself, then walked sulkily along the beck, reciting her poem in a loud and impatient voice.

Hild ran to catch up with her, to calm her down, but stopped when she caught sight of a little patch of red. She shouted to her sister and pointed ecstatically at the grass.

'It's come out of you! Have you seen? You're of age! It's blood!'

'Rubbish!' said Hereswid, but couldn't help going back to look. She gazed at the blood with huge round eyes.

'Has it really come out of me?'

She put a hand between her legs, then held it up. Blood.

Hild jumped up and down in excitement.

'Can you check?' asked Hereswid, as she sat down on the rock with her legs apart and pulled up her skirts. They both looked, as discreetly as possible, and it was indeed true.

Hereswid had come of age. From now on she would wear adult clothes, have a place in the hall among the grown-ups and sit on the Eostre-bench in the women's room when she had her bleeding-days. Her mother could speed up the marriage negotiations.

'You've got to do the same for me,' said Hild. She'd already settled herself on the rock.

'What?' said Hereswid.

'Just like I did—appeal to Frig. Otherwise I'll be stuck by myself with all the little ones.'

Hereswid went along with it. Being the first was good, but it was also good to have someone to keep you company. She mumbled long invocations to Frig while walking round the rock, upon which Hild sat, rigid, eyes screwed tightly shut, waiting for the miracle to happen.

Hereswid didn't use stones or flowers; she made holy crosses from the longest blades of grass and placed them at the four corners of the world. To the east she put three in a row. Hild watched what she was doing through an almost invisible slit in her eyes. Hild's inquisitiveness had often got her into trouble and made Hereswid angry, but she simply couldn't control it. Now she could both feel and see the sun coming out again. A good sign. She was certain their ritual would work—until, that is, Hereswid dropped her arms and kicked her grass composition.

'I won't do it when you cheat!' she shouted, heading homeward; and there was no way she could be persuaded or enticed to try again.

Hild's coming of age thus kept her waiting for over a year, and Hereswid often lectured on the dangers of cheating in such matters. It was highly likely that Frig would now miss Hild out and leave her childless and barren for the rest of her days.

'Just like a mule,' said Hereswid, and Hild shuddered.

She loved her sister. Hereswid had been the wisest, the most beautiful, the boldest, the most inventive of them all. Hild missed her so much that she ached all over.

She picked Frigyd up and hugged her tightly. The little girl's warm body calmed her, a different kind of calmness than the babies could provide, they were too fragile to be hugged.

'My sister lives in the kingdom of the East Angles, and maybe she's had a child too by now.'

Frigyd gave a satisfied smile. She liked, best of all, to listen to Hild talking about her sister and her childhood at Ad Gefrin; although she never said anything, very occasionally she laughed out loud. Hild guessed that Frigyd had also been part of a large flock of children who had run in and out of all the buildings on the farm and dashed around in the fields and in the forest, found birds' nests and collected stones and played hide-and-seek between the trees, wriggled on their stomachs through the high grass, caught frogs and inspected anthills. When listening to such tales from Hild, Frigyd had a contented and conspiratorial air of tranquillity.

But there hadn't been any slain children in the house. Perhaps Frigyd's playmates only existed in her dreams. On farms of this size, the children usually took part in the work as soon as they were able, free-children and slaves alike. Hild knew that her childhood freedom to play and roam was a privilege of the very wealthiest, and this was a medium-sized farm.

She stroked Frigyd's hair and spoke about her home at Mædeltun. When the unrest was over, they would go back there and Frigyd would be brought up with all the happiness Hild had enjoyed in her own childhood. And she would learn to read and write. Hild was certain that Frigyd had once been able to speak just like other children, and that one day she would do so again. She had told Hild her name, and she was a bright child.

There was no more bread in the house. They ate porridge made from crushed oats and barley left to soak overnight, then covered with honey, of which they had plenty, and Frigyd laughed at the amount Hild used. The cow had more milk than they could drink and the rest was put out for the wights. There was still a whole side of smoked bacon and a vat of salted meats. The farm had been well run. Everything was clean and orderly and, apart from beer, they had enough to last the winter. It was too early for the winter slaughter, so there were undoubtedly pigs and sheep and goats grazing the surrounding land.

Hild didn't go outside to investigate, and she told herself that her lack of interest was because they had enough provisions indoors. When she had to go out, she did so quickly and furtively, and she spent a long time listening for hoofbeats and the sounds of human activity before she scurried down to the well and filled the pails. On the way back, she was always in such a hurry that she spilt half the water.

She stopped counting the days, so she didn't know they were now in the month of sacrifice. The only thing she did know was that she must soon set out and find her husband in Mercia. When the babies were robust enough.

Wilbrord and Frigyd were coughing. Hild had to get up in the night and carry Wilbrord around until he coughed up the badness. She wrapped the lion's jawbone in his swaddling clothes, and realized she'd have to keep the doors closed as the autumn storms were blowing hard. The stench inside was going to be unbearable.

She had never taken part in a slaughter, and the thought of cutting up the dead cows was distasteful to her. Not to mention the large man who had as good as melted across the floor.

She tied a cloth around the lower part of her face and set to work. It took her two days to get the cows out, and then she had to bury them so their remains wouldn't attract wolves. She had long since consigned the dead people to the earth.

And then there was the man. Frigyd helped. She must have forgotten the connection between her father and this putrefying heap of flesh on the floor, and it was indeed difficult to detect. She took to the task with the same enthusiasm she had shown when helping Hild with the cows.

It made a difference to the air, even though it was harder to dry the babies' linen now the wind no longer blew through the house. But Wilbrord and Frigyd were still coughing. The old remedies of putting sick children on the roof or warming them in the oven were of no use here. She mustn't give the outside world any sign of their presence.

She lit the fire anyway when darkness fell. Sat Frigyd down on her stool next to the hearth and drew a circle of ash around her. She placed Wilbrord in the middle of another ash circle and lifted Hundfrid onto her lap. He had begun to smile. She sang to them, a nonsense mixture of holy words, names of flowers and whatever else entered her head, to the melody of an old heroic song. She told them about her mother and her sister, and her father who had been poisoned while Hild still lay in her mother's womb. And about her husband Eadfrid. He never came home empty-handed from a wild-boar hunt. He was an intrepid hunter, was their father. He could teach them a lot when the time came. Hundfrid babbled along when she talked about their father. They must both be longing to see him.

The water in the well didn't smell good. Hild thought the odour clung to the linen after it had been washed. Even patient Star drank tentatively, giving Hild a look that said this cow has known far better days with far better water.

'I know,' she said, patting the cow, 'but I'm doing the best I can.'

She kept Star's coat smooth and glossy, and she mucked out twice a day. She hadn't known a cow could give such joy.

One day, there was a shoe in the pail; a child's shoe, maybe a three-year-old. She leant over and stared down into the well, her eyes slowly growing accustomed to the darkness. She could see a lot of other things floating around down there.

Hild had to sit for a while before going in to the children. She lifted Frigyd onto her lap, rocking her backwards and forwards, clasping her firmly in her arms.

From now on she would have to fetch water from the beck. She couldn't wash the little ones in the water from the well, nor their clothes. The evil might pass into them.

Star would have to put up with it, given that a large cow couldn't walk to the beck without being visible to any passers-by for a good part of the way. But when, a few days later, Hild hauled up the pail and saw a length of linen in it—the kind she used to swaddle the babies— she let go of the rope and vomited.

She found a new bucket in one of the outhouses, and now she had to drag the water all the way from the beck. She preferred to do it as darkness drew in. Frigyd wanted to go with her, but Hild daren't let her outside, so she brought home surprises for the little girl to play with instead—a few twigs or stones—as a reward for looking after the babies.

Frigyd was delighted with the presents. She placed them in a circle and tried to tell the grass snakes that this was their home, even though they went where they pleased. They drank the milk she put down for them in the circle, but they never drank from Frigyd's bowl.

Hild was uneasy about this, but she convinced herself that believing children were ensured a long life if grass snakes ate from their bowl was just a deep-rooted superstition. Paulinus would definitely have called it superstition and paganism. He had thundered against all the old notions of what constituted a sign of good fortune or of ill fortune. The will of the Lord would prevail anyway, said Paulinus.

But how, then, can grown men throw small children down a well? thought Hild, looking at her own infants. Tiny little children who can do no harm to anyone—how can that be the will of the new god?

There was a lot she didn't understand. And now she no longer had Paulinus to turn the incomprehensible into the comprehensible.

# HOUNDS, HARES AND LIONS

*– wergild for Frigyd –*

One evening, when Frigyd sat warming herself in her ash circle and Hild had just settled down to suckle the babies, they heard hoofbeats. Far away, but there was no mistaking the sound. More than ten, fewer than thirty horses.

'Strangers!' she cried out to Frigyd, and doused the fire with the bucket of water she always had ready for just such an occasion. There was also a basket prepared for the children, which she forgot all about as she ran from the house with a baby in each arm and Frigyd close on her heels. She had long since explained to Frigyd what they had to do if strangers approached, and she'd explained so many times that Frigyd was beginning to believe they were the only people in the world—because no one ever came.

Now she ran energetically alongside Hild, who she had started to call 'mother', but she simply didn't understand why they weren't allowed to welcome the guests. She was used to strangers being given a proper greeting, even if there was no ale to offer them. And, just think, they might have dogs!

Hild had decided on an escape route the very first day she had been in the house. She glanced at the track every time she went to fetch water, although she had never dared find out where it led—partly from fear of disappointment, and partly from dread of leaving the children on their own in the house, but mostly because she didn't feel safe wandering around outdoors. Inside the house with all the good-luck snakes, it was as if nothing bad could happen. The wights were well-disposed towards them.

Now she discovered that the escape track, having passed through the thicket, led up to a large enclosed field. They ran across and clambered over the wall at the far side, but couldn't find a path. She cursed the wet weather—their footprints would be easily visible in the mud—and prayed that the drizzle would turn into a torrential downpour and wash away their tracks. Through the rain she heard the hoofbeats come to a halt by the house and the sound of men shouting. Frigyd was out of breath and could hardly keep up, even though Hild was carrying the twins. Their firm little bodies gave her the strength to keep running.

She shifted one baby so that they were both in her right arm, and grabbed Frigyd's little palm with her left hand.

They couldn't run any further, but had to force their way through a dense scrub of brambles and stickyweed filling the gaps between tall and small trees. Hild had to use one hand to bend the branches aside, so Frigyd followed behind, tightly clutching the skirt of her 'mother'. And so they walked for a long time, through unchanging undergrowth, but the Lord had granted her prayer and sent rain; a heavy autumn storm made the trees howl, buffeting the one against the other. They were soaked through and Frigyd was coughing. If they startled a wild boar they were done for.

Hild made a sort of lair from broken branches with her outer skirt on top, like a tent. Frigyd enjoyed sitting with her while she suckled the babies; between coughing fits, she rested her head on Hild's knee. It was so dark they couldn't even see one another. The rain was a blessing.

Hild closed her eyes, and when she opened them again the rain had stopped. She was frozen stiff. She woke Frigyd and they started on their way; Frigyd was still half-asleep, but Hild could feel the little tug on the back of her skirt as she forced her way through the scrub.

Frigyd walked with eyes closed, thinking about the big hounds that had come with some strangers who once visited on a very hot sunny day. She'd been allowed to play with the dogs, they had soft warm fur. One of them had fetched the twigs she threw, even though hounds actually preferred fetching twigs for adults who threw further. She could still remember the smell of the reddish-brown fur, and the feel of it kept her warm as she trudged along in the darkness behind this new mother.

They were brought up short by the smell of burnt wood. They must be close to a farm. Hild flushed with happiness. Then she stopped. There would be people.

'We'll wait until it gets light,' she said to Frigyd, and made ready so they could sit in their tent again. Frigyd had no idea what was happening, she was so tired, she just leant against Hild and slept. She dreamt about the big warm hound.

Wilbrord woke with a little cry, but settled down as soon as she put him to her breast. She fed both twins; she wanted to stay awake so the very first light of daybreak would reveal if they could go up to the farmhouse or if they would have to keep walking. She started praying for her husband, and for all those fallen in battle; for her slain cousin, whose silver ring she wore on her finger, for her wetnurse and her cupbearer, for her handmaid and for her swordbearer, everyone who had travelled with her from Mædeltun, and for Frigyd's dead family.

She could see them all, dancing in the sunlight on a succulent pasture covered with yellow marsh marigolds. Everyone was there, her sister and mother, all of her kin and all of Edwin's kin. Eadfrid offered Hild his hand in the dance, and even her missing brother was there. He was sitting on a fallen tree-trunk, waving at them. He was too young to dance, but Hild's cousin picked him up, swung him round until they both tumbled over on the grass and he shouted loudly in delight. Wilbrord and Hundfrid had grown; they were playing dice with their paternal grandfather Hereric, who now had a long silvery-white beard.

It was the life eternal that Paulinus had told them about, and Hild was getting a foretaste while she thought she was keeping herself awake and vigilant.

She awoke with a little jolt. Frigyd had leapt up and was running off. Hild shouted at her, but Frigyd didn't have time to stop.

'They've come home,' she shouted breathlessly. 'Hurry, mother, they've come back home!'

Hild stood up quickly and looked around. She covered her eyes with her hands and spoke her god's name out loud, but when she looked again the picture was the same: in front of them, in the early dawn, she saw Frigyd's thatched farmhouse.

The building was surrounded by men, the field was full of saddle horses, and she couldn't stop Frigyd, who had nearly reached the house.

She saw Frigyd bend down, pick up a stick and fling it into the air, and she heard the baying of beasts and saw three large greyhounds bounding towards the little girl. And then the baying of the dogs turned into one long howl.

Hild screamed at the dogs, gathered up the twins in one arm, grabbed a stick in her free hand and raced bellowing towards the house. She paid no attention to the men who came running, she only saw the three huge hounds fighting over Frigyd's body. She as good as threw the twins onto the stone wall and started beating the dogs' heads with the stick. She shouted with all her might, her voice easily matching the clamouring of the beasts.

One of the dogs sank its teeth into her calf; she yanked its tail backwards until it snapped. The dog wailed and let go. A man ran towards them with a whip and beat the dogs off. Others stood looking on in horror.

Frigyd was slumped on her side; there was a lot of blood. Hild bent over her. The little girl's blue eyes were staring straight ahead and her mouth was half open, almost in a smile.

Hild smoothed Frigyd's eyelids shut and lifted her up. She weighed next to nothing. Hearing an infant crying, far away, Hild looked towards the sound, but she really didn't know if it had anything to do with her.

Some of the men had crowded round the two babies on the wall; she saw one of them pick up the whimpering Wilbrord. Without letting go of Frigyd's limp little body, Hild charged at the man, roaring, and wrenched Wilbrord from him.

The man made no attempt to hold onto the baby, he had merely intended to hand him to Hild. One of the others was going to pass Hundfrid to her, but changed his mind and stepped away. The men drew back in silence to make room for the woman.

Once she had a firm grasp on both her sons, she looked at the men. They were Britons, maybe Welsh. Two were still just boys, and one was over forty. Being the eldest, he stepped forward and addressed her in a language spoken by the Britons, slowly and respectfully.

'We have little to offer—but if a lady traveller might be content with what there is, then we can provide food and shelter for her and her babies. And I pledge my word that the wicked actions of the hounds will be justly punished.'

His kindly voice and sincere brown eyes were too much for Hild. She had to look at the ground, and she didn't struggle when he gently took her elbow and guided her into the house.

He signalled that she should keep quiet. A tall, thin man was slumped across the table, fast asleep. His hefty man-at-arms sat alongside, polishing his sword, but glanced up when she entered and then moved on to his master's sword.

Hild was shown to a bench, where she had so often sat before. The old man was wandering around looking for something; he found it, in a corner, her basket, and gave it to her. She put it on the floor by her feet, keeping the babies in her arms. She had carefully laid Frigyd next to her on the bench. Star's place was empty.

The men walked quietly in and out, going about their business. One was boiling up porridge and getting breakfast ready. The thin man was snoring loudly, his head resting on his outstretched arms.

He was wearing a scarlet tunic, a woad-blue cape of fine linen around his shoulders. All filthy. The cape was edged with a gold-worked bright-red border; his boots were new and had spurs of silver. He had longish raven-black hair, which fell across his face and his arms.

Hild could hear dogs howling and the sharp cracking of a whip; in no way, to her mind, could that be called justice for Frigyd. She would demand wergeld, real blood revenge. Someone would have to pay with their life for Frigyd, she didn't care who, but Frigyd's death had to be compensated.

The old man approached her, asked who she was.

'I am Hildeburh,' she replied, 'daughter of Hereric and Breguswid, and wife of King Edwin's son Eadfrid.'

The man just stared at her.

'And these are my sons fathered by Eadfrid: Hundfrid and Wilbrord!'

The man's face took on an expression of pity, and he trudged over to the man-at-arms seated next to his sleeping master. They whispered to one another, glancing at Hild in disbelief. They obviously came to some agreement and the old man walked to the hearth and prepared a hot drink, which he carried back to Hild.

'You need something,' he said, and patted her head. He encouraged her to lie on the bench and rest. He vouched with his life that nothing would happen to her or the babies. And her daughter there, he was sorry about that with the daughter. Someone had brought along those wretched hounds from Mædeltun; they shouldn't have, but some people were like that—they couldn't pass up on a single thing, not even a couple of unruly curs. Personally, all he was looking forward to was a calmer state of affairs. Benchoer in Gwynedd—that was his home.

Hild was listless from the drink and the heat from the fireplace. She didn't know the drink was a magic potion intended to bring back her senses.

The men whispered and stared at her with a mixture of terror and pity. They weren't used to being in the same room as people whose territory they had seized. A shout, a couple of slashes, job done—that was how they consorted with these foreign persons. It was quite another story to have a young woman sitting there with her children, and to see for themselves how her wits had left her. They didn't like being reminded that just last year they had found their own women in the very same state after Edwin's campaign of punishment. They shuddered at the thought, and avoided looking at the foreign woman's impassive face.

Hild closed her eyes and thought back to Edwin's hopeless attempt to abolish blood feuds—after he'd been baptized—then things had started going wrong.

The older folk had objected straight to his face, some had even laughed out loud. Who, they wanted to know, would enforce justice if the family didn't immediately retaliate in kind—who? And what would keep people in their place? What would prevent them pillaging each other's property and killing one another? 'The king!' Edwin had shouted, with a look that made them save their protests for later.

Edwin had decreed financial compensation for the loss of family members, in accordance with their rank and status, and he imposed banishment for blood feuds. But given that he couldn't be everywhere at once, the king's justice often made a rather sluggish journey around his extensive realm and, as had been customary, the people had to take matters into their own hands, which was where they sat best—as Edwin eventually began to realize.

The king's justice simply led to the shrugging of shoulders. Regions that had never heard about the king's ban on blood feuds were spared the wave of violence that hit areas within reach of the king's sword—for the latter no longer knew the difference between justice and injustice: you could stab an enemy and pay your way out of it. Many old enmities boiled up again, and the rich certainly didn't hold back. Paying wergeld was nothing to them, but if they or their sons had personally had to pay with their lives, then they'd have been able to behave themselves.

Edwin had set off a veritable bloodbath with his ideas about peace. Paulinus had put them into his head. Paulinus' vision was to build a Christian realm.

'It's just a passing phase,' said Paulinus. 'That will always be the case during a period of transition.'

When Paulinus' words were quoted at funeral feasts, the ideas of this foreign monk with a clean-shaven circle on the top of his head were greeted with resounding laughter, and planning got underway as to how this particular death should be avenged.

As Hild sat there on the bench in Frigyd's house, invited indoors by the little girl's slayers, every fibre in her body knew that Paulinus' ideas were a betrayal of all human decency. A fantasy, an unnatural and foreign fabrication flouting and pouring scorn on all bonds of kinship and love, dispelling all solidarity between people and making the world a cold and desolate place. Neither land nor silver nor all the treasures on earth, nothing other than blood itself could compensate for Frigyd's blood.

More troops turned up during the day. Some arrived pulling a barrel of beer on a cart, others had brought along a big cask of mead. A pig and a young sheep were caught; there was to be something to suit every taste, and they had already slaughtered the cow. While everything was being made ready for roasting, bread was baked and preparations for a feast got underway.

The young men outside were making a lot of noise and showing off their booty. One of them had gold and silver rings up his entire arm; he had swapped his way to most of them, and he was trying to exchange a fur-lined cloak for a garnet-studded gold ring now in possession of a man from another troop. They negotiated at length, and by mid-afternoon the deal was done—they swapped horses too. The young man couldn't live without that ring, so he'd rather continue the campaign on a scrawny hack.

Hild took her twins in the basket when she went out to bury Frigyd. The old man, her protector, went too, and helped with the digging. Hild would have liked to give Frigyd her favourite stool, but she didn't dare defy Paulinus' warnings about what happened to people who had been buried with grave goods. She could see the sense in this; all those objects would just weigh down the soul and get in the way at the time of resurrection.

Frigyd had been wrapped in a fine cloth, washed and clean for the meeting with her Lord, pale and delicate. The hounds hadn't got as far as her head, there was just a little wound on her chin. Hild placed a thin piece of fabric over Frigyd's face, said the Lord's Prayer and threw soil into the grave in the name of the Father, the Son and the Holy Spirit. Five of the men had come along; their eyes were wet when they shook Hild's hand afterwards, which she could have done without. She went back indoors so she could sit in peace and plot her revenge.

The old man cut a holy cross into shape and put it on the grave. He was glad to do it; it felt homely to have time for that kind of thing, especially after hacking so many to death and just leaving them to the wolves and the ravens.

Their king, Cædwalla, hated the unbelieving foreigners and wouldn't let anyone be buried because—as he said—they were on their way to Hell anyway, and the wolves had to live too.

He was right about that, the old man thought. Not only was he their king, he was right too. Because, apart from this lady and her children, most of them were heathens and worshipped their own forefathers. Worshipped themselves, actually. They turned people into gods, shaped them in wood and stone and sacrificed captives to them. These coarse and savage people, who had spent the last few generations stripping his people of their land with unprecedented cruelty, disgusted him.

Perfidious, they were. What despicable reward had King Edwin given his foster-brother Cædwalla, whose father had taken him in when he was a child. At the royal estate in Aberffraw, Edwin had allowed himself to be marked with the sign of the cross, and had sworn blood fraternity with Cædwalla. But once Edwin had taken power in Northumbria, he had fallen back to the odious practices of the pagans. He had sacrificed Cædwalla's brother, his own foster-brother, to Woden! Hung him from a tree. To buy good fortune.

People in Gwynedd would do anything to erase the memory of Edwin. Their king had invited a viper into his home when he took in and fostered the banished boy.

Now the Lord had punished Edwin. He had let him see his eldest son fall. And if there was any justice in the world, then, on his way to Hell, Edwin had also caught a glimpse of his second son, Eadfrid, surrendering—surrendering to the slayer of his father and his brother. Edwin certainly deserved to see that!

And while mulling this over in his mind, the old man went indoors and made another magic potion for the pitiful young woman.

Cædwalla woke with a jolt, and got up straight away. He shook himself like a dog would, and then he was awake. The declaration went out: the king was awake. The people greeted him with loud cheers.

As he went outside to relieve himself, he walked past Hild, but he didn't see her. His man-at-arms followed him like a shadow. He came back indoors and ate with a good appetite—milky porridge with honey, freshly-baked bread—while the leaders of the newly-arrived troops gave their reports.

Hild looked at his water-blue eyes, almost luminous against pale skin and black hair. She had heard a lot about Cædwalla, even though Edwin had forbidden all mention of his name; the long arm of Edwin's authority couldn't stop people whispering. Hild knew that Edwin had loved Cædwalla with a passion he hadn't harboured for any woman, but blood-brotherhood had turned into enmity. And Cædwalla had thrown himself into his passion for gaming.

Hild was so enraged by Frigyd's death that she completely forgot to concern herself about her own life and her children. The option to prostrate herself before Cædwalla and plead for safe passage to Mercia plus an accompanying entourage simply didn't occur to her. Her thoughts were entirely focused on the possibility that the men would drink themselves into a stupor this evening, and then she could bolt the doors and set fire to the whole lot of them—or might they be smart enough to post sentries? Considering the way they were knocking back the drink, they didn't seem particularly concerned about their enemies. There probably weren't any left in these parts anyway. Except her.

The arrival of these men was the sign she had been waiting for: Eadfrid needed her. His captivity was beset with sorrow and darkness. She knew him so well. Once she had set fire to the thatched roof, she would take two horses and leave.

The men weren't surprised when they saw Hild packing up linen and clothing; they were only surprised that the Lord had kept her safe for so long. She obviously hadn't encountered any kind of hazard, or she wouldn't be wearing that gold holy cross around her neck.

Two more barrels of beer—of unusually fine quality—had turned up. Men with hunger in their eyes crowded the room; skewered above the open fireplace in the middle, Star had become a sizzling roast, making everyone's mouth water—those who hadn't known her, at least.

The pig and lamb were carved and chunks handed round. Hild hadn't tasted fresh meat since she left her home in Mædeltun; she had always been fond of the fatty cuts of mutton, the shoulder and breast. She sat alone, next to the door, and helped herself to plenty, and to the beer and fresh bread. She hadn't been able to give Frigyd such a good meal. She felt the need to put something on Frigyd's grave, in the way they had always done when she was a child—she immediately prayed to her god, asking forgiveness for such a thought.

Hild rubbed a small piece of bread in a drop of beer, and gave it to Wilbrord, who ate it with an astonished expression on his face, looking around to see where it had come from. Hundfrid spat his out, and she couldn't make him eat it. He screamed every time she tried, so she had to place him at her breast. She wasn't too keen on sitting here amongst strangers breastfeeding him like some kind of wetnurse, but she had no other option.

The men showed no surprise. Where they came from it was quite normal for free-women to breastfeed their babies themselves. The young lads found it a little disconcerting; they could almost remember how it felt, the warm stream of sweet milk hitting the roof of your mouth. The memory made them miss the smell of their mothers, and they started shouting and bragging about all their great deeds.

The noisy eating and loud belching that had filled the house was as silence compared with this competition for attention. A roar from Cædwalla, and the only sounds left were the crackling of the fire and Hundfrid's sucking. The men now took it in turns to brag. One by one, they told the tale of a tremendous feat; if they inflated their role too much, the next man took over.

Hild had nothing against hearing about bear hunting and bare-fisted brawling with wolves, which was preferable to hearing about how many of her compatriots they had put to death. She knew most of the names mentioned. Cædwalla's tale was a happy exception. He told them about the successful theft of a week-old eaglet from a rock ledge on Môn. Hild sat with bated breath as she pictured him climbing across the rock face, a stone giving way under his foot. Had a companion not grabbed hold of his belt, he would have plunged into the abyss and certain death. While hovering over the void, he had seen both an angel and the Devil himself, and he had promised he would be a faithful warrior of the Lord. He ended his tale by thanking his god for helping him at that time and particularly now, when he had granted them the good fortune of defeating heathen Northumbria.

When he sat down, the cry rang out: 'Rout the heathen Northumbria!' Everyone stood up and joined in the shouting. They then spent some time toasting their good fortune in battle.

Hild closed her ears when the next story started; it was so dreadful a tale that she had to hum a little tune to Wilbrord. She wasn't sure how much he understood; he picked up everything with his eyes. But when she heard her husband Eadfrid's name, her ears could no longer remain closed.

A stout manservant was recalling the day he took a king's son prisoner. Most of the assembly knew all the details, but enjoyed them all the same and howled with laughter when he imitated Eadfrid's rather delicate voice: 'Spare me, spare me!' And when the man raised his arms in the air and cried out, first to the right, then to the left, 'I surrender! Take me to your king!', the thatch roof nearly took off. They roared with laughter, stamped the floor and hammered their fists on the tables in applause.

Hild bowed her head, her cheeks and eyes aflame. Wilbrord stared fixedly at her. She had tried to obscure the circumstances by telling her children that their father was alive, and by comforting herself with Paulinus' words. But Eadfrid's cowardice couldn't be explained away. Not with a whole year of words.

'While we're on the subject of Eadfrid,' the next man began, and she couldn't block out the sounds, 'the proud prince!' . . . and here he was interrupted by roars of laughter.

'Yes, yes, that's what was said of him until recently, but then I started thinking about his manhood . . .'

This caused much merriment, and the men started talking among themselves, most of them familiar with the story.

'His manhood, yes,' the man continued, louder this time. 'Because it was also said that his wife was expecting. So I was thinking . . . she must have been in such a hurry when they hastened from Mædeltun that she forgot to tie the pillow to her belly!' He looked around in triumph. 'Or maybe she lost it by riding at such speed—and she had to be fast if she wanted to escape us. Because there certainly wasn't any baby in that belly, on that you have my word of honour!'

A murmur of astonishment from the few who hadn't heard the story before, and the man held his head high.

'I was actually one of those who found her and her retinue at the Welburn ford—down here, where we passed by today, it was. So, there they stood, gawping, like they had all the time in the world. But then their fate overtook them, it did. And I'll put my head on the block, I will: there was no babe in that stomach! Nor had any man been in her!'

With these final words he looked around again, with an air of self-importance, and was pleased to note that with just this one sentence he had managed to shed light on the king's son's lack of potency and on his own vigour and experience. He nodded and gave a little shrug before sitting down and accepting the well-deserved drinking horn.

Hild scooped up both babies and forced her way through to the middle of the hall, a raised arm signalling that she wanted to say something. She turned to face the man who had just spoken, lowering her arm to point at his crotch: thumb and three fingers gathered in her palm, middle finger bent; an age-old curse, which might be punished by amputation of the finger or—if the curse worked—the whole hand.

The man grabbed his crotch and shouted for the witch to be sent away, but her voice drowned out his cries.

'This slander will not go unanswered! No vilification can be made of my husband's manhood, and I am holding the very proof: two healthy sons have I borne him—two!'

She held two fingers aloft and was so furious that she didn't notice the old man, her friend, rushing up to the king and whispering in his ear.

'I am Eadfrid's wife, and the maiden you violated was my cousin. And you could have left the plait on her head—cutting the hair from a corpse does no one any credit!'

Turning to the whole assembly, so all could hear, she continued: 'You can say what you will about my husband's fighting spirit. But his manhood will not be besmirched. For it is superior to most!'

And looking at the man who had spoken, she added: 'Yours is a thing of the past, that's for certain.'

Hild returned to her seat by the door. The old man came to fetch her, on the king's command. As they forced their way through the crowd, she still had no inkling that she was in danger. She had spent her entire life under Edwin's protection, and she was unaware that once his protection had gone so too had the order of things she took for granted. She was still angry, and not in the least frightened, when she stepped in front of King Cædwalla—who could end her life with a flick of his finger.

Cædwalla smiled broadly. He was glad to have a little digression from the usual running order. He knew the stories in and out, and even though everyone did their best to serve up something new—as they had been told to—they seldom succeeded. He was bored by these undigested narratives that hadn't passed through the workings of a skilled bard, calling them 'squits'—mediocre tales listing the number of heads and the number of well-aimed spears. Good bardic art, on the other hand, he could listen to for hours, days even, without a moment's boredom, and he rewarded it handsomely. Bards flocked to his court.

The storytellers at these bragging sessions wanted to show themselves in a good light, hoping to win the king's favour. But Cædwalla preferred songs that gathered all the deeds into one big tribute to his leadership. The Lion of Gwynedd, that was him! And he looked forward to getting home and hearing if anyone had made a new song in praise of the lion. Now he had more worldly goods than ever with which to reward them.

This expedition had become tedious. You could hardly call it proper battle anymore. Just run-of-the-mill pillaging, which was boring in the long run. Like living off good fresh pork every day; he missed some seasoning. The demented woman was therefore a welcome diversion; maybe she could tell them something about the misty realm in which she found herself. Delighted, he made the unusual move of proffering his hand, but to his surprise she didn't respond to the royal gesture, acceptance of which would have safeguarded her life, but just stared fixedly at the new ring on his little finger—the ring he had been given by Samson from Caer-Segeint. She was well away in the mists, maybe too far to call back.

It was a lovely ring, thick pale gold, two large oblong garnets inset crosswise. Like glinting lion eyes, Samson had said, and therefore rightfully due the king of Gwynedd. Cædwalla had rewarded him handsomely. It was apparently also a magic ring, given that it had completely paralysed the young stranger, this woman who had been shouting loud enough a few moments ago. He was now even more pleased with Samson's gift, stroking the red stones with his forefinger.

'Do you like my ring?' he asked kindly, disregarding her offensive behaviour in not taking his outstretched hand. She continued to stare at the ring, and he was suddenly intensely annoyed that he couldn't see her eyes. He was overwhelmed by a ferocious need to see the colour of her eyes. They had to be green. Yes, definitely green.

The green eyes of a woman drove him crazy, he was virtually addicted to them. Momentarily forgetting his aversion to nursing women, this straight-backed green-eyed woman took on the aura of a Queen of Saba. He had never worried about madness being transmitted by sex. On the contrary, deranged women held a singular attraction and he'd never yet been infected. Playing with fire was his speciality, his utmost craving, and if there were green eyes under those lowered eyelids, then he wouldn't be alone in his bed tonight.

The woman reached out and grabbed hold of his ring. He gasped, desire rushing through his body. Her conduct was unprecedented.

'That is my ring, give it to me,' she said, lifting calm and steady eyes to look straight at him. They were deep blue.

Blue eyes had never been of any interest to him, but she was still the Queen of Saba. Her eyes were very dark, and he shuddered with delight as he felt himself being sucked down into their dangerous depths of madness. This was the first time he had ever experienced such feelings for a blue-eyed woman, and he was surprised. He wasn't exactly a youngster, he was forty-nine years old, so he'd had about fifteen years more than the usual span, and now, in his old age, it seemed he was indeed going to be obsessed by a pair of blue eyes! Dizzy with joy and munificence, he blissfully abandoned himself to the blue depths and forgot everything around him.

'I demand my ring,' she said, loud and clear.

'Tell me who you are, fair one,' he smiled, 'and then I'll consider your request.'

'Demanding the return of one's rightful property is not a request,' she replied. 'I also demand wergild for Frigyd, ripped to pieces by your hounds. My name is Hildeburh, daughter of Hereric and Breguswid. King Edwin's son Eadfrid is my husband. I am travelling to Mercia and will share his captivity. One request I shall make, however: the provision of horses and attendants for the journey. The ring and the wergild are not requests.'

The old man at her side paled and started to tremble. It had suddenly occurred to him that perhaps she had been speaking the truth all along and, if so, guaranteeing her life with his own was quite a different matter. No one would touch a demented person, they brought misfortune, but if she really was the wife of a prince then things weren't looking at all good for him. He tried to wink at his master and signal that her words shouldn't be taken at face value, but he merely managed a few jerky little movements and a hapless shaking of his head. Cædwalla was far too preoccupied to notice anyway.

'Her words are, of course, untrue,' he finally managed to get out, and attempted to smile persuasively.

The woman turned to him in surprise.

'Why would I speak false words?'

And there was something about her that made him feel the rope tightening around his neck. He was almost certain she was speaking the truth.

Cædwalla snapped his fingers and gave an order to the attendant who had appeared instantaneously. The man fetched a board game and placed it in front of his master.

Hild had never seen so magnificent a gaming board. Elaborately inlaid with the palest straight-grained wood alternating with a deep-brown knotty wood; and different, in that it was raised up on lion's feet carved from a yellowish wood. It was very beautiful, but the gaming pieces were even more astonishing, carved from a twisted unicorn horn. One set of pieces had a thin gold strand inlaid in the twisting, the other a strand of verdigris copper that accentuated the pale cream colour of the unicorn horn.

'You choose the game,' said Cædwalla. 'If you win, you are Hildeburh and will have your company for the journey to Mercia.'

'I want my ring back, too,' said Hild, 'and wergild for Frigyd!'

'You will get what you want, but otherwise you will accompany me!'

A chair was brought for Hild and goblets were filled before the game could start. The men crowded round. Hild didn't know any of the more complicated board games, but when they were children their mother Breguswid had taught them a game she always won: Hare and Hounds it was called, and the hare had to slip past the four hounds. Hild and her sister had taken a year to work out that the hare didn't stand a chance—not, that is, if the she-dogs knew how to play the game.

Hild chose Hare and Hounds in the hope that the game hadn't reached Walas. It had been Breguswid's own invention, from the time before she lost interest in this world and her children.

Unlike most of her compatriots, Hild had no great interest in games or gaming, but this particular one was ingrained in her very marrow. All those eyes watching her every move didn't unsettle her, and there was really only the one way to steer her hounds: in closed ranks. Cædwalla made his moves just as swiftly and with just the mistakes he was meant to, and within no time she had forced him into a corner.

'That was the first round, we'll play three,' said Cædwalla, and turned the board. He steered his hounds forwards as he had seen her do, leaving no openings. Her hare was cornered.

'Third round,' she said calmly, and turned the board. This time he thought out his moves, and twice broke her advance, but she eventually got him in the top corner.

He wasn't angry, which surprised his men because he didn't like to lose, but he stood up with a smile and pulled the gold ring off his little finger. He held it aloft for all to see, before presenting it to Hild with a sweeping gesture.

She received it with an equally sweeping gesture, put it on the third finger of her right hand, held her hand up in the air and the men cheered.

She felt a deep connection with Cædwalla; he had not gone back on his word, even though he had seen through her ploy at the gaming board. She would have done the same. She elbowed her way through the men to the basket where the babies lay, and took out the jawbone she had found in the cave. Wilbrord's cold was much better and, besides, amulets were a bad pagan habit.

She presented the bone to Cædwalla, bowing deeply.

'In gratitude for the entourage that will accompany me to Mercia,' she said, 'and, unless I am very much mistaken, this is the jawbone of a lion!'

Cædwalla's hand trembled as he accepted the gift. He had to place the lion's jawbone on the table and sit down so as not to be utterly overwhelmed.

He already owned a lion's canine tooth, sold to him by a Persian merchant ten years ago. Very expensive, but not too expensive. And on his journey to the land of the Visigoths, King Sisebut's son had given him a dagger as a farewell gift, the sheath covered with lion's pelt, yellowish and bristly. He was the only person in the whole realm to possess lion effects of any kind. Many were envious, so he always carried the objects about his person, clearly visible. He was convinced they were the reason for his good fortune in war. He wore the tooth on a gold chain around his neck, and he knew its shape so well that just one glance at Hildeburh's gift was enough to tell him this was indeed a large portion of lion. He was overcome by gratitude and had no idea what he could do in return. Her ring and her life were so little in comparison. He decided to do what he could to get her husband released from captivity. He would, if necessary, purchase the man's freedom.

Gratitude had completely quenched his desire, which had already cooled somewhat since he had started to doubt the authenticity of her insanity; and had cooled even more when he saw her dispassionate approach to gaming. She was one of those women who give pleasure as an associate. Not a woman for the bed.

'Hildeburh,' he said, with a slight incline of his upper body, 'wife of King Edwin's son Eadfrid, I invite you to accept whomsoever of my men you might consider right and proper wergild for the girl!'

Hild thanked him with equal formality: 'King Cædwalla, Lion of Gwynedd, son of the renowned King Cadfan, I offer gratitude for your good grace! Which, I ask, of the king's men might have presented the king with my ring?'

Cædwalla's eyes flickered, and he hoped that Samson from Caer-Segeint would simply vanish. He abhorred blood revenge, and right now he'd had enough blood to last him for years. He had expected Hildeburh to select a good young freeman as her slave. He was reluctant to abandon Samson to a dishonourable death, and was unable to utter his name; but he stared at him, and at the dark patch spreading across his trousers from the very spot into which Hildeburh had pointed a curse.

Hild followed the direction of Cædwalla's gaze, and homed in on the man, recently so boastful. She saw the expanding damp patch, she walked slowly across to him and was just about to voice her demand when she saw his face turn ashen and drenched in sweat, saw him clasp his chest, and saw him collapse screaming.

'Thank you, Lord Jesus,' she whispered, as the man doubled up on the floor, graceless and convulsive, and breathed his last. The Lord God had granted her vengeance. Now Frigyd and Hild's young cousin could rest peacefully.

She turned to Cædwalla, satisfied.

'I want Tancwoystel, the red-haired young man from Walas. He needs a new cap, by the way. The seam has come apart by his left ear.'

Cædwalla bowed deeply, and ordered Tancwoystel to be brought before him. The young man had spent the evening in the barn, along with his mates, because there wasn't room for everyone in the house.

Cædwalla made a sweeping gesture and declared that if Hild wanted Tancwoystel's life then he would be hanged immediately. This lad, whom he hardly knew, was of no concern to him. He didn't want any scores left to settle with a woman who was clairvoyant and could kill with a glance.

But Hild wanted him alive. She gave him the name Talcuin, with the byname Frigyd-geld, and promised him new clothing. Late in the evening, when she lay down to sleep on the bench, he settled on the floor near her head. From then on he followed her like a shadow.

She set forth the next day on her journey to Mercia, accompanied by an entourage of twenty-four armed men and a letter from Cædwalla to Mercia's commander Penda.

# THE LONGEST TALE

*– how Hild's father died and Edwin became king of Northumbria –*

Hild was two years old when Edwin became king of the two realms that made up Northumbria: Deira north of the river called Humbre, and then Bernicia stretching from the river Tese all the way up to the realm of the Picts.

Bernicia was huge, its hilly and rugged terrain making travel difficult. Three generations back, several kings of the Britons had approached an Angle famed for his expertise in warfare and asked for his help to repel the rampaging Picts and Frisians. The Britons gave the man Bebbanburh on the coast, and under his leadership the enemy was kept in check—as were the Britons themselves, given that the Angle had soon subjugated the whole realm.

Deira had been inhabited by Angles since they had first arrived from across the sea seven generations ago. They had found a pleasant, green and hilly country crisscrossed by becks and rivers, more precipitous than their own fair Angeln on the Baltic coast, but not so different that they couldn't cultivate the soil using their customary methods.

The only problem was the native Britons, grudgingly subjugated and ousted. On the other hand, the clashes provided the Angles with captives aplenty, and the incomers all soon became freemen with Britons as slaves. The royal dynasty in Deira and in Bernicia alike could be traced back to Woden, the mightiest of heroes, their great forefather who granted good fortune in battle or inflicted famine and disease, as fancy took him.

Edwin's father, King Ælle, reigned over Deira. When Edwin was seven years old, news arrived from Bernicia that Ædelfred, a grandson of the skilled battle strategist from Angeln, had overthrown his brother-in-law the king. Ædelfred now demanded to be principal king of Deira, to hold King Ælle's two sons as hostages and to take his eleven-year-old daughter Acha as his bride.

For young Edwin, the day was filled with anxiety; he couldn't work out what was going on. His father was having a meeting with the elders, who had arrived on horseback from all over Deira, and the royal settlement was seething with apprehension. He usually turned to his older sister, Acha, but on that day she stayed in her mother's chamber and no one was allowed to enter except the nurse and servants, who rushed around packing up silver vessels and the very finest red and blue glass. The most beautiful of the wall hangings in the hall were taken down and the whole lot was carried out into the yard and stowed on carts—the same carts that usually came home bearing the spoils of war or the goods paid in taxes—and Edwin didn't understand why all these things were now being loaded up and sent away. He wandered around in a state of perplexity, until finally he found his eighteen-year-old brother Eadfrid in the stables, getting the horses ready; Edwin tugged doggedly at his brother's tunic until the older lad led him into a corner and explained the situation.

'There's no need to be frightened,' said Eadfrid. 'The council of elders won't accept any of it, and then we'll be off to battle!' It would be the first real battle he'd taken part in, and he couldn't wait.

Edwin didn't understand much of what Eadfrid was saying, but he felt a little reassured. He stayed with his brother for the rest of the day. Acha was still locked away. Then his wetnurse came to fetch him, and she dressed him in her son's shabby clothes. He was instructed to sit among the lowest ranks at table and absolutely not reveal his true identity.

Edwin's parents had pale faces when they entered the hall. Acha sat in the place of honour alongside the envoy from Bernicia; she was dressed like an adult woman. She deported herself with an air of importance that was completely new. Just once, she gave Edwin a quick little wave and looked as if she had momentous things to report.

King Ælle stood up and announced the decision of the council: they would gladly acknowledge King Ædelfred's peaceful neighbourliness and they asked him to accept the princess as a sign of their friendship.

Acha blushed when all eyes turned to her, but then she held her head high and smiled proudly to everyone in the hall. Edwin was on the brink of leaping up from the bench to join in Acha's happiness—she had always shared everything with him—but his nurse held him back.

King Ælle continued his speech. He and his wife took great pleasure in complying with Ædelfred's request to welcome their eldest son into his residence as well.

Edwin saw his brother bow his head.

Young Edwin would follow later, Ælle said, providing fate spared him; his frailty would not permit the long journey to Bernicia. They hoped he would survive the winter.

Edwin stared at his nurse. She put an arm around his shoulders and pulled him in tightly to her copious bosom, the safest place in the world. He suddenly felt at death's door.

'I'm going to be sick,' he said, and she took him out of the hall.

'Now you know how the land lies,' said the nurse. 'You'll be going to your mother's sister in Gwynedd.'

Edwin's entourage was saddled and ready. His mother came outside and gathered him into her arms. She would come and visit as soon as the unrest had settled down.

Then Acha came out, her new status already giving her greater poise. She handed Edwin her favourite doll; he had always envied her that doll. Below the edge of her adult headdress, her eyes had an unfamiliar shine, but when she picked him up and pinched his bottom, she was suddenly her old self again.

'So I'll be the queen of Bernicia,' she laughed, 'and you'll come to visit me in Bebbanburh!'

She danced a few steps with her little Edwin, as she called him, and then King Ælle came out into the yard and placed a hand on his son's shoulder.

'They can teach you to be a great warrior in Gwynedd. When the time is ripe, you will return.'

Edwin was lifted into a rush basket on the flank of a horse, and the last he heard was Acha shouting excitedly: 'Come and visit me in Bebbanburh, little Edwin, come and visit me in Bebbanburh!'

Edwin never spoke about his childhood, but Acha's words echoed in his ears until the day he died. He knew he had to avenge the wrong done to her and all his kin.

His older brother had been obliged to marry Ædelfred's crazy sister; she had been less than straightforward with him, and he'd had to endure many a taunt when a baby arrived three months after the wedding. But he had loved that baby, and defiantly insisted he was the father; he had nothing else that was his, in his exile, and he didn't see much of Acha. He named this son Hereric, and the boy would grow up to father Hild.

Acha was pale and shed tears during her wedding feast; the king she was to marry wasn't as she had imagined. He was big and stocky, drank a lot of mead and spoke in a loud voice. His right hand was stiff and twisted and looked like a dead bird's claw. His head only had a scanty covering of hair. Cutting across his forehead and down into his eyebrow, he had an irregular welt that had damaged his right eye and made his face lopsided. He proudly guided his bride's fingers along the jagged battle scar and laughed loudly when she pulled her hand away in alarm. He ate an extraordinary amount of food and grunted as he stuffed his mouth and stomach with roast meat, swilling it down from the drinking horn. He leant back and belched loudly and methodically, counting out the belches in a blaring voice. When he reached five, he got stuck back into the food and drink.

Acha stared at the mountain of flesh that was her bridegroom; she quickly looked away, disgusted by the sight of so many greasy chunks of meat disappearing down his throat. Her father was a handsome man, and she had thought other kings would be like him.

Acha's predecessor, Bebba, upon hearing that her husband had slain her kingly brother, had plunged to her death from the fortress she had been given as a morning gift. She had left just the one son, so it suited Ædelfred well to have a new and very young wife. He wanted lots of children.

He therefore defied time-honoured custom and took her that very first night. Even though she screamed and cried out for her wetnurse and her father and mother, he pinned her down and forced himself into the narrow opening between her thin thighs. He was used to women screaming, and he was proud to have a wife with temperament. Her resistance and the dark glances she gave him during the day were irresistibly arousing; he hadn't felt in such good shape since he was seventeen.

The nurse gave the young queen a bottle of flaxseed oil and taught her how to daub it between her legs; but Acha was having none of it and flung the bottle away.

'I want to go home,' she shouted. 'I want to go home to Eoforwik!' And she wept some more and called out for her mother and her little Edwin.

She eventually accepted the nurse's guidance, and was then able to walk and stand and sit. The sensation of having a hedgehog up her crotch disappeared, but not her aversion to her husband and his intrusive shaft. She'd have to learn to live with that, said her nurse.

No children were forthcoming. No curves appeared on Acha's body; no breasts, no hips, and no menstruation. Her brother had already produced three children with Ædelfred's sister before Acha had her first woman's bleeding. The blood came as a great relief—once she was pregnant, days could pass between his 'riding trips' as he called them, and she was left alone completely for the final fortnight. Acha was seventeen when she gave birth to her first child. He was far too big for her body, and she was in labour for three days. But it became easier year by year, and eventually she gave birth as effortlessly as if she were simply relieving herself.

Edwin also shed many tears. When he and his entourage arrived at the Aberffraw royal estate on the island of Môn, he refused to climb from the basket and he ordered his men to return to Eoforwik. He screamed when they lifted him out, and thereafter he cried himself to sleep every night. It took a few months before he stopped calling out for Acha and his mother.

He never let on how much his aunt reminded him of his mother; if he closed his eyes, her voice was almost his mother's voice. He slipped away from any attempt she made to touch him, and he sat mute and hunched whenever she was nearby. But he stole a scarf from her chamber, and kept it with him at all times. He didn't bat an eyelid when his aunt's handmaid was sent packing, blamed for the theft. Every last one of them could disappear for all he cared, except his mother's sister—and, after a while, his foster-brother Cædwalla.

Edwin didn't know that his foster-parents had given wilful Cædwalla a choice: he could either take the despondent little boy in hand or he could be sent to the king of Elmet, a realm held by the Britons, for his upbringing. Cædwalla, who was only interested in birds of prey and knew all their haunts around the royal estate, had chosen the lesser of two evils. Now he had to take Edwin along on his expeditions hunting for birds' eggs and chicks, up in the highest branches, out on the sheerest cliffs.

During the first year, Edwin didn't leave a single nest untouched, even though Cædwalla thrashed him for doing so. But gradually he made do with imagining how he would come back and fling every little twig and every blade of grass into the abyss; and sometimes he did just that. Cædwalla could always see it on him afterwards—they had become so close—and then they would fight, with a savage love, and wouldn't stop until the blood flowed or one of them begged for mercy. They were an even match, as Cædwalla was slightly built.

When they were older, their brawls were caused by a new interest—girls—until the day Cædwalla hit his head on a rock and didn't get up. Edwin sat by the bed until Cædwalla's spirit returned. And then they vowed that nothing, not the most beautiful woman, not gold or falcons or saddle horses, nothing at all would ever come between them. To seal their pact, each drew a blade along his wrist and they made a blood oath.

Cædwalla's appetite for girls was greater than Edwin's. To Edwin's eyes, none was as beautiful as Acha. Whoever he was looking at, it was always Acha's image that glowed within him. But he didn't even tell his blood-brother about his mother's loveliness: the softness of her lap; the scent in his nostrils when he burrowed his face into her hair; her clear voice; her easy laughter filling the whole settlement with the sound of sunshine. She died the year he was sent to Gwynedd, three months after the death of her husband Ælle.

When Edwin turned sixteen, he was sent into the service of a king in Mercia, and this king's eldest daughter, Cwenburh, became his wife; her younger sister, Breguswid, married Edwin's nephew Hereric. Breguswid and Hereric named their children Hereberht, Hereswid and Hildeburh.

Edwin was so taken by Hereric that he almost forgot about Cædwalla. He had found his lineage again and, what was more, he was now his seven-year-younger nephew's brother-in-law. He named his second son Eadfrid after his brother—Hereric's father—and hoped he would be more energetic and active than his brother had been.

The two brothers-in-law sat together for nights on end, hatching plans. Hereric would help Edwin take back Deira, and they'd take Bernicia too while they were at it.

Edwin didn't know much about Bernicia, but Hereric's tales whetted his appetite. The spring and autumn festivals there lasted seventeen days, with competitions in the use of all sorts of weaponry and who could jump and swim furthest, drink most, run and ride fastest. However, yuletide was the best, as it wasn't the orgy of drunkenness and whoring that it had become in many places—neither activity holding any great interest for Edwin. At yuletide in Bernicia, they held bardic tournaments lasting far into the new year. The best bards gathered in Ad Gefrin by the river Glene, and the record for the longest tale was held by an old woman from Magilros. She'd talked three sittings of listeners to sleep with an uninterrupted tale lasting three days and two nights before she had collapsed.

Competitors were allowed to eat, as long as they carried on with their story between each mouthful; they could also relieve themselves, if the listeners went out with them and the break was no longer than thirty breaths. What was more, the story had to be good and listeners weren't to fall asleep because of boredom. Many bards were booed off when they started repeating themselves or drivelling on about things that were of no interest to anyone.

It didn't matter if the listeners already knew the story. Suspense was but heightened by fresh examples of the giants' extraordinary stupidity, or a new take on what Brynhild had said when she realized that Sigurd was the man to whom she had sworn fidelity, back in the days when she was young, and now she'd married someone else.

It wasn't just a matter of choosing a different word, but of coming up with something that could make the story even more dreadful and heartrending. If the listeners wept or laughed, the time was added to the total. The most skilled bards could jump nimbly between the various phases of Brynhild's discovery of Sigurd's deceit and her final act of vengeance, making the listeners doubt or sometimes even fight about whether or not an incident had already been narrated. A quarrel in the audience would give the storyteller a little breather, but it was also risky—you might then be booed off.

The oldest listeners had priority; they were in the first group, then they could have a sleep while the next sitting listened, and wake up to hear the part where it got really exciting. A tale seldom lasted for more than two days and one night. Hereric had himself taken part in these bardic tournaments, both as listener and as storyteller. But, he had to admit, he'd been too young.

Edwin loved stories, and the thought of being able to sit and listen for days on end fired him up to conquer Bernicia—none of the realms he had visited held that kind of bardic tournament.

Once he got Bebbanburh under control, he would hold them, that was for sure, oh yes he'd hold bardic tournaments all right, and they wouldn't be forgotten in a hurry. Along with Hereric, he'd make Northumbria the gathering place for the best bards and entertainers and storytellers in these isles. They would never be able to outstrip the southern realms in richness from the land—his soil was too acid and poor, he'd seen for himself how the corn grew in Kent and in the fields of the South Saxons and the West Saxons—but in the art of poetry they would be triumphant, Hereric and him.

Edwin often abandoned himself to reverie. Hild's mother, Breguswid, thought Edwin probably cared more for his dreams than for reality and therefore he hesitated to put them into effect. His actual reality was something he conjured up during the night, she said, and then during the day he found things so grey and commonplace.

But Hereric knew what had to be done. He planned his own and Edwin's trips to visit the kings who would support them in winning back Northumbria. Ædelfred had many enemies, he was getting too powerful.

It was on one of these journeys that Hereric met his fate. After lengthy negotiations, he had convinced the king of Elmet that Edwin was the man of the new era. The king had promised his support, provided Edwin got the mighty King Rædwald of the East Angles on his side.

The king of Elmet had been very cautious during Hereric's stay. He thought he knew which of his people were spies for Ædelfred—but that's where he had been wrong. When Ædelfred heard what was brewing, he sent his men to deal with the situation. They hadn't had to spell anything out for the king of Elmet; his eyes darted between the guests from Bernicia and a crumpled Hereric, squirming on the floor in spasms and a desperate attempt to spit out the poison. At that moment, the king realized that Elmet's geographical position didn't lend itself to political experimentation, and Ædelfred's men returned home without having to take any further action.

Elmet wasn't a major player, but East Anglia was, and Edwin stayed there for quite a while, drumming up support for his cause. King Rædwald wouldn't be tricked like that, and anyway his security measures were the best in the whole land. He had many enemies.

Ædelfred therefore offered Rædwald three bushels of gold to hand over Edwin, five bushels of pure silver, a white bearskin from the North and a bushel of the big and much sought-after Bohemian garnets—an exquisite batch that had just arrived: red as blood and large enough to be cut into slivers and inlaid in jewellery and weapons.

Nothing went so well with gold as garnets, and nothing was so beneficial for fortunes in war. If you stared at a garnet-studded sword and took a deep breath, its potency entered your blood and a red mist engulfed your eyes. Then you were certain to go into a frenzy, rushing forward and not stopping until the red mist was replaced by actual foaming blood. Rædwald always used garnets before battle to work himself into a rage. His weapons and horse tack were densely studded with the red stones, of which he owned many, but he had never thought he owned enough, nor did he have enough gold and silver, even though he had more than anyone.

What really preyed on his mind was the thought of being able to hang a white bearskin above his seat in the hall—that was an offer you only got once in a lifetime. He'd heard that white bears were found in the furthest reaches of the North, far bigger than their own brown bears, and far far more dangerous. But the only single piece of white bear he'd ever seen was a claw belonging to the king of Dyfed, who'd had it inlaid in the hilt of his sword and no one had since survived an encounter with *that* weapon.

Rædwald's nights were full of dreams about the enormous white bearskin. He would have huge garnets put into the beast's eye sockets, he would put a gold chain around its neck and maybe a shackle on its one foot, to show he had subjugated the creature. One claw would enhance his sword, and perhaps one would adorn his helmet, at the front, between his eyes. Or should he use two, one on either side at the top? Or a little lower down, closer to his temples?

Rædwald was already leading his men, the bear claws fixed to his helmet, and he let out a roar as he rushed forwards, sword held aloft—and was woken by his wife Rægenhild, who had been disturbed by his bellowing.

She lashed out at the mare riding his chest, striking him three times. She leapt out of bed and walked around it three times with her besom, while muttering a formula to Loki asking for the mare to be recalled—it was jumping on her husband at night with increasing frequency.

'What has it pressed into you?' she asked.

Rædwald wouldn't say; he was quite familiar with his wife's thoughts on that topic. He considered telling her it wasn't a matter of killing Edwin or handing him over, just a question of leaving a tiny little chink open for Ædelfred's men, but he had lived with Rægenhild for twenty years.

'Is it Ædelfred's offer, is that what's bothering you?'

He couldn't reply yes or no, as he'd never once been able to deceive her. He closed his eyes and imagined his own burial: his wife and children and retainers and all sorts of bigwigs stood, screaming, in a circle around his sword-slashed body outstretched on a large long-haired white pelt. The bearskin. Stories would be told about that.

He had unfortunately given up the possibility of grave goods, having recently been baptized to the new god while visiting Cantwaraburh. Grave clothes or something to lie on weren't forbidden, though—well, at least he hadn't heard they were.

He just needed that bearskin so badly. He simply wouldn't be able to live for more than half a year without it. Not one man in the whole land owned such a pelt. He trembled at the thought of drawing his fingers through the long stiff pile, white and quivering, perhaps twice as thick as the fur of their own bears. He could already smell beast of prey in his nostrils, pungent and rancid, and couldn't stop a moan escaping.

Rægenhild sat on the edge of the bed, staring into space. Her husband had become a man whose word and hospitality could not be trusted. His vanity had made him forsake everything that gave human life coherence. He had insulted their forefathers' fidelity to the gods by following this alien god—a new whim from Kent. Power had gone to his head, so he now thought a man could make his own laws and disregard what their forefathers had held in respect. By so doing he undermined his own power and dignity; lacerated the bonds that joined people together and united the whole realm. It was the beginning of the end. And he was dazzled by his greed for power.

She rose from the bed and stood in front of him.

'I tell you, Rædwald, I had never thought I'd be wife to a knave. If you wait just one more day to spurn Ædelfred's impertinence, you will no longer find me here!'

'But he's threatening war, Rægenhild!' Rædwald never liked admitting he had been mistaken.

'Is he really?' Rægenhild's eyes narrowed in contempt—that was surely the most pathetic attempt to explain something away she had yet heard from her husband.

'Yes, yes, well, as you wish,' Rædwald mumbled, turning over with a grunt.

The delegation from Northumbria had to get a move on when they found out Rædwald had summoned his men. King Ædelfred was always campaigning against someone—either Mercia, the Picts, the Irish to the west or some other Britons—and sometimes his men were fighting on several fronts at once. Rædwald's best chance was to take them by surprise.

Most surprised of all was Edwin, over his case taking such an abrupt turn. He wandered around in a haze and couldn't sleep at night, and that was when his nightly discussions with Breguswid began. Following Hereric's death, she had come to join Edwin, as he was her late sister Cwenburh's widowed husband and now her closest family. Her three children were happy in East Anglia; they stood alongside Rægenhild and all of Rædwald's household waving to the men when they set forth. Whereupon all the children rushed out to play battle games.

Rædwald and Edwin met King Ædelfred by the Idle river in Mercia. Ædelfred hadn't marshalled even half of his forces. When the armies were deployed and were waiting for the signal to attack, Rædwald rode across to Edwin.

'That white bearskin of Ædelfred's—I'd like to see it in Rendlæsham, as thanks for helping you!'

Edwin would have given anything for Northumbria—his wife, his children, his right arm. Everything except Acha, his beloved Acha. He was taking revenge for her as he hacked his way through Ædelfred's men. She had been dead for six years. She had reached the age of thirty, by which time she had long since learnt to live with her loathing of her husband, but to Edwin she was still the tender eleven-year-old girl with the shining eyes. The girl who had laughed to him, lifted him in the air and given him her best doll as a parting gift.

The doll was his token of Acha's love, his only tangible tie to the world and the assignment that had been placed on his shoulders, a child's shoulders. He treated it like a relic, and not even his children were allowed to touch it. Tucked under his chainmail, on the left-hand side, it wasn't in the way but would protect him and bring him good fortune in the battle.

It did just that, quite literally. An arrow penetrated Edwin's armour, its head was blocked by the hard oakwood body of the doll, and when the news that Edwin was invincible spread among Ædelfred's men—that he was fighting on with an arrow in his chest—they knew there was sorcery involved, and many fled.

Once his entire personal troop had been slain, Ædelfred too was killed. Rædwald had lost eighty-seven men; one of the fallen was his fourteen-year-old son.

One hundred and forty-eight of Ædelfred's men had fallen; nearly one hundred swords were retrieved, and the slain men provided unusually rich pickings of gold and silver. Rædwald smiled when he thought about the wisdom of his wife's words; all this far exceeded Ædelfred's offer, and even more could be expected when they moved on throughout the land. What was more, the wool up here was of better quality than they were used to back home.

Cloaks and tunics and hose were salvaged too, making the clearing-up easier for the ravens who had alighted on the ground during the first din of battle—a flock of hoarsely screeching spectators. It was said they had flown along from East Anglia once they had seen the empty carts roll out.

Rædwald and his men accompanied Edwin all the way up to Bebbanburh, encountering next to no resistance on the way. Now the realm was his, Edwin would have preferred them to refrain from running amok, but he kept that to himself—a spot of looting was the least he could allow the men from the south in return for their help. And Northumbria proved to be a wealthy kingdom; it hadn't been plundered for a long time.

They didn't find the white bearskin. Ædelfred's family and household had moved northwards and must have taken it with them. Rædwald couldn't hide his disappointment, and Edwin promised himself he would get hold of it even if it meant conquering the Picts' entire realm. He had yet to learn just how doggedly the Picts held onto their land.

Edwin's first undertaking in Bernicia was to make a sacrifice at Acha's grave; he knelt in front of the mound and wept for the first time since he had been eight years old.

'Here I am, finally come to visit you, dear Acha,' he said over and over.

Maybe he was just as overwhelmed by the emotion of so suddenly achieving the goal of his dreams. He'd had no idea Bernicia was such a beautiful country. For some strange reason, he'd never tried to picture the landscape up here—just the fortresses and royal settlements, grand halls and bardic tournaments, not the endless swathes of forest, gentle hills and long, long valleys.

The beech was the only tree already in leaf when they rode up through the kingdom, and its intense light greenness was a shock to Edwin's senses. He felt as if he had never seen a beech forest before. It took him unawares. Bernicia made him feel like a jealous lover, suspicious, alert.

Before setting out on the return journey, Edwin's entourage held a large sacrificial ritual as was befitting after such a rewarding campaign.

Rædwald chose Ædelfred's estate at Ad Gefrin as the best setting. It was situated slightly inland from the coast, by the river Glene, and bonfires blazed on all the beacon hills for three days and three nights to signal that the lines of communication had been re-established and a new era under a new king had begun.

Edwin would have preferred to do without human sacrifices. His Welsh foster-family had been Christians for several generations, and he had also been influenced by what he had heard in Kent and by the priests in East Anglia. He thought a couple of oxen and some of the booty would have been sufficient, but he didn't want to clash with Rædwald—after all, he had him to thank for his kingship.

Rædwald was fully aware the new god didn't like human sacrifice, but he wasn't thanking this new god for the victory. He owed his thanks to Tiw and Woden. No one surpassed the old gods when it came to fortune in battle; this new one was more about securing eternal life.

He personally selected three of the best captives for the ritual—the kind who could only be overpowered if five or six men circled them with their shields pressed together. One of the three was a warrior from Ædelfred's personal troop, and it suited him fine to follow his lord; he hadn't wanted to look anyone in the eye since his king had been slain.

The other two were princes of the Britons: a red-haired northerner from Rheged and a black-haired Welshman from Gwynedd. Extremely handsome men, they had been Ædelfred's vassals and had only turned up as the battle was drawing to a close. Their horses would also be sacrificed. Woden, in particular, appreciated horses.

It was a beautiful sight: the red-haired prince on his chestnut stallion and the black-haired prince, dressed in black, on his pitch-black gelding; standing between them, the fair-haired and uncommonly robust warrior, clad entirely in white.

Afterwards, Edwin was glad he'd let Rædwald have his way. No finer sacrificial ritual had been seen in living memory. Now he could be certain the gods would help him rule this extensive kingdom.

Edwin was a harsh king in Bernicia. In Deira, on the other hand, which he knew and to which he was rightfully entitled after his father, he went about things in a gentler fashion; he had confidence in the people's loyalty here, almost as a matter of course. But in Bernicia he saw conspiracies everywhere, and many a freeman was executed under suspicion of wanting Ædelfred's kin back in power. Edwin missed Hereric and his innate political talent. He had trouble trying to work everything out for himself.

When Edwin's strategic and political deliberations met an impasse, he summoned Breguswid. A manservant would fetch her from her bed, and she would hurry to Edwin, who sat staring into the fire. Having sent everyone else away, he would whisper to her: 'What do you think Hereric would have done?'

He explained the various pros and cons in detail, any recent shifts in the balance of power here or there, regions weakened by a bad harvest, new alliances and marriages, all the connections between mighty men, be they the source of dispute or of mutual support.

Breguswid lacked Hereric's flair for politics, and as the years went by she became increasingly detached from the world; but that was of no consequence to Edwin. The important thing for him was that she was Hereric's widow and as such had a direct link to his astuteness and know-how. Breguswid usually replied that she would have to sleep on it. Next day, having in deepest secret consulted with her daughters, she could advise the king. She relied heavily on her two daughters, trusting their judgement: they had her memory and their father's strategic mindset. Sometimes, if very tired, she would rouse one of the daughters and take her along to the king; he would barely notice the girl sitting there, supposedly asleep. A yawn or a stretch signalled to her mother that more information was needed, and then Breguswid would have to see if she could elicit the missing pieces.

Hild and Hereswid had thus acquired intimate knowledge of the political and financial affairs of the kingdom, and they developed an unerring awareness of what was possible and what was not possible. They hadn't advised Edwin to embark on great campaigns of conquest westward—that had been Paulinus' strategy, thinking the realm should be of an imposing size before it could be turned into a model Christian territory.

Breguswid's death put an end to the girls' counsel. They had looked on with concern as increasing numbers of freemen fled up to the Picts, to Mercia, Gwynedd, Rheged, Dalriada and the other neighbouring territories controlled by the Britons. As Edwin's policies became harsher, the realms wishing to escape the burden of his taxes grew all the stronger. They welcomed all exiles, and had by now become so numerous that they had succeeded in throwing off Edwin's yoke.

Edwin and Paulinus might well have created an almost perfect kingdom on earth, but in so doing they had allowed their enemies to outgrow them. And now they had grown so huge that they had smashed the whole of Northumbria to pieces.

# PLAGUED BY DEMONS

*– Eadfrid in Mercia –*

When Hild and her entourage came over the crest of the final hill before Tamoworthig and saw Penda's royal estate below, bathed in the last pink winter light, her heart lurched and she wanted to spur her horse to a gallop and roar Eadfrid's name across the landscape.

She saw the gate open and people come out, but he wasn't among them. Penda's wife bid her welcome, Penda wasn't home. Hild asked her to provide a wetnurse for her babies, where was her husband?

They led her across to a guest outhouse on the periphery of the settlement. A man was sitting in the darkest corner, but it wasn't Eadfrid.

They closed the door and left her alone with this stranger. He stretched out a hand to her. She took a step forwards and gazed at the blue eyes in the lean face. Everything shattered when she recognized her husband.

He didn't stand up to greet her. He waited until she had walked across to him and then grabbed her hand. He lowered his head and wept.

She wanted to help him up; it wasn't seemly to sit on the floor crying. She got him up on his feet. He stood weeping onto her shoulder.

'I'm here now,' she said, 'with your two sons. Everything will be fine now.'

She couldn't bear to see him like this.

'Everything is over,' he responded.

'Hundfrid and Wilbrord are longing for their father,' she said.

He gazed at her and shook his head. She had to send for the babies. It was only when he actually saw them that he believed her. He beamed with proud wonder.

'Hundfrid looks like you,' said Hild, 'and Wilbrord is just like your brother Osfrid.'

Eadfrid's face darkened at the mention of his slain brother's name.

'Osfrid, Osfrid, Osfrid,' he murmured. 'Osfrid!' he shouted, punching the wall.

Hild knew full well why Osfrid hadn't found peace in his grave and continued to plague his brother. She shouldn't have spoken his name.

'Eadfrid,' she said loudly, 'you now have two sons, and they will help us avenge your family.'

Eadfrid glanced at the infants and gestured to the slave Talcuin that he should take them back to their wetnurse.

'Cædwalla will help us get you released,' said Hild. 'I bring a letter from him to Penda.'

'Cædwalla?' Eadfrid scoffed. 'Help us?!'

Hild took out the letter. He grabbed it and threw it in the fire. She leapt forward, pulling it swiftly from the flames, but it kept burning.

'So you've lain with Cædwalla, have you!' Eadfrid shouted and gripped her wrists. 'Better with that lion, was it?'

Hild didn't understand what had happened to her husband, the way he was glaring at her, his eyes almost popping out of his head. She wrenched herself free from his grasp.

Not much of the letter had survived. She examined the remains, but couldn't bring herself to throw the scraps back into the flames.

'So that was the letter to Penda,' she said, as if they had shared responsibility for an accident.

'The upstart!' Eadfrid sneered.

Hild couldn't take her eyes off the sooty fragments that should have brought them freedom.

'Just look at it!' she said.

'So you think Penda is open to persuasion, do you?' Eadfrid's voice oozed contempt.

'He's a human being, isn't he,' she retorted angrily.

'That's more than can be said of you,' he yelled. 'Scurrying all over the place, sucking up to this and that king while your husband is left here to rot!'

Hild couldn't believe her own ears.

'What are you talking about?'

'Why didn't you come immediately? Was it that lion, kept you busy all that time, did he?'

'I don't know what has come over you, Eadfrid!'

She turned away from him. Now she felt no desire to tell him what had happened.

'He was perhaps better than your husband? You just couldn't get enough, could you? Couldn't let him go?'

He had grabbed hold of her again, but this time she couldn't get away. He pushed her down onto the bed, loosened his hose with his free hand and forced himself into her.

She could have shouted, could have called out for her slave, but that would have been too humiliating. Both for Eadfrid and for her own pride. So she kept silent and let him have his way, even though the act itself was forbidden given that she had breastfed the babies right up to this very day. Anxiety about breaking that taboo was almost worse than the pain and the mortification he was inflicting.

This was not how she had imagined the reunion with her husband.

Hild didn't spend as much time with the babies as she would have liked; Eadfrid became anxious if she was away from him for too long.

She had asked for the services of a wetnurse, and of course it was of paramount importance that the infants were thriving, but when Hundfrid had tummy ache and would only be comforted by his nurse, it felt like a stab to her heart.

The nurse brought the children across every morning. But when Eadfrid was in *that* mood, the visit would be very brief.

'My husband is in agony with toothache,' said Hild. Next day the nurse came with a little bag of herbs to place on the tooth; Eadfrid flung the bag into the fire.

Hild explained to the nurse that her husband never consumed anything other than the meals served in the hall. Not that they suspected her, but that was how he preferred it now. In these times, you couldn't be careful enough. The wetnurse nodded and hurried away with the babies.

'Fool!' Hild snapped at him once they were alone.

Eadfrid was on his feet.

'Who do you think you are, spewing out all that tosh about toothache. You are the most meddlesome female creature I have ever come across!'

'Can't you get it into your head—we don't want people saying you're just stretched out here brooding!'

'Well, what people might say is my concern, isn't it. And the more you interfere, the worse it'll get.'

'But don't you understand?'

'Why don't you look after your own affairs? Don't you think you've ruined enough for me?'

'I haven't the slightest idea what I could have ruined for you!'

'Oh, so you don't know?'

'No, on my honour, I don't know.'

He walked right up to her and hissed in her face: 'Was it not you who came running and couldn't leave me alone the night before battle?'

'I just wanted to say goodnight.'

'And for you there's only one way to say goodnight, isn't there?'

Eadfrid's voice was menacing. He had nearly reached the point she had come to fear.

'On my oath, Eadfrid, I wanted nothing other than to say goodnight.'

'And so you rub yourself all over me like a wheedling kitten and offer yourself like some hussy!'

'I'm your wife, Eadfrid. And it is not seemly to speak to me in that way.'

'Nor is it seemly to offer yourself when your son is just about to be born! Or do you think it is?'

'Listen to what I'm saying—I simply wanted . . . '

'Or to drain your husband of all the strength he needs for battle? You think that's perfectly seemly, do you?' he shouted, grabbing her firmly by the wrists.

'Of course I don't think that, and it wasn't meant like that, as well you know!'

'You meant and you meant! Full of waffle you are!'

With these words, he flung her against the wall and left.

As the weeks passed, Hild's body became heavier and heavier. Sometimes her legs could hardly carry her, and she had trouble raising her arms. She was bearing a heavy burden of guilt. She gazed at the trees and knew that all she could do in her defence was to explain things away; shameful attempts to avoid staring the truth in the face.

She was the cause of Eadfrid's misfortune: her recklessness, her wantonness, her amorousness and her lack of forethought. Not that she had come asking for it, because the possibility simply hadn't occurred to her, but when it had happened, she had enjoyed it. And when she really thought it all through, then she had always been someone who put herself first.

Yes, she had enjoyed his embraces, which she had long been obliged to do without, and it hadn't for a second crossed her mind that he wouldn't have strength for the battle next day. No matter how deep she dug, there wasn't one single excuse for her thoughtlessness.

She simply wished she could have borne the punishment alone, without it affecting Eadfrid, her own husband. For that was the harshest punishment: watching her husband disintegrate before her very eyes, day by day, fading more and more, torn to pieces by indignation, tears, rage, self-pity, contrition, resignation and pure madness.

The demons were wrestling with each other to have a stab, and there was room for them all. She tried to hold them at bay, but they kept on coming and she was no match for them. They were the stronger.

'I don't understand why you've brought the children with you,' said Eadfrid. 'Why didn't you find a foster-family for them in Deira?'

'I couldn't,' Hild retorted.

She was almost at the end of her tether, all his sowing of doubt about her decisions. He could even criticize the way she had played when she was a little girl, her close relationship with her sister, the way her mother spoke. No stone was left unturned; her family and everything she had ever done were dissected and held up as early signs of her pride and deep-rooted selfishness.

He was right, time and again he was right, but her body froze when he started digging around in the past. She was so acutely aware that, regardless of what had happened and why, there was only one path to follow now, and that path went forwards.

'I don't want my sons growing up without liberty,' Eadfrid pressed on. 'You must ensure they return to Deira.'

'But Deira is not at peace.'

'Nonsense! There's no more conflict than usual.'

'We don't even know who's still there,' she protested.

'Our people do not retreat in the face of someone like Cædwalla,' Eadfrid insisted, 'a beast from the wilderness!'

'Well, it doesn't matter anyway,' she said, 'because the children are staying here.'

She had been accustomed to discussing every little thing with Eadfrid. Now it was virtually impossible. He didn't listen to her, or he instantly twisted her words into an attack on what she had meant. Nothing was straightforward any longer. Everything could be turned into its opposite, and nearly always ended up in violent criticism of her and her family. She couldn't recognize herself in the woman her husband was constantly belittling; she sat alongside her body while it was being drenched by his vilification.

She couldn't recognize him either—just occasionally, and that was what made it so painful. Then he would beg her forgiveness for the wrong he had done her, but she wouldn't talk about it, now it was over and done with, and they discussed everything, like they used to, and Hild was so happy to have him back that she instantly forgot what it had been like the day before. And he was upright and dignified and spoke in a clear voice. They could laugh too, and when they lay together she felt desire for his body, an abandoned lust for him that she hadn't felt before. She threw herself joyfully into his arms, surrendered herself and showered him with caresses. Then she felt sure the evil providence had vanished; they could soon go home to their estate in Mædeltun.

Such closeness, however, was always followed by the rage, returning with greater and greater force. After a few months, she was frightened to lie with him. The sunny days were always followed by the dark days. But she couldn't stop herself. Closeness with him was the only thing that could assuage the intense privation she suffered on the dark days. All he had to do was take hold of her with his familiar, firm arms and all the grief evaporated like dew before the sun, and she sang lustily and talked about the sunshine outside and the days getting longer and longer; she invented new patterns to weave and embroidered birds and intertwining flowers on his tunic.

He had hit her in the face. For the first time since they were children, he had hit her in the face. And for the first time, it was impossible to ignore yesterday.

Talcuin, her slave, had to fetch food. She couldn't show herself in the hall, with the red-and-purple swelling. She knew how many days an eye like that could last.

'Hild,' said Eadfrid, sitting down on the bed, which she rarely left at the moment. 'You've got to help me get away from here, I can't take any more.'

She sat up.

'Everything's going wrong,' he said, putting his head in his hands. 'Something has taken away my powers. You have to get me out of here!'

'Yes,' she said, taking his hand.

'May the Lord forgive me for what I have done to you,' he said quietly. 'And Lord grant me a time to make it up to you.'

He wept without knowing. He brushed away the tears running down his cheeks as if he were scratching an itch, but they kept on coming.

They started eating in the hall again. Hild held her head high and looked calmly into all the eyes staring at her. Her mother would have done just the same.

No one said anything, but from the way they looked at her, Hild could tell they more than suspected her husband was in a bad way—or that she was.

She smiled and jested and was extra forthcoming. It was strenuous, and she was grateful to Eadfrid for always leaving company early—often in a bad temper, it was true, but he was nonetheless easier to deal with than all the unfamiliar faces.

The children were an ongoing subject of disagreement. Eadfrid remained adamant they could only grow up to fulfil their destiny if they lived in Deira; they shouldn't be living in confinement, shouldn't be seeing their father as a captive, but should be growing strong and trained in bearing arms so they would be able to avenge their family line.

They were developing well, and could almost sit up. They no longer merely settled for the wetnurse's milk, but happily ate porridge and wheat bread. Wilbrord, in particular, was partial to solid foods.

Hundfrid was still as happy as always when Hild sang to him, and he warbled cheerfully along with her tunes.

'Are you a little bard?' she laughed to him, until she was interrupted by her husband sending the babies back with the wetnurse.

'You'll ruin them with all that nonsense!' he shouted, slamming the door behind the nurse. 'Hundfrid will turn into a wimp if you carry on like that.'

Hild didn't know if he was right. She sang less and less and took greater care about which little games she played with them, but temptation occasionally got the better of her and she would sing and hum along with Hundfrid while walking the nurse home.

She felt so very lonely when she went back to her hut alone.

They were sitting on the bench outside the guest hut, warming themselves in the early spring sunshine.

'Do you know why your father hadn't summoned the freemen from Bernicia?' Hild asked Eadfrid. Today they could talk; it was one of the sunny days.

'Why should he have? We were plenty without them.' Eadfrid didn't know why they had been so few men.

'You're right when you say your father wasn't his usual self the last few years,' said Hild.

'And you just sat in Mædeltun twiddling your thumbs, thinking more men should be sent out.'

'It might have turned the tide of the battle.'

'There was a time when the women didn't sit by idly while the men marched off to battle, but you've undoubtedly never heard about that.'

'Do you mean the Valkyries?'

'You know nothing!' he exclaimed. 'I mean in olden times. When women were equally capable of bearing arms. They didn't sit at the hearth gorging themselves and playing board games once they'd sent the men off to battle. They fought too.'

'But I was heavily pregnant!' Hild objected.

'Yes, you always know how to wheedle your way out of things.'

Eadfrid stood up and walked away. He could no longer bear being anywhere near her. He was so sick of all her excuses.

Penda came home in order to prepare weaponry and equipment for the next campaign. He was informed that Eadfrid's wife had arrived; he sent for her.

Hild presented herself immediately. She sank to her knees and recited a few phrases commending his hall and his friendship, all in all expressing admiration for his skills. She'd once heard an envoy from Kent greet King Edwin with these refrains, and the words had been well received. She'd been practising them all the way over to the hall.

She didn't know what else to say. She remained where she was, head bowed; all she could hear was her own breathing—his, too, after a while, and a pair of cackling jackdaws outside.

She looked up. He was an impressive man, tall and sturdy. In his hands he held their lives and their honour.

He sat with spine straight and shoulders back, silently staring at her. He was not unaffected by her elegant words. On the other hand, he'd heard it all before. He wanted to hear her speak again, he liked her voice—and the rest of her. Eadfrid's wife was a beautiful young woman, of highest descent and the finest rearing. Penda, who had seen his fair share of women, knew these attributes were to be valued.

'It is said you can read and write,' he stated, having cleared his throat.

'Our mother tongue and also Latin,' she responded.

'That being so, I would like you to teach my children some of this skill.'

'My grateful thanks,' she said.

And as he said no more, she bowed and left.

Hild was honoured and, what was more, she was proud that her knowledge—which she had been keeping to herself and feeling ashamed of, thanks to all Eadfrid's accusations—could nonetheless be put to use. She knew Eadfrid would be against it; he was against everything about her as a simple reflex. Walking back to the guest hut, she thought over what she could say in her defence.

'Penda is a man of honour who will reward a service, perhaps by granting your freedom.' Or: 'Penda is protective of his honour. He wouldn't look kindly on a rebuttal and might even punish us.' Or: 'Perhaps Penda's children, through learning, will be won over to the true faith, and perhaps Penda will want to be baptized too. That could lead to the conversion of the whole kingdom.'

As she arrived back at the hut, however, she realized that the only workable arguments were those involving personal gain.

She was wrong.

'Do you think Penda will let us go—ever—if you're of use to him here?'

'Well, his goodwill is certainly of greater benefit than his anger,' she replied.

'Do you really think you can turn *his* head too?'

'It's his children I'll be teaching,' she answered, and span round to leave; she suddenly couldn't bear being anywhere near him.

As she started to walk away, she felt a sharp tightening around her neck, a little snap as the gold chain broke, a crunching sound as her foot trod on the gold holy cross, crushing it.

She screamed and leapt aside. Standing stock-still, she stared in horror at the wreckage on the floor. She stooped down and carefully picked up all the pieces, placing them in the palm of her hand. One arm of the holy cross had broken off, the rest was bent, two of the inlaid garnets had fallen out, and the filigree border around the large circular garnet in the centre had folded over.

She put her other hand over the fragments, like a lid.

'The baptismal gift from your father,' she whispered.

'That's how it goes when you pander to a pagan,' he said, and sat down in his corner. 'So what—Penda doesn't like holy crosses anyway.'

Hild didn't like to think of her husband as a man possessed by demons, and the thought of seeing him undergo an exorcism made her sick to the heart. But that possibility seemed increasing likely and he had, after all, asked for her help.

She stared at him, sitting in his corner, slumped and thin. His father, the king, had given him a name that meant wealth and peace, and now he had come to this—lethargic, morose and so scrawny the fleas could hardly be bothered to pay him a visit. He hadn't been destined to live this life; something had come between him and his happiness. Or else his parents' hopes for their son—all their fine thoughts and endeavours—had been nothing but idle fancy.

It would take more than optimistic hope to turn his fate around. Hild asked Talcuin to find a holy hermit, in the last resort just a wise woman, who knew about demons—and to do so in secret.

He came back with an old woman, a hermit living in the great forest to the west, over towards Walas. Hild spoke with her in private.

'Tell me, mother,' said Hild, 'can a foreign spirit take abode in a man?'

'If that man's own spirit has moved out, then it can happen,' the hermit replied, 'and more than one might enter.'

'And are you certain this is not superstition, mother?'

'Yes,' she replied. 'Jesus Christ exorcized spirits from a man. They leapt across into a herd of swine rooting around atop a steep slope near the sea.'

'Indeed,' said Hild, 'but that was a long time ago, and far from here, and I was thinking perhaps it doesn't happen anymore, not here, not among us, not today.'

She held onto a steadfast hope that she would get her husband back, the proud Eadfrid she had married and had known since childhood.

'How long has it been going on?' the hermit asked.

'Four months, six perhaps.'

'Did it happen suddenly?'

'I wasn't present, but I think so.'

'Yes,' said the hermit, 'if the body is moved rapidly from one place to another, the spirit can't always keep up. And that's when the Devil seizes his opportunity.'

'If the man goes back to that place, will his spirit then find him again?'

'Perhaps,' she replied, 'but the evil spirit will not capitulate voluntarily. Take care it doesn't leap into you if it becomes homeless. Wear a holy cross around your neck day and night, and remember to say the Lord's Prayer. Furthermore—if both of you journey back—do not do so on the thirteenth day of the month, nor on the ninth.'

She opened her travel bag and asked Hild to step aside. Mumbling unintelligible incantations, she mixed a drink from the pots and bottles, the contents of which were her secret.

'Give him this at full moon. Speak sparingly that day, the two of you, and remain silent for a good while before and after he drinks. Otherwise, it will merely make matters worse.'

Hild fell to her knees and thanked the old woman.

'Give thanks to the Lord, my child,' said the hermit, 'that your husband lives. And pray for him. That is the best advice I can give you.'

This advice was borne of experience. Twelve years previously, her husband had been possessed by a demon so stubborn it would not be cast out. So brutal were the measures necessary, her husband had died; only then had the demon left his body, in the shape of a bat.

She had thereafter devoted her time to studying gentler forms of exorcism. Herbs could be effective if taken in the correct manner. Without the Lord's help, however, nothing was of any use.

Eadfrid refused to swallow the herbal drink.

'I don't need it,' he said, 'but others undoubtedly do.'

He held the beaker to her mouth, pressed it against her lips. Perspiration pouring down her temples, she had to sit, her head between her knees; he laughed.

'You can't get rid of me that easily,' she heard him say. She stared into his eyes, again glassy and distant. When he had those eyes, her husband was gone and this stranger hardly knew who she was.

'Drink it!' he shouted. He had suddenly lost patience, and she knew what that meant. She drank, her heart churning frantically as if it were trying to tumble out of her body.

Now I'm going to die, she thought, and Wilbrord and Hundfrid are far too young; this can't be covered up, and Eadfrid will hang. She struggled to breathe, and she was sitting in a warm and sticky puddle. She had let go of everything, and it stank.

'Help me, Eadfrid,' she whispered. She refused to budge from the stubborn conviction that her husband would return.

'You always survive,' he said. 'So I have no doubt you'll survive the poison you wanted me to drink!'

'It isn't poison! I swear, it isn't poison!'

She regretted her prevarication, because he was now someone else entirely, and with one leap he was on her, pushing her head back and forcing the rest of the liquid down her throat.

'Jesus, have mercy on me,' she gasped, and then it all came spewing out in one great cascade, splattering his tunic.

Wiping away the splashes with his sleeve, he stared at her in disbelief.

'You are sickening!' he exclaimed, suddenly looking exhausted.

He opened the door and took a few deep breaths of fresh air; then he washed his hands and face in the bowl, threw her a final sneering look and lay down to sleep.

Hild's mother had been half-sister to Eadfrid's mother, and they had grown up together not far from Tamoworthig. Perhaps that was why neither Hild nor Eadfrid found the landscape unfamiliar. It also reminded them of fertile hilly Deira, stretching from the white chalk cliffs by the sea, southwest to the Humbre river, carrying on down through Lindsey. When spring arrived, the flowers growing in the light soil looked nearly the same as the ones they had so often gathered for the spring festivals at the old shrine in Godmundingaham. In the good old days, before the new god made his entry and divided the people.

That, at least, was how Eadfrid saw it. He intended to take part in Eostre's festival, and his wife would too. She had to realize that by genuflecting before the new god she bore a large portion of responsibility for Northumbria's misfortune. She had been completely uncritical in her admiration of the new notions, and in so doing had thrown out the old order, insulted the customs and hard-won wisdom of her ancestors, and broken away from her own father and mother in order to seek better reward for herself from the new god. Breaking away from family was unnatural, and it became clearer to him by the day that she was only out for herself. She'd had no idea what she was stirring up when she went so eagerly overboard for Paulinus' twaddle. No wonder the gods had withdrawn the good fortune in battle previously granted to their family.

'Just look at Penda,' said Eadfrid, 'why do you think he's always got fortune on his side?'

'Because he's the best strategist,' answered Hild, 'and we haven't seen the last of it yet.'

She knew whatever she said she'd get a twisted version flung back in her face, but she wouldn't let the demons manipulate her. She was baptized in the name of the Lord Jesus, and she would obey no one else.

Eadfrid shook his head at her stupidity.

'And you've already forgotten that it is Woden who grants his people skilfulness in battle strategy, have you?'

'I know the pagans say so,' Hild replied sharply. 'But however many battles Penda might win with the help of his false gods, there is only *one* true god great enough to descend into the Land of the Dead and bring back the lost souls. And we are both baptized in the name of that god, whatever you say.'

'In the rashness of youth,' Eadfrid added. 'A lord who helps his people here on earth is of greater worth.'

'In allegiance to your father who knew what served us best,' Hild went on.

'Nonsense!' cried Eadfrid. 'Now we'll go to the spring festival to become friends with Penda, so he'll grant me my freedom. It is not befitting to be absent from the king's spring sacrifice, and if you let me down you'll regret it. After all, it's your fault we're here in the first place.'

'I will not let down the lord in whose name I was baptized along with you and your father!' said Hild.

Eostre's lilies were already in bud, and as Hild rode off she was transported to the country of her childhood, to Deira and Ad Gefrin.

The gold holy cross around her neck was the baptismal gift from Edwin. Penda's wife had ordered the goldsmith to piece it together. King Edwin had ordered a holy cross for each of the most distinguished people who were baptized alongside him.

At that point, Breguswid had again started to show an interest in her daughters' futures. Both girls were so excited by all the new learning and fascinated by everything Paulinus said. Breguswid wouldn't stand in their way. Although she suspected the future did indeed belong to Jesus Christ and his campaigners, for her own part she politely declined the offer of baptism. She didn't want to embark on something new; she would continue to serve that which she and her husband had served together. She was in no doubt that Paradise was a lovely place, as Paulinus said. However, she didn't want to risk losing the possibility of seeing her beloved husband again, even if that meeting took place in the cavernous deep or—as Paulinus maintained—in Hell. It was not in her nature to seek out better lodgings than those allocated to her husband. Their fates were joined.

Hild was thinking a great deal about her mother: what had gone through her mother's mind and what she had hoped for when she was young and frequented these very same places. She was glad her mother wasn't here to see the misfortune that had befallen the family line, but she would have liked to see her with the infant boys, and to show her all their new skills.

Sometimes she wept with longing for her mother. A need to throw herself into her mother's arms, curl up like a small child, lay her head in her lap, have her hair stroked and listen to her mother's soft lulling voice while she simply closed her eyes and forgot all about the challenges she faced. She couldn't actually remember if she had ever sought such comfort, because she had spent so many years in the maternal and protective role for her mother.

She felt an aching need for Breguswid's small blinking eyes looking out from below the grey tufts of hair, her sing-song voice, her swift bird-like movements. Every evening she prayed to the Lord to show mercy and take her parents to join him in Heaven, and Hereberht too, if he was dead—they'd never found him. Hild didn't believe he had died, and she always imagined they'd meet again, in life: one day he would come walking towards her, flinging out his arms. Her brother.

Now it seemed as if childhood had been one long summer, interrupted only by a spot of fragrant spring, with lilies, like now; and just before the leaves appeared, a white covering of anemones across the forest floor; and later, corydalis, purple-mauve with succulent stems, good for tying garlands. Eostre's festival was full of corydalis.

It was a complex flower. If she found one first, Hereswid would pull it apart, much to Hild's chagrin. Hereswid would not be satisfied until she had seen its insides, as she put it, and she also used to eat a bit of the plants she found. She didn't only eat them in the spring, when it was normal to feel a need for green shoots given that you'd spent a long winter putting up with porridges, salted pork and dried meat—then it was bliss to sink your teeth into crispness itself and suck the life-giving juice from the new green life—everyone did. But Hereswid ate the flowers too; just a little of each, chewing slowly and thoughtfully, not for the taste, because that might be very bitter or sour, but to appropriate their very essence. She had to know how it was possible to lie in the black sod, dead and decomposed, and then, when the hour came and the skylark was singing jubilantly high above the earth, to rise again in splendour and glory—the bird warbling and twittering and calling the flowers forth in a magnificent green resurrection.

Spring belonged to the lovely Eostre, not even Paulinus had refuted that fact. When her month arrived, Eostre finally prevailed upon herself to return from the insides of the earth—where she had spent the cold period sleeping in a very deep and distant cave, in the arms of a slumbering bear. The previous autumn, yawning from fatigue, she had settled down to rest in the embrace of a white bear she had chanced upon in a cave far to the north. Snorting, the bear squinted out of one eye and, discovering itself in the fine company of Eostre, it slapped a protective paw across her breast and sank back into its winter slumber.

That had been one of their best games: Eostre and the white bear. Hild and Hereswid played it when the boys weren't there; it was their favourite in springtime. Courting Frig had been a good game too; they could play that at any season.

It was all so long ago. Now, surely, other children would be running around playing the same games in the hills surrounding Edwin's royal settlement at Ad Gefrin, with no thought to the fate outlined for them, with no experience of separation, grief and loss. She and her sister had been looking forward to grown-up life: being married ladies and sitting in the place of honour, receiving guests from distant lands, filling their beakers from the large horn—they'd seen Queen Edelberg, Edwin's fair-haired young wife from Kent, doing just that. She was known as Tata, and being allowed to comb her long golden hair was the best thing ever as far as the girls were concerned. They thought she looked like one of the big angels Paulinus talked about.

Queen Tata's good fortune had lasted until the previous year. The Lord had granted her eight years as queen; how many years would he give her as widow? Now she had to accept her brother's bread, and every evening she had to thank his wife for the food she had eaten and for her seat by the table at the far end of the hall.

# THE SPARROW THROUGH
# THE KING'S HALL

*– when the kingdom of Northumbria decided to serve the new god –*

Tata, Queen Edelberg, was deserving of great credit for guiding her husband along his path to the Lord—she had the Pope's own word for it, but reward would first befall her in Heaven.

In the meantime, she must be grateful for the opportunity to spend her widowhood living with her brother, King Edbald of Kent—and thank Paulinus' presence of mind for the fact she was alive at all. When the news of Edwin's defeat arrived, Paulinus had swiftly ensured that the remaining members of the royal household boarded a ship he had waiting on the river called Use. And by the time they saw the first plumes of smoke rising above the landscape, they were already out in the Humbre estuary. Paulinus had also saved the golden chalice, the big gold holy cross and four holy books—all of which he had packed the moment the army had ridden off.

Hild never forgot the days between the arrival of the Pope's letter and the announcement of Edwin's imminent baptism. Everyone at the royal settlement had suffered along with Tata. They had prayed and made sacrifices to their gods, hoping this young queen would keep her life. However strange and foreign she might be, they had accepted and embraced her and wanted her at Edwin's side, not under the turf.

The Pope's letter had filled the queen with terror. While Paulinus read it aloud, she screamed; when he reached the end, she lost all self-control. She sprinted through the gate, improperly dressed, and had to be brought back by force. Whereupon she ran off again and locked herself in her chamber, only allowing Paulinus and her handmaid access. She paid no attention to the costly gifts the Pope had sent with the letter: a silver mirror and an ivory comb inlaid with gold. She lay outstretched in prayer for days on end. All Paulinus could tell Edwin was that Tata was determined to fast and pray until her husband resolved to receive the Lord God.

Twelve days and nights—that was how long it took Edwin to come to his momentous decision. He never did anything rashly, and he always consulted with Hereric's widow Breguswid, and with the elders. On this matter, being absolutely certain in her mind, Breguswid didn't ask her daughters' advice—even though she was very fond of the young queen and would like her to keep her life. The king had become less melancholy after his marriage, and less inclined to seek Breguswid's nocturnal counsel. Not because he was a man who urgently desired to lie with his wife—he wasn't like that—but his mood had improved, particularly once the queen started getting pregnant. He was very partial to having children.

Hereswid filled Hild in on all the details; she had, as usual, been listening at the door. Two passages in the letter had thrown the queen off balance: where the Pope expressed doubts about the extent to which her marriage with Edwin could be called a true union, and his concluding words about the longingly awaited salvation 'of you and yours'.

Tata could hardly articulate her anxiety, not even to Paulinus. Had her salvation not been ensured through baptism? And had the men of the Church not given her their word that marriage to the king who might not yet be baptized, but had accepted the sign of the cross, wouldn't get in the way of her salvation?

Summarizing Paulinus' reply gave Hereswid some trouble. On the one hand, he had stuck to the validity of baptism as admission to Heaven, and also accepted that her marriage was totally valid—after all, he had blessed it himself—but, on the other hand, he neither would nor could contest the seeds of doubt sown by the Pope.

'The Lord judges us, and all we can do is endeavour to ensure that the judgement will be merciful,' he had said.

'And as well you know, Tata,' he had added, 'conversion of the king will provide you with a great and favourable cache, one you can take along when you meet Saint Peter!'

Tata understood. She was utterly dependent on the mercy of the Lord. Both her parents were in his Heaven, and her brother King Edbald of Kent would also be allowed in; were she to spend eternity elsewhere, she wouldn't have the companionship of a single family member.

She dismissed Paulinus and looked at her reflection in the Pope's big round silver mirror. Looked for a sign. She was so pale, so very pale.

She would be even paler when the icicle hand of death ripped dust and spirit apart and blew the warmth from her heart. Paler yet, far paler yet.

She slammed her hands against the mirror. Her fingers were already icy cold. She could hardly breathe.

The Lord had counted her days, and her husband's days. He could call them home whensoever he might choose, and she'd just been tra-la-la-ing through life. Since her marriage, she hadn't given eternity a second thought; she had been so absorbed in her new grandeur—and in her husband. Especially his night-time embraces. Especially them, yes, there was no point lying to the Lord. Her husband's gentle lingering embraces had made her forget everything about eternal salvation.

The Devil comes in many guises, she thought, and now he has used the pleasures of the flesh to lure me from the path of life.

When she mulled it over, however, she knew it wasn't the pleasures of the flesh during Edwin's embrace that made her see shining moons and sparkling flashes, thousands of tiny shooting stars, sometimes causing her to scream with delight. No, her rapture was caused by the thought of being able to give her husband an heir. She knew how much he prized heirs, and she wanted to give him everything—everything.

She also wanted him at her side in Heaven. She was twenty-four years old when she married Edwin, and now she knew what it meant to be with a man. She didn't want to spend eternity going without—her first twenty-four years had already been too many—there, like here, he should rest in her arms. She wasn't going to give him up.

Queen Tata fasted. She only let Paulinus into her chamber, and the handmaid who brought water and emptied the privy bucket. She left her room every third day; she sat at table in the hall, drank a beaker of water while the others tucked into the pork and beer, and then she withdrew early—with a little swing of her hips as she walked past her husband.

Swaying her hips like that was wasted on Edwin, he simply didn't notice. He could see how pale she was, and he feared for her life. He had difficulty doing any kind of justice to the food, and he grew hollow-cheeked.

He hastily summoned the council of elders: now they simply had to make up their minds about this new god. Every evening, while waiting for them to arrive, he asked for Hereric's widow to be brought to him—she was the wisest person on the estate. She often had messages from her husband; they came to her in dreams or from the birds or the way in which a hare ran past. Breguswid was in regular contact with her husband in the hereafter, receiving many useful guidelines, which she passed on to Edwin; she was his invaluable support. But in this matter she stood firm. She didn't even have to think things over; she could immediately and simply state the opinion held by her husband and herself: no!

Edwin had also taken delivery of a despatch from the Pope—the highest accolade he had yet received. Paulinus had read it to him, and his own scribe had verified it. The Pope called on Edwin to break with the worship of idols and receive the gift of baptism, plus the accompanying articles: a tunic with gold embroidery and a cloak from Ancyra.

Edwin was eager to take the gold-embroidered tunic into immediate use. It was woven of silk and the most finely-spun wool ever seen on these shores; completely white, but with a soft reflection in the silk threads and, on the chest, embroidered with many thin gold threads, a large holy cross.

'No,' said Paulinus firmly, 'only those who have been baptized are allowed to wear the holy cross!'

Edwin dropped the tunic as if his hands were ablaze, but a moment later he was again stroking the magnificent fabric—the finest and softest he had ever felt in his entire life.

He pulled back his hands, and then picked up the cloak and sniffed it. When he pressed it right onto his nose, he could see distant lands: the palms and camels of Ancyra, grandiose processions of kings and emperors, sages and the high priests of foreign religions, clean-shaven on the top of their heads like this Paulinus, all dressed in gold-embroidered tunics made of shining silk fabrics, adorned with trimmings of otter pelt and more gold embroidery, their men-at-arms wearing caps of marten hide and silk, garnet-studded swords in their hands, silver vessels containing scented oils, multi-coloured enamel patterning on gold jewellery, glistening helmets, the horses' gilded bridles and strap buckles gleaming, the freemen raising their swords in allegiance to the king, sitting on his throne high above, higher even than Woden himself, with eagles at each ear keeping him informed about the fidelity and deceit of his people.

To be a part of all this—the letter and the wonderful gifts from the Pope held that promise. All he had to do was agree to be baptized.

Ancyra, Ancyra. The very sound of the word made Edwin light-headed; he could almost sense the aromatic fragrance of Byzantium, of Rome, of the Mediterranean, the old imperial power, times of greatness and wisdom. In comparison with all this, he knew his own magnificence was but a heap of shoddy and shiny trimmings. The ostentatious imitation of the upstart.

Edwin could not read.

All he could do was write his name in Latin letters, next to his real name in runic letters. That was as far as he'd got. He hoped his children would learn to read and write, so they could comprehend more than he would ever be able to.

He had a feeling this Paulinus was onto something—something that had passed them by in this country, something fundamental and vital. But he didn't know what it was.

Perhaps it was the fragrance of Mediterranean grandeur, the sagacity and perceptiveness of distant times affecting his heart in a way that both provoked him and made him want for more. Perhaps he would grasp it all if he were reborn in the name of their god, washed clean in holy water and born anew.

His forty-two years weighed him down; he understood but little of life's mysteries, and he thought he understood less year by year. It seemed to him that most human endeavours were in vain; a person was able to achieve so little, and what little they did achieve was soon forgotten. So what was it worth, all that labour under the sun? It pained him to think that all his toil in consolidating the realm would be forgotten as soon as a wind had blown its course across the land; no one would know it was his place anymore; he would be gone like the grass.

He had recently heard Paulinus saying something very similar to the queen. And he was aching with hunger to partake of whatever it was Paulinus had on offer. Paulinus said that when you accepted baptism in the name of his lord then you were never forgotten. Your name was written in his god's book in the heavenly kingdom he ruled, and it could never ever be wiped out again. His god remembered everything, absolutely everything, and especially those who served him.

So however many winds might blow across Northumbria, if his days on earth should be but the same as those of the grass, if all his companions and family died and no one knew of his whereabouts anymore, he would nevertheless be remembered for all eternity thanks to the written entry in this book Paulinus' god kept at his side. And now he had personally heard of King Saul and the renowned King David for the simple reason that they were written about in the thick book Paulinus kept at *his* side, and which was obviously familiar to everyone in Ancyra and the surrounding territory—just not here, on this remote island, where the light had trouble breaking through, as Paulinus said. Probably because of all the rain.

Yes, they ate the flesh of the fine and healthy beasts they sacrificed to Woden, and that gave them strength too, and helped their understanding of the world. Paulinus, however, served the flesh and blood of his own lord to those who served that lord. He served up the flesh and blood of his lord—at the command of the Lord Jesus himself.

What an abyss separated this Jesus from their Woden! What would Woden have said about being served up to his people? Edwin couldn't resist a cheerful little smile at the thought of Woden's fury if he saw his own flesh and blood on the table!

This Jesus thought along very different lines—that was what was so awful about him, and it was starting to drive Edwin mad. It was incredible to think he was willing to lower himself so deep that he became one with human beings. There was something utterly indecent, intrusive and almost being crippled, something downright distasteful about it. A god who wouldn't settle for being a god, who wanted to be a person too. Not to trick and annoy people, like Woden did, but because he loved them. That's what was shocking about the story: this god loved people!

And hearing that, well, you just had to laugh, because who had ever heard of a god who loved anything other than himself and the sacrificial offerings he received? In good company, the very idea seemed womanly and ridiculous, and was the source of many an indelicate word. But afterwards, alone in your bed, or with just the stars for company, then the words kept ringing in your head and even echoed in your dreams. They took liberties, they couldn't be brushed aside, they came crashing down with such force from the hereafter that you had to give way and every muscle went instantly and completely limp. You could breathe out all the air inside and then breathe it in again as easily and calmly as an infant in its mother's arms; could almost feel the ground was safe and good to walk on—that you were being held, in the midst of darkness, by the gentle and strong arms of a god. And suddenly it all fell into place: he was with you and he didn't give up on his children, the fruit of his loins—which was just how you felt about your own children.

If he really loved the world like that, then he must have created it. Just take a look! You could only have those feelings for your own children—fully aware of their shortcomings, but nonetheless loving them just as they were. You couldn't feel like that about anyone else.

But could that kind of a father be a real god? Would he have enough strength to keep Northumbria's enemies in check?

Territories controlled by the Britons had been Christian since before Edwin's forefathers had arrived, seven generations back. Their fate wasn't exactly a good testimonial, but Kent had grown more powerful under the new god; he'd seen that for himself when he was in exile.

Had Edwin thought the essence of a man could be infused through the gut, he would happily have sacrificed Paulinus, slaughtered and devoured him in order to partake of his knowledge, his culture, his terminology, his linguistic ability, his proficiency in reading and writing, and above all: his key to immortality.

He was sure Hereric, had he lived, would have shared this desire, and he didn't understand how Breguswid continued to receive signs from her husband telling them to stay away from the new practice.

This much Edwin knew: Paulinus was onto something that he wasn't, something that defied his understanding. And he didn't think he could live with that any longer.

By the time the elders had gathered in Eoforwik, the queen had been fasting for twelve days.

The king outlined the problem. He started by telling them that when he married the princess from the Christian realm of Kent, he had promised her brother the king to give the new god a proper chance in his deliberations. He had already taken a step in that direction by allowing his new-born daughter to be baptized at Whitsuntide last year. After all, Paulinus' prayers had made sure the queen was safely delivered of the child, no one had been in any doubt about that.

Paulinus had also given him to understand that God's providence had saved him from the murderer sent by the king of the West Saxons at the last festival of Eostre. The manservant Lilla had thrown himself between his king and the poisoned dagger, and had saved him with his own life. Edwin had therefore promised Paulinus that if the new god could procure him revenge on the West Saxons, he would again consider following in his service. Everyone knew how fulsome Edwin's revenge had been: he had slain five chieftains. After that, he had stopped making sacrifices to the old gods. The realm remained free of misfortune, but decisions about the final step would be left to the wisdom of the council of elders in the light of the case presented by the old gods' own high priests.

He cleared his throat and gave the word to Paulinus, who now had his first chance in this realm to make a public presentation in favour of his god. Unfortunately, he wasn't a particularly skilled speaker.

Paulinus carried in his big bible. He showed them how packed full of words it was, and explained what it said: his god had created the world, and all its animals and plants. It had taken five days, and on the sixth day he had created people in his own image. He had created them as woman and as man. Out of clay. And breathed his spirit into them. On the seventh day he had rested: it was a sun's day—so that was when his people should have their day of rest, not on Thunor's day.

But the people forgot who they had to thank for the abundant riches of the earth and the progeny of the lineage. Time after time they lapsed and started worshipping pieces of wood, which they carved into shapes and claimed were gods. And, every time, the Lord punished them by sending years of misfortune, famine, enemies and pestilence—he stretched out his arm, the waters divided and mountains were shaken to dust. But when the people did penance, he forgave them. He was, after all, their father.

One night he had turned himself into a man, born as Jesus Christ to a virgin, so he could live the life of a man among his people. So no one could come and say: 'He doesn't know what he's talking about!'

He had healed people who were blind and people who were paralysed, had walked across the surface of a lake, turned water into wine, brought the dead to life, and undertaken many other powerful deeds. He had taught people that if they were baptized in his name, they would not perish, but would have shelter for evermore in his grand realm high up in the heavens. And every word he had said was written down in this holy book.

This is how the Lord had ended his days on earth: he let himself be nailed to a wooden cross in order to redeem mankind, of his own free will. Therefore, no further sacrifices would be necessary. He had sacrificed himself, once and for all. Then he travelled down to the realm of the dead, broke open the gates and released the captives. Three days later, he rose from the dead, a sun's day in Eostre's month. Whereupon he ascended into Heaven. And that was where he sat now, deciding who should spend eternity in his great hall, and who should be cast into the flames to burn.

'Everything is in his hand,' Paulinus concluded, 'our fate, too. His hand holds the earth steady, and makes the sun revolve around it, he holds the water in the seas and makes the seed corn put forth shoots. And not a sparrow falls to the earth without his hand upon it.'

When Paulinus fell silent, a sparrow flew in through a smoke-hole in the east side of the hall, flapped around under the rafters and vanished out through the smoke-hole in the west gable.

The elders nodded to one another. This stranger served a powerful god; not all of them could have produced a sign like that.

The next to speak was Coifi, the high priest from Deira's largest temple at Godmundingaham. He was a tall scrawny man. He paced back and forth on the speaking-area, adjusted his long beard before bowing to the assembly and beginning his speech.

'O king, let us carefully consider that which is now preached to us; for I declare to you what I have learnt beyond doubt: the religion which we have hitherto professed seems of no worth and no authority. For none of the king's people have applied themselves more diligently to the service of our gods than I; and yet there are many who receive greater favours, and are more preferred than I, and are more prosperous in their undertakings. Now, if the gods had any power, they would rather forward me, who has served them with greater zeal. Therefore, say I, if upon examination you find those new doctrines better and more powerful, then we will hasten to receive them without any delay.'

To emphasize the authority with which he spoke, Coifi raised his arms in the air, as if he had just dispatched a sacrificial animal; he again paced the length of the tightly-packed benches, took his seat and accepted the quality mead warranted by his contribution to the debate.

The discussion was open to participation. First there was a little thinking and muttering on the benches. Then a highly respected farmer stepped forward in front of the assembly. He owned all the land east of the upper course of the river Derwent and lived in the gentle vale near Hacanos. On Thunor's day he usually rode out to rough Hræfenclif to get a perspective on his view, and to check if the path leading into the sea was still there. He was one of the old guard and, like most sheep-breeders, he didn't waste his breath. Whatever came from his mouth had been well chewed over and digested, and was weighty as silver. He launched into the longest speech he had ever made.

'O king, if we compare the present life of man upon earth with that time which is unknown to us, then it seems to me like the swift flight of a sparrow through the king's hall wherein you sit at supper on a winter's day with your nobles and attendants, the fire blazing in the midst, and the hall warmed, while wintry storms of rain or snow are raging outside. The sparrow flies in through one door and out through the other. While inside, it is safe from the wintry storm; but after a few moments of safety, it immediately vanishes out of sight, out to the wintry world whence it came. So does this life of man on earth appear for a short moment, but of what went before and what is to follow—of that we know nothing. If, therefore, this new doctrine brings us any more certain knowledge at all, then it seems to me we ought to follow it.'

Whereupon he sat down with his mead and didn't speak again until he arrived back in Hacanos next day and said good afternoon.

There were women in the assembly, too, widows of the chief men or representatives of freemen who had lawful absence. One of the former was the mistress of Hæafuddene, the swampy stretches of marshland north of where the Humbre started its course.

She cleared her throat and stepped forwards.

'What is a human life,' she began, 'other than a moment here on earth, feet on the earth's crust and head in the air? In the left ear we hear snarling from the ogre we escaped by being born, in the right ear we hear growling from the bear that will devour us when we no longer have the strength to hold our head aloft. When our legs give way, we are easy prey to the ogres.'

She paused briefly before continuing.

'This much I can say: I would but wish that my husband, who fate took from us this summer, had been informed of the new doctrines. If they truly have the means by which to fetter the wild beasts that lie in wait for us in the darkness, then we must immediately accede to them.'

A farmer from Hæselertun then stepped forward. He was guaranteed to be the grouch of any gathering, and a cause he advocated would instantly lose quite a few of its supporters. He stood in the middle of the floor and pointed a steady finger at Paulinus.

'You say your god has created everything there is in the world. Anyone can say that. Why should we believe you more than any other stranger who travels around dishing out stories?'

Paulinus stepped forward holding his bible aloft.

'Because it is all written in this book, which has been dictated by the Lord himself. Here, for example: the first human, Adam, and the woman was called Eve. And here: when Jesus Christ was born—when light shone upon the world and everything was changed. That is why we count the years from his birth. It was six hundred and twenty-seven years ago.'

The farmer's long finger again pointed at Paulinus.

'So perhaps you can also tell us when the world was made?'

'I can,' replied Paulinus, and decided to use the old reckoning worked out by Sextus Julius Africanus in the early third century. He had said the world was created in the year 5502 before the birth of Christ. Paulinus knew there were forces within the Eastern Church trying to change this to 5508, but he couldn't believe the Pope would follow the lead of the Eastern Church in such a matter.

Now he could really feel how far away he was from home. He was among barbarians; not only were they illiterate and had never heard the Latin tongue, but they couldn't calculate in numbers beyond how many sheep or children they had, never with any accuracy anyway. Lots! they said, making a sweeping gesture, maybe a few times. But he had never heard anyone other than the kings use precise numbers over one hundred, and that was when they counted their soldiers and their fallen—and the number was never correct.

5,502 plus 627, that made 6,129. He tried again and came to the same result, then raised his head from his hands, where it had been resting while the huge numbers fell into place.

'It is six mille, one hundred and twenty-nine years ago,' he said. 'You see, a mille in Latin is ten times one hundred.'

As he could still see open mouths and gawking eyes, he started again, this time enlisting the help of his fingers.

'You take one hundred, do so ten times and that gives you a mille. Then you take six of the mille, then one hundred, then twenty-nine. And that number comes from the fact that the world was created five mille and five hundred and two before the birth of Christ. If we add them to the six hundred and twenty-seven years we have lived in grace, then we reach six mille and one hundred and twenty-nine. That is how long ago the Lord created the first people.'

Coifi leapt to his feet and was about to say something, but he sat back down shaking his head. He was dizzy from all those years and didn't understand how the foreign high priest could keep track of them. Those mille, as he called them. What Coifi did understand, however, was that it must be a very powerful book he had in his hands, and that it had more uses than just reading. He stood up again and walked forwards.

'So tell me, stranger, is there anything in that book about when we can expect the end of time?'

'Of course,' replied Paulinus without blinking, 'but that is knowledge privy only to the few. This much I can say: the second coming of the Lord should be expected at any moment. Then he will call his servants to the eternal banquet. The rest will be cast into Hell, a seething sea of fire, where there will be weeping and the gnashing of teeth, for all eternity.'

Paulinus' bad omens caused quite a stir. Many felt an urgency to get that baptism over and done with. Coifi had stepped forwards again, red blotches on his throat, cheeks burning.

'This eternity you talk about—is it one hundred years long, or perhaps several *mille* long?' He had some difficulty pronouncing the peculiar foreign word.

'That, I *can* tell you,' replied Paulinus. 'Eternity is mille and mille and mille, a mille times! It is so long that no man can grasp it. As many years as there are grains of sand along the coast, and as there are stars in the sky. And then just as many again. For eternity has no end. And once you have descended into Hell, then there is no way out! And do you think the torment stops when your skin is really *really* well-singed?'

He looked around at the frightened faces and went on in a gentle and earnest voice.

'No, as the milles pass, it gets worse and worse. But by then it is too late to beg for forgiveness! Once the Lord has passed judgement, he sits down to supper with his servants. There is no shortage of either mead or anything else, it is the eternal joy where hunger and thirst, cold and sorrow and death are vanquished, and where happiness is your companion from early morning to late at night. There you are neither tormented nor burnt as you would be in Hell. The wisest move is thus to be baptized and be guided by the Lord's command. Then you know where you will be spending eternity.'

Paulinus had warmed to his subject, seeing all the faces staring at him, greedy to hear more. This was the hour for which he had been waiting, and he beseeched the Lord to assist him.

'Must be a pretty big hall,' someone mumbled.

'Incredible,' the man next to him joined in. 'All those years! You can't get them to fit in an ordinary head!'

Coifi had to step forwards again. He tugged at his beard and stood deep in thought, until the benches creaked from impatient shifting.

'Could Paulinus not tell us about the years in a different way? In this country we don't count in *milles*. Perhaps Paulinus could say how many generations ago this Jesus lived, and how many generations that was after the world had been made?'

Paulinus' mind set to work. He estimated four generations to a century. He held his forehead while he ran through the calculation, and hoped he had added it up correctly.

'Jesus Christ was born twenty-five generations ago. And by then two hundred and twenty generations had lived after Adam and Eve. So, all in all, there have been two hundred and forty-five generations on earth since the first people.'

He held up his fingers and showed them what he meant by two hundred and forty-five.

Edwin wasn't the only one to pale at the news. There was a stir in the hall; even those of highest rank couldn't trace their lineage further back than to Woden, and that was fourteen generations. There hadn't been any real people before then, but there had been people in this foreigner's kingdom for so long it was impossible to grasp inside a human mind. More than two hundred generations, that's what he'd said.

Yes, he had. Over two hundred.

Edwin thought that when you were dealing with such quantities it was ridiculous to speculate about whether it was one hundred or two hundred and forty-five generations. No one could grasp that kind of time-span anyway.

A young man from Driffeld stepped forwards. He would like to know if Paulinus could specify some cases in which, having entered into the service of this lord, people had seen an improvement in their lives. 'And I've noticed that you drag one of your legs slightly, so I wondered: did the injury happen before or after your baptism?'

'Before,' Paulinus replied without hesitation, 'for it occurred while I lay in my mother's womb. She was a devout woman, and the neighbour cast evil eyes upon her. They thought I would never be able to walk. However, the miraculous baptismal water purged me of the evil, and I suffer almost no ill-effects whatsoever!'

He pulled up his loose trouser leg, and everyone could see there was nothing wrong except that the right calf was a little thin.

'So your mother didn't have to put you out,' said the lady from Hæafuddene once she had felt his leg.

'No,' said Paulinus, 'and I was her firstborn.'

'What joy for her,' exclaimed an older woman from Loidis who had once had to part with a bewitched son.

'But then the Lord gave her two more,' said Paulinus. 'They too are in the Lord's service. My sister in Scholastica's convent. Scholastica was sister of the holy Benedict of Nursia, founder of the monastery at Monte Cassino near Neapolis. Her convent is not far from Monte Cassino. My sister and my brother both write books, like this one.'

'What sorrow for your parents!' the woman from Loidis exclaimed. 'So there is no one to carry on the family.'

'We are all sisters and brothers in Jesus Christ,' responded Paulinus. 'A family on earth they did not have, but a huge treasure in Heaven for which they thank the Lord. For what use are gold and many heirs, if the gates of Heaven are closed to you?'

He threw out his arms and then slammed them together to demonstrate what he meant by a closed Heaven.

'For as is written in this book here: everything perishes, but the steadfast love of the Lord never ceases.'

'So maybe your sister wrote the book for you?'

'Yes,' he lied. 'It was her farewell gift when I left my native soil for the sake of Jesus Christ.'

Paulinus had to adjust a few details in order to accommodate the barbarians, given that they had a completely different perception of everything. He would have to remember all the modifications for which he must ask forgiveness at prayer this evening, even though he was doing it in a good cause.

He saw no reason to tell them that in the year 589 Monte Cassino had been destroyed by the Lombards and had only recently been rebuilt, on a much smaller scale. They would never believe in a god who wasn't able to protect his own possessions. Or that his mother had actually died of grief at having to give up her children—no, he wouldn't be telling them that either.

'So you get messages from your kin back home?' asked the young man from Driffeld. He'd like to travel out into the world, but would hate to lose touch with his family.

'My sister sent me this tunic, which she wove herself,' Paulinus lied, hitching up his peasant's coat, giving everyone a chance to admire the embroidered borders. Women and men alike crowded round to take a closer look at the material and feel it.

'I have never seen such fine linen!' exclaimed the mistress of Hæafuddene. 'Perhaps it grows differently down there?'

'It is not flax linen, mistress,' replied Paulinus. 'It is from the seeds of a plant we call cotton. And I can assure you all, this is a rough type of cotton. Far far finer varieties are available, and it can be dyed in the most glorious colours. What is more, it is a great deal softer than flax linen.'

'Indeed it is,' said the woman from Loidis. 'Perhaps you have others like this?'

'I do not collect worldly goods,' replied Paulinus, 'and had this tunic not been a gift from my sister, then I would have preferred to wear the coarsest wool. Like John, who baptized Jesus—he never wore anything other than a camel-hair cloak of the roughest making. John gave notice of the coming of the Lord, and he paid for it with his head, cut off on the orders of the evil king Herod.'

Now he had made a mistake: telling them about people who had suffered misfortune in the service of the Lord wasn't going to guide them onto the true path. Information of that category would have to be imparted little by little.

On the other hand, he knew they always appreciated a good story, and one of them would soon be asking him to tell the whole tale about the man who had been beheaded. They were like children in that respect. If he had the energy to narrate the entire Old Testament, they would sit still for hours on end, mouths gaping and those incredulous round eyes, which were currently staring fixedly in his direction. And then later he would be confronted with the most hair-raising versions of the holy stories. That's how it was with these children he had been sent to teach, but their tendency to dramatic exaggeration was both good and bad. The old stories could be used as an opening into the core of the matter, but it was often tricky to involve Jesus without his listeners starting to yawn or pick fleas off one another—or simply falling asleep, accompanied by loud uninhibited snoring. He'd had to put up with that in Kent, where people were otherwise more civilized than up here. As far as Jesus was concerned, they were only interested in the miracles; his act of redemption was of no interest. But the difference between Hell and the great king's hall—they understood that all right.

The Lord had sent him to a crude people, but he was grateful for the burdens this mission placed on his shoulders—they lightened the weight of the cross Paulinus had carried with him to the disbelievers.

What he'd said about his leg wasn't true either, but what other answer could he have given? The palsy that had destroyed some of his muscles when he was seven years old was a child's plague, seldom survived, and only as an invalid. It had carried away his youngest brother and many other children in Neapolis. On the other hand, that his mother was a very devout woman was true. Once she had been widowed, however, there was only one way in which she could support a family. Given that she was neither young nor particularly beautiful, she could hardly earn enough for her children's footwear. She had handed them over to a monastery, otherwise they would have died of hunger. She had then lain down to die, unable to endure her trade.

The actions of the Lombards had left many children fatherless, so back then the monasteries had been able to pick the brightest and most dutiful; after a trial period of a year, more than half were sent away again. It could hardly be called home, even though the monastery continued to use that term. Paulinus and his siblings managed to hold their own; they were diligent, quick to learn and good-looking. His sister in particular had been talented, both academically and musically. They wouldn't have got through it without her.

'Everything has its price,' he later told himself. The price he and his brother had paid was a lifelong sense of guilt about their sister, who had sacrificed her opportunities in Heaven in order to procure bread at the monastery table for her brothers and herself.

The look in her eyes, and the curses and incantations she muttered for the rest of the day after her weekly one-to-one lesson with the superior of the monastery, an elderly abbot who had bad legs and trouble walking—that sight haunted Paulinus in his dreams. And it was the reason he had enrolled for the dangerous and thankless task up here in the remote North, among primitive people in an inhospitable land where the rain and the wind seemed never-ending. And the same reason made him avoid any contact with prepubescent girls; the very sight of one was distasteful to him: there was something of his sister about them, which made his guilt cling like boiling oil.

This was the cross Paulinus had carried with him to the Island of the Angles. Oppressed by its weight, he remained seated when the king stopped the meeting to offer refreshments before a verdict was reached. According to Edwin, major decisions should not be taken on empty stomachs.

Paulinus was too affected to stand up. The warm hand of the lady from Hæafuddene tingled against the skin of his leg, poorly since a childhood. There was a gentleness about her that reminded him of his own dear mother, and he wondered if she too was afflicted by great sorrows. This woman had never seen the filthy alleyways in Neapolis and she was probably unfamiliar with the stench from the sordid underbelly of this world, but her sympathy did his heart good. The only people in this country to have shown any interest in him as a person were the brethren in Cantwaraburh; together they had discussed the loneliness of exile and the homes they came from. Paulinus hadn't told them everything. They came from families of rank, bringing with them a good portion of land to the monastery chosen by their parents as the best place of education for their sons; that, at least, was what they had given him to understand, but perhaps they too carried crosses they couldn't share with anyone but the Lord.

Paulinus had worked resolutely and energetically on Edwin's conversion. He had spoken with him when he was in exile with King Rædwald, and he had asked to accompany Queen

Tata on her journey north. It had been a difficult and lonely time, and now, when the goal seemed within reach, he felt immensely tired, as if he would never again stand on his weary legs.

Taking his hands from his face, he stared straight into a girl's large round eyes.

'Hild is bringing in some food!' Hereswid reassured him in a concerned tone intended to be soothing. She scanned the hall and bit her lip.

'Does Paulinus feel better now?' she asked gently.

'Yes, yes,' he mumbled, and wished she would go far away. Hild came running in with bread and pork.

'So there's no beer for him?' hissed Hereswid.

'I couldn't carry it,' Hild apologized and ran straight back out to fetch a cup.

'Paulinus looks better now!' Hereswid stated once he had eaten. 'Paulinus has perhaps fasted too much.'

She gave him a stern look, and it wasn't the first time he had felt as if he was being kept under surveillance by these annoying lasses, who weren't content with his twice-weekly lessons. They were forever under his feet on the pretext of this or that. He was grateful for the beer, however, and when he drained his cup the girl rushed off to fetch more. All that talking had made him thirsty.

When the meeting resumed, the participants had cast all hesitation aside and turned into a highly vocal gathering. A good many wanted to speak in the decisive round, but it was Coifi who was given the floor.

'I have long acknowledged that our worship is empty; for the more diligently I sought the truth, the less I found. Now I publicly declare that the new teachings clearly reveal truths that will grant us the blessing of life, salvation and eternal bliss. Therefore, noble king, I permit myself to hold the opinion that the temples and altars we have consecrated, to no benefit whatsoever, shall immediately be desecrated and burnt.'

Edwin was pale when he stood up, his hands in tight fists at his chest.

'But who, Coifi? Who will do it?'

Coifi looked down at the floor, and everyone else looked down too. Then Coifi stood up slowly and stepped forwards, arms aloft.

'I, my king! I, who in ignorance have worshipped idols, I will do it, for the sake of my salvation!'

Whereupon he rode to Godmundingaham, threw a spear into the shrine and set light to the sacrificial grove.

People screamed in terror and thought Coifi had lost his mind. He bellowed loudly while he desecrated the temple and everything he had held sacred. Nobody intervened; they had no idea what to do against such an act of disgrace, which simply could not happen—the action was unprecedented and went beyond their powers of imagination.

Some wept loudly, others were struck rigid with horror, yet others shouted to the gods to come and protect their property; many flung themselves to the ground and clung to the earth, shaking with fear that their foothold would vanish and they would suddenly be hurled upwards and outwards in a fall without end. They awaited retribution from the gods, lightning and crashing thunder, the whole world in flames, the day of fire and blood, the earth collapsing in on itself.

But nothing happened. They just heard Coifi's menacing laughter and the loud crackling of the flames. Where were those gods now, the ones who allowed such a disgrace to occur in front of their very eyes as if it were nothing but a fly being squashed?

The world had lost all coherence. There was no longer any consistency, no framework to rely on. Chaos had taken the reins, and there they were, standing with their drooping shoulders, no longer knowing what they should hold onto.

One of the men who had been lying on the ground now stood up and did something about it: he leapt into the saddle and galloped to the king.

He was not even given an audience. He was told the king's council had decided to serve the new god from the south. The gathering of elders had put this new god at the helm, in command of the realm.

The man couldn't believe his own ears. He dared not return to Godmundingaham; he would wait until it all turned out to have been a bad dream. Walking back and forth in front of the gate through which he had been dismissed, he saw Coifi return, heard his demented laughter and saw him stagger into the king's hall. And then the man wept and staggered off home.

Coifi had downed a drink or two on his way home. It was a big day for him, the biggest of his life. He had found a worthy master. He had proven the idols were nothing but dry wood, impotent and with no connection whatsoever to the power of the earth. They burnt well, these images executed by skilled artisans, the work of human hands and nothing else—maybe with a faint touch of abomination, given all the crackling and smoke, he couldn't deny that. But there was certainly not one grain of divinity.

Thus began the new era in Northumbria: with flames spreading horror and dividing the people.

Coifi had dropped dead a couple of years later, and Woden had gradually deprived Edwin of his good fortune in war.

Hild just hoped Woden had now taken what he wanted, so peace could again descend upon the realm of Northumbria.

# THE BELL IN DOLWYDDELAN

*- Cædwalla brings the twins to Deira -*

Cædwalla was grateful to the Lord for helping him cast off the yoke of Edwin. The many realms Edwin had made his vassals were now free, and the exiles could return. They hailed Cædwalla as their liberator and thanked him with impressive gifts. Among those who returned were Ædelfred's children; Edwin hadn't managed to persuade the Picts to kill them or to hand them over, not at any price, and he'd made a good offer.

They met Cædwalla in Eoforwik and celebrated peace with a Mass in Saint Peter's church, built on Edwin's orders for his baptism. Ædelfred's children had been introduced to the new doctrines by the Irish monks on the isle of Iona, and they too were baptized. They had also learnt to read and write. Ebba, the daughter, wanted nothing more than to continue her studies in the service of the Lord. Cædwalla gave her Coludesburh on Bernicia's brown rocky coast in remembrance of his brother, martyred by Edwin. They recalled the terrible ritual sacrifice with which Edwin had celebrated his victory, and thanked the Lord that this barbarism was finally over and done with. Nothing like that must ever happen again.

Cædwalla didn't want power; he had more than enough of that in the kingdom he had inherited from his father. He simply wanted justice, plus a virtually symbolic tax from the new kings, because he would need a little extra in order to rebuild his realm after Edwin's last ravages.

A united Northumbria would be too mighty a neighbour, as the people from Lindsey and Mercia thought too. Cædwalla followed Penda's advice to reintroduce the natural division of the realm that had been in force since olden times: Bernicia was again allotted to King Ædelfred's line, with Cædwalla suggesting that Ædelfred's son with Bebba, called Eanfred, should be made king, and he was duly selected by the elders of the land. For Deira to the south, Cædwalla advocated a man from King Ælle's kin: Edwin's cousin, called Osric, who had also been obliged to go abroad during Edwin's rule. He too was selected unanimously. Now the good times—the pre-Edwin times—could return.

They did. The new kings quickly realized that if their power was to endure, they would have to go back to the practices of their forefathers, as had the others who had returned home. For the Picts and the Britons, the Lord God reigned, so there it had been right to serve him. Here, however, the old gods reigned, and therefore it was fitting to serve *them*. The new kings steered clear of human sacrifices, since it was such a sore point with Cædwalla. They couldn't, of course, ban others from carrying them out, and they themselves sacrificed many good horses and oxen. Things were looking bright for them.

They didn't see any reason why they should pay tax to Cædwalla. In any case, they thought he had demanded too much, and so they agreed to free themselves of the man, kill him if necessary.

The stipulated taxes failed to materialize. Cædwalla stayed in Aberffraw, waiting a month before mobilizing his best men and setting forth for Tamoworthig to consult Penda who, in the month of Eostre, had been chosen as king of Mercia.

Penda advised him to get straight down to business, although he couldn't personally offer any assistance as he had his hands full further south. He gave Cædwalla a large pitcher of his best red wine and wished him luck. Cædwalla would just have time to celebrate the midsummer festival first.

'You simply have to do what you can, Hild!' Eadfrid entreated her. He was depending on her.
'Yes,' she answered.

He gave her hand a firm squeeze and looked earnestly into her eyes.

'I mean *everything* you can. Get him all excited if you want!'

'Nonsense, Eadfrid.'

'I know he's infatuated with you. We mustn't throw away this chance.'

'There's no guarantee he can do anything. Hereswid and her husband haven't been able to, have they.'

'You can make him, Hild. I know you can.'

He kissed her brow.

'And I'll withdraw early. See if you can talk to him in private.'

'I haven't got anything to say that can't be heard by all.'

'Just this once. For my sake,' Eadfrid implored, pulling her hands hard against his chest.

Hild smiled as she ran back to the guest outhouse later that night. The sky was light, the singing echoed inside her, her feet were still dancing. Eadfrid's eyes would pop out of his head when he heard what she had achieved.

The candle had been snuffed out, but he wasn't asleep. He was sitting in his corner, half undressed, as if he had wanted to get ready for bed, but hadn't been able to finish the job. She put the lantern on the table and dismissed Talcuin. Eadfrid didn't move, but in the weak light she could see *that* look in his eyes; she was happy in the knowledge that perhaps this would be the last time the evil got a hold on him.

'It worked, Eadfrid! Cædwalla will bring the children home to Deira!'

He didn't reply.

'Are you listening? Hundfrid and Wilbrord are coming back to Deira with Cædwalla! Now you can sleep in peace, you don't have to worry about them anymore.'

She started undressing, her pale arms shining in the semidarkness.

'Comes naturally to you, doesn't it?' he said from his corner. 'Taking your clothes off in front of a man.'

She stopped mid-movement, then carried on.

'Should I perhaps hide myself from my husband's eyes?'

'So you got what you wanted!'

She turned to face him and said calmly, with emphasis: 'What *you* wanted, yes! And I can inform you that Cædwalla has pleaded our cause with Penda. He has asked Penda to release you. Maybe just a couple of months, Cædwalla says.'

She reached out, drawing him to bed. He knocked her hand away.

'Come on, Eadfrid, it's late.'

'Why didn't you stay with *the lion*?' he snarled. 'Then you wouldn't have had to undress and dress so many times.'

'No!' Hild whispered, as if needing to tell herself that what she had just heard hadn't been said. She took a very deep breath.

'Go to bed, Eadfrid; everything is looking brighter for us, you hear?'

She didn't like going to sleep before he had settled; she risked a very abrupt and unpleasant awakening. It was better to talk to him until he calmed down, and if that didn't work then it was best to let him have his way. He usually fell asleep once he'd got it out of his body.

'You have sold our honour—that's what I hear!'

He had stood up so quickly that she leapt backwards. The look in his eyes told her the perverting spirit had taken over, the one standing between them, making it impossible to get through to him.

So when his fist slammed into her left cheekbone and sent her flying sideways into the wall, she knew it wasn't Eadfrid guiding the hand. And when she heard him shout 'Get away from me, Satan!' she looked up in the desperate hope of seeing the evil spirit rush away from her husband.

But he was talking about *her*, and the clenched fist landed with a dull thud in the middle of her face, sparking a white streak of light, pouring out of her in waves that slowly lost their force, became sluggish and slack, and took on a red sheen, redder and redder, heaving dark red, unremitting and piercing; she had to hold her hands to her face, so great was the stream.

She sat up in bed that night, alongside her sleeping husband, and stared out into the midsummer semi-darkness. The dawn came early.

As the first cockcrow sounded she got up, wrapped a scarf around her face and threw Eadfrid's old cloak around her shoulders. She didn't want to be recognized.

The nurse let out a little cry when she saw her mistress standing in the doorway of her pit house. The woman was already prepared for the journey. She guided Hild onto a stool, and fetched water and cloth.

'I was far too tired,' Hild explained, 'I walked straight into the door when I came home.' She couldn't speak clearly, her lips were swollen.

'That can happen,' said the nurse, carefully dabbing Hild's face with cold water.

Hild thought she had washed, but she'd only managed to smear the blood around her face. She hadn't wanted to wake Eadfrid. She jumped when the nurse's finger slid down her nose.

'Thought so,' the nurse mumbled, and took a pot from the shelf above the window. 'This is the best bone ointment you'll find in the whole realm!'

'Hundfrid and Wilbrord!' Hild gasped, while the nurse rubbed in a good helping of ointment around her nose. She wasn't crying; the water just wouldn't stay in her eyes when her nose was touched, given the state it was in.

'You can be sure of one thing,' said the nurse, 'they'll want for nothing.'

'Send word when you get there,' Hild requested.

The nurse fetched the infants; they had been made ready for travel and then both had gone back to sleep. Hild started singing gently to Hundfrid, who lay grunting and twitching, but her throat rasped and her voice evaporated.

'Don't forget to sing for him,' she croaked.

'You've heard my voice,' said the nurse, 'but I'll get the women up there to sing, don't you worry.'

Hild couldn't stop herself; she lifted both children onto her lap. Hundfrid started crying, and the nurse had to put him to her breast. Wilbrord sat on Hild's knee, staring at her with his deep-blue eyes. She became self-conscious under his thoughtful gaze, and lifted him up to her shoulder. She rocked him back and forth and hummed a little—tried to comfort herself by thinking about all the good things they would experience in Deira. They'd have a proper upbringing there, learn the use of weaponry and everything. She took hold of his hot little hand and thought about how big it would have to grow before it could grasp a sword. He started pushing with his legs, practically stood up, bouncing, and she thought: good legs he's got, he'll be a skilled horseman.

She was overcome by the warmth from his body. They were so tiny, her boys, and she wanted to keep them with her until they were old enough to ride on their own—or until they could walk.

'Strong babies, aren't they?' she wept.

'They're certainly the strongest and healthiest babies I've ever seen,' said the nurse confidently. 'You just wait and see what they grow into, say I!'

The nurse knew what she was talking about; her last baby had been a changeling, and they'd had to put it out.

They heard the horn sounding in the yard, the signal to go to the horses.

A dense mist had settled on the land as they walked across to Cædwalla's entourage. Everyone was ready for the journey, and most were already on horseback. The nurse mounted a grey mare; Hundfrid and Wilbrord were stowed away in two large baskets on the flanks of a brown gelding. The farm staff stood in the yard holding burning torches. The sun would soon break up the mist.

Hild saw Cædwalla striding up from the privy. His red travel cloak shone brightly in the glow from the flames. She walked towards him, but then remembered the state of her face and pulled her scarf up higher.

She was going to tell him that he had to give her a horse, that she had to come with them, that she couldn't let her babies travel, that she couldn't stay, and she started to say something, but it all came apart; she walked closer to him and mumbled into the scarf, cleared her throat and started again from the beginning.

Cædwalla mounted his horse and raised his hand; his man-at-arms blew three blasts on the horn and she started running towards him, to shout and stop him; his eyes glanced at her briefly as he rode past.

She was left staring at the long column of horsemen, the ones at the front already encircled in mist. As the last one rode through the gate, she could still have pulled him up, could still have told them who she was, pulled the scarf aside and shouted that they had to take her with them—but she couldn't.

The torches were extinguished. Hild stood rooted to the spot, her arms hanging limply at her sides. The sound of hoofbeats was soon engulfed by the mist. She stayed put while all the others got going on the day's work, while the mist slowly dispersed, while the eastern sky turned yellow and light green, and she saw the sun emerge, large and luminous yellow.

She pulled the scarf up and went home to hide, but when she reached the guest hut she couldn't make herself go in.

She followed the beck, away from the estate, down into the forest. Having walked a short distance, she saw a stooping figure sitting on a rock at the water's edge. It was Talcuin: his head was resting in his hands, but he glanced up as she approached. She stopped alongside him.

'You would perhaps have liked to travel with them to Deira?'

'It's my father,' he said, shaking his head. 'I have received word that he's ill.'

'So why are you sitting here? Shouldn't you be on your way to him?'

He looked at her in surprise.

'May I?'

'Of course you may.'

Talcuin leapt up and rushed off. Hild called him back.

'Couldn't I . . . I mean, may I . . . wait a moment!'

She wanted to ask him to take her along, but it was too hard to ask for help, and she could feel the tears building up in her eyes. She cleared her throat and took a deep breath.

'Well now, Talcuin: go in quietly and fetch my travelling clothes, I'm coming with you. We'll meet at the horse paddock.'

She turned her back and waited until he had left.

'I'm free, aren't I?' she said out loud across the beck. 'I'm not the captive. I can just leave!'

Her legs dragged heavily while tracing a wide arc around the guest hut, and she had trouble hauling herself up to the paddock.

She couldn't go inside, where Penda's wife would see her, but she couldn't leave without letting him know. She sent Talcuin in with the brief message, saying that she was leaving for Gwynedd, thanking him for the loan of a pair of horses; she would be back within a month. Penda's wife insisted on sending six men with her, and they left it at that.

They rode fast, only taking brief breaks. Hild urged them on and pushed the horses to their limit. She knew it was wrong to leave her husband like this, but at the same time it was vital she got away—she felt as if she had next to no breath left.

Galloping for mile after mile, she now felt a growing sense of joy. She saw everything along the route as if for the first time. She was twenty years old, and even though her head was aching, life was returning to her body. Feeling the horse responding to her commands, seeing the yellow and white flowers at the edge of the track, hearing the skylark and the curlew, the sun prickling her face, being treated with kindness and respect. She smiled into the wind.

She pulled up abruptly and turned to one of Penda's men.

'Ride back with this message for my husband: that I had to leave suddenly, that I wish him well and I shall return within a month at the latest. And this message for your mistress: that I wish her well and request that she take care of my husband, he being afflicted by toothache. Talcuin's father, Evan of Dolwyddelan, son of Gwerful, awaits us on his sickbed.'

The rider repeated the message word for word before turning his horse.

Eadfrid was struck down by a toothache that locked him inside a circle of pain. Such was his befuddled state that he showed no surprise when Penda's wife sent a handmaid with poultice and hot drink. He lay in a stupor for several days, the badness in his backmost molar swelling up into a large bulge in his cheek. When the usual measures didn't help, the doctor and his effective herbs took over; two days later the boil burst.

Eadfrid was soon able to move onto solid foods, and he had many days' catching up to do. The handmaid brought him roast wood pigeons and the greenest of spring shoots steamed in butter; the colour returned to his cheeks. He grabbed at the girl, which cheered him up.

But the badness wouldn't leave him completely; the poisoned tooth had to go. Eadfrid drank mead for hours on end before they could get started. He needed greater quantities to reach the desired state these days, after idleness had led him to drinking himself to sleep—it was the only thing that could stop the voices.

It took six men to hold him down, and the tooth came out in fragments—it didn't want to relinquish its place. Eadfrid was given a herb compress and the wound healed slowly, but the badness was drawn upwards and settled in his ear. He was soon racked with just as much pain as the tooth had caused. The handmaid had to speak into his left ear as he could hardly hear anything with the right one.

'He needs his wife, I reckon,' the young woman said to the others in the hall. She had nothing against looking after the prince, but her husband was starting to look less than kindly on all her visits to this man from far away.

Penda's wife sent word to her husband: she didn't know what plans he had for the captive, but he certainly shouldn't be allowed to wither away like this.

A Christian missionary was immediately summoned to work on Eadfrid's treatment alongside Penda's own doctor. Everything had to be consecrated and blessed before it was used on the Christian prince. Penda reckoned that, for the most part, all the gods probably helped their own, like people do—so he wasn't going to take any risks.

He knew how he could use Eadfrid. He had to think long-term. He'd had his way with Northumbria, and for as long as he had a say in the matter, Deira and Bernicia would each have a king. There was no risk the two lineages would join forces, but if one of them gained power in both realms and started eyeing up Mercia, well, Penda was prepared. He knew it wouldn't take long before people started remembering the good aspects of Edwin's rule, and they would be kindly disposed to his son Eadfrid—whom Penda could supply with an army whensoever might be necessary.

Awareness of this circumstance ought to stop the new kings getting too greedy, and Penda would thus have the peace and quiet to improve his position to the south. He was in the process of subjugating the Hwicce territories: good land, which would provide another route to the sea. At the moment he only had the Mæres river, but the Hwicce regions would give him access to the waters south of Walas via the Sæfern river. He planned to expand trade with the Mediterranean countries; he loved their sweet red wine, their gold-work and their fine cloths.

Wool and flax had many uses, but they couldn't be dyed to take on the strong colours of the foreign silks. Powerful colours were fitting for a king, not faded green, not woad blue or brown, but crimson and purple; no other colours could provide such a splendid background for jewels and gold borders. His impressive belt clasp with its interlaced animals—where he kept his casting lots—certainly deserved appropriate clothing.

The thought made Penda smile, and he fingered the imposing clasp on his belt. He raised his drinking horn to Eadfrid, who was slouching at the long table on the right, tortured by the flying venom in his ear. The man wasn't much good for anything, and Penda hoped it never became necessary to deploy him. He wouldn't be able to hang onto the realm for more than a year, and then Penda would have to think up something else. For the time being, he could just spread rumours about how keen Eadfrid was to return to Deira. Whenever there were visitors from Deira or Bernicia, he would keep Eadfrid out of the way as much as possible, send him off on a good hunt. And he had commissioned a song in Eadfrid's honour, which was already beginning to circulate.

Eadfrid lit up when he heard the new heroic lay celebrating his deeds. He looked forward to Hild hearing it, then she'd have to take notice, he thought, straightening his back.

He hardly slept in her absence. He lay on the bed with his eyes closed or sat in his corner with his hand over his ear, and all he could hear was her deep soft voice, as if she were just outside.

Her voice was what he loved most about his wife. She could sing so the bench under you literally vibrated, and her stock of songs and ballads was inexhaustible. She only needed to hear a song once and she could sing long passages from it; having heard it twice, she knew it perfectly. Everything stuck so easily in her head, as if it were a never-ending space. He didn't have nearly as much room up there, and he envied her; but most of all he envied her rich voice, so he never praised it. He so wished he could sing, but all that came out was an uncontrollable growling sound. He hadn't been born with the gift of music; on the other hand, he'd been gifted her.

Her absence tormented him, and taking the servant girl into his bed didn't help: her body was too plump and too short, and she was beginning to get on his nerves, especially her voice, so fast and clipped.

He had no idea what kind of urgent errand his wife had in Gwynedd, and he didn't understand how anything could be more important to her than staying with her husband. Nor did he understand why he couldn't sleep, and he didn't know what he had done to earn him such painful earache.

Hild rode up alongside Talcuin.

'Isn't it wonderful the giants built roads like these.'

At first Talcuin didn't understand what she meant, then he lit up in a smile.

'The Romans built this one,' he said.

Now it was Hild's turn to be confused.

'You mean the people from Rome? Where the Pope lives?'

'Yes,' he replied.

They rode on in silence for a while.

'But why would they do that—so far away?' asked Hild.

'Because they lived here. They built lots of roads. A lot of fortifications, too. Like Eoforwik. And Mædeltun.'

'Well, the giants built the stone houses in Mædeltun, that's for sure!' Hild said brusquely. She lived there, didn't she, and she didn't think it was appropriate for Talcuin to tell her who had built their cowhouses and sheepfolds—because they certainly weren't fit to accommodate people.

Talcuin shrugged.

Hild was annoyed; he obviously knew something that had passed her by.

'And who says the Romans built those gigantic things?'

Talcuin had to think about this.

'It's one of those things we know. And it's written about in our monasteries. The Romans came here after the death of the Lord and before the destruction of Jerusalem. They built the Great Wall in Bernicia, too, against the Picts.'

'Well, that was built by giants, of course, because people can't build things that big. That goes without saying!'

Talcuin didn't respond.

'And what else, according to you, did the Romans build?'

'All the paved roads we call giant's way or king's way. And the fortifications. And the town walls, like the ones around Eoforwik. And whole big towns like Bathum, and Burh on the banks of the Humbre, and Legaceaster, as you say. We call it Carlegion. And Viroconium, which we passed yesterday. And a fort at Caer-Segeint in Gwynedd, lots of places. All built from stone.'

'But how do you know all this?'

'From my teachers, from books. Everyone knows.'

'So why haven't you told me this before?'

'You haven't asked. You and your people just say all those things were made by giants. None of my business.'

Talcuin's father had been visited by two angels. He was tired, and it suited him to meet his maker. Two of his sons had been killed by the intruders, one taken into slavery, and a daughter had died in childbirth. The world had gone awry, he no longer had any business in it, now the grandchildren would have to take over. All he wanted to do was meet his family and his maker in the hereafter.

He motioned all those who had gathered at the farm to come closer. Hild approached too, and received his blessing; she needed all the blessing she could get.

She awoke early next morning to the sound of something metallic, something brittle and very delicate, steadfastly resounding across the valley. She hurried out of bed and into the yard, where she instantly heard the wailing. She ran into the house and threw herself onto the floor next to the deceased, wailing, along with the other mourners.

The family was already gathered, so they buried Evan of Dolwyddelan two days later. The funeral procession was led by a priest carrying the small clanging metal thing they called a bell, and the wailing of the mourners blended in rhythmically. More than one hundred people followed him to the little graveyard by the church, taking turns to carry him so that everyone had the chance to show the deceased man their goodwill. They prayed for his soul, in Welsh and in Latin, and they asked him to intercede for them with the Lord. The prayers were recited in unison, as they were accustomed to doing in church. Hild had never heard such a large gathering reciting all the prayers without hesitation and without mistakes; they sounded as if they understood what they were saying.

Talcuin's father was lying in an open coffin, on a bed of mixed ferns. The followers also carried ferns; the hours between death and burial had been spent fasting, praying and fetching ferns: royal fern, polypody, brittle bladder-fern, buckler fern, hard fern, moonwort, bracken, ostrich plume fern, spleenwort, lady fern, hard shield-fern, wall-rue, pillwort and adder's-tongue fern. As many varieties as possible, and as large as possible. It was the same where

Hild came from. Ferns were beneficial for their preserving qualities, for their scent and for the closely-set spore cases indicating a fertility that could doubtless contribute to eternal life. Moreover, good ferns were available almost all year round. Now he was lying restfully and delicately, as if on feathers, embraced by the aromatic scent of fertility.

When they reached the entrance to the churchyard, the wailing stopped and everyone followed the coffin into the church to the steady clanging of the bell. The whole interior was decorated with carvings and painted in brilliant colours, patterned with the circles and spirals favoured by the Britons—for clothes, jewellery, weapons, domestic utensils, buildings.

Hild held her breath when the singing started. She didn't know the hymn, but managed to pick up most of it; she'd ask Talcuin to repeat it for her later. Most impressive was the force with which they sang. Even the children sang at the top of their voices, as if they had learnt it in their mother's womb and the rhythm had become the rhythm of their own heartbeat. They stood swaying, coaxing the song forth with their whole bodies, deep rounded notes pouring out of them with no apparent exertion, as if they were simply breathing.

They formed circles around the grave. The heavy carved wooden cross, which had been carried just behind the priest, was lowered three times over the grave. Everyone held their breath, because this required a lot of muscle, and people sometimes overestimated their strength; but that, too, passed off without incident.

The priest stood at the west end of the grave, arms outstretched, praying loudly. Hild had been given a place of honour, in the second row, just behind Talcuin, and she could see the bell close-up when it was swung again. She'd never seen anything like it and never heard such a lovely sound. She couldn't help wishing she owned a bell like that, even though it was only for church use. She would certainly have to find an opportunity to touch it.

The coffin was lowered into the ground while the bell tolled, three short beats and then just as long a pause. The priest held the bell aloft so everyone had a view. It was splendid.

Talcuin told Hild the bell had been brought along by an Irish monk. They'd called him the little Irishman because of his lack of height. He had carried himself with extraordinary dignity, but by the time people recognized his true stature the name had already stuck. He had founded the church when Talcuin's father was a child, and Talcuin informed her that it was the beguiling bell that had inspired people to provide land and whatever else was needed. The little Irishman had told them the bell could be heard all the way up in Heaven, because the holy Brigid of Cill Dara had touched it.

Brigid had founded the monastery in Cill Dara, and the holy Ibor had anointed her bishop. She was the women's favourite. Her convent was the foremost in Ireland, and an eternal flame was burning there, one hundred years after her death, tended by the nuns. No man was allowed close to the flame; but women could approach it, and share in Brigid's power, which blessed the larder, ensured the cows gave milk three times a day, prevented the butter turning rancid and could generate life in a reluctant womb.

Indeed, much blessed abundance came from Ireland, thought Hild, unable to take her eyes off the little bell. She would have the forge make one for Hundfrid; its ringing would make him laugh, would help him forget his colic and everything that might be causing him pain.

She missed Hundfrid and Wilbrord so much it hurt. She had to keep occupied to ward off the longing for their warm little bodies, their prattling and their loud exclamations of surprise when they experienced something new. The small dogs at Tamoworthig had made them shriek with delight. During the first few days in Gwynedd, Hild had looked away when a child was nearby; now she chatted with all the children, gazed into all the cradles, exchanged stories with the mothers.

On the other side of the grave, in the third row, she spotted a very small infant's head leaning on a young woman's shoulder. Hild thought the mother should have put a bonnet on the child to protect it from the strong sun, and from everything on the loose before the dead man was completely buried.

Clynnog Fawr was a sacred place at the coast, built for the Lord by the hermit Beuno. For a generation, he had conducted baptisms and received people who were suffering, either in soul or in body. Talcuin had made a pilgrimage to this place when he was a child, to the hermit's miraculous hands and the spring waters, and he had been cured of a malady that his mother couldn't control. His strongest memory of the trip was seeing the coastline of Ireland far away across the sea.

Now Talcuin was taking Hild to Clynnog Fawr. Beuno was dead, but his reputation and his sacred place lived on, and right now his niece Gwenfrewi, whom he had trained, was visiting from her own monastery.

There were long queues: sickly and pregnant and possessed and bewildered people. The short queue was made up of those just wanting to be baptized. Tents had been pitched for anyone who couldn't pay to stay in the guest huts.

Talcuin approached one of the brethren and told him the identity of the distinguished lady he was attending; she was allowed to enter ahead of all the others.

Hild confided details of her misfortune to Gwenfrewi, and asked for help. How could she atone for her guilt? How could she make the demons release her husband, as he was paying the penalty for her offences and was no longer master of himself? Moreover, she thought a new baby was on its way; she feared for the health of the unborn child.

'If the infant is immediately baptized, there is nothing to be afraid of,' said Gwenfrewi. 'The idea that the demons can leap from father to child is sheer superstition. It's only the mother's demons that can be dangerous. Demons don't like being alone, they always try to summon more of their kind. So it's important that you keep them at bay, through prayer and fasting, but in moderation given that you are with child. If you refuse to acknowledge the demons, then they have no power over you.'

Gwenfrewi gave Hild a herbal tonic to take home, and then blessed her. Within a year at most, things would change a good deal; until that time, they would have to be patient and trust in the mercy of the Lord. Their lives depended on their allegiance to him.

Hild wept as they rode away, for Eadfrid was leaning more and more towards the old beliefs—and she couldn't talk him out of it.

# CÆDWALLA'S CALLING

*– the paupers' army –*

Riding up through the green hills of Mercia after the midsummer celebration, Cædwalla's thoughts turned to Hild. He wondered why she hadn't come out to wish him a good journey. He admired the proud and forthright woman who had given him a lion gift, his joy, now his finest ornament, which he'd had set in gold and wore around his neck at all times.

He wished she'd been his sister, so close did he feel to her, and he was glad he could help her. He couldn't see any reason for Penda wanting to keep her husband in confinement. Penda now had control of Lindsey, surely he couldn't wish for more. For his part, Cædwalla just wanted to get his business in Northumbria over and done with as quickly as possible. He had a pair of young falcons born last spring, and they needed putting to the test.

He reached Eoforwik a few days later, and sent for King Osric—who sent his son, Oswine, with a message saying the king would present himself shortly.

Oswine was a Christian man with the future on his side; he was also so beautiful that the sight of him could be quite startling. His well-mannered and gentle disposition appealed to Cædwalla, and he decided on the spot to entrust Hildeburh's twins to this handsome prince. No better foster-father would be found in Deira. Cædwalla offered him Penda's wine and gave him an arm-ring of light gold; Oswine then left with the twins, returning home to the wife he had recently married, a red-haired beauty of the royal line in Lindsey. The nurse was happy with Cædwalla's choice; the boys would lack for nothing in Oswine's household.

Cædwalla had to wait for three days before King Osric presented himself. And when Cædwalla saw the army Osric had brought with him, he closed the Eoforwik town gates.

Osric did not request negotiation, but simply deployed his army in a ring around the town. He would rather use a little time starving the inhabitants into surrender than burning down his own royal settlement. However, he was caught off guard one moonlit summer's night:

Cædwalla's men made a lightning-fast sortie, killing Osric and many of his troops, some in full flight. Not many came home from the siege of Eoforwik.

Cædwalla was not well pleased. When he had liberated Northumbria, he had clamped down on Edwin's supporters; now he would have to weed out Edwin's enemies too—the very people he had installed. It seemed they had already forgotten their debt to him.

Cædwalla went off by himself to think. He visited a holy hermit in the forest at Elmet, intending to fast and pray while he reflected and awaited a sign from the Lord.

'Come with me to the sea,' said the hermit.

They rode northeast, along the solid Roman roads, and the hermit didn't utter a single word. They rode past Eoforwik and spent the night in Mædeltun. Following the Roman road northwards, they crossed the broad tract of marshland up to Piceringas. Thereafter, the road led up into the highland, covered in its ancient dense forest; oak and lime and elm looking as if they had been there forever, nearly impenetrable alder thicket in the danker patches. The old Roman road cut straight through it all. They didn't know a broad strip had once been cleared alongside the road, they simply noticed a difference between the ancient forest and the airier new forest surrounding all the roads and buildings: ash, birch, some beech, hazel, buckthorn and small oaks.

Having ridden across the high hilly country in silence for several hours, they rode downhill until they crossed the Esca river, following it out to the sea, to Streonæshalch, a good little port Cædwalla had heard about. It was late afternoon and he thought they had reached their destination, but the hermit pressed on. They crossed the Esca river again, in the centre of the town, and now headed southwards along the coast, following an old bridle path.

Cædwalla was comfortable riding alongside the sea as he had grown up by the coast, on the other side of the country. To him, the sea represented freedom. Fish. Steep cliffs with birds' nests. Mussels. Hunting ducks. The missionaries had come by sea from Ireland, bringing the Lord's word. Tradespeople had arrived with rare goods from the Mediterranean countries. Cædwalla loved the sea.

As dusk fell, they rode southwards until the hermit pulled up and pointed across a wide bay to a high projection, just visible against the lighter sea and the summer sky.

'There!' he said.

And that was where they made camp.

Cædwalla was woken by a feather-light finger touching his shoulder. He got up and went out, at which point his man-at-arms leapt to his feet and grabbed wildly for his sword.

Cædwalla's men brought cushions and rosehip tea for their lord and the old hermit sitting outside on the ground, gazing out to sea.

A thin layer of cloud on the horizon, light yellowish, gradually took on more colour from the rising sun. When the luminous disc slid up behind the edge of the sea, the birds started singing: terns, gulls, skuas, ravens, ducks; on land, larks, yellowhammers, finches. The sun had called the earth back to life.

The mist hanging over the land gradually faded, and to the north the bay emerged: the coastline was a horseshoe-shaped hollow, surrounded by wooded upland. The forest was patchy with large clearings, barrows and the occasional farmhouse, smoke already rising into the air.

Their vantage point was on the roof of the world, looking down on the birds. A red-backed falcon nosedived and flew up again with a chaffinch in its beak—the little bird hadn't even had time to register danger. The tide was coming in; you could see each new wave sliding a little further up the shore than the one before. Two small rocks, on which a few gulls had been resting, disappeared under the persistent caress of the waves.

Having sat there for so long that Cædwalla had lost track of time, the old man stood up and bowed to the sun. Cædwalla did the same. They walked across to a ruin, most of its old stone tower rising up from the rubble. They climbed up inside the tower.

A raven flapped into the air, croaking. It had been monitoring the strangers sitting down there on the grass, but now it had to leave its hoarsely protesting young in the nest. They stretched their necks and cackled at the approaching creatures; as the huge figures drew closer, the chicks cowered, pressing themselves flat on the twigs and tufts of heather at the bottom of the nest. Cædwalla stopped and stared at their black beaks with the air of an expert. It would have been easy to plunder the nest, but there was no time for that. He lashed out at the raven mother when she dived at him, and then he followed the hermit to the other side of the square tower, cautiously, so no more heavy stones crumbled away. The big bird landed smoothly on the rim of the nest and watched them distrustfully.

The ravens had given the place its name: Hræfenclif, it was called.

'All this,' the old man said, with a gesture indicating a wide arc across land and sea.

The coastline to the south jutted out, drew in again, jutted out even further, then inward, and far in the distance another projection, chalk-white and sparkling.

Cædwalla gazed down into the depths; the sea had started to pull back. From the tip of the promontory a narrow track led out into the sea, straight and paved with darker stone.

'Where to?' he asked the old man.

The hermit turned and descended from the tower.

Stumbling on the foundations, Cædwalla saw a stone slab meticulously covered in hewn letters, which he tried to decipher. The tower was a link in the chain of warning beacons along the coast, built by the Romans when the Saxons had been threatening attack. The names were the easiest to read: Justinian and Vindicianus. But they hadn't been able to keep the intruders out.

Cædwalla had to get down to the sea, had to taste it: was this eastern water the same as the sea back home at Aberffraw? Having journeyed to the land of the Visigoths, he knew that not all seas were the same; the Mediterranean was salty, and you could float on it as easily as a log.

He clambered down the slope, criss-crossing carefully: the ground was very unstable with alternately loose and solid patches. The soil only slipped away under him once, and he slid some distance before regaining his footing.

By the time he got to the bottom, the tide was out. Pebbles and boulders as tall as a man were spread around a rocky terrain. He looked up at the tower, but it had vanished behind a promontory.

The sea was quite a long way off. The narrow paved track led into the water, uniform square stones placed in a furrow on the seabed—by the Romans, presumably, for who else could have built something like that? Cædwalla knew everything had a natural explanation. The track had undoubtedly been laid to reach something no longer in existence, a chapel or a stronghold washed away by the sea. He knew all about the mighty power of the tide from his home coastline, but in the Mediterranean it didn't have anything like the same force—probably because of the salt, which made it thicker, more sluggish.

He walked towards the water. His body felt light, as did his heart, and his strides were brisk. Seen from the top of the slope, he would probably just look like a little red spider going about its business. He belonged here, sea and rock were his element, and he felt a kinship with the brown rocky ground underfoot. Hearing a tantalizing buzzing in his ears, he quickened his pace. The sea was still quite a way off.

The sound grew slowly louder, swelling to a rumble that rose to the thunder of avalanches and landslides, a roaring from the depths of the earth, perhaps from the fires of Hell itself.

Cædwalla was dizzy: he had to crouch on the stone track. The edge of his cloak dragged in the shallow water. He lowered his head and breathed heavily. The din was coming from below his feet; he twisted round until he was sitting in a little pool, and now everything was getting wet. He could just spot the hermit's brown cloak at the very top of the tower.

A crab scurried off sideways, hurried past his foot and flopped into a little lagoon, right next to a snakestone. The snake had curled up around itself, like they did, and had lost its head. Cædwalla put it in his pocket; the bigger they were, the greater the evil they could cure, and this one was almost as broad as a hand.

He crawled out of the pool and sat on the dryish rock, collecting his thoughts. He scooped up a handful of the water; it was a little saltier than back home, but nothing at all like the Mediterranean.

The tide had turned, and he started heading back. He made for the stone track, but the dizziness and roaring overcame him again and he had to get away from it.

He was nearly back on land when he encountered the most terrible sight he had ever seen: a dragon in the cliffside. About ten feet long, certainly large enough to snap him up in two mouthfuls. Pitch-black and horrifying, it didn't move: maybe it hadn't noticed him yet.

Without his sword and without his man-at-arms, he was naked and helpless. He bitterly regretted his solitary walk, took a couple of steps backwards and tripped over a rock. He looked around for another route up the cliff. The dragon still wasn't moving. His throat was dry; he picked up a few stones as quietly as he could and then remembered the snakestone, maybe that could put the dragon out of action.

When he looked again, it moved slightly, but Cædwalla was quick; he ran forwards a few steps and hurled the snakestone at the dragon's head. Something snapped off, but it didn't move.

He advanced very very slowly—it might be a trap—and could see that half the head was missing. He took another step forwards. And another. And one more, then he stood still and stared.

The dragon had been struck to stone. The snakestone had crushed its head and turned it into its own kind, and with such force that the dragon had become part of the cliff where it had been lurking. Soon it would probably sink right into the rockface.

Cædwalla plucked up his courage and examined the rock, looking for blood to smear on his body as the Angeln hero Sigurd had done. But there wasn't a drop, it was completely dry.

He tried to console himself: bathing in dragon's blood hadn't made Sigurd Fafnersbane invulnerable anyway; a spear had struck him in the back, at the very spot where a fallen leaf had stuck to his skin.

Cædwalla had found an awe-inspiring weapon, so dangerous that he shuddered to think of the possible consequences. It must never fall into the wrong hands.

There was only one problem: the weapon had vanished. He searched and searched an ever-expanding area, in the pools and finally under the rocks. He couldn't believe it had been swallowed up by the cliff. Hope faded, and the only likely explanation seemed to be that it had come to life and slipped away. The dragon's life must have jumped across into the snake.

When the high tide started lapping at his ankles, he had to abandon his search and clamber up the cliff.

Cædwalla's men had set up camp at a fair distance from their master. They took it in turns to keep watch; they brought tea and water and in the evenings a thin vegetable soup, the only nourishment permitted during the fast.

It was raining on the fourth day; the men erected a shelter so Cædwalla and the hermit could sit in their usual place to pray and contemplate. Given that two characters of their calibre were countering the power of the elves and demons that swarmed around such a desolate area, the men weren't afraid. They passed the time playing board games and telling stories, they polished their weapons and made the horses gleam, and they did a bit of hunting.

Cædwalla and the hermit fasted. They spent their days in prayer and contemplation, sitting at the top of the tower, the sea below and the land stretching away to the sides. Clarification gradually came to Cædwalla, and day by day his understanding became sharper.

The misfortunes befalling the land were caused by those who came from afar—as his forefather Ambrosius Aurelianus had known when he had brought the native Britons together and forced the outsiders down into the most south-easterly corner of the land, where they had stayed for more than a generation, until the Britons started their infighting again. When Cædwalla's father was a boy, the intruders had started moving around again and their settlements had sprung up all over the land like molehills. They had spread like a putrid fungus, like a plague.

Now it was the Britons who were being ousted—forced onto the poor soils of the hilly regions to the west, up into the harsh highlands of the Picts, and out to Walas, which in truth had never flowed with milk and honey. Gwynedd and Dyfed didn't have the resources to support the influx of refugees. The proudest asked for nothing, and immediately set off for other shores—in a sea-going vessel if there was one, but otherwise taking their chances in coracles, small wicker-framed craft covered in hide and sealed with tar, suitable for use on lakes and becks, or in flat-bottomed dinghies which, like the coracles, could be carried on your back.

Many had thus reached Ireland or Armorica and further down the coast of Gaul; some even got all the way to the north coast of the land of the Visigoths. Most ended up at the bottom of the sea, fish food. But they would rather commend themselves to the Lord while sailing on the waves than toil like a slave for the unbelievers.

The worshippers of idols spared none who refused to serve them. They had laid monasteries waste, had bound the people of the Lord hand and foot and dragged them behind the horses until they were bloody lumps of flesh. Those of highest rank had been sacrificed to their brutal forefathers. They had burnt book collections, even throwing holy books into the flames. Books were just convoluted drawings on stiff hide, as far as they were concerned. They didn't know what parchment was, could neither read nor write, had never heard Latin, had no books and no art of any merit. Everything they produced was crude and boorish—just like they were. They could only express themselves through the sword—they didn't understand anything else.

Now they had brought misery upon the whole land with their carnage and ignorance.

When the sun rose above the sea on the fifth day, it was of such a light golden colour that you might have mistaken it for a moon. The clouds in the far distance took on a greenish glow, and the air was filled with a tremendous chorus of birdsong.

Cædwalla saw God alight from the sun.

He approached Cædwalla in a straight line, as if he were being pulled by a rope. In his right hand, raised high above his head, he was holding Gabriel's flaming sword, which he passed to Cædwalla: God had chosen *him* to follow in Ambrosius' footsteps. As Moses was once called to lead the people of Israel, now God was calling his servant Cædwalla to unite and lead the divided Britons. The battle would soon be fought, here in Northumbria. The outsiders had to be expelled; the paved track leading out into the sea showed them the route.

Cædwalla was almost knocked off his feet by the magnitude of the task the Lord had placed on his shoulders. He pleaded to be spared, he was not worthy of such an assignment, but God was relentless and vanished into the air.

Cædwalla threw himself to the ground and wept.

The hermit turned to him.

'Do you remember the massacre at Carlegion?'

Cædwalla nodded, he couldn't speak for tears.

'I was one of those who escaped,' said the old man, and Cædwalla grabbed him by the knees and lay prostrate before him; and there he stayed for a long time.

It had been twenty years ago, and felt like yesterday. Cædwalla had been journeying in the land of the Visigoths—King Cadfan's final attempt to interest his youngest son in scholarship, given that he had shown no talent for the business of government. King Cadfan was a highly educated man who spoke Latin as easily as his native language, and his reign had seen life at the monasteries flourish and bards flock to his royal settlement. His two eldest sons read and wrote elegant Latin and were happy to discuss philosophical and political topics with their father. But all this had bypassed Cædwalla—just two Latin words had sunk in: FALCO and LEO.

King Cadfan had links to the Britons in exile with the Visigoths, and also with the royal family there, so he had sent Cædwalla down to multitalented King Sisebut, a man who could write hexameters about the influence of the stars on human lives, who persecuted the Jews and the heretical Arians, and who succeeded in extending his realm. Cædwalla learnt a lot from King Sisebut—including Latin. He was sitting in the shade of an orange tree, eating olives, drinking spicy wine and discussing the errors of Arianism with two of the monks who taught him, when a message arrived from home.

King Ædelfred of Northumbria had been rampaging his way towards Walas when, at Carlegion, he had been confronted by King Cadfan and other Welsh kings. Men and women from the monasteries had also turned out, standing at a distance, fasting and praying for victory over the unbelievers.

'If they call out to their god in opposition to us, then they are fighting against us, even if they are not bearing arms!' Ædelfred had bellowed, and gave the order to cut them down before all else. More than two hundred of the Lord's unarmed servants and handmaids had been slaughtered—only fifty escaped.

The message had arrived via Cædwalla's former tutor, who had been one of those who got away; he had fled to the land of the Visigoths, promising to make sure Cædwalla received news of the massacre.

Cædwalla visited the tutor on his journey home, but by that time the man had turned his back on this world. He sat under a canopy of leafy branches in the depths of the forest and had stopped speaking; not even his eyes revealed any recognition of his former pupil.

On board the vessel taking him home, Cædwalla had a dream: the nonbelievers would overrun the entire land of the Britons. Not a mountaintop, not a rock would they leave untouched as they swarmed, like the locusts of Egypt, throughout the landscape and drove the Britons into the Irish Sea, which would slowly be transformed into a fetid pool of venom covered with lifeless bodies: men, women, children and beasts sloshing around in a chaotic mess, broken bird wings, fish with their bellies in the air.

They would abuse this beautiful green country until it turned into one big dunghill, under a cloud of stifling black smoke so dense the sun seemed in perpetual eclipse. Not a pasture would remain, and the animals would die.

Cædwalla now realized this had been the first sign from God about the task he had to undertake—but he had never been interested in politics. His oldest brother, and then the next brother down, were the ones destined to follow in their father's footsteps, as they had an aptitude for leadership and had been brought up to rule. They had both, nonetheless, ended up as vassals of King Ædelfred the year before he was defeated by Edwin and Rædwald.

Cædwalla's second oldest brother fell in the battle, having fought honourably. The oldest brother was strung up in a tree, an offering to Edwin's forefathers in gratitude for victory over Ædelfred.

Edwin had later sworn on his forthcoming life eternal that he hadn't known the man was his foster-brother. This foster-brother had been too proud to speak up; he and Edwin had, after all, gone to Mass together in Aberffraw.

King Cadfan hadn't had the power to avenge his son; he died of shame, and on his gravestone Cædwalla wrote: King Cadfan, most wise and renowned of all kings.

He had the words hewn in stone because he knew Gwynedd would never again have so great a king—he personally wouldn't hit the mark, that was certain. He would happily have done without the royal crown: board games and falconry, that was enough for him.

Now the Lord had given him victory over Edwin and vengeance for his oldest brother. Another sign. And today he'd handed him the sword of flame, for a task that was infinitely greater than his father's. He'd have to get a move on if he was going to make up for lost ground.

He released his grip on the hermit's knees and stood up. The old man blessed him, and Cædwalla gave him a horse and a golden cup as a parting gift, then he left Hræfenclif and rode back to his army in Eoforwik.

Following his father's death, Oswine had fled; Cædwalla thus assumed Hild's twins were in safety and he wouldn't have to spare anyone.

His army spent the autumn advancing victoriously throughout the country, burning farms and crops. Initially, some slaves attempted to defend the property of masters who had fled, using harvesting implements and kitchen utensils; gradually realizing where their best interests lay, however, slaves started to join the liberation army.

It was an army made up of the poorest of the poor. Cædwalla didn't turn away anyone who offered to enter his service: lame, stooped, undersized or deformed, they could all be used, particularly as yuletide approached and not many men capable of bearing arms were left in Deira. He even let women and children join his following; he didn't have the heart to leave them without protection and food. As it turned out, many of the women became excellent warriors.

Those born into slavery had never held a weapon. Hang a sword at their side and they straightened their backs, discussed their kit and compared patterns and sheaths, studs and fittings. They were also very interested in the fine clothing they seized along the way, and were constantly swapping and gaming for the weapons, clothes and other equipment seized from freemen.

The moment of fulfilment had finally arrived, and old scores had to be settled. They all had something to avenge, and weren't too bothered if the hand now paying the penalty was or wasn't the very one that had cracked the whip and only allowed a starvation ration of cabbage soup; the important thing was the repayment of injustice.

They became increasingly well-armed, all had spears, most had swords or long-bladed knives, nearly everyone had a shield, lots of chainmail, and one man had even seized a helmet—but Cædwalla demanded he hand it over; it wasn't fitting for a slave to wear a helmet, freedom or no freedom.

It was often difficult to get people to move on; they gazed with longing at the granary, at the pigsty and the milk-yielding cows, while Cædwalla's soldiers forced them to set fire to it all and leave. They simply couldn't miss the opportunity by walking away from all that goodness, so they dragged along hens and sides of pork. They were never quite sure where the next meal was coming from. Most only knew the feeling of a really full stomach at yuletide, when their masters celebrated the winter solstice. Eating your fill of meat day after day was not within the scope of their experience; they had never done so before and they couldn't digest all that meat, but nor could they resist the temptation when they spotted an animal ripe for slaughter. Now they marched from binge to binge.

Cædwalla had to eat on his own. He couldn't cope with all that vomit and the stench from loose stomachs. He had to take bark extract against his increasing loss of appetite; he fasted with increasing frequency.

At yuletide they held a much-needed break. Having been slaves to the heathens for so long, they could now at last celebrate the birth of their Lord in a befitting manner. They celebrated for a whole month, in Eoforwik, while Cædwalla was in Tamoworthig on some pretext or other. Upon his return, he gave orders for departure; staying in the town was untenable now.

When spring arrived, and pickings were becoming scarce, Cædwalla realized their task in Deira was done. He decided to head for Bernicia.

Eanfred, the new king of Bernicia, came to meet him at Cetreht. He had left his army behind and arrived with twelve unarmed men pulling three carts loaded with gifts far outdoing the agreed-upon tribute: pitchers of sweet spiced wine from the Mediterranean area, three tall drinking glasses from Egypt, a gilt silver dish from Anatolia, large quantities of bronze receptacles, a finely-carved ivory box filled with heavy gold jewellery, thirty reindeer hides, thirty wolf skins and fifty marten skins from snared beasts, all excellently tanned and whole.

Cædwalla took a gold ring and held it up: a rough shape and coarse decoration, executed with the Angles' usual lack of elegance; it could easily be melted down and re-worked.

King Eanfred promised twice as much if he would make peace.

'Taste the wine at least,' he smiled, handing Cædwalla a sealed earthenware jar.

Cædwalla resisted the temptation. The Devil has many faces, he thought. He would no longer be deceived. He raised the jar and let go; the red wine splashed up their legs and spread across the floor.

His first thought was to have them slain by the sword, but then he pictured his hanged brother, so he had them hanged too, one by one, from an ash tree that was only half in blossom.

Cædwalla then defeated King Eanfred's army; once that was done, he felt so sick of everything that not even a long-postponed falcon hunt could raise his spirits.

He commanded his army to set forth and ravage Bernicia, to burn down Bebbanburh and the reconstructed royal fortress of Ad Gefrin. He then fasted and prayed for three days, imploring the Lord to release him from this hard calling. On the third day, God took pity and gave Cædwalla to understand that he should enter a monastery and thereby fight the fight of the good. The evil was too overwhelming to be contested with the sword. By prayer and fasting he should bring forth goodness, peace, justice, expulsion of the outsiders. But just as Jesus had wandered for forty days in the wilderness, so must Cædwalla continue his calling in Northumbria for a further forty days.

His army spent those forty days marching through the realm on a crusade of justice. Liberation of the Britons was at hand, first in Northumbria, then in all their territory.

The army continued to increase in numbers, and it wasn't easy to find food and shelter, especially when the Angles started burning their farms before heading north.

A plague broke out, carrying off many of Cædwalla's people. Every time they made camp, they had to dig a mass grave.

The army was no longer the biggest ever seen on the Britons' terrain, but Cædwalla's soldiers still spread the word of its invincibility.

In the realm of the Picts, Oswald—half-brother of the murdered King Eanfred, and Ædelfred's eldest son with Acha—gathered an army of freemen who had fled from the south: people who had always had enough to eat, who knew how to organize a campaign, use weapons, find provisions, plan and bring off a battle. All had good horses and were equipped with weapons they knew how to use; in number, about a twentieth of the ragged army, but as seasoned as mercenaries. And they wanted their land back.

Cædwalla's soldiers had moved south to build up their strength, and had set up camp just north of the huge wall. It had turned unnaturally warm, and the stench was dreadful. The sick dragged themselves to Mass several times a day, praying for an end to this plague. They nearly all had loose stomachs, and it was impossible to stop them relieving themselves right where they stood, so quickly did their insides move. You couldn't walk through the camp without constantly stepping in big brownish-yellow splodges, crawling with white worms.

Cædwalla had kept careful track of the days: he had to remain at his post for two more. He lashed out to get rid of a swarm of bluebottles trying to settle in his hair and on his head. Holding a scarf to his face, he hurried out of the camp.

He found a slightly cooler spot up by the wall, where he managed to get rid of the flies by calmly letting them settle, and then striking.

He had swatted nearly forty now—his magic number. He arranged them on the ground, little heaps of five placed in a straight line. Having squashed the fortieth, he looked up and caught sight of two of his scouts approaching at a gallop.

They drew up in front of him: Oswald's army had gathered just a few miles to the north and would attack the next day.

Cædwalla simply couldn't handle going back to the bluebottles and the stench from the brownish-yellow sloppy puddles. He sent the scouts home. He trusted his subordinates; they would have to do what needed doing. Now was probably the time to instil some discipline—and some battle skills. Perhaps those who were very ill and any pregnant women should be taken to a safe place. Somewhere or other. Yes, and the children too.

It was all a bit much to deal with. He couldn't keep his thoughts together for any length of time, could only think about his prayers, his fasting and Mass. The Lord was on their side—that was the crucial thing.

Cædwalla sat at the highest point of the wall, waiting to watch the sun set behind the forest. The swallows were flying low, the evening was orange-golden and calm; the sunset breeze had brought along a wonderful coolness and he saw a new sky and a new earth and realized that a new Jerusalem was already on its way down from Heaven.

When the bats started swarming, his manservant came to take him back to camp. He listened to all the proposals as to how best the army should be deployed; he nodded to all the plans.

He was no longer very interested in worldly things. He spent the night in prayer, stretched out on the ground, and thanked the Lord that his task would soon be at an end.

There wasn't any actual battle. Oswald's soldiers advanced in an unbroken straight line and lost just one man. The encounter was brief.

Oswald had forbidden any kind of looting. Some of his men gazed wistfully at the crimson silk cloaks, edged with fur and trimming shot with gold, which they found around lean shoulders and swollen bellies. They thought the aftermath of putrid guts could be washed away, but they didn't dare defy their army commander. Oswald ordered everything burnt, even weapons and jewellery and costly domestic utensils.

They found more food than any other goods. The freemen shook their heads in dismay and shock as they worked through the camp finding sacks of flour that had turned into sacks of mealworms, half carcasses of pigs almost completely devoured by maggots, stockpiles of mouldy green bread under canvas, big chunks of meat secreted everywhere and taken over by mites and grubs.

Having gone one third of the way through, the stench forced them to turn back. Oswald gave the order to torch the camp; it made no great difference to those who couldn't move whether they were burnt or hacked to death.

Anyone fleeing was chased down, and none were spared—not even the children. They had been part of this satanic destruction of the realm and its natural order, had seen slaves boasting of gold and witnessed women using weapons. Unnaturalness had a way of sticking; evils of that kind were as infectious as the plague.

When his personal troops realized the battle was lost, Cædwalla was hauled up onto a horse. Without a look to either side, they whipped the horses into a gallop along the Deira Way.

They managed to ride seven miles southwards before being overtaken by the enemy's fresh horses. Cædwalla hadn't really sensed what was going on around him; he had held on with half-closed eyes while his man-at-arms guided the horse homewards.

In spirit, Cædwalla was already handling birds of prey in his Lord's eternal hunt. He barely noticed when a spear pierced his back. He was so happy that his mission in Northumbria had finally come to an end.

# A RED-HAIRED DAUGHTER

*- a monk named Aidan -*

Eadfrid wasn't particularly pleased to get his wife back from Gwynedd; he said he'd been much calmer on his own. But he was worried—they'd had no news of the children.

'Didn't you tell the lion to send word?' he asked.

'I told Cædwalla,' Hild replied, 'and he promised.'

'You should never have left our children to someone like him.'

'No,' said Hild, 'but it was your choice.'

'I presumed you knew what you were doing,' said Eadfrid.

Hild hadn't known she would miss the children so much it hurt, physically. Part of her body was missing; she could feel she had shrunk, even though her belly was growing around the new baby.

Her life now had just the one purpose: to save their blemished honour from further harm. To do so, she must protect the little life growing inside her, and stop the filth and vermin from prospering on her husband: make sure his hair, beard and nails weren't allowed to grow unchecked and keep his demons at arm's length.

The latter task was beyond her, but she refused to let them prevail. She doggedly continued to talk to her husband as if he were still the man to whom she had pledged her troth, as if he were still master of his own house, and occasionally he replied in his old voice.

His eruptions lost their dramatic force. It wasn't that they became less violent, quite the contrary, but they no longer had the power to throw her off balance; they had become rather trite.

Mostly he just sat in his corner. He'd got into the habit of holding his hand over his mouth while speaking, so she had to get up close in order to hear what he was mumbling—but standing at a safe distance.

Just before the sacrificial month, it was rumoured in Tamoworthig that a quite exceptional monk named Aidan was travelling in the area. Preachers usually only came visiting in the summer, but this man paid no attention to summer or winter, he set forth when he thought the time was right. He'd come from Dalriada, from the monastery on Iona, where they followed their holy father Columba's example and teachings. Columba had come from Ireland, and the king had granted him a little island, whence he conducted his missionary work. He had even converted Brude, king of the Picts.

The monastery on Iona was famous for its scholarship, and crowds always gathered around servants of the Lord who came from the isle. They were also sought after in Mercia, for their wisdom and for their powers of healing. People who had heard the words of a holy man had often avoided the epidemics that usually raged during the winter—even if they weren't baptized.

Hild tried to persuade Eadfrid to go with her, but he had earache and wasn't in the mood for anything. She went on her own, accompanied by Talcuin, and when she heard the man speak she realized that, indeed, he was an exceptional man.

She had brought a finely-woven tunic and a good-sized goose, which Penda's wife had given her to take along, and asked if she could be heard in confession.

To her surprise, the monk simply gave the choice goose away, to a thin and haggard woman in the crowd. Her skinny arms hugged the fat goose while her eyes darted around anxiously, in case this sudden wealth should just as suddenly be taken away again. He gave the tunic to a slave boy with scab all over his face. Hild hadn't expected her excellent gifts to be squandered, or she would have brought something else. The tunic would be ruined within ten days on that boy; it wasn't a work garment. But given was given.

Then it was her turn. She confessed her offence: she had drained her husband's powers, so now he was a captive of the very king who had slain his father and his brother.

Aidan gave her the Lord's forgiveness, but pointed out that human forgiveness was a different matter—one she would have to sort out with the persons concerned.

'We are all in debt to God and to our neighbour, and the one probably no more than the other,' he said. 'If your husband continues to throw this blame in your face, then he makes himself to blame. No person and no lineage is an island: we are all linked one to the other, for good or bad, and there is nothing to choose between the one or the other. You have received God's forgiveness. Now you must forgive yourself and then your husband. And your husband must forgive himself and then you. Tell this to your husband! On the Day of Judgement we must all answer for our sins, and then the Lord will judge us. But during the brief life we have here on earth, it is our duty to forgive one another. Just like the Lord forgave us when he was born a man here on earth. Do you understand?'

Hild looked unsure, so he continued: 'If we cannot forgive, we forge a yoke for one another, the heaviness of which will weigh us down to the ground like exhausted slaves. And then we have disparaged his act of salvation. Jesus Christ died to deliver us from slavery. Do you understand now, my child?'

'No,' she said, 'because if no one is judged here on earth, then injustice will have free rein.'

'Injustice must be judged and punished,' said Aidan. 'And thereafter it must be forgiven. As our Lord said: Let him who is without sin cast the first stone. Kings and executioners must therefore strive for purity and justice, and forgive the people they are set to punish.'

'Yes, but that's not how it is,' said Hild faintly.

'That's how it must be,' said Aidan. 'And if you remember to say your prayers, then you will notice that every day takes you closer to God's kingdom. The day will come when kings cast themselves in the dust at the feet of their slaves, and executioners will ask the severed heads for forgiveness. Just you wait and see!'

'When will that day come about?' she asked.

'Not today, and not tomorrow. When the time is right. When the kingdom of God comes and Christ returns to earth with his servants from on high. Therefore, as he says: Pray and watch, for none know the day or the hour!'

And then he broke into a song that caused all talking to die away. It was a familiar spring song, but instead of thanking Eostre for the green and the freshness, he thanked the Lord. Apart from that, the words were the same.

Hild was confused. Her own worries had now been replaced by all the thoughts Aidan provoked.

'I didn't think that was allowed!' she exclaimed when Aidan's song came to an end. 'Paulinus always said we should keep away from the old songs.'

'Have you been baptized, my child?' Aidan asked.

'I was baptized by Paulinus, when I was thirteen years old, together with King Edwin, an Easter day,' she answered proudly.

'Then sing any song you choose,' Aidan smiled, patting her head. 'Just remember to remove all mention of the pagan idols. Nothing pleases God more than the sound of people singing, of that you can be sure.'

He broke into a new song, his voice becoming even richer, and people couldn't help but join in. Hild was delighted to sing at full volume once again; there hadn't been much singing lately.

'May I write to you?' she asked when the song was over.

Aidan looked at her sceptically.

'Have you a scribe?'

'I can write. Our language and Latin . . . '

'Be alert to conceit, my child. You write Irish too?'

She nodded.

Aidan was not familiar with her language, and their conversation had been in Irish. He could read Latin, particularly if he had heard what was written read aloud, just once, but he was reluctant to write it. He knew that humility and good deeds led to God, not letters written with a quill—they led all over the place. And as the Lord had said: Only one thing is needful.

'Write to me as often as you like,' said Aidan. 'But remember, it is prayer that leads us to the Lord, not the skill of writing. You must say David's psalms—every day!'

'Thank you, father,' said Hild, bowing to him.

She took great comfort from having met this holy man.

The sense of anchorage that Hild found in the psalms of David and in her connection with Aidan stopped her drifting away from reality.

She recited the psalms every day, all one hundred and fifty of them, and if she was interrupted by Eadfrid's demon, she started from the beginning again. There were a few passages she hadn't been quite sure about—the priest in Dolwyddelan had helped by reading them with her. Paulinus had also stressed the importance of saying the psalms every day.

She recited them rhythmically, as Paulinus had taught her, sounding slightly different to the bards when they spoke verse. This way fitted in with the rhythm of her weaving.

> O Lord my God,
> by day I cry out and even at night;
> let my prayer come before you,
> turn your ear to my clamour;
> for my soul is distressed,
> my life drawing close to the realm of the dead . . .
>
> If I say 'The darkness shall hide me,
> light shall be night around me!'
> then the darkness is not dark for you
> and the night will shine as the day;
> the darkness is as the light.
> For you have made my inner parts,
> woven me in my mother's womb.
> I shall thank you, for I am most wonderfully made.
> Marvellous are all your works
> as my soul knows right well.
> My bones were not hidden from you
> when I was fashioned in secret, in the depths of the earth;
> your eyes saw my creation, being yet unfinished,
> and in your book all my parts were written,
> the days decided before a single one as yet was formed.
> How precious are your thoughts to me, O God,

*how great is their sum!*
*Should I count them, they are more than the sand,*
*when I awake, I am still with you.*
*Surely you will slay the wicked, O God.*
*May the men of blood retreat from me,*
*they who speak against you wickedly,*
*and your enemies who take your name in vain.*
*Do I not hate them, O Lord, who hate you?*
*Am I not grieved with those who attack you?*
*I hate them with perfect hatred;*
*they are my enemies too.*
*Search me, O God, and know my heart!*
*Examine me, and know my thoughts!*
*See if I am on the path of torment*
*and lead me on the path of eternity!*

The baby arrived at yuletide, a good year after the twins had been born. It had come too soon, and some of its skin was rubbed off during the birth. The midwife thought it had been dead for a while. Hild was ill until springtime. It had been a girl; red-haired like the others. She couldn't even be baptized.

Another case of someone else having to suffer for her transgressions. The Lord could not have chosen a harsher punishment: her unborn baby had paid the price.

# THE LORD GAVE ...
# THE LORD TOOK AWAY ...

*- Hild and Eadfrid in Elmet -*

Hild grieved for Cædwalla. She found it hard to believe all the details she was given about his behaviour in Northumbria. Surprised by her husband's sudden vitality, she wondered if the demons had just been a dream.

Eadfrid was now too busy to sit in his corner. He sent word to his father's old allies: he intended to return and present himself for selection in Eoforwik. He spoke sensibly and coherently, you could hear what he was saying and he had started smiling.

Penda assisted in word and action. He was well informed about the state of affairs in the neighbouring kingdoms and would rather see Deira under Eadfrid's command than united with Bernicia under a man like Oswald; for Oswald had learnt more than Christianity and writing on Iona, and he had waited a long time to get hold of his father's realm.

It was as good as a done deed that Bernicia would choose Oswald, but Eadfrid's chances were favourable in Deira. After the horrors of recent years, people had realized that Edwin's times had been the good times after all. Edwin's lineage had grown popular.

It was a lovely summer's morning when Hild and Eadfrid took their leave of Penda and his wife, who had housed them for a good year and a half. The children ran alongside, unhappy to be losing their teacher.

Everything had been agreed: Eadfrid could govern with Penda's blessing, and had in return promised to give up Lindsey—even though the realm had been under his father's command.

Laughing, Eadfrid had declined Penda's offer of an entourage of one hundred men. 'I want them to know that I bring peace!' he'd said, voicing his wife's heartfelt desire. Hild had smiled; her husband's spirit had finally returned and now he had the opportunity to show the world that he really was Edwin's son, not only in name.

Penda had, as was his custom, read the signs for their journey, and had told them what to expect. But they knew how he interpreted his signs; they laughed and thanked him.

Superstitions belonging to the olden times were not going to hinder them now. They would soon be entering their estate at Mædeltun, or what was left of it; the buildings would have to be repaired, and the royal settlements in Eoforwik, Driffeld, Cetreht and by Loidis would have to be rebuilt. They talked about hiring some of the good woodcarvers from Bernicia to come and work on decorating the gables. Their royal estates would not be inferior to Edwin's burnt-down settlements.

'And spirals on the interior posts,' said Hild, when they retired after the first day of the journey.

'All over,' Eadfrid laughed, pulling her close, 'all over!'

They travelled along the Ryknild road, an ancient giant's way. Penda had insisted on giving them two of his big Gallic horses, but Hild had asked to ride an ordinary horse. When it trotted, you hardly noticed you were riding at all. Gallic horses were more for processions and royal appearances. They had accepted the two for their entry into Eoforwik, but undertook the actual journey on the more comfortable mounts bred by the Britons.

Another day on horseback took them across the Isara river and into Elmet, the kingdom of Britons that Edwin had at one time obliterated and incorporated into Deira, in revenge for Hereric's death. A good many Angles from Bernicia and Deira, liberated slaves, had been moved down here and had started to clear the ancient forest. These settlers fell foul of the natives, who were forced further and further into the forest. The new masters demanded taxes, and many of the Britons had thus sold themselves into slavery or left the area completely.

Eadfrid and Hild entered a farm high up in the hills, with a view across forests to the north and south. The farmer was beside himself at the great honour and organized a splendid feast. Deira's coming royal couple were to lack for nothing, and he didn't want to lack their friendship.

'Wasn't it here?' asked Hild, looking around.

'Yes,' answered the farmer, 'but I built all this myself. The royal settlement was where the farm buildings are now. Yes, eighteen years ago.'

'Twenty-one years since my father was poisoned,' said Hild. 'I would like to see his grave.'

The burial ground wasn't far from the old royal settlement. They had removed the Britons' graves, but kept those of the best Angle families. Hild prayed at her father's grave and made an offering of one of the costly pitchers of wine Penda had given them.

Once mounted, they were confronted by two ragged families of Britons who threw themselves to the ground, the largest of the men with a raised hand indicating he had something to say.

'Stand and speak!' the farmer ordered.

The man obeyed with thanks and came nearer. Using elegant phrases with many words of praise about the farmer's reputation for goodness, and with the most courteous of gestures, the man offered himself, his family and his sister's entire family as slaves. All were healthy, his wife's weaving was unsurpassed, his sister was known for her excellent bread, and he and his sister's husband were splendid woodcarvers and experts in livestock farming. Moreover, they were skilled in snaring—animals and birds alike.

The farmer had been staring into the air for most of the man's speech, and had started scratching himself here and there. Now he turned to Hild, laughing.

'He can certainly sing, can't he?'

And to the man's bowed head he shouted: 'We don't appreciate that kind of gibberish here! If you want to say something, then you'll have to learn a language people can understand!'

He smiled to his distinguished guest and was about to ride on, but drew his reins in again when Hild started translating the man's speech word for word.

'We don't need any more slaves at the moment,' he replied. 'Tell him to come back at harvest-time.'

Hild translated, but the man was not to be dissuaded. They would build their own huts, they would bring eight pigs and fourteen goats, and the children were good at watching over them.

'I have spoken!' exclaimed the farmer in annoyance once Hild had translated the last part. 'But they are obviously deaf.'

Whereupon they rode off.

'He thinks he can save himself by being the first to turn up,' the farmer explained, 'because in a month they'll come pouring out of the forests, and then you'll be able to get a whole family for nothing.'

'But,' he added a little later, 'if they can't even be bothered to learn the language, then of course we have no use for them.'

Hild didn't respond. The price of slaves had risen enormously and would undoubtedly keep on going up now the freemen had returned home and re-established themselves. Purchasing his slaves was this farmer's own business, and she wasn't queen yet.

Once she *was* queen, she thought, then she'd teach him a thing or two—including a little respect for the natives. Her nurse had been a Briton, and many of the servants, so to her the language felt almost as natural as her mother tongue. And she valued their songs and stories just as highly as those of her own people. In Ad Gefrin, the Britons' language had been heard just as often as her own, and it was also spoken in Tamoworthig. Remaining ignorant of the language spoken by your slaves was hardly a wise move—they might be talking ill of you behind your back and making all sorts of plans.

Yes, the natives were different, but they were a people of sorts too, created by God in his own image. She knew many Britons who were actually not as bad as they were made out to be.

Once she was queen, she would invite this boastful farmer to one of her evening revelries, and make sure the entertainment consisted exclusively of songs and stories from the Britons. Perhaps she would present him with a very small bronze ornament, patterned with the natives' interlaced spirals; she certainly wouldn't be giving him anything made from silver.

His purchase of slaves might not be her concern, but his stupidity was—once she was queen.

She had actually only intervened with her translation because the youngest child—too young to have learnt how to behave—had carried on staring steadfastly at her while all the others bowed their heads, and she thought she could see something of Hundfrid's dreamy smile in those eyes.

Not a particularly good-looking child, nearly bald with protruding ears, nowhere near as handsome as her own twins, but with a lovely smile.

The thought warmed her all evening. Perhaps she would send word that she wanted to buy the child, so her own infants could learn how to employ a helper from the outset—always supposing the little staring Briton was a boy, of course.

Eadfrid reached for his wife, but she was too tired and pretended to be asleep.

He smiled into the darkness, let out a happy little sigh, and placed an arm and a leg over her sleeping body. Now she would see what he was made of; he would finally be able to provide her with a life of true honour and happiness. She wasn't born to a life of captivity, and she would be glad to get the twins home. The thought that she might begin to sing again, her strong deep voice, warmed his body. She no longer spoke much; when she did, she rarely looked you in the eye, you could hardly hear what she was saying. Soon she would stand up straight and conduct herself with her old dignity. Deira would have the wisest and proudest queen ever.

Eadfrid gave his wife a careful little hug, and fell asleep with a contented smile on his lips. A sunny, delightful dream came to him: Deira's freemen greeted them with shouts of joy as he and his proud wife rode into Eoforwik, in the luminous glow of golden rays and with the unnaturally slow movements of dreams. 'Long live King Edwin's son!' they cried out. 'Long live King Edwin's son, our King Eadfrid!'

He was awakened by his man-at-arms—an urgent message had arrived from Penda. He hushed the man so as not to disturb his wife, gently stroked her hair and left the bed.

Hild awoke from brooding dreams. She had been standing next to the mighty ash tree in the sacred grove of Godmundingaham; had tried to embrace the blessed tree, pressing her arms against its furrowed bark and gazing up at its crown. Then she had seen herself as the titmouse hopping effortlessly between the highest branches, looking down at the earth, encircled by light green leaves swaying gently in the wind.

She turned to her husband; he had come back to her, free and proud as he'd been before misfortune had befallen them. She moved to nestle against him, but his side of the bed was empty.

She got up and went out. It wasn't light yet, but the blackbird had begun to sing, perched at the top of a large ash tree, deep tones welling from its throat.

That was a good sign—to be greeted by tranquillity and the warbling of a single blackbird in the early morning. A blackbird was often one of your kin who had come to wish you well. If only she could return the greeting half so beautifully, she thought, and smiled to herself.

She moved closer to the tree—a gentle breeze rocked the leaves, and a delicate rustling came from the poplars on the other side. She stood quite still and, for the first time since the misfortune, she felt free, endlessly free, and the future lay before them bright and full of promise.

To the east there was a faint blurred glow: the day would be dry and bring good weather for the journey. When they rode into Eoforwik the streets would be filled with people waiting to greet them. She wouldn't make her entrance in travelling clothes; today, from early morning, she would wear her new red ceremonial dress with its gold-wrought trimming, Penda's magnificent farewell gift, and the golden cap with long fluttering ribbons and high crown that Penda's wife had sewn for her. They wouldn't enter the capital of Deira looking like paupers—thanks to Penda's friendship.

She drew herself up and took a deep breath. Fortune had been hard on them: the Lord had bowed the proud mind; her husband had paid the penalty for her arrogance, as had their little daughter with the red hair. Now Hild would be a queen to Eadfrid, a queen of whom he could be proud, so she could pay off her debt of guilt.

She was Hereric's daughter. This was the place where he had been so shamefully murdered, and this was where she would now restore the dignity of his family—as the blackbird had come to attest. Perhaps her new position would enable her to find her brother; she knew he was alive, somewhere, either here or in Bernicia where Oswald would become king. Oswald would help her, he was a Christian man, and the son of Edwin's sister, Acha.

The thought of once again holding Hundfrid and Wilbrord in her arms warmed her. Their small snug bodies, their little prattling sounds, the fragrance of babies—she gasped for air and laughed to herself. How she would sing for Hundfrid; every hour she would sing for him, the little minstrel.

A cock crowed. She turned and was walking quickly back to the house when something caught her foot, causing her to stumble. Her right arm landed on the chest of a large prostrate body; as her weight pressed down on the chest, blood spurted out of the man's open mouth, sounding like vomiting or a deep sigh, over her face and over her hair. She rolled off down his right-hand side and thrashed around in the grass before struggling to her feet.

It wasn't the gruesome sight of the almost severed right arm, it wasn't the blood oozing from a slim fatal wound in his breast—a clean incision with a sword—nor was it being splattered with blood that made her stiffen and then relax all her muscles, a warm dampness running down her legs and filling her shoes; it was that she had immediately recognized him: Eadfrid's man-at-arms. He would never desert his lord.

She put her hands to her face as all the strength seeped from her body; she sank to the ground without a thought for the puddle she had made and in which she was now sitting. Her left hand clutched the sleeve of the man-at-arms and tugged it back and forth, the slash becoming more and more exposed: a pink chasm of flesh, no more blood flowing from it. Her feet squeezed in under his body, seeking protection from the raw morning air. She leant forwards and pressed her forehead against his chest; he was their protector, after all, a gift from Penda. He had given them one of his very best men for the journey into their new life.

She huddled as closely as possible into him, seeking security and a little warmth, but there wasn't much left.

She had fallen into the hands of the living god; and now she knew he wouldn't release her until he had burnt to ashes everything she called hers, until her pride had been rubbed away and she was able to submit to him in praise. Just like Job had done.

Would she be able to? What was it Job had said?

'The Lord gave, the Lord took away, the Lord gives to me again.'

No, that's not how it went, quite wrong.

She sat up. 'The Lord gave, the Lord took away . . . '

That much was certainly right. And then what? Something about praise? Yes. She said aloud, into the air: 'The Lord gave, the Lord took away, praised be the name of the Lord'—and turned her gaze upwards.


He had one shoe missing. Only the left foot was wearing a shoe; the right one just hung there all naked. Almost like the day it had come into the world.

'What have you done with your shoe, Eadfrid?' she called up to him cautiously.

When there was no reply, she started to search. It had to be somewhere. A shoe doesn't walk off by itself.

'No, no,' she laughed, 'a shoe can't walk, it has to *be* walked. A shoe can't do anything except sit still until someone puts it on and walks off in it. Wait,' she called up to him again, 'I'll find it for you.'

And she found it, not so very far away, on a flattened patch of grass. She examined the area closely and gave the shoe a stern look.

'Was it you, naughty shoe, did you trample the grass? What has the grass ever done to you, might I ask. Why have you stamped it down like this, that's what I'd like to know.'

And since no reply was forthcoming here either, she slapped it hard.

'You think you'll get away with this, do you? Think you can trick fate by staying silent, eh? But just let me tell you, the living god sees everything and knows your most secret thoughts. You'll not trick *him*.'

She pinched the shoe hard, but it still didn't reply; all she squeezed out of it was a little moisture.

'I see, so you think you'll be let off, do you? You think fate will be won over by tears? Then just let me show you something.'

And she pounded the shoe hard on the ground, to beat the evil out of it. Once it was limp and motionless and had given up all resistance, she walked back and stood under the ash tree.

'I've found your shoe, Eadfrid. Do you want me to put it on you, or what? Would you rather do it yourself? No, that won't do.'

She would have to think this through carefully because Eadfrid's wrath could be terrible. It was even more important to take care now that the demon had left him. It could return soon enough.

'I don't know, Eadfrid—shall I put your shoe on for you? Or perhaps you prefer just wearing the one?'

You never could tell with her husband. Having worked something out with the utmost care, it could easily transpire that things should have been done differently after all. So what you had done was just terrible and the floodgates would open and you were all but knocked over by the venom gushing forth.

She transferred the shoe into her other hand, straightening it out a little.

'There are shoemakers in Eoforwik, Eadfrid, you say so yourself: shoemakers who have no equal in the whole of Mercia. Isn't that right, you say so yourself?'

She started pacing uneasily up and down. By this point, she should long since have been told to hold her tongue, or that she was quite fundamentally mistaken, or that his ear was aching. He should also have thrown something at her.

It was all very wrong indeed.

'I didn't do it to be mean, Eadfrid,' she said, looking up at him. 'I just thought you'd like your shoe back and so I found it for you.'

She stood still for a while, gazing at his body, which was hanging so absolutely bolt upright—apart from the head, which was tilting forwards and slightly to the side.

That must be because of the rope. Tied in a noose around his neck. He'd always had a way of holding his head a bit on the slant. Particularly when he was cold. And it was cold now.

'But if you're freezing, then your shoe's here, you know,' she called out.

She wouldn't dream of saying anything about the imprudence of going out without hose. She'd stopped that kind of 'babying', as he called it, long ago. She thought her thoughts, but didn't say any word to Eadfrid that might cause the demon to jump out at her.

Now she was freezing, shaking even, and the shawl . . . where was her shawl? Surely she hadn't come out wearing nothing but this nightshift? She'd like to go indoors, but wasn't sure whether or not Eadfrid would be furious if she left his shoe, and she couldn't reach up to him. She daren't simply put it on his foot. Nor did she dare put it on the ground; the grass was wet with dew and it would just start weeping again, so that was out of the question.

She paced up and down under the tree and considered her options. Finally, temptation got the better of her and she called up to him.

'I'm cold now, Eadfrid, and, if you don't mind, I'm going back to bed.'

He didn't answer.

'Is it all right then, if I go back up? I'll leave your shoe here, in case you want to put it on.'

She found a big stone, which she dragged over and positioned underneath him; she placed the shoe on the stone and left.

When she was halfway to the house, she ran back and grabbed the shoe.

'I think I'll take it up with me after all, Eadfrid. It's far too cold out here.'

She crept down under the cover, but couldn't find any warmth. She missed her husband's body. Much could be said about him, and there was much that she thought about him too, but the warmth from his body was lovely—and it wasn't at the mercy of the demons; only his arms, and especially his mouth, might pounce on her.

She got up, she had to find him, she really needed a little warmth and, yes, they were on their way to Eoforwik, on their way home to Deira! It suddenly dawned on her, what had she been thinking? He was rid of the demons and their new life had already begun. She must have been dreaming. Yes, she'd been dreaming about the huge ash in the sacred grove—of course she had.

Pulling on her cloak, she opened the shutters to the new day. Their new day. At that very moment she heard stealthy footsteps come up the stairs and walk into the next-door chamber.

'Talcuin,' she called, 'come in here.'

Talcuin presented himself, somewhat ashamed at being found out.

'And where were you, Talcuin?' she asked.

He looked down, unwilling to divulge the woman's name. She slapped his face, first with her right hand and then with her left hand, making the palms sting. He winced a couple of times, but didn't move.

'Go, slave!' she commanded in a voice he'd never heard before. He noticed she was shaking, was sweaty and pallid. He left, as instructed.

She stared out of the window. Dawn, the sun was about to break through.

Just in front of her, no more than fifty, sixty paces away, hung her husband. She stared at him, but he was looking down, a little lopsided.

A breeze sprang up, as so often at sunrise, causing him to swing very gently. The leaves joined in, they said something, swaying there in the wind. She couldn't catch what they were saying, and perhaps they were talking to him anyway.

'But Eadfrid, why are you hanging in that tree?' she asked, finally.

She'd been wondering about this for a quite a while now. She just hadn't dared say it until she was well inside the house, and not so close.

In the chaos that followed, Talcuin was the only one to keep his composure. He had spent a night of intense passion with a raven-haired woman whose husband was away in the forest with the cattle. As such an event occurred but rarely, he hadn't slept a wink. He had actually heard some commotion, but had presumed it was the usual fighting that went hand-in-hand with such a lavish feast.

The gatekeeper stated that he had been awakened by four men bringing an urgent message from King Penda; they had demanded to speak with Eadfrid immediately. He had called Eadfrid's man-at-arms, instructed his relief gatekeeper to take over the watch, and had then gone to bed. The relief claimed he hadn't been roused; it was surmised that heavy intoxication had prevented him from waking up. This applied to everyone; the mead had been unusually good.

The lord of the estate lost all semblance of self-control. He ran from the one to the other, enquiring about their movements, dispensing blows with his stick, curses with his tongue and promises of rewards if the culprits were found. The more the negligence of his own people became apparent, the more frantically he lashed out, promising floggings and vowing that, at the very first opportunity, he would sell the slaves who should have raised the alarm—which was actually all of them.

He eventually collapsed from fatigue, muttering prayers to the Lord and invocations to Woden. He, too, had spent an exhausting night.

Talcuin took no notice of the man. Instead, he rode out and found that at least ten horses had come to a halt just beyond earshot of the estate. The tracks led away to the west, which could be a diversionary tactic. He asked the lord of the estate to send out a few reliable men to follow the hoofmarks.

His mistress lay prostrate and delirious, mumbling about the sacred ash and her husband's shoe, which she was gripping firmly in both hands. When they tried to take it from her grasp, she screamed like one possessed. It was impossible to get any information out of her; her condition was critical, that much Talcuin could see. He arranged for a canopy to be fixed over one of their carts, and they carried the screaming Hildeburh out into the yard. They put their lord's corpse on another cart.

Talcuin's plan was to travel back to Tamoworthig that very morning, and he curtly brushed aside the protestations of the estate lord: that he would walk straight into the arms of his lord's murderer, that he was risking his mistress's life, and so on.

If Penda was behind the murder, then he must now be satisfied and would help Hildeburh, reasoned Talcuin. If, on the other hand, Oswald was responsible, then Hildeburh should still be in fear of him. And what the doctors in Deira were like, well, Talcuin didn't know. But Penda would provide the best for Hildeburh, immediately, that much he did know. They set forth, retracing their route, with a pledge from the lord of the estate that he would send information about the destination of the horse tracks.

Hild lay on the cart, wrapped in the finest marten pelt, unaware of what was going on around her. The lord of the estate had insisted on presenting her with the precious fur in an attempt to make good for having so poorly discharged his responsibilities as host.

Standing in the gateway, wringing his hands as the guests rode out, he tried to console himself with the thought that at least the feast had wanted for nothing. The problem was just that his wretched servants had swilled down the lot. And for that they would pay.

# Penda's buckle

*– a deal with Woden –*

Hild's life hung by a thin thread. Only the Norns knew just how thin—they had spun it.

Runic incantations were tied around her ankles, wrists and head. The nine effective herbs were hung from the ceiling, and a bunch placed in each of the four corners of the world, filling the chamber with an aromatic smell. Penda's own doctor was in attendance: she shook her head. A Christian missionary was summoned: he called for yet another so they could take it in turns to maintain an unceasing flow of prayer. Eadfrid's slayers must have poisoned or bewitched her.

What had happened that night remained unclear. It was certainly true that Penda had sent an urgent message; he had observed new omens, which clearly divined a huge misfortune on their journey: the white cow he had planned to sacrifice for their future fortunes had been found dead in the cattle shed, and there was something odd about a flight of birds. Penda had sent his men with the message, which they had delivered to Eadfrid and then immediately returned home, as instructed. They hadn't noticed anything untoward.

Talcuin didn't leave his mistress's side. He slept on a rug next to her bed.

Penda's wife started her contractions and the midwife was summoned immediately; this baby was arriving slightly early and its mother had always had difficult labours. Her screams echoed around the royal settlement. Everyone crept about their business as quietly as they could; communication would have to be conducted in whispers for as long as it took.

The baby wanted to come out, but then couldn't make up its mind; it hung on inside its mother's womb, not wanting to see the light. The contractions came in quick succession, too quick, but there was no power in them. After two days she was exhausted, the only sounds her panting and whimpering.

Penda ordered the sacrifice of a white ox, personally selecting the right one. The hewn carcass of the young bull was hung on stakes in the middle of the royal settlement, but the pagan priest didn't divulge the omens he had read in its entrails—and Penda didn't ask.

Another day passed, and Penda's wife had nearly used up all her strength. She was sallow and hollow-cheeked, her eyes protruding like those of a woman possessed.

One of the midwives took a strip of fabric from her travel bag; embroidered with Eostre's name in several types of rune, it was only ever used as a last resort. She signalled to the woman with the most muscular arms and together they lifted Penda's wife from the chair and placed her on a bed; draping the fabric across her belly, they pressed downwards from either side.

'Let him go now!' they cried. 'Press as hard as you can so the boy can get out!'

But she didn't have the strength.

*They* did, however, and they put it all into the job, stretching the runes until a few threads snapped. Her belly now had that pointed shape, indicating the baby was on its way.

'Come on!' they shouted, and she did what she could—which wasn't much. They would have to apply the fabric again. Sweat poured from their brows.

Penda's wife let out a gasp, and they heard the sound of something bursting, followed by the sight of a gushing stream of fresh bright blood. They grabbed pieces of dry cloth and crammed them inside her, but nothing helped; she lay in an ever-expanding pool that didn't stop until there was next to no blood left in her.

The bed was red, she was whiter than white. The baby's indecisiveness had cost them both their lives.

'Often like that with sons,' said the midwife, folding up her stained runic cloth, 'but the ones who finally make up their minds are often the boldest of all.'

Hild opened her eyes and stared straight into Penda's belt buckle—the large and ostentatious gold ornament in which he kept his casting lots. Stylized animals wound into themselves, so ingeniously that you really had to look hard to work out where the one beast stopped and the next started. Penda had the best goldsmith in the land—in his opinion, at least.

Hild saw only one shape in all the intertwining: the letter H. Blinking several times to wake up and refocus her eyes, she then spotted an O shining out from the pattern. She closed her eyes, just for a second, and saw a large L, then the prominent O appeared again.

There he stood, stooping as he mumbled an incantation to Woden, unsure as to whether or not his supplication would be heard.

She sat up in bed. His buckle now revealed a perfectly clear F and, at such speed she could hardly keep up, an E, R, N, another E and then an S. She gazed at him, never having seen him in that light before: Holofernes.

The tyrant looked pale. He feared for her life.

'Hildeburh,' he whispered, as if he was afraid he might scare her back into the land of darkness, 'are you awake?'

'Awake, yes,' she said. 'I must get up!'

She didn't want him standing there doing tricks over her. She had seen who he was: her husband's slayer, Holofernes. And if his plan was to take control of her, then she'd show him a thing or two. She might be a widow, and her sister might be the only family she had left, far away in East Anglia, perhaps their brother too, but even without help from her family she'd show him who she was: the daughter of Hereric and Breguswid, the wife of Edwin's son. And he wasn't going to get away with the murder of her husband. She called for Talcuin, and a worried Penda withdrew.

She didn't know how long she'd been lying there, but now she had recovered her health and told Talcuin to fetch her clothes. As she got out of bed her legs faltered, unable to bear the weight of her frail body. Talcuin carefully helped his mistress, guiding her to a chair. She insisted on getting fully dressed, even though it took a long time. He supported her as she tottered across to the window and opened the shutters. She took a deep breath. The sun shone on the dark August leaves; the warm summer air was good for her and she sent Talcuin to fetch bread and beer.

A magpie was hopping around on the ground; it tugged at the remains of some small creature, perhaps a mouse. Pulling long slivers from the little belly, the black-and-white bird was so concentrated on its work that it didn't notice the goshawk, which swooped down without warning and took but an instant to give the magpie a brutal peck and fly off with its prey.

This was the second sign Hild had received, and now there could be no doubt whatsoever. She closed the shutters and sat down. She had been assigned a major task, which filled her with a sense of resolution and quiet satisfaction, but first she had to restore her strength.

She set about this task with determination. Given that large chunks of meat, whole slices of bread and brimming mugs of milk filled her with an overwhelming nausea, she asked to be served very small helpings. She gradually managed—by stealth—to consume four paltry portions at a sitting: while chewing and swallowing, she concentrated all her attention on gazing out through the open shutters. Four, however, was her limit; any more and it all came rushing up again, defeating the purpose of the exercise.

The doctor came every day and could but shake her head, now in wonder over what was happening. Her medicines didn't usually work this swiftly; someone else must have a hand in it. And it was a mightier power than the one she had invoked, that was certain. Maybe those missionaries were onto something after all.

There was nonetheless a look in her patient's eyes that troubled the doctor: a zealousness, abnormal and only seen in the profoundly possessed. She was afraid of infection, and started coming less frequently. She had no idea what to do with those eyes, so the wisest course of action was to close her own to the problem.

Hild was already able to walk a short distance unaided, and it suited her to go out among the dark-green trees. She didn't think much and she hardly spoke. She felt safest when she was completely encircled by very dark leaves. Her cheeks had filled out a little, and some colour had also returned.

She visited her husband's grave. As they walked, Talcuin had to tell her all the details of his burial.

'That's exactly what I want, too, when my time comes,' said Hild. 'At Eadfrid's side, and exactly the same.'

Talcuin nodded.

There was another new grave at the royal burial place, and Hild now learnt that Penda's wife had died. Another sign.

She gazed at her husband's grave and imagined his body down there. The last time she had seen him, Eadfrid had been so very upright—except for his head. She wasn't sure where he was now, given that his Christian faith had been extremely limited and hardly adequate to get him all the way to Saint Peter's gate.

It was what she hoped for, however: that he would go to Woden's realm—if Woden would have him, of course, with his version of warrior credentials—or to some other subterranean place. So she would never again have to see him, never again hear his strident voice haranguing her; the very thought made her ears ache.

It would undoubtedly also suit him best to spend eternity in the corner of a dark cave, muttering into the hand held in front of his mouth, occasionally scratching in the wake of the fleas he couldn't be bothered to catch. Pointing to where the fleas were, that's all he'd managed, and it was her job to catch and squash them, which she had done, as she had done so many other things for him.

She pounded the ground, and continued her hammering while a howl of lament rose in her throat.

Talcuin sat at a little distance. He didn't want to interrupt the torrent issuing from his widowed mistress; his mother had sounded just the same when his father died. It was normal. He sucked a blade of grass, wondering about the hunting potential here, even though it was holy ground.

Hild lay across the grave, praying to her god. She entreated him to send Eadfrid to Woden's place, where he could live in dignity, or to somewhere similar—just not to his Heaven, because she'd like to live there in peace and dignity once she had done what she had to do here on earth. And she asked him to forgive Eadfrid for his malice over recent years, because she wasn't personally able to forgive him. But everything is possible for the Lord God, she knew that. She also asked him to protect Hundfrid and Wilbrord and, when the time came, to unite them with her in the kingdom of Heaven.

When she felt comforted and certain her prayers had been heard, she stood and said her thanks. Then she opened a pitcher of wine and poured it on the grave, for Woden. She negotiated, promising more if he would take into account a heroic deed she would soon be undertaking—one he could count in Eadfrid's favour. They were, after all, of one flesh.

'Because you know', she said to Woden, 'how courageous he was before the misfortune. You remember how bold he was in the battles against the Irish in Dalriada; he cut down many good men. But since it was my fault he lost his power, then let me be the one to restore his reputation as the mighty warrior he once was! Let him revel in battle among all your other champions!'

When she felt sure Woden had heard her entreaty, they rode back.

Hild requested an audience with Penda. She took great trouble with her attire. She asked permission to resume teaching his sons and daughters, managing to insert appropriate remarks about what a pleasure it was to tutor such intelligent and quick-minded children. Penda's eyes lit up; yes, he would be happy for his offspring to receive tuition from her.

She missed no opportunity to discuss the children with him, praising their progress. The girls were interested and quick to learn, but Penda only really wanted to hear about his sons. So she concentrated on the boys and let the girls take care of themselves, which evened things up a little. She taught the boys to write elegant words to their father, filling him with immense gratification.

'Were you not born to be wife and ruler, you could have earned your daily bread working as a bard—and there would be some extra gold into the bargain!' he laughed.

'You make too much of my efforts', she whispered, bowing to him while tightening the muscles in her neck to produce a becoming blush in her cheeks.

That certainly had the desired effect. They spoke at length about his bright children and much more. He was loath to let her go; she withdrew while he was still aflame.

It was true that Penda exaggerated her skills as a bard. She had done a slight rewrite of a couple of laudatory poems to a Roman emperor—Paulinus had taught them the originals—in Latin, it must be said.

On the other hand, he could have praised her ability to write their native language in Latin letters, but that didn't occur to him. This skill was of her own making, an improvement on the alphabet she and her sister had used for secret messages and for fun when they were children. Paulinus had forbidden it, and warned them in the strongest terms that the Latin letters were only applicable in the Latin language. Their native tongue should be written with runes, which was a matter they would have to learn elsewhere. Latin was not to be treated frivolously; it was the key to the holy scriptures, to the doctrines of the fathers of the Church and to much more of benefit. If they wanted to be flippant they must do so with runes, and not in his classes—the latter remark made after he had looked at Hereswid's wax tablet and seen a Latin rendering of: *Eadfrid loves Hild. Osfrid is a drip.*

He had been outraged to see the Latin letters misused in this way, and had it not been for the queen's insistent directive to get some kind of learning into these children's heads, he would long since have given up on them. These girls were chastisement from the Lord: a far too corporeal reminder of his debt to his sister.

Hereswid and Hild had nonetheless blithely continued their experimentation, quite undeterred by Paulinus' scruples—and Hild was now deriving the benefit.

They weren't the first people to use the Latin alphabet for their own language. The laws in Kent had been written in this style a few years before the girls had even been born, as Paulinus well knew given that his first years among the barbarians had been spent in that very realm. He just couldn't accept the practice. Hild, however, had never seen anyone write in this way, as the few letters King Edwin had received were always written in Latin. More often than not, word was brought by messenger, and verbal communication ensured the message was understood.

'Do you think I should appoint a scribe?' Penda asked.

'Why?' said Hild. 'I would be happy to write for you, should you consider me worthy.'

And so she did. Hild now had plenty to do since Penda would want a letter sent somewhere nearly every day. When he couldn't think of anyone to write to, he consulted her. The messengers had to learn the letters by heart, so they could also deliver the content verbally, because the recipients wouldn't be able to read and seldom had anyone in their service who was literate.

Penda found it hard to let these fine letters go; they always had to wait a day or two, so he could really enjoy them. He also took pleasure in watching his skilled scribe as she sat at her work, head bent over her parchment, producing the most delicate squiggles. He had no qualms about procuring the best materials available: calfskin parchment, many different pigments for her inks, he even ordered liquid gold from Kent—she wanted to use it for his letters to other kings, and he liked that idea. He signed in red ink, thinking this most appropriate for his status, and she was in complete agreement.

When he initially practised signing his name, she had to guide his hand. Getting this thin quill to glide smoothly was quite unlike holding a good knife to carve runes in wood. The trick was to keep a tight rein on your muscle power, and he found that difficult. He squeezed the frail writing feather and moved it around with his whole arm, well aware that such a big signature looked clumsy in contrast to the neat little letters of the message. But Hild praised his writing. It was fitting for the king's signature to have a certain magnitude, she thought, differentiating it from the smaller characters written by the king's subject. He could see the logic in that, and asked her to guide his hand again so he could practise a muscular flourish, a more vigorous and a weightier version of his signature. She was happy to do so, carefully leading his hand through expansively lavish strokes. A lock of hair touched his arm when she leant over him, and her breast brushed against his shoulder a few times, which could hardly be avoided.

'So cold,' Penda murmured, and raised her hand to his cheek. 'And no husband to keep it warm.'

Hild did the tightening movement with her throat muscles that caused her to blush, and he looked up at that very moment and took great pleasure in what he saw.

'And you still don't come to warm yourself in the hall of an evening?' His voice sounded thick and parched.

'That would not be seemly while I am in mourning,' she said softly, and lowered her head.

'I could . . . perhaps you could . . .' he murmured, her hand still resting against his cheek, 'you could perhaps come and dine in my chamber, just a light Lenten meal, as is proper and seemly?'

Hild bowed deeply.

'That would be a great honour, lord king,' she whispered, and the blush now spreading across her cheeks had flared up of its own accord. She asked permission to leave and hurried off.

Hild was busy. She hadn't left with such haste simply to prevent Penda from regretting his invitation. She asked Talcuin to prepare the horses, gathered a few things and they rode out.

They stopped by a beck, and Hild set Talcuin to stand guard while she bathed. The water was cold and not particularly pleasant. It wasn't like sinking into a hot tub at home, the handmaid scrubbing your back. Today, however, wasn't washing day, and she didn't want anyone involved in her business.

As usual when assigned this task, Talcuin suffered the torments of the damned. It wasn't right to spy on his mistress, or to think the thought that always came to him on these occasions: when clothing was removed, very little gave away a person's rank or occupation. Not even the most noble lady was much different from the dairymaid back home in Dolwyddelan, not in terms of beauty, at least. His mistress was more fearless and prouder than anyone else, no doubt about that, but still—they had the same luminous white buttocks, the same lushly curving thighs, which he found absolutely the most breath-taking part of womankind, well, perhaps apart from . . . no, when he really thought about it, nothing surpassed that extraordinary roundness of a woman's thighs. Nothing.

He got his usual two or three glimpses of his mistress's nakedness, but this time he saw something to make him gasp, and amazed him as much as the sight of the luminously pale dairymaid: his mistress's shame was shrouded in fiery-red, as bright and radiant as the hair on her head, like molten copper or a newly-opened poplar bud.

Feeling quite dizzy, he had to walk away; he sat down, head in hands. This was the punishment for peeking; now he would never be able to look at her without thinking about just *that*. He wished he could go out and find another job, but he was her property: wergeld for little Frigyd.

He had thought—if he thought about it at all— her pubic hair would be dark, almost black like his own; they had the same colour hair on their heads, after all. It had never occurred to him that you could have the same bright red colour down there as well.

Still—he was glad he'd seen it. The Angle's Frig must surely look just like that when bathing in the beck in springtime; yes, that's exactly what she would look like.

As they rode off, Talcuin avoided looking directly at Hild, so he didn't notice her energized state.

They visited Eadfrid's grave. He sat at a distance while she spoke with her god, at length and earnestly, asking for strength to fulfil her task. She also offered a pitcher of Gallic wine to Woden, again entreated him to overlook the one time courage had deserted her husband, and confirmed she would redress this lapse if Woden would accept Eadfrid.

'And remember what I have said,' she told Talcuin as they rode away. 'I want to lie next to my husband, no matter what happens.'

'I shall remember,' Talcuin replied.

Once home again, she wrote to Hundfrid and Wilbrord. She explained what a great man their father had been, until misfortune struck his father's kingdom, but all that had now been redressed. Deira belonged to them—that much was definite—and maybe they could also take over Bernicia, which had been their paternal grandfather Edwin's, so they would each have a realm.

'Beware fratricidal conflict,' she wrote, 'for nothing is so wretched as a family feuding with itself. Hunger can indeed be a torment, but only a fool eats his own flesh. Queen Hereswid in East Anglia is your maternal aunt: her help would not be sought in vain. You are both baptized in the name of Jesus Christ: hold that in high esteem. And learn to write, I tell you—without the skill of writing you will achieve very little in the new era. Learn to fight, learn to pray, learn Latin, and do not forget those who came before. And know this: the days of a man are like a flower in the grass. A wind passes over and it is gone—and no one remembers where it was. Remembrance of the bold man, however, is never erased, not if his reputation was won deservedly. A good name weighs heavier than gold. Neither Deira nor Bernicia have known kings of greater justice than your father's father Edwin. He ignited the Lord's light in the realm, and his descendants must follow in his footsteps. Your mother gave birth to you in a cave, and protected you from wolves. We saved our lives by means of King Edwin's gold holy cross and by means of a lion. May the Lord always protect you, until the day of our joyous reunion in the kingdom of Heaven. You were to be raised as freemen, therefore our ways had to part, but the Lord God seeks again that which is past.'

She wrote all this—and more—on particularly fine parchment, which she had kept for this very purpose. Love for her two children flowed through her like a warm current. Their lives would not be swept away by the evil fate that had struck their parents; they could now follow in the footsteps of Edwin and Hereric and, as free princes, demand their realms and rally support to take them. The thought made her smile.

Reading through the letter, Hild saw she had written 'My dear little hatchlings'. She was about to cross out the words when she realized she had no time for corrections—they might not like the expression, but they *were* nonetheless her dear little hatchlings.

She handed the letter to Talcuin, instructing him to make sure her sons received it should anything happen to her.

And then she dressed for her evening appointment. Neither grand nor humble, neither immodest nor dreary, she dressed as befitting a young royal widow, still in mourning, who had been invited to supper with the king in his private chamber.

# 'THERE WAS A LITTLE MOUSE . . . '

*– supper with Holofernes –*

Hair combed for lice, lips and cheeks massaged into a becoming blush, eyes given softness and depth by warming the surrounding skin with hands that had been furiously rubbed together. Hair almost concealed under the blue widow's cap, but no more fastened than a single flick would release bright copper cascades, which were always kept at just the length to cover her breasts—as Queen Tata's chambermaid had taught them. The gold holy cross, now twice repaired, hung in such a way that a hand wanting to study it at closer quarters would also have to make acquaintance with the soft firmness of her breasts. Throat, armpits and groin rubbed with Gallic lavender oil, its bluish fragrance providing a more youthful air than her twenty-one years, something almost virginal. Thus Hild walked through a fine drizzle in the dusk to the back entrance of the hall, where Penda had his private chamber, accompanied by his two pages and her handmaid, the latter concealing a cloth for their booty. Penda had now been a widower for forty days.

She had repeated the words so many times that they coursed through her mind even when she was asleep: 'Help me now, God of Israel!'

Walking this route, however, she started to have doubts. Was it really the God of Israel she should ask for help? She wasn't an Israelite like Judith; she was an Angle and came from Deira. Perhaps she should invoke the god of Deira. But if she did that, would the Lord God then reach out his hand and increase her strength? Could you reasonably claim Deira as a Christian country?

No, you couldn't. And Woden would never help her in this undertaking: she had left his service.

When they reached the door, she tensed the muscles in her upper arms while murmuring her mantra, having decided it was sound: 'Help me now, God of Israel!'

The room was brightly lit; he stood in the middle of the floor and took a step forwards. She bowed deeply, only straightening up when he gently took hold of her arm and indicated the bearskin on the bench, inviting her to take a seat.

The bed was where it should be, visible through the doorway into the next chamber. The sword hung where it should, in its sheath on the wall above the bed.

Everything else was wrong.

He spoke to her and offered her the drinking horn. His hands holding the aurochs horn were so vibrant; they weren't the hands of Holofernes, nor was it his voice—softer and more melodic than she had ever heard it before. A voice to close your eyes to, lie down to, and let your breath go all the way out and all the way in, deep and calm, to its own rhythm. A voice that snuggled warmly around you, filling the space between ceiling and the soft hides and woven hangings on the wall.

She straightened her shoulders and tried to shield herself from the sorcery with a swift Our Father. Even though it was coming from Penda's mouth, this wasn't Penda's voice. She fixed her eyes on his belt buckle, and in her mind she murmured the mantra that would give her strength.

The buckle, however, was merely a buckle, with interlaced beasts made of gold and inlaid with the black nielo. It wasn't giving off any signs at all; the curves didn't even reveal one single letter of the alphabet, just an organized chaos, and not the slightest hint about the truth of the matter.

She had seen it—once—and now she had to hold on to her secret knowledge. She mustn't let his voice cast a spell over her, no matter what ploy he might use.

'Do you like my belt?' she heard him say. She nodded and couldn't take her eyes off the clasp, willing it to speak to her again, to give her power, to replenish the strength steadily seeping away.

He undid his belt and offered it to her. She held the buckle close to her eyes—nothing changed; she turned it, breathed on it, rubbed it with her sleeve, but she could still only see intertwined beasts.

'You can't work that out, now, can you,' he laughed, his pride obvious.

She looked up into his amused eyes. They shone, even though they were brown, dark brown, the markings almost black, and so deep she had to struggle back to the surface and catch her breath.

'Help me,' she whispered, head bowed.

'It's on the back,' he said cheerfully, and took the belt from her hand. 'Look—like this!'

With a little push and a click, he opened the buckle and held it up to her. She looked into the golden cavity, saw the small pale sticks that the pagan priest carved for him every spring from the new ash twigs. These were Penda's casting lots, used for all major decisions, and when the belt was opened, they had arranged themselves thus: the largest two lying so close together that they almost became one, the two smallest on top at an angle, and the other four, medium-sized, spread randomly at the other end of the cavity.

She could feel the blood rushing to her face, and was afraid to look up. He expelled a sort of gasp, and she was relieved to hear the food being brought in at that very moment.

Penda cleared his throat and took a step backwards.

'What I was going to say,' he began, stroking his beard, 'was wergild for Eadfrid!'

Hild didn't respond.

He passed her a fowl and took one for himself; small quails, snared, spit-roasted and now golden-brown, and just the sight of them made her nauseous. She was burning inside, as if on fire. The flames, however, weren't interested in food, but her month-long training in eating against her will enabled the chewing and swallowing of small morsels, slowly and by thinking about Hundfrid and Wilbrord, their warm little bodies. The mead helped. She glanced sideways and saw one piece of fowl after another vanish into Penda's mouth.

'Because surely you haven't all abandoned the old ways to such an extent that you have forgotten obligations to family?'

There was a touch of scorn to his voice.

'We have not,' she answered. She was still prodding the thigh of her first little bird.

'So why haven't you demanded wergild?' he asked, helping himself to his fifth. He ate everything, thoroughly chewing the wings, only leaving the largest bones, which he gnawed and sucked before placing them in a neat pile on the table.

'I think blood should be avenged with blood,' she replied.

He glanced at her and then carried on eating, wiped his mouth and took another quail.

'You won't get far with that when talking to a king.'

When she didn't respond, he threw out his arms: 'Where are your people, where are your kin, where is your army?'

Searing humiliation galvanized her; she could barely remain seated. She had to control her hatred: restrain the urge to rip into him, tear his fine tunic, dig her nails into his flesh, grab his hair and his beard, and pull with all her might until his skin peeled off; hit him, smash him to pieces, stab the life out of him with his own sword, hack him all over, not just hack his head off with a clean slash—she would do that at the very end. First she wanted to see his blood, a little trickle and then gushing, wanted to see his guts heaving out, his great big body lying as silent and powerless as her own people when she had shooed the ravens away from them down by the ford. As immobile and inarticulate as Eadfrid hanging from his branch in the ash tree.

This man in front of her—she could thank him for all her misfortune. And she would.

'The Lord will help me,' she answered firmly.

'I certainly hope so,' he smiled. 'But it wouldn't hurt if I gave a little assistance too, would it?'

'My husband's death cannot be redressed with land,' said Hild, 'nor with gold.'

'Think of your sons.'

'I am thinking of their honour,' she replied.

'A little patch of land has never harmed anyone's honour,' he said. 'I would think a measurement of five hundred hides would be suitable.'

An enormous penance, and Eadfrid hadn't even been king. A pleasant chill ran through her, a deep contempt for his baseness. He could happily give five hundred hides in penance, twice as much too, and feel magnanimous in the face of her powerlessness, the powerlessness for which he alone was to blame. She didn't want any of it, not his land!

'Had Eadfrid lived, he would have been king,' Penda went on, munching, 'which would have served Deira better than that hothead Oswald.'

'You mean Eadfrid in Deira and Oswald in Bernicia would have served *you* better,' Hild couldn't stop herself responding.

'Of course, but Deira too. Now there will be unrest and conflict. And they are so fond of peace and harmony,' he laughed scornfully.

'Had it not been for the clever merchants of Deira, Penda would not have owned this tunic,' she answered quickly, giving his imported silk tunic a little tug: a splendid red garment, his wife had edged the sleeves and neckline in darker red trimmings interwoven with gold. His mania for all things red was ridiculous. Eadfrid had been right: Penda was an upstart, there wasn't a grain of majesty in him, he always had to overdo everything.

He smoothed the fabric where she'd plucked at it, and also smoothed the other sleeve with an expression of great satisfaction.

'I have always had good links with Deira.'

'Have had, yes,' said Hild.

'In future we'll be dealing directly with the Mediterranean merchants,' he said proudly.

'I didn't know you Mercians were fond of the open seas.'

'It will all be fine,' he assured her, patting the back of her hand.

He was old enough to be her father, and she could have bitten his hand off. But it had to be done. She thought about all the children his hefty body had fathered. He'd already had two wives, and probably quite a lot of women besides, and no doubt he already had his eye on the next—one from the south, given that he was so keen to extend his reach down there. She wasn't sure if any of the West Saxon princesses were ready to be bedded, but he was certainly enough of a barbarian to marry a child.

'Yes, yes,' he said, 'we'll sort out the penance to be paid.'

His hand had rested long enough on hers to burn an imprint on her skin, and she suppressed her urge to rub it clean. He picked up the mead horn and drank.

There was something nimble, effortless and all too vibrant about his hands which continued to intrigue her. So supple and so agile, they didn't fit in with his sturdy body, but matched the brightness in his eyes, with their almost bird-like alertness.

He had been a magpie in the sign she had been sent, but now he seemed more like a goshawk.

No matter what, she would soon exact restitution for the swift movements of those hands, and for the sorcery radiating from his eyes.

She gave him a quick glance; she didn't want to be ensnared by his eyes. Looked at from the front, he seemed stout; here from the side, however, he was a slim man. His height and his powerful bone structure gave the impression of something bulky and solid. He was actually a handsome man, his unusual eyes shining brightly in all their darkness, and his thick flaxen hair hanging to just below shoulder level. All his children had inherited that splendid mane of hair.

Hild felt inviolable, as if sitting on a cloud, reigning over his final hours. Her only concern was his moderate drinking, which did not fit the picture. Holofernes had drunk himself into a stupor even before Judith had been brought to his private quarters. She had left unsullied by the tyrant's seed; he had passed out drunk before anything had happened. It had been easy for Judith to slip out of the tent with his head wrapped in the maid's cloth.

The evening wasn't going to proceed quite so straightforwardly here, and as she wasn't the hostess she could hardly press him to drink. The only option was to lead by example and drink more, which she did, but to no great avail.

'A good mead you serve here,' she said.

'I'll have a cask brought over, since you rarely come to the hall,' he replied.

From where she was sitting, she could see into his sleeping chamber, his wide bed and the sword hanging on the wall above. A good sword, neither too light nor too heavy, but just as it should be. Today she hadn't had time for her daily exercise in the forest, snapping branches of increasing thickness by hammering a heavy oak stick onto boughs she had laid across two tree stumps. She had improved, and was now good at it; Talcuin had taught her how to put the whole weight of her body, not just her arm muscles, into the force of the blows.

In fact, the only element that was amiss was this man. He wasn't really the Holofernes providence had once revealed to her, and were it not for the signs she had received, she wouldn't have any idea how all this fitted together.

Apples preserved in honey, served with blackberries and nuts, thick cream on top, all slipped down more easily than the rich dish of fowl. He encouraged her to eat more, several times, and she realized that she was actually enjoying the warmth, the light, the sweet fruits, mead, even his voice. She had to remind herself that someone who has everything can easily make things pleasant for others.

'At your age, all I thought about was performing great deeds,' he said. 'That's how we thought in those days. It's different for you youngsters today.'

'Why should it be any different?'

'Well, so much has changed. Things were more unpredictable back then. Now the world is more organized. People don't have to create everything for themselves, from scratch, as it were.'

'I don't think there's much predictability now, the way the world is today,' she said.

'Depends what you're comparing it with,' said Penda. 'There was more unrest back then; you never knew if you would get to harvest the soil you'd sown. We had to flee many times when I was a boy. Moving, they called it, but it was the unrest that forced us out. It's not like that anymore. Not in too many places, at least.' He took a draught from the horn. 'But if it's better . . . I don't know. Lots of young people today think they can just sit back and do nothing. But that will get you neither wealth nor honour.'

'Perhaps, these days, people think for themselves more,' suggested Hild, trying to come up with some kind of defence for her indolent generation.

'Possibly,' he replied. 'I just don't think the conclusions to all that thinking add up to much. Bards such as Taliesin and Aneirin—you don't come across the likes of them today! I never turn a bard away, you know, because one fine day maybe a song bearing comparison with Y Gododdin will crop up, or even one with just a *touch* of the old quality. And I give them gold and testimonials so they can see a bit more of the world—because it operates in far stranger ways than you, sitting here, can possibly imagine.'

Hild had to give this careful consideration.

'Well, perhaps only Taliesin's *good* works are remembered,' she eventually said. 'He might have written lots of hogwash too, but that's just been forgotten. When he was young—I mean, he had to learn his trade first.'

'No,' he said, 'Taliesin never wrote any hogwash, and I have that on the authority of King Cadfan of Gwynedd, Cædwalla's father.'

'Well then, when he was *very* young!' Hild didn't want to abandon her brainwave.

'I speak with absolute certainty,' said Penda, 'because my mother's father was one of King Maelgwn Gwynedd's manservants, and he told me about Taliesin. He was very short, did you know that?'

Hild shook her head.

'Yes,' Penda continued excitedly, 'no taller than a woman, my grandfather always said, but mighty of mind. And when he sang his verses in the king's hall in Aberffraw, well, then he grew so he nearly reached the roof ridge. And no one ever dared so much as to touch him. Not even the king. Even though he said what he meant, straight to the king's face.'

'He even dared give notice of the king's death,' Hild added to the pool of information, and spoke the verse she had heard on her journey to Dolwyddelan:

> *The marshes of Rhionedd*
> *produce dangerous creatures;*
> *severe be vengeance on*
> *the sins of Maelgwn Gwynedd.*
> *Its hair, its teeth,*
> *its eyes, all afire*
> *—it will put an end to*
> *Maelgwn Gwynedd's days.*

'That's what I mean,' Penda enthused. 'Where, in our day, do you see a bard who dares do anything other than heap praise on the king who happens to be right in front of him? One who has balls and ambitions—other than just rattling off all the old songs and bedecking himself in gold! I tell you, the number of appalling songs I've heard at Cædwalla's—enough to make you sick! I liked Cædwalla a lot, you know, but where songs were concerned he had no taste whatsoever. Everything else was good enough, but the bards he kept—pitiful!'

Penda straightened up and sang in a mangled voice:

> *The lion of Gwynedd*
> *plays with the mouse*
> *mighty in magnificence*
> *glittering in garnets*
> *wealthy in words*
> *loudly plays the lion.*

Hild laughed. She knew the song.

'Yes, have you ever heard anything so ridiculous as a lion playing with a mouse? What, might I ask, is heroic about *that*?' Penda wasn't going to let the subject drop.

'Perhaps he means that as Cædwalla's enemies are so small and scared in comparison with the great man, they seem like little mice?' she offered.

'I don't know what he means,' said Penda, shaking his head, 'but if that's the case then he should just state it properly. Playing with a mouse—that's no verse for a king!'

He pulled a scornful face and burst into laughter.

'Here comes the little mouse,' he warbled, walking his right-hand forefinger and middle finger from Hild's knee along her thigh. 'Up to its little house!' Then across her lap, up over her left breast, ending with a brief caress of her earlobe. Slapping his thighs with both hands, he laughed long and loud.

'See,' he shouted, pointing at her, 'there's not much lion in you.'

Hild sat bolt upright, her face a deep red; his conduct was not seemly and, what is more, he had given her a fright.

On the other hand, they were on the right track. She just hadn't pictured their time together like this; she had thought it would be more dignified. She was in the process of carrying out a heroic deed, and this kind of silliness didn't fit in with her currently undivided heroic spirit.

You could kill a tyrant, but you couldn't kill this big playful boy without turning the heroic endeavour into an act of villainy. There had to be more gravity to proceedings.

She didn't have long to dwell on her problem before Penda started talking about the great sense of loss he had experienced when Cædwalla died.

'He was very fond of you, you know that? In some strange way. He was concerned for your wellbeing. Didn't think Eadfrid treated you properly. That time you fell down the stairs, he kept saying I should send you over to his wife in Aberffraw, or to his sister in East Anglia. Funnily enough—when I think what you looked like!'

Hild turned her drinking horn between her fingers, studying the silver-gilt rim. She didn't like being reminded of her appearance back then.

'What you really needed was rest and quiet to recover, as I told Cædwalla,' Penda went on. 'A woman like Hildeburh, I said to him, she won't put up with anything she doesn't want to, she's not just some slave; you've heard for yourself how she can hold her own, I said to him.'

Shame and anger ripped through Hild; she didn't want to think about that period and tried to put an end to the subject. 'No, back then I could hardly have sat on a horse,' she said curtly.

'And you were so incredibly clumsy,' he laughed. 'Imagine—tripping over your own feet,' he nudged them a couple of times, 'because you're usually so supple and nimble.'

'Thank you,' Hild replied.

'And one time Cædwalla said: Thank God, her eyes are blue! But are they? May I see if that's true?'

She looked him straight in the face, staring at him as steadily as she could, but she quickly had to look away to protect herself from the sorcery that was causing everything to seep out of her; she could feel the dampness quite clearly. And he would soon feel the power of her god, making short work of any kind of magic powers. She wasn't afraid of his tricks, whatever they might be.

There was a knock at the door; the servant's head appeared.

'Just a moment,' said Penda, and the boy vanished.

'Listen, Hild,' he said in a serious voice, and she was a little flustered because he usually used her full name. 'Would you like me to sort out the penance?'

Those deep luminous eyes casting their spell; she had to look at the floor.

'No,' she replied and, realizing the audience was approaching its end, hastily grabbed her necklace and held it out to him.

'This holy cross, it's been ruined, perhaps the new goldsmith could . . . just look!'

Penda looked at it, but kept his hands to himself; he'd rather not touch a holy cross.

'It's a lovely piece,' he said, 'you can just send it over to him.'

'But here,' she persisted, 'it's broken.'

'He can easily mend it,' Penda reassured her, and stood up. There was another knock at the door, she also rose from her seat and just stood there, arms hanging at her sides, staring at him.

'Thank you for coming,' he said and held out his hand. She placed a cold limp hand in his; it nearly vanished.

'Still so cold,' he murmured. 'I could also sort out the matter of a new hus . . . '

'No thank you!' she exclaimed, retracting her hand.

'As you choose,' he said gently, squeezing his hand ever so lightly around her upper arm, 'exactly as you choose.'

She looked up at him, wanted to slap his face, and wanted to throw herself against him and ask him to hold her tightly in his arms. The floor wobbled and her strength drained away; she felt deathly tired and had no idea how she was going to get out of there.

Eventually she managed to turn on her heel and walk away.

'Good night,' she heard as she left.

The servant was waiting outside with her maid. The rain was pouring down heavily now, and as they turned the corner she spotted the other servant taking shelter under the eaves—along with the lady's maid who had served Penda's wife. Once Hild had passed, they stepped out onto the path and walked back in the direction whence she had come.

She couldn't stop herself, she knew it wasn't seemly, but she couldn't do anything else: she ran back and caught sight of the edge of the maid's cloak in the light from the hut just as the door closed behind her.

# CAPTURE THE FOXES, THOSE LITTLE FOXES!

*– the laughing dwarf –*

Hild had finally fallen asleep, but woke with a start. She was in great danger, and the terror had paralysed her. She wanted to leap up and beat the evil away, call Talcuin, save her life, but not a muscle would move.

A dwarf-creature had crouched down on the floor at the head of her bed. It was poised ready to jump, its large head pressed down between its shoulders, fighting back silent, persistent laughter. Laughing at her fruitless attempts to make her body obey her commands, it enjoyed watching her flounder in the net. It wasn't going anywhere in a hurry. She couldn't move her head, not even her eyes, but she could hear it—and even if she hadn't been able to, she would have known it was there, crouched and cackling in delight at her torment.

Her terror was boundless and indescribable. Her final second lasted an eternity, waiting for the dwarf to spring, her muscles aching from their futile exertion. Her thoughts were in turmoil, the terror had struck them too, running round and round in circles, unable to find their way along the tracks that would set her free; they dashed around in a little sealed room, hunted by wolves, and couldn't find a way out, couldn't even gather themselves to try one place at a time, raced on round and round, senseless with panic. If only she could come up with an incantation to ward off evil and chant it in her mind, then she would be saved, but she couldn't even think of the first little word of any single appropriate incantation, and she knew many. The more her mind struggled to find the liberating words, the louder the dwarf laughed, cackling and malevolent. In the very next moment it would throw itself upon her, and she couldn't even lift her arms to shield herself and her life.

But this next moment went on and on, there was no end to it; an eternity, several eternities passed and the night just went on its endless way, a relentless night of horror, refusing to end.

As he had done before, Talcuin now had to sleep on a rug on the floor at the head of his mistress's bed, in the dwarf-creature's place. The dwarf, however, had found new methods: it stood by the foot of the bed, it hung off the ceiling above her, once it sat on her left foot. She could never feel safe.

She had to give Talcuin strict orders: he must not sleep so much as a wink. But the dwarf tricked him by making itself invisible.

Hild was again becoming hollow-cheeked and pale. She suspected the demon from Eadfrid was trying to find a permanent home in her. Not even the holy cross could keep it away.

One day it started to rain in a strange and unnatural way, an almost totally black cloud covering the sun; the light turned to dusk and large drops of rain poured from the sky, as if coming from every direction. The branches couldn't decide which way to bend, flailing this way and that. And the holy month had only just begun. Hild was gripped by panic; throwing herself to the ground and praying, she remained prostrate until the cloud dissolved and the sun returned. A slight muddiness was all that remained as testimony to the ominous occurrence.

*I slept, but my heart was awake: hear—my beloved knocks on the door, saying: 'Open to me, my sister, my love, my dove, my pure everything: for my head is filled with dew, and my locks with the drops of the night.'*

*'I have taken off my coat; how shall I put it on? I have washed my feet; how shall I soil them?'*
*My beloved put in his hand through the hole of the door, and my heart trembled.*

*I arose to open to my beloved; and my hands dripped with myrrh, and from my fingers poured liquid myrrh upon the handles of the bolt. I opened to my beloved; but my beloved had withdrawn and was gone: my soul failed me: I sought him, but I could not find him; I called to him, but he did not answer. The watchmen going about the city found me, they struck me and wounded me; the keepers of the walls took my shawl from me.*

*I implore you, O daughters of Jerusalem: if you find my beloved, tell him that I am sick of love.*

Hild tossed and turned in bed. She had dozed for a moment, and the incubus had immediately taken its chance to leap. Talcuin watched her with concern; he was keeping guard, and she could settle down again.

The Song of Songs, Solomon's sacred canticle had come to her. The Church yearning for its master, Jesus Christ. A good sign; she hadn't lost her way completely. She closed her eyes and dozed off again.

*By night on my bed I sought he whom my soul so loves: I sought him, but I did not find him. I would arise, and go about the city, in the streets and in the squares I would seek he whom my soul so loves: I sought him, but I did not find him, but the watchmen going about the city found me. To them I said, 'Saw you him whom my soul so loves?' I had only just passed from them, when I found him whom my soul so loves. I held him, and would not let him go until I had taken him to my mother's house, and into the chamber of she who conceived me.*

*I implore you, O daughters of Jerusalem, by the roes and by the hinds of the field: stir not up, nor awaken love until it pleases.*

Now she was awake again. The incubus had made itself invisible, but Talcuin was keeping watch. She said her Our Father three times, and fell asleep.

*His left hand is under my head, and his right hand embraces me. I implore you, O daughters of Jerusalem, by the roes and by the hinds of the field: stir not up, nor awaken love until it pleases.*

*The voice of my beloved! See, he comes leaping across the mountains, skipping across the hills.*

*My beloved is like a roe or a young hart: see, he stands behind our wall, he looks through the windows, shows himself through the lattice. My beloved spoke, and said to me, 'Arise, my love, my fair one, and come away. For now the winter is past, the rain has stopped, it is over and gone. The flowers appear on the earth; the time of the singing of birds has come, and the voice of the turtledove is heard in our land. The fruit of the fig tree ripens, and the blossoming vines smell fragrant. Arise, my love, my fair one, and come away.'*

*My dove, sitting in the clefts of the gorge, in the secret places of the cliffs, let me see your countenance, let me hear your voice; for sweet is your voice, and comely is your countenance.*

*Capture the foxes, those little foxes that spoil the vines: for our vineyards are in blossom.*

*My beloved is mine, and I am his: he shepherds his flock among the lilies. Until the day be cool, and the shadows long, turn, my beloved, nimbly as a roe or a young hart on the mountains of Bether.*

Now she could feel him, his head against her shoulder, he was whispering and murmuring to her; she answered him in the same tone, she grabbed his head, pressed it down against her throat, her eyes filled, his hair was in her nose, his long bristly flaxen hair; she stroked her hand across his shoulder, neck, down his back, squeezed him to her until her arms ached; fulfilment, it came so very naturally, at long last, and that's how it had to be, it had been so long in the coming.

Talcuin behaved as if nothing had happened. She searched his face next morning; it revealed nothing.

'Did you sleep?' she asked.

He looked at her in surprise, and answered genuinely and without hesitation: 'I was keeping watch.'

'Were you there all night?'

'Throughout, my lady.'

'Then go and sleep,' she said roughly, to hide her confusion.

The next day she asked: 'Was someone here?'

'No one, my lady.'

'And you didn't cheat?'

'Not for a moment, my lady.'

She no longer knew what to believe. She knew the Devil has many faces; that much she did know. But she hadn't been visited by a devil— far from it.

What did he look like, the man who had used his magic on her? She was familiar with the thick flaxen hair, and his bulky outline, but she couldn't picture him. She probably wouldn't even be able to recognize him if he were standing right in front of her.

There was a certain logic to all this: by letting his body seep into hers, he would have to die, as it were, have to dissolve as body. He couldn't be both there and here, however many tricks he might know.

She sat in the hall listening to the bard's version of the story of Ingeld. It was evening, her cheeks were feverish, and it was as if the game of their childhood had been played just yesterday. Hereswid's authoritative voice: 'And you're Freawaru, and I'm Ingeld, and Osfrid is leader of the Danes, and Eadfrid is leader of the Hadubards.'

And Osfrid had leapt to his feet and roused his people to battle against the Hadubards. Hild had again been given the not particularly desirable role of Freawaru, daughter of the Danish king Frode, who had to sit and express devotion to her husband Ingeld, and the rest of the role consisted of allowing misfortune to cascade all over her without any real possibility of intervening.

The story belonged to Ingeld, caught between the vow of fidelity to his wife and the duty to avenge his father's death. He had tried to settle the lengthy conflict by means of this marriage, but now it had all flared up again and he had to make a choice—and that would entail breaking one of his sworn pledges. But which one? The decision depended on Hereswid's mood. The boys would always choose to keep their promise to the family lineage, and so Hild, like Hereswid, varied her choice in order to add some variety to this boring predictability.

Had it been today, she would not have hesitated: Ingeld would have to avenge his father; anything else would be but delusion and make-believe. Ingeld had also come to this realization, albeit reluctantly—with such a lovely wife, and a baby already on the way.

The Devil had many faces back then, too, thought Hild. She always carried a knife now, a strong and sharp dagger.

# JOY AND DISGUST

*- overpowered -*

Penda had finished his dictation: a somewhat foolish letter requesting information about prices and delivery options with regard to rare animals and birds, plus finely-bound books, preferably without a holy cross on the cover. And he couldn't even read!

Hild had guided his hand through the brazenly crude signature. The heat from his hand was loathsome and hard to shed; she hated him, could hardly draw breath in his proximity.

They had finished, at long last, and he sent a servant off to the messenger with the letter. They were alone; he didn't move, but looked at her with a serious expression in his eyes.

'Hildeburh,' he said, 'you have to demand wergild. You owe that to Eadfrid, and you owe that to your sons.'

'And what is it I should claim, King Penda?'

She bowed to him, so deeply he found it a little embarrassing.

'Five hundred hides of land, I would think,' he said, the second time he had made this suggestion.

She stood up and looked him straight in the face.

'I have a better suggestion, lord king, should it be fitting for me to submit a proposal.'

'Only your hesitation is not fitting,' he replied impatiently.

'Good,' she said. 'I demand the head of the king on a platter. Preferably a silver platter.'

Penda shook his head.

'But should the king find gold more appropriate,' she went on, 'then I shall be happy to accept.'

He didn't like the way her eyes were shining. Some madness had entered her, which might be understandable, but wasn't particularly useful.

'I've said it before: he is too powerful for you. You can't touch him. Land—*that* you can get.'

'Can't touch him?' she said slowly, accentuating each word.

She had that bewitched expression in her eyes, the one he didn't like, and a strange little smile on her lips—and at that very instant he fell backwards.

Stumbling on the hem of the long cloak when he attempted to get his footing, he fell to the floor in an awkward position, promptly and irritably noting a rip near the fastener at the shoulder and the knife she was pointing at him.

He leapt on her, had no trouble seizing the knife and turning it against his assailant, but abruptly stopped, looked at the sharply-ground blade, its worn antler handle, and threw it aside. With one arm around her, gripping her shoulder, he could smell the lavender fragrance from her hair. He held her out at arm's length, studying her face.

Her look of hatred was unaltered and there wasn't the slightest hint of fear in her eyes. She stood stock still, as she had done before attacking him, and didn't move at all when he loosened her cap and let it fall to the floor, loosened her hair, ran his fingers through her locks, inhaled their fragrance, and pulled her head to his chest, making her gasp for air.

Holding her at arm's length again, he studied the curved lips, slightly apart, her eyes, almost black, her pink nostrils breathing rapidly in and out, red flushes shining on her throat. He leant forward and pressed his lips to her artery. Her head slipped a little to the side, baring more of her neck. His teeth brushed across the skin, biting very lightly. She trembled as he pulled her into his arms. Through all the layers of fabric she could feel his aroused manhood and heard something that sounded like a sigh or a moan.

'You can have my head,' he murmured in her ear, 'but the wergild you will have to get from Oswald.'

He looked into her eyes, but made no attempt to hold on when she twisted free and took a step backwards. She was ashen, staring at him with wide eyes: 'Oswald?'

He shook his head.

'How could you believe anything else?'

He shook his head again.

'How on earth could you believe anything else?'

He reached out and cautiously stroked her hair. He picked up the knife, the cap too and smoothed it, sighed deeply and handed her both items; the tip of the knife blade pointing at his chest.

'Hildeburh,' he said, 'you really don't know me.'

He remained where he was for a moment, as if undecided, but then turned and left.

She was unable to move, just watched as he walked swiftly through the doorway, head bowed. She felt dizzy, staggered to the bench and clung to it while the room swam before her eyes.

She didn't know how long she'd been lying there when she heard footsteps and the door opened and his hands were on her back, around her hips.

He pulled her up onto the bench; it didn't take much strength, then she was half sitting, half lying across his lap and his hands were not slow to slip under her skirts—her thighs had separated of their own accord—to find the warm and wet place where she most longed for him.

She loosened his belt, his hose came off easily; so very easy, it was, as she lay down and pulled him across her, and it was all so simple: they just slipped smoothly together and became one flesh; such was their design, that at exactly the spot where she needed him most, that was exactly the spot where he most needed to be, with exactly the body part she missed so intensely.

It was so amazingly easy, without words, sightless and incredulous: almost like two simpletons, they left it to their bodies to work it out, for themselves and then each other, as is the nature of bodies.

He sat gazing at her body, lying naked and defenceless, lifeless in appearance, but breathing gently, and his fingers slipped tenderly through her pubic hair. He pulled the skirt down over her nakedness; and as fast as he had removed his clothes, he was in them again and out of the door.

A jolt coursed through her body as the door slammed. She leapt to her feet and stood rigid, unmoving, gave herself a shake and stood still again, adjusted her clothes and hair, and then rushed out with only one thought in her mind: she had to go to Eadfrid's grave.

Later, she stayed in her hut. She wasn't feeling quite well, Talcuin announced, so teaching and letter-writing would have to wait.

Inside the hut, Hild was pacing back and forth, patrolling the room like a caged animal, in restless motion from one wall to another. Wringing her hands, she implored her god to let her escape the shame, to take her now—but he did not respond.

She crumbled like old bread and no longer knew who she was. Every thought and idea she had ever had dissolved into a chaotic torrent of fragments incessantly changing colour and consequence, and refusing to join together. One moment they seemed to be like this, and the next moment they were the exact opposite, but at no point were they all involved: some gave her the slip and then turned up the next day sneering at her, lay in wait and assailed her at unexpected moments, woke her at night with the dwarf-creature's cackling derisive laughter. She didn't have a moment's peace.

One evening, she dismissed Talcuin and tied her belt firmly to a ceiling rafter. She stood on the stool and knew that one little step into the air would release her. Paulinus appeared in her mind's eye: there was no forgiveness for this sin—for everything else, yes, but not this.

She pulled the nail from the rafter, threw it out into the dark night, and burnt her belt. She would have to await the Lord's mercy.

Perhaps he had heard her prayers after all, because the life force trickled out of her in a never-ending stream—not blood, but the pure life juice, clear and transparent.

On the first night of the month of the winter full moon, while the geese were migrating south and burnished leaves swirled in the autumn storm, Hild was awakened by Talcuin. Penda's servant was outside: he had been told to fetch her.

Fuming with rage, she sent him home. He was barely out of sight before she grabbed her cloak and hurried after him.

That night she lay in Penda's embrace and took Penda in her arms; that night she gave herself to Penda and took possession of Penda; and she was filled with joy, and also with disgust. She no longer knew what she should believe and think, or what she felt, saw and heard. Even the constants—what is up and what is down—no longer seemed certain.

She clutched him tightly and wept, her caresses fierce and direct; he was heavy and big and gentle, endlessly gentle; he wept as he lay upon her breast, and she was at a complete loss.

He pledged his love and promised his fidelity: he wanted her as his wife, immediately, now, at once. She thought it unseemly, so very and utterly unseemly; she hit him hard in the chest and couldn't live without him. She pledged her love and promised her fidelity: she wanted him as her husband, wanted to share bed and home with him, wanted to live with him every day and every night, for her god and for humankind.

They planned their wedding festivities then and there, in bed; they would be married on the first day of the sacrificial month, and the invitations were issued the following morning.

# GOLD GLADLY GIVEN . . .

*– wedding in Tamoworthig –*

A great deal of drinking went on at their wedding—from real glass beakers, Penda's imported luxury goods, which were only taken out of the storage chests for the most exceptional occasions. Green glass for the guests, dark-blue for the guests of honour—Penda owned fifteen of the latter glasses—and then for the bride and groom: ruby, splendid works of glass art looking like garnets, but blown, not cut like garnets, blown with a convex lip and little dots fixed in a ring just under the rim.

Once the guests had gathered, the bride and groom gave one another their hands and pledged their fidelity, as was the age-old custom.

After a toast of sweet and strong elderflower-beor, drunk in the presence of the guests, and with their arms entwined, the marriage was sealed.

Hereswid made the journey to attend the wedding. As she dismounted, she wept with joy and embraced her sister. Their childhood dream had finally come true: that they would visit one another, accompanied by a large entourage, would tell one another about everything they had seen in the big outside world, all the strange people, all the exciting places.

Hereswid wasn't offended by Hild's decision to get married before her year of mourning was over.

'Life is so short,' she said. 'You'll be happy with Penda.'

The sisters were now also neighbours, as Hild's morning gift of Rotanland bordered on East Anglia; Penda had recently captured this sizeable and bountiful patch of land from Hereswid's husband, who had hitherto been collecting taxes in the area.

'Not too much,' said Hereswid, 'and not too little!'

Hild was an excellent match for Penda. He could now stake a claim to rule Deira until his wife's sons reached the age of ten. The boys had closer ties to the throne than Oswald, the hothead, no doubt about that, even though Oswald had already been selected.

There was one more gift. When Hild opened the shutters on the morning after the wedding, she saw it sitting on a branch in a big elm; it was screaming with such piercing horror that she simply stood in amazement staring at this unnatural-looking feather-clad creature. Clearly not one of the Lord's creations, it seemed to undermine its own existence and had a tail that must make it impossible to provide food for itself.

Its body was even bigger than that of a capercaillie, a bit straggly, and when it dropped to the ground and strutted across the grass she could see that the tail was more than three times as long as the body. The creature was covered in countless large blue eyes—it must be able to see everything! Its head, neck and chest were a shiny metallic blue, in an un-birdlike way; the blue was far darker than a kingfisher's back, but the kingfisher was a bringer of good fortune, and it was very dark.

She had a shock when it emitted a strident and penetrating screech, almost like an infant or a randy cat, but metallic, more terrifying than beseeching. It wasn't a bird, that was clear enough: it was the Devil himself, dressed up in plumage and come to fetch her, an abomination blaring out across the entire royal estate.

Hild slammed the shutters shut and put her hands over her ears. So fate had caught up with her anyway, she conceded bitterly, you couldn't run from it.

Penda put his arms around his wife, glowing with pride.

'Do you like it?'

She buried her face into his chest and wept. She hadn't expected to be parted from him quite so soon, but now the hour had come when she must pay for her deeds. She clung to her new happiness and sobbed.

Penda laughed and opened the shutters again.

'A morning gift for the king's wife! No one else in the whole country owns such a bird.'

He pulled her along until they were standing outside and she could see for herself that it was indeed a bird—with a slightly more natural-looking mate. A Frisian merchant had procured these rarities; they hadn't come cheap.

'There's one more gift,' Penda confided to her. 'But that won't arrive until the time is right.'

Hild smiled, relieved the day wouldn't be bringing any more surprises. His joy in giving was the greatest joy for her; he was obviously desperate for the other gift to announce its impending arrival.

'Did you know Oswald was responsible for Eadfrid's death?' asked Hild.

Hereswid pulled her thinking-really-hard face.

'Who, apart from Oswald, would have an interest in his death?'

'Well, indeed,' said Hild, embarrassed to reveal her stupidity, 'but for a while I thought it was Penda.'

'Penda's interest had been far better served with Eadfrid in Deira, surely you know that.'

'I received a sign, so I thought no more of it.'

Hereswid slapped her thighs.

'Do you rely on signs?'

'Not exactly,' Hild floundered. 'I'm not on the look-out for them. But if they appear, well, you can't just ignore them, can you.'

'Not if they fit in with what you've already worked out, but they mustn't ever be the only guideline. That's what the heathens do, so they don't have to bother to think for themselves and take responsibility. They can always blame fate for their blunders. That's the pagan way of interpreting signs. Once you've been baptized, Jesus Christ is with you in everything, but you have to take responsibility on the Day of Judgement, and you can't pretend to him. And if you . . . ' Hereswid stopped in the middle of her lecture. 'What sign?'

Hild didn't really want to say.

'There hasn't been anyone I could talk with about such things. And on your own you think so many strange thoughts.'

She adjusted her skirt.

'Tell me. What sign?'

Hild squirmed on the stool.

'Penda's belt buckle. So many winding curves—that's where I saw the writing. All the letters in order, clear as anything: *Holofernes*, they said. And so I had to slay him. Like Judith had done.'

Hereswid was deliberating the matter, her face completely puckered up.

'I've always thought there was something evil about that buckle,' she admitted.

'It can open up; that's where he keeps his casting lots.'

'I knew there was something about it,' murmured Hereswid.

They sat in silence for a while, then Hereswid straightened up.

'Firstly, you must never read signs from things that belong to heathens. Secondly, you ought to have known there was something wrong with the sign, given that it was so inconsistent with your common sense. Penda is no villain; you should have thought about that!'

'He's a heathen,' said Hild. 'And Oswald is a Christian man.'

'Ha!' said Hereswid, and they fell silent again.

'There's something I've been thinking about,' said Hereswid. 'When my husband was baptized, many people followed his example—like they did with Edwin that time—but it doesn't always seem to be the best people who turn to Christ.'

'Perhaps they're the ones most in need of the grace of God?' Hild suggested.

'Possibly,' said Hereswid, 'but if so, they don't show it. Did you get any other signs?'

'A goshawk swooped down on a magpie pecking at a mouse.'

'And how did you interpret that?'

'I should kill Penda, who had killed Eadfrid.'

Hereswid nodded, the furrows deepening in her brow.

'How about: Penda will kill Oswald, who killed Eadfrid?'

A smile of comprehension spread across Hild's face. She leapt to her feet, and hopped up and down.

'Yes, yes, of course, that's it!'

She clapped her hands and couldn't control her joy, but then stood stock still, eyebrows raised.

'To lie with a man who slew a husband! While that husband lies in the earth—unredressed.'

Hereswid shrugged.

'Just like breaking in two,' Hild continued.

'Had that been the case, well, you wouldn't be the first.'

'Eadfrid's demon . . . it tried to cross over into me when it lost its abode.'

Hereswid really didn't want to say this, but it just flew out of her mouth: 'If you say your Our Father the demons don't stand a chance! And confess your faith.'

'That's not what Paulinus said!'

'No, but Sigebert does, and he knows just as much as Paulinus. He's studied in Gaul, and he knows more than anyone else in this land.'

Hild sat motionless; she almost couldn't say the words, just thinking them brought tears to her eyes, but she managed to get them out: 'Eadfrid lapsed,' she faltered, staring into space. 'Everything I did failed. I thought the Lord had turned away from me.'

'Don't say that!' Hereswid was wide-eyed.

'I know. And if I say it again, he might do so. But that's how I felt.'

Hereswid shook her head.

'Don't you think he knows what goes on in your mind? You'll have to do penance for that! And in future, couldn't you just settle for thinking: The ways of the Lord are past understanding? That's not remonstrating with the Lord, but it might well make him think twice.'

'The ways of the Lord are past understanding,' Hild repeated. 'Yes, that would be good to think.'

She repeated the phrase to herself several times, so it would stick in her mind and later emerge automatically and prevent her from saying anything wrong. She signalled to the slave that he should put more wood on the fire and fetch candles. He brought them immediately, along with some coltsfoot tea, which they hadn't asked for, but enjoyed anyway.

'This man Sigebert, who knows so much,' said Hild, 'have you asked him about our brother?'

Hereswid nodded.

'What does he say?'

'He says people can't see into that which is secret.'

'Can't he either?'

'God seeks out that which is past, he says, and that is not a matter for humankind. He says that if anyone claims they can see into that which is secret, then they are the children of Satan and we must shun them. Their words are poisonous vermin. That's what he says.'

'Good thing Paulinus didn't hear that!'

'God is in Heaven, he says, and we're on the earth. And we shouldn't believe we can fly like our god, he says.'

'Paulinus doesn't believe he can fly, but he can certainly see into that which is secret, as you have witnessed.'

'I'm not so sure anymore. He said he could, but at home in Rendlæsham I've heard the missionaries claim all manner of things to impress the heathens. They do it to serve the Lord, not to extol themselves, and it's helped them bring many to baptism. But Sigebert is having none of it. If he hears of someone getting up to what he calls *trickery*, then he throws them out.'

'Paulinus saw Hereberht playing in a meadow!'

'Maybe he dreamt it. And dreams can just as well come from the Devil as from the Lord.'

'Not Paulinus' dreams,' Hild protested. 'I believe he saw him, and I believe he lives in Bernicia, perhaps by the river Glene or the Tuidi, on a farm with good pasture—that's how he appeared to me in a dream. I think Oswald knows where he is, and I think we should write to Oswald and say that if he releases Hereberht then he can keep Deira, and neither Hereberht nor my sons will lay claim to what is rightfully theirs.'

Hereswid's thought-furrows reappeared; her response was a while coming.

'Deira is ours.'

Hild waited a moment.

'You think he's dead, don't you?'

Hereswid was reluctant to answer, but she took a deep breath and looked Hild straight in the eye.

'Yes, I do, and I have for a long time. Because I can't think of one single reason for Ædelfred to have let him live. And neither can you.'

'No, but so much could have happened. They might have lost him in the forest and a hermit took care of him, or one of Ædelfred's men could have found him a family to stay with, and then they slaughtered a lamb and smeared the blood on his clothes so Ædelfred thought he had been slain . . . can't you picture it?'

'I don't know,' said Hereswid evasively.

'So now he's a slave and doesn't know he can lay claim to Deira and his family will help him—he doesn't even *know*. Can't you see it?'

Hereswid's face was sombre as she straightened her back.

'If he has grown up in the position of a slave, what do you think he looks like now? Do you think anyone would choose a man like that to be king?' She paused, but didn't take her eyes off her sister. 'Maybe all his teeth have been knocked out, he has never heard the word of the Lord, his back is bowed and crooked, his children die of hunger, and all he dreams about is to eat his fill. He gets meat when his master makes an offering to his god, a tiny little scrap of horsemeat, and only because his master wants Woden to keep his slave alive. To be quite honest, Hild—why would you want a brother like that?'

'I want him!' Hild shouted, leaping up from her stool. 'And I couldn't care less about Deira, I just want my brother; he won't have to work or anything, and he can have just as much food as he can eat, and pork and legs of mutton, he just has to be here and be my brother!'

She sat down, exhausted from her shouting fit.

'Yes, fine,' Hereswid said at length. 'But it seems to me that by waiving your sons' claim on Deira we do the family a disservice. We owe Ædelfred's kin nothing but retribution. And you can't negotiate with a rogue like Oswald; his words carry less weight than those of a slave. Well, I'm sorry, perhaps our brother is an upright man, if he's alive, but Ædelfred's lineage certainly isn't.'

Hild couldn't speak.

'Hild, listen: Hereberht would have become a powerful man who made Oswald's life a misery; perhaps he would have fought, so Edwin would still be alive; but the Lord took him, and if he's playing in a meadow somewhere, then it must be in Paradise.'

'He wasn't baptized!'

'No, because the word of the Lord hadn't yet been proclaimed, but had he lived then he would have been as true to the Lord as you and I, and our god knows that.'

'Nonsense,' said Hild, 'that's unheard of.'

'It's what Sigebert says,' Hereswid assured her. 'And had it been otherwise, then indeed there would be no justice. Christ the King broke open the gates to the Land of the Dead and released the lost souls.'

'What about our mother, then?' Hild asked, seeing a glimmer of hope.

'I've asked about that too. Sigebert says there is no forgiveness for those who do not receive Christ. But he also says that the greatest sin is to forsake your kin.'

'So what does he think?'

'Well, both the one thing and the other, it seems.'

Hereswid was not satisfied with her own inadequate answer.

'Does the Lord accept her or does he not?'

Hereswid sighed, and stated flatly: 'He doesn't know. I don't think he knows.' Then she added, in a firmer voice: 'But I know it helps if we pray for our parents—that much I know.'

Hild nodded, and they sat in silence for a while. Darkness had fallen outside and for the first time in ages the owl hooted, very close, perhaps even from the ridge of the roof.

Hereswid resumed her lecturing; she wanted to show that she had learnt a thing or two from Sigebert. He wasn't completely ignorant, her husband's half-brother who had returned home from Gaul.

'If you read signs, you can only do so from something the Lord has created—never from something made by people.'

'What about horses?'

'Not from Woden's beasts, of course, you must never do that! Never horses, and never anything with the number nine, that goes without saying.'

'I know, but didn't the Lord create horses? Like everything else?'

Hereswid was one big thought-furrow.

'Well yes, that must be so. But then Woden must have taken the reins of horses, as it were, so they became impure. I mean: they are the Lord's creatures, but they've been infected by the idolaters. So we Christians can't eat them without dying. But there's no harm in using them for everything else.'

Hild shuddered. Talcuin had recently told her about a slave woman from Gwynedd who had been sold to a heathen farmer in Mercia who had forced her to take part in the sacrifice of a horse and she'd dropped down dead—on the spot.

'What about ravens?' she asked. 'And owls?'

'Never ravens—are you out of your mind! You have to use your sound judgement, at all times and in all situations. And your sound judgement tells you that ravens are just as defiled as horses.'

'Owls?' asked Hild, delighted to be on the receiving end of all this knowledge.

'Well, owls are Hreda's bird and I think it's possible, with the application of a little common sense, to glean some information through them.'

'So what's this one saying?'

It hooted again, penetrating and hollow—seven times.

'Maybe it's saying that you and I will meet again soon,' said Hereswid. 'Well, definitely something about women who are going to meet.'

'All this you say about *sound judgement*, where did you get it from?' asked Hild. She had to extract all the learning she could from Hereswid during their brief time together.

'Sigebert says so, but Bishop Felix says: Unto the pure all things are pure! He learnt that from the apostle Paul. But he also says it has no practical significance because we aren't pure and so we should do as Sigebert says and use our sound judgement.'

'Yes, but how is it sound?'

'Sound because the Lord has created it in us so we can distinguish between good and evil. So we don't just follow our noses like animals—and heathens, who don't bother to think but just call it fate when misfortune strikes.'

'Aren't we made pure in baptism?' Hild asked.

This was actually a foolish question, because she knew the answer; but she so enjoyed hearing Hereswid talk about her teachers and the right path that she just had to make her say more.

'Yes we are, but we are constantly being defiled. For one thing, we have inherited sin from our forefather Adam; and for another, we are endlessly subjected to temptations by the old enemy who is trying to draw us back into his troops. You'll have to see if you can get a teacher—even though you're married to a heathen. It's contagious, as you know.'

'Isn't there some way to protect yourself? I usually write to Aidan on Iona, but if Sigebert has told you something, then ...'

'The Lord's Prayer,' answered Hereswid, 'and the confession of your faith. Three times every evening and every morning, and when you're sitting at the loom. David's psalms are good, too. You don't forget to do that, do you?'

'No, no! I just wondered if there might be something else.'

'Reliquaries,' said Hereswid. 'Sigebert carries a little bit of soil from Radegund's grave as an amulet—it's the most effective he's had. She was a very great saint, of course. Perhaps you could get hold of a nail or a few strands of hair from one of the travelling holy men, and they might be able to sell you something from Saint David or Illtud or Samson or Beuno or someone like that.'

'Aidan might be able to get me something from his master, the holy Colomba. What more does he say?'

'Who?'

'Sigebert, of course!'

'What about?'

'Doesn't matter. Just something he says.'

Hild waited in suspense while Hereswid thought.

'He says—yes, now I'll tell you the best bit—he says: If I spoke in the tongues of men and of angels, but had not love, then I would be a noisy gong or a clanging cymbal. And if I had prophetic powers, and understood all mysteries and had all knowledge, and if I had all faith, so I could move mountains, but had not love, then I would be nothing.'

Hild had been holding her breath; now she sighed deeply.

'And if I gave away all that I have to the poor, and if I delivered up my body to be burnt, but had not love, I would gain nothing. Love is patient, love is kind; love does not envy; love does not boast; it is not arrogant or improper, does not insist on its own way, is not irritable or resentful, it does not rejoice at wrongdoing, but rejoices with the truth; love bears all things, believes all things, hopes all things, endures all things.'

'Bears all things, believes all things, endures all things,' Hild repeated, thinking of Penda.

'And then it goes: Love never ends. As for prophecies, they will sometime pass away; as for tongues, they will cease; as for knowledge, it will pass away.' Hereswid's eyes glowed. 'And listen to this, I think this is really good: For we know in part, and we prophesy in part, but when the perfect comes, the partial will pass away.'

'But when the perfect comes, the partial will pass away,' Hild repeated, and was overcome by a burning sensation in her crotch.

'And what about this, the absolutely best bit: Now we see things imperfectly, like puzzling reflections, but then we will see face to face; now I know in part, but then I shall know fully, just as I am known fully.'

She raised her voice, as if to emphasize her equation: 'So now faith, hope and love abide, these three; but the greatest of them is love.'

Hild sat with her hands pressing against her chest and tears in her eyes; she was trembling with emotion. Sigebert's words about the blessings of marriage were the truest she had ever heard.

'Didn't our mother say something like that?' she asked, having cleared her throat a few times. She couldn't quite remember the phrase their mother had always used.

'No, that was about something else entirely,' Hereswid brushed Hild's question aside.

'What then, what was it she said?'

'Do you mean about having a husband?'

'Yes, how did it go?'

'It wasn't something she had thought up, it's just a phrase you say.'

'So what was it?'

'Is it: Gold is gladly given for a husband's loving embrace.'

'Yes!' exclaimed Hild enthusiastically. 'Gold is gladly given for a husband's loving embrace. That's what I was thinking of—and so many years a widow!'

'It's not the same,' Hereswid stated emphatically. 'Sigebert is talking about love of the Lord, and that has nothing to do with men.'

Hild was both disappointed and embarrassed, which she tried to cover up by pressing her point. 'Love is surely love, and Jesus himself said: Little children, love one another. And Paulinus said that earthly love helps us envisage the love of our god. Yes, he said that.'

'Sibling love, yes, and maternal love, but not the bodily type, not the kind with men! Paulinus has never said that!' Hereswid shouted.

'I've heard it with my own ears. He didn't say it to us, because we were too young, but he said it to the adults—he did!'

'That's not true!' Hereswid snapped. She was familiar with Hild's tendency to embellish the truth.

'I heard it with my very own ears: I was standing behind the door—listening!' Hild shouted.

It was too late to back down. Now she'd have to stick to her story until the day she died— and so she would, she already thought she could hear him saying the words.

The wedding celebrations went on for a week. Every evening, they drank a toast with the guests and were congratulated and wished a happy life together.

On the third evening, Hild spat out the wine; it had hardly passed her lips before she realized it was poisoned. She rinsed her mouth meticulously with beer, spitting it out on the floor.

She summoned the steward, pointed at her glass and asked him to drink. Sweat and nausea instantly swept over him—he blanched, sought out Penda's eyes; with a curt inclination of his head, Penda merely indicated Hild's glass.

The steward promptly picked up the glass, downed it in one and asked permission to leave. Penda nodded and the man walked quickly out of the hall, nothing about his gait suggesting poison.

He was never seen again, and after a one-year period of mourning his wife was free to re-marry.

'Should I have let him off?' Hild asked Hereswid next day.

'Certainly not,' she replied. 'You have to show them who is in charge. Some of them might not have wanted a queen who adheres to the new faith.'

'I'll have to appoint a cupbearer,' said Hild.

'As you should have done long since,' said Hereswid. 'The chief men are not to be taken lightly.'

'Should we write to Oswald?'

'There's no point,' said Hereswid. She had considered the matter and rejected the idea. 'We'll never get Oswald to admit anything! Not the one nor the other.'

'Penda thinks I should demand land measuring five hundred hides for Eadfrid.'

'Five hides or five times five hundred—we won't get so much as a fastening pin out of him. Oswald is sly, and he's too powerful for us. We might just as well forget it,' said Hereswid, and thought the case was closed.

'I'll get him, you can be sure of that,' said Hild.

They had hoped Hundfrid and Wilbrord could have attended the wedding. Penda had sent some of his best men to Deira to find them. They were just over two years old now. The men returned empty-handed on the fourth day of the wedding festivities; they hadn't found any trace whatsoever of the children, nor had they been able to find the nurse.

Penda suggested that Talcuin should be sent to search for the boys, with an appropriate company of men. He had more than once taken note of Talcuin's quite special alertness. Hild was surprised, but agreed to the suggestion; she couldn't come up with a better idea.

Talcuin thanked them for the honour and asked for a little silver to procure co-operation where needed. Having received what he asked for—and more—he set off via Elmet, where he made his own investigations into Eadfrid's death. Finding no trace of the children in Deira, and that none of Cædwalla's troops were left alive, he moved on to Bernicia. In the yuletide month he, too, had to return home empty-handed.

Hereswid had already prepared Hild for the worst.

'Maybe you should accept it,' she had said, 'like with Hereberht. And we'll pray to the Lord that he might give you some other sons.'

'You can only say that because you don't know them!' Hild had cried. 'You don't know what kind of sons they are. And I don't want any other sons than those two boys.'

'No, no, of course not,' Hereswid had said.

When Talcuin eventually returned, Hild wished Hereswid was still at her side, so she could weep and weep on her sister's shoulder.

She was at a loss as to how she could find her children. She wrote to Aidan seeking advice. Not for a second did she doubt they were alive, and she also knew the Lord would bring them all together again—it was simply a question of when.

# BEFORE SEVEN SUMMERS HAVE PASSED

*- King Oswald's kiss -*

During the next few peaceful and happy weeks, Hild often wondered what she had done to deserve all this.

So much joy! New pleasures every day, new discoveries, new delights. Intimate nights in bed with Penda's warm body next to or on top of or under her—she could never get enough of him. Morning, noon and night, she accepted his gentle caresses and returned them with an intensity that startled her. Such abandon couldn't come from inside, it must come from outside, stronger than her, coursing through her; she was no match for its ferocity, and after a while she stopped trying.

It could come over her in the middle of the day, in the brightest sunshine, and run through her like a feverish shiver. The slightest glimpse of Penda—just the thought even—made her come apart at every seam, the life force draining from her almost like a menstruation. She feared for her health and made an effort to eat and drink plentifully; her body filled out, became shapely, which was befitting for her position.

Her new eminence caused her to hold her head high. She was consulted for advice, and she was always able to answer; born to be queen, providing counsel and giving orders came naturally.

She felt as if she had never been married before, as if she had been a maiden when she gave herself to Penda. Time and again, she was overcome by such happiness that she had to drop what she was doing and just smile. She laughed a lot, from the depths of her being, which was something she hadn't done for many years. There was a sprightliness about her, her movements and her plump body. She sang at the top of her voice when standing at the loom, the shuttle flying back and forth.

At night, however, the bad dreams could get such a grip that her screams woke Penda; he would take her in his arms, cradle her, hold her tight until her sobbing stopped.

'Can you explain?' she asked. 'Why do grown men throw young children down a well? Tiny little children who couldn't do any harm to anyone?'

Tears filled her eyes again—she could see a very small hand and the back of a slightly bigger child's head.

'I don't know,' said Penda. 'War is war.'

'Maybe so, but children have no part to play in that, and they can't even defend themselves.'

'A lot goes on in a war,' Penda muttered, picturing the frenzied rampages, but he didn't think that appropriate to explain to his wife. 'Now we have peace, what's done is done and no one can undo it. Don't think about it, Hild. Let the dead rest.'

'But they don't give me any rest,' she protested. 'Perhaps it would have been different if I had pulled them out and given them a burial.'

She couldn't forgive herself; she had simply turned away, hadn't been able to keep the contents of her stomach down whenever she approached that well.

She had never discussed the matter with Talcuin, and therefore she never found out that he was the one who had thrown the children down the well. He hadn't done it in a frenzied rampage or with cruel malice—on the contrary, having walked among the corpses of their family, he simply hadn't been able to bear the sight of those terrified little faces and the knowledge that they would now starve to death. He decided it was better to make short work of it and curtail their suffering.

Talcuin had always been on the soft side, and tormented by far too many thoughts. He had taken care of the situation while his fellow warriors were busy helping themselves to what they could find indoors. One of the children had given him the slip, but there hadn't been time to catch her, they'd had to push on northwards.

Another picture plagued Hild's nights: her husband's body dangling from the big ash tree. Consummation of the curse on Edwin's kin, or punishment for marrying his second-cousin, daughter of his mother's half-sister.

Paulinus had warned her; he wouldn't forbid the marriage, given that it had been agreed upon since before Hild was born, but nor would he bless it. So they got married according to the ancient custom, which had pleased Hild's mother.

'Penda,' said Hild one night, once more overwhelmed by the picture, 'when will punishment strike, the price to be paid for marrying Eadfrid?'

Penda was angry.

'And when will you start using your own sense instead of listening to all the nonsense those foreigners tell you?'

'It's not nonsense,' she insisted. 'Their predictions are often better than your signs, as well you know.'

'Now you just listen here!' he exclaimed, sitting up straight. 'Was it not settled between your father and Edwin that you would marry Eadfrid and together you'd rule Deira after Edwin?'

'Yes,' Hild nodded, 'but my father didn't know the law of the Lord.'

'The law of the Lord!' barked Penda, leaping out of bed. He paced up and down, as was his habit when infuriated. 'Have you completely lost your mind to that foreign hogwash? Couldn't you try to use your head and stop falling in line with all those rules they make up to manipulate everyone? Scaring you into bowing to their power with all that talk of eternal fire!'

For the first time, he seriously considered expelling the missionaries allowed to travel his realm speaking freely. They were doing a lot of damage: causing people to lose their good sense—even his wife, who was otherwise sound of mind. Earnestly, and stressing every word, he said: 'Is this the daughter of the renowned Hereric, sitting here blubbering because she followed the wishes of her deceased father? Who thinks she could have wangled herself a better lot in life by listening to the new-fangled nonsense brought in by outsiders, and insulting her murdered father?' Walking into the adjoining chamber, he turned in the doorway: 'I didn't marry a timid gullible baby hare: I married a daughter of Hereric and Breguswid, who are still spoken of here in Mercia.'

Hild was ashamed of herself when Penda left her like this at night. She tried to straighten out her thoughts, but they ran round in circles and she couldn't get them under control.

Just one thing was certain: Eadfrid had to be avenged.

It was just before yuletide when King Cynegils of the West Saxons decided to be baptized. Hild was among the high-ranking persons invited to attend; she gratefully accepted.

Cynegils' conversion had come about in a rather unusual way, and was actually attributable to Oswald who, being son of Ædelfred and Acha, was Edwin's nephew. Oswald had started the process to avenge the attempted murder of Edwin, ordered ten years previously by the West Saxons' king but thwarted when a manservant called Lilla threw himself between the king and a poisoned dagger. Edwin's subsequent victorious revenge attack on the West Saxons led everyone to presume the matter closed; Oswald, on the other hand, was eager to stake his claim as Edwin's rightful successor, Northumbria's Christian king number two—not in reputation, but in chronological sequence.

So now he was going to show the West Saxons just who they were dealing with, and at the same time reward his men. As had been the case at the battle against Cædwalla, he didn't cross the Humbre river with a particularly large army, but with a troop of good men who knew what they were after and knew how to fight for it. Some of them were not natives of Northumbria, and they were happy to be paid for their services with land in the south; the rest could be paid with any movables they could loot. He owed them that, and he owed it to his maternal uncle and eminent predecessor, Edwin.

Oswald pushed on through Lindsey at such speed that Penda didn't have time to stop him, and he arrived at the West Saxons' royal settlement before Cynegils had time to gather an army.

Cynegils consulted his council of elders and a missionary called Birinus, sent by Pope Honorius a couple of years earlier. Offerings were made, and signs were read—the results were not reassuring. Birinus saw his opportunity and preached with great urgency and confidence: only the king's conversion could avert disaster.

As nothing better was suggested, this remedy was put into action and an enquiry was sent to Oswald as to whether he would do King Cynegils the honour of being his sponsor at the baptism, plus accept one of the king's daughters as his wife—the choice was his—to seal their good relationship.

Oswald was livid about this trick being played on him. He strode furiously back and forth in front of the tent, refusing to speak with anyone and throwing his food and drink in the faces of those who brought it to him.

The next day, realizing he would have to find somewhere else to reward his men, Oswald conceded defeat. He sent a magnificent delegation to Cynegils with grateful thanks for the offer, which he was happy to accept.

During the two weeks now left before the baptismal ceremony, Oswald stayed with Cynegils as his guest, taking the opportunity to weigh up the daughters.

He chose Cyneburh, a plump and red-cheeked calf-like fourteen-year-old with dimples. He would have taken the youngest, because the younger they were the easier they were to mould, but the ten-year-old walked with a slight limp, which he noticed even though they tried to conceal her defect, and the eleven-year-old didn't look quite healthy: her skin was rather sallow, not exactly appetizing in appearance. They all had their father's somewhat protruding eyes, but Oswald's advisers confirmed this was not a symptom of any disorder.

The only real drawback with the chosen bride was her ready laughter: she would suddenly burst into the most unseemly overexcitement, as if everything were boiling up and bubbling over inside. This wasn't a major problem, however, as it was a tendency of which she would soon be cured. She had good and wide hips, which was of greater importance, and her breasts appeared to be acceptable, her age taken into consideration. The latter feature could, of course, be faked; it wouldn't be the first time, but breasts weren't decisive. The decisive issue was her state of health: she was simply bursting with energy, like a young mare yet to be broken in. Oswald knew all about breaking in young horses, and he took pleasure in doing so—he didn't like mounting a horse someone else had ridden.

So once Oswald had recovered from his fury about Cynegils' conversion, he actually started looking forward to training this unruly young mare, to having a fling with her white skin, her pink flesh.

As the days passed, he warmed more and more to the thought. She'd have to be baptized first, of course, along with her father. He didn't want an unbaptized female in his bed; he'd had a few of those when there hadn't been any other convenient option—and it had led to trouble every time.

Cyneburh was beside herself with pride and excitement. On one and the same day, holy baptismal water would render her a new person and she would receive a great king in her bed, which would make her queen of the vast realm of Northumbria.

She couldn't sit still during the intensive baptism instruction Birinus had to give in great haste—to her, to her father and the closest retainers who would accompany him. Time and again, Birinus' lessons were interrupted by her loud eruptions of laughter. She put her hand to her mouth and blushed scarlet with shame, but it wasn't long before she was overcome again and her laughter spluttered out.

She found it much easier to concentrate on guidance given by her nurse and by her older sister—information she would need about this, that and the other. They were relieved to establish that her maidenhead was healthy and intact, so there was no need to teach her squeezing techniques or how to use the little sponge soaked in pig's blood. She was taught how to use flaxseed oil: not too much, not too little. The nurse would be going with her up north anyway, plus two maids and some other servants.

'At first, you don't understand why they talk so much about that thing and what on earth it's for,' said Cyneburh's big sister. 'But let me tell you this: without it you wouldn't get any heirs. So you just have to relax completely and think about the children you'll have, and the more you think about them, the less it'll hurt. And remember the flaxseed oil!'

'Always inside the lips,' added the nurse, 'and men appreciate that too. But only use as much as sticks to one finger—or perhaps two, to start with. Yes, try two.'

'You soon get used to it,' her sister went on—she had been married for three years now.

'You do indeed,' the nurse said emphatically. 'And eventually you can't do without it. Then you'll do anything to get a young buck in your bed; just look at me. I . . . ' She blushed and fell silent. She had been about to reveal how she lured the young men with mead and goodies from the king's table, but this was neither the time nor the place for sharing such confidences.

'Well, it certainly improves as the years go by,' her sister said to the nurse, 'I'll give you that.'

Cyneburh shook her head over all these new and strange activities into which she was being initiated; she was glad the nurse was going with her. And then she had a sudden fit of giggles, which developed into violent weeping, and the two women exchanged meaningful looks across the top of her curly hair.

'There there,' said the nurse, 'it'll all turn out fine.'

Hild was full of praise for Birinus' beautiful Gospel Book. She asked if she might be permitted to take a closer look, and Birinus was happy to oblige. He had always thought it a rather rough copy, but with the queen's words of praise his book grew in stature, and he could see that the parchment was indeed really very fine. He willingly told the Christian queen about the forthcoming ceremony—which pages would be read and which page the two kings would kiss as a representation of their reconciliation in Christ.

The big day came, and everything went as it should: King Oswald was sponsor to King Cynegils; Queen Hild witnessed his marriage to Cyneburh; and when the ceremony was at an end, Oswald had kissed his own death warrant.

Hild had placed a thin sheet of parchment under the kissed page; on it she had written: *Before seven summers have passed, he who has slain Eadfrid will pay with his head.*

It was first written with Latin letters in the Latin language, and then in the native tongue, with runes. Below the writing, two raven feathers were fixed across one another with glue made of toad blood, crow spittle and the gall of young shrews, which had been expensive, but not too expensive. She had been fortunate enough to carry out the work at full moon, and had said three Our Fathers while writing the words.

Hild stood with a blissful smile on her lips as she witnessed the marriage of Oswald and Cyneburh.

'The will of the Lord be done!' were the words she said to them, and Oswald thanked her; he thought she put it beautifully.

When Hild got back home to Tamoworthig, there was a letter waiting for her from Hereswid, with an invitation to visit. Her husband Ecgric now ruled the whole of East Anglia, and they spent most of their time in Rendlæsham. King Sigebert had entered the service of the Lord at the monastery in Beodericsworth, which he had founded at the start of his reign. The school he had established continued its work; Bishop Felix was in charge, Hereswid and two monks were the teachers. Hereswid enjoyed teaching; it brought back memories of the lessons given by Paulinus. The children she taught reminded her of her younger self and the ideas she'd had back then—so she didn't take quite such a tough line with the errors of their ways. The light of the Lord was still new to the kingdom.

'Do you remember Frig's Seat?' she wrote, and Hild felt a sudden rush of warmth, a memory of sun and wind and running at speed through sweet-smelling grasses. Frig's Seat. She wondered who would be sitting on it now, hoping to get out into the world and experience all its splendour.

Radiant with joy, she read the letter aloud to Penda. His eyes lit up when she read Hereswid's account of the unnatural frost that had covered the swampy marshlands with a thick layer of ice.

'Would you like to visit your sister?' he asked.

Hild was surprised that Penda seemed to want her to go away; he never usually interfered in her day-to-day activities, and they were not long married. In this matter, however, he was resolute: she should leave immediately and return in four weeks' time, not a day later.

Hild was happy to oblige, as there was nothing she would rather do than visit Hereswid.

# UNDER THE WIDE OPEN SKIES

*– Penda's expedition to East Anglia –*

On the homeward journey from East Anglia, Hild was full of plans. She would send word to Aidan asking him to come and take charge of a monastery she would establish—the first in Mercia. She would have Eadfrid's mortal remains moved to the monastery, where daily prayers would be said for his soul. Sigebert had told her this was the best way to ensure her husband was at peace in his grave, and she shouldn't worry about meeting him again in Paradise as the peace of the Lord prevailed there and no one would ever raise their hand or voice against another.

She looked forward to having Aidan nearby. If necessary, she would use her entire morning gift to build the monastery; the thought made her smile—she was a woman of not inconsiderable means.

Entering Mercia, she saw signs of upheaval. They made a rest stop, where they were told that all the freemen had been called up: Penda was planning a campaign, the call-up had been issued roughly one month previously.

Hild immediately wrote to Hereswid: 'Spring has come to Cantwaraburh. Do not let your children forego Eostre's lilies. May the Lord bless you.' She sent off her swordbearer with the letter, ordering him to deliver it into the hands of the queen; she hoped Hereswid would understand. She then hurried home to Tamoworthig, which was crawling with men and horses.

Penda was going to attack East Anglia.

Once the army had left, Hild got ready to travel again. There couldn't be much doubt about the outcome, but if her god intervened, then . . .

She lay prostrate on the ground, praying to the Lord God. She prayed that Penda would lose the battle but keep his life, so he would return home and abandon his war campaigns—and perhaps turn to her god.

She knew she was praying for the impossible, but everything was possible for the Lord, as she also knew.

Four days later news arrived that Penda had been victorious and had succeeded in totally disbanding Ecgric's army, the men fleeing in all directions once their king had fallen. Sigebert, too, had fallen.

Hild couldn't believe her ears. She had spoken with Sigebert just ten days earlier, and his monastic pledge hadn't seemed mere pretence. She refused to believe that this humble and self-possessed man could have broken his vows and taken up arms. He who, like Saulus, had turned from the sword and renounced all secular power in order, like Paulus, to fight the divine fight—could he really have taken on the robe of Saulus again and entered the earthly battle?

She also knew he had a belligerent temperament and had taken part in an attack against his own brother, King Rædwald's eldest son, who had seized the throne after their father. Sigebert had thus been obliged to flee to Gaul; he had been brought home after his brother's death, to be appointed king.

'You're lying!' she told the messenger. 'Sigebert wasn't there. He must have been slain in the monastery.'

'Sigebert was there, and both kings have fallen, my lady. Had the thaw not set in, King Penda would have slain each and every one of their men, my lady.'

Hild was perplexed by the ways of the Lord.

'And where are Queen Hereswid and her children?'

'In Cantwaraburh, my lady. Penda has sent for them and granted them safe passage to the burial ceremony. He also requests the presence of his wife.'

Hild set forth, taking with her ten round silver bowls with cruciform decoration, which she had recently acquired from a Frisian merchant who had bought them from a well-to-do family that had fled—in the year of Hild's birth—from the Persians' attempt to win Byzantium. She would donate them to Sigebert's monastery, along with a favourite large hanging bowl, at the bottom of which an enamel-inlaid trout with red garnet eyes had been set on a little pin, so when the bowl was full it seemed as if the fish was swimming. And if you rocked the bowl, the fish spun round. She only used it for the sweet white wine, and only ever for the most distinguished guests. It had been handled roughly at the wedding, trapped between two of Penda's bodyguards and a guest from Bernicia who they thought was getting a little too close to the king. Hild had recently had it repaired. It had been a gift from Cædwalla, sent by his widow who knew that her deceased husband and Hild had shared a taste for red colours; they had both thought red went best with bronze, and as the widow didn't share their view, she had no difficulty parting with the bowl.

Hild was so fond of this bowl that she would give it to Sigebert's monastery, along with the silver bowls, which she was having second thoughts about—they were a little unstable. These donations would buy requiem masses for the fallen kings.

She travelled via Beodericsworth and found the monastery intact. The abbot was grateful for her gifts; the hanging bowl was much appreciated, his finger traced the spiral patterns.

It was truly an uncommonly beautiful piece. Only the Britons could shape spiral patterns, and with such elegance. In comparison, there was something hopelessly coarse and clumsy about the Angles' objects, no matter how much gold and how many precious stones were lavished upon them. Hild now realized—just as she was parting with it—that the bowl was actually the finest piece she had owned.

The abbot tied a wick to the fish, filled the bowl with oil, and used it to illuminate the sacristy. The fish was no longer visible, which annoyed and upset Hild, but she had no say in something she'd given away.

The abbot offered her a beaker of wine. He could but corroborate what Penda's messenger had said. It had happened thus:

Thirty armed men on horseback had arrived at the monastery and asked Sigebert to take charge of their campaign. Without him they would not venture into battle. Even though their army was greater in numbers than Penda's, they lacked experience when it came to fighting. And against Penda they also lacked fighting spirit. No one matched Penda when it came to good fortune in war—wherever he got *that* from. He had never lost a battle, however numerous the opposing forces. There was such belief in Penda's good fortune in war that King Ecgric feared mutiny. The chief men had therefore decided to call on the services of Sigebert, who was known to be a mighty warrior, an outstanding strategist and, moreover, a man of the Lord, and would certainly ensure good fortune in war.

But Sigebert had refused; he couldn't go back on his monastic vows, he said. He had devoted himself to the Lord, and he would never again carry a sword. The abbot had whispered to him that the Lord would give permission for this battle against the heathens, but Sigebert wouldn't listen. When the men realized that nothing would make Sigebert break his vows, they were overcome by panic and dragged him out by force.

Several of the monks had clung to their brother, but they were knocked aside; one was killed, and then Sigebert left voluntarily. He had also mounted the horse unaided. But when they handed him his weapons, he had just dropped them. It had been impossible to make him hold a sword or a spear, even when they threatened his life. Then the abbot went to the blacksmith's pile of iron waiting to be forged into other objects and fetched an axe-hammer Sigebert had brought with him from Gaul as a curiosity. It was an elegant attempt to make an iron tool that could serve as both a hammer and an axe, and was of no use as either the one or the other. When they put it into Sigebert's hand, he held onto it—at the wrong end. And the abbot had heard him say that this iron stick was half of his holy cross, and he would soon get the other half.

Terrified by this, the men hadn't tried to make him do anything else; it was enough that he rode into battle with them. They'd have to work out the strategy themselves. By all accounts, the people had taken heart when they saw Sigebert's standard fluttering in the vanguard, and they had thrown themselves into the fight, bellowing loudly. Sigebert's presence had at least prevented the mass desertion of men the king had feared.

The abbot finished his account by making the sign of the cross. Hild asked why, then, the army had fled anyway and hadn't even attempted to avenge the fallen kings.

The abbot gave her a wry look.

'Well, you know how . . . '

He shook his head and stared gloomily at nothing.

'Times will be hard for the faith now.'

He stood up and started to pace back and forth.

'No one believes what we say—when they can see with their own eyes that Penda's gods are stronger than Christ!'

He had clenched his right hand, punching the fist rhythmically into his left palm.

'When the Lord won't send us better signs! The whole monastery has done nothing but fast and pray since we heard Penda was on his way. And Sigebert, that . . . ' He couldn't get the words out.

'What about Sigebert?' asked Hild.

'Oh . . . well . . . ' The abbot's clenched fist pummelled harder and faster, and he was on the verge of blurting it out, but he pulled himself up at the last moment.

'Well, just that I think he would have been in better standing with Saint Peter if he'd acted like a decent warrior, instead of being all pedantic about that monastic vow. If he'd shown the people which side is the strongest.'

'And break his vow?'

Hild almost couldn't believe the words she was hearing from the abbot's mouth.

'And save the realm from the misfortune he'd saddled it with in the first place!'

The abbot had raised his voice, and Hild didn't know what he meant.

'Is it a misfortune for the realm that the king is a servant of the Lord?'

'No, no!' He made a deflecting hand gesture and his pacing grew faster and heavier. 'But sin is sin!' he erupted, turning defiantly to face Hild.

'That it is,' she responded calmly. 'And so what?'

He glared at her.

'I have no more to say,' he eventually stated in a flat tone.

And once he had spoken these words, Hild took her leave.

He did, nonetheless, have more to say, because as she prompted her horse into action, and the vanguard of her entourage had already ridden out of the gate, he called after her.

'Ask your sister! If you bump into her, that is!'

She spent the rest of the journey mulling over this conversation. That the abbot as an individual exasperated her was one thing, and of no relevance in this instance, but what was this secret he wanted her to be acquainted with? She had to push it out of her mind, because she could find no resolution to the issue.

We owe the Lord thanks for the thaw, she told herself. Without it Ecgric's entire army would have been annihilated, but now they had been able to use their old tactic of spreading out across the marshland, where they knew their pursuers would sink and drown.

Penda's men were not at all familiar with how to advance swiftly through marshy land, but many of them could never resist chasing after enemy in flight, it was in their blood—and it killed them.

Hild knew the East Angles couldn't really be blamed for fleeing the field where their king had fallen, because they hadn't done so out of cowardice or lack of loyalty to their master. On the contrary, it was a strategy that had proven to be the cruellest manner in which to avenge the death of a king—because the enemy would always set off in pursuit and then die in the swamps.

This was a cunning tactic, and the kings themselves had ordered it, much against the will of the elders. It wasn't particularly manly, getting assistance from nature because you couldn't deal with the enemy yourself. Hild had to admit Penda was right in that respect. Even King Rædwald had used the method, and it had given the East Angles a reputation for slyness, some would say sorcery. The gods ruled differently out here where the land was so flat and the sky so mighty and overwhelmingly close at hand, with demons and water spirits everywhere, which was why it had always been necessary to be on good terms with these powers. Until Sigebert arrived, enemy captives had still been sacrificed—something Penda had never done.

In East Anglia, however, the demons were so firmly entrenched that no one had succeeded in driving them out. Not even the holy men from Cantwaraburh and Ireland and Gaul, given land by King Rædwald to fight the Lord's fight, had managed to expel them. Even after his baptism, Rædwald had been obliged to make sacrifices both to the one and to the other, as Hild had heard him explaining to Edwin, who didn't think you could serve two masters at once. Rædwald had agreed, adding that he only served the Lord God but had to keep the others happy or they wouldn't leave him in peace.

Hild had more respect for Penda: at least his fidelity to the ancestral line never wavered, and his forefathers seemed to reward him well, with plenty of good fortune in war.

She was relieved the monastery hadn't been torched. Penda didn't usually spare the monasteries, so her small ember of hope glowed brighter. If he did convert, at least she would have done some good by marrying him, and the thought filled her with joy, a feeling that lasted the rest of the trip to Rendlæsham. She saw quite a few burnt-down farmhouses along the route, which was understandable—the people would want something in return for their efforts.

Hild reflected on all these matters in order to avoid thinking about her sister, who had lost everything except for her children: a three-year-old daughter and her son, Aldwulf, who was barely two.

Hereswid returned on her own, leaving the children in Kent. She didn't trust Penda's word when it came to a king's son such as Aldwulf, but Hild thought her sister was doing Penda an injustice. Her husband might well be a pagan, but his word was just as good as that of other rulers, and certainly better than Edwin's had been, as she knew for fact.

Nor had Penda torched the royal settlement at Rendlæsham. He sat at the high table and received his wife; they sat there together and received Hereswid when she returned. A tall, thin figure, but below the headdress her eyes still gleamed a clear blue. Just looking at her, you couldn't tell she would be giving birth in four months' time.

Some of King Ecgric's men had already sworn allegiance to Penda; when they saw their now former king's widow enter the hall surrounded by a tight circle of her own men, they averted their eyes and stared intently at the floor. Penda made no attempt to force Hereswid's men to swear their allegiance to him—he had too much respect for his wife's sister for that to be necessary. Hereswid's husband and the monk-king would be entombed with every possible honour and splendour. Her husband had been a valiant warrior, who had slain several of Penda's best men before he fell.

The monk-king! Penda's mind wouldn't let go of the monk-king, and he had already asked for the story to be repeated several times: what Sigebert had said in the monastery, why he wouldn't carry a sword, why he had abdicated the throne, how he had ridden between the opposing troops without so much as blinking, and had let himself be slain without offering any resistance whatsoever.

This final point in particular was the strangest thing Penda had ever heard, but as to its veracity, well, he had now heard it told from many mouths. Sigebert had not so much as lifted his hand when Trumhere from Wodensburh raised his sword against him. According to both Trumhere and several others who had been right there, Sigebert hadn't even blinked when Trumhere's sword pierced his throat and cut through his artery.

A remarkable man, and a very brave one too, Sigebert would be talked about for a long time to come. The story already noted that a white dove had flown into the air as he fell to the ground. Trumhere and the others could not corroborate this detail, but nor would they contradict it—given that there were plenty of men ready to swear they had seen it with their very own eyes.

Penda couldn't get Sigebert out of his mind, and speculated intensely on how he could honour him with the most magnificent of interments, with a burial mound even visible from out at sea. Foreigners arriving by ship would know that here lay a king the like of whom had not been seen before.

Penda looked around the long table, hoping for inspiration as to how this splendour could be achieved. Trumhere sat hunched over, staring down, scratching the surface with his thumbnail. Penda asked Hild to fill his drinking horn.

Trumhere had drunk a lot, but he was still full of melancholy. He proposed a toast to Penda, and as he did so the corner of his mouth twitched; he bowed and asked permission to retire, he wasn't feeling so good; he had tears in his eyes.

Penda was startled. He walked across to Trumhere and accompanied him out of the hall, his arm around the man's shoulders; he gestured to the servants following them that they should stay where they were.

The two men stood outside in the cold air; the frost had set in again, which was even less natural, here at the beginning of Hreda's month. The sky was so wide and clear in these parts, and there were far too many stars up there. Staring at them this evening made your head swim and you nearly disappeared into them, they were so close you could almost reach out and touch them.

'Yes,' said Trumhere, and shook his head.

'Yes,' Penda answered.

They stood in silence, their breath hanging in the air.

'And he didn't even blink?'

Penda had grabbed hold of Trumhere's belt, and leant in towards him.

Trumhere shook his head.

'Not even once,' he faltered, rested heavily against Penda and wept. Collecting himself, he blew his nose and brushed down his clothes—at length, even though there was nothing to brush away. He looked at his master; dark and empty eyes staring from a thin grey face.

'Fortune has deserted me,' he said quietly. 'And I don't think it will come back.'

Penda couldn't refute this. Considering the way in which Trumhere had wasted away over the winter, it was obvious he wasn't any Lucky Man.

'Well, you don't lack good fortune in war,' said Penda, trying to offer some kind of comfort.

'I do,' said Trumhere, 'for there is no good fortune in slaying a defenceless man.'

'You have served me loyally,' said Penda, 'and for that I shall reward you.'

'I have brought misfortune upon you!' Trumhere shouted, his hands to his face. 'And upon your entire kingdom.'

'Do not say that,' Penda threatened, making a deflecting gesture to the gods.

'It's no use,' Trumhere cried out, beating the air with both hands, 'for misfortune has already set in. And now it will swoop down on us all.'

'I don't know what you're talking about,' Penda replied dismissively, turning to leave. But Trumhere couldn't stop, he leapt in front of Penda.

'I thought I was carrying out your will,' he whispered in anguish, and stared Penda straight in the eyes.

Penda felt a sharp pain in his chest, and put his hand over his heart. He couldn't stop Trumhere.

'I thought I was serving you by bringing down the swine, I didn't know you'd marry her—a queen who isn't true to the gods . . . and draw down the wrath of the gods . . . '

'The wrath of the gods!' Penda shouted, and hit Trumhere across the face, causing him to fall backwards. He immediately regretted his action and helped him up.

The pain in his breast had moved out into his arm, his entire left side hurt, and he was having trouble catching his breath. He had to sit on the ground, on the stiff frosty grass.

'Say no more,' he stuttered out, pressing his hands hard against his chest. 'I don't know what you're talking about, and I don't want to hear any more.'

Trumhere went to help his master stand up, but his outstretched hand was knocked away. He looked around in alarm to find help, saw nothing but closed huts, the unrelenting stars and the flat frosty ground, withered grass, otherwise just darkness all around.

'Go!' he heard his master say in a voice he didn't recognize. 'And bear your fate like a man! Go home to Wodensburh if you're not up to the job! This is a campaign of conquest, and we have triumphed. And it is of no interest to anyone whether a man blinks or laughs or farts when he falls. I will not see blubbering women around me, you hear? Get out of my sight!'

During this tirade, Penda had been huddled on the ground in great pain, and he feared the East Angles' marshes would engulf them before they could get away. He regretted embarking on this campaign and would have surrendered all the booty to be back in Tamowrthig.

He had also mixed everything together, and was talking more to himself than to pale and stooping Trumhere, who received his master's curses and then hesitantly took himself off as he had been ordered.

Penda slowly recovered his composure; he was usually a cool-headed man who didn't let his emotions get the better of him.

He had to get away from here, but they couldn't leave before the interment. He clutched his head and tried to think. There were two problems: Trumhere and the burial. He took his casting lots from his belt buckle and threw them on the ground—that was Trumhere done, now there was just the interment to sort out.

The monk-king had to be properly honoured. Like the other East Anglian kings, he had been a notable shipmaster and wasn't afraid of the open seas. He should be buried in a ship—a large and magnificent seagoing vessel, one of the best in the East Anglian fleet—and the grave goods would surpass anything ever seen before. Remembrance of the remarkable king would live on forever. The only problem left was whether or not there should be a funeral pyre.

He cast lots: no funeral pyre, but a slow voyage to the hereafter.

So the problems were resolved, and the cold had penetrated right into his bones. He stood up laboriously and tottered back to the hall, where his wife greeted him in the doorway: Hereswid wanted to make a request.

He settled himself on his chair, frozen right through and out of sorts, and indicated that he would now listen to what Hereswid had to say.

Hereswid was very pale, but composed; she stepped forward, stood in front of Penda and bowed deeply. Straightening up, she spoke in a loud, clear voice.

'I request the King of Mercia, my sister's husband, to grant me one wish, which will cost you nothing but will for ever be to your credit.'

'Speak out,' said Penda, 'I shall do what I can for my wife's sister and valiant King Ecgric's queen.'

'I ask that my husband and King Sigebert might be buried in the monastery at Beodericsworth.'

Hereswid kneeled, her head bowed. Penda didn't answer. Hereswid remained kneeling in front of him, everyone waiting in anticipation, the only sound that of crackling from the fireplace. Eventually, after a lengthy interval, Penda shook his head.

'I would give you gold, I would give you land, and everything else you might request. But the interment cannot be changed. I have cast lots.'

Hild leapt from her chair, stood for an instant before sitting down again, heavily, and stared up into the smoke-hole.

Hereswid showed no reaction. She stayed on her knees for a few moments, and then, as if nothing had occurred, she stood up, bowed to the king and walked back to her place, her bearing as upright as when she had stepped forward.

Conversation gradually started up again in the hall. Hild sat staring up into the smoke-hole for a long time before walking across to sit with Hereswid and pouring her a beaker of wine.

'I'll come to you tonight,' she said. She didn't know if her sister had heard her words, but Hereswid soon left the company.

Hild stayed where she was. The thought of these great kings being buried in the pagan way, and not partaking of the heavenly joys they, more than any, deserved, was incomprehensible. Their souls would perish, and neither of them would rise from the dead. When the Lord came again and summoned his servants, he wouldn't know the names Ecgric and Sigebert. Their souls would have disintegrated—dissolved like those of the heathens—and all their allegiance to the Lord would have been in vain.

Hild rested her head in her hands, which helped steady these impossible thoughts.

Sigebert was the finest-looking man she had ever seen, and the most attractive. Strong and supple, skilled at fighting and all manner of physical contests, and he controlled a sailing vessel as surely as he controlled a horse. Be that as it may—he wasn't the only one with those skills—but there was a gentleness to him, eyes that showed they had seen the world and a voice that was as one with the words it spoke. When he talked you just wanted to close your eyes, lean back and let the sound float in: your whole body would settle down and relax at the sound of his voice.

You could almost envy the Lord for having a monopoly on Sigebert in a monastery, and you might think a woman should also enjoy the pleasures of his loins, his hands. A man like him should have heirs.

He had told her about Gaul, about monasteries he had visited, towns he had lived in, strange trees and animals that didn't live in this country. He mastered Greek and had taught her to count to ten, and he knew Latin perfectly. He had told her about the holy Queen Radegund—a story so wonderful she had asked him to repeat it, word for word, the second time she visited the monastery.

Radegund was a princess from the kingdom of Thuringia, deep in the endless Germanic forests. At the age of twelve she had been taken captive by the Franks, who had taught her the true faith. She was so beautiful and wise that King Chlotar married her when she was eighteen years old. But her goodness was lost on him; he continued his impious life and indulged in all manner of excesses involving young women, murder and deceit, killing Radegund's brother and taunting her for her childlessness. After six years of marriage, she left him and became a nun in Noviomagus. She later founded a monastery in Pictavis, which received an invaluable relic from the Holy Land: a piece of Christ's cross. The monastery was now known as the

Abbey of the Holy Cross, and it had become a centre of learning with nuns whose Latin and writing skills surpassed those of most. Two hours a day were dedicated exclusively to study, and those who were particularly good scribes spent additional hours making copies from the Holy Scriptures. Moreover, Radegund never ceased her endeavours to bring about peace: even though she had renounced this earthly existence with the luxury and splendour of her former life at court, she was tireless in her mediation between parties warring over their earthly affairs—nothing was too big or too small to receive her attention.

She had died fifty years ago, but Sigebert had met people who had known her—one being the nun Baudovinia, who had written about Radegund's life. He had also visited her monastery and paused by her grave, where many miracles had occurred, praying that he might return home from exile. A few years later, this wish had been granted. Sigebert had ended both accounts of Radegund's life by making the sign of the cross and saying a short prayer.

Sigebert. His bearing, his way of moving, his eyes and his voice—it wasn't for want of experience or pleasure in the flesh that he had renounced the carnal life, that much was clear. It must have been because his need for the eternal life was even stronger, or it was something else entirely, something she didn't understand.

Penda's pagan thick-headedness had now closed the door of Paradise on Sigebert, and she would never see him again.

She felt intensely angry with Penda. She looked at him sitting there, staring down at the table, grey-faced, hunched shoulders—almost like Trumhere, scratching the table with his thumbnail. She knew Penda already regretted the whole campaign, and that he would have given a lot to grant Hereswid's wish. He was a prisoner of his own idiotic superstition, and he couldn't extricate himself from it, was afraid to think and act for himself, didn't use his *sound judgement*, as Sigebert called it, always consulted pagan priests and others who read signs, and when a swift decision was needed, he cast lots. Those stupid little sticks of his.

And so that was how it had to be: nothing, nothing in the world could change the decision, not death—nothing. He simply refused to use the sound judgement given to him by the Lord, which was strange because he was perfectly able to use it in other matters. He was uncommonly sharp-minded and quick, eagle-eyed, with a remarkable memory; he could describe each and every stone, every tree, every building, every bend in a road he had ridden, crops and their qualities, and he didn't forget a single detail. People, too, even if only seen fleetingly: he could describe them from top to toe—their clothes, all the features of their jewellery, the colour and cut of their hair. He remembered every word spoken, and events of thirty years ago were no less important to him than those of yesterday.

Hild admired this ability. His head was also exceptionally large, with a very broad forehead—probably half as broad again as hers—so in that respect she was no match for him. He'd also had quite a few more years than her in which to train his memory.

'Are you ill?' she asked.

Looking as if he was waking up from a deep sleep, he shook his head.

'I'll go to bed now,' he replied listlessly.

# NINE TIMES AROUND THE BURIAL MOUND

*– Sigebert's legacy –*

Hild found Hereswid sitting on the bed, fully clothed. She sent the slave to fetch milk and sat down on the stool.

'Penda won't be staying here long,' she said. 'In a few months, you can remove both Ecgric and Sigebert and have them buried where you like. Take notice of how they fill in the mound, and work out the best way to do it—you know who you can ask for help, the abbot in Beodericsworth, for instance, and maybe Anna, Eni's son.'

'Anna is a weak man,' said Hereswid.

'All the better, then,' said Hild. 'But he's been baptized, hasn't he. Tell him it will be to his credit when he gets to meet Saint Peter!'

Hereswid nodded.

'Penda will probably want Eni's son on the throne,' Hild went on. 'He can control Anna—at a distance, too. I think Penda's had enough of East Anglia.'

'Yes,' said Hereswid.

'Don't bring the children home until things are more settled. Wait until you know where Anna stands.'

'Of course,' said Hereswid.

They were silent for a while.

'I'll give Aidan land for a monastery, where they'll offer prayers for Ecgric and Sigebert, and for Eadfrid too. I thought it could be a monastery dedicated to the holy Radegund.'

'Radegund, yes!' Hereswid brightened up at the idea. 'Sigebert was very fond of Radegund. He would have appreciated that.'

She fell silent for a moment.

'Sigebert always said that Radegund was the greatest of women, after Maria.'

She was silent again.

'But it was of course different with Maria,' she added.

'Yes,' said Hild, 'it was different.'

Hereswid was thinking; her wrinkles appeared.

'He also had high regard for the holy Brigid of Cill Dara, but not in the same way as with Radegund. I think it must be because Radegund is of our day—more real.'

'And she was the one who had him brought home from Gaul,' said Hild.

'Yes, indeed. And he had her relic around his neck.'

Hereswid fell into another short reverie.

'Although—I think he should have stayed over there. It was hard to come home after so many years. Everything had changed.'

'And he had too, I suppose.'

'Yes, and he did what he could to move the kingdom on from the old practices. But he never really settled in.'

'Perhaps he yearned for the kingdom of the Lord,' Hild offered.

'I think he yearned more for Gaul,' said Hereswid quietly. 'And for his youth. He had a woman over there. He was very sad to be parted from her, but he wouldn't take her with him.' Adding, with a quick glance at Hild: 'Well, he hasn't always been a monk.'

'I wouldn't mind going to Gaul either,' said Hild, 'after everything he told us about it.'

She fiddled with her shoe and thought about strange trees. One in particular she would like to see with her own eyes: the Judas tree. Sigebert had said it was the tree in which Judas had hung himself after he'd betrayed his master. That's why it had blood-red flowers, growing directly from the trunk. Not because it had a shortage of branches and twigs to support the flowers, but because of its shame. It wanted to remind posterity of Judas' treachery and the Lord's heroic death on the cross. Now *that* was a tree she would very much like to see, and stroke with her own palms.

Hereswid took Hild's hand.

'Do you think there is any hope for Sigebert's soul?'

Hild thought carefully. She then spoke, in as convincing a voice as she could muster.

'I think so, and I shall pray for his soul. Our god sees everything, and he can also see why Sigebert and Ecgric are being buried in this way. They are baptized in his name, and he won't let Penda keep them from him.'

This was contrary to everything she had learnt. She had heard priests and missionaries thundering—hundreds of times—against all forms of grave goods. While voicing the words, however, she became convinced they were true, because otherwise the new god was not the

Lord himself, but just a petty little idol who danced to Penda's tune, like everyone else. But the Lord God wasn't like that.

Then she started thinking along practical lines again, because perhaps there were people in need of help.

'Did Sigebert leave any children?' she asked.

Hereswid turned her face to the wall.

'Do you know if Sigebert has any surviving children?'

Hereswid cast a furtive glance at Hild.

'Aldwulf,' she eventually whispered. 'My son Aldwulf!'

Then she pointed at her stomach and said, her face turned away: 'And this one here.'

Hild swiftly withdrew her hand and jumped up from the stool. She stood staring at her sister for a moment.

'I see,' she said, and started pacing the room, back and forth, back and forth, looking by turns at the ceiling and the floor.

Maybe she had simply had her eyes closed. She had presumed Hereswid's devotion to Sigebert was an expression of her feeling of affinity in their work towards conversion of the kingdom—as Hild, too, had felt. But this spiritual affinity obviously hadn't been enough for them!

She couldn't deny the hot prickles of envy: her older sister had embraced Sigebert—that wonderful and devout man with his soft voice—and she had done so more than once. His voice, which could make ice melt, had whispered sweet words in Hereswid's ear. His open and frank eyes had gazed upon her, and she had been able to stroke, kiss, caress, fondle and clasp his lovely, lovely body. She went weak at the thought and shook her head.

'Was Ecgric not a good husband to you?'

'He was,' Hereswid replied without looking up. 'It wasn't that.'

To mask her envy, Hild had resorted to indignation. She caught a flea and dropped it into the venom bowl by the window.

'I see,' she said again, and sat down. She was very well aware that Ecgric had been a good husband to Hereswid, loyal and considerate, without one single little sparkle. Dreary until death, and not particularly good-looking. An excellent king, indeed, even though it would seem he had also walked around with his eyes shut. Or had he?

She caught another flea and then curiosity got the better of her.

'Was that why Sigebert entered the monastery?'

'No,' Hereswid replied, 'that wasn't the reason.'

Hild had recovered her composure and went back to thinking practicalities.

'Does anyone know about this?'

'Only the abbot in Beodericsworth. Sigebert went to confession with him. He had started doing penance. He'd been fasting for three months when Penda arrived. And the abbot whipped him every Saturday.'

'The abbot is a worm. Do you think he'll hold his tongue?'

'He hates me,' said Hereswid. 'I go to Felix for confession.'

Hild contemplated dropping a word in Penda's ear about the well-stocked monastery and all its treasures.

'Maybe it doesn't matter,' she said, as if to herself. 'Anna won't seek anybody's life.'

'Anna is a weak man,' Hereswid said again. 'You never know with him.'

'Aldwulf must be raised with King Edbald in Kent—and the next one.'

'Yes,' said Hereswid, adding in a whisper, 'if it is a child.'

'Just look after yourself properly,' said Hild sternly. 'You know, there aren't nearly as many changelings as you think. Sometimes it's just because they haven't had enough nourishment. There is so much superstition mixed up with the whole notion. It's very important you eat well. Round things—onions and hearts and testicles and apples and berries—you're not forgetting that, are you?'

There was all good reason to fear for the baby, but now it was a matter of keeping a cool head. She launched into a long explanation about how she had made many parents in Mercia hand over children they suspected of being changelings. And if she managed to get an infant into good shape within fourteen days, the child would be found a place among Penda's people. She made use of good wetnurses. There were, of course, cases when she instantly knew the child would have to be put out, but that was uncommon—as were cases of people asking to have children back once Hild had declared them normal. Once put out, then out they stayed, but they were by no means all changelings, nor bewitched.

Hereswid started to weep, quietly and desolately. Hild broke off the lecture and took her hand.

'At least promise me you won't put the baby out, whatever you might think of it. Send it to me, so I can try with a wetnurse first.'

She looked earnestly at her sister. Hereswid nodded.

Hild had spoken with her husband and asked Hereswid to accept his offer of moving in with them. If she preferred, she could have her own estate in Mercia.

'Thank you,' said Hereswid, 'but it would not be fitting for my children to grow up in the kingdom that went to war against their father and killed him. What is more, they must be brought up among Christians, so I shall ask King Edbald of Kent to accommodate us, for Sigebert's sake.'

'You should rather keep Sigebert out of it,' said Hild. 'The less you say about him, the safer the children. Wait until they have grown up.'

'I shall,' said Hereswid. 'And I shall travel to Gaul and enter the service of the Lord. In a year or two. Sigebert knew I would follow him on his monastic path. We had to be together.'

'Can't you wait?' asked Hild. 'Just until the children are a little older?'

'And let Sigebert's soul perish?' Hereswid exclaimed aghast. 'I think they are better served by me praying for their father's soul.'

'Yes,' said Hild sadly, 'undoubtedly, that's how you will serve them best.'

A ship-burial with all the pagan magnificence on show—this decision could not be changed. Hereswid could have everything else exactly as she wanted.

One of King Ecgric's officials would be responsible for the ceremony, and Hild was permitted to assist. They agreed to give the burial as Christian a quality as was feasible under the circumstances.

Once messengers had ridden forth to invite kings, bishops and other eminent persons, the ship chosen for the ceremony was dragged from the river Deope—an operation requiring ingenuity and considerable man- and horse-power. The ship was huge and heavy and had been rowed by forty men. It had to be dragged on rollers, numerous men and horses dropping under the strain; the oxen couldn't cope with the gradient, so once they'd fallen they had to be abandoned.

Hereswid embroidered day and night. Sigebert's sword would rest on his chest, its hilt well and truly bound with strips of cloth to prove it hadn't been drawn from its scabbard when he was felled. She embroidered tiny letters of the alphabet into the strips: a written message to the Lord, telling the whole story and with inserted prayers and promises, including a pledge to dedicate her life to his service.

Once the ship had been lowered into the deep trench that had been dug for it, a chamber was constructed in the central section, and there the two kings would rest, side by side.

The emblems of royal power would be placed alongside their heads—in that respect, they had been equals. The first article was the sceptre, on which the king's people made their vow of allegiance. In olden times it had been used to sharpen sword blades, so it was still hewn as a whetstone even though its use was now purely symbolic.

The second article was the royal standard, used to display enemy heads after a successful battle. With room for four, hung by their hair so they looked out to all four corners of the world, the standard was as tall as a man, and when carried forth, supported in a shoulder holster, it towered above the crowd for all to admire the trophies. When the standard was carried in front of the king, it was adorned with the Wuffingas family colours: red and yellow plumes, and long strips of golden and red material fluttering in the breeze.

These two objects were placed at the west end of the chamber, so when a new king was selected he would have to procure his own symbols of power. There were no more descendants from Rædwald, so his brother Eni's family would probably take over.

Sigebert and Ecgric were laid out in the Christian manner—if the Lord should show mercy, they would be able to rise again facing eastwards. Ecgric was wearing his splendid helmet; it had not been damaged, the mortal wound was to his chest.

Looking at the items Penda had set aside for the burial, Hild was startled to see Cædwalla's beautiful hanging bowl, with its red enamel clasps and the swimming fish at the bottom, and the stack of silver bowls she had just given to the monastery in Beodericsworth.

'Ah, well,' said Penda cagily, 'it can't do any harm to have a few Christian goods in there. I brought some holy water, too. Hereswid wanted some of that.'

He pointed at a large wooden vat he'd had transported all the way from Beodericsworth on a cart; it was still half-full of foul-smelling water.

'I think they use it for their baptisms, or for healing—so it can't do any harm,' said Penda.

Hild thanked him, but felt she had to find out if Penda had acquired these items lawfully, because that was one ruling the Christians shared with the pagans: the king's burial peace had to be observed. Whatever earthly disputes there might be, they had to wait until the fourth day after the end of the funeral feast. No one, at least, was to be slain; not even executions could be carried out before the dead king had arrived at his destination.

'We haven't killed anyone,' Penda assured her. 'But that abbot might not make quite such a fuss next time he receives visitors. He's not a particularly generous man, it has to be said! I think those holy crosses will please Hereswid, don't you?'

He picked up one of the silver bowls and studied it with admiration.

Hild caught herself wishing they had killed the abbot. If it slipped out that Sigebert had fathered two of Hereswid's children, those children would be exposed to even greater dangers than royal offspring always had to expect. She would have to talk with the abbot on the return journey—let him know her husband had torched a monastery on more than one occasion, and meanness in respect of the kings' burial was not appropriate. Under the given circumstances, holy crosses were an essential, as was whatever else there might be in the way of ecclesiastical gifts.

She was pleased with the holy vat and had it placed behind Sigebert's head. Penda had also taken two silver spoons from the monastery, one with the name Paulus, the other with the name Saulus, both engraved in Greek letters. Sigebert had shown them to her when she had visited him, the occasion on which he had also taught her the Greek alphabet, and how to count to ten. He had written it all on a wax tablet, which he gave to her; she would never erase his writing, even though she had long since learnt it all by heart. Sigebert hadn't been an ungenerous man, either with his learning or anything else.

The cross-adorned silver bowls were put just behind Sigebert's head, along with the spoons, which would surely convey what kind of man he was. And behind them was the large vat of holy water, and then, right at the back, the sceptre and the royal standard. Behind Ecgric's head was his ceremonial shield, a beautiful piece covered with pale buckskin and finely decorated with a falcon, a dragon and other fittings. Ecgric had been just as enthusiastic about his falconry as Cædwalla.

Penda had taken other objects from the monastery, too. A heavy bronze vat brought to Ireland in olden times by a merchant who claimed to have purchased it from a monastery in Egypt, where the very first monasteries to the Lord had been built. The vat had reached Ecgric via a somewhat circuitous route, but he gave it to Beodericsworth when Sigebert renounced the kingship—thus forging a connection between those following in Christ's footsteps: the monks' watery Lenten soup was made in a vessel that had held Lenten soup drunk by the brethren who had gone before.

'Not much of a gift!' Ecgric had said, but Sigebert had been deeply moved. Earlier, when he first thought about fighting the Lord's fight, he had wanted to visit those regions and pray at the holy Antonius' grave: Antonius, who had taught them the monastic life, following the example of the Lord. Looking at this vat, which might have come from Antonius' very own monastery—the possibility couldn't be ruled out—Sigebert had thought the circle was complete. Antonius had suffered in his desert and resisted the Devil's many temptations. Sigebert himself sat in the swampy East Anglian marshland, sorely tempted by the whims of the old enemy; he had sometimes resisted, sometimes not.

On the occasions he hadn't succeeded, then he'd gone to the fireplace and pressed his hands against Antonius' vat until he lost control over his arms and they sprang back from the searing hot bronze, leaving sooty slivers of his palm flesh. This was to teach his hands to avoid the path of sin. He had no other way to rein them in when temptation approached: the woman he ought to look upon as his sister. He had already desecrated the plank bed in his cell with her, and thus sullied the whole monastery.

Hild had the bronze vat placed in the corner, furthest to the left of Sigebert's head. Penda had examined the royal weaponry stockpile and selected five spears and three particularly fine little javelins. Hild took the three javelins and stuck them through the handle on Antonius' vat: another way in which to show that Sigebert's appetite for battle had been shackled through his love of service to the Lord, and also that Antonius had been his guide and leading example.

On top of the vat, she placed Sigebert's lyre, wrapped in a beaver-pelt bag. Sigebert had been a great singer, and although Hild had never heard him sing, Hereswid was not alone in praising his talent. Some of the pieces in his pre-monastery repertoire were translations he had made of songs he'd heard in Gaul, and some were his own compositions. All had been secular tales of battles and conquests, so the lyre had not accompanied him to Beodericsworth.

She stuck the spears firmly into the ground, and then they too were wrapped. She had a nail driven into the wall and hung Cædwalla's beautiful bowl with its swimming fish above the spears.

King Ecgric was laid out with a magnificent purse in his belt, made for him by his own craftsman, who had come from the kingdom of the Swedes. The man had also made the helmet and was responsible for many of the king's personal ornaments. He was an expert at cutting garnets into shape and inserting them into a cellwork frame, the cells often lined with silver- or gold-foil, which shone through and made the garnets sparkle in a variety of nuances. He also used enamel and blue colours, pale and dark, and under large pieces of garnet he might hatch a crisscross pattern into the foil, which made the stones twinkle.

Penda was stunned by the quality of the pieces and had tried to persuade the craftsman to enter his service, but the man declined: he'd had enough of this country and wanted to return to his native land. He had been glad, however, of the opportunity to study Penda's belt buckle; he would never have been able to devise that closing device himself, he said, and his praise for this favourite piece made Penda swagger with pride.

The craftsman had not been baptized, and although his suggested motifs for the design of Ecgric's purse had not been in keeping with the new faith, the king had permitted him to make it anyway.

Two pictures on the purse particularly impressed Ecgric: a bird of prey, roughly the same as the eagle on his shield, holding a smaller bird in its claws; and a man wedged-in between two ferocious wolves. The wolves have placed their paws on the man's shoulders, and they are growling into his ears, jaws open. He's trying to push away their paws, but it is a hopeless task, even his legs are locked apart by their tails. He has been caught, utterly, and he knows it.

'And that,' Ecgric had said, 'is our lot in life: surrounded on all sides by ogres, and we know nothing more about whence we came and where we are going. I want a purse like that.'

'But Christ slew the ogre when he gave himself for us!' Hereswid had protested.

'And therefore we are baptized in his name,' her husband had replied, 'and for that we give him thanks. But we have yet to see anyone who wouldn't rather stay here in the light than go into the darkness, however Christian he might be!'

The purse was made, and Ecgric used it to hold a treasure Sigebert had given him when he chose the way of the Lord: thirty-seven Frankish gold coins Sigebert had collected in Gaul, each from a different mint, some old and some new. In Gaul they used these specially-struck coins as a means of payment, which had impressed Sigebert: another area in which Gaul was more civilized than his home land, where payment was made by bartering things or cutting a suitably-sized chunk of precious metal from a bowl or a piece of jewellery.

'It takes forty men to row the ship,' said Penda, 'and there are only thirty-seven pieces of gold! And what about the kings themselves?'

'Nonsense,' said Hild, 'all this payment talk is simply superstition, and you can see for yourself: that ship isn't going to be rowed anywhere!'

'A burial is a burial,' said Penda, and sent a message to the craftsman that he should make three gold pieces of the same value as the others, and two slightly different and more costly pieces for the kings' ferry passage.

Hild shook her head, but she wouldn't interfere. Everything was in confusion anyway, and she was feeling overwhelmed by weariness. She had sat up all night with Hereswid, embroidering cross after holy cross on a fine woollen cloth that was to be wrapped around Sigebert's sword before it was sheathed and sealed with Hereswid's letter.

She had listened to her sister's inexhaustible stream of praise for Sigebert and all his virtues, and had gradually felt a little aggrieved that Hereswid made no mention of her husband. Ecgric hadn't treated her badly.

Hereswid had yet another good idea: they should put Sigebert's writing stylus on top of the wrapped sword. He'd had a very fine ivory stylus with silver fittings, inlaid with garnets, and this would be an additional way of presenting the man who had given up the sword in favour of the weapon of learning. Hild had immediately sent Talcuin and a couple of big lads to collect the writing stylus—with kind regards—they had just enough time to get back before the ceremony.

She looked around the burial chamber. The two large drinking vessels made from the horns of aurochs were placed at the men's feet, together with six small wooden beakers on two blankets they could use to keep warm at their resurrection. After that, Sigebert's ring-mail armour, folded and packed up with the long red cloak he had worn as king, a costly otter-pelt cap and various finely-woven undergarments. Placed among these objects, another roll of embroidered letters from Hereswid—each sentence ending with a holy cross.

Leather riding trousers, coarsely woven cloaks, thin leggings and tunics, hose and kirtles in a multitude of colours and weaves, a pair of shoes each—they would want for nothing should they one day be called back to life.

The peculiar tool Sigebert had carried in battle was laid next to the clothing: a vulgar object for a royal grave, its only function being that of testifying to the truth.

There were also some large silver plates and a beautiful ladle, goods imported from the eastern Mediterranean countries, as was all the silver. A lot of pieces had found their way onto the market at the moment, thanks to the turbulent conditions down there, and the Anglian silver wasn't good enough for Penda. They placed a few personal items in one of the silver bowls: combs, knives, nightcaps, wooden pots with bone ointment and various other salves, a box of pulverised unicorn horn—the most powerful remedy against virile weakness—and a set of gaming-pieces made of sperm-whale tusk. Ecgric had also shared Cædwalla's passion for gaming.

They decided to move the gaming-pieces up to Ecgric's shield; they had, after all, been among his most cherished possessions, inlaid with copper and beautifully carved.

At the very back were a number of cauldrons and buckets, and a lovely and ingeniously wrought chain for suspending the cauldron from the beams in the big hall. The vessels were full of food and drink, and on that point Hild let Penda and the master of ceremonies do what they wanted; she saw it as purely symbolic. It was obvious that the beer and the roast joints and all that bread would fester long before the Day of Judgement.

'Is that it?' she asked her husband once she had inspected the arrangement. The floor was covered with buckskin, the symbol of the Wuffingas family, and the walls were hung with fine fabrics. Now all that was missing was Sigebert's writing stylus.

Penda wasn't satisfied; he thought Ecgric looked too bland alongside Sigebert. Maybe it was the pale-leather cuirass that took the shine off him, even though the shoulder-clasps were magnificent. A properly red cloak would be more becoming, and would also cover more of his fatal wound, in Penda's opinion. Besides, it was only fair that the royal tunic worn by the kings in turn didn't look as if it belonged exclusively to just one of them; it ought to lie between them.

Hild nodded in approval, to be finished with the job, but Penda still wasn't satisfied.

'The sword!' he exclaimed. 'King Ecgric hasn't got his sword!'

'No,' said Hild firmly. 'Hereswid has put that by for her son, Aldwulf, for what has he otherwise inherited from his father?'

'Ah, well,' said Penda, looking at Ecgric from every angle, 'then we'll have to think of something else.'

He thought long and hard; Hild was ready to drop with fatigue.

Penda eventually took a momentous decision. Loosening his belt, he asked Hild to hold his trousers up while the ceremony master was sent to fetch a length of cord. Penda leant forwards over Ecgric—in her attempt to hold onto his waistband, Hild very nearly toppled him onto the corpse, with herself on top—and laid his precious belt with its cherished buckle across the dead body of the king.

How very beautiful it looked against the bright-red cloak and the elaborate purse. Penda straightened up with pride and Hild fell backwards, scrambling around in the fabrics by the wall, unable to hang on to his waistband and keep his trousers up. He stared at her in astonishment as she battled her way out of a huge cloth that had tumbled down to cover her.

'What about helping me instead of standing there gawping,' she hissed.

He tottered across to her with difficulty and held out his hand to help her up. She noted with satisfaction that her husband's undergarments were by no means inferior to those of the dead kings: fine woad-blue linen—she had woven the fabric herself.

The writing stylus arrived, and the guests arrived. Even King Oswald presented himself to honour his colleagues. The royal family and the bishop came from Kent, along with numerous people from the monasteries. Hild had never seen so many notable figures from the various kingdoms gathered in one place. The brethren and sisters sang hymns and rang bells—the first time Hild had seen a bell since Gwynedd. Nine East Angles sounded long horns, and the volume of screaming women was overwhelming.

Candles had been lit in the burial chamber, both in the hanging bowl and in a whole row of small lamps. The finest of the guests filed past while the brethren and sisters sang and the plaintive choir reached unprecedented heights. The Christians handed out a few silver pieces to the poor people of the realm; not wanting to be outdone, the followers of the old faith gave a few more. It was a day to remember for the paupers of East Anglia.

The funeral feast was magnificent, beyond reproach. Penda had to acknowledge that the financial yield from the campaign was probably quite a lot less than first assumed, but that didn't bother him: the acclaim he harvested from all sides for holding such a lavish burial and such a majestic repast was of far greater importance. Almost made you wish you'd fall in battle against him, one of the guests had remarked.

The only drawback was the weather. The day before the actual solemnities, the thaw set in with intense rain throughout the night, which turned the excavated area into one big swamp. They had laid out planks so the guests wouldn't have to wade through the mire, but the rain made them slippery and some of the guests ended up in the mud anyway.

The rainwater also started running down into the burial chamber before everyone had finished filing past. The buckskins on the floor were awash, and some of the fabric hangings had soaked up so much water they plummeted from the wall. The people filing past had to be hurried along, and the damage had to be swiftly repaired before the grave could be sealed.

The entourage stood shuffling their feet in the pouring rain, and a stiff westerly wind forced them to pull up their cowls so they had difficulty watching the climax of the ceremony: Penda and his best men rode nine times around the burial mound, with drawn swords and echoing roars. The final three circles were to be ridden at a gallop, but during the penultimate circling Penda's horse slipped so awkwardly it couldn't get up again. Penda wasn't hurt, but the ritual had to be repeated—somewhat slower this time, although it was still a most dignified ending to the solemnities.

Afterwards, stepping into the king's warm hall felt so much the better and—despite all the coughing and sneezing—all those juicy roast joints and all that fine mead made you fully aware that you were still in the realm of the living.

'You mustn't let Oswald get away with it,' Hereswid said to Hild that night, her eyes shining brightly. 'He killed Eadfrid, I could see it written all over him, and he's not to get away with it.'

'Nor will he,' said Hild.

'I'll go back to Kent with King Edbald,' said Hereswid. 'I've never liked East Anglia.'

'Kent's more affluent, isn't it?'

'More affluent, yes, and far more civilized!'

Hild handed her sister the round loaf and the chunks of meat she had taken from the table. If Hereswid carried on like this, the outcome wasn't going to be a normal child, that was for certain.

Before leaving for home, they paid another visit to the craftsman's workshop. He was pleased with Penda's interest and happily showed them his moulds and sketched patterns, some of which he had brought from his homeland, some he had designed later.

'This one,' he said, holding up a mould from which he could hammer a metal fitting, 'I suggested to King Ecgric, for his helmet. But he didn't want to wear a picture of deceit. Make a picture of loyalty! he said. So I did.'

He showed them the mould for one of the motifs in Ecgric's helmet: two warriors standing next to one another, their adjoining arms crossing, holding swords aloft; their outer hands holding two crossed spears each, forming a wall to either side; two crossed spears between the two men. As long as they hold their loyalty, nothing can strike them, but if they give way, they will be run through by the crossed spears between them.

Hild looked at the rejected mould. You could imagine the two warriors, just a moment earlier, standing exactly as they were on Ecgric's helmet; but here one of them had turned towards the other, broken the wall on his side, and transformed into a monster with tail and wolf's head. His right hand was already grasping the sword he would pull against his sworn blood-brother, who was trying to run away, even though he was still holding the spear upright—he wasn't the one to have broken the wall and allowed misfortune to leap in.

'I would have preferred the other one, too,' said Penda. 'Treachery isn't something you would want to carry around on your helmet—that would almost be asking for it.'

'Well, it has more to say than the other one,' said Hild.

'Indeed it does,' Penda conceded, 'but what it's saying is wrong. And you shouldn't put thoughts like that into people's minds.'

The craftsman showed them another mould he hadn't used here: a man wedged between two bears that have risen on their hind legs and seized hold of him from each side. Their legs are wound around his, their jaws are open and they are growling into his ears. He looks helpless and bewildered; they will soon devour him, but he has thrust his sword into the stomach of one of the monsters.

'But that's Jesus!' Hild exclaimed eagerly. 'He who has vanquished death!'

'Well, that wasn't my plan,' the craftsman replied, somewhat offended. 'But I didn't actually draw it myself. It was Queen Hereswid's idea.'

'Yes, yes it is,' Hild pressed on. 'Can't you see: Jesus triumphed over death, and thus we shall no longer fear the monster!'

'Well, I wouldn't know,' said the craftsman, 'nor have I heard that baptized men are braver in battle than the rest of us.'

'You're right about that,' said Penda, drawing himself up, 'nor are things getting any better for them, it seems.'

'Sigebert was a great king,' the craftsman confided to Penda. 'But he shouldn't have abandoned the gods of our ancestors. That's caused a lot of strife in this kingdom, I can tell you, and just see what's happened!'

He made a sweeping gesture with his arm.

'And that's why I want to go home, too. Back home, they don't let foreigners come in and turn people's heads. Life is just how it is, and they can't change destiny, no matter what they say.'

'My offer still stands,' said Penda, 'and you can state your terms.'

'I had a dream,' said the craftsman, 'so there's probably nothing more to discuss. But I thank you for the offer. Who knows what fate has in store for me back home?'

'No,' said Penda, 'no one can control destiny. But my wife and I wish you the best of luck.'

With that they made their farewells and left East Anglia.

The marshland was alive with lapwings and curlews, their swiftly warbling calls reverberating through the air. Spring had finally arrived. The first cowslips stood smiling along the road—Hild hoped Hereswid had seen them.

# HILD'S MARE AND THUNOR'S POWER

*– spring in Tamoworthig –*

The cowslip was Hereswid's flower. On the way home from East Anglia, Hild was greeted by its spring-yellow brightness. Hereswid had declared it her own when she was just seven years old, and Hild had ever since had to make do with simply admiring it, as she couldn't really appropriate it. She used to sit on the ground watching her sister study the flower meticulously, count its filaments and then slowly chew the petals and swallow the yellowness.

'Five filaments,' said Hereswid, 'five again. Why are there always five?'

'What does that matter to you?' said Hild. 'Surely it's enough to find them there at all!'

'Yes, but the Lord must know why they're made like that,' Hereswid persisted, 'given that he created them.'

'It was so long ago,' said Hild, 'and Paulinus says that we people can't know everything.'

The love of cowslips—cow teats, as they called them—had taught Hereswid to absorb the flowers by tasting them, pulling off the blooms and sucking out their honey. When no one was looking, Hild did the same. Hereswid would lounge across the Eostre-bench during her ceremonious women's bleeding days: 'Fetch me some cow teats, will you?'

Off Hild would rush to gather the flowers for her beloved sister who was in need of cow-udder honey to recover her strength. The flowers always worked, but they were only to be found in early spring, just when everyone needed something fortifying and went foraging along the edges of forests and in ditches. The cow teats were in great demand. Grown-ups used them to make their sweet amber beor, which you didn't just knock back, but served in small cups to the women on the Eostre-bench. The liquid relaxed the womb and counteracted dragging spasms in the thighs: after a cup of beor you could close your eyes, pull the blanket up under your chin and doze off for a while, then everything should feel better when you woke up.

Hereswid had already left for Kent and undoubtedly helped herself to plenty of cow udders, but Hild still felt as if she was committing an offence against her sister when she sucked out all the blooms she found in the edge of the forest when they had a rest stop on the journey—the cowslip had, after all, never been her flower.

But it was lovely.

She awoke at home in her own bed, and had no idea where she was—until she saw her husband standing by the open shutters, staring out.

He let out a happy little cry and leapt back into the bed, on top of her, and rained kisses on her.

'Congratulations!'

He was bursting with expectations, and was as radiant as a little sun.

'Your birthday present has arrived.'

'Oh,' she said, turning her face into the pillow, on the verge of tears. She had prayed to the Lord God to let her forget about it, but he obviously hadn't listened because it had been the first thing to flash into her mind when she had woken up in the early hours: my birthday! Whereupon, by confessing her faith over and over again, she had managed to fall back into a heavy and dreamless sleep.

But he had remembered.

'You know, Penda,' she started, but had to close her eyes, 'we Christians don't like remembering our birthdays.'

He rose from the bed and stood, arms dangling at his sides, gazing at her as if she had taken away his greatest treasure; even his beard seemed to droop more than usual.

'It's from Merewald too,' he said, as if matters were improved by the gift also being from his eldest son.

Hild couldn't hold back a tear. Merewald, of all people, she was so very fond of him.

Penda sat on the edge of the bed and stroked his wife's hair, and now she couldn't control her weeping at all. Of all the practices in a Christian life, this was the hardest: to disregard your birthday and only mark the day of your baptism. Every single year she forgot to forget, and Hereswid had confided it happened for her too, even though she spent the day reciting the psalms of David.

'The ways of the Lord are past understanding!' Hild wept.

'Seems like it,' said Penda, and didn't know how to salvage the situation. He had arranged a celebration for the evening, but he could, of course, just change it to an ordinary homecoming festivity, and remember to tell the bard so he didn't ruin the evening with a birthday song.

'It's in no way a birthday present,' he said to his wife. 'It's a perfectly straightforward springtime gift, as everyone can see. It arrived today purely by chance. But it didn't actually, because it arrived several days ago, and it has nothing whatsoever to do with your birthday.'

Hild wiped her nose.

'Well, what is it?'

'You must see for yourself,' he said proudly.

She couldn't contain herself any longer, jumped out of bed and ran across to the window.

'Oh,' she sighed, and now she wept with pleasure.

She had never seen anything so lovely. A circle of cowslips, a huge garland of flowering cowslips in the grass. And inside the garland: H + P.

She shook her head in delight.

'How?' she asked.

Penda glowed.

'Merewald,' he said. 'So it turns out the lad's good at something. Do you like it?'

Hild threw her arms round his neck and kissed him; never had she received so wonderful a springtime gift—nor birthday gift.

'Thank you, Penda, thank you!'

And they celebrated spring by hopping back into bed, while it was still warm.

Penda was really quite alone in his appreciation of the new queen, as nearly everyone else was afraid and some were angry.

A queen who would not participate in the communal sacrifices, but who, last year, had left when the pagan priest slashed the throats of the white cows with his knife, and had only taken part in the less crucial parts of the winter solstice festival, but not the mutual laying on of hands, the communal singing and the eating of the sacrificial beasts.

A chain is no stronger than its weakest link, they said. A queen who did not stand shoulder to shoulder with her people was not going to bring good fortune to the kingdom.

Hild had already lost one cupbearer, which had made her more careful, and now she didn't go anywhere without Talcuin and two bulky attendants. In order to prevent her allegiance to the Lord God from splitting the kingdom or making a martyr of her, she realized she would have to do as Jesus had said and give what was theirs to her god and to the emperor alike, while trying to keep a pure heart.

She hoped Aidan would come soon, so she could receive both guidance and the Lord's forgiveness for the times she was obliged to desert her faith a little, at least to appearances. Many day-to-day issues caused her uncertainty as to the correct way in which to proceed.

When the spring festival arrived, she sat at her husband's side knowing that her every movement, even the tiniest glance and twitch of her face, would be scrupulously monitored. She cheered like everyone else when the white cows were driven into the square in front of the hall, and the largest of the bulls was let out to join them.

The queen's presence was important for the procreativity of the bull, the pagan priest had informed her. Mounting all five ensured a good harvest, managing four was no cause for complaint, three meant a so-so harvest, but two or one would most likely result in the army having to fetch winter supplies from elsewhere.

There was jubilation when the third cow was covered, and even more cheering when the bull mounted the fourth, but then it seemed to forget what it was there for, and the jeering started. The beast raised its head at the sound of loud booing, and looked around angrily before launching itself onto the fifth cow. The euphoria was never-ending and Hild received a nod of appreciation from the pagan priest—a good sign.

Then it was the turn of the horses, and Penda's chestnut stallion was led in. To have your mare mounted by the king's stallion was not only a sign of favourable standing, but also a symbol of alliance, confirmation of solidarity between the highest in the realm and his subjects. As was only fitting, Hild's mare was chosen to be the first, a demonstration of the royal couple's marital unity and verification of Hild's integration among the people of Mercia.

She prayed her mare would be willing; her life could depend on it. Neither chief men nor more humble subjects would look benignly on rejection of their king's stallion.

Penda's groom gripped the reins extra firmly as soon as the chestnut horse had registered the mare's scent. The stallion reared and neighed loudly, kicked up the earth with its large hooves, and revealed its thick and immensely long penis.

Where had that been? Had it been hidden inside the stallion? Or were the old folk right when they said Thunor breathed power into it, and without his intervention nothing at all would happen, because he and he alone was responsible for the blessing of fertility?

Hild didn't believe this explanation, because she knew the old gods didn't possess anything like the power attributed to them. She knew the Lord God was behind all forces of creation on earth, including that of the stallion and of the bull.

Her prayers went to the Lord; partly to forgive her participation in the pagan festival, and partly to ensure the mating occurred as it should. She had been to the stable several times in an attempt to instruct the mare, talking, stroking and praying, and the day before she had—surreptitiously—sprinkled holy water on the entrance that had to open up for the stallion. Talcuin had to assist her, but he had been baptized to the service of Jesus, and the mare was really quite flighty.

Talcuin it was who led in Hild's cream-coloured mare, accompanied by cheering from the crowd. The mare was startled and reared into the air, but Talcuin calmed her down and then gave her free rein to run. It wouldn't be good if she just stood there and let it happen; some fighting spirit would help, and would show the king's stallion to its best advantage.

Penda stood loudly admiring his stallion, which had started to overtake the mare, but she didn't seem particularly willing. Hild also rose to her feet as, with bated breath and praying with all her might, she watched the mare run round and round the yard.

The stallion, with a gigantic swaying penis, had been released by the groom and was now right behind the mare, looking as if he was just about to mount her, when she kicked out her back hooves and escaped. She turned and faced the stallion, which was digging up the earth with its front hooves. The stallion threw back his head and neighed, walked cautiously towards the mare, was allowed to get so close that he was almost touching her muzzle, stood still for a moment, and then sprang round behind her. The mare whinnied as she threw back *her* head and sped away.

The scene repeated itself, the crowd shouting so raucously that Hild couldn't hear what Penda was saying, but his eyes shone with excitement.

Now the mare had the upper hand. She looked as if she was laughing at the stallion's efforts and was having fun enticing him over to her and then scurrying off at the last moment. Hild couldn't keep her pride in check and she wanted to laugh too, but she gave no indication of what she was feeling while praying that the mare would eventually submit to the stallion.

Time was passing, and the crowd was seething with excitement. Hild noticed little smiles tugging at the lips of quite a few women; some were simply laughing and calling out in recognition of the situation. The men were wide-eyed in wonder or narrow-eyed with indignation; some were red in the face and shouting very loudly. The temptation was becoming too strong and a few of them were openly hurling abuse at their king's stallion.

Perhaps the pressure was overpowering, because now the stallion looked as if he was giving up. Thunor had apparently lost patience, because the penis went limp and seemed about to vanish altogether. A sigh of disappointment rose from the women's side; from the men's side there were angry shouts, and Hild stole a glance at her husband. His face was scarlet and he was staring at the ground; such shame had never previously befallen him. She sought his hand and smiled encouragingly, but deep down she was now scared. He gave her a look so sombre that she winced. The mare had gone too far—such teasing behaviour went way beyond the bounds of propriety.

The stallion was now more interested in the grass. The mare stood watching him, and then she walked tentatively towards him, bit off a tuft of grass, walked on, turned her hind quarters towards the stallion, stopped right in front of him and carried on grazing.

The stable master looked up questioningly at Penda, wondering if they should abandon the show and move on to the cockfight. This situation had never arisen before, and the disgrace was unprecedented, but Penda—now totally ashen—was staring downwards and didn't look back at his stable master.

Hild prayed like a woman possessed. She clutched her holy cross and promised her god the moon and anything and everything if he would grant her prayer, and she vowed to have the mare destroyed if it didn't soon do what it was meant to do.

The mare stood, legs apart, munching grass, demonstratively positioned right in front of the stallion, which now had nothing but grass on its mind—it gave her backside a quick sniff, and then continued grazing. The mare walked around the stallion and sniffed his behind, but he just continued grazing and was not to be disturbed. She lowered her head and sniffed at the place where Thunor had let his power vanish: absolutely nothing of interest left, so the mare kicked up her hind legs and trotted around the yard. She came to a halt and nipped the stallion's ear, took another turn of the yard and nudged his neck with her head, rubbed her forehead against his chest and nipped his other ear.

The stallion looked up, flung back its head and whinnied loudly. The power of Thunor had returned, and on no lesser scale than before. The women gasped, breathless with admiration, and the men drew themselves up.

Then the stallion got a move on. He chased the mare around the yard, caught up with her, nipped, snorted, and was just about to mount her when she ran off again, the stallion at her heels; he caught up again, jumped towards her, lost his grip again, was after her, on her, and his penis was just about to enter her when she sprang away from him, rushed halfway round the yard, came to a halt, head held high. The silence was deafening as he mounted the mare and let the power of Thunor sink into her, thrust by thrust. She bellowed loudly when it could press no further—there was no way of knowing if it was too much or too little for her, thought Hild, but she certainly wasn't resisting.

Penda squeezed Hild's hand so tightly it hurt; the colour had come back into his face, and his eyes shone.

Thunor had also paid him a visit, that much was quite obvious, as was the case with most of the men, which was as it should be, a sign of a good year and many children. Hild could happily have lain with him right there, on the spot, but they weren't beasts of the field, they would have to wait until the midday rest hour. She laughed appreciatively at his power, and took a deep breath.

'The Lord be praised!' she exclaimed.

When the stallion slipped off the mare, Penda sank onto the bench in exhaustion, wiped his brow, smiled at her, worn out but proud. Now she was indeed his wife and Mercia's queen, and now no one could dispute her status. He was more relieved than she was, because he knew how the chief men operated.

Had there ever been a spring as lovely as this? Hild thought not. Then again, she couldn't really recall the previous spring—it just seemed to have turned into summer, suddenly very hot and oppressive, at least that was how she remembered it, with some violent thunder storms.

Exactly when the beech had come into leaf, however, she couldn't say, but this year she had seen them unfold like luminous yellow-green flecks above the forest carpet of anemones and corydalis. The elder had come even earlier, but it didn't shine, it just grew leaves that couldn't light up the dead forest. There was no splendour about elder until its fragrant clusters of flowers blossomed and later its good black berries hung on the branches. The lower branches of the beech came into leaf first, and the trees around the farms were almost stripped by people hungry for green—they needed it after the winter.

The royal estate was buzzing with activity. In the mornings, the men went to the fields to finish sowing the seed; a few women went with them, but most were busy with the washing. Woollens and all the bedding had to have their monthly going-over, the wall coverings had to be shaken and beaten, and fresh sprigs of wormwood and juniper had to be laid out against wool worm and other vermin.

Repairs had been done during the winter, but if anything needed painting or if the thatching had to be mended, then now was the time to do it, and to erect any new buildings required.

Eight couples were going to get married at the midsummer festival, and the groundwork was already being dug out for the round huts where they would live. A larger hut for the women's weaving and sewing had also been planned, and a mill down by the beck, alongside the washhouse.

Laundry was done several times a year: slaves were allowed two washes in boiling water, free people four washes, masters and mistresses had their washing done every month. Penda appreciated freshly-laundered clothing.

As usual, Hild spent the morning with the steward. Each month had its schedule, and she had yet to find out about all the jobs that went on, so she had decided to study the processes on the estate and then she would be able to take charge of the work—just like Queen Tata had done, and as she had done at home in Mædeltun. This household, however, was larger, many things were done differently, and she wanted to know about every aspect of the estate before she intervened.

When she saw a farmhand tear down a swallow's nest, however, she couldn't help but speak up. Not only did the swallow bring good fortune, it also kept the air clear of flying beasts. The swallow was Eostre's bird, as she had learnt when she was a child, and those who didn't keep on a friendly footing with it might well be struck barren.

This was news in Tamoworthig; they had always seen the swallow as a bird of fickleness, just there for the good times, because it disappeared at the end of every summer.

Ravens and magpies were a different matter: their nests had to be removed. Not the jackdaws' nests, however, because they brought luck to the home, and Hild liked their prattling. She considered the jackdaw to be the brightest of the birds, after the raven of course, and she wouldn't allow it to be cooked and served, which caused some grumbling because even children could catch young jackdaws. Hild was adamant, although she did slightly increase the meat ration—an extra pig per family per month—so there could be no excuse for hunting jackdaws, and punishment was set at five blows with a stick, to be carried out promptly.

She later increased the annual ration of beans by three butts. She thought the slave children were too skinny and they didn't do enough work, and the adults would also be of greater value if they had a bit more weight on them. She was in a position to make this change after she had travelled the kingdom with Penda and seen the amount of produce, and thus what she could afford to allocate.

There had been some good years. Penda had conquered numerous territories, and others had voluntarily acceded to his rule. His kingdom was more loosely put together than either Bernicia or Deira, and his various territories were governed by a minor king or a nobleman, who were allowed quite a free rein. On the other hand, these governors would have to supply troops at just a few days' notice when so required, and had to maintain roads and bridges, take responsibility for law and order, and give the king and his men suitable board and lodging when they visited the area.

Penda's sub-kings were utterly loyal, and they demanded the same steadfastness from their own men. This was one of the secrets behind Penda's good fortune in war: there were no cowards, courage simply didn't fail them, for that would be punished by death.

So a hero's death on the battlefield was a better option—for the bereaved at home, too. A good reputation was the best legacy; property and gold were all very well, but they could vanish in the toss of dice, in flames, enemy attack or any other whim of fate. However richly adorned a shield might be, the story of how it was won was worth more than double its actual value. A story lived on long after the shield had perished from age, and it might well be the greatest treasure the descendants possessed: a reputation admirably won would never perish.

That was how it was, and it had been no different in Bernicia and Deira, but Edwin hadn't been able to trust his men in the same way, as had become apparent in his last battle. He had taken away people's belief, split them by turning to the new god, so he was no longer the people's representative to Woden, no longer took the lead at the important fertility festivals and sacrifices. Many had wished him dead; you couldn't forsake what had held the kingdom together from ancient times and expect to go unpunished. Edwin had lost the best of his men when he got baptized, and was left surrounded by bootlickers, the kind of people who will instantly just say yes to the latest scheme.

Hild could see all this far more clearly today, and she understood why Edwin had been obliged to rule with a much heavier hand than the one Penda used. It seemed he hadn't discussed every single issue with Hereswid and Hild, via Breguswid. He had pounced hard on the slightest suspicion of disloyalty: land was confiscated, and men had to flee or be sold into slavery along with their entire family and household. This policy might have expanded the crown holdings, but it also increased the danger of rebellion in the surrounding realms, which couldn't both pay tax to Edwin and house so many refugees without expanding their own territories or plundering other areas.

In that respect, Penda was a far more prudent king than Edwin, as was becoming increasingly clear to Hild.

It soon became general knowledge that the new queen might well pay up to double price for slave children. Families who had lost their property because of crop failure, or because their beasts had been bewitched, their land plundered by outsiders, or by gaming or betting, and had thus been forced to sell themselves into slavery, could sometimes pull through by selling one of their children to the rich queen.

Hild had to turn down many children, so great was the demand. Nor would she buy a child unless the family was in really serious distress—not simply because the father wanted to buy some more cows. She also flatly rejected any child who was obviously the bearer of misfortune, and in such cases the impoverishment of the family was of no consequence, they would have to dispose of the child elsewhere.

Being sold to the royal estate in Tamoworthig had its advantages over most other places: you would learn a skill, you wouldn't be beaten quite so often and you would be better fed. It was said that some few had even learnt to read, but that probably wasn't true—and if it was, then they must have cheated their way to it.

Hild also paid parents to bring her any infant they suspected of being a changeling and who would otherwise be abandoned deep inside the forest. She didn't pay them much, but enough to make the journey to Tamoworthig worth their while.

There were many reasons parents might want to get rid of their children, and Hild was often of the opinion that the parents were lying. Maybe they simply didn't like the child, because it resembled one of the parents too much or not enough, and then they would claim the infant was bewitched, which every impartial onlooker could see was nonsense. If a child looked too much like someone who had met an untimely death or had in some other way brought shame on the family, then the parents would be reluctant to say so, but would refer to poverty, gaming debts, bad omens and evil eyes. In such cases, Hild sometimes ordered the parents to be flogged before she sent them home without payment, but she always kept their children, reasoning that fate would have less power over them if they weren't told about the cruel fortune awaiting them.

Hild was outside in the summer warmth, where she could devote every daylight hour to her new weaving project: a cloak for Penda, flax linen to be dyed with colour from the madder plant, alternating use of thick and thin threads to produce a pattern of her own composition.

When the sun shone, her maid moved the loom to the shady side of the house, and Hild could stand there all day, birds singing and chilly wind blowing. Towards evening, thrush and blackbird dominated the singing, their calm timbre warming her all over. Her father sang to her through the large blackbird that nearly always perched in the crown of an elm tree just before sunset. She tried to respond in the same whistled tones, but she could never replicate his sound accurately.

She knew all the birds around Tamoworthig, could distinguish between their songs and knew where they usually built their nests. For singing, she liked the thrush and the blackbird best, but for appearance she preferred the wren and the robin, plus the hedge sparrow, which also bustled around. Always alone, hopping about in the lowest branches and on the ground, rather like a mouse, the hedge sparrow's legs were set far apart, like old women's—and like the legs on Penda's eldest son, Merewald: Penda's sorrow and shame.

While Hild stood weaving, the birds would come right up close, look at her, heads cocked, then hop away searching for food without taking much more notice of her. When a robin chose her as the object of its glance, she felt as if fortune was smiling on her; she hadn't forgotten the time her mother came in the shape of a robin and showed her the way to Frigyd's house. The cats in Tamoworthig weren't allowed to hunt robins.

She had to keep her yarn in lidded baskets so the little birds couldn't steal lengths of fibre to build their nests, or to do repairs long into the summer. The goldfinches were the worst; as soon as you had washed the sheepskins and put them out to dry in the sun, then there they were, pecking at the wool for their nests, and a maid had to stand alongside to keep them away or they'd stain the clean pieces. No other bird was as faithful as the goldfinch, never more than a couple of wingspans from its mate.

Hild was also fond of wood pigeon, mostly the young birds, plucked and roasted on a spit. They ate a lot of those in early summer; there were rarely enough for everyone, but always for the king and his wife. Sweet foods were served too, fruit or berries preserved in honey, a cake or other treats, also for the children, and any leftovers were generously shared between the queen's maids—they knew whose turn it was to have something sweet, and the lucky ones bowed in gratitude to the master and mistress.

The Lord had granted her a good life when he led her to Tamoworthig and into Penda's gentle and strong arms. Life here in the solid new houses was far happier than it had been among Mædeltun's sinister ruins. She didn't know if she would ever have become accustomed to the giants' crumbling dwellings. Even though many of their old buildings were serviceable for sheep and cattle, the spirits never really left the stone and the shepherds tried to steer clear of them when they had to spend a night in the area, during lambing time or if a cow was ill. They had taken Paulinus out there to drive away the spirits with holy water, but that hadn't proved sufficient. The buildings would probably have to be pulled down, or given to the servants of the Lord so their prayers could overcome the evil. She didn't know who was living at their farm now, using their giants' cowhouses; maybe it had all been burnt to the ground.

She wove in three-ply twill, very difficult and time-consuming, but appropriate for a king's daily-wear cloak. She had no need to be ashamed of her husband's clothing, neither his everyday nor his ceremonial outfits. He didn't own one piece of clothing that hadn't been embellished with multi-coloured edging: for everyday use, this might be tablet-woven in various colours and patterns; for the finer items, she wove narrow bands, which she then sewed on in winding patterns, and although these might look identical at first glance, actually they always had small differences. Her latest idea was to make one length red, then go on with one length yellow, then a length of green, and then another in red. She attached the bands in curves forming a red, a yellow and a green section of circular interlacing, and they really did come into their own when put against a woad-blue background. She had also had success with interlacing multi-coloured bands sequentially, so a yellow section was wound together with a green, and a black with a red section.

The front of Penda's most recent ceremonial cloak had been a great success. The cloak itself was madder-red, and at the top she had added small yellow squares, followed by a row of medium-blue and white intertwined bands, the white ones dotted along the edge with red thread. She had sewn little glass beads onto the yellow squares, accentuating the diamond-pattern and sparkling when he moved. The whole front section was covered with coiled ribbon interlace and tablet-woven triangles and squares. She had used yellow thread to embroider intertwined animals on the border, in the same style as the belt buckle he had sacrificed. That cloak was almost a living object.

They had recently received visitors from Deira, and one of the men wore a dark-brown cloak covered in very narrow pale-yellow ribbon interlace. She wanted to make something similar for herself, but in a lighter colour and with slightly narrower bands, varying the colour intensity here and there. She was going to weave some very long ribbons, then she would sew them into patterns, some forming a holy cross on the back of the cloak. Maybe she should wait a while with the last step—it would be seen as a provocation—but she could test out the technique with a square. A cloak like this would certainly be heavy to wear, but any discomfort would be more than offset by its beauty; anyway, you could always sit on horseback and not have to walk very far.

She paused at the loom to enjoy the sight of clumsy fledglings hopping on the ground or screeching until their parents rushed in with worms and other tasty morsels, mites and grubs, seeds and shoots and whatever else they had managed to gather, and crammed the food into the mouths of the greedy little ones, which were almost as big as their parents, just more dishevelled.

Birds wouldn't entertain the notion of being brought up by strangers; only human beings could think up something so unnatural. In the birds' world, blood was still thicker than water.

Hild was becoming ever more puzzled by the way human beings arranged matters, and she found ever more cause to criticize and effect change.

'It's unnatural!' her mother had said when she could find no other way to account for her aversion to the new ideas that would unsettle her world. She had found the new faith, in particular, impossible to accept; it was unnatural to flout what their ancestors had venerated, to think you were wiser than them, to withhold the offerings to which they were entitled, it was all unnatural and would surely bring its own punishment.

'Sooner or later it will come back to us,' Breguswid had said. 'But by then it will have turned against us, and I do not wish myself or my children to witness that day. For it will be a day of fire and blood.'

She never said in detail what she actually meant by that, but it was alarming enough as it was—just seeing her face when she spoke the words.

A day of fire and blood, Hereswid explained to Hild, was the day on which the whole world would start to burn, so intensely you wouldn't be able to fetch water anywhere at all because the lakes and the rivers would have boiled away, such was the force of the fire. Small holes would appear under people's arms, certainly, and under the soles of their feet, and all their blood would run out, leaving a bloodstain for every step taken. But you might just as well stay where you were, because there was nowhere to go, not even on the swiftest horse. The whole world would be in flames, even the Humbre river and the wide expanses of sea.

'But—how do you know?' Hild managed to whisper.

'Everyone knows that!' Hereswid answered, taken aback by her younger sister's ignorance— and she always did everything she could to enlighten Hild!

It was the most hideous thought Hild could have in her head, and Hereswid had been able to get her to do anything at all simply by threatening to tell her about the end of days, the day of fire and blood. Hild had wept and pressed her hands to her ears, but Hereswid just came closer and shouted louder, and Hild knew the story far too well to be able to shut it out of her head with her hands. So she might just as well give in to Hereswid straight away.

Penda thought like their mother, and when he ran out of arguments, he would say: 'Because it goes against nature!' To his mind, nothing was above nature, and Hild had long been persuaded by that line of thought, but now she was beginning to be unsure if people were *nature* at all. The Lord had created them when he had finished with the things that *were* nature. He had created them in his own image, and he had set them to cultivate the earth for him—a kind of tenancy—until they broke faith with him and he had to expel them. And then they'd had to make their own way in the world, to cultivate the earth as they saw fit and get from it what they could. That's what the Lord God had told them.

Hild had recently started wondering if the problem might be that humankind hadn't risen far enough *above* nature: maybe they still had too much of the animal in them to be humans at all, and maybe they lacked the courage to take on the huge challenge laid down by the Lord and to rule freely *over* nature.

They still fancied that the forest spirits and water demons and wights and trolls had more power than they did, and maybe that was just cowardice because they didn't dare shoulder the responsibility when it came to the Day of Judgement. Face to face with the Lord when he took out his book, they would rather try to talk their way out of it with excuses about a malicious fate, a couple of demons who had got in their way, evil eyes and so on and so forth.

But the Lord had set humans to manage his possessions, until he returned from his Heaven—that was what the writings said. Once he had seen how badly the humans were coping, he had come again and told them they should be their brother's keeper, should love and do good to their neighbour, shelter widows and the poor, protect family and children— and then he would reward their faithfulness, when his eternal kingdom came.

Hild stopped her weaving, again overcome with shame. She lowered her head and tried to make the picture of her hanged husband disappear. His death was still not avenged, so poorly had she protected her lineage. She was a sinner, guilty of many misdeeds against her family and countless others.

She resolutely returned to her weaving, and not even the little birds could disturb her daily recitation of David's psalms.

# WAR AND PEACE

*– Merewald's garden –*

'Edwin was a strange king,' said Penda pensively. 'He wasn't very promising as a young man—I had more faith in your father, actually. He appreciated the fight and a good song and he had a better head, they both knew that. Edwin was a dreamer. I was surprised he held on to power for so long. Some of his advisors must have had more sense than that Paulinus.'

'Me,' said Hild, 'and Hereswid.'

Penda stared at her. She explained about Edwin's nocturnal conversations with Breguswid, and how her mother had been baffled by matters concerning anything other than the new god.

Penda rocked with laughter.

'Had I known that,' he cried, 'I'd have recommended a rebellion against Edwin much earlier.'

'Things went very well,' said Hild.

'He was too weak,' said Penda. 'He was never keen on going to war.'

'That was Breguswid's influence,' said Hild. 'My mother would say: Whetted knives— wasted lives.'

'Wasted lives, no,' said Penda, 'but battle is necessary.'

'Peace is better.'

'Peace?' Penda was puzzled. 'Yes, well, we don't fight every day. But you can't base a kingdom on peace.'

'It worked all right for years.'

Hild had dug in her heels. He looked at her and shook his head.

'I don't know what it is with you women. You're always talking about peace and you make an awful fuss when we prepare for battle. At home, though, it would be hard to find anything less peaceful. And you don't say no thank you very much to the booty.'

'Corpses are of little use, we say. War is dangerous.'

'Dangerous?'

He tilted his head and thought for a moment. This was a trait she valued in her husband: he always mulled over her words and didn't simply dismiss them as nonsense, even though they disagreed on practically everything.

'How do you mean—dangerous?'

'People get killed—that's what I mean.'

'Oh,' he smiled jauntily. 'So I've been killed, have I?'

'Lots of others have,' she replied, her hackles up.

'When they don't take care, yes, that stands to reason. But if you keep your wits and eyes about you and know the job, then I don't think you can say it's dangerous. You just have to know what you're doing.'

'You're not going to deny that many were lost in East Anglia?'

'They were,' conceded Penda. 'But you have to remember there were a lot of new men, they're rash. Yes, your first battles can be a little risky, I'll grant you that. But as soon as you've got the hang of it, then it's no more dangerous than anything else.'

'That's not what the widows say,' Hild persisted.

'No, but widows always exaggerate because they want the wergild, that's natural. Widows of men who die felling trees and hunting, they don't make such a fuss. But those jobs are far more dangerous.'

'Felling and hunting are necessary,' said Hild. 'War isn't.'

'Funny how often you women say that,' said Penda, scratching his scalp. 'Maybe because you're not involved, maybe that's it. But you can see how necessary it is from what happened to Edwin.'

'Killed in battle, yes,' said Hild.

'Killed because he was reluctant to fight,' Penda corrected.

'Paulinus wanted *a realm of peace*. And Edwin shared the opinion that whetted knives make for wasted lives.'

'And therefore ended up a waste of a corpse himself,' Penda insisted. 'We couldn't pay the taxes he burdened us with. And then it was easy enough to get all his territories to join against him. We couldn't simply sit back and watch people work until they dropped, and children die of hunger, just because the neighbouring king had got ideas about peace. If it's human lives you're thinking about, then many more were sacrificed during Edwin's peace than at any normal time. Maybe you think Mercia and Gwynedd and Lindsey could feed all his scribes and minstrels and everyone he paid to inform on the others—arse-lickers, we called them.'

'You could have discussed it with him,' tried Hild. 'Perhaps you might have reached a settlement.'

Penda laughed loudly.

'You should have suggested that to him on one of your late nights—I'm sure he'd have been most appreciative.' He then quickly added, somewhat bitterly: 'When you have power, there's not much to discuss. There's no alternative but to take up arms. Edwin knew full well how many slaves we lost that winter the birds died. But the taxes had to be paid. No discussion there. Yes, that was a costly peace.'

Hild racked her brains to think of something that would refute his allegation. She knew she was right, but it was hard to prove.

'It was a transition,' she said. 'As soon as everyone has got thoughts of war out of their heads, the armies can all be sent home and everyone can live off the land without coveting their neighbour's crops.'

He gazed at her as if he had not believed such stupidity possible, and then he burst into loud laughter again.

'You're quite right: it was a transition, and what a transition! With many, so to speak, transitional deaths. Many freemen in Mercia had to plough their fields themselves that spring, and their wives had to do the milking and churn the butter, there were so few slaves left. Yes, a fine transition that was.'

Hild paced up and down.

'Paulinus said the kingdom needed peace and law and order.'

'And very cosy it was for him too, when he was in the king's service and could just sit back and fill his belly with food from the conquered territories. Everything depends on where you're standing. And very cosy indeed it must have been for Edwin's men, who could sit back and polish their swords and pour mead down their throats and boast about past bravery. Men like that—you might as well send them home. Their bellies get too heavy and they get scared of dying. And, as you very well know: where was Edwin's personal troop when it counted? And Eadfrid would never have surrendered if he hadn't been left standing there all alone when his men took to their heels. At least he didn't run away. Yes, they were a pretty shower. Real transitional warriors Edwin had got hold of there.'

Hild didn't know how to respond. Her husband knew far more about these matters than she did. She shrugged and pulled a face.

'War is so primitive.'

'Primitive?'

Penda shook his head. He settled himself comfortably and explained to his wife the different ways in which to wage war, hand-to-hand combat on foot and on horseback, the factors to be considered when drawing up an army, how this army should be deployed in the terrain, the timing and who should take up the various positions. He tried to teach her a little about the advantages and disadvantages of different kinds of weapon, how the weather could come to your assistance when, for example, the sun shone in the enemy's eyes. He'd once seen a rain squall pour down on the enemy while not a drop fell on his troops; the enemy hadn't wasted any time in making themselves scarce, the quickest retreat he'd ever seen, and he had seen a few.

Penda laughed happily as he spoke. He liked talking about the battles he had fought, and by the time they'd been married a year Hild knew about them all, down to the tiniest detail.

He explained to her that these battles were the best form of wages, the best training and the only way to ensure that the best people applied to be in the service of the king. Unlike Edwin's policy, which led to the best men fighting against him. At the end of this lecture, which she had also heard before, he smiled triumphantly and, head cocked teasingly, asked: 'Or should Edwin rather have sent all his men home to twiddle their thumbs?'

'Yes,' answered Hild promptly, 'if everyone did.'

Penda laughed. 'Well I won't, of that you can be sure.'

'Yes, but what if you could get all the other kings to do it too?'

'Never! Nor would I ever try. I like fighting, remember!'

When she didn't respond, he nudged her with his foot and smiled.

'You must be completely mad, little Hild.'

It hurt her to be spoken to in this way. Mad she was not, but it would seem there were others who were.

'You're mad yourself!' she cried. 'You can hardly look at a piece of jewellery or hear about a good stretch of grazing land before you have to get your hands on it. Greed plucks you by the nose, you just can't see it.'

'See? I can't see? Who is it that's blind as a bat and never notices what's going on right in front of her nose, hardly notices what people are wearing? Who does that remind you of, if I might be so bold?'

She had to stay firm so as not to be side-tracked by his diversionary tactics. The point was: he had said she was mad. She countered instantly: 'And if using little wooden sticks to make decisions about things you should work out in your own head isn't madness, then I don't know what madness is.'

'No, that's exactly what you don't know,' he shouted back, 'being stark staring mad yourself. You walk around in the clouds, totally oblivious to the real world. It's a good thing your father didn't live to see what a foolish daughter he'd had.'

'Foolish, yes, that's you all right,' she shouted, tears in her eyes. 'And your father was a fool too, and a serf!'

She had finally hit him where it hurt. He held his breath for a second, and then said quietly: 'He was not a fool, but a serf, yes, he was for a time and I don't deny it. But he was not a fool, he was better than any slave I've ever met. He earned his freedom, and perhaps that's more worthy than those who just take it for granted and scarcely know what to do with it. It's easy for you to talk, you've never known anything other than dishes of pork in the warmth of the king's hall. I've always known there are some things you have to fight for. And for that I thank my serf father.'

He had regained the advantage; she found it extremely irritating that he always seemed to be in the right.

'Why, then, did you order the minstrel to make a song about your fine ancestry?' she asked cuttingly.

'Oh, you know what people are like.' He was calm. 'They don't believe a serf can beget a king, you must know *that*. I honour my father by promoting him a little. He would have been very proud of me had he lived, of that you can be sure.'

He smiled and pinched her cheek.

'And you can be sure he'd have been proud of his daughter-in-law. He'd have scuttled along at your heels, day in, day out, like a little dog. I'd never have been allowed to have you to myself.'

Hild couldn't help but smile at this dubious compliment: walking around with a toothless dotard in close pursuit didn't strike her as being particularly dignified. She laughed and ruffled his hair.

When Oswald had become king, he had asked for the services of a monk from Iona. The fathers of the monastery had selected a man who was then ordained bishop and dispatched to Oswald's estate. A few months later he returned, fuming, to Iona. He could see no purpose, he said, in preaching to the broad backs of Oswald's soldiers; unless protected by a circle of these men, he was barely allowed to open his mouth.

The people of Bernicia had seen the new god in action, they said, and they were not about to be told, for the second time, that he was more powerful than the gods of their forefathers. They had put up with a lot because of him. First, Edwin's increasingly peculiar way of ruling, then his defeat, then the ravaging campaigns of the Christian Cædwalla. They had no need of further instruction from above.

'There's no salvation for them,' the bishop stated, back home on Iona, about the perverse barbarians who had derided and intimidated him and been completely impervious to the word of the Lord, even though he was considered a skilful missionary.

'You have to speak gently to the perverse,' one of the other monks had said; this was Aidan, Hild's mentor.

'Perhaps you've been too harsh,' he continued. 'You should have followed the example of the apostles by first giving them the simple milk of learning, and then gradually nourishing them with the word of the Lord until they are capable of comprehending more of Christ's higher teachings.'

Hearing this, the fathers on Iona became aware of Aidan's exceptional wisdom, and they nominated him bishop. They ordained him and then sent him, at the mercy of the Lord, to the barbarians—and accompanied him with their prayers.

Aidan took over Oswald's gift to his predecessor, the little tidal island of Lindisfarena just north of Bebbanburh, and from here he set out on his missionary journeys around Bernicia. Aidan spoke only Irish, so at first Oswald had to assist with translation. This suited Oswald, as it provided him with the opportunity to improve upon Aidan's preaching, which was, to his mind, far too mild.

After a while, however, he realized that Aidan's method had a lot to commend it, and so he bought the freedom of a couple of slaves who could translate for the missionary and teach him the local language. Seeing that Aidan was completely inoffensive, the people of Bernicia then stopped mocking him and even started to visit him, voluntarily, for his healing powers. As time passed, more missionaries came south to Aidan's monastery, and the people in the area admired them for their temperate way of life. It seemed they actually lived according to the rules they preached. They never spurned paupers, and when those who had been healed thanked them with gifts, these riches were immediately passed on to others. Such was the strength of their trust in the heavenly Lord, believing that he would continue to provide for their needs, as indeed he did.

Not that their needs were great, given that they dressed simply and ate extremely frugally. You were never eaten out of house and home if you invited them in, and you were left to drink the mead yourself. It wasn't from impoliteness that they refused the better dishes, but in order to follow the example of their Lord Jesus and thereby prepare themselves for the ultimate meeting with him. He would judge them and, according to how they had lived their lives, he would either send them down to an eternal underground fire or send them up amongst his friends in a heavenly hall where no one ever went without, or so they claimed.

Aidan had therefore been obliged to decline Hild's invitation to Mercia. He offered to find a suitable replacement, and she accepted. Although, if Aidan himself was unable to come, she wrote, then she would be grateful if he would send a man who could teach her more Latin and, if possible, some Greek would be appreciated.

Hild looked forward to improving her skills, but for the time being she had to continue teaching Penda's children to the best of her abilities.

The children were a mixed bunch. The first wife had borne Merewald, now sixteen years old, the rest had died at birth and the mother had herself died during a pregnancy. From his second marriage, Penda had two very intelligent and precocious daughters: Tibba, aged twelve, and Eadburh, aged eleven. And then there were the sons Bothelm, Gefmund and Peada, aged ten, eight and five; these three would inherit the realm from Penda given that Merewald could neither ride, hunt, fight, nor do anything else expected of a candidate for king.

His legs were all wrong. He couldn't be called malformed, but there was definitely a flaw: his backside jutted out, and in order to move forwards he had to swing his legs slightly outwards. But onwards he marched, as his wetnurse had always insisted, just not far enough to be a warrior, let alone a king.

Tibba and Eadburh were fascinated by the process of reading and writing, but teaching the three prospective kings was a somewhat harder task. Their main interests were hunting and war; so Hild made up little stories in Latin about horses and swords, war expeditions, boar hunting and falconry.

This suited the boys perfectly, apart from Merewald who wasn't in the least interested. It was all the same to the girls; they were interested in everything and could deal with any subject. Besides, the main purpose was for the boys to learn something, at least the 'king's sons', as Penda called all his boys except Merewald.

More than two years of marriage passed before Hild bore Penda a son. The baby was heavy and healthy and she named him Wulfhere—as Hundfrid still hadn't been found. A wolf was a kind of hound, and the name befitted a king's son.

Penda just nodded when she told him that the boy was Wulfhere. She had known as soon as he came out. Penda sat on the edge of the bed and took her hand. He didn't care about his son's name, his only concern was that both his wife and son were alive and that his son was big and sturdy. The way he clutched Penda's finger—he promised to be a real warrior.

Apart from their names, Hundfrid and Wulfhere had little in common. If Wulfhere resembled anyone it was Wilbrord, in those eyes that never missed a thing; they could see straight through you.

Hild thought he resembled his father more than his mother, and Penda had no argument with this. He thought all his sons looked a lot like him, apart from Merewald. Three king's sons wasn't much, so he was more than happy to have another sound one.

Penda preferred not to dwell on Merewald and the way he always kept himself to himself, never thinking about anything but plants, without putting them to any useful purpose. He just looked at them and brought them home to put in a garden he had laid out, and there wasn't one single plant you could eat or spin or derive any benefit from whatsoever. Merewald was Penda's shame and sorrow.

Hild set great store by Merewald and everything he taught her about plants: where they grew, what they thrived on, how they propagated, how they were constructed internally, externally and under the soil.

Just like Hereswid, Merewald would take the plants apart in order to discover their innermost essence. Not a plant in his garden withheld a secret; he knew about their roots, number of filaments, preference for a lot or a little water, heavy or light soil, if they wanted to be exposed to the sun or to stay under cover of the trees, if they had relations of a different colour, which ones were eaten by which beasts, how their seeds were dispersed to new sites, and how some used rootstock so their progeny shot up all around the mother plant.

'They're just like everyone else,' he explained to Hild, 'they want a big family too.'

He showed her the dandelion's flying seeds, the sticky seeds on the goosegrass, the touch-me-not's jumping seeds, the bird-spread seeds of the rowan, the poppy's sprinkle-seeds and all the variations in between.

Ferns held a special interest for Merewald. No other plant had its seeds on the underside of the leaves, without pedicels, just sort of sitting there. Merewald had various kinds of fern in his garden, and he admired them all unconditionally.

Of course he also knew—more than most people—about the uses for a plant's seeds or root or fibre or leaves or sap or flowers or pollen, and so Hild also learnt valuable information on this point. And raw materials: her basket of medicines was more extensive than the one carried around by the woman who dispensed remedies, and Hild was often asked for advice before this doctor was consulted.

For Merewald, however, the medicinal use of plants was merely a by-product, as was any other application. His interest was in pure observation, the satisfaction of his own curiosity. It was possibly not a particularly noble trait, and obviously not one which could be indulged by anyone other than the outcast son of a king, but, as Hild said in his defence to Penda: would it be better to set traps for tiny songbirds and kill wolves and bears for their skins, of which they had plenty?

Yes, in Penda's opinion, that would definitely be better. You could never have enough good skins, they could be sold or bartered for foreign goods, whereas he had yet to hear of a trader who was on the lookout for dandelion seeds.

Hild couldn't contradict that contention.

Merewald had been slow to learn his letters, nor was he interested in the word of the Lord or tales of war. But when Hild told him about some writings she had heard Paulinus mention—Plinius' *Naturalis historia*, in thirty-seven volumes, and a new work by Isidorus of Seville, *De natura rerum* in thirteen volumes, about animals and plants all over the world— Merewald suddenly showed some activity. It hadn't ever occurred to him that little written squiggles could serve any useful purpose whatsoever.

Admittedly, Hild had never seen Plinius' or Isidorus' works, nor did she know if they could be found anywhere in the country, but with sufficient resources it would surely be possible to procure them through one of the traders who frequently offered wares for sale at the royal estate.

The last one had offered to get them an elephant from the land of Africa. Penda had considered this at length, a faraway look in his eyes, cheeks burning, but in the end he'd had to decline. Purchase of an elephant would have called for the proceeds of a more than extremely successful expedition, and an elephant wasn't the only thing he needed.

He did, however, ask the trader to let him know if anyone else in the country ordered one. Should that be the case, he would hate to be found wanting.

If a trader could procure an elephant, thought Hild, then surely he could get hold of a natural history book. A single volume, they could afford that.

It was botany that brought Merewald to the Lord. He spun round when Hild told him everything had been created by the new god, who wasn't actually new, as was said, but had always existed, since before there even *was* a world, and who had then undertaken the creation of the world.

And with such wisdom, thought Merewald: this god had been able to think up something to grow on every single patch of land, however indifferent the quality, however wind-swept or swathed in darkness. Nothing had gone to waste; such inventiveness—inconceivable in humans, who otherwise dreamt up the strangest things—and such profusion.

What impressed him most was the orderliness of the creation because, he thought, if he'd done it himself it would have been one big muddle. He would have forgotten something here and overdone something else there. He would never, not in all his life—even if he lived to be eight hundred years old, as they said Methuselah had—he would still never have achieved that breadth of vision and clear-headedness combined with the fertility of imagination necessary to make just one tiny little flower like the scarlet pimpernel.

Well, actually the scarlet pimpernel was probably the one he *could* have worked out, but that would have been all: not the dandelion, and certainly not something like the toadflax or corydalis, which needed a slightly heavy insect for pollination, because you didn't only have to plan their structure, but also how they functioned, like devising a tool.

The more Merewald got to know the plants, the more certain he was that they were all service-plants, if not directly for humans and livestock, then for some beast or other. At any rate, he had yet to see a plant that was not used by, for example, spiders or very small vermin, and no flower was so ugly as to be shunned by flying creatures, nor did any of them seem to have seeds that the birds rejected, and even ants were happy to crawl on them.

He had heard a missionary preach on a text from Ecclesiastes, and he would never forget those words. He said them to himself every day as he wandered in his garden: 'I know that, whatever God does, it shall be for ever, nothing can be added, nor anything taken away; and God does it so that men should fear before him.'

He could see for himself that this was the truth. Every year the Lord let the world be resurrected in all its green splendour, every year he stripped the leaves from the trees again; he let the grass wither and the wind rush across the land, but he always let new tufts peep out when the time was right for them.

Merewald simply couldn't understand why there were still people with eyes so closed they couldn't see this—especially his father, worst of all, his own father lacked eyes with which to see.

He'd tried to show him once, had taken him all round the garden, had painstakingly shown and explained everything to him, concluding that this orderliness was due to the wisdom of the Lord. At which point Penda had stared at him with an odd expression on his face and then, shaking his head, had gone indoors to his chamber.

Merewald put his trust in his father's new wife: she could put him on the right track, if anyone could.

Hild was outside, working at the loom on a bonnet for Wulfhere. It had turned out to be a fine day; as the sun broke through, the birds all burst into rejoicing. The scarlet pimpernel opened its tiny head and made you laugh, which was how it had got its nickname: laughter-bringer. Its life was often cut short, because mothers and wetnurses with sullen infants would pick it optimistically and put a little bunch in the cradle with the baby. If that didn't help, you could give the child a sprinkling of dried laughter-bringer in its food—that would certainly do the trick.

Hild had put a small spray of scarlet pimpernel at the foot of Wulfhere's cradle. Not that he was especially sullen, and he was already smiling, but sullenness could easily develop so it was better to get in first. Wulfhere was thriving; his wetnurse had plenty of milk and his cheeks were filling out daily.

Hild kept an eye on a pair of goldfinches who had built a nest far out on a branch in the holly tree. An unusually messy little affair, almost as shoddy as the wood pigeons', but it had stayed firmly in place throughout the stormy weather of late spring. The first brood of young would be ready to fly the nest by the onset of the mild months, then they would sit in the elm screaming as they waited for their parents to bring more food. This continued until the female was again sitting on her eggs; in a good summer, they would have three broods, after which the dapper little goldfinch parents would be looking rather dishevelled.

Hild was working through David's psalms. The hay crop had far outstripped normal expectations and she hoped they would be able to collect many more head of cattle than usual. They had much for which to thank the Lord.

She usually accompanied Penda on his trips around the realm to collect the dues. During the plant month they collected corn and during the month of the winter full moon they brought home cattle.

The method of paying taxes was unfair, in Hild's opinion: in good years people had to part with more, but in bad years they had to part with the same amount as in normal years, unless things were so bad that they only had enough for seed grain.

She had spoken about this with her husband, and he didn't disagree. But she must understand, he had explained, it wasn't a question of arranging things as fairly as possible, but of getting the greatest possible returns. In the long run this was to the benefit of all, because if the king and his men couldn't get by, then the outlook was bleak for everyone else. If you gave a reduction in lean years then some would be tempted to say: 'It's been a bad year, lord king!' And who would gain from that? No, as the system stood, everyone was encouraged to do their best.

Penda had never speculated about such matters before. It was all so straightforward as it was; and, as far as he knew, that was how it had always been.

Nor would Hild have worried over these concerns had it not been for Paulinus, who had spoken at length about justice and peace. She could see the logic when Penda explained how these ideas had brought about Edwin's downfall. Unnaturalness, he called it, contrary to the order of the world and life itself. But she still couldn't abandon the ideas, even though it was true they hadn't been successful for Edwin. One day they would flourish, when more people had their eyes opened to the true path. Penda's children would certainly not wander in ignorance, for they were told the truth.

It was fortunate that she was in a position to teach them. One day Mercia would be a Christian realm, and Merewald had already asked his father for permission to be baptized. Hild smiled at the thought.

There wasn't a cloud in sight, but it would have to rain soon if the corn harvest was to be good. She would pray to her god about the matter, rather than wait for the pagan priest to start on his rain rituals, in which she would have to participate.

'Only the most necessary, and with a pure heart,' Aidan had written when she made enquiries about the extent to which her participation in the pagan ceremonies would influence her salvation.

If she could sort out the rain herself, she would avoid this obstacle on the road to Paradise.

# MEREWALD AND THE FILAMENT

*– Penda marches against Oswald –*

Penda returned from a successful expedition: he had conquered the Magonsætan. His kingdom was growing year by year, he never lost a battle, and his opponents knew it.

'What do you want with all that?' asked Hild, surveying the booty spread out over the tables in the hall.

'Mercia is growing big,' answered Penda.

'Northumbria's bigger,' said Hild, 'and one day Oswald will attack.'

'That's why we've got to expand,' said Penda.

'Oswald isn't as favoured in the fortunes of war as you,' said Hild. 'You could defeat him tomorrow if you wanted.'

'All in good time.'

'My husband still lies unredressed in his grave,' said Hild. She turned away to give the steward instructions about decking the hall with red rugs for the evening's victory celebrations, but stopped mid-flow.

She had caught sight of a round brooch, large and radiant: gold filigree, pale and dark garnet inlay, countless cobalt-blue stones making it leap to life, almost animate, and glistening silver—the latter for variation, not thrift. The goldsmith had obviously had access to every material he wanted. There were holy crosses and circles, entwined animals in gold filigree, garnets on scraped gold foil shining up through the redness of the jewels. And that intensely potent blue!

A shade of blue akin to that of the cornflower, but she had never before seen it in a stone. The blue of Cædwalla's pendant and Sigebert's gold ornaments hadn't been nearly as penetrating and lustrous.

It was a sumptuous piece of jewellery; in craft and design, materials, size and weight, it was far superior to her own necklace.

She clasped her hands tightly behind her back, swallowed hard a couple of times and walked away, trying to recapture her focus on the decoration of the hall. But her legs returned and turned into pillars of stone refusing to budge. Oh, that brooch would be so beautifully set off by her red hair and blue eyes.

She forced her gaze away and her feet onwards. That piece of jewellery was just so gorgeous it made your heart ache.

She would not have any of his war booty.

'You have to understand,' said Penda when they had gone to bed. 'If we're going to fight Oswald, we need more troops, from a wider area. And we must have peace with the West Saxons. No one could deal with unrest on four fronts.'

'The people in Walas are no threat,' said Hild, 'and certainly not East Anglia and Lindsey.'

'Not at the moment,' said Penda, 'but if they join forces with Oswald they will be.'

'Northumbria has always been surrounded by unrest, on all sides,' said Hild, 'and no one can say they've suffered unduly.'

'We've not seen the end of it yet,' said Penda. 'Oswald has better contact with the Picts than anyone's had before. Of course, there's the occasional uprising to the west, but the only threat there is to Oswald's cattle. He demands too much in dues. It won't be long before he takes Lindsey, as far as I can see.'

'Unless you defend Lindsey.'

'Which I don't think I'll be doing,' said Penda. 'Not until my army is bigger, at least. And until such time, I think I can keep on good terms with Oswald.'

'You wouldn't let him take Lindsey, would you?'

'Rather than lose a battle, yes, I would. It won't be difficult to get it back. Once I've dealt with Oswald.'

'Yes, yes,' she said, 'you're in command, not me.'

'So you say,' said Penda, 'but actually I think fate is in command.'

'You and your fate,' she laughed, and pulled him towards her. She was in a much better mood. It was all only a question of time.

'And you with all your talk about peace,' mumbled Penda, stroking his strange wife's hair.

'What do you mean by that?' she exclaimed, sitting up abruptly in the bed.

'You say such contradictory things,' he smiled, shaking his head.

'I certainly do not,' she countered sharply. 'I say that Eadfrid has to be avenged.'

'And then you keep on saying we have to stop waging war. Is that not contradictory?' Hild's eyes were almost black.

'I'm talking about honour,' she said angrily, 'not about getting yourself a whole lot of booty.'

'War is war,' said Penda, 'and honour and booty can't be separated like that. Besides, the method's the same.'

'Honour and greed are two very different things,' Hild stated emphatically, lying down, her back to her husband.

Sometimes his pagan idiocy was just too much to bear.

Penda's power grew, even though Oswald soon took Lindsey from him. Penda's good connections with Lindsey continued, however, and—come the day of battle—he was confident that Lindsey's allegiance to Oswald would be less than forthcoming.

The regime laid down by Oswald was far too severe: he had ordered the burning of sacred places and harsh punishment for all forms of idol-worship, as he called it. Of all Oswald's actions, this, in Penda's opinion, was the most foolish. If the gods didn't take revenge, the freemen of Lindsey would, as soon as the opportunity presented itself, and that opportunity would arise courtesy of Penda, when the time was right.

Two years after the birth of Wulfhere, Hild produced another son. She named him Ædelræd, and now Penda had five king's sons who looked promising. Wulfhere had inherited his mother's red hair and was already a crusty little warrior.

The daughters, Tibba and Eadburh, were fully occupied with their studies, and both planned to continue them in the service of the Lord. This meant they would have to be baptized, but their father had yet to give Merewald his permission.

From Hereswid's letters, Hild understood that the Gallic monasteries were the best places for study. Better than Lindisfarena, which was a double house, for both men and women; but Aidan had hardly any books, and he placed greater emphasis on prayer and missionary travels. The example and pure lives of the communities converted many, but Penda's daughters were more interested in scholarship than in imitation of the Lord.

According to Hereswid, her own monastery of Cale and the neighbouring monasteries were very good places of education both for women and men—with abundant and steadily expanding book collections. Study and transcription of the holy books took up almost as much of the day as was spent in prayer and singing psalms of thanksgiving. Where was there such a place in Hild's realm?

Penda eventually left for Northumbria. It was the month of thanksgiving, the harvest had been good and there was the prospect of a huge quantity of booty. Hild had embroidered three small holy crosses inside the hem of his kirtle.

The army was away for four weeks, and did indeed bring home an enormous booty, but Oswald had eluded them.

He had retreated to Bebbanburh. They had laid siege to him, but knew it would take years to starve him out. Penda decided to smoke him out instead: the church and surrounding farms were pulled down, and all the timber collected was built into an enormous fire at the foot of the mighty basalt formation on which the stronghold was sited.

The wind changed direction, however, and nearly poisoned Penda's army. The pagan priest and wise men had tried to entice the wind around, but all to no avail and they had to accept that they were up against more powerful forces than they could handle. This hadn't caused outright panic, but they had withdrawn in great haste and had to make do with plundering whatever they came across on the homeward journey.

Hild gazed at the fallen, laid out in rows of equal length on a covering of fern in the hall. Among them was Trumhere from Wodensburh; incredible how much blood there could be in one person, thought Hild. He'd been in the forefront and had been struck by an arrow in his neck. His wife would not be happy, she thought, but perhaps she would feel relieved:

Trumhere had been acting strangely since the expedition to East Anglia, had shunned people and stayed indoors—until this campaign.

'The Lord protects his own,' Hild murmured to herself, and inspected the rest of the dead. This was the punishment for slaying a man like Sigebert.

'You must understand,' said Penda next day, 'when Oswald is killed, then the trouble will begin. One of his brothers will become king and they won't look kindly on his death, as well you know.'

'Of course,' said Hild, 'we must be prepared. What about Merewald?'

'What about him?'

He was always slightly annoyed when he didn't immediately understand what she meant.

'I mean Cynegils' daughters. Marry Merewald to one of them.'

'Oh, I see,' said Penda, with an expression of distaste.

'Well, he is the son of a king,' said Hild.

Penda looked doubtful.

'I've been thinking it over for a long time now,' said Hild. 'Merewald could do with a wife.'

It was Hild who approached Merewald on the subject. He had recently turned twenty-one and still showed no interest in anything other than his garden.

'Now you mention it,' he smiled, looking lovingly at a bracken, 'have you seen Cynegils' daughters?'

'There's nothing wrong with them,' said Hild reassuringly, although this was not strictly true, as Oswald had taken the only really healthy one.

Merewald set forth. He didn't find any of Cynegils' daughters to his liking; he felt stared at by the protruding eyes they had all inherited from their father; they sniggered at his jutting-out backside and he heard them whisper 'cripple' behind his back. So he moved on to the South Saxons, but found nothing here either, so he moved on to Kent.

In Kent he found what he was looking for. He found her in the garden, admiring a patch of teasels, which she grew so the goldfinches would have winter food. She showed him her flowers as a matter of course, and he knew that he had found the one for him.

She was sixteen years old and her father, who was the brother of the new king, Erconberth, would have preferred the elder sister to be married off first, but Merewald wouldn't give way—he would have his choice, or no one.

Negotiations about the morning gift and dowry were set in motion, if it really was going to be Ermenburh. The elder sister would come with a considerably larger dowry, and although Merewald had no understanding of such matters, his attendants did. Everything, however, had to be sanctioned by Penda.

Merewald returned home radiant, his stooped back a little straighter and his legs tottering swiftly forwards at a speed never previously seen.

'A fine arrangement you've made,' said Penda to Hild. 'What use is Kent's friendship to us?'

'It might prove useful,' said Hild, 'and as to the West Saxons, well, you've got five other sons.'

'You don't think my king's sons will take a woman rejected by Merewald, do you?' snapped Penda.

'It might prove necessary,' she said. 'And anyway, tastes differ.'

'Nonsense. Rejected is rejected.'

'Yes, otherwise you'll have to go courting yourself!' she laughed.

'It will probably come to that,' said Penda, and he couldn't see anything to laugh about.

Merewald's wedding plans made slow progress as Penda kept finding fault with details in the Kent offer. He hoped Merewald would grasp the political realities and resign himself to one of the West Saxon king's daughters. If Penda made himself sufficiently uncooperative, the king of Kent might withdraw his offer and find a better match.

In this, Penda showed how little he knew his son. Having made up his mind, Merewald would have waited until his death rather than take another. He hummed the beloved one's name as he wandered around the garden taking care of his children. Perhaps these tiny, dumb and immobile beings were all that would be allotted them, which gave even more reason to be solicitous. He had moved some small apple trees in from the forest, and he was anxious to see if they would bear fruit under the more sheltered conditions of the garden.

She had given him teasel seeds, and he sent her little bags full of seeds from his henbane, corydalis and the tall yellow aconite—and a pot of royal fern, polypody and moonwort leaves, thickly studded with seeds. He had never yet been successful in germinating fern seeds. It was a modest plant, intolerant of any intervention in its propagation, but multiplying excellently if left to itself—perhaps his chosen bride could bring about the miracle in the warm soil of Kent.

Hild had long been aware that Merewald was ruminating on something, a matter of greater weight than wedding plans. She didn't disturb him because she knew that, if left in peace, the delicious fruits of his mind were well worth waiting for.

One day in Hreda's month, he asked her to accompany him into the garden; he had made a discovery and could no longer keep it to himself.

In a breathless and disjointed account, he tried to share it with her: he had found a regularity, an order, in the Lord's creation, of which he now, at last, had proof. There was a correlation between the number of seed-leaves produced by a plant and the number of its filaments, petals and sepals.

Last year he had made note of which seeds germinated with one leaf, and when they flowered he found that they bore three, six, nine or twelve petals, sepals and filaments, perhaps stigma. Always a combination of three. Now he had made a study of those that germinated with two leaves. And their flowers were always in a combination of five.

Hild had to rack her brain to picture a seedling at all.

Merewald went on to explain that in this there was a profound testimony. First a seed-leaf emerges. For our Lord is one and all-encompassing. Subsequently the plant, at every stage, is formed in combinations of three. Because later the Lord became man, on earth, and the Holy Spirit descended: the Holy Trinity! The fully-grown and fully-developed plant signalled the Holy Trinity itself.

'And which plants do you think I'm talking about, Hild?' asked Merewald, taking a step backwards and watching her with bated breath.

Hild thought, but couldn't remember how many petals there were on an anemone, or a primrose for that matter.

'The dandelion, perhaps?'

This was a shot in the dark because she had never counted its petals, so very many it had, and she'd caught the habit from Hereswid of thinking that if there were more than ten, then there were a lot and you didn't have to count the rest. Merewald, on the other hand, obviously had the required patience.

He shook his head and couldn't resist helping her out.

'Who sacrifice themselves for humans, by allowing themselves to be eaten?' he asked momentously.

'Barley?' asked Hild. 'Or wheat or rye? Oats, maybe?'

Merewald beamed—at last, someone who understood him. He nodded slowly and continued: 'And what about grass? Eaten by our livestock so that we can eat them, and thus the grass also gives its life for the sake of humans. And what about this: we know that our Lord created everything in the way he thought it should be. And do you know what, Hild? The way he made the plants, he proclaimed his gospel right there. He wanted to show himself to us through the plants. So that we could acknowledge the Holy Trinity—which, although it's made up of three, is as one in flesh and soul—and to signify that he himself sacrificed his body for us.'

Hild was dumbfounded, overwhelmed by the idea that the Lord had, so to speak, put his signature on everything he had created.

'Surely even my father must be able to see it,' said Merewald eagerly. 'Even pagans like him have been given plants by the Lord, so they can get to know him, can't you see? Even people far away, who have never been visited by missionaries, might be able to understand a little about the will of the Lord when they look at the plants.'

'Yes,' Hild was moved, 'as long as their eyes are open. And your father—have you told him about this?'

Merewald glanced down and shuffled his feet, then he grabbed her hand and looked at her beseechingly.

'I'd be so grateful if you would explain it to him. At least then he'd listen.'

Hild consented, but first she wanted to see Merewald's evidence. When they had been through the entire garden, she had to sit down, overcome by the knowledge Merewald had unveiled for her.

There was no mistaking it: the Lord had revealed himself through his very creations. And not even Paulinus had known, with all his learning.

'The ways of the Lord are past understanding,' she murmured, thinking, not least, that the Lord had selected Merewald, the absurd and despised son, to break his code and open people's eyes. The ways of the Lord were indeed beyond all understanding, and once again, as the Lord had prophesied, the last would be first and the first last.

However grand and powerful her husband might be, and however sharp his eyesight, he didn't have a tenth of the understanding Merewald gleaned from just, in Penda's words, sitting gawping.

Penda followed grudgingly into Merewald's 'fool's farm', as he called it. He listened to his wife's lengthy explanation, turning aside so as not to be confronted with Merewald's eagerly nodding head—so much obstinacy and nonsense in one head! His invention was boundless when it came to acquainting his own father with the truth about the way of the world.

Of all the many indications that the world was about to go out of kilter, the clearest sign was the egg believing it could teach the hen.

Yet Penda also knew that he had himself brought these unnatural ideas into his home by marrying a woman of the new faith—and allowing her to teach the children.

If only she could have stuck to the alphabet, but she persisted with her claim that it wasn't possible to learn the alphabet from its letters alone. Writings were necessary, she said, meaningful writings, and as there were no writings from the old faith, she had to use the new—even though she said they were very old.

'Beer,' he said, 'barley and hops. So the same goes for them, does it?'

'Yes,' said Hild, but Merewald pulled her aside and whispered that he wasn't entirely sure about hops.

'In all probability,' said Hild, 'but your son wishes to conduct a further experiment with hops before he can be completely certain. Barley is definite.'

'Rye and wheat?' asked Penda.

They both nodded eagerly.

'Beans?' asked Penda, and Merewald blushed. Once again he pulled Hild aside and explained to her that the bean was an exception, the exception that proved the rule, so to speak—as far as he could tell from his studies to date.

'One or two seed-leaves?' asked Penda impatiently.

'You know, Penda, you can't have a rule without an exception. And that's exactly what you've just demonstrated. The bean is the exception to prove the rule, and it's quite incredible that you should point it out yourself,' said Hild, with an admiring glance at her husband, but he wasn't about to fall for her flattery.

'What rot!' he snapped, spun round and stalked back to the hall. This was the kind of futile speculation bred by idleness.

In his rage he decided to attack Oswald again. Then they would see whose gods you could depend on.

Once the hay had been gathered in, he summoned his troops, now numerous and in good condition. His two eldest king's sons, Bothelm and Gefmund, were sixteen and fourteen years old respectively, and it was impossible to find one single good reason to leave them at home. Each lad was provided with his own escort of hand-picked men, the best Penda had.

They set forth for Northumbria.

Hild could do nothing but wait. Never before had he been away for so long on an expedition, and the messages she received about his movements seemed curious. She had never been afraid when he was away: he knew what he was doing and he had fortune on his side, but many weeks had passed.

She had spent a few rainy days indoors embroidering a boar on a cloak for Penda and when, on the first sunny morning, she had the loom carried outside, a transformation had occurred.

It had become strangely quiet. Something odd and threatening hung over the whole estate, and didn't lift even when the sun had warmed everything through. The air was thick with foreboding, as if her god had withdrawn and left the world to look after itself. She became seriously anxious for her husband's wellbeing, and went down to Merewald in his garden on the pretext of needing a little valerian.

'What's happened?' she asked, once she had her valerian.

'Nothing that I know of,' he answered. 'What do you mean?'

'It's as if everything's dead,' she blurted out. She didn't dare voice her fears: this must be the first portent that good fortune had deserted their estate—should they start packing and try to escape to East Anglia?

The last message from Penda had arrived several days previously, and she didn't understand his movements. Nine-year-old Peada would be left to avenge him, and four-year-old Wulfhere and two-year-old Ædelræd—and Hundfrid and Wilbrord, once they were found.

Merewald obviously couldn't sense the evil; he looked completely untroubled.

'It's so ominous, such silence,' she said, hoping to prod Merewald in the right direction.

'Oh, that,' smiled Merewald, and made his familiar gesture, passing his fingers over his forehead to give a quick click up in the air where they rested momentarily before returning to their customary position: thumbs in belt, first and second fingers drumming on his stomach, his usual stance when inspecting his plants.

'You mean the birdsong,' he said, relieved to grasp what she meant.

Hild looked around, to spot a bird and catch its song.

'I don't know. Is that what's wrong?' she asked doubtfully.

'A week before the dog days, they stopped their summer song. Isn't that what you're talking about?'

'Oh,' she said, and continued to look around until she caught sight of a starling and then a sparrow and then two great titmice. She couldn't have been more disappointed had he told her they were dead, each and every one. If only that was all!

'Is it over then? The summer?'

He nodded, and pointed at a flight of swallows winging its way over the meadow.

'They've already started gathering,' he said.

'Ah,' she sighed, 'it doesn't usually end so early.'

It was as if the whole summer had just slipped by, without her really noticing it. She had been so worried about her husband's enterprise, but if things were taking their normal course, then it wasn't necessarily a bad omen.

'You know,' he smiled, in an attempt to take the edge off her grief, 'it's actually the same every year. But they'll be back.'

'Yes, yes,' she said, 'no doubt they will.'

And she shuffled from foot to foot.

'If our god so desires,' she added, just for the sake of saying something. She didn't want to voice her anxiety, for fear of giving it substance.

'He usually does,' said Merewald. 'After all, it's his own scheme he's following.'

'So it is,' said Hild emphatically, and there was some comfort in being told this once again.

There was a whizzing, slightly hoarse sound from the lime tree, and they saw a flycatcher hurl itself into the air and catch a cabbage-white butterfly, whereupon it immediately returned to its lookout on the outmost low branch.

'But look, they're still here,' said Merewald. 'It's just the singing they've finished with.'

'Yes,' said Hild, 'but do you know why they stop?'

'Well,' said Merewald, 'there's not much left to be joyful about, now that it gets light later and dark earlier.'

'That's true,' said Hild, thinking how early they already had to have torches indoors if they wanted to work.

'Perhaps they're running out of food as well?' she offered.

'No, they've got plenty,' said Merewald, 'but maybe so much they don't really appreciate it.'

'That's probably what's wrong,' nodded Hild, and looked up at the birds with disapproval. 'And then they forget to say thank you.'

'Yes,' said Merewald. 'Birds, they soon forget winter cold and hunger. And then they think life's nothing but sunshine and cabbage-whites.'

They watched two blackbirds fighting over an earthworm, the battle ending with them tearing the worm in two. The flight of swallows returned, sweeping over the meadow.

'Do you know where they're flying to?' asked Hild.

'Gaul, I think,' answered Merewald. 'Because I've heard there aren't any left in Kent during the winter.'

'Did Ermenburh tell you that?'

'Yes,' beamed Merewald, 'and soon we'll be married.'

'Marriage is a good thing,' said Hild. 'And without it the lineage would quickly die out.'

'Really?' said Merewald, and gave a little laugh. 'The plants survive all right. And the birds.'

'But they're not human,' said Hild, 'and I dare say they have their own way of getting married.'

It surprised her that this big scraggy man of a Merewald thought about such matters. She simply couldn't imagine him in a matrimonial bed, but on this very topic there was just no telling, with anyone, she mused.

'It's not true about Gaul, though,' she continued, 'because my sister has written to me that the swallows desert them too. They fly south. I've wondered if perhaps they pay a visit to the Holy Land.'

'A sort of pilgrimage?' asked Merewald with interest.

'Yes, of sorts.'

Merewald's gaze followed the swallows, enchanted.

'I've always thought there was something special about them,' he smiled. 'They're so happy in the air. You can't help but think of the Holy Spirit.'

'That's true,' said Hild.

She had never thought of the Holy Spirit in this context. Talking with Merewald was just so inspiring, you came away with so many new ideas.

# OSWALD'S HEAD

*– Eadfrid finds peace in the grave –*

Penda was following a plan to which no one was privy. He marched quickly up through Deira and forbade looting.

He encountered Oswald's men near Cetreht; he routed them, let them go and followed them. He then laid siege to Oswald at Bebbanburh, and when Oswald made a sortie Penda took flight, to the great displeasure of his men who were ready and eager for battle. He continued to retreat—slowly enough for Oswald to keep up and yet quickly enough to prevent him doing much serious looting—down through Deira, Elmet, Mercia and west towards Walas.

Penda had laid his plans so carefully that the army from Gwynedd didn't have to wait for more than four days before Oswald and his men arrived—and then Penda struck.

Of course, there would have been greater honour in defeating Oswald without the Gwynedd men's ambush. However, Penda wanted to make quite sure this time, not just in killing Oswald, but in wiping out his army, which would then give him a breathing space before Northumbria once again became really dangerous.

Early in the weed-month, news reached Tamoworthig that Penda had been victorious: he had slain Oswald.

Hild was quite giddy with happiness. The cheering was ear-splitting and endless as Penda rode into the courtyard at the head of his warriors and the long heavily-laden train of carts.

She bade her husband and his men welcome home as was seemly, even though she was so hoarse she could barely speak.

As was customary, the best pieces were laid out on tables in the hall, so that everyone could enjoy the sight before the king rewarded his men. They had brought back a most wondrous booty, every item taken from those who had been slain.

Hild walked around admiring swords and spears, chain mail and shields, bridles and harnesses, cooking utensils and a large quantity of jewellery and costly clothing. Despite the season, there was quite a lot of good quality imported fur, merely in need of a clean to remove the rust-brown battle stains.

There was also a beautiful helmet, kingly and protective, which she hoped Penda would keep for himself. Every other second she paused and thanked the Lord for returning Penda to her, and for giving Eadfrid peace in his grave.

'You haven't seen the best yet,' said Penda, embracing his wife, his eyes sparkling.

The thanksgiving festivities had been under preparation since word of victory had arrived. A very fine bard had come from Gwynedd, and it was hoped he would have completed a new song in time for the celebrations, so the victory could be recalled in a fitting manner.

Hild dressed in her best clothes: a new bright-red silk gown with narrow white ermine edging; at her breast she wore the big round gold brooch with red and blue inlaid stones, a gift from Penda after his last expedition. He had noticed her lingering near this fine piece and he'd hidden it away until her baptism day, a brooch wrought for her alone, and oh, how it sparkled.

She put on an orange-red silk cap, nearly the same colour as her hair, with twisting gold embroidery, lighter in tone than the fabric, and three large garnets sewn onto the back. Finally, a pair of new red kidskin ankle-boots, dyed to match the dress and lined with young lambskin.

She was usually active in the preparations for such festivities, arranging a little here, rearranging something there. Mostly she dealt with which hangings should be used to deck the hall; they had to suit the occasion and complement one another. For this particular evening, the colour scheme she had in mind started with black, moving on through brown to deep oxblood, scarlet, orange, and concluding with a potent corn yellow outside the entrance to their private chamber.

When she was ready to go into the hall, she found the chamber servant blocking the doorway: his lord's express desire was that she should first make her appearance when everyone was seated; the fact being, there was a surprise for her. She could hear laughing and giggling; they were in high spirits, exhilarated.

She gave instructions as to how she wished the hangings arranged, and then withdrew. To pass the time while waiting, she went outside to see to her peacocks. She'd grown fond of them, and always took something for them to eat, wheat bread being their favourite.

The male was sitting in a tall ash tree, screeching, and fluttered to the ground as soon as he saw her. He stood at an appropriate distance, gabbling until the bread appeared. The female came running; she was not as impressive as the male and, as usual, didn't get to share the delicious titbit.

Hild was told she could now come in: everyone was seated at table. There was still the wound-up atmosphere that always followed a successful expedition, and the king's distribution of gifts was eagerly anticipated.

She wasn't allowed to enter by her usual route, through her chamber, but, with meaningful looks, she was led around the outside of the hall and up to the grand main door—as the king had specifically requested. She was escorted by the guild master from Peaclond and a young prince of the Magonsætan; the door opened and, as they stepped through it, the horns sounded.

Hild was confused by this great mark of respect; after all, the warriors were the ones who should be celebrated, not her, she had just sat waiting. Twiddling her thumbs, as Eadfrid had always said, while the men fought for her honour. This time more than her honour had been at stake, because if Penda hadn't been victorious, then the whole of Mercia would have been overrun.

The hall was decked just as she had wanted: it was a magnificent sight. An ox and a couple of lambs fizzed and spat over the central fire; the hall was filled with flaming torches, the delights on the table sparkling at one another in the glow. Following old custom, the men were still dressed and equipped as they had been in battle, and they hadn't yet washed. Wounds, however, had been bandaged, something Hild had instituted; some had to participate lying down. The expedition would only be considered finished once the booty had been distributed.

Penda stood up and came to meet her. He reached out his hand and led Hild to the long table at the far end of the hall. The plunder completely covered all the tables, but she spotted something tall and red at her place; as she drew closer, she could see it was some sort of tent, sewn of the finest flax, trimmed with a darker red.

Penda was bursting with pride and flung out his right arm, rather too quickly for the slight wound he had received on the upper part, and he winced.

'This is for you,' he said thickly, in an emotional voice she hadn't heard for many years.

'Thank you,' she said, giving him a little bow. 'How very fine it is.'

'There's something underneath,' he whispered, making a careful gesture.

He wanted her to examine her gift, although it was really quite enough in itself—a noble little tent exactly like their own, just right for use in the field, hung on poles and with overlapping front flaps.

She loosened one of the flaps and lifted it. She could see something black: black hair. She loosened the other flap and looked again: more black hair. Perhaps it was for her loom, horsetail or the mane from one of the worthiest horses in the battle—she used all sorts for her weaving—and then she spotted a large gold ring.

Everyone followed her movements, everyone was in just as much suspense as she was, their eyes popping out of their heads. Her heart leapt at the thought that perhaps it was hair from Oswald's horse, and her mind raced to think how best she could use it.

'You can lift it off,' whispered Penda.

Using both hands, she took hold of the poles at the top and lifted.

The crowd in the hall let out a gasp, as did Hild. She crushed the red tent to her chest, crumpled and crushed and scrunched it, forgetting it was a little work of art; one of the struts snapped.

'Oswald!' she whispered.

Penda quivered at the sight of his wife's great emotion. His face flushed, his eyes flashed, he nodded in acknowledgement to the guild master from Peaclond who, smiling, nodded back.

'Turn it round so the others can see,' he murmured to his wife, and she carefully turned the silver platter until all she could see was the splendid mane of black hair. She closed her eyes for a moment and swallowed, came over a little faint, and felt her husband's unscathed arm around her shoulders, a firm and secure grip.

He signalled the throng to step closer and inspect the trophy.

'See how pale he is!'

'He didn't even have time to close his eyes.'

'Probably too busy praying to his god.'

'Well, that's put a stop to his havoc!'

'He's always been a bit pasty-looking, hasn't he?'

'I can't see!'

'Neither can we. Can't you move, up there at the front?'

Hild hadn't taken her eyes off that most hated head, hated above all else, hated even more than the Evil One himself. She stepped forward, dropped her red gift and grasped the head, a firm grip under the back of the jaws, and lifted it up. The large gold ring, which had been lying on the hair, rolled off and fell to the floor, to be picked up by one of the men at the front, who made haste to put it back on the table.

Oswald's long black hair, his pride and adornment, which many had, with good reason, envied, tumbled down over Hild's arms, covering them to her elbows. The people gazed at the victory trophy in dumbfounded concentration. She held it aloft and turned it in all directions for as long as her arms could bear; it was strangely heavy, and when she put it back on the silver platter she noticed that there was hardly any blood.

The king's sons Bothelm and Gefmund walked proudly around the hall. It had been their first proper expedition. Bothelm, the sixteen-year-old, had previously taken part in a minor skirmish, but this time he had been in the thick of the fighting, whereas Gefmund had been positioned much too far back. Nevertheless, it was Gefmund who had been wounded, not seriously, but still a quite legitimate flesh wound from an arrow in his arm.

Bothelm couldn't make a similar boast. He'd been so tightly surrounded by his personal troop that he hadn't even been able to use his new sword. He stole envious glances at his brother's bandage and promised himself that next time he'd show them all right.

'Where's the body?' asked Hild once they had retired for the night.

'Didn't you see it? Hanging in the yard. Did you really not see it?'

'I think I'd like to give Oswald's head to Bishop Aidan on Lindisfarena. If you don't mind me giving your gift away, that is.'

'Do as you please,' said Penda. 'Oswald's head is yours.'

'Will you give me his body too?'

Penda hesitated. The corpse of a man like Oswald was not something you gave away just like that. His kin would give a lot to have it returned, and Penda was not at all keen to miss out on the glory of having it hanging here. He wasn't sure.

'An arm, perhaps?'

His wife was not easily put off when she had set her mind on something. He had a heavy head from all the fine mead and the lingering smoke that hadn't been drawn out into the still night air.

'Yes, yes, take an arm then,' he said, pulling her into his side.

'Now Eadfrid will find peace in the grave,' she whispered. 'Thank you, Penda, thank you!'

When she finally fell asleep, she slept soundly and undisturbed, which she hadn't done since Edwin's time, in the good old days.

Next morning, she went out to the courtyard with a sense of immeasurable peace and feeling utterly refreshed. In her hurry last night, she hadn't noticed anything at all.

Now she saw it: tall stakes, not the usual poles used for sacrifice, but thinner and taller stakes holding up parts of the enemy king's body. Arms each on their stake, legs on two others, and the torso hung in triumph on the gable of the hall building. The male parts had been cut off and fixed alongside the torso—they weren't much to look at and Hild smiled at the paltry little things.

Not only had he been slain, Oswald, he had also been destroyed, finished, and never would his power return. His limbs looked so pitiful hanging there, severed from life and severed from their body. A pale pair of legs and a hairy pair of arms; they could have belonged to anyone.

While Hild was preparing to travel, she had the head and an arm placed in a herbal extract to keep them fresh and protect them from the ravages of time. The day before she was due to leave, Penda decided she could actually take it all with her as he no longer derived any personal satisfaction from the trophy—they could have it back in Bernicia.

Very little remained to reveal the repute and rank of the royal limbs; the skin had been flayed patchily right into the bone, and the odour wasn't pleasant. Some very large ravens had visited; maybe Woden's own Hugin and Munin had pecked out their share. What was left wasn't really of any use; Hild had it packed in a box crammed with bracken, so they could transport it without any great inconvenience.

This plan was, however, thwarted by the pagan priest; just before Hild was due to depart, he rushed in and told them about a dream he'd had. Hild barely listened, nor did she make a fuss or mention breach of promise or anything like that—such issues could not be discussed with Penda: an omen was an omen, and that was that. Any suggestion that the pagan priest might be following his own agenda in the advice he gave the king was met with a blank stare. Penda simply could not imagine anything coming between himself and the divine signs—a belief with which Hild could not come to terms.

She wasn't exactly enthusiastic about his offerings to Woden; but at least she had been familiar with the practice since childhood, and it seemed natural. She knew it was wrong and pernicious, because she had been instructed in the matter and had seen the error of their ways, thanks to the teaching of Paulinus and later Aidan—and Sigebert. However, if the Lord hadn't been born in Jesus Christ and his glad tidings spread among people, then the people wouldn't have known, of that she was sure. Because the old people found it natural to make these sacrifices, just as natural as delighting in their grandchildren, and wishing them the best, the very best.

It was simply wrong to make offerings, of that she was certain. Something wasn't right just because it was natural, as Penda thought—no, they could never agree on that.

Theft, for example, was something she could understand, even though it was a dishonourable act. It was, nonetheless, natural when a poor person was hungry and a rich person had plenty, and the poor one took from the rich one, and the rich man defended his property and killed the thief. It was all natural, but that didn't make it right.

Adultery, too: natural and understandable—after a few years, at least—but still undeniably wrong.

She had recently been discussing these issues at length and somewhat stridently with Penda, because he was now considering marriage with one of the West Saxon princesses—on condition the king down there would marry his sister.

Hild was perfectly aware that concluding peace with the West Saxons was a matter of urgency. Oswald, as godfather and son-in-law to King Cynegils, had sent for help while marching southwards to fight Penda—and had got it. Unfortunately, Cynegils had then fallen in the battle. The men from Gwynedd had been uncontrollable; many of them had gone into a frenzy, and Penda hadn't been able to stop the fighting.

With the neighbours both to the south and to the north intent on revenge, the outlook was bleak for Mercia. Hild was the first to see the political necessity, and she also knew that even one of the king's sons wouldn't be sufficient to secure peace with Cynegils' son.

Penda's sister was totally accommodating. Her husband had fallen in an earlier battle against Oswald, she owned much land, and she was—albeit her childbearing days were over—an advantageous match for the young king. She had good political insight and was famed for her embroidery; she would happily be the peace-weaver, and she had the aptitude for the task. Hostages would be exchanged, too, possibly one of the princes, just to be sure.

Hild was against the plan, even though her arguments were weak: all she could say was that it was an insult to their marriage, not legally, but morally.

Penda insisted it was for the sake of the whole realm, and also for her sake, and that of course he would continue to sleep with Hild. He wouldn't spend much more than the wedding night in bed with his new bride; young girls like her weren't to his taste, he insisted, but needs must. The pagan priest had received favourable auguries about the plan; if they didn't carry it through, then Hild could pack her belongings and head off for East Anglia—because Mercia would very quickly be ravaged, and she wouldn't be spared either.

The royal couple did not, therefore, have a particularly tender or moving farewell. Hild wept a little once she had left, but she soon stopped: destiny could not be changed.

She wept again later—when they rode up through Deira and she saw her home region. Deira's gentle hills were just visible from the giant's road running up through the middle of the country. Having passed the road leading to Eoforwik, looking eastwards she could see Deira's scrub-clad upland, at the southern foot of which she had given birth to her twins, cherished above all else. She still pictured her silky-soft boys as prattling infants with wide eyes, even though she knew they were nine years old, like Peada, and could undoubtedly ride and shoot and read. If, that is, they were being fostered by decent Christian folk. Otherwise—and the painful recurring thought entered her mind—they might now be tending swine somewhere, bow-legged and hollow-chested from undernourishment. Most of the time she was able to think of them as princes of a sort, living in the best circumstances.

Travelling northward through Deira, she started looking out for boys their age. A couple of times, she thought she saw lads who could well have been the twins, but when she reined in her horse and questioned them about their background, she quickly realized they were not of her people—as soon as they opened their mouths and spoke.

She also saw boys who made her realize that if this was the kind of life her sons were leading, then she would prefer they were dead, rather than covered in scabs and rashes from the lice, emaciated and dull-eyed, hands outstretched, hungry begging faces. Her sons were born to freedom, not to the yoke of bondage; their father had said as much, and that was non-negotiable.

She had sent word in advance and had been granted safe passage by Oswald's brother, Oswy, who was as good as king in Bernicia. His men met her at the border and accompanied her up to Bebbanburh, the last stop on their journey to Lindisfarena. The weather was clear when they arrived, and they could just glimpse Aidan's monastic island to the north. They could see the rocky Farne islands, where the monks occasionally withdrew in order to be closer to their god.

Oswy received her with honour. He had the same raven-black hair as his brother, but none of his brother's beauty: there was something wrong with the proportions of his face, and his voice had a jarringly metallic edge. She felt an instantaneous aversion to him.

Next she greeted Cyneburh, Oswald's widow. She was now twenty years old, and they hadn't seen one another since Hild was witness at her wedding. In the meantime, Cyneburh had given birth to two daughters and a son, Ædelwald; a second son had died shortly after birth.

The two women embraced, and Cyneburh thanked Hild for bringing a small portion of her husband's mortal remains back to where they belonged. She and Oswy and Aidan had discussed the matter and agreed that the arm should by rights remain at Bebbanburh, whence it had wielded its power, and the head should be interred in the monastery that had been the subject of his love and his thoughts.

After the evening meal, with all its ceremonial courtesies, the two women withdrew to talk in private; as soon as they had closed the door, Cyneburh wept.

'I told him so many times,' she said. 'They who live by the sword will die by the sword. It is written thus, I told him.'

'And what did he say to that?' Hild enquired, with compassion in her voice.

'He asked how I thought King David would have got by if he hadn't known how to use a sword. He also said that I read the wrong passages in the scriptures. He could always find a section saying the opposite. And he said the only language heathens understand is that of the sword!'

'I saw many churches and wooden holy crosses along our route,' said Hild, 'so he did make some headway.'

Cyneburh walked across to the door and peeped out, but no one was listening. She leant close and whispered to Hild: 'You should see how many sacrificial offerings have been made since he fell. And before, too, but very secretively. I have my own sources. My husband had idolaters hung by the neck—you know that, don't you?'

Hild nodded. Mercia had received quite a few refugees because of that particular policy, and not just the lowest of the low either. Penda had been well pleased—also in having his contempt for the modern hypocrites, as he called them, corroborated.

'That's not the way to usher in the kingdom of Christ,' Cyneburh exclaimed with sudden vehemence. 'That way leads to the kingdom of Satan!'

'I don't know,' said Hild, 'but the new ideas do indeed destroy a good deal. Even though our god is the life and the truth. And worshipping the pagan gods is wrong—as well you know!'

'They're crazy, all of them,' Cyneburh mumbled, shaking her head. 'All they can think about is war and plunder and rape. Call it what they will!'

She stared gloomily into the distance.

'I was widowed at twenty-one,' said Hild after a while. 'And my twins, my sons, they were sent to be brought up in Deira. With Cædwalla. And now I don't know where they are.'

'How old are they?' Cyneburh asked.

'Nine. And they weren't even one year old when they were sent away. I'm certain Oswald knew their whereabouts.'

'I don't think so,' said Cyneburh with conviction.

'He didn't tell you everything, did he?'

'No, but there were some things he always told me. And if he'd known the location of a rival for the throne, then he would have . . . yes, I'm sure he would.'

'Got rid of that rival?'

'Indeed. Even a babe in arms. Girls, too. I'm sure—and he would have told me about it.'

'The children of my husband's brother? Osfrid's children?'

'That was Oswald, yes.'

'Even though their mother fled all the way to Gaul with them?'

Cyneburh nodded.

'You see, my husband was a very cautious man.'

'Yes, and unfortunately mine wasn't!' Hild exclaimed bitterly.

'He was a little foolhardy,' Cyneburh suggested. 'Or was he just naïve?'

'Well, he was certainly no villain!' Hild shouted wildly, rising swiftly from the stool. 'Not the type who ambush people and string them up in trees!'

Cyneburh looked at her sympathetically.

'No, of course not, I know he wasn't.'

And then all at once she realized what Hild had meant.

'No!' she cried in astonishment. 'You don't believe Oswald murdered Eadfrid, do you?'

'Who else?' asked Hild grimly.

'Yes, who else?' said Cyneburh in a calmer voice. 'There aren't that many possibilities.'

'There are no other possibilities—just Oswald!'

'More than enough, as far as I can see,' said Cyneburh, a little surprised. 'And Oswald—he would have told me. Once we had retired for the night. If you understand . . . it was always there that he disclosed such matters. I've heard a great deal—a very great deal.'

'You didn't know him back then,' Hild persisted.

'He told me about things that happened much further back,' said Cyneburh. 'He couldn't carry those memories alone. From time to time he would tell me something that I thought he must be making up. Just to shock me. And then he wanted us to pray for the souls of the dead! It was, of course, just a pretext to . . . well, it's over and done with now.'

She fell into a reverie.

'But Eadfrid—no, he never mentioned him, not with a single word! And he certainly wouldn't have wasted a chance.'

Hild felt nauseous. She walked to the window and pulled aside the shutters; the fresh night air helped her breathing.

She didn't doubt Cyneburh's sincerity, but everything else had become dark and swampy, like bog water.

# LARK SONG

*– back to Frig's Seat –*

Word of Oswald's death was received with jubilation in Deira. All the larger towns—Eoforwik, Mædeltun and Cetreht—celebrated for three days and three nights. The old sacrificial stakes, which had been stowed away in lofts, hidden under straw and dilapidated furnishings, were restored to favour. A few days after the joyful news became common knowledge, Deira's horse population had been reduced by approximately one tenth.

The chief men, those who adhered to the old faith and had sought refuge in Mercia, now returned and ousted Oswald's toadies from their farms, although most had already fled in great haste. Hatred of Oswald, and of Ædelfred's family, who had no business in Deira but belonged by rights in Bernicia, was vast. People who had been friends with Oswald and his kin also had a rough time. This hatred had not only been provoked by his zealous persecution of those who stuck with the old ways, but equally by the heavy-handed way in which he executed his royal power.

For a trading nation such as Deira, it seemed totally unreasonable that they had to pay tax on every single shipload of goods brought home to the kingdom at risk of life and limb. Interference on that scale was neither natural nor of benefit to the commercial enterprise underpinning the prosperity of the kingdom. That's how they saw it.

News that Oswald's brother Oswy was after the throne met with outrage, and to such an extent that Oswy's advisers warned him to stay away from Eoforwik, as a precaution.

Having returned home, the chief men of Deira recommended submission to protection by Mercia; then they would be able to trade unimpeded across the entirety of this large and affluent territory and only have to pay a modest tax to Penda. His wife Hildeburh was cited as justification for the choice; her husband would have been king, had he not met with a nefarious death on his way to the throne. What had previously been whispered was now spoken aloud: Oswald had put Eadfrid to death. It was thus only fair that Eadfrid's widow now became queen.

King Penda was the sole alternative to Ædelfred's lineage. The worthy arguments were completely superfluous as not a single voice ventured to advocate Oswy's candidature, and Penda was elected without any contest.

Hild stayed away for longer than she had planned. She accompanied Aidan on his mission, visiting small settlements where he preached, baptized, heard confessions, administered Holy Communion and exorcized spirits.

At first, however, she found it physically arduous. She wasn't used to walking, to sleeping wherever they found hospitality, and to the simple food. Every evening her maid had to comb the lice from her scalp or try to find the fleas hiding in the seams and fur trim on her clothing. When night fell and they were far from any inhabited settlement, they would pitch little tents in which they slept on rugs on the ground—nothing like Penda's roomy and comfortable tent.

Hild felt a deep sense of satisfaction. Every day spent with Aidan was full of small pleasures, and she could put all thoughts of what was going on back home out of her mind. The simplicity of Aidan's way of life appealed to her; the plain and humble fare did her good, and after the first couple of days, when she had missed the rich and juicy roast meat from Penda's hall, her body felt sprightlier.

They woke, drank water, relieved themselves, washed, ate and slept, following such a regular pattern it was as if they had brought along a sundial. Aidan seemed to have one built in; he didn't need to look at the sun to judge the hour, and the three daily prayer times were always observed. The eternal and unceasing hymn of thanksgiving to the Lord could not be stopped by bad weather, good hospitality, negotiation of marshy terrain. When the hour came, he drew to a halt and led the singing and prayer, and thus you were always united with the brethren in the monastery, wherever you might be, said Aidan, and with the brothers and sisters in the whole of Christendom. He told Hild there was nothing wrong with praying alone but, whatever the circumstances, you still had to observe the daily times of prayer. This was not simply because by doing so you helped intensify the overall stream of thanksgiving to the Lord, but also because being part of the entire community of Christendom gave you strength. By training in regular prayer, she would soon experience what Jesus had revealed: in him, all people here on earth are united.

'No family is an island,' Aidan said. 'We are all created for one another, regardless of birth, sex, language, wealth, honour and health. Even the leper and the slave are the Lord's children. Everything is created by him, beautiful and in its season. Even the wolf is of his creation, so we know to beware the Devil.'

They had been on a northward trip, up to the Tuidi river. Now they were embarking on a new journey. Hild had wanted to revisit Ad Gefrin, her childhood paradise, climb up to the high hilltops and look out across the country. Above all, she looked forward to Frig's Seat—to sit down and close her eyes.

Aidan had no objection to walking to Ad Gefrin. He didn't follow a fixed itinerary; he spoke with the people he met and stayed as long as he thought best. Even if he came across a group of children or swineherds, he might well start telling them about the bliss of Heaven and Jesus's heroic death on the cross. He would continue on his mission from place to place while Hild visited Ad Gefrin.

'When will the end of time arrive?' Hild asked.

'You ask as a child would ask,' Aidan smiled and patted her cheek. 'Are you not aware that a man or woman comprehends nothing, neither of the first nor of the last.'

He quoted Ecclesiastes, which she now knew by heart, but which always took on a new and weightier meaning when recited in Aidan's deep voice.

'. . . then I looked at all the work of God, and realized that man cannot fathom all that is done under the sun: because however much a man labours to seek it out, he shall not find it . . . We just don't know, dear Hild, and if you meet a man who says he knows, then shun him like the Devil, for he is the Devil's man. Are you concerned about the days of your own lifetime? Then remember the words of the Preacher: Behold, what I have seen to be good and to be appropriate is for a person to eat and to drink, and to enjoy good in all his labour under the sun, all the days of his life which God has given him: for this is his portion. And every time God has given a man riches and wealth, and has given him power to use of it, and to take his portion, and to rejoice in his labour, this is the gift of God. For he shall not much think on the days of his life, because God answers him in the joy of his heart.'

Aidan instructed Hild in these matters as they walked along the narrow sand causeway linking the holy island with the mainland at ebb tide. First they had to cross a little bridge, which had been built on Oswald's orders. Eider seaducks swam in the water, while oystercatchers gathered food from the drying mud. The eiders were the blessing of the Lord upon the place; the monks plucked them and filled pillows with the soft feathers and down, which they then sold and thus had more to give to the poor folk. The monks didn't use such a luxury item themselves, but were happy for the guests to use them. Hild slept wonderfully well with one of these down pads under her head; she decided to buy a few and take them home, both for guests and for her bed with Penda.

'The Lord created the world,' said Aidan, 'and Jesus has taught us what to do. He has opened our eyes and shown us the difference between the evil and the good. Before him, no one could see the difference. People lived like the beasts, who only gather food for their own family and frighten off any strangers.'

'At least they looked after their kin,' said Hild, 'and that's happening less and less today.'

'And stole from everyone else,' said Aidan. 'Conquest, they call it. And anyone who didn't belong to the family was sent away.'

'Yes,' said Hild, 'that's no different now.'

'They could lie down and die outside the gate without anyone being in the least concerned!'

'Indeed,' said Hild, 'but not all pagans are like that.'

'Not if it's a festival day or the husband thinks he's received some kind of sign! But, as a rule, that's what happens when people turn up and can't really account for themselves.'

'They're always thieves,' said Hild, 'and runaway slaves! If slaves could just up and go and seek better shelter, there would soon be chaos. You surely don't mean we should give protection to thieves and runaway slaves and all sorts of drifters.'

'Yes,' Aidan insisted, 'I do mean that, actually. I think they should be forgiven, so they can make a fresh start. Jesus, too, was a drifter, don't forget.'

'But not a criminal!' Hild objected.

'According to the law of the land, he was exactly that. He was executed, because he insulted the god of the Jews. He knew blasphemy was punishable by death. Yes, indeed he was a criminal.'

'But not in *our* sense,' said Hild, 'and he certainly wasn't a runaway slave.'

'To him, runaway slaves were as good as anybody else,' said Aidan, 'and that is how we should see them. As soon as I get the king's permission, I shall welcome anyone on Lindisfarena—irrespective of what they might have done!'

It was a pleasant day, with a light breeze, more cloudy than sunny. Hild pulled her headdress right down across her forehead to protect her skin, fearing her face already looked like a slave's now that it had been exposed to so much sun and wind. They didn't have mirrors on Lindisfarena, neither the nuns nor the monks, but she hoped she could regain her whiteness before she got home.

She looked across at Aidan. His face had a slave's furrows and was weather-beaten, but he didn't have the wretchedness of a slave scratched into his features, no grief and greed. He was the most handsome man she had ever seen: gentler than Sigebert, more dignified and calmer in his movements than Penda. Her heart flinched when she thought about her husband; she would rather not think about him at all, and tried to concentrate on all the wonderful things Aidan could tell her.

They walked up across the terrain and reached the first ridge, where most of the monastery's beehives were arranged in long rows. They rested here awhile, looking out across the water and the tidal island. When they walked forth, it would be long before they could see home again, as the other monks said—but not Aidan, the whole world was his home.

Frig's Seat.

She spotted it in the clearing and ran, stood in front of it, and looked: bird droppings and a little moss, new trees growing around it, putting the seat in half-shade. She smiled at the thought of birds enjoying the large rock, so it wasn't just left standing there, to no purpose. She brushed the biggest droppings away and sat on the stone, settling herself on the seat as best she could—it was no longer so large, and her backside was no longer so little.

Hild closed her eyes. The rock felt warm against her body; it wasn't comfortable anymore, but promised endless security when she leant back. She could hear Hereswid's voice authoritatively commanding: 'Right, now Osfrid is Ingeld, and Hild is the Danes' leader, and Eadfrid is Freawaru, and then I'm the Hadubards' oldest warrior . . . '

A game—playing and training. Sometimes Ingeld had chosen to take the arm of his devoted wife; sometimes he had chosen to go to war with her people. Whatever he chose was wrong and caused many tears and much bloodshed.

That's what made the story so good, and why it could be played over and over again: always new complications. Hereswid had been an expert when it came to finding new points of dispute; now she had resolved them for herself by becoming the Lord's handmaiden.

For Hild, however, life was still one big chaos and she was increasingly unsure as to what was true and what wasn't. Even the more basic issues—the path of the sun and the moon around the earth, for example, or the origins of the winds, the germination of seeds in the soil, how the water withdrew from the shore and then came back again, why elephants existed, and what was the point of Eostre's lilies—over the years, all such matters had become ever more mysterious to her mind. And what about her own life: she ought to be contented, now that Eadfrid had been avenged, but Oswald's head hadn't been the deliverance it had initially promised to be—she was glad she'd given it away, and yet she felt as if Oswald's blood clung to her.

How odd—there had been so little blood.

Her intellect told her that she had done the right thing, because what was a person anyway if they didn't safeguard their family and remembrance of the dead? If they weren't bound by the ties of duty and love, but simply let their loved ones be slain with no form for retribution? No, then the human community would disintegrate and people would be no different from the fish that eat their own fry. Just infinitely more wicked.

All this she knew but couldn't feel. She wished—however unnatural it might be—that Oswald's head was still attached to his ugly neck, and that he was still at large, tormenting the life out of people.

A preposterous thought, and so she abandoned it; there was no solution to that particular problem. She longed for the childhood version: the fallen only dead until mealtime, when the next game would turn out differently and they could all race homewards together, moments after being mortal enemies.

Something had broken, not just in her but in the kingdom and the whole land. Perhaps the old folk sitting in Edwin's hall of an evening were right when they said the mistake had been in leaving Angeln, the fair country they never tired of praising—even though no one had ever seen it. Tales of the loveliness of the country had been told them by their grandparents, who had in turn heard about it from *their* grandparents. Stayed put on Angeln and stuck to the old gods, that's what they should have done! The latter point was made loudly during Hild's childhood; after Edwin's baptism it was just whispered, or mumbled during a hefty bout of intoxication, and next day—when Paulinus came asking—no one had any recollection whatsoever of anyone at all mocking the new god.

Perhaps they had been right, even though it was blasphemy. Blood was thicker than water, as everyone had always known, but looking at her life you'd think she was a sparrow rather than a human being—just see how she'd taken care of Hereric's and Breguswid's kin . . . the twins, their soft little prattling mouths, strong fingers and watchful eyes, their sweet baby fragrance . . .

For a while she had hated Eadfrid for the loss of the infants; for a while she had hated Oswald and all Ædelfred's family for her loss; and then for a long, very long time she had hated herself for her weakness—that she hadn't stood up to her husband, but had simply given in to his demand in order to be left in peace and to save her own skin.

Now there was just grief, nothing but a dark well of grief. She could no longer picture them, and for the first time she had begun to doubt if they were even alive, but she couldn't imagine them dead. To her they lived in a shadowy actuality, an existence beyond the visible world, motionless, mute and desolate.

She hadn't even been able to track down her own brother; she had tried everything, but hadn't unearthed one single trace of him. It was as if he had never existed, and even Hereswid believed he was dead.

But she knew he was alive. She had his wooden horse, and a singlet that Breguswid had kept. Her relics. And she had a tiny thin lock of intertwined hair taken from Hundfrid and Wilbrord. That was all.

No, in Hild blood wasn't thicker than water. In her, life-juice was the thickest, the life-juice that seeped out of her when she looked at Penda, her husband, and she no longer knew if she hated him or loved him.

The thought of another woman embracing him and welcoming him in her bed—it left her cold—made her feel nothing, nothing except it was an impossibility, almost physically impossible, and cancelled out all the years of happiness they had shared.

Bodily intimacy, her unreserved devotion to him, winking at him across the supper table and finding him hidden under the bedcover.

To stand in wait behind the wall hangings in the bedchamber and then leap out when he was searching through the bedcovers in the chest, to jump on him, tumble him onto the bed and pull off his hose before he knew what was happening.

To walk past him with the swaying of her hips that made him drop whatever he was doing and instinctively follow her to the chamber.

To feel every seam come apart when he stood looking at her in that particular way, making her just want to lie down on the spot, part her thighs and invite him in.

Never again.

Eadwacer—that's what she'd called him for fun when his greed for gold and pastures new became too much for her to bear. And he was Eadwacer now: no longer her roe, her young hart on the mountains of Bether, but an administrator of riches, a watcher of wealth, a coveter of gold, who would happily sell their love for political profit. *That* wasn't Penda—that was Eadwacer, and now he was living up to the name.

She stood up abruptly; it was too painful to sit thinking about Penda, or Eadwacer, or whoever he was. Her husband—she would give her right arm for him, her every possession, her very life if need be—but she no longer knew who he was; he was evasive, couldn't be pinned down or defined, she would never get wise to him. And yet they were one flesh.

Aidan had taught her that it was wrong, downright reprehensible, to exact vengeance through death. 'Revenge,' he had said, 'is not the business of men. It is a matter for the Lord alone.'

Paulinus had said the same, and she had bowed her head to escape further reprimand. She knew in her heart this only applied to people like Aidan and Paulinus: they had parted from their earthly family and sworn fidelity to the Lord God, and then the Lord would take on the responsibility of avenging every wrong done to his subordinates. It didn't apply to people like her, however, because she hadn't renounced her kin and commended herself to the service of the Lord God; *she* would have to protect her family.

Hild walked across to the beck and bent down to watch the water flow by, quietly and sluggishly. She couldn't see any caddisfly larvae, but remembered that the larvae only appeared in the spring. Maybe they were actually still there, just not now; maybe they were there and weren't there—simultaneously. Impossible, but perhaps that's how it was.

She drank from the beck and then set out on the trek: she would walk all the way up the Hill of the Goats and look out across the dale, her childhood realm. The track on this side was overgrown, although the trees were still scattered and small, so it shouldn't be too hard to pass through—but it was an uphill climb, steeply uphill.

Looking through the trees, she could see the bare summit surrounded by the solid stone wall. The soldiers had been on the lookout up there; Edwin's men, those with the sharpest vision—their hawk's eyes had also caught sight of Hild and her sister playing their springtime game. The sentries had reported back, and Paulinus had taken the matter very seriously. Or maybe she and Hereswid had just chattered too loudly about Frig's Seat, because one day Paulinus had ordered them to take him there so he could exorcize the evil spirit; and he had forced them to promise they would never visit that place again and never speak Frig's name again—otherwise he would have to cease his teaching.

Hild had simply stared at Hereswid, trusting her sister to find a way out of their predicament, because personally she couldn't see one at all. Hereswid had agreed to guide Paulinus—wearing Mass vestments, carrying holy water under one arm and his precious holy cross under the other—and a group of high-ranking officials as witnesses, to Frig's Seat. Hild walked alongside her sister, holding her hand tightly, while silently entreating with all her might that Frig would come to Hereswid's aid and send her strength and resourcefulness.

Frig did not forsake her faithful children: she inspired Hereswid with the idea of leading the procession up onto a hilltop just north of Frig's Seat, to a spot they rarely visited— renouncing it wouldn't cause them any distress, and in the circumstances it was a sacrifice they made willingly.

They continued to hold hands when ordered to bend down and each receive three blows from a stick. Paulinus hit harder than their mother, but as Hereswid was wont to say: 'Nowhere near as bad as a wasp sting!'

As the stick swept down, Hild thought: nowhere near as bad as two wasp stings! And gritted her teeth.

Afterwards, they had to lie on the ground praying with the witnesses while Paulinus walked around the entire area, holding his holy cross aloft and sprinkling holy water; he then declared the place baptized. The mountain of the holy Gregorius, it was to be called—and should anyone call it anything else from that day onwards, they would receive five blows of a stick, one for each of Christ's wounds. No idols and devils were to have their domain at such close proximity to the seat of a great king.

Paulinus avoided uttering the name of the fair one; when speaking of the old gods, he used terms such as 'devils', 'tempters', 'spirits' and 'demons'. To speak their names would have granted them existence and a dignity to which they were not entitled.

Hereswid's cheeks were a flaming red when they eventually walked away, hand in hand, and Hild didn't dare say a word. The falsehood was their shared responsibility: Hereswid had carried it through, Hild had got Frig to inspire her. It was a sin they couldn't admit at confession; they would have to shoulder it alone, with one another, and with lovely Frig who rewarded her handmaids with exquisite dreams and visions.

This was the first time Hild realized there were matters you had to shoulder on your own—a lesson she was now grateful to have learnt.

Talcuin had followed his mistress at a suitable distance, knowing she liked to feel as if she were alone and could walk in her own thoughts. He had now belonged to her for so long that he knew her slightest wish: she barely had to raise her hand before he was next to her with the wheat bread they had brought along, and if she stood still for a moment looking at the ground, he would immediately step in and spread out his cloak.

When she stood scrutinizing the beck so carefully, he had feared she was planning to bathe. The memory of what he had once seen scorched through him, causing him to hang further back than usual in an attempt to keep any unseemly thoughts at bay.

He had done everything he could to get the picture out of his mind, but it had stuck far too resolutely. At regular intervals—even when his mistress was more than decently dressed—he still saw the fiery-red tuft of hair and where it was placed. Not one single red-haired woman had since walked past without Talcuin doing his utmost to arrange a closer inspection, and given that they travelled widely and he was a handsome and courteous man, well dressed and carrying plenty of silver, he didn't have much trouble finding a warm bed.

Some of the women had been surprised when he turned up with a burning rush light, but they had never objected, and the slightly older ones had even found pleasure in his enthusiastic interest in the particulars of their bodies. A few had taken the opportunity to study him in similar detail, which he didn't like: it wasn't seemly to observe a man when he was in that state, but he now knew there were women who possessed neither delicacy nor decency; he shuddered at the thought of Queen Cyneburh's nurse.

She was the closest he had come in his hunt for the fiery-red tuft of hair. It wasn't because of beauty that he had accepted her invitation—and she could easily have been his mother—but because of her red hair: dark auburn, not a single strand of grey, very thick and long. He couldn't tell if she used a dye.

True to form, he crawled up the ladder, rush light in hand, and she . . . yes, she'd simply pulled the cover aside and there she was: outstretched on the bed! When he didn't move, she had very slowly turned towards him, head propped up on her left arm, right leg angled slightly upwards, so there could be no doubt whatsoever.

He felt an emotional lump in his throat and was no longer in control of his actions. Her heavy white breasts, round and engorged with milk, the plump belly with a dark stripe up to the navel, the broad well-rounded hips, the magnificent curve of her strong womanly thighs, and the red hair—radiant shining bright-red hair surrounding her nakedness.

He sank to his knees and buried himself in the red tuft, forgot all about his burning rush light, which the nurse fortunately had the presence of mind to snuff out with her hand, sank deeper and deeper into her redness. And when her dexterous fingers started to peel off his tight trousers, and she did to him what he had just done to her, he had no strength to resist. Yes, she did, she licked and sucked on his secret until he didn't know which way to turn and collapsed with a little moan against her soft white flesh.

Never had he been so vulnerable and lost, and never so sparklingly blissful as amid all this unseemliness. It was all he could do not to laugh out loud from delight as he embraced her pale flesh tightly with his arms and legs, and could feel favour returning—the favour unbelievers called the power of Thunor. He laughed to her in the darkness as his hardening penis swelled inside her; she murmured sweet words, clasped her legs around his loins, and he again forgot everything as he became engulfed in the red mist.

Next morning, she had to push him out of bed: Talcuin, the man who always returned to his quarters, and before dawn too. Today, however, he couldn't drag himself away from this glorious helping of womanhood. He wouldn't leave until she had promised to receive him next evening.

Her reservation was only for show, of course. It had been a long time since she'd enjoyed a man like this one, but she knew the young lads needed to prove their mettle when it came to satisfying their appetite; without a touch of resistance and a little preciousness it didn't really count.

Those were the rules of the game; now she'd learnt them, it didn't bother her. It was like pike and old trout: you pulled them in, slackened the line, tightened the cord, but at no point did you let it go. That was her method, she'd worked it out from experience and it very rarely failed her; not with the young men, at least, and they were her preferred catch.

This one, whatever he was called—Talcut or some such name used by the Britons—was obviously a really lovely specimen with his copper-coloured hair and freckles all over his cheeks. A lad like him didn't knock on her door every day, and he could get even better, as she also knew from experience.

Such were the nurse's thoughts—the nurse who had accompanied Queen Cyneburh from the kingdom of the West Saxons nearly seven years ago, when Cyneburh married Oswald.

Talcuin went hot and cold when he thought about her. Next time, he'd really show her who he was.

His mistress had reached the summit of the Hill of the Goats and was looking as if she wanted to sit down, so he hurried up the track. There was a fierce wind blowing, and she had to sit in the lee of the wall. Talcuin spread out his cloak for her and signalled to the rest of the entourage that they could take a break, and the carrier could bring food and beer.

Hild drank in silence. She shooed away one of Oswy's soldiers who had taken position blocking her view of the dale; she wanted the vista for herself. She wanted to revisit the happy days of childhood, when an entourage of ten highly-trained men hadn't been necessary.

There had been sentry posts, of course; and if the guards had been on duty earlier, well, she would still have had her brother. Afterwards, Edwin's sons had been accompanied by a couple of armed men no matter where they went, which wasn't strictly necessary when all the summits were so well manned, in a system running throughout Edwin's entire kingdom. Edwin wasn't going to take any risks, however: unlike now, robbers weren't the problem back then—the problem had been Ædelfred's men.

Hild stood up and counted the summits, all the way around; not just the real mountain peaks, but also the hills and every kind of crest visible from up here. She made it twenty-six, but there ought to be twenty-seven. She re-counted, and reached twenty-nine, so she asked Talcuin to count, and he said twenty-seven, then pointed them out to her—the number tallied.

'At least something remains unchanged,' she said.

'Indeed,' said Talcuin.

She invited him to drink with her, and he accepted with thanks. He was thirsty after the trip, but he wasn't keen on drinking from becks, as his mistress was in the habit of doing. He simply didn't like water. When he had been a free young man in Dolwyddelan, they'd always had beer at home; the slaves had drunk water, of course, except at festival times. That was another bonus of working for his mistress: she didn't begrudge him his beer, and all in all she treated him like an employed freeman.

'It was a long time ago,' said Hild.

'It was,' Talcuin responded, looking down at the dale, where you could just make out the black remains of Edwin's burnt-out royal settlement. He thought she was talking about Ad Gefrin.

They had examined the ruins carefully, and when they moved on his mistress had been wearing a sombre expression; bad memories, no doubt.

It had been a magnificent place back then. Maybe the largest hall in the land, certainly the most impressive he had seen. What carvings, and what colours on the gable! Filled with trophies! The walls inside the hall had been hung with the finest cloths, probably gifts or plunder from the Picts. He would have liked to take one home to his sister, but their leader, Cædwalla, had commandeered them all. Anyway, Talcuin had enough loot, so that wasn't the issue, but they didn't have any fabric like that in Gwynedd; he could have got a horse for one of those wall hangings, a really good horse, but Cædwalla had the same idea.

Yes indeed, it had been a long time ago, and the site seemed smaller without the palisades. It hadn't been easy to capture. True, it had been poorly manned, but the actual fortifications had been good and it could be defended by a really quite small unit. The north side faced the Glene's marshy river valley, which was impassable. Cædwalla had sent a man out there, and he had been instantly sucked down—so they were forewarned. Had the royal settlement been fully-manned, they would have been obliged to starve them out, but that would have taken far too long because Ad Gefrin had adequate supplies to last many men quite a while, and two deep wells.

Deciding they weren't numerous enough to venture a direct attack, they had burnt their way in through the palisades. Ad Gefrin's archers had already felled too many of Cædwalla's men—they were damned skilled, those bowmen! Their reputation was well deserved.

Setting fire to the palisades had been something of an achievement. The besieged men and women had filled every vat and bucket, so the flames were extinguished even before taking hold, and every time they tried to get the flames going, those archers let fly a few arrows—every time.

Talcuin could justifiably brag that he had been the one who advised Cædwalla to focus the enemy's attention on the west gate while he and two others shot burning arrows at the east gate, which set off a slowly smouldering fire. By the time the besieged folk noticed the smoke, it was too late. Terrified, some of them had wanted to surrender on the spot, and opened the gate from the inside, which had so enraged the others that they had attacked the cowards. When Talcuin and his squad entered through the gate, there was hardly a man still standing, and the living ones were so weakened that they couldn't actually offer any resistance.

In that respect, the conquest of Ad Gefrin had been one of the most varied campaigns he had taken part in, and wasn't the usual charging at poorly-armed people who were barely even aware there was a war going on at all. He was so very tired of those campaigns, and they hardly had enough carts to drag along any more plunder anyway, so when Cædwalla gave him away in wergild, he hadn't been unhappy about leaving the military life. No, he hadn't, and he hadn't had a moment of regret about it since. Not that anyone had asked him—but still.

He studied his mistress's profile, thinking that if he had killed her back there in the cave—as he would have done had he not seen her two little babies—then today he would have been a freeman, prosperous too, and able to go wherever he wanted and marry whenever he wanted.

Still, no one could escape their fate, he thought, and then immediately started wondering how much Cyneburh's nurse would cost. Had he been a freeman he would have bought her for sure, he would have, yes. A tremor ran through him, he turned to jelly, and he didn't even know her name.

Hild was resting, and Talcuin fetched a cloak from the guards and tucked it around her. Just looking at her elicited a huge rush of tenderness; he would defend her with his life—and not just because it was his duty to do so. He loved his mistress, and that was that. Had it been possible, he would happily remove every stone that might ever obstruct her path; he would do anything for her.

Hild had fallen asleep and been transported back to the Ad Gefrin of her childhood—but back to the most painful of memories.

The earth was bathed in bright light, raindrops on blades of grass and little pools of water reflected the springtime sun, and the whole world was fresh and new. Hild and the other children stood in the doorway listening to the birdsong striking up again, the warbling of the lark so clear. The children hurried out and jumped around in the puddles in the yard, high-spirited and happy after all the hours spent indoors. It was time for the sentry change, the rain-drenched men coming in to dry by the fireplace with a lot of banter and shouting.

Through the gateway, the children had a clear view of a puppy running around beyond the fencing. It was playing with a piece of pelt, caught it, tossed it up into the air, tumbled on the ground.

Noticing the sentries were distracted, the children sped out through the gateway and across to the puppy, but it ran away with strange slithering movements. The children raced to catch the puppy, which was already quite a way off down by the road. Eadfrid was first, Hild number two, but she slipped and fell in the mud and was overtaken by Hereswid and by Osfrid and by her brother Hereberht. They didn't have time to help her as they had almost caught up with the puppy, but it kept on moving away, sliding sideways in the wet grass, whimpering in protest, and as Hild struggled to her feet she saw the cord pulling the dog and could see that it stretched to the grove where two strangers stood with their horses, one of them already on his way up into the saddle and holding both sets of reins.

She screamed to the others, but they weren't registering anything in their desperate chase to be the first one to reach the puppy. She screamed louder, and now the man ran forwards and grabbed the first two children, throwing one—Hereberht—up to the other stranger who immediately rode off through the grove; Hereberht's screams mingled with Eadfrid's—he was the second child—and now he was lying across the stranger's horse, which thundered off spattering earth and turf in its wake.

The noises gradually faded; the children were left standing stock still, silent, the only sound now the penetrating springtime song of the lark. And then they heard shouting and horses' hooves pounding through the gateway; five sentries galloped past—they hadn't had time to saddle their mounts—and while the children just stood together in a huddle, a unit of soldiers rode out, at such speed that the children were left almost unrecognizable, covered in spattered soil and mud. Soldiers ran out from the yard: one stopped abruptly and yelled angrily, shooing the children back.

They were fetched in, everything was in total uproar, and they couldn't answer the agitated questions. Osfrid hadn't seen anything before he saw a dragon fly off with his little brother; Hereswid wept and hadn't seen anything other than the little puppy with the white patch by its ear, and afterwards had heard horses; and Hild insisted through her sobs that she had seen two men, strangers, ride away with her brother and the king's second son.

Edwin walked back and forth, hands behind his back, pacing the floor, but he couldn't contain himself. He gave orders to bring his horse, and once he had ridden off, with an entourage of thirty men, the royal estate was quieter than they had ever heard before.

The only sound came from the lark, which continued undaunted with its warbling, high up in the sky, filling the whole landscape with its singing and making the stillness so very audible.

Never before had she heard her own heart: it was hammering in competition with the lark and with Hereswid's breathing, even though they were sitting in silence behind the door.

Hild leapt up from the ground and hit out in confusion. She felt surrounded by a swarm of evil spirits, but then recognized Talcuin and knew where she was. She stood still, breathing deeply, no lark singing now.

Back then, she had absorbed it as some kind of hope, reassurance that not everything was falling apart even though her world was disintegrating. But it was also a mockery, indifference to their misfortune. The lark had just gone on singing its joyous song, unconcerned, while everything had utterly changed for her kin, and the old world could never return.

She heard a pulsating sound and looked up; a large flight of greylag geese was heading southwards.

As she looked out from the Hill of the Goats, across the twenty-seven summits for one last time, a deep sense of tranquillity came over her.

Fate had done what fate should do: Oswald's father, Ædelfred, had poisoned her father and taken her brother, and Edwin had slain him; Oswald had slain her husband, and now he had paid with his head.

It was right and proper, and she could let it lie. It was as it should be. Now they were even.

# ONE WIFE TOO MANY

*– extract of unripe plums –*

The autumn storms arrived and ripped the leaves from the trees. The monks had returned home after their summer of missionary work and Hild took her leave of Aidan.

She said goodbye with a heavy heart, because her god was all around Aidan, you could feel the presence when you accompanied him. You were never completely alone; you could truly sense the firm grasp holding the world steady and preventing fate from knocking you over.

She knelt before Aidan and kissed his shoes, the right one and then the left.

'We'll meet again,' he said, helping her up.

'If our god so wills,' she replied.

'He will,' said Aidan, and kissed her forehead.

When they were a two-day ride from Tamoworthig, Hild sent a couple of men in advance.

Penda rode out to meet her. Spotting his standard fluttering above the camp, all her worries untangled. She dug her heels into the horse's flanks; she couldn't get there fast enough, and she laughed out loud with happiness. Now she knew who he was: her husband.

She arrived gasping for breath, calming her mount, which had reared up when it saw the other horses. Penda reached up and caught her as she slid down.

'Such slim hips!' he laughed, and steadied her on the ground.

'When there's no one to keep them plump!' she smiled.

His hair was greying, but perhaps she simply hadn't noticed before, and the deep furrows between his eyes seemed deeper than ever. She had both hands in his hair, feeling the shape of his head; pulled his head down and breathed in the heady scent of his hair—it took her breath away. She was already weak at the knees, the life-force seeping out of her. He embraced her tightly, and there could be no doubt: he was her husband, and they were one flesh.

'Come,' said Penda, taking her hand and guiding her into the prepared tent.

It had always been this way; they didn't have to size one another up first. This was how their reunions always proceeded, as was proper for a husband and wife who had no objection to validating their alliance.

'You have to understand,' Penda said afterwards, 'with Oswy in Bernicia!'

Hild was silent. She'd known it all along, but coming back and seeing him again she'd thought maybe it was just a bad dream.

How could he have embraced her as he did, had their lovemaking not cancelled out all the other business? She curled up under the bedcover and wished he'd stop talking about it, so she could just forget it again.

'There was no other option,' he persisted, 'and you've just got to help me make it work. If she goes back home, there will be war.'

'I didn't know it was necessary to forsake one's wife in order to maintain peace,' said Hild a little later as they mounted their horses.

Penda didn't respond, but after they had ridden for a while he said, darkly: 'I believe it to be in my wife's best interests that I safeguard her life and property.'

'Which wife?' Hild exclaimed, and bit her lip. As she couldn't unsay the words she had spoken, she went on: 'You don't have to worry about me. I'll cope.'

Upon which she dug her heels into the horse's flanks and rode ahead. He caught up with her, face glowering with anger, and grabbed her arm.

'Fine thanks I get for avenging your husband!'

She wrenched herself free and rode from him again.

The servants had gathered in the courtyard and welcomed their mistress home. She was touched—such warmth, and she had yet to be greeted with such honour in Tamoworthig.

She was still the lady of the estate, queen of the realm, King Penda's foremost wife, mother to two of his sons. She was suddenly happy to be back: this was her home, and this was where her work lay. Even though she'd been away for a long time, and a thing or two had happened, she hadn't lost the respect she had built up among the people here in recent years—despite her faith—and she held her head high.

Having greeted them all and blessed the new-born babies, she asked in a loud voice: 'And where is Princess Cynewise? I would like to greet the princess and bid her welcome.'

She was told that Queen Cynewise was indisposed.

Hild went straight to the women's house. A young woman was sitting on the Eostre-bench; she was pale and in great pain, her face a greyish-white. By nature, she was uncommonly fair of complexion and despite her condition it was clear she was growing prettier with age—the slightly protruding eyes were no great disfigurement—but she was still no match for her sister, Cyneburh.

Hild greeted her politely, introducing herself as Queen Hildeburh.

'I imagine you have already met my sons—Wulfhere and Ædelræd?'

The young woman nodded in pain.

'Haven't you taken anything to help?' Hild asked with sympathy.

Cynewise shook her head.

'It's not our way,' she whispered.

'No, but nor do you use Eostre's bench! Or do you?'

'Some use it,' Cynewise side-stepped.

'You are baptized, are you not?'

Cynewise blushed.

'They said it would be best if I sat here,' she said faintly.

'Have you tried saying the Lord's Prayer?'

'It didn't work,' Cynewise whimpered, as a cramp struck.

Hild sent everyone out, ordering a servant girl to fetch boiling water. Slowly, and with great care, she lifted the bunch of keys hanging from her belt and went through them all, stopping when she reached the little key to the chest in which she kept her medicinal plants and various infusions.

'There are some matters I prefer not to share with others,' she explained absent-mindedly as she held the various pots and bottles up to the light. 'I'm sure you'll see the sense in that when you're a little older.'

She contemplated the pot of henbane seed in her hand, but put it back, as she did the grey powder made from black nightshade, which would be detected instantly. Then she settled on a concentrated extract of unripe plums and put a good portion in the elm-wood beaker brought by the servant girl—that would certainly speed it along.

'It is said you were not a maiden?' she said, holding out the beaker.

Cynewise's eyes, large and round, stared intently at the hot drink, her hands trembling so much that she spilt a few drops.

'Don't you worry,' Hild reassured her, wiping the drops of liquid away rather vigorously. 'Drink up!'

Cynewise held the beaker in both hands and sniffed the contents, looking at Hild with eyes that seemed to be on their way out of her head.

'It's not true,' she faltered.

'Well, I don't know how the Saxons go about things,' Hild continued, in the same matter-of-fact tone, 'but our custom up here is for the bridegroom to send the bride home if she has taken a head start to the pleasures in store.'

Cynewise blushed in all her pallor.

'So, there's a dash of colour in you after all,' said Hild appreciatively, 'or is it shame? Yes, it's ancient practice—a man wants to make sure he isn't providing for another man's offspring.

And who can blame him. Especially when there's inheritance involved. A natural reaction, don't you think?'

She walked across to the peephole and looked out.

'But maybe it's different where you come from. Every place has its own practices.'

'It's not true to say I wasn't a maiden,' Cynewise protested. 'I have never been with a man before!'

'Well, you can never be sure, can you,' Hild went on, 'about a woman who lies with another woman's husband.'

'I'm his wife too,' said Cynewise.

'So they say,' said Hild, now pacing up and down.

'God is my witness!' cried Cynewise.

'Let's hope so,' said Hild dispassionately. 'But then he is also witness to you resorting to Eostre's bench when in difficulty.'

'And our marriage was blessed by my own priest!' Cynewise called out.

Hild came to an abrupt standstill, but quickly resumed her pacing. Her own wedding had taken place according to ancient custom, and there had been no blessing. It pained her to the very core that Penda had agreed to a blessing, because now his marriage with Cynewise had a different kind of validity, she thought. She took a deep breath.

'Then it won't be a problem, will it, with another man's offspring,' she remarked, nodding towards Cynewise's belly. The girl blushed again.

She was eighteen years old, and her father had turned down many offers for her hand because the plan had always been for her to marry into Mercia, but with one of the sons, not the king himself.

'You perhaps don't produce as many children in your family?' Hild asked sympathetically.

'Probably just as many as in other families,' Cynewise replied. 'But we don't usually send them off with foreigners.'

Hild ignored the latter comment and carried on undaunted: 'Your sister was certainly upset only to have given Oswald the one son.'

'She has written to tell me she's expecting,' said Cynewise, her head now held high.

'Well, well,' said Hild, impressed. 'She wasn't when I saw her at Bebbanburh. Then again, some men get their heirs a whole year after they've died.'

'You should know,' came the prompt retort from Cynewise, 'given that your mother was a widow when you were born.'

Hild froze and had to do some adding up; she'd never considered this possibility before. As she started to pack away her pots and bottles, she stole a glance at the young woman and met eyes stormy with anger.

'How old are you anyway?' Hild asked.

'Old enough to recognize a witch when I meet one,' Cynewise answered, more colour in her cheeks now. She held the beaker aloft and poured its contents on the floor.

Hild carefully locked the medicine chest, took her time replacing the key in the bunch on her belt, and called for the maid who would carry the chest back. Then she left, without looking at Cynewise.

Negotiating peace had been a costly affair for Penda. Cynewise's brother, King Cenwalch, had made it a condition that his sister would be provided with a new royal estate, and until this was ready her place would be at the king's right hand. A huge morning gift of land bordering the West Saxons' kingdom was agreed. The bride would be bringing fifty of her own people, for whom suitable quarters and arrangements would have to be made. In addition, Penda had to pay a considerable wergild for King Cynegils and also for Cynewise's older brother who had earlier fallen in battle. Penda surrendered two of the territories he had recently captured from the West Saxons, and paid a chest of silver to the new king. Cenwalch also wanted to receive one of the 'king's sons' as hostage, but at the last moment Penda had this changed to four of his most trusted men.

The disputes thus settled, a lasting peace was woven with two brides: Cynewise and Penda's sister.

Cynewise didn't meet the same kind of resistance Hild had initially encountered. Things had now been going well for quite a few years with a queen of the new faith; actually, things had made progress in terms of wealth, territory and status.

Cynewise nonetheless appointed a cupbearer, but that was due to fear of her co-queen rather than fear of the chief men from whom Hild had been obliged to protect herself.

Hild kept her cupbearer, for the same reason.

What goes on inside a girl like that, Hild wondered when she saw Cynewise's pale face in the hall of an evening, her slightly protruding eyes moist and expressionless.

Hild observed her furtively, and noticed that the young woman was doing the same with her; both quickly glanced away when they realized their curiosity had been detected.

Cynewise had taken her place at Penda's right hand, and Hild had to make do with his left hand. She compensated by quickly rising from her seat and taking mead round to the guests, thus retaining a little of her status. Cynewise tried a few times, but she wasn't quick enough, so she abandoned the contest and remained in her seat of honour all evening.

And there she sat, her delicate little dog on her lap: a wedding gift from her brother, bought at great expense for the occasion. No one in Mercia, nor any of the West Saxons, had so fine and so small a dog. Cynewise had to put a stop to all the puppy-making it was asked to do: the dog couldn't cope with all the jobs, however honourable they might be. It had needed help mating; it couldn't reach up to the calf-sized gundogs, however eager it had been.

Hild simply couldn't understand why Cynewise would let her little dog mate with all sorts of bitches. It would soon lose its value. If she also let it mate with its own medium-sized progeny then she was simply too stupid, even taking her age and everything else into account. She might just as well give her valuable rarity away.

She felt an intense urge to go over and stroke the little creature's strange tightly-curled coat. Everyone else did, and then went all soppy, as if greeting a new-born baby. She certainly wouldn't do that; there was, after all, a difference between a human baby and a little dog, and she could easily control herself. She noticed an empty cup and busied herself filling it up; never before had Penda's men been served so well.

Nor did the art of the bard seem to make an impression on her young co-queen. Hild wondered if she even heard the magnificent songs, or perhaps she simply had no feeling for song. Some were descriptions of triumphant campaigns against her father, and mostly involved listing the chief men slain by Penda's soldiers and the plunder brought home.

Perhaps Cynewise had known these people, and had seen the celebrated helmets and magnificent swords while they were still carried by their West Saxon owners, but her face gave nothing away, not even during a song about the killing of her own brother.

Penda, on the other hand, was embarrassed. He remonstrated with the bard, and singing about memorable battles against the West Saxons came to an abrupt end. They went back to the old repertoire, especially songs about the battles with Bernicia and Deira. The warriors sat hammering their beer mugs on the tabletop during the long song about Penda's victory over Edwin and his sons. The song about Oswald's defeat was another favourite, and laughter echoed to the rafters when the bard shifted into falsetto and mimicked Oswald's piping voice: 'Dear God, have mercy on them!' Thus had he prayed, it was said, for his men lying dead all around him.

Hild wasn't particularly fond of the song about Edwin's death, but she had heard it many many times before and it no longer had much affect, merely describing what always happened in battle, and it didn't deny that Edwin had been a great warrior in critical situations.

However, she disliked the section about Eadfrid's surrender, which wasn't fitting in a heroic song, in her opinion; besides, you shouldn't speak ill of the dead—she certainly never did, whatever went on in her mind.

The bards, however, were afraid of neither gods nor devils, not even of fate. They dared say whatever they wanted, which was what they were paid to do—by Penda at least—but they probably shouldn't count on a reward from Jesus.

A passage like that—about Eadfrid's surrender—well, then it was time to go out and breathe in some fresh air; the smoke in the hall could get quite dense.

A few months later and Cynewise was expecting. Hild didn't think it suited her; the young woman was even paler, if that were possible, and her eyes were far too protruding—as if they were about to fall out of their sockets.

But pregnancy was a natural condition for a young woman, and not anything to make a big fuss about. If Cynewise was one of those who couldn't deal with it, well, she should have thought about that earlier.

On the other hand, Cynewise's pregnancy didn't seem to be totally natural. Hild simply couldn't get her mind around how Penda, her own husband, could make this insipid specimen of womanhood pregnant; nor could she get it *out* of her mind.

The thought haunted her day and night: her husband lying with the pallid princess. What pleasure could he get from *that*?

She was on the look-out for signs of change, but everything was as normal. Except for her own behaviour, that is, wanting him to be with her the entire time, and in bed too. If, of a morning, he managed to sneak out of bed in the belief that she was still asleep, she immediately pulled him back and excited him with loving words and actions. Penda was behaving exactly as usual, and she didn't understand *that* either.

She looked at him almost exclusively in terms of lying with him now, and her body had turned into a kind of frame supporting a greedy, virtually insatiable desire. Whether she saw him in conversation with strangers, at supper in the hall, playing a game of dice or on horseback, everything was always overshadowed by the picture of his arousal—the picture that had been her secret and had sweetened so many years: her seven happy years.

This gnawing hunger between her legs wasn't the happy anticipation of good days gone by; it was a craving that could never be completely satisfied, which pushed her around and drove her into one more humiliating situation after another. She hated her desire; it had disempowered her, and rendered her one big hole that he alone could plug.

Of course, he couldn't spend day and night doing just that, he had to devote time to other pursuits too—Cynewise, for instance. Fortunately, pregnancy was making her so ill that she wasn't troubled about sleeping alone at night.

Hild had told Talcuin to court Cynewise's maid; and thus she was kept informed, although relations between Cynewise and Penda didn't sound as if they posed any threat. Cynewise might sometimes tell him about her swollen ankles, and it seemed Penda dutifully sympathized with her infirmities—undoubtedly to avoid other matrimonial duties, Hild surmised.

She just hoped this unnatural pregnancy would endure and preferably be the death of the fragile woman—a scenario that wouldn't bring the West Saxon army down on them.

When Penda was hunting, she would ride out to meet him, with such impatience that she often had to wait half the day before he turned up, at which point she was ready with their red tent and everything prepared for his arrival.

She was still able to play a part in much of his business, as she had in the early years of their marriage. Keeping meticulously abreast of the affairs of the kingdom, she was happy to counsel her husband. Some of the matters to which she had earlier devoted her efforts—the children's schooling, taking on infants who would otherwise be put out to die, buying slaves and giving advice to people who were in difficulty—were now somewhat neglected. She could only be in one place at a time, and she would rather be with her husband.

Cynewise's belly grew larger, but she made no attempt to conceal it by her choice of clothing—quite the contrary.

There was something a little unseemly about the way in which she displayed her pregnancy. On several occasions Hild heard her refer to the baby she was expecting as 'our son', which sounded like a rather uncompromising challenge to fate. Firstly, the pregnancy was still developing; secondly, you didn't get a son every time, whatever the doctor might say about belly shape and the expectant mother's eyes. Yes, Hild had given birth to sons—every time—but you couldn't just count on that outcome.

Hild could have helped Cynewise feel better; she had more herbal medicines than the doctor, and far more knowledge too, in her opinion, but she wasn't going to risk being blamed for anything. Anyway, no one had asked. She was very careful never to show her aversion to the fatuous young woman.

When Penda spent the night with Cynewise, the bad dreams visited Hild. She wouldn't tell him, because over the months she had used so many ploys to keep him from Cynewise's bed that she was disgusted with herself. So she had Wulfhere brought to her from his nurse. He was five years old now, and even though he slept rather restlessly she found some respite in his warm softness. She breathed in the scent of his red summer-hair and tried to think about cowslips and bright beech leaves.

Talcuin watched over her, ready to put the incubus to flight. It usually tried once or twice a night. The old incubus had found her again; huddled, cackling, by the bedhead, it struck her with horror and she couldn't move so much as a muscle. When it was really bad, she wasn't sure if Talcuin was keeping watch at all, because she couldn't see anything. At other times, she might catch sight of the dwarf-creature when it scurried out and closed the door just after she had torn herself loose. She never managed to catch it, but she came to know its ways and was thus able to elude its power.

She could wake up, having just fallen asleep, in an abyss of horror, knowing that the incubus was poised to leap. Sometimes she could hear it laughing, and then in her thoughts she would say: 'It is the incubus, it has returned. It is trying to gain power over me. In the name of Jesus Christ, it will not succeed!'

Whereupon she calmly and almost imperceptibly started wriggling her toes up and down—very cautiously, it mustn't notice—for a long time, without panicking. Then her foot, and once her foot was free it wasn't long before the whole leg was set free, quickly followed by her arms, and then it was the turn of her head, and she could sit up and get out of bed.

She mustn't lie down again too soon, because first the incubus had to be softened up. She usually sent Talcuin to fetch beer, or she'd wake Wulfhere and tell him stories. By the time she had sat with her drink, woven a little and thought about other matters, the incubus had given up and gone off elsewhere.

'My beloved sister!' wrote Hereswid. 'Great was my joy upon reading your last letter. The shame upon our family has finally been rescinded, and we can again raise our heads. I would request you convey my gratitude to your husband, who has at last restored our honour. The Lord be with him.

'Some time ago I had a dream that filled my thoughts for several days and nights. I saw a darkness that was suddenly lit up by a clear radiant glow. It imbued me with happiness, but given that I was not able to interpret the dream, I long pondered its meaning. Only now have I understood: the darkness from Oswald's tyranny would disperse and our family rise again in dignity. For the dream visited me at the moment our enemy received his retribution.

'What a wonderful divine sign! . . . '

The new royal estate was under construction, but was constantly struck by misfortunes so severe that a good many slaves fled the site. They would rather sustain themselves in the forests and risk the penalty of death than continue working on those cursed buildings. Even careful men plunged from the scaffolding—whosoever might be the cause.

Cynewise sent her priest to exorcize the evil. Work ceased while he spent twelve days at the site, praying and fasting.

Cynewise was the price to be paid for Oswald's head. Hild knew this, although sometimes she knew it more than at other times, but she made an effort to be polite and stopped referring to her as 'the princess', but she simply couldn't bring herself to use the word 'queen'.

In the afternoon, she would invite Cynewise into the sewing room, so they could embroider together. It was easier to be obliging now that she knew she would soon be the only mistress of the estate. They talked about times past—first in general, and then gradually in more personal terms.

Cynewise spoke about the preparations for Cyneburh's marriage with Oswald; she had listened at the door, and hadn't envied her sister this great honour.

'But it still didn't stop *you* from getting married!' Hild exclaimed spontaneously.

'It was so long ago,' said Cynewise. 'And anyway, you want to find out what it's like. Besides, we need people willing to be peace-weavers.'

'Yes,' said Hild, 'still, it can't have been easy—marrying the man who had made your sister a widow. And had slain your father, and your brother.'

'Well, so the penance got paid,' said Cynewise, staring hard at her embroidery. 'Have you got any blue silk thread? I think it must be far worse to marry a man who had made his bride a widow. Don't you?'

Hild stiffened, but immediately started searching for the thread.

Cynewise thought it was too dark, so Hild found one in a lighter tone.

'Yes, that can't be easy,' she said casually.

'It happens,' Cynewise went on.

'So it's said.' Hild accidentally stuck a needle in her finger. 'Of women who have had no choice,' she added.

'Well, I don't know much about it,' said Cynewise, without looking up, 'but they say it can make a witch of the best woman.'

'Indeed, so it is said.'

'By the way, how is the pagan priest's horse?' asked Cynewise.

'No change, it seems. I heard yesterday that they were thinking of slaughtering it.'

'Well then, at least the *horse* will have been freed of the evil,' remarked Cynewise.

Hild searched her brain trying to think of another subject.

'They'd be better off slaughtering the woman who bewitched it,' said Cynewise.
'Undoubtedly.'
'Otherwise there's no knowing where it will end,' Cynewise continued.
'No, that too,' said Hild.
'Once she's taken the first, then she'll be going for the next,' Cynewise persisted.
'Indeed, that could well be the case,' Hild replied.

When summer was at its height, Cynewise received word that her sister had died at Bebbanburh. All of a sudden, King Oswy reported, the Lord had taken Cyneburh, her two daughters, the barely seven-year-old son and the infant daughter to be with him, united with Oswald in eternal salvation. A raging fire, and just before the daughter was to be baptized. None lamented this more than Oswy, who hereby sent Cynewise his heartfelt sympathy.

Cynewise had a difficult time, with nightly visits from her dead sister. Cyneburh's spirit didn't find rest until Cynewise promised to name the unborn child after her or her son.

This all happened while a troupe of entertainers was visiting from further north. They came every year, and were happy to work for King Penda; there hadn't been many pickings at Bebbanburh.

On their first evening in the hall, the oldest of the women performed a peculiar little play, which initially no one understood. The audience enjoyed themselves trying to guess what was going on; when they misunderstood something, she would repeat the scene until everyone had got the point. Penda was greatly entertained by her skill and enthusiastically joined in the guessing game. Without any warning, Cynewise gave a piercing scream, tried to stand up, fainted and had to be carried out. Hild had to force herself not to offer help—but then again, no one had asked her. When Penda came back into the hall, he was as pale as Cynewise had been. He strode straight over to the woman performer and grabbed her by the arm.

'Where is he? Tell me—where is he!'

At first the woman claimed not to know, and insisted all this was just something she had heard and nothing she was mixed up in, but she was gradually convinced that the king bore her no ill will, and so she promised to fetch the boy—on condition that Penda staked his own son's life as guarantee for the boy's safety.

'Soldiers have I none,' she said, 'but I've learnt a thing or two from my mother, and if anything happens to the lad . . . ' She pulled her finger across her throat, a gesture putting that very throat in jeopardy had she been in the company of a less magnanimous king.

When Penda—in front of the entire assembly—guaranteed the boy's life with that of his own son, the woman left the hall, immediately reappearing with a lanky black-haired boy, whose only point of similarity with the itinerant troupe of players was his clothing. His royal descent was written all over him, and neither Penda nor anyone else was in any doubt: this was Ædelwald, Cyneburh's son with Oswald.

Hild, who had seen the boy when she visited the year before, could but confirm his identity. It pained her to see how his face resembled Oswald's. She embraced the boy, and he was happy to see someone he had met before, talking with her readily and openly; he longed to get home to his dog, and to his mother, he said—he'd got a new little sister.

The woman now told the whole story: she had always received a warm welcome from Queen Cyneburh, who took a lively interest in their skills, their dancing and juggling, and had asked to learn a few of them, and her son had also learned a little; it was apparently one of their few pleasures.

With King Oswald dead, the travelling entertainers had faced difficult times in Bernicia as only the dowager queen carried on paying them. When they had last been there, the widowed queen had looked closely at the woman's delicate grandson: dance and perform he couldn't—not with that club foot—and he was too slow-witted to clown or speak verse. What was more, he had recently developed a bad cough, perhaps the same one that had taken his parents.

The dowager queen had asked that her son, Ædelwald, should join the troupe and learn their skills—this was his deepest desire, she said—and in return she offered to take in the woman's ailing grandson and help him recover.

At first the woman turned her down, but when she sensed there was an underlying agenda of something serious—and the dowager queen even slipped her a gold ring—she didn't ask any more questions and they left the next day. She didn't hear about the fire until much later.

Ædelwald's pale-blue eyes gazed at Hild.

'What fire?' he asked, and she had to tell him. His mother and his sisters, the new little sister too, were now together with his father in the Lord's enormous hall in Heaven. Then she took him to her chamber, and let him sleep alongside her in the bed.

Penda paid the entertainers well, and gave the woman a gold ring for her loyalty. Ædelwald's appearance at the estate was of great benefit to Cynewise's condition, and once he had spent some time with her, he was sent to the West Saxons' kingdom, where he was raised by his maternal uncle, King Cenwalch.

With the approaching arrival of Cynewise's baby, Hild moved up to the little monastery she'd had built on a patch of land Penda had given her, north of the royal estate. She could thus avoid helping at the birth.

She took part in the monk's observance of canonical hours and made sure she constantly had high-ranking company, so it could be testified under oath that she had not performed any magic. The most dangerous outcome would be for Cynewise to survive and the baby to die; the best outcome would be for both of them to die.

They both survived. Cynewise gave birth without any complications to a fine and healthy daughter; boys were generally more troublesome to bring into the world.

Hild kept away until Cynewise had moved to the new royal estate, and then she didn't visit the mother and baby until she was invited, which wasn't until after the child had been baptized. She was a big baby, not particularly pretty, and not recognizably a daughter of Penda.

Later in the autumn, Hild had other things to think about: she received word from her kinsman Oswine; he wanted to speak with her—he had news of her twins' whereabouts.

# A BLESSED PLACE

*– Hild's twins –*

Silvery-white patches of light dappled through the foliage, making the air thick, almost milky, and totally tranquil, slanting columns slicing through the vertical lines of the trees. The forest floor had been covered in anemones; now they were dying down while wood sorrel and true lover's knot were taking over.

The horses' hooves thudded on the sparse grass covering of the track through the forest, mingling with the thrush's song and the cooing of the wood pigeon. In the distance, a cuckoo; the cuckoo tells you how many years you have left, or how many kisses you have coming to you from the one who fills your thoughts.

Hild counted: she had thirty-six years left, or perhaps she had thirty-six kisses coming her way. From Hundfrid, and from Wilbrord—thirty-six from each.

No, no, there would be many more kisses after all those years: hundreds.

A bend in the track, a dale opened out in front of them and they rode round the north side to avoid its marshy basin. To the south, through the trees, glimpses of the wide wet plains they had passed by; to the other side of the marshy land lay Mædeltun, where they had spent the night, and some of the richest land in Deira, with farms dotted all along the hillcrest where the land rose from the marshy river valley.

It was a fine kingdom, Deira, as you really realized once you'd been away for a while. The good soil of Deira, and the enterprising towns. The people up here weren't dependent on Frisian merchants; they simply set sail and fetched the goods themselves. There wasn't a single thing you couldn't get in Eoforwik, they had everything.

Deira was a good place, a realm with great prospects for the future, and she felt not the slightest sorrow about having given it up—not the slightest. Softly rocking on the trotting horse, feeling no need to urge it on, she knew that each swaying step took her closer to her fulfilment. She was imbued with such gentleness, and every so often she just had to close her eyes and breathe in the scent of forest floor, as if she were wrapped in the very softest lambswool and was brimful of honey and thick cream.

They passed a band of forest workers. A whoosh sounded throughout the forest when a mighty elm toppled to the ground, and axes immediately set to work removing its branches. The thudding song of iron axe striking wood followed them until they had crossed the next hilltop.

Her belly wasn't getting in her way yet. She was only five months pregnant, and this time it would be a girl. A little sister. What would they think about having a little sister? And about the two brothers who had already arrived, Wulfhere and Ædelræd?

Hild looked across at Oswine, the handsome young man she had made sure was chosen king of Deira. He was of her own lineage, the son of Edwin's cousin Osric, slain by Cædwalla at Eoforwik ten years ago. There was something sad about Oswine's mouth, something reminiscent of Edwin, which made her cherish him even more.

'Is something preying on your mind?' she asked, as she rode up alongside him.

'No, no,' he said, eyes firmly on his horse's mane. Then he turned to look at her and attempted a smile. 'I had perhaps abandoned hope of getting Deira.'

'It's turned out for the best,' she said, 'and the kingdom remains in the family.'

They rode a while in silence.

'What use is a kingdom if you have no sons?' she asked.

'Indeed,' said Oswine, 'but you've had two sons since.'

'They belong to Mercia. And Hundfrid and Wilbrord belong here in Deira. I plan to give one of them the estate in Mædeltun. And perhaps you could take them into your service. When they're a little older.'

She mulled over her plans for the future with some thought to potential wives, even though it was rather early, they were barely eleven years old—but still.

'How old are your daughters?' she asked.

They were ten and seven and three.

Given that Oswine didn't have any sons—yet—it seemed a good idea for their lineage to be bonded even closer, which would also prevent future disputes about dominion and render it harder for Bernicia to make claims. The children were not so closely related as to cause any kind of ecclesiastical protest.

'Actually, I would have given most of Mercia to get my sons back,' she laughed to Oswine.

He smiled at her.

'You would, yes, but your husband undoubtedly wouldn't have!'

'I think not, no,' she laughed. 'But he is quite satisfied with our agreement.'

'I'm glad it finally got cleared up,' said Oswine, 'so we could settle matters.'

Hild nodded; the negotiations had taken time, but that was all irrelevant now.

After Oswald's death, an idea had suggested itself to Oswine, but his investigations had taken a while. He had sent word from Dalriada, where he was in exile. The matter really got going when Hild offered young Oswine the throne of Deira—if he found her children unharmed. She would speak in favour of his candidature, and the selection would be a formality.

Penda accepted his wife's dealings; Deira was hers more than it was his. Oswine had been a hair's breadth from finding the twins, but nonetheless had to postpone the search until after his selection because the boys had been moved several times when Oswald was thought to have discovered their whereabouts.

The road wound uphill, and when they reached the top and could see across the next dale, Oswine signalled that they should make a halt. Hild would have liked to carry on, but she could wait. To the right of the track, a long series of high earthworks rose all the way up the side of the hill—clearly man-made, because they didn't follow the direction of the water.

'What is that?' asked Hild, once she had been up to the summit and looked out to both sides.

'Must be something Woden built,' said Oswine, 'or the giants.'

Hild laughed. She knew the Romans had built everything they called giants' towns and giants' trenches and giants' roads, but had they also made huge earthworks like these?

Talcuin didn't know. He paced out the area and noted the foundations of two towers at the foot of the embankment. He thought it was perhaps something the Britons had built to defend themselves against the Romans.

'Or they might be even older,' he said. 'There's always been a need for defence.'

'Lust for gold!' said Hild.

'Maybe just for food,' said Talcuin.

'And such plenty there is in this realm!' Hild pressed on.

'For some, yes,' said Talcuin.

'Is it not correct,' Hild went on to Oswine, 'that if everyone could be satisfied with what is theirs and leave their neighbour's property in peace, then there would be ample for all of us in this land?'

Oswine wasn't sure.

'You have to think about your family,' he said, pulling off tufts of grass, 'that you leave something for them.'

'You're right about that,' said Hild emphatically, 'because without that we wouldn't be people. We'd be like the beasts, who only think about their own survival. And what would life then be worth?'

Oswine didn't reply, and Talcuin didn't feel the question was addressed to him, although there was plenty he could have said to his mistress: her idea about peace, and the one about lust for gold being the source of all misfortune, well, it was all starting to get out of hand, he thought, but she hadn't asked for his opinion.

'This much I can tell you, Oswine,' Hild continued, 'the older you get, the more you discover the significance of lineage. You don't think much about it when you're young. But the person who doesn't take care of his or her family is like a tree easily felled by the wind. And I'm glad you are of the same mind. I knew you would be as soon as I saw you: *he* is of Edwin's line, *he* is my blood relation! There aren't many left. My sister is serving the Lord in Gaul, and I haven't seen her since she was widowed. You can miss your family, even if you've got a husband and children. Now and then you wonder: where are my own people?—which is why I was so happy when you sent word. I knew it would bring good fortune. And just see what has happened!'

She stood up and shouted to the entourage, spread out on the grass in small groups: 'Stand and drink to King Oswine!'

The men scrambled up, stiff after the long ride, and more beer was passed round.

'A toast to our kinship, and to our friendship,' she called out, 'and that includes my husband, and on our honour we will henceforward support King Oswine in all his endeavours. May the Lord send good fortune to King Oswine and Deira!'

She raised her drinking horn, and a chorus of voices rang out across the dale: 'Good fortune to King Oswine and Deira!'

They would happily have drunk a toast to anything, for the beer was good and the sun was hot and they had yet to reach their destination; but Oswine wanted to press on—he wasn't feeling at his best.

Talcuin was irritated by the second-rate horse he was riding. His own mount, or at least the one he usually rode, was ailing and they'd had to leave it in Mædeltun. He hoped it would be back on form by the time they returned, and that they would take the same route home; the horse had served him well for so many years.

He hadn't toasted Oswine, just brought the horn to his mouth and pressed his lips together.

He was very fond of his mistress, and would neither voice nor think a bad word about her, but when it came to men she had neither good taste nor sound judgement. Not to his mind, at any rate. There was something about this Oswine that reminded him of Cædwalla. His mistress had also been besotted with Cædwalla, but Talcuin had been in his service and knew him better—nothing to cheer about there.

Talcuin never spoke of his soldier days under Cædwalla's leadership. Everything had happened at such speed back then, and he'd been young. Now he didn't like thinking about it, and had to be particularly vigilant when he was eating because those memories could strip all the joy from a good roast, especially if it wasn't quite done. In Penda's hall they didn't eat their meat well-roasted; they wanted to show how good and tender it was, which hadn't been the case back home in Dolwyddelan.

Penda was a decent man, however, and a great king, no doubt about that. Unlike her first husband! Thank goodness he'd died on her. It had made you sick to see how he treated her, and see how she didn't hit back, but just got weaker and weaker, her voice and everything.

Talcuin had been forced to keep himself under control, to hold back from stepping in and flattening Eadfrid. Someone else, however, *had* stepped in, had done something about it. Yes, the ways of the Lord are past understanding; or maybe it had been fate, he reasoned, because the Lord doesn't act through heathens, does he, even though he has everything in his power.

He was happy about that, having so little power himself.

During their rest, they had been looking out across the dale of the trout beck; they didn't ride down into it, but headed northeast through the forest. A light and leafy forest with oak and ash and rowan and hazel, a few beech trees shining brightly with their intense yellow-green foliage. The oak still had a little way to go before it came into leaf, and the ash had only just shed its black bud-scales.

'The ash doesn't seem to have noticed that spring has arrived,' Hild said to Oswine, laughing.

He gave her one of his lovely melancholy smiles, the kind that went straight to the heart. She felt safe with him at her side, almost like being a child again and riding out with Edwin. What a happy time that had been, childhood!

'You've probably wondered about their names, too, haven't you? Why I didn't name them after Edwin or someone in the family. But that's just how it turned out, as soon as I saw them I knew who they were. And they were Hundfrid and Wilbrord. I hadn't thought it through beforehand. As soon as I saw them, I just knew—knew who they were.'

Oswine smiled gently, and Hild continued: 'Did you feel like that with yours too?'

'I don't think so. I had decided on their names in advance.'

'But did you then think they suited those names when they arrived, your daughters?'

'I don't know. I obviously didn't give it much thought.'

'No, because a name like Wilbrord,' Hild went on, 'well, you might think it sounds strange for a son born to Eadfrid and me, but it fits him perfectly. He really is Wilbrord.'

Oswine watched a wood pigeon.

'Those eyes,' said Hild, 'they looked straight through you. That's probably what I'm most curious about—if they're still the same: Wilbrord uses his eyes, and Hundfrid loves singing.'

She wasn't bothered by Oswine's lack of response, because it just showed his kinship with Edwin—he'd thought more than he spoke too, a man of few words, that was Edwin, but his words had carried weight.

'You're just like him!' she exclaimed.

Oswine turned his head to look at her: 'Who?'

'Edwin. Your father's cousin.' She smiled at him appreciatively.

'A better king Deira has never seen,' she said. 'It was a good time.'

He stared ahead.

A bit of a challenge would do him no harm; Edwin had liked it when someone pinned him down.

'Or what do you think?' she asked, and as he didn't look as if he was about to answer, she pressed on: 'Perhaps you think Oswald's day was the best time? Or what?'

Oswine cleared his throat.

'Your father's day, perhaps?'

A huge responsibility had been placed on his young shoulders, but he'd have to get used to being interrogated even if he was feeling quite weighed down by it all.

He cleared his throat again, and then it came out: 'I was in exile.'

'Ah,' said Hild, 'but not under Edwin?'

'Under Edwin, along with my father in Dalriada, and after my father had been slain I was there on my own. Along with my first wife.'

Hild didn't understand a thing.

'No, surely not!' she exclaimed. 'You're not trying to tell me you lived up there because you were afraid of Edwin!'

He glanced at her and then returned his gaze to the track.

'My father was perhaps mistaken,' he said sullenly, 'but I don't know who else would have sent a hired sword after us. Twice.'

Hild was dismayed.

'No,' she said, 'Edwin wouldn't have done something like that. Not against his own kin!'

It pained her that the young man could think like this; he had clearly been through a lot.

Oswine shrugged. 'My father might have been mistaken.'

'I certainly think so,' said Hild.

After they had ridden in silence for a while, she exclaimed: 'Because, you know, Edwin wanted peace. Peace and justice, he said, especially in the later years, after his baptism. And in my opinion it has to stop at some point, all these wars over gold and land, because what do we get out of them? Whetted knives—wasted lives, my mother Breguswid always said. And it becomes increasingly obvious to me: what use are goods and gold if you lose your kin and forfeit your admission to Paradise? The lust for gold deludes people! They think they're wise, but they're just foolish. I ask you—chasing around after gold! And when they stand there in front of Saint Peter, and he asks: What have you achieved on earth?—what are they going to say? His friendship can't be bought, no matter how much gold and goods they've managed to pile up, and there they stand! Should they say: I have deceived my neighbour and stolen his goods, I have killed a hundred men and begotten two hundred bastards with their widows, and I've brought along this stolen hoard of gold as the payoff for my soul?! And what do you think Saint Peter would say to that?'

She was so caught up in her own train of thought that she didn't wait for an answer, but just carried on: 'Be off with you! says Saint Peter. See if your gold will buy you anything down there among the flames! he says. And then believe you me, Oswine, there will be some who repent. But it'll be too late. And that's what people can't get into their heads: life is so short, and what is done can't be undone. But when the Day of Judgement comes, well, then you'll see them wailing: but we believed, but we thought, but we didn't mean it like that—and all that snivelling. Then there'll be no end to their good intentions. But by then it's just too late!'

This outpouring had left her short of breath, but looking at Oswine's pale beauty, she couldn't help laughing.

'Yes, yes, you probably think I'm crazy, with all that talk of Hell while we're here in the sun and spring and all this happiness.'

He shook his head and smiled.

'It's because I'm so happy,' she said. 'That's how it feels today—as if everything is floating.'

They rode on in silence. She had no need to say anything else, having experienced the intense happiness of being able to share her thoughts with someone who understood: a kinsman in blood and in mind, a man who didn't make sacrifices to Woden or eat horseflesh. She shuddered at the thought of Penda—such matters were simply beyond his comprehension.

Oswine reined in his horse; they had reached a crest from which they could see far to the north, across a stream flowing swiftly downwards between the forest-clad slopes.

'The Deorwent river,' he said.

Up here it was still just a brook, but once it had gathered water from all the other upland streams, it would become the mighty river that flowed past Mædeltun.

Riding downhill, slowly and carefully, they turned eastward and saw the slope on the other side of the river opening into a dale, from which a brook flowed out into the Deorwent.

'There!' said Oswine, pointing.

Before them lay the most delightful hollow, branching out into narrow fingers encircled by forest: as if an enormous giant, perhaps the Lord himself, had pressed his large and irregular five-fingered paw into the hilly landscape before it had finished setting and taken shape; as if he wanted to make his final mark before resting after his work.

'A hand!' Hild laughed, and Oswine stared at her.

The slope was covered with cowslips, yellow cowslips everywhere. The flowers had lasted on these northerly and easterly slopes, and were the most wonderful sign Hild could be given: these little yellow heads had brought a greeting from her faraway sister.

'Cow teats,' she murmured, captivated, while they rode downhill. She wouldn't stop to look, however, because Oswine had said this was the place, and there would be time enough later for cow teats. Her nerves were jangling all over as they rode across the ford and into the wrist of the paw-print.

In the palm there was a farm, a good and big farm, a prosperous farm. It had come true, what she had always hoped and what had meant so much to their father: for their sons to grow up in circumstances befitting their status, not in one of Penda's little guest huts, like captives, but here in the forest and fields, free, learning to hunt and doing all the things the sons of a king should do.

Hild had tears in her eyes as, for the first time, she realized how much she had wronged Eadfrid. He had taken the difficult decision to send their sons to Deira, but how right he had been to let them grow up in a place like this. She understood that now, and silently asked him to forgive her anger, and her short-sightedness, her selfishness.

'What is this place called?' she whispered to Oswine as they rode towards the large farmhouse.

'Hacanos.'

'Blessed by the Lord,' said Hild.

'It is a good farm,' Oswine replied.

They had hardly reached the fencing before the gate was opened, and when they rode into the yard, the farmer was waiting to receive them.

'A blessed place!' Hild said to him.

'Many thanks,' the man replied.

She looked around, expecting to see the two boys running towards her.

'Are they waiting indoors?' she asked.

'I shall take you there,' the man replied.

'Was this not the place?' she asked Oswine.

'Yes, yes,' said Oswine.

The farmer's horse was already saddled.

'It's not far,' he said.

They rode off again, across a brook and a little way uphill, into Our Lord's forefinger, cowslips to all sides under the trees, pale yellow, butter yellow, springtime yellow.

They drew to a halt before they reached the summit, dismounted and walked into the forest. There was a clearing ahead; it looked like a burial place. Perhaps the man wanted to make a sacrifice before he handed over the children. He led them to two fresh graves.

'Here!' he said, and pointed.

Hild stared at him. She didn't understand. She stared at Oswine, but he was gazing rigidly at the graves and didn't look up. The graves were covered with fresh flowers and bracken.

'I'm sorry,' the farmer mumbled, looking at the ground. 'Both at once like that. A wild boar. Hunting. And just last week. Yes, just last week it was.'

Talcuin, again, had to supervise his mistress's homeward journey. He had to forget about fetching his horse in Mædeltun; they would have to get home as quickly as possible—he was worried about the child on the way.


A girl, just as she had hoped. Well, the childbirth helper told her so, but Hild never saw the baby. She hadn't been fully developed, and was buried near the monastery, as close as possible to consecrated ground. Baptism was out of the question, but Hild gave her daughter the name Radegund, hoping the holy Frankish queen, from her place near the Lord's throne, would assist her little namesake. Although it didn't really comply with the rules, Hild nonetheless added her daughter's name to the list of those the monk prayed for every day, along with Hundfrid and Wilbrord.

# THE VIXEN IN THE TRAP

*- Hild's and Cynewise's trickery -*

Hild recovered but slowly from the miscarriage. She watched Wulfhere and Ædelræd, and simply couldn't take in that she had given birth to them. The memory of Frigyd often visited her, and she wept; the passage of time hadn't lessened the pain of recalling the little girl's brief life. Penda was right when he said the dead should be left to rest; she would gladly have let them go, but they wouldn't leave her alone.

The dead came to her at night, but she no longer feared them: her mother, Paulinus, Frigyd, Edwin, and a stooping young man she didn't know—their brother perhaps, or her father. Kinfolk, that was certain, but no Hundfrid or Wilbrord.

Breguswid muttered inarticulately, her hair was even greyer, and sometimes she laughed quietly, but she didn't hear Hild's questions. Well, she didn't answer at any rate. On one visit, she arrived with her arms full of yellow irises she had picked down by the river Use. She intended to offer them to her daughters' god, but Paulinus was standing in the way, and Breguswid couldn't get rid of her flowers; the big yellow petals withered away in her hands.

Paulinus always showed himself in profile or walking away, never his face. Frigyd would sit playing with the small gifts Hild had brought indoors for her.

They wanted to tell her something—but whatever that might be wasn't clear yet.

She spent most of the time in her monastery, and joined in the monk's prayers for her family. Prayers were said every day for her parents, her brother, Hereswid, her children, for Eadfrid and all his kin. The list was long and also included Sigebert, Paulinus, Cædwalla,

Frigyd, people who had died while in Hild's service plus, to her surprise and strangest of all: Oswald.

She hadn't wanted to put him on the list—and his brother, King Oswy, undoubtedly organized plenty of praying for him up north—but the thought haunted her, and she eventually took the consequence and ordered Masses for the repose of his soul. She'd had her revenge, there was no more unfinished business between them, and now she just wished him peace in Paradise.

She wrote long letters to Hereswid and to Aidan, who was still her guide and spiritual adviser.

Eadburh and Tibba, Penda's daughters, often visited, to her great delight and comfort. They didn't want to miss out on lessons and continued to make good progress; they brought greetings from everyone at the estate, and often a plant or a few seeds from Merewald.

'I am your husband, you know,' said Penda one night after she had excused herself on an exceptionally thin pretext.

'Cynewise's husband, that's what you are,' she said quietly and without anger, 'but my god does not see us as husband and wife.'

She put her head on his shoulder, an arm across his chest, eyes closed.

Penda lay motionless, staring at the ceiling. He was shocked she could think like that about their marriage, which was as fully valid as his marriage with Cynewise, but just hadn't been blessed by some priest. It was beyond him that it should mean so much, because if her god saw everything, then he must also see the love they had for one another, and had always had, yes, from the first time he had seen her.

Such piercing tenderness for her, and an aching, burning desire. Just the one of those feelings might have been all very well, but taken together they had turned into a hurricane that had nearly blown him away, and which he would gladly have done without.

It had possessed him with a force more powerful than he could control, driving him to actions he would not have thought possible. He had given in to this force, well aware that it could ruin his lineage and the whole realm.

Marrying a woman of the new faith hadn't been without cost, but he had known the price and had never been surprised by the opposition their marriage had provoked. Nor had he at any point thought it would bring good fortune either for him or for the kingdom. But every single happy day, every good harvest and every battle won had filled him with an incredulous delight, a new-born gratitude for . . . he knew not what.

He had taken on a dangerous option, had done so with eyes wide open, and it had turned into good fortune—for him personally, for his kinfolk and for all of Mercia.

He stroked his disheartened wife's hair, thinking how nothing could eradicate their seven years of happiness. The hair at her temples was already streaked with white, and the singing that used to ring out wherever she walked had all but ceased. She stooped slightly, her eyes a little dull and distant.

He would do anything and he would give everything he owned—which was a lot—if he could turn good fortune her way again. No one, however, could control destiny, and now events would just have to run their course. Not even the king of Mercia was the master of fate, as he had always known—unlike those kings who professed the new faith and thought they could bribe fate with prayers and gifts for the monasteries, thought they could make themselves masters of their lives and then just order it around. Ridiculous, they were, simply ridiculous: as if their god was above fate and could give it orders!

Of course, the gods should have their share: you needed to stay good friends with them so they didn't actively go out to make trouble for you. They should have what they were entitled to, plus a little extra; they didn't like tight-fistedness. In that respect, they were no different from anyone else, which was understandable.

Whatever the gods might have in their power, not a single one of them could control fate. Fate—it went without saying—was above everything and everyone.

Besides, who his people chose to serve was no concern of his, as long as they knew to whom they owed taxes and for whom they went into battle: providing they served their king, then as far as he was concerned they could serve whatever else they wanted. They could worship a stone, or a cabbage, it wasn't any of his business—or even this new foreign god, and his Jewish son who had been executed.

The gallows-bird, as he called him when Hild wasn't listening. What a peculiar idea they had, worshipping an executed criminal, and the whole notion that a god would do something as ludicrous as becoming a man! If he was in possession of all the bliss in Heaven and everything in the whole world, why would he let himself be crucified? Very odd way to go about things, in his opinion, and not in the least appropriate for a king. A shabby way to govern—no matter how many times he might have risen from the grave.

There was, however, one thing in their holy book he agreed with, something said about the gallows-bird once he'd been nailed up: 'If you really are the son of God, then get down from the cross and show us what you're worth!'

And someone else had said: 'He says he's hanging there and saving all the people in the world. But he can't save himself!'

Strange they'd written down something like that and then even went around telling people! That really was making a fool of yourself, and making things easier for your opponents. He would never have included that part of the story if he'd been telling it.

They were thoroughly peculiar, those people. You couldn't really do anything but smile, or shake your head, and even that didn't seem to bother them—extremely odd.

And then the final argument, which Hild always presented with the most solemn of expressions, and which always made him laugh out loud, even though he'd got better at hiding it: Our god created the world!

Well, what a mess he'd made of that job! You'd have to search long and hard to find an unruly chaos to match it!

Penda couldn't stifle his merriment any longer; he started to chuckle, his chest heaving.

'What is it?' asked Hild, who had been woken by her head bouncing up and down on his shoulder.

'Oh it's nothing, you just sleep on,' he said, but now he simply couldn't hold back any longer and had to sit up in bed to finish laughing.

'But what is it?' she insisted. His merriment was infectious, she wanted to join in.

'Oh, just something they said, something about a goat that had given birth to a kid lamb—it's nothing.'

Hild's eyes darkened.

'Where did this happen?' she asked, filled with misgiving.

'Pure nonsense,' Penda reassured her. 'Of course it's not true, it was just something they said, don't concern yourself, go back to sleep.'

'But what if it *is* true?' she whispered uneasily.

'I swear, it's a downright falsehood,' Penda promised. He lay down and pulled her head back onto his shoulder.

'Just forget it, it's utter twaddle.'

'Yes, because it could mean the end of times,' whispered Hild.

'It could, but it really doesn't mean the one thing or the other, because it hasn't happened at all,' said Penda, stroking her hair soothingly. It wasn't long before her breathing told him she had fallen asleep.

He always felt so strange when he was with Hild—and it was because *she* was strange. Cynewise was quite normal, and he found her company really very boring; she wasn't stupid or unbalanced, no, it was just that her line of thought was simple, undemanding and absolutely predictable. And that was the joy of living with Hild: her peculiar way of turning everything upside down had given him so much amusement and such great delight.

He didn't fear the bad fortune that had descended upon them. Fate had changed course before and given him things he hadn't asked for, things he couldn't have imagined, and now it had changed course again, as was its nature.

The thread of fate spun between them had woven them together, in lust and in loss. She had grown into his bones, and when he had to do without her, well, she was still there, embedded in him for ever; their fate had become one.

He was dozing off; it was always like this when he slept with her: his breathing and his heartbeat settled down, found rest alongside her sinewy old body—the unison singing of their bones and the mutual sympathy of their blood were having their customary effect.

Then he fell asleep.

The vixen was caught in the trap.

She had no idea what had happened, but one thing she did know: she had to get away. As the tension in her swollen teats increased, one thing more: she had to suckle. Above all, she knew the cubs had to be kept away.

The vixen had a young hare—had sunk her teeth into its neck, but not taken a single bite. The cubs had to become familiar with the scent of a hare; they couldn't eat it, but they could lick a drop or two of blood. Scent was the important factor, and they had to be taught about it, just like *her* mother had taught her.

A couple of chicken wings had attracted the vixen's attention: at the very moment she grabbed them, she was stuck. The pain in her leg was shocking, and when she pulled and pushed with her other legs, the pain became paralysing. Escape was not an option.

After all her exertion, she dozed off, and when she woke up she'd forgotten about the cubs, and ate the young hare and what flesh there was on the chicken wings. A little strength returned, but the pain in her leg had increased, and the tension in her swollen teats was now almost unbearable.

The den was very close; she could hear the cubs romping around, and every so often they would interrupt their game to call out, start playing again, stop again. Their whimpering intensified; she could hear every sound they made, through the wind whispering in the trees and the blackbirds rustling in the dry leaves. She closed her oval eyes and waited in silence. Not far off a mouse moved—she tensed, ready to leap, and took off.

Afterwards she lay distraught with pain. Recovering slightly, she licked her leg, then heard the big cub coming towards her. She pressed herself flat against the cold object gripping her leg, but she could already see the cub's head sticking through the blackberry runners, heard it bark loudly as it threw itself upon her. She tried in vain to shoo it back, pushed harder against the cold object so the cub couldn't get at her teats, snarled and snapped at it, but the noise attracted the smaller ones and they were soon tumbling out of the thicket, yapping eagerly with excitement and hunger.

There were five of them, and she soon had to relent. She rolled wearily onto her side and let them do what they wanted. They stumbled around, fighting over the teats, nipped a little here and sucked a little there, before abandoning themselves to the warm milk.

Then it was just a matter of the leg. Once the tension in her teats had been relieved, it was purely a question of the leg. It was bleeding from the spot where the object clenched tightly, and she licked the congealed blood; more blood oozed out, she licked that too. Her fur had been ripped off and shreds of flesh jutted out; she bit them off, licked the wounds, and bit again, until the pain was too excruciating. The cubs had fallen asleep, some still teat in mouth; she licked them clean and rested.

Hearing the sound of large creatures approaching, she pressed down against the earth. Then came the sound of the big dangerous beasts around the henhouses and the food store and everything that was good. Her heart was thudding at double speed; she tried to cover the cubs with her body, but merely succeeded in waking them: they whimpered and then started tumbling around again. Stuck where she was, she had no way of reprimanding them.

The large creatures were very close now, and fear was about to be the death of her; they came nearer, a pungent stink and such sickening sounds they made. She managed to toss one of the cubs aside so it fell towards the den; another ran after it, but the other three just pressed more firmly against her belly.

The smell of the huge dangerous beasts was overwhelming, far worse than the smell of the ones who trotted and did no harm. She had to give up trying to shoo the cubs home and settle for pressing herself flat and invisible against the earth. A shadow fell across her, she closed her eyes, paralysed with fear, could feel the blood forcing its way up her throat, could hardly breathe, pressed down on the cubs.

Peering through narrow slits, she saw the huge dangerous beast leaning over the hard object that was holding her down. She launched herself and bit with all her might, heard a scream more jarring than a chased hare, and she held on tight. The taste of blood, noise and a crack on the head.

When she woke up, she was free. She limped back to the den, jostling along her little cubs.

Hild refused to turn back. They were so close to the monastery, and letting a vixen change your resolve could lead to misfortune. Heathens behaved like that, not Christian people. Today, it was nine years since fate had caught up with Eadfrid.

Talcuin's protests were half-hearted—his abrupt insubordination hadn't led to any good.

They pressed on in silence, but when they reached their destination Hild had to make do with a brief prayer and the customary pitcher of wine. She had to let Talcuin look at her hand; he raised it to his mouth and sucked and bit and squeezed until she screamed.

When they passed the place where they had spotted the red pelt amongst the white bladder campions on the forest floor, she just had to stop and have a look.

The vixen and the cubs had gone—Hild had no regrets. On the return journey, she kept picturing what she hadn't seen in reality: the vixen lying in her den, plump bluish cubs suckling at her teats.

Soaking the arm in hot water, herb poultices, camomile tea, coltsfoot, ointment—Hild's entire arsenal of cures was deployed, but the swelling grew larger, a dark line ran up her arm from the wound, and she was delirious. The doctor hung the nine effective herbs from the ceiling, and Talcuin spent the nights on a stool next to her bed, alternately pleading with the Lord and cursing himself.

He hadn't refused to comply with his mistress's orders because he was scared of the vixen, but because he knew it was Cynewise's trap, and they had troubles enough as it was.

'She can have a marten pelt instead,' his lady had said, whereupon she had gone to it herself and thrown the snare open.

One fur more or less wasn't important, but Hild's lack of respect for Cynewise's property *was*, and Cynewise took the violation most seriously, pointing out that her god obviously felt the need to set Hild an example. She would not accept the offer of a marten pelt, but demanded that from now on Hild stuck to her own business.

Penda promised on Hild's behalf, which he could do quite safely as he didn't think his wife would recover. He didn't understand what was going on inside her, and Talcuin's explanation sounded bizarre. Had Hild become so petty-minded that she begrudged her co-wife a fox fur? They could both have bear and marten and otter, whatever they wanted. They had some sable too, come to that, so why fight over a fox? He simply couldn't understand.

However, he did something he had never thought he would: he prayed to Hild's god—locked the door to his chamber, lay prostrate on the floor and implored her god to make her well—because this was a matter in which neither the pagan priest nor Woden could help.

While Hild languished, Cynewise gave birth to a son. A splendid son with everything just as it should be, and thick black hair. He shrieked like a madman the moment he came out, and he had a huge appetite: a real warrior, and sturdier than Hild's sons had been, it was said.

Penda rode back and forth between royal estates. At the one he sang and tickled the baby, at the other he sat slumped on a stool with Hild's hand in his, or lay on the floor and prayed.

Two weeks, and then Hild opened her eyes and called for Penda. She couldn't believe he was lying on the floor next to her bed, praying, and he could hardly believe she had come to herself again. He danced with joy, and Hild laughed.

She was sitting up in bed drinking soup when word arrived from Cynewise's estate that Penda must come immediately, so he kissed Hild and set forth.

By then his son was already dead.

They couldn't find any cause; he had been asleep, everything had been fine and then, in an instant, he was dead.

He hadn't even been baptised, even though the agreement with Cynewise's brother said that their children should be baptised.

Unnerving, the way fate might just snatch away a prince, and one it had only just bestowed—as was the subject of much discussion in the days that followed. This unnerving phenomenon soon took on an added dimension: the son had died at the very moment Hild's life-force had returned, from wherever it might have been. Particularly unnerving, it had to be said, but perhaps also a natural explanation for the otherwise inexplicable death. Cynewise wasn't slow to grasp the doctor's insinuation.

Penda usually went red in the face when he was angry, but now he was ashen, and he sent everyone from the chamber. His anger was of a type Hild had not encountered before; she was scared, which made her inadvertently laugh—a piercing and nervous laugh that stopped as abruptly as it had started—and she had to concentrate all her efforts in order to understand what he was saying.

'Cynewise is demanding restitution for our son. From you. Otherwise she will return home.'

'Why should I pay a fine?' asked Hild, once she had eventually grasped what he had said.

'Because you are to blame!' Penda roared.

'Why on earth should I be to blame?' asked Hild. She had no idea what was going on, but she could tell it must be serious.

'While your spirit was elsewhere, they are saying, then, they say, you took the life-force out of him—when you yourself were unable to go on any longer.'

Penda sat down heavily, shaking his head.

'Well, I don't understand either,' he added.

After a while he looked up at Hild.

'And that was the reason you wanted Cynewise's fox skin, they say—for trickery.'

'But that's madness,' Hild eventually responded.

'Possibly, but you'll have to do it nonetheless.'

'Never! I can't atone for something I didn't do.'

'You have to take a broader view. Give her what she wants. It's the only way to stop her leaving.'

'Well, she'll just have to leave,' said Hild. 'I can't pay for something of which I am not guilty.'

Penda sat in grim silence.

'So—you cling to gold after all, do you?' he snarled.

'I cling to my honour, as you well know.'

'Your *honour* and your *honour*—to your Hell with that accursed pride!'

He hammered a fist into the tabletop, and his face was paler than she had ever seen before—was this her husband, Penda?

'Then I'd be admitting it was me—and it wasn't,' she whispered, finding it hard to catch her breath. 'I don't know who killed Cynewise's son, but it was not me, that much I do know.'

'And *that* is really not the point,' said Penda. 'Because he's dead anyway. But you are the only person who can make her stay, and here you are talking about your honour!'

'Why would I want to make her stay when she's making up a story like that?' Hild asked frostily.

'Because otherwise the peace will be broken,' Penda bellowed, 'as well you know!'

'Apparently it has been already.'

Penda took a deep breath and said bitterly: 'I seem to recall you talking frequently and at great length about peace—but that was perhaps just talk, idle talk.'

Hild bit her lip.

Penda stood up and started pacing back and forth, deep in thought; he eventually came to a halt, and addressed her calmly.

'How many men, in your opinion, should we sacrifice for your pride? Have a think about how much it's worth. And don't forget that Oswy will attack swiftly from the other flank. So—how many families should have their land laid waste, how many warriors should be slain, how many crops should be scorched—work it out! How many lives is your pride worth?'

Hild sat stony-faced. His questions were meaningless, and she refused to be spoken to in that way. It seemed as if Eadfrid's tormentor had now taken up residence in Penda. The whole conversation was absurd.

'One hundred,' she said.

'Fine,' he shouted. 'If you can limit the devastation to one hundred lives then you're a greater sorceress than they say. Be my guest. Then you can take over and rule the realm! If you can limit it to one hundred lives, then well done you!'

He rushed towards the door, but turned round.

'A piece of good advice: you had better muster an army immediately.'

The door slammed.

The metallic taste of blood in her mouth, the pain in her clenched hands and arms as she pummelled the table, kicked the stool, screamed in agony, pounded the walls.

She knew, had known all along: this was the price for Oswald's head, and it might well increase, but there was no way back.

Hild rode to her monastery, fasted and implored the Lord to send her a sign. She had ended up on a dead-end track, closed and impenetrable to all sides, feeling as if the Lord had released his hold on the strands of her destiny and was letting them snake around her so she could neither go forwards nor backwards.

He simply had to give her a sign, an opening, a tiny little doorway, so she could find the way onward.

*O Lord, my God,*
*I have cried to you day and night;*
*let my prayer appear before you,*
*lend your ear to my cry!*
*for my soul is full of suffering*
*and my life draws close to the grave . . .*

*Save me, O God, for the waters reach to my soul;*
*I have sunk in unfathomable mire*
*where there is no foothold.*
*I have come into the deep*
*where the floods overflow me.*
*I am weary of my crying, my throat burns,*
*my eyes fail while I wait for my God . . .*

*O God, you know my foolishness,*
*my sins are not hidden from you;*
*let me not bring shame on those who hope in you.*
*O Lord God of hosts,*
*let me not bring disgrace*
*on those who seek you, O God of Israel!*

Talcuin knocked on his mistress's door. She had spent five days in prayer and fasting, and he thought that was enough. She had refused to talk to anyone, but now she would have to listen to him.

He came straight to the point and told her what he knew: Penda had married her against all the warnings and appeals of the pagan priest; even Penda's own casting of lots had spoken strongly against marriage; the council had made an unsolicited statement, and Penda had told them to hold their tongues—for the first and only time.

Hild had never known Penda to act against a lot he had thrown. She was stunned and mystified.

'How do you know this?' she asked eventually.

'You hear a thing or two,' Talcuin shrugged, mumbling evasively.

She knew he was telling the truth.

'Leave,' she said quietly, and he left.

She sat motionless for a while, staring into space, and when she finally stood up her legs gave way. She fell to the floor, her entire body shuddering with sobs.

'Forgive me!' she cried, doubling up. 'Forgive me!'

How wretchedly she had rewarded this man; the Lord had led her to him, had let her see him, so closely it had nearly blinded her, a man more genuine than anyone she had ever met, who had sacrificed everything in order to have her at his side! He had yet again risked his life and the security of the realm in order to restore her honour, and she had repelled his love through her pride. Her pride, which was nothing other than pettiness, vile and dishonourable pettiness.

Never had she known such a magnanimous man as Penda. Compared to him she was so small, so very small. Were it still possible, she would do everything in her power to atone the harm she had done him, the man who was her life-blood, her lungs, her muscles and sinews, father of her sons, the songbird in her bed, her love, her life.

She hurried home to Tamoworthig, to be told that Penda had left on horseback; she immediately rode off after him and found his horse by the sacred grove, to which she was not allowed access. She sent one of the unbaptized men to fetch him.

'Get out of here! Sorceress! Witch!'

It was Penda's voice, and she flinched.

'Penda,' she shouted, 'let me talk with you!'

'Never,' he shouted back, 'you have brought enough misfortune. Go away, or they'll string you up!'

'Never,' she shouted back, 'I must talk with you.'

'There's nothing to talk about,' he shouted, 'apart from rallying an army.'

She sat on the grass and waited. She stayed there for a long time, until she finally heard him approaching and ran to meet him, threw herself to the ground in front of him, clutched at his feet and begged his forgiveness.

'I know I have caused misfortune for you and the realm. Forgive me, so I can make amends,' she begged.

He pulled her up from her far too servile supplication, held her at arm's length and then hugged her tightly.

'I'm afraid it's too late,' he said. 'Cynewise is unlikely to forgive you.'

'You are the one who must forgive me,' Hild went on, 'for what I have done to you.'

'I forgive you,' said Penda, 'everything and always. But that is not enough to safeguard your life. Cynewise is set against you, as you know.'

'She can have her own way, whatever she wants,' said Hild, 'as long as she doesn't separate us.'

'I'll talk with her,' said Penda. He lifted a corner of her cap and breathed in the scent of her hair.

'My darling old wife,' he whispered, 'darling little old wife . . . '

Hild wept in his arms—her flesh, her love, her song thrush.

The air was heavy and oppressive; flies buzzed in the hot dust and the birds only managed an occasional feeble twitter.

Hild leant across the well and hooked the bucket onto the hoist. Neither before nor since she had stayed at Frigyd's house had she been obliged to fetch water; she looked down the well and quickly glanced away.

The watching crowd silently and inquisitively followed her every movement. She didn't look at anyone while she fixed the bucket onto the yoke—it was heavier than she had expected—straightened up and walked slowly and resolutely towards the hall, without spilling too much. The door was open and with steady little steps she entered and progressed all the way along the fireplace to the top table where Cynewise and Penda were sitting.

She squatted slightly until the buckets rested on the floor, removed the yoke and prostrated herself in front of Cynewise. In a loud and firm voice, she said: 'I entreat Queen Cynewise to forgive my despicable deed! I pledge to abstain from all sorcery and to behave with propriety to King Penda's wife.'

Then she waited, but something must have gone wrong with the agreed performance because no answer was forthcoming. When she thought she had been lying there long enough, she stood up and carried the bucket across to a silver dish, which she filled.

She bowed to her co-wife and asked leave to wash her feet. Cynewise nodded in silence. The handmaid passed Hild a vessel of oil, which she poured into the water. Slowly and fastidiously, she rubbed the solution between the toes and around the edges of the nails, to remove the dirt that wasn't there, ran her hand from the instep to the back of the heel and back under the arch, rubbed and stroked the feet of a stranger, her hands becoming hot and the feet almost scalding despite the chilly water, and she felt queasy in the heat transmitted by the young woman.

Perhaps Cynewise was capable of more than they knew, given the heat passing through Hild's hands and arms and spreading throughout her body; she could feel it all the way down to the soles of her feet, melting away the last scraps of her old pride. She looked up at Cynewise's face and thought she could see the hint of a smile and a little nod.

Hild didn't look at Penda, who had put his arm around Cynewise's shoulders, which, strange to say, didn't bother her. All she could see was the smile on Cynewise's beautiful pale face; she felt burning hot and bowed her head, blushing.

She reached for the towel and methodically and meticulously dried Cynewise's feet. First cautiously, then massaging them more vigorously; pink as dog roses they were. She took the right foot firmly in her hand and pressed it to her mouth.

At this point, she ought to have stood up and walked away—that was the agreement—but she stayed lying on the floor, Cynewise's foot to her lips. She stayed there, even though first Cynewise's voice and then Penda's ordered her to stand up. The otherwise so dignified and well-implemented scene was threatening to unravel.

Hild stayed where she was, holding onto Cynewise's foot. Eventually, Cynewise stood up and helped Hild from her prostrate position on the floor.

Hild pressed a light kiss on the young woman's forehead, bowed to her and walked away, head held high. She then rode back to her monastery.

Hild was a changed woman. When she leant over the well, she thought she could see a little hand down there, so very small and clenched. It could almost have been Hundfrid's chubby little hand, but when she looked more closely, it had vanished.

She knew this was a sign sent by the Lord, and that she must heed its meaning. She sank more and more into herself, never asked about her husband and didn't seem particularly interested in what he was doing.

It was said she was getting old, and that was indeed how she felt. Her woman's bleeding became increasingly sporadic, which was probably rather early, but suited the widow's life she led.

Her first husband had been avenged, and two healthy sons were thriving at Penda's court. She had seen Hundfrid and Wilbrord once in a dream, playing in a meadow, just as she had seen her brother long ago. Now she was content in the knowledge that the Lord had taken them to be with him: they had been baptized, so nothing in the world could cut them off from his love, as Paulinus had always said, and Aidan had also said. There was nothing more she could do for them.

Her husband Penda was married to a woman who could have been his grandchild—but that couldn't take away the seven years of happiness she had spent with him. A long time ago, a very long time ago. Their union had never been blessed by a priest, but fate had bound them to one another, no matter what happened. She wished him nothing but good fortune, and for herself she wished peace.

Her years of happiness were over, but perhaps he could have seven new years of happiness with his young Cynewise. She was a good and prudent wife to him, none better, more mature than Hild had been at her age. That was how it had turned out, and that was for the best.

# THE HUNGER FOR ACTION

*- Penda's princely sons -*

Penda rode to visit Hild. He still hadn't been able to decide whether or not to accept Merewald's baptism, so the wedding had to wait. He had long since abandoned any hope that Merewald would marry into the West Saxons, but that was no longer such a pressing matter anyway, even though it would have been pleasing.

He was vacillating because of pressure from his other children. Tibba and Eadburh also wanted to be baptized, and before he knew it his princely sons might want to as well and then, after his death, the kingdom would be converted to the new god. More and more kingdoms were doing just that, and it was causing much strife, but he wanted his princely sons to inherit good kingdoms with no more friction than the inevitable.

Moreover, it seemed to him that followers of the new faith had forsaken some of the absolute prerequisites for a healthy realm: initiative, the spirit of self-sacrifice, the hunger for action.

Many of the kings who served Jesus Christ spent their time forever praying and were only concerned about the salvation of their souls. They granted far too much land to the monasteries, thereby reducing the crown territories, but worse still: the unity of a kingdom was split by allowing another regime to operate alongside the royal regime. In Penda's way of being king, he was the leader of his people when dealing with foreigners and gods alike, whereas the kings of the new faith had to compete with the people of the Church. In particular, missionaries from the south were trying to assert themselves—in Kent, he'd seen how the king had proved his legitimacy by being anointed and blessed by the Church people.

It hadn't been like that in olden times when the Britons were the only ones serving the new god. The kings and the monastic people had taken care of their respective areas, and the holy ones hadn't wanted to own anything other than a little patch of land on which to subsist. Many holy people still lived in this kind of isolation, without the claims of the material world; they didn't evangelize and would hardly even talk to 'the new' as they called people like Penda, whose family had now lived in these isles for eight generations.

The Church people's lust for power seemed to be growing at the same time as their followers seemed to be losing their resolve to deploy everything, life included, for their honour and the reputation of their lineage.

Many people were quite content simply to have eternal life in the hereafter and felt no obligation to accomplish any mighty deeds in order to win immortality through the reputation they left behind on earth. Instead, they became possessed of a strange obstinacy. Baptized slaves would refuse to help at sacrifices, they treated Thunor's day as any other workday, and often insisted on having the sun day off. You could flog them and threaten them with that which was worse, all to no avail. When the Christians had to choose which of two masters they would serve, the celestial one always prevailed. The only thing they really feared was Hell. He never bought Christian slaves—unlike both his wives—which was rather practical, because the pagans worked on sun days too.

In Kent, he'd also seen how the monasteries actually fed people who had fallen into hardship, and he'd heard that Aidan did the same in Lindisfarena. People knew they could just gamble away everything or be negligent with their work and let the slaves put their feet up, thank you very much—if they lost the farm they could always get their bellies filled in some monastery or other.

A system like that wasn't going to make people work to build up their prosperity and plan carefully. In the old days you had to go from farm to farm if you got into hardship and didn't have kin to help you. Maybe you'd get some food, maybe not. Maybe you and your family would be bought, maybe not. You just had to carry on until fate found you a place—or let you perish along the way. That's how it was, and you would perhaps think twice before gambling away everything you owned.

People didn't care about anything today. They could just get baptized, and then they'd be handed everything other people had been obliged to fight for all their lives. It wasn't a healthy attitude: one baptismal ducking in the river and you'd never vanish and be forgotten, food readily available from the monasteries—all without lifting a finger.

Not in Mercia, you didn't feed vagrants here, not yet, but you did everywhere else. Indifference was spreading slowly but surely, and Penda didn't want his princely sons to inherit that kind of kingdom.

'You can say what you will,' he told Hild, once he had settled in and had something to eat, 'but the desire for gold is what drives the world onwards.'

'Greed, my dear Eadwacer!' she corrected him tartly. 'I think you mean greed for gold.'

'No—desire, the pleasure in acquiring it,' Penda insisted.

Hild shrugged.

'Well,' said Penda, 'call it what you will. But without it, we'd still be sitting on Angeln twiddling our thumbs.'

'Which might have been preferable,' said Hild.

'You might think so, but it wouldn't have suited me, that's absolutely certain. Nor my sons.'

'Merewald wouldn't have objected.'

'Ah, Merewald—no. I'm referring to my princely sons.'

'I've thought it over, and I mean what I say. This lust for gold and power has been the death of my father and almost my entire family,' said Hild. 'Where's my brother? Where are my twins? My sister's husband was slain, my own husband murdered, our friend Cædwalla was slain. Edwin was slain, and his people, there had been two previous attempts on Edwin's life, three of my cupbearers are dead, Sigebert has fallen, my own kin Oswine has forsaken me—what good has come of it?'

'I don't know—when you put it like that,' said Penda. 'But Mercia has expanded during the time you're talking about.'

'And others have become proportionally smaller,' Hild retorted. 'Were you not king, it would be called theft.'

Penda didn't understand.

'Well, if you'd taken bread or cattle from others,' Hild tried to explain, 'you'd be hung. But when a king takes a stretch of land, it's called conquest and considered a good thing. Can't you see?'

No, Penda couldn't.

'Won in a fair fight—and that is a very long way from being theft, when you sneak up and hope no one notices.'

'Yes, there are differences. As there are differences between falling in battle and being ambushed as Eadfrid was!'

'Leave him in peace, Hild,' said Penda. 'He has been avenged.'

'And then there's one more widow to add to all the other widows,' she responded. 'That's what I mean: who gets any satisfaction from *that*? One day it might be your turn to be killed—and then there'll be two more widows. And were it not for this never-ending strife, our marriage wouldn't have been ruined by one wife too many.'

'It's only because you can't adapt to how things really are. If you weren't so damned proud, you would have adjusted to the situation. My mother did. She made no comment when my father took an extra wife after he became one of the chief men.'

'It was a different time,' said Hild.

'It's just *you* that's different,' said Penda. 'You walk on a little cloud up in the air! You don't know anything, nor could you care less! You're more concerned with how you think the world *ought* to be than how it actually is. *That's* what makes for all the problems.'

'No, it isn't,' she answered, 'and it won't be any more true however many times you say it. Greed for gold makes for the problems. It's almost impossible to find my husband Penda now. You really are turning into Eadwacer—a watcher of wealth!'

Penda made a sweeping gesture.

'That's what people are like, and you may just as well accept it. What's more, you benefit from everything I bring home. I don't think you'd be particularly happy to wear undyed linen every single day, the same dress, and no food on the table? And get frostbite when you have to fetch firewood in wintertime?'

Hild fumed at his underhand trick.

'That's not what I'm talking about!' she shouted. 'What I mean is: if everyone could just settle for what is theirs, then there would be enough for us all!'

'Well, my darling,' said Penda, 'you are quite at liberty to become a slave. Whensoever you might choose, you can sell yourself into slavery. Why not try it, instead of talking so much? I'll buy your freedom when you weary of it all, don't you worry.'

He laughed.

'Unless, of course, you're completely done for. And I'm telling you: no men in your bed! Otherwise I won't buy you back!'

Hild snorted—she didn't find him anywhere near as funny as he thought he was.

'You know exactly what I mean: everyone should have food to eat and clothes for their children. And don't always twist what I say.'

'No no, but I think you could start by granting your own slaves their freedom. And you could give away your marten-fur cloak and your silk dress, and your otter cap, and your little red boots, plus all your gold jewellery, or just the round brooch with all its shiny blue—what do you need it all for? The possibility cannot be ruled out that the world would indeed be a better place if you gave it all to the first beggar who crosses your path! Just like Aidan does.'

He laughed loudly, enjoying her ordeal.

'That might very well be the case!' she countered defiantly. The thought of her red boots and otter-fur cap broke her heart, and the round brooch and the gold holy cross from Edwin. She could perhaps give everything else away, but preferably not that holy cross—nor, come to think of it, the ermine-edged red silk dress, no, she wouldn't be happy to let that go either.

'Oh, you women,' Penda laughed. 'Finger on everything, what's wrong here and what's wrong there—but your own part in it all, no, that's much harder for you to spot!'

'You say that every time,' said Hild, 'but when everything is added up, we get less happiness than misfortune out of it, and I really mean that.'

'I see, so you would rather live in less comfortable circumstances?'

He had raised his eyebrows. Now he was going to ensnare her in her own trap.

'Yes, I would, if in return I could have kept my father and my brother and my twins, and had been spared the co-wife, yes, I would!'

'You forgot your husband Eadfrid.'

'Him too,' Hild lied—she had to.

'All right, then,' said Penda. 'And then you would have sown and harvested the crops yourselves, you and Eadfrid, and done the milking and churning, carding the yarn and spinning, and everything, would you? Because you wouldn't have had slaves to do the dirty work, now would you?'

'No, we wouldn't, and we would have managed; it's been seen before.'

'It has indeed,' Penda smiled, 'and those people didn't exactly live a long life. But that doesn't count for much, or what—the desire to live?'

'You should be the first to know that honour means more than a long life,' Hild snarled.

'Of course, of course, it's just difficult to see the honourable element in what you're suggesting.'

'Because you're blind,' she shouted, 'totally dazzled by your desire for gold!'

Penda was still having fun, which annoyed her intensely.

'Why don't you go home to Angeln,' he asked, 'so you can see what a lovely time they all have over there? Perhaps you could learn to twiddle your thumbs, in the right direction!'

Hild stared at him with disdain.

'One would think that was a muttonhead balancing on your neck! Or a head of cabbage!'

'Never mind,' he said, leaning back, 'I don't use it anyway!'

'No, as long as you have your casting lots, right?'

'Exactly!' he replied, and then they started laughing.

It wasn't the first time these words had been exchanged, but now they were both aware of that one time Penda had defied his lots. Hild walked across and pressed his head to her breast, smoothed back his hair and kissed the skin behind his ear. He put his arm around her waist and pulled her close. She sat again and they were silent for a while; she smiled, amazed by the sense of peace she felt through this man who was of such an unfathomably and fascinatingly different make-up.

She picked up her train of thought: 'Listen, it's obvious. The island is rich and fertile, lots of good pasture, which can be extended when we clear more forest and drain the land. Gold and silver and tin and copper—all can be dug from the ground. The brooks are full of fish, the forests teeming with game, birds of every variety and everything we people need. Why can't we just say: let's share it! Instead of fighting over it! And then we'd all be taken care of.'

'Firstly,' said Penda, 'you would never get the Picts to share anything with anyone.'

'Keep the Picts out of it, I mean the rest of us—down here.'

'Secondly, I don't think I'd want to live in that kind of kingdom. It would be far too big. We wouldn't know who was who, who you could count on. Also, it would be too boring. People don't thrive if there's too much prosperity. It's not healthy to have such a heavy belly you can hardly be bothered to stand up. Everything you say—well, you can think all that because you've never had to fight for your needs. You don't know what it means to face hardship and hunger. You lament the loss of your twins, but I don't know what you would have thought if you'd had to bury them when they'd died from hunger, or if you'd had to put them out. Or choose which boy should have food and which boy should die. And that's how it would be if your ideas were ever put into practice. The corn wouldn't be sown, but even if it were then it wouldn't be harvested. Everything would come to a standstill if we didn't fight a constant battle for survival. Just look at the beasts! They don't live with a teat in their mouths—they have to go out and find their food, even before they want to. And most of them perish. It might not be fair to *your* mind, but that's life. And no thought-up ideas can change that.'

He took another piece of pork and drained his beer.

'And I'm content with things the way they are,' he added.

Hild didn't respond, but mulled this over for a while.

'That's probably the decisive point,' she said eventually. 'But I'm not content with things the way they are.'

'No,' said Penda. 'But then you've got your Heaven to look forward to. Maybe up there things are sorted out as you'd like them to be.'

He said this without malice, as a kind of comfort, and Hild understood.

'Yes, yes,' she said. 'There's no knowing how things are sorted out up there. But it's certainly lovely, that much I know. And more fair-minded.'

She kissed his cheek, tugged his beard, and resumed her weaving. When the monk rang the bell for prayers, she poured a mug of fresh beer for her husband before leaving to pray for her kin.

His scribe had suddenly been taken ill, and therefore it was too late for action when the information finally reached Penda that Cynewise had sent a letter to her brother, King Cenwalch: she could no longer accept the conditions she was offered in Mercia; she would return home with two daughters, her morning gift and her jewellery.

The scribe's duty to keep the king informed was one of the security precautions Penda was compelled to maintain. Hild was the only person on the estate who could write, so Cynewise and all the others had to use the scribe.

Penda hurriedly sent some marten pelts to his dear brother-in-law, as he addressed him in his accompanying letter, with the very best wishes and hoping all was well with them, just as all in Mercia was in the very best shape. With greetings from his honoured and beloved wife Cynewise.

Due to a storm, which held up the message for three days, the gift did not arrive before King Cenwalch had taken his own precautions: rather than sending an equivalent gift of friendship, Penda's sister arrived, dressed in the most basic of clothes and only accompanied by her maid and very few men. Her people had been taken by surprise, and the rest of them were now being held hostage by her husband, King Cenwalch.

Cenwalch had seized her morning gift and substantial dowry, had banished her from the realm, and, in addition to all that, he had not allowed her to take her own jewellery and clothing.

An unprecedented disgrace, and a violation of every law, old as well as new.

Penda paced the floor. Had it not been for the extravagant feasts he had only just held to show Cynewise and the entire kingdom that she was his rightful queen and was entitled to the respect commensurate with her position, then he would instantly have sent her home, with less dignity than his sister had been afforded. He had no personal reason to keep her.

Reciprocation, however, wasn't enough to re-establish his honour: he would have to exact revenge.

Cynewise's people were disarmed and locked up. Cynewise and her daughters were taken to Tamoworthig where they were kept under guard by Penda's men, who plugged their ears with wool and kept their eyes averted from the forceful young queen. Now she could scream all she liked, and no one had to pay any attention to the curses and predictions that usually accompanied her fits and kept everyone at her beck and call.

Penda, of course, had spies in the courts of those kings he had to reckon with, and thus he knew that Oswy had his hands full with some of the Britons, tribes trying to recapture a little of their lost land in the west. Penda could safely attack the West Saxons.

His seventeen-year-old son Gefmund wasn't quite ready for action, having come too close to a wild boar; the wound hadn't healed, but there was nothing wrong with his fighting spirit. He begged his father to let him take part, but Penda thought it would be enough to take his other son, Bothelm, who was nineteen years old and had already proved his ability in battle. Gefmund asked Hild to intercede for him with his father, and Penda reluctantly agreed to take him along. Twelve-year-old Peada didn't even ask for permission.

It was a large and well-equipped army that set forth against the West Saxons. Hild and Cynewise looked at one another once the last horseman had vanished over the crest of the hill; they didn't really have anything to say. Hild was ready to run, fearful that Cynewise would have one of her fits and make some appalling predictions—but she didn't, so now they could just sit twiddling their thumbs while they waited for the outcome of the battle.

'Well,' said Cynewise.

'Well,' said Hild.

They went each to her chamber and prayed to the same god, with the same fervour, and the same faith that he would hear them. The only difference being that the one prayed for victory to the man the other wished dead.

It was the middle of the second mild-month and, while they waited, the same deadly stillness settled on the estate as had descended when Penda had gone to battle against Oswald. Hild had to visit Merewald several times, to hear him speak quite calmly about the cause of this stillness. He wasn't in the least apprehensive, and took it upon himself to instruct his father's wife as to the erroneousness of interpreting the manifestations of nature as auguries. She should have reprimanded him, but didn't as she, too, knew it was wrong. When necessity called, however, she couldn't stop herself from clutching at every last straw within reach. Anyway, he had merely been repeating her own instruction about how people should not think they understand the will of the Lord.

Ten days passed before the first horsemen returned: Penda had been victorious and had ousted Cenwalch; Penda was unharmed. That was the message.

Hild gave thanks to her god, but she couldn't understand why Penda hadn't come home yet; he was usually one of the first to arrive.

The following day, a procession of carts started rolling up across the hills. Hild scanned the arrivals, but couldn't see Penda anywhere; his red cloak usually shone out from the throng. She suddenly screamed and started running: she had spotted the cloak, on a cart, wrapped around a curled-up and motionless man.

She met the procession at the foot of the hill, and ran frantically towards the cart. An ashen face with flaxen hair stuck out of Penda's cloak: Bothelm, the eldest of the princely sons. His eyes met hers, but they held little promise.

She looked around and saw Penda riding alongside the cart, as ashen-faced as Bothelm, but he hadn't even seen her. She rushed back to the settlement, gave instructions to boil water and bring clean cloths, and ran to fetch her box of medicines.

Bothelm was carried in and put on their bed. He wasn't keen on the idea, preferring to lie curled up, as he had been on the cart, which kept the bleeding to a minimum, but he had no option.

Throughout the journey, his man-at-arms had tried to hold the wound closed with his fingers, because it was too deep and too long to be held together by a dressing, and the flies had to be kept away so the wound didn't get infected by maggots and flying venom.

Hild's ointment had been boiled up in wild boar lard—the most powerful of beasts. It consisted of extract from the testicles of bull, stallion and ram, and nine types of purifying and healing plants, with the addition of a drop of holy water from the spring at Clynnog Fawr. There was no better ointment in the country; it was her own formula, and she didn't have to tell anyone about the holy water.

Bothelm whimpered as she washed around the wound: a quiet wheezy lament sounding more like an injured animal than a man. His gut was blueish-white, encased in a thin layer of whitish fat extending under the thin flesh of his stomach muscles. Nor was that much different from an animal, thought Hild.

Does an animal know it's going to die? Does it know its life has been too brief, and does it dread eternal oblivion given that it hasn't had time to achieve anything memorable?

She wiped his face with a cloth from the cold-water basin. Bothelm was sweating and his breathing was rapid and laboured, even more colour had drained out of him, and now he almost had the whitish-yellow hue of a corpse. She put a finger to his throat, trying to feel his heartbeat—it was racing along far too swiftly.

She looked at Penda, slumped in the corner, staring at his son with glassy eyes.

'The boy needs blood,' she said. When it was obvious he hadn't heard, she put her hand on his shoulder and said it again; he shuddered and looked up at her blankly.

'Bothelm needs blood,' she said loud and clear. 'You must tell the pagan priest—maybe the best would be from one of the young bulls.'

'Yes, of course,' said Penda, standing up. He stood, arms dangling, but couldn't take his eyes off his son and seemed to have forgotten what Hild had said.

She turned to the man-at-arms.

'Quickly, tell the pagan priest to come immediately with blood from one of the young bulls. And sacrifice the rest. Quickly, run!'

The man-at-arms was also just gaping; she had to hit him before he understood what she was saying and then he ran, with all his might.

Hild took Penda by the shoulders, guided him to the stool and made him sit down; he didn't resist or grumble. She sat next to Bothelm and took his hand.

'They speak of your courage in battle,' she said loudly. 'Your feats will long be remembered.'

His eyes brightened a little, and the corners of his mouth twitched in a slight smile, but he was no longer sweating, which was not a good sign at all.

'Your father says you fought like a lion,' Hild continued. 'And many of the old folk say they have never seen such a young man show *such* bravery.'

The brightness in his eyes flickered a little again, and maybe there was a hint of colour in the waxy cheeks. She couldn't understand why they were taking so long to get that miserable creature slaughtered. And where was Gefmund? She had neither seen nor heard anything about Gefmund. She gazed at her husband, but dared not ask. Many more carts would undoubtedly be arriving—a campaign of this sort wouldn't end without plundering—plus cartloads of the fallen.

A fly settled on Bothelm's downy cheek, and she flicked it off. Wailing could be heard from the yard, and the sound of a rattling oxcart drawing to a halt. She thought she recognized the voice of the woman married to Gefmund's man-at-arms, and couldn't stop herself from looking at Penda. Because if Gefmund's man-at-arms had fallen . . .

Where was Gefmund? Dread crawled up her spine and settled between her shoulder blades.

Where was young Gefmund? Penda's pride and joy, the delight of his old age, the boy with the pale flaxen hair and the brown eyes, the boy who outdid everyone in vaulting and throwing the javelin, who had been prophesied a glorious future and whose personal troops were invincible? No better men were to be found in the whole land, and if they hadn't been able to defend their young prince then there must have been sorcery at play.

Maybe nothing had happened. Maybe the man-at-arms' wife was wailing so ear-splittingly about someone else entirely, her brother perhaps—he'd been in the battle too. Hild collected herself and sent the maid to fetch mugs and more boiled water, which she used to make a strengthening drink for her husband whose lips were cracked and covered in a layer of crusty white spittle. He drank it without protest, and she then gave him a beaker of camomile tea, which he sat holding until she said he should drink, and he drank as obediently as if he were a child and she his nurse.

The silence in the room became so audible in contrast with the ever-increasing volume of wailing from the yard. Hild couldn't bear it any longer; she sent the maid to find out where the blood had got to and to enquire, quietly, about Gefmund. Because where was he, the naughty lad who had always played so many tricks on them, where had he got to?

The maid had only been gone a moment when the pagan priest came rushing in with a pitcher of blood.

'The Lord be praised!' Hild cried, and managed to get Bothelm propped up against some pillows so he was almost in a sitting position. He didn't complain; maybe he could no longer feel what was going on around him.

Hild stirred the blood vigorously, filled a beaker and held it to his mouth, but he didn't even know it was there.

'Penda,' she asked, 'wake up and tell your son to drink!'

She had to shout before she could make Penda stand up and lean over Bothelm.

'Drink, son!' he implored, and it seemed as if Bothelm revived a little. He gazed around, spotted his father and then collapsed again.

'Bothelm, my son, drink! In the name of Woden, drink!' Penda cried out.

Hild held the beaker against his lips. Bothelm opened his mouth a little and she let the life-giving liquid flow in. Holding her breath while he tried to drink, she beseeched the Lord God to save this boy, and Bothelm managed to swallow by himself. It was at the very last moment; she could no longer feel his heartbeat, and he was cold, far too cold. Was there a little more colour in his waxen face? She wasn't sure, but she could feel some kind of pressure from the hand she held in hers; he was really making an effort. She held the beaker to his mouth again, and poured a drop between his parted lips.

She had to wipe away the blood when it spilled down over his chin. And there they sat, in the stale stillness while the screaming outside became ever more urgent.

Penda took Hild by the hand.

'Try,' he implored. 'See if your god can help him!'

Hild nodded and made the sign of the cross in front of the boy's head, chest and mortal wound.

'In the name of the Father, and of the Son, and of the Holy Spirit,' she murmured.

She prostrated herself on the floor, arms outstretched to the sides—the way you prayed when you didn't have to do it in secret. She prayed with all her might, while Penda and the pagan priest did what they did.

They stopped when they heard a gurgling sound from Bothelm's throat. The blood was coming up again, his jaw hung slackly, then there was no more.

Blood can be washed off, thought Hild, as she gazed at the young princely son, it comes off easily with cold water, and Penda will have his cloak back, as good as new, but he won't get a son like this back again, not a son like this, so bold, so loved by all.

Penda didn't believe what the others were saying; he thought he could feel a very faint heartbeat, and he wasn't icy cold. Once they had removed the bloodied cloak and washed Bothelm's face, he was certain the spirit would return to his son; it had been seen before, and the others couldn't contradict that fact, there was always a chance.

Penda went into action: he moved Bothelm, placing him flat so he could breathe more easily. At first Hild helped, then she sat down on the stool, just as Penda had before—gazing glassy-eyed at her husband's sudden activity. He spoke to Bothelm's spirit, bargained with Woden and promised generous gifts if he would send the spirit back. When he proposed that Woden should take one of his other sons instead, Hild felt uneasy.

'Penda,' she said, 'fate has taken what it wants. It cannot be undone.'

But he didn't hear her.

She went outside to find Wulfhere and Ædelræd, and she made the sign of the cross over them. Then she was told that Gefmund had fallen, one of the first, and she locked her sons indoors, instructed Talcuin to guard them, and joined the large group of wailing women around the dead.

Penda pottered around his princely son for more than two days before he acknowledged his son had become a corpse. The stench was unmistakeable.

He went to the privy hut, whereupon he went to Cynewise's chamber.

Cynewise had been standing on the hill watching the army return, their shields held aloft. Recognizing the shields of her home land, she had entered her chamber and bolted the door.

'You owe me two sons!' Penda shouted, but she didn't unbolt the door—it had to be forced open. Cynewise's screams mingled with the wailing screams of the mourners.

Hild tried to drown them out by screaming even louder. It wasn't hard; she was now screaming because her husband had lost his mind, and she knew he wouldn't let Cynewise's bed grow cold until she had borne him two sons.

# SEVEN GOLD RINGS FOR EADFRID

*– after the years of happiness –*

Hereswid wrote to Hild:

> . . . There are rumours that Oswald was a saint. It is said that miracles have occurred at the place where he fell, and that many have been cured by consuming a little soil from that spot. Personally, I have always considered Oswald to have been a villain, but given that I don't know if the rumours speak the truth, I have not initiated others into my perception of him.
>
> Here he is only evaluated on the basis that he was Christian, and as your husband still serves the old gods, he, of course, enjoys little sympathy. Are you making progress in guiding him along the true path?
>
> Well, I no longer know what is right, and we have misjudged people before, have we not, and had to realize that the lowest were the highest and, as the Gospel says, the last will be first.
>
> Could you investigate the matter for me? The rumours come from the brother of Abbess Telchildis at our neighbouring monastery, the monk called Agilbert, who recently visited us here and seemed to me a highly trustworthy character, albeit somewhat conceited. Again, not my words . . .

Hild wrote to Hereswid:

> . . . As far as Oswald's holiness is concerned, I can answer that these rumours are also circulating here, and that people who offer plants and remedies for sale now also include soil from Oswald's place of death among their wares. When I received your letter, I bought a little and tried it out on a slave who suffers from acute arthritis and is barely in a condition to work. And still isn't, unfortunately. Next, I attempted to cure my cold, and it lasted for two weeks

as is usual. My final test was upon my horse, and it died—be that from illness or something else I cannot be the judge.

We nonetheless constantly hear these rumours. And I cannot say whether or not they are untrue, because I have yet to meet any reliable character who can verify them. Nor can I tell if it was the authentic commodity that I purchased. But I usually do business with this same merchant, and there has never been anything wrong with his goods before.

Here it is also said, with awe, that Oswald's arm is as pristine as the day on which it arrived at Bebbanburh. That is because I had Oswald's remains prepared with a herbal infusion before I took them up to Aidan. Otherwise I wouldn't have been able to take them along for the stench of the corpse, as I tell everyone who can be bothered to listen. But apparently people would rather listen to nonsense. Do me the service of passing this on. Fortunately, the Lord's people prefer the truth to babble and superstition.

And it is indeed true, as you write, that we humans know not who are the Lord's chosen. But can a man who has an innocent strung from a tree—without other reason than that he covets his throne—can a man like that be a saint? Well, I know I am not the right person to pronounce judgement on this matter. But I can tell you that Oswald's wife Cyneburh, all honour to her memory, did not give him many chances for eternal life. Although, again, she will not be the one judging him on the last day.

Likewise, I can inform you that there was great joy in Deira over Oswald's death. My husband was greeted with much enthusiasm, and I am certain that—even without marriage to me—he would have been chosen as their king. The realm needs peace and respite from upheavals. Deira and Lindsey will not soon forget Oswald's cruelty. You can tell that to those who continue to talk about his holiness! You can also tell them that my husband might well stick to the old gods, but he also sticks to the old virtues. Upon my soul, I guarantee that he is a man of honour who keeps his word and takes care of his people. And that cannot be said either of Oswald or of his brother Oswy, even were they to be baptized three hundred times . . .

Hereswid wrote to Hild:

. . . Do you remember the dream I had when Oswald died? I recently reported it as an example of a divine sign, and I was sternly reproved by the abbess who was of the opinion that I had misunderstood the sign. On the contrary, she says, the dream means that someone of quite exceptional holiness is on their way to eternal bliss. Thus the light.

She instructed me to do penance and called my interpretation unacceptably self-centred, saying: There is more to the world than your kin! And she reminded me that my mortal family no longer has significance, because I now have all the Lord's people as sisters and brothers. I, of course, understood this and have already done penance for my selfish interpretation.

Blood is thicker than water, but thickest of all is the life-giving baptismal water, which you too, my sister, have received. The abbess asks me to send you greetings and to tell you that every day we pray to the Lord to assist you in the conversion of your husband, so that both he and the people of Mercia will in due course be able to enjoy the divine joys with us . . .

At yuletide the following year, Cynewise gave birth to a son, an infant almost as healthy and robust as the first one had been.

Hild was relieved. One more son and her marriage would again be normal, as normal as it could be, that was.

She did not grieve when, five weeks after the birth, Penda left her bed in order to concentrate all his procreative power on Cynewise. Hild rode to her monastery and hoped he would quickly make the woman pregnant; they had enjoyed their time together during Cynewise's last pregnancy.

Cynewise hadn't: her legs had swollen as never before, and she had been huge. The stoutness suited her, even though it made her somewhat immobile. The final month of her pregnancy had been spent either in a chair, with her feet up on a stool, or in bed—she just didn't have enough energy to walk on those legs, she said.

When Penda returned, however, the flesh fell off her. Whenever he had a free moment, he called her into his chamber and did his best. He was tireless, despite his age, and could take her several times a day.

She grew so thin you might have thought her a maiden—if you ignored her eyes, which were listless and never really focused on anything. She was held in awe and had many supporters among the mightiest men. The prophecies she voiced during her fits did not make pleasant listening, and the previous year her predictions for the harvest had come true.

Hild saw Cynewise at the baptismal feast. She hadn't been invited to the baptism itself, but seeing the emaciated young woman made Hild decide she had to remonstrate with Penda. If he carried on like this, she was going to say, it wouldn't be sons he'd be having but a funeral, more like. Then she changed her mind—a funeral was perhaps the best solution anyway.

In the month of Eostre, when the cowslips had finished flowering and the birds were singing in competition for a mate, Penda arrived on horseback at Hild's monastery. She ran to meet him, thinking he had finished getting Cynewise pregnant and now she could go home to pursue her normal life in Tamoworthig. He didn't even remove his cloak, however, or his gloves, before he grabbed her, roared and shook her so everything came loose inside.

Thus it took a while for her to understand what had happened, and when it finally sank in, she was so horror-struck she could neither think nor speak—as if it were the day of fire and blood, when everything comes back and has turned against you.

'No, no, no,' she moaned.

Worst of all, Penda, her own husband, also believed that her sorcery had taken the life of the newly-baptized boy, because it had happened in exactly the same manner as with the first son: one morning he had been found dead in his cradle, and there had been nothing wrong with him.

'So they were indeed right,' he bellowed at her, 'and this time you won't get away with it!'

She closed her eyes and could see the axe, saw the scaffold and the big raven that always turned up, and felt dishonour run icily through her body. The daughter of Breguswid and Hereric, fulfilment of the curse upon the family.

Talcuin's testimony wasn't considered valid, and the monk's wasn't allowed. She hadn't kept any other company, and she had spent much time alone. She didn't have a chance. What about Wulfhere and Ædelræd? Penda couldn't allow them to execute the mother of two of his princely sons. Or could he? Did he think Cynewise's womb could carry on producing sons? He could do what he wanted, as well she knew; what he wanted, however, she never knew, even after all these years. His mind followed its own path.

'I am with child!' she blurted out.

'You're lying,' he replied just as promptly.

'With a son,' she continued.

He stood still and looked at her, stepped back and studied her again.

'Let us go indoors,' he said.

He took off his cloak and walked around as he did when he was mentally positioning his troops for battle, tugged at his beard and murmured unintelligibly to himself, then turned his gaze on her.

'You do know that will be the proof against you, don't you?'

'No—well, yes,' she faltered.

She realize that in thinking she had saved herself from the axe, she had actually placed it at her feet.

'But, but it was longer ago!'

'I don't believe you,' he said, having thought it over for a moment or two.

'No,' she said faintly.

'Because you would have told me straight away.'

'Yes.'

'So it happened last time?'

'There is no child.'

'Indeed,' he said.

He sat drumming the table with his fingers, then stood up and continued his unbearable pacing.

'I could send you away,' he murmured. 'Instead.'

'No!' she exclaimed.

'Would you rather die?'

'There is no honour in running away.'

'Nor with the other option.'

'True,' she said, and stared at the floor.

'But for princely sons there is less dishonour in having a mother who has escaped.'

'Yes,' she said. 'But I doubt anyone would receive me, matters being as they are.'

'You could go to King Anna, in East Anglia.'

'He's hardly in a position to refuse.'

'Hardly,' said Penda, 'and you would have the company of King Cenwalch!'

'That's not a life,' she said a few moments later.

He shrugged, not moving his expressionless gaze from the fireplace.

'How long?' she asked.

He had to sit down. Eventually he replied: 'Well, for ever.'

Penda accompanied her a little way into East Anglia. King Anna's people were to assume responsibility for her safety during the last part of the journey, and they were waiting, as arranged.

All that remained was to say goodbye.

Evening was already drawing in—a thin layer of ground mist covered the low-lying land and wolves could be heard in the distance—so they would have one more night.

The tent was pitched, their red field-home, draped with the rugs they had brought along. Hild wanted it like this, even though they could easily have spent the night more comfortably on a farm, as Anna's people would, but she didn't want that.

A lean, hazy moon rose in the sky; it was waning, slender as the stroke of a nib. The bats had begun to swarm around.

Hild felt as if she was nothing but eyes: she had looked at everything for the last time, and she knew she would never again ride through the gentle hills of Mercia. Her packing had been done while the beech trees were bursting into leaf, while the birds were busy with their nests and all things green were welling up from the soil. Merewald's garden was beautiful as never before; his apple trees were in blossom. New life was beginning in Tamoworthig; her life was ending.

Wulfhere and Ædelræd. She had heard them calling out from the hilltop, but she wouldn't turn round; over was over, she had taken her leave. They were healthy boys, there was nothing more she could give them now; they would be warriors, like their father—which is how it should be.

She took a last look at the crescent moon; next time it appeared in that form everything would be different. It was hard to imagine she would ever see it again. Tomorrow, when Penda left, her life would be over but, for just a moment more, he was there.

She lifted the flap and went into the tent. He was lying on the pallet and pulled her down, hugging her tightly, but there was no fervour in him: his body seemed to have dispersed. They were like two big clouds side by side, full of the knowledge of what had been, laden with sorrow, and there was nothing left to say.

And yet, as they lay there close together, Penda still had something to tell her; she knew from his occasional little shudder.

'What is it?' she asked, and stroked his hair, which had grown thin and streaked with grey.

'Yes,' he said, 'I've got to tell you. Because there won't be another opportunity.'

'No,' she said, 'fate has decided that we should not be together after all. What have you got to tell me?'

He couldn't quite bring himself to say it.

'It's Oswald,' he said. 'It's that he . . . it wasn't Oswald who ordered Eadfrid's death.'

Hild frowned; she didn't understand what he was saying.

'What are you trying to tell me?'

She stared at her husband and wondered if he had gone mad.

'It's just as I say,' said Penda, taking her gently by the arm. 'Oswald did not have Eadfrid slain.'

'How do you know?' she asked incredulously.

'I know because . . . because I know who did.'

'Then why haven't you told me before?'

She paused to catch her breath before she could get the question out: 'Who was it?'

She could no longer contain her dread.

Penda sank his head against her breast and mumbled something she couldn't hear. He held her so tightly it hurt, and when he finally let go and sat up, his face was completely drained of colour.

'Tell me, if you really know!' she exclaimed with an intensity that took even her by surprise.

'I'll tell you because I have to,' said Penda. 'But you're not going to like what you hear.'

'What's wrong with you?' she cried. 'Can't you just come straight out with it instead of all this evasion?'

She suddenly wanted to hit him. Gone were the tranquil tenderness and the silent sense of gently melting into him that she had been feeling all day. What kind of game was he playing with her?

Penda felt under the pillow and pulled out seven gold arm-rings; he thrust them towards her.

'A paltry wergild,' he mumbled. 'Take them.'

The gold shone in the glow from the tapers. They were engraved with animals, and one of them was in the same style as the buckle Penda had put with Ecgric and Sigebert in their grave; another was inlaid with small garnets, and a third was more modern, interlaced birds with long bills and talons. Two were in the style made by the Britons, with the ingenious spiral pattern Hild prized so highly. She could suddenly no longer bear to look at them. She hid her face in her hands and was unable to utter a word, neither of thanks nor the contrary. She was also incapable of pushing the rings back to him, so there they lay, between them, glittering in competition with one another.

Her only thought was: it's not true. At the same time: Eadwacer—lover of possessions! Hoarder of riches! Coveter of gold!

The air had become stifling, it was hard to breathe; Hild was hot and cold and wet and she was freezing.

He carefully took hold of her wrists; she pulled her hands away and looked straight at him.

'Why?' she asked quietly.

He shook his head and stared into the distance, at something that wasn't there.

'Why?' she asked again. 'I have to know, Penda. Why? Why?'

'I couldn't sit by and watch it any longer,' he replied quietly, 'the way he treated you.'

Then he told her how it had happened. He had wanted Eadfrid to be King of Deira; it would be to his own advantage and he had also thought that kingship might restore Eadfrid's manliness and put a stop to his dishonourable behaviour towards Hild. But he had grown to hate Eadfrid. The last time Hild had been absent from the hall for several days, and had then eventually appeared with a face still bearing the mark of having walked into a door or fallen down some steps or whatever she chose to call it, Penda had to leave the hall for fear of losing control of himself. It made his blood boil to see Hereric's daughter so dishonoured. He had set great store by Hereric, and also Breguswid; he had secretly adored her, but his status had not been suitable for a king's daughter like her.

Having heard Cædwalla's account of Hild's fearless conduct at the farm up in Deira, and having finally got to see her for himself, it was obvious to him that all his future happiness rested with her. Even though reason told him it could only bring about misfortune. He dreamed about her at night and he lost all pleasure in his wife.

'You were so fresh,' he said gently, and stroked her cheek, 'like a young trout in the beck. Or a goshawk just beginning its training. Something about your eyes. There was a lustre about you. Yes, that was it.'

Hild didn't know what to believe. Everything whirred around her, drawing her in and up to flap about in little pieces in the air. She put her hands on her head, holding it steady, and after a while she raised her face to him.

'If you wanted to get me away from Eadfrid, why didn't you say? Why didn't you help me? Why didn't you ask me to marry you?'

'Why? You know very well you wouldn't have listened. And anyway, I was married.'

'No,' she said after a moment's pause, 'I wouldn't have listened.'

'You couldn't have left him, the state he was in. It would have brought you disgrace for the rest of your life. But a widow, that's a different story, she can marry.'

'Yes, that's a different story.'

They lay in silence for a little while, and then Penda continued: 'I could have had Eadfrid slain. And then I'd never have got you. You were going to be queen in Deira, that's what you were born to. I hoped something might turn up, because I knew, from the moment I saw you, that fate had destined us for one another.'

He paused and took a deep breath before beginning to tell her about the evening after she had set out with Eadfrid to the royal selection in Eoforwik.

Penda and his men had been drinking hard. They had been in the hall since noon, and the excellent mead had been on the table throughout, but the more he drank, the more hopeless it all seemed. He was bound hand and foot.

'Can no one rid me of this dastard?' he had cried out across the hall, and that was the last thing he remembered. His men had carried him to bed when he had collapsed, but Trumhere had risen to his feet, as Penda learnt the next day, and had ridden out with twenty men. They were gone for four days, hunting boar, but they only managed to catch one.

'Now you know,' said Penda, 'that's what happened.'

Hild bit her lip.

'You told me quite another story.'

'I didn't know what had happened myself. Not until I heard it from you, and then slowly I began to believe it. Trumhere told me in East Anglia. He thought I'd known all along.'

'As indeed you did,' she said bitterly.

'Perhaps,' he replied.

And presently he added: 'I suppose I did, yes.'

Through the canvas they could hear the erratic crackle of the fire, keeping the wolves at bay. A sound that usually gave peace of mind, now it felt as if the world was ablaze and Hild could already see little tongues of flame flickering all around. She jumped up and rushed out into the cool air.

Everything was calm and normal. The people sitting around the fire turned their faces to her: was there something they could do for her? The food still needed a little longer over the flames.

She went back into the tent.

'And you know the rest,' Penda continued. 'For three weeks your spirit was elsewhere. I was at your bedside when my wife died. And I got a sorceress to recite incantations over you. Not even Talcuin knew that. She got a gold ring when your spirit returned.'

He sat in silence for a long time.

'Did you reward Trumhere too?' she eventually asked.

'Yes,' answered Penda, 'but not with gold.'

'With land?'

'Not with land, no. I couldn't have him near me any longer. No one has served so faithfully as him. I rewarded him poorly, I . . . '

He had to clear his throat a couple of times, before he could continue: 'I let him go in front when we tried to storm Bebbanburh.'

Hild closed her eyes and took a deep breath. Bebbanburh could not be stormed, even a child knew that. Its location on the high, steep cliff, its strong stockade, Bernicia's feared bowmen—any attempt would be sheer suicide. As everyone knew.

She remembered Trumhere as he had looked when they brought him home after the campaign. Wounds from three arrows: one in the stomach, one in the shoulder and one in the throat. The last one had killed him; there had been a lot of blood, the arrow had pierced his artery.

'You said he had fallen in battle!' she exclaimed bitterly. 'Fine thanks for his loyalty to you, Penda.'

'Yes,' he said. 'Fine thanks indeed.'

A little later he added: 'And I know, after all you've told me about your god, that he would never forgive me for what I did. But Woden does, I know he does. Maybe he would have done the same.'

'That's not true,' said Hild vehemently. 'My god forgives everything. He's forgiven me many things, I know he has.'

'Because you've repented and prayed for forgiveness,' said Penda. 'But he can't forgive me. Because I'm not repentant.'

'No,' she said quietly. 'Then he can't forgive you.'

Talcuin called to them from outside the tent: the food and everything were ready. They sat by the fire and ate in silence. Hild gazed into the flames and drank more than she ate. It didn't put the world back together, but made it easier to draw breath amid the chaos of disintegrated fragments.

'A heap of rubble,' she said into thin air.

'What?' asked Penda.

'I don't know.' She held out her empty meadhorn for Talcuin to fill.

# Latin for 'a fly'

*– a former queen –*

'Amo means: I love.'

Aldwulf suppressed a giggle. Hild asked him to repeat what she had said; he did so, blushing. Hereswid would have been ashamed to see her son behaving in this way.

She went on to the other forms: you love, he-she-it loves, we love, you—plural—love, they love, and the imperative: love!—which was ridiculous, because how could you tell someone: 'Love!'? It was just an example, of course, to help them learn their Latin verbs of action, but it was of no practical use, nor could you say: 'Don't love!'

King Anna's son had dozed off. Hild whacked him on the head and was immediately sorry, because why shouldn't he? Sleep was probably just as useful as learning grammar.

She lashed out at a fly as it buzzed noisily past, the children watching its flight path. And why shouldn't they? Learning about flies was undoubtedly just as useful as learning these pointless Latin words—which were so old, so very old—when they couldn't even write their own native language.

Should she have stood up to King Anna? A man who could neither write his own language nor understand a single word of Latin. He wanted his children to speak Latin, and only time would tell if they would grow up to have their own scribes. Who knew what would happen? She'd had scribes, and teachers; now she had to do both jobs herself.

'A fly,' she said, 'in Latin . . .' and her mind went blank, although the word had been right there a moment ago. Anna's son saw his chance.

'What do you call a fly in Latin?' he asked.

All the little eyes homed in on her confusion.

'I've just told you,' she blustered, 'while you've been fast asleep! I shall be telling your father you don't pay attention.'

The boy cowered, but Ædelthryd—that little truthsayer—piped up: 'You did actually forget to tell us what a fly is called.'

'Well,' Hild replied curtly, 'a fly is a fly, whatever you call it. In Rome, too, they fly around leaving their little worms all over the place. They're the same everywhere. You would all do well to think twice before you speak.'

She thought the lesson had been going on for an eternity, but it had only just begun. The children seemed uncooperative and not particularly bright—the ones at home had been far more intelligent—but then again, Anna wasn't the most quick-witted man she'd ever come across.

'King,' she said, 'what is a king called in Latin?'

They gawped at her.

'Rex,' she announced. 'Write it on your slates: R—E—X. Rex!'

And there they sat in all their stupidity and couldn't even write an R.

She gave up—she'd had more than enough for one day.

Were the people of this kingdom hard of hearing? She'd been trying to attract the steward's attention for an eternity, but it was as if no one could hear her. It had never been necessary to shout at home: a small hand gesture and they would immediately leap into action, ready to act on instructions. In this place she had to shout loudly, and then they just carried on as if she hadn't said a word.

She leant back on the bench and sighed in defeat, half-closed her eyes and took deep breaths; it was difficult to breathe in this humid, stifling air.

East Anglia wasn't a pleasant place with all its marshes and wetlands, its omnipresent demons. The people were sullen and odd, lacking the spryness of folk in Deira, lacking the pride of Bernicia, the adroitness of Mercia. They were heavy and taciturn, as if fearful the spirits would fly into any mouth, albeit one only opened a hair's breadth.

When Hild had visited Hereswid, she hadn't noticed the strangeness of the people. No wonder her sister had gone to Gaul: why would you stay here when the world was full of other places? Which was surely why all these slow-witted people had ended up in this spot: they wouldn't have coped in the inhabitable areas of the world.

It was impossible to believe that Sigebert had come from so morose a people, or that Anna was of his kin—although quite far removed, it had to be said.

King Anna—probably in the belief that he was netting gold rings in Heaven—had accepted the delicate baby Hereswid had borne after her husband's death, and adopted the girl as his own: Ædelthryd. The most peculiar child Hild had ever seen, Ædelthryd was utterly devoid of Hereswid's instinctual strength and could well have been the issue of cobweb: so pale, so very pale, with eyes so pale-blue they were almost colourless, just a glow. Hardly surprising when you considered how the girl had been begotten, and all the thoughts running through Hereswid's mind during her pregnancy. But the child was no changeling, no, she wasn't; although she wasn't completely normal either.

The eldest daughter had died a few months after Hereswid had left. She had simply stopped eating once her mother had gone, they said, and even trying to force food down her hadn't helped.

Hild was sweating; the summer was too hot, and they hadn't seen any rain for four weeks. You couldn't go outdoors during the day without the company of a cloud of horseflies, and in the evening a swarm of big mosquitoes. The horseflies were the worst. The hall doors had been opened because of the heat from the roasting fire, and everyone sitting at the long tables in the hall was scratching. Hild felt a bite, it smarted, and she swatted the horsefly. It had a shiny green head, the body of a bluebottle, and brown-and-white patterned wings; a strange creature, with that long sucking nozzle—like an elephant, if what they said was true.

If she'd stayed in Mercia, she might have owned an elephant, but things had turned out differently. What would Merewald have said about the horseflies? Would he have explained to her that they, too, were a kind of utility creature? She'd never had occasion to ask him—horseflies weren't a bother in Tamoworthig.

She heard a loud buzzing and then felt a fresh bite, on her neck. Maybe she should leave the hall before supper; in her house, she kept the doors and shutters closed. No one had died of heat yet, and when winter arrived they'd undoubtedly change their tune. Hild stood up and walked across to the steward.

'Those doors let in the horseflies,' she said. 'They shouldn't be left open.'

The steward looked at her briefly, then went to the queen and whispered; the queen spoke to King Anna, the three spoke quietly to one another, their eyes all turned to Hild: six eyes, one pair each, just above the middle of their faces. She nodded and tried to smile at them.

The steward got on with his work, and Hild swatted two more horseflies.

Preparation of the food had now reached the stage where the royal couple could start eating: roast lamb, one split head each. They cut out the contents with knives, scooped up the brains with silver spoons, then moved onto the next course: liver and roast kidneys.

Hild gazed wistfully at their delicacies while fighting off the flies on her sinewy little piece of lamb neck. The bread wasn't the best she'd ever had, nor the beer, which was weak, tasted of yeast and gave no satisfaction—she would have let it brew for at least another two weeks.

The meal was a speedy affair on Hild's part. She could have had more bread, and more beer too, but she would rather go without. All she could do was observe the royal couple while they consumed their sweet course: what looked like egg yolks with honey and beor, accompanied by more beor in small deep-blue drinking vessels.

She was kept busy swatting insects. The king and queen had a man on either side, fanning the flies away. The steward walked down to Talcuin and spoke to him; they both turned and looked in Hild's direction.

'He says it isn't befitting for strangers to give orders to the servants. And guests shouldn't interfere in the practices of the king and queen,' said Talcuin, with little enthusiasm for passing on the message.

Hild was not obliged to contain herself when dealing with her slave.

'So he says that, does he? Then you must tell him it is not befitting to serve such weak beer to guests, and the lamb is scrawny and was slaughtered too early. And they should find themselves a better baker. Furthermore, it ill befits a steward to reprimand a . . . a former queen . . . and widow of a prince. Yes, you tell him that!'

'The message came from the queen, my lady,' said Talcuin, reddening. 'The steward merely passed it on.'

'Then tell the queen that she keeps an improvident household and should relay such messages personally to her guests without involving the servants.'

Talcuin was now shuffling his feet.

'I'd really rather not, my lady,' he managed to mumble. 'It wouldn't make our stay here any more agreeable.'

Hild was overwhelmed with weariness. Was she really meant to enter into a discussion with her own slave? Had she no longer command over anything at all? How low was she meant to sink?

'Go, slave!' she hissed, and he hurried off.

She went to bed. It was too early to sleep, but what else was she meant to do?

Talcuin had to get a move on. The last time he'd heard his lady utter such words had been in Elmet, and then her spirit had departed as soon as she had spoken them. He had only the one option: get on good terms with the doctor woman. She hadn't been in the hall this evening, but he knew where she lived. He was already well acquainted with one of the milkmaids, and before long he was standing outside the doctor's door holding a little pitcher of cream—and who would sneeze at the offer of fresh cream.

Talcuin had worried unnecessarily, as Hild's spirit had not left her at all. It was, in fact, bustling around with such force that she had to get out of bed again and sit with her weaving in an effort to calm it down.

She was seething with anger. What kind of hospitality was this? They had never treated their guests like this in Tamoworthig. King Anna and his wife were treating her like any other underling, just some teacher in the king's service—not like a queen, and sister to the former queen of the realm. Hereswid's husband had known how to treat guests according to time-honoured custom, as had his paternal uncle, Rædwald, who had organized hunting parties and instructed the bards to celebrate his guests, just like Edwin had. There had always been more than enough of everything, and the beer had been more full-bodied than anywhere else, tastier and a little stronger. The beer they served here would have been given to the slaves in Tamoworthig; she wouldn't have drunk a drop of it and she certainly wouldn't have served it for her guests—such a measly table would bring dishonour upon a queen and her housekeeping. Did Anna not know what was befitting for a king?

There had been no enmity between Hereswid and the royal couple. Hereswid hadn't thought highly of King Anna, it was true, but her appraisal had been quite accurate: Anna was nowhere near as mighty a king as Ecgric had been, and he even still paid tax to Penda and couldn't do anything without asking his permission.

Over and above Penda, King Anna lived in fear of his god. Everyone on the estate had to line up for Mass three times a day, even if they were in the middle of sowing, reaping or slaughtering. In itself, this suited Hild, because she had much catching up to do in that respect, but it was hard to see how all the necessary tasks could be undertaken at the same time—a royal estate could hardly be compared with a monastery. Perhaps this organization of time explained the weak, under-brewed beer and the tasteless bread.

She pictured the evening meals in Tamoworthig, and her mouth watered. The food and beer had been first-rate, yes, but so had the songs and the travelling entertainers who were always welcome in the hall, and every evening had its festive element. Penda was the greatest king in the land, as everyone knew, and he in turn knew how to hold a feast, take care of friendships and behave in a royal manner. He didn't hold back on the food, for a king's words had to be reinforced by a visible weightiness: if a king was forever fasting and losing flesh, people would start doubting his strength.

They needed to be certain he was a man who could and would reward their loyalty, certain he wasn't going to seek his fortune elsewhere, with a foreign god, without his people, in some kind of forthcoming world. The life of the king and the people—they were one and the same. A spring sacrifice without the king was no spring sacrifice. He had to lead his people, also by pleading their cause with the gods and sprites and all the forces at large, otherwise the kingdom would fall apart. That went without saying, as Penda was wont to say, and, as he had also always said: if it was the kingdom of the Lord God you were after, then you should just seek it out—like Sigebert had—nothing underhand about that.

Penda's admiration for Sigebert had not diminished over the years. Given that he could no longer ask Trumhere to tell the story, Penda had supplied a bard with all the necessary details, so he could sit in the hall and hear the tale as often as he wanted. It had become one of his favourite songs, after the songs about himself, that is, and especially the ones about his lineage: how his father was a true descendant of Woden, through Offa of Angeln, King Wermund's son, who had so heroically fought two Saxon warriors at once, on an island in the Eider river, the border between the two kingdoms.

Offa had slain them both, with King Wermund's magic sword, the iron forged by dwarves in olden times. Thwack! the sword sliced through the air and then the skull of the Saxon warrior. Thwack! it sliced through the next one, who had hardly drawn his sword from its sheath. All this Wermund had heard from his seat on the river bank, age having taken his sight. He had then calmly lain down to die, safe in the knowledge his son was man enough to rule over the realm, even though this son hadn't spoken a single word up until that day. As Offa said, it hadn't been necessary to speak while his father had said everything that needed saying—any more words would have been too many.

Yes, Penda was well satisfied with the songs he had commissioned about his forefathers; they reflected well on him personally and on his ancestors.

Hild smiled at the memory of Penda sitting with his hefty head slightly tilted as he listened to a song. She realized this was the first time she had been able to think about her husband without the raging sorrow seizing her and shaking her and making her scurry between bed and chair and loom, weeping noisily and pounding the bedcovers, then easing up in an attempt to calm herself down. Sorrow could sweep over her when she least expected it, and about one matter she remained at a total loss: that their marriage was over. Surely, she thought, providence must somehow have got the wrong end of the stick.

More than once, after one of these brutal evening frenzies in her room, she had packed her belongings. She just *had* to be with him again; he was her life and anything else was merely a dead shadowy existence. No matter if she lost all dignity and respect, the secondary-wife of her husband's slayer, risking a death in disgrace and an eternity burning in the scorching flames of Hell, she simply had to lie in his arms and feel the beat of his heart, his steady breathing.

When morning came, she could see the hopelessness of her project. What about Wulfhere and Ædelræd? She had to consider their future, but she preferred not to think about them, it hurt too much. Wulfhere wasn't going to have a trouble-free life anyway, even without her standing in his way; he had a frail body and a tricky mind, and she hadn't been able to put any of it right, no matter how hard she had tried.

It swept over her again, the despair, the raging sorrow about everything she had thrown away; she had taken such poor care of her family and now her life was over and she couldn't say: See, this is what I have achieved. Most grievous and painful of all, however, was her craving for the husband she missed so unbearably.

'Penda, Penda, Penda,' she whispered, curling up on the floor.

*His left hand is under my head, and his right hand embraces me. I implore you, O daughters of Jerusalem, by the roes and by the hinds of the field: stir not up, nor awaken love until it pleases.*

When she sat up, she thought: Where does the salt in the sea come from, if not from the tears we weep? But why would they end up out there? They dry on our cheeks, she reasoned, or are wiped away on our sleeves, so how does the salt get into the sea?

Hild made a little pile of crossed sticks, which she walked around three times while murmuring Cynewise's name. Now they'd find out if Hild really was a witch or not. No one could accuse her if Cynewise suddenly started wasting away, and Penda knew where he could fetch his wife.

Her curse on Cynewise was the only regular feature of Hild's daily schedule. She executed it every evening, whereas all her other undertakings, even her teaching, could be moved around, and might easily be cancelled if Anna came up with some other plan.

She was grateful for this one fixed point. Cynewise has taken my husband, she thought, and no greater offence is possible: what our god has joined must not be split apart by a human being. The Lord put Penda and me together, and neither Cynewise nor anyone else has any business coming between us.

At the same time, she was well aware that Cynewise had stepped onto their board as a very inexperienced gaming piece: she had changed hands, not against her will but nonetheless without any idea of what the moves meant. This did not exempt her from blame. Cynewise was a harbinger of ill fortune, and no matter how many male babies providence might grant her with Penda, those sons would be tormented, this much Hild knew. Not a scrap of good fortune had been bestowed on Cynewise—and even if it had, the little white sticks would get rid of it.

Despair pitched her to the ground again, and there she lay until the cock crowed.

Hild didn't know how she could carry on, with the sorrow—and Oswald's blood—sticking to her and refusing to be washed away no matter how vigorously she scrubbed.

She had written to Aidan asking for advice: was there some way in which she could atone for her guilt, or was she already damned to the flames of Hell? She would give everything she owned to the Lord, after paying off Cynewise's claims, but would that be sufficient?

The messenger returned and told of Aidan's horrified dismay and agitation: he couldn't simply set a routine penance, but would have to give the matter due consideration. 'So much innocent blood for the sake of her pride!' he had said. Her offence was so much the graver since it had become increasingly clear that Oswald had been a holy man. Many people had been cured of their ailments by means of soil from the place where he had died, and his arm had been displayed at Bebbanburh—the march of time had left not a mark on it. Bernicia was now suffering under the command of his brother, Oswy, and Oswy wasn't the type of man who donated land for monasteries, the messenger confided.

Hild had lost much flesh to the fast she had imposed upon herself. Fearing the Lord might summon her to judgement before she had atoned for anything at all, she now decided to keep herself alive by eating. This strategy proved difficult, however, as she wasn't hungry and nothing on the table caused her mouth to water. Every morning she had to force her legs over the side of the bed, where they often just hung for quite a while before she got up.

Talcuin spoke to her gently and harshly, and she ordered him to keep silent. Not even teaching gave her pleasure, and she realized her talents had forsaken her, including her talent for Latin. The years had consumed her accomplishments, along with everything else.

A letter arrived from Hereswid. Hild cancelled lessons and rode out to Sigebert's grave, the only place where she could find some degree of calm and where she could lose herself in her sister's voice—across the long long journey dividing them.

The burial mounds lay like swellings on the flat landscape, overgrown with grass and low scrub, and the month-of-sacrifice sun made them seem bigger than in summertime. She noticed a couple of rabbits on the south side of one of the old graves; they had obviously found a good spot since the mound was riddled with their burrows.

Nature was no respecter of the dead, she thought, and thus it was so much the more necessary to safeguard remembrance of them, no matter which god might have been invoked at their burial.

She gazed across the flat areas flanking the wide mouth of the river Deope; the lapwings were still flapping around, crying shrilly, even though the time of singing was over—for birds too.

But people seek out so many schemes—she added, addressing Sigebert's grave in the hope he would understand—which make them forget the dead.

Hild sat on a rock and took out Hereswid's letter, written, as always, on the finest parchment. How they made it like that—thinner and softer than anything Hild had written on in Mercia—she had no idea. She broke the seal and started reading:

My beloved sister! What are you doing in that little backwater when a world of opportunities lies ahead of you? Sell your belongings, travel to Rome and then come to us. Our lives are filled with study and prayer, and the abbess would be happy to see a queen of the Angles as her successor. Beloved foolish little sister, the swamps of East Anglia discharge despondency, but here the sun shines, and however long we spend on our writing, our fingers never stiffen from the cold. My dearest, one and only on the earth, why do you linger? Are you still waiting for Penda to change his mind and cast his second wife aside? Then you will linger long. If he wants sons with her, he will have sons with her. And until such time, he won't stop.

Listen, dearest sister of the flesh, and maybe one day also in the Lord: our god stripped you of this world's fleeting benefits in order to prepare you for a far greater position, should you open your eyes to the joy that does not perish, neither of rust nor of age, but which endures into eternity. What are all the gold rings and queenships in the world, men's sweet words of love and the fervent embraces of their bodies, in comparison with the love of Jesus? I know of what I speak, and the advantages were as honey to me while they lasted. But I assure you, compared with the heavenly crown that the Lord grants his handmaidens, the crown of the queen of Mercia is but dazzle and rusty iron.

My dearest Hild, do not let the loss of gold and the esteem of the people embitter your mind. Time is well advanced, and who can say when the Lord will summon us? The Day of Judgement can be expected whenever it might be, and woe betide the one who did not seize her opportunities. Should the Lord then say 'I know you not!' when you, full of trepidation, step before his seat of judgement?

Your eyes will open wide when you see how much learning and how many deep thoughts have been written down here. When the neighbouring monastery receives a new book, we borrow it to make a transcription—thus our resources suffice for three times as much learning. We make the parchment ourselves, and I have yet to receive one single letter from you written on parchment that compares favourably with ours. Do you not agree?

Could you not, for the sake of my love, enquire in Cantwaraburh about a queen named Boudicca who ruled East Anglia at the time when the Romans conquered our country? I cannot believe what is written about her! Here in Gaul the women fight all they can against the men's strife—as everyone who does not let judgement be hampered by prejudice has to acknowledge. Of course, the men speak of peace, but I have never heard of any man who puts peace higher than his own power. I have never met men like Bishop Aidan here.

We learn more in this place than we dreamt of as children. Every day I marvel and thank my creator for granting me the ability to read and opening the door to all this magnificent learning. The more I learn, the more my ignorance is revealed to me. For what, all things considered, do the living know except that we shall eventually die? As is written in Ecclesiastes.

I am sending you a section of a work we received from the religious community established by Isidorus' sister in the land of the Visigoths. It is written by a certain Plinius at the time of the Roman Empire, and it is years since I have learnt so many things about this world. Our abbess was far from pleased, and of the opinion that they had made poor return for our precious embroidery. According to her, the work has been superseded by Isidorus' *De natura rerum*. Anyway, it is made up of thirty-seven books, and I know how eager you are to partake of its learning. As I am eager to see you, my dearest one. The abbess gave me permission to make this copy and she sends you her greetings. We pray that the Lord will guide your feet to this place—your very own, your Hereswid.

Hild had stopped several times while reading the letter, to catch her breath or to dry her eyes. Now she wept wretchedly, hugging Hereswid's letter to her breast and murmuring her name. When she noticed the parchment was getting wet, she anxiously wrapped it all together.

She blew her nose and took a deep breath, stood up, gazed out at the flat landscape. Despondency, yes, but she couldn't decide whether it was she who discharged despondency across the land or if it was the other way around—although it was certainly something they shared. She wouldn't be able to live in a bright light under a hot sun; being wrapped in heavy clothing gave a sense of security. Nor could she cope with the thought of a long journey and all the preparations involved, no matter how much she yearned to throw herself into her sister's embrace.

She would seek out the information Hereswid had requested, find out as much as she could, and she would travel to Cantwaraburh straight away, tomorrow. The yearning for Hereswid spread like a warmth within her breast—it had been so very long ago: Hereswid's laughter, her frank and cheerful manner, even in the company of the finest people.

Then, as usual, she walked around the burial mounds and prayed for Sigebert and for Hereswid's husband, which calmed her down enough to concentrate on Hereswid's gift.

She glowed all over when she took it out: Plinius—she had never managed to get hold of anything written by him before. It was the best book she had ever held in her hands, it exuded wisdom, and this was only a small section of the whole. Hereswid was able to copy it all, she could just walk to the book collection and choose a book: a book about animals and plants, the way in which the world was put together and the Lord's scheme with it all, reflections on the Gospels, on the Song of Solomon, Ecclesiastes, Paulus. They paid for books with their embroidery and surplus from their farm, and with gifts they received from wealthy women, both when they entered the monastery and when they wished to show their gratitude to the nuns for saying intercessory prayers on behalf of the realm.

Hild sat for a while, enjoying the sense of suspense, before she started reading. Her eyes raced across the pages, her cheeks were now burning and she had to stop occasionally to catch breath, her head swimming.

She closed her eyes, and when she opened them again she could see a herd of elephants lumbering peacefully towards her from the river bank. They vanished. She continued her reading: the description of their composition and colour was followed by a section about their habits. She read to the end, sighed and closed her eyes. There was so very much about which she knew nothing! Hereswid was right in saying that ignorance seemed to increase with the years.

The elephant's modesty was fascinating: this huge animal was more civilized than humankind, herself included! Purer of body and thought, closer to its creator's purpose.

People also like to couple privately, she thought, unlike animals—except, that is, the elephant—but since the Fall, the human body has become full of desire, and we don't indulge in the ways of the flesh solely for the sake of breeding. She had with Eadfrid; not with Penda. The thought of Penda's body made her wince. What she knew with her intellect was utterly incomprehensible: that Penda's eagerness to lie with Cynewise was more agreeable to the Lord God than his instinctive desire to lie with Hild.

Losing the status accorded a queen was nothing when compared with losing her king's body. The thought of his embrace could make her wail to the heavens, her screams mingling with the autumn wind blowing across the flat landscape and its mute overgrown burial mounds.

# Elephants and Apricot Trees

*– Hild makes preparations for her journey –*

They could tell her little about Queen Boudicca in Cantwaraburh, and it wasn't until Hild put Talcuin on the case that the investigation started bearing fruit. He questioned the old Britons, and some could inform him that Boudicca had fought for the Britons' freedom. Hild was now so determined to unearth more information that she took Talcuin with her to Walas, where the stories about what had happened before these people had been driven west might still be remembered. She spoke with people at the monastery, he spoke with people elsewhere.

She was not pleased by what she heard. Boudicca, it seemed, had been a queen of the Brittonic Iceni tribe over there in the eastern realm, and she had led the most vicious uprising ever seen in these islands. The king, her husband, had entered an alliance with the Romans. When he died, however, the Romans simply invaded, ejected people from their farms, killed, raped and took survivors as slaves. When Boudicca protested about their actions at her royal estate, they killed her servants and raped her two daughters. And when she cried out and cursed them for so doing, they tied her hands and put her to the lash.

Terrible, of course, but was it really acceptable to let the whole of Colneceaster pay the penalty? And then Lunden, which at the time was already a town inhabited by thousands of people? The Romans hadn't defended the town, because their soldiers were on the island of Môn destroying the rebels' stronghold and sacred place. Lunden was burnt to the ground. Boudicca's army marched from town to town, but they didn't take prisoners: no, everyone they came across was slain—on the gibbet, the cross or by fire, it was said—and this was the part Hild found so hard to understand.

More Brittonic tribes, and yet more, had joined forces with Boudicca: the foreigners would be sent back across the sea. Her army was said to number two hundred thousand men—impossible.

The largest army Hild had ever heard about was Cædwalla's paupers' army of two thousand men—an enormous troop, which had proved impossible to maintain. One hundred times as many men was simply not feasible, but now she had heard the tale from three mouths.

Exploits had a habit of expanding as the years passed, and all this had taken place a very long time ago, just a couple of generations after Jesus Christ had laid down his life. The army had undoubtedly grown every time the story had been told.

The catastrophe occurred when the Britons went into battle pulling their heavily-laden carts behind them—carts full of booty and children, and totally incompatible with any kind of combat. Somewhere in Mercia, each and every one had been slain. They had blocked their own escape route with all the goods they had brought along. Boudicca managed to get away and she rode home, where she and her daughters took poison.

A dreadful fate. What had gone through her mind as she saw her people being massacred? Given that she herself had led them into disaster in order to avenge her daughters. But had ended up handing them a poisoned chalice. Amends and retribution for her daughters had been beyond her reach—instead, she had offered an honourable departure from their abasement. They hadn't served a god who forbade his people from using such a method, and in that respect life had been easier back in those days.

How could Hild explain to her sister that she had personally been no better? That she, Hild, had spoken of peace, just like the men in Hereswid's letter, while at the same time she had incited war.

Boudicca had fought against a foreign tyranny, Hild against an innocent man of the Lord whose imperishable arm continued to bear witness to her offence.

How could she write all that to Hereswid?

The investigation put her on the track of another queen from Boudicca's day. Many Brittonic tribes had joined in the uprising, but not the Brigantes up in Bernicia; their queen had stuck to her alliance with the Romans because without their support she couldn't hang on to power. The Romans had sent troops to rescue her when her rejected husband had invaded the kingdom to oust the 'traitor queen', as she was known.

Cartimandua was her name, and she had been given her byname after betraying her ally Caradoc from Walas. He had been fighting against the Romans for eight years, and eventually sought sanctuary with Cartimandua, who had him put in chains and handed him over to the foreign forces.

Cartimandua was becoming of greater interest to Hild than Boudicca had been. Hospitality, she had always been taught, was inviolable, and from olden times it had been law. Not even gold-greedy King Rædwald had been so despicable as to contravene the rule of hospitality when it came to the young Edwin—even though King Ædelfred had offered him a great deal to do so, Sigebert had told her. Even he wouldn't have minded seeing a white bearskin adorning the hall at Rendlæsham, but was nonetheless glad that his father had placed more importance on the old customs.

Cartimandua's action might well be incomprehensible, but she had obviously prospered for a long time afterwards. Hild wanted to know if Cartimandua's husband had always been against the alliance with the Romans, or if he had turned against them when she rejected him. She couldn't track down a clear-cut answer; every time she got one aspect settled, two or three new questions emerged. The more she found out, the more gaps appeared in the story.

This queen obviously had no integrity, but whether she acted for the sake of power or of peace remained a mystery to Hild. One fact did become clear, however: life in olden times had been just as complex as it was today—and even back then you couldn't simply say: This is what you have to do, this is right!

Hild sought counsel from Bishop Felix, who had once assisted Sigebert in his undertakings to convert the realm. She told him about her difficulties in finding the right path; confided that she often thought about the song concerning pagan Ingeld who had to choose between forsaking his wife or forsaking his duty to avenge his father; admitted that she felt like him: whichever path she followed was wrong.

She thought this also applied to Queen Boudicca and Queen Cartimandua: one had followed the path of family honour, and slain thousands of people; the other had pursued the path of peace, and forsaken the most fundamental notions of integrity. Both had acted wrongly, but how could you have acted correctly in that situation?

'If the Lord really loves us,' she said, 'then why has he made it so difficult to be a human? He has given the animals a far easier life.'

'Humankind wanted it thus,' said Felix. 'They could have stayed in Paradise. But they wouldn't settle for just *hearing* about things from him, they wanted to experience them for themselves. Like all children do—or were you different?'

'Had I been, then perhaps much would have been better.'

'I think not,' he said. 'Your children also need to experience things for themselves.'

'I am not with them,' Hild whispered, 'so they have to.'

'Whatever you might tell them, they need to learn for themselves,' Felix emphasized. 'We are all the children of Eve, who ate from the tree of knowledge, and hence we are not like animals. We can tell the difference, and guilt sticks to us until Jesus takes it from us. Don't forget to say David's psalms! Then your mind will gradually be directed along the right path.'

'I have said them every day throughout all the years gone by.'

'Then say them twice,' Felix suggested, and assigned a very mild penance for letting her thoughts wander to the old pagans.

'Tell me one more thing,' she said. 'What is the most powerfully effective penance of all?'

'To work in the service of the Lord,' said Felix. 'And, if you have the resources, to do penance at the apostles' graves.'

'Is that powerful enough to benefit the family lineage too?' she asked.

'Such a journey would naturally add more weight to your prayers,' Felix replied.

'Good,' said Hild, 'so that is how it shall be!'

She asked him to help her find a companion for the journey, and to give her instruction until the time came for her departure. Having now heard his magnificent Latin, and having realized she was barely able to keep up with his young pupils, Hild didn't think her increasingly home-grown Latin would be acceptable when meeting educated people.

She wrote to Hereswid's community requesting to be admitted. There was nothing left for her in this island.

The abbess's reply arrived together with an enthusiastic letter from Hereswid. The abbess would like to know how much Hild could bring in dowry to the Lord. Hild would have to find out, also the cost of a pilgrimage. Bishop Felix explained that a dowry was only required if she travelled directly to the monastery; if she used her resources on something so laudable as a visit to Rome, she didn't have to worry about the dowry.

Hild sold her land and property in Rotanland—the generous morning gift from Penda—and payment was made in coin stamped with the head of the king of Kent. This had become quite normal practice in recent years, even though it was hard to see what purpose these coins should serve; you couldn't wear them, you could just give them away in exchange for land or real gold for personal adornment.

She sat up in bed, surrounded by all the pieces of gold coin; her fingers ran through them. She held a handful aloft and then let them cascade down over her, clinking one against the other.

'No husband in the bed,' she said to herself, 'but enough pieces of gold to buy an entire kingdom.'

She soon tired of the coins, they gave no warmth. She got up and spread her treasures across a cloth on the table. She had accumulated a fine collection of large and small gifts, which she would sit and enjoy of an evening: brooches and clasps with inlaid garnet, silver rings with nielo animal decorations, belt buckles and fastening pins of gold. A good deal of first-rate fabric, too, which she had bought both to wear and to give as gifts. She spread the fabrics across the bed and chairs while wondering what might be lacking from her collection.

The brightly-coloured sight pleased her. When she really wanted to luxuriate in it, she instructed Talcuin to walk around the room carrying an oil lamp in each hand, so the light flickered and sparkled in the precious metals and stones and in the small pieces of silver sewn into the fabrics. The big rock-crystal bead in a silver mounting, allowing it to be hung from a belt, was for the abbess of Hereswid's monastery. Queen Tata had owned a similar bead, which Breguswid had greatly admired, and if Breguswid could see her daughter's treasures now, she would be proud—although probably not about her general situation.

She had dismissed Talcuin for the evening, so she had to carry the lamps herself. The bright gold sparkled and shone right into the corners of the room.

One of the merchants who came to Tamoworthig had said there were black slaves in Gaul. Proper slaves, who could do everything required of them, it was just that their skin was as black as night. He could get hold of one too, he claimed, but he wanted some of the payment in advance and that wasn't how Hild handled her transactions. First the goods, then the payment—when it came to trade, she didn't trust the word of honour. Penda did, however, and when a merchant didn't return, he would continue to believe the man's ship had sunk, or he had been killed by robbers. He was such a principled man, her husband, and he simply couldn't imagine a merchant would deliberately cheat. She smiled at the memory of his blank expression when she had said the merchant had undoubtedly taken the gold and run.

On several occasions, she had asked the merchants to find her a copy of Plinius' *Naturalis historia*, but now she wouldn't have to search for a single book: the library at Hereswid's monastery had Plinius' entire work on its shelves, and much more, yes, more learning than she could possibly imagine, all the learning in the world gathered in one place.

If she worked hard, she could become a scribe like Hereswid, and she would drink in every single word. Whenever she fetched a volume from the bookcase, she would brush her hand across the adjoining volumes; she could always pretend she was just a little confused.

'Amo, amas, amat, amamus, amatis, amant!'

Felix was the first person since Paulinus to give her proper lessons, but she had forgotten to ask him how to say 'fly' in Latin. There was so much she didn't know, and it was a staggering thought that it was all—and all at once—within her reach.

'Musca! That was it—Musca domestica, the common housefly.'

No husband in the bed, but a firm grasp of the Latin for 'housefly'.

The world might well be out of kilter—that much, at least, was certain—but she was going to see it anyway. She was looking forward to the journey: to seeing the Judas tree, its flowers blossoming on the trunk itself, elephants, perhaps, orange trees, apricot trees. Hereswid had written to her about the apricot trees—just imagine, such trees exist!

She had dreamt about apricot trees last night; she had held a warm and downy fruit in her hand, sunk her teeth into its bittersweet juicy flesh, and licked its oozing nectar.

Of all the wonders Hereswid had reported, the apricot tree was the most impressive. Its blossom floated like a little white cloud just above the ground; later, intensely green leaves appeared on a reddish stem; and then the branches hung heavy with fragrant, golden, enticing fruit. The taste defied all description, Hereswid had written, having tried many comparisons, but it was different, completely different. Hild would have to come and see for herself, see it growing, all year round, a little living miracle.

The summers were warmer over there, the wine sweet and delicious, and vegetables appeared earlier. They only had to light a fire in the writing room during the harshest of winter months. Now Hild could really feel the dankness; it had been raining all day and yuletide was just about to start.

In the Holy Land it only rains in wintertime, Hereswid had written, having read a book about all the holy places. That was going to be the first book Hild would read when she got there. And King Anna didn't own one single book!

'Well, that's what they say,' Talcuin finished.

'It's good you keep your ear to the ground,' said Hild. 'Continue to do so!'

She was angry, seething, and would have to make a real effort or risk losing everything. You couldn't let rip at a man like Anna, and there wasn't even any point in telling him what you thought in a nice friendly manner. To get what you wanted, you had to make him believe it was all his idea. A rotten apple, that's what he was, distrustful and self-important in all his weakness.

The cutting wind cooled her mind as she walked across to the hall. The yuletide month had arrived with gales and rough weather.

When it was her turn, she made the most elegant of curtsies, almost lying on the floor at the king's feet, where she stayed until he requested her to rise. She thanked him.

'As King Anna is aware, it is my intention to set out on a pilgrimage to Rome,' she started.

He nodded benevolently.

'The future of the children is therefore a matter close to my heart, and I would ask King Anna if he would be so kind as to inform me of any plans he might have in that respect.'

'I would indeed,' Anna replied, 'and as good fortune would have it, I am currently in negotiations as regards Ædelthryd's future.'

He made a rhetorical pause to accommodate her approval, which was promptly expressed.

'Well well,' she said appreciatively, 'what news, to be sure!'

'Indeed,' Anna nodded. 'And you are perhaps interested to learn with whom I am negotiating?'

'Most certainly, my king.'

'Well, an excellent man,' said Anna. 'An excellent man—with the exception of his loyalty, which has fluctuated somewhat. Given the location of his kingdom. He's actually more Penda's man than mine. He thinks he can operate as his own man, taking a little here, a little there.'

'Does he really?'

'In a word, it's Tondberht, chief of the Southern Girvij. Upon marriage, he will commit his loyalty to me.'

'That sounds promising. Are there any plans as to when the engagement will take place?'

'At Easter,' he replied.

'An excellent idea,' Hild exclaimed, 'for then he can be baptized first. Which was of course your plan: a man who is not baptized—his word cannot be trusted. And then we would have no way of knowing if he would keep his promise to leave her in peace until her body is ready for a man. Marriage is a serious matter for us Christians. I myself was eighteen years of age when I married King Edwin's son. And to the best of my belief, sixteen years is the very earliest age at which a woman can partake of the matrimonial pursuit.'

Anna looked confused, obviously thinking as hard as he could.

'Exactly!' he eventually said. 'Just what I was thinking, yes. Our thoughts precisely.'

'And Ædelthryd's morning gift—not a matter of trifles, I imagine?'

'Not likely,' said Anna, 'but it's a surprise. For you, that is.'

'Ædelthryd herself does actually say that she wants to be a nun like her mother—like my sister Hereswid. And, obviously, should she really wish to do so later, then she must have the possibility. And so—I think—her morning gift must be large enough to pay for the building of a monastery. That's the thing about us Christians: we recognize the liberty of the individual person; we won't just *use* our fellow humans, we want their happiness and their redemption. Yes, above all, their redemption, and seen with our Christian eyes it is a sin to marry off a young girl against her will. Only pagans could act in that way these days.'

'You are right,' said Anna, 'you are so infinitely right, and that's exactly what I was thinking too.'

'Although Penda will probably not be pleased,' Hild smiled.

Anna laughed in delight.

'No, probably not,' he confided to her, 'because when the Southern Girvij pledge their allegiance to me, Penda's foothold here will be a little less firm. He won't be able to trample all over us when Tondberht goes over to King Anna!'

'He'll certainly find it harder to do so,' said Hild.

'That he will,' Anna laughed.

'I don't know if you have already decided who should sponsor Tondberht,' said Hild humbly, 'and I in no way expect to be taken into consideration, now that you have been so magnanimous as to assume responsibility for Ædelthryd, so my kinship is not what it would have been had her mother not followed the great calling . . . '

'I had actually thought to ask you to be sponsor. It would be an honour for Tondberht.'

'My humble gratitude,' she said. 'That is nearly too great an honour.'

'Not at all, not at all.'

'Then I proffer many thanks for your favour,' she said, bending her knee to Anna. 'I have always known that Hereswid was right in letting her children be *your* children. I would have liked to raise them myself, but as she said: I don't want my children to be fed horsemeat—they must live among Christian people. And how right she was.'

Anna nodded graciously when Hild again bent her knee to him.

She left well-pleased. That King Anna had sold her eleven-year-old niece to a fifty-five-year-old one-eyed drunkard, with a reputation for violence against his three earlier wives, was a non-negotiable transaction, but Hild now had the opportunity to protect Ædelthryd—to some small extent, at least. She would initiate this ruthless husband in the punitive measures available to the Lord when anyone failed to follow his commandments. She would also tell him about the nature of Christian conduct: he must not lie with his new wife before her body was ready for a man and not before the wedding; he must never raise a hand against her, and she should receive a sizeable morning gift.

These prerequisites would help Ædelthryd find a better husband when this one dropped dead from drink—or from Penda's revenge. Tondberht was a worthless good-for-nothing in every respect.

'Hereswid!' Hild spoke into the air. 'You are a fool!'

Regardless of horsemeat and spring sacrifices, the children would have been better off with her and Penda. Not many Masses, admittedly, but they would have learnt to read and write—and Latin, to the best of Hild's ability.

Sigebert had turned Hereswid's head, and after he had come into the picture all they ever heard was 'Sigebert says . . . ' and 'Sigebert thinks . . . ', 'Sigebert *this*' and 'Sigebert *that*'! Hereswid had suspended her judgement in order to repeat the words of her beloved and she had even echoed his great respect for 'sound judgement', without a thought to exercising her own.

Where sex enters, sense leaves, Hild said to herself. Had Hereswid been married to the splendid Sigebert, she would soon have rediscovered her sound judgement, without a doubt. It's not healthy with all that daydreaming—no matter how delightful it might be while it lasts!

'Hereswid!' she called into the air, which was now filled with loose white flakes that melted the moment they settled. 'A little horsemeat does no one any harm. Stupidity like Anna's is far more dangerous. It could prove fatal to your children!'

Penda would never have sold Ædelthryd for political gain, and definitely not for a payback that was merely a visual illusion. He knew how to differentiate between the long and the short view, and between advantage and flattery. This deal would be a very short-term advantage for Anna. How on earth did he imagine he could take on Penda?

If he decided to exact revenge for this stunt, Penda would spare Hereswid's children—Hild knew him well enough to be sure of that—but as of yet, Ædelthryd didn't even know what Anna had planned for her.

# AFTER THE FALL

*– three letters to Hild –*

One day in the month of Hreda, three letters arrived for Hild.

The first two were brought by messenger from Cantwaraburh, and Hild ripped open the long-awaited communication from Bishop Honorius. He wrote that, following consultation with Bishop Felix, he had selected a well-educated Gallic monk to escort her to Rome. She could come straight after the Easter festival; the man was ready for departure.

Hild cried out with happiness. Finally! Her own preparations had long been completed and today was the last day of the Easter festival. Talcuin was put to work with the packing, her things and his own: he would, of course, be accompanying her.

Then she sat down with the second letter; she didn't recognize the handwriting. It was from the abbess at Cale. She reported that Hereswid was dead, or rather, as she expressed it: had entered the true life. During her final hours, she had prayed for her children and her sister and for one of her former teachers. The abbess was enclosing Hereswid's gold holy cross—a baptismal gift from King Edwin—and the hope that she would soon receive Hild as a bride of Christ. At the monastery in Cale, they valued the presence of a well-educated queen from across the water, she wrote, and now they were without one; Hild need speculate no further on the matter of the dowry.

Hild gazed at the cross, the same kind as her own. She wondered if she should pop it in her mouth and eat it, or bury it at Sigebert's ship-grave. She could trample it to pieces, or give it to the first beggar who crossed her path.

No, Ædelthryd should have it. What else did this translucent girl have left of the mother she couldn't even remember? Even though she persisted in regaling Hild with the most moving incidents from her childhood, what her mother had said and what her mother had done. Each and every time, Hild knew that Hereswid would never have said such a thing; besides, Ædelthryd was not even a year old when Hereswid had followed her calling.

She sat with the ornament in her hand, staring into the world of red garnets; it was as though they came to life when she turned the ornament in the light. And thus she sat as evening drew in and Talcuin was still packing and the third letter arrived, brought by a monk from the north. She didn't have the energy to break the seal, and asked Talcuin to tell her what the letter said.

It was from Aidan. He asked her to come, asked her to abandon her journey and come north instead, to help spread the faith.

'We need you,' read Talcuin. 'Superstition has gained ground since Oswald's death. We lack enlightened souls to lead the people along the right path.'

'He says they need me?' asked Hild.

'That's what he writes, yes.'

'Fortune doesn't smile on me,' she said quietly. 'In my footsteps there is nothing but grief and death. They must have made a mistake.'

'Well, anyway, that's what Aidan writes,' said Talcuin. 'He writes that he has had a dream: if you convert people in Northumbria, the Lord will forgive you and embrace your kin as well.'

'What an idea,' she said.

She sat for a while, staring into space, then she shook herself and began pacing up and down. Finally she turned to Talcuin.

'Does that mean King Oswine too?'

Talcuin found the passage in the letter and read it again.

'He doesn't say who, he just writes: your kin. No names. He must mean your mother and your father.'

'And my brother, perhaps?'

'Undoubtedly, yes, your brother as well.'

'Indeed,' she said, and asked Talcuin to fetch Aldwulf and Ædelthryd and order elderberry syrup, their favourite drink.

The children sat on the bench in front of her and waited for her blessing, now that she was going on a journey to Rome. Ædelthryd had picked the first primroses of the year, most of them still in bud; she knew Hild was very fond of them, just like her own mother, her beloved nun-mother. Hild must take half the bunch of primroses to her nun-mother in Gaul.

'And when I grow up, I'll come over to join you,' she said, beaming with joy. 'And be the bride of Christ,' she added proudly. She had grown recently, had drawn herself up during the betrothal party and her future husband's baptism.

Hild stroked the girl's hair and breathed in the fragrance of the pale yellow petals.

'The abbess of your mother's monastery has written to tell us that your mother has gone up to Jesus. Now she's in Heaven, rejoicing in your beautiful flowers.'

'That is not true!' Aldwulf shouted, jumping up.

'Yes, it is true, and now I'll read the letter to you. Or you can read it yourselves; you're both so good at reading.'

She passed the letter to Aldwulf, who shook his head and pushed it away, fighting back tears.

'You try, Ædelthryd,' said Hild, and Ædelthryd began. She managed, with a lot of help, to get through the letter, she was proud of her skill. Aldwulf stood stiffly and refused to look at the words.

'It is not true. It's just something she writes,' he said defiantly.

'I think it is true,' said Hild, 'and I wish it were otherwise. Now we must pray to our god to receive her kindly in Heaven. For your mother was a wise and strong woman, and she will not be forgotten. Neither in Gaul nor in this country.'

'You said she was in Heaven already,' said Ædelthryd.

'And so she is, because she was a handmaiden of the Lord and she has secured a treasure for herself, which no one can take from her. But we'll pray for her anyway, so she knows we're thinking of her. And remember, one day, when we go up there—then she'll be waiting to receive us.'

'I'll go in a bridal gown,' said Ædelthryd eagerly.

They lay on the floor and prayed for Hereswid's soul. Aldwulf sobbed loudly. Hild had no idea what to do with him; he had always been a self-contained child, and wouldn't let anyone touch him.

When they stood up, he threw himself upon her, weeping, burrowed his face into her shoulder and clung to her. He was fourteen years old, nearly as tall as she was.

Ædelthryd pulled gently at his cloak and gazed up at him with her big bright eyes.

'She's an angel, Aldwulf, don't you understand? She's looking after us from up in Heaven now, isn't that lovely?'

Her luminous eleven-year-old face was full of wonder at the fuss her brother was making. Personally, she felt greatly reassured to learn that her mother was in Heaven rather than in Gaul, about which she had heard many strange things.

'You've got to stay with us, you've got to!' cried Aldwulf, and shook Hild by the shoulders. 'You've got to, you've got to!'

Hild was glad there were no witnesses to Aldwulf's behaviour, apart from Talcuin. Aldwulf would, after all, be king one day. He was a grown man—should be, at least. And now she was going to weep too.

'Aldwulf,' she said, 'remember, your mother was a very good and wise woman, and your father a great king. A very great king, I tell you, and a very devout man. Now you have to follow in their footsteps, you and your sister. They are sitting together up in Heaven and they rejoice over your happiness and weep over your grief. And they want you to carry the lineage forward—that is what they expect. You must not bring dishonour upon them.'

Aldwulf nodded and took a deep breath, wiped his nose on his sleeve and cleared his throat. Ædelthryd was radiant.

'And our whole lineage will be angels one day, up in Paradise, won't they, Hild?'

'We certainly hope so,' said Hild, attempting to smile. What on earth would become of this strange child?

A violent rage suddenly welled up in her, against Hereswid, sitting up there, everything fine, leaving them in this chaos. Couldn't she have stayed? Why had she gone to Gaul in the first place?

She immediately repented her unreasonable thoughts, for no act is greater than serving the Lord.

'Have a drink now,' she said to Aldwulf, 'it'll do you good.'

He nodded and obediently gulped down the syrup.

Hild woke during the night. Hereswid stood at the foot of the bed, blood running from her eye sockets, down her cheeks, down onto her dress, which was completely soaked a dark red. She wrung her hands at her breast and, in a strange dry voice, repeated over and over: 'Pray for me, Hild, pray for me, Hild.'

She had a deep wound across her brow. It was the mark left by the holy Peter's key—he had struck her face when she presented herself before him.

'I know you not!' he had cried in a tone that had caused Hereswid's eyes to burst from their sockets and her voice to sound so very strange.

She had been sent back to earth, to bear witness to her sins, so people could see what awaited them if they defied the word of the Lord. From now on, she would spend her time roaming the world and tormenting people with her dreadful testimony. Until their prayers redeemed her. All the way into eternity—or until the end of eternity.

Hild sat up in bed, stretching out a hand to her sister.

'Forgive me, Hereswid, forgive me.'

But Hereswid paid her no heed; it was even impossible to tell if she heard, her eyes looking as they did. She just kept repeating, in her peculiar voice: 'Pray for me, Hild, pray for me.'

'Every day of my life I shall pray for you, I promise, Hereswid. Listen to me: every day I shall pray for you.'

Hereswid's body dissolved in front of Hild's eyes, just slowly disappeared. When she got up and felt around the room there was nothing to be found. Such was the nature of phantoms—they can't be felt physically, as well she knew.

She flung open the door and peered out into the darkness. A shadow vanished between the trees.

'Hereswid!' she shouted, and rushed out into the night, but there was nothing to be found among the dark trees, apart from thick shrub and wet ferns.

She stood still and listened. Nothing to be heard, just a gentle sighing in the treetops. She jumped when an owl screeched, discordantly, like the howl of an afflicted child.

She clutched her head and the owl screeched again.

So, they would soon meet, she and Hereswid, either here or there. She felt cold to her bones, recoiling when the owl screeched yet again.

'Hereswid!' she shouted from the depth of her lungs. 'Every single day of my life I shall pray for you. Listen to me. Every single day!'

The owl was silent.

She walked back, wet from the night dew and completely exhausted.

Talcuin met her in front of the house; he hadn't been able to find her in the darkness. He wrapped her in a cloak and lit the fire. When the flames were blazing, he went to fetch mead.

She drank without looking up, and reached out for more.

'Help yourself,' she said, and he was pleased at the offer. He didn't like the taste of King Anna's beer either; he had been converted to mead.

'Yes,' said Hild, 'that's the way it is.'

Talcuin didn't answer; he didn't suppose the words were addressed to him, and in any case, there wasn't much to say by way of response.

'Our god is in Heaven and the people on earth,' said Hild, as she stared into the fire and took a deep draught from her cup. 'But why is it so difficult to please him?'

The look she gave Talcuin made him flinch.

'The ways of the Lord are past understanding,' he replied. This was the only real solace he knew, and it was certainly true. He also thought his mistress was past understanding.

This came from his great love for her.

She sat silently for a long time, falling into a reverie.

'Talcuin,' she said finally, 'are you a person?'

She looked straight at him, and he didn't understand her question.

'What else could I be?' he asked self-consciously.

'Come,' she said, and reached out her hand to him. 'I want to see if it is true.'

He found this rather embarrassing, but complied, as always, with her wishes. Her hands felt cold when she pushed them up inside the sleeves of his jerkin and pressed into his skin.

'Yes,' she said, as if from another world, 'of flesh and blood indeed.'

She placed her fingers on the pulsation in his wrist and his neck and shook her head doubtfully. She felt his head and his shoulders, his chest and his legs, and he stood stiff as a post and understood nothing.

'I wonder why the Lord created us like this?' she murmured to herself. 'What on earth can he have had in mind?'

She was now on the other side of Talcuin, and she pressed his back with one hand while holding him firmly by the arm with her other hand. She placed both her hands on his hips and pressed. Talcuin gasped when she put an arm around his waist and ran the other down his spine, her whole forearm at once.

'Yes, indeed,' she said, 'that's the way it is.'

Had she rested her brow on his shoulder blade? Or was she sniffing his armpit?

'And yet one understands nothing,' he heard her say, 'nothing, one understands nothing.'

'No,' he said, 'but perhaps it isn't for *us* to understand.'

'Nevertheless, we continue to ask,' said Hild.

'We could have stayed in Paradise,' said Talcuin, 'then there wouldn't have been so much to wonder about.'

'Would you rather have lived there?'

'Me?' Talcuin shook his head quickly. 'I don't know. I don't think so. But I was never asked.'

'Bishop Felix says the story of Adam and Eve is every single person's story. The Fall, too. That it's something we've all wanted.'

'I don't know,' answered Talcuin, 'but just to stay there eating fruit from the trees—I think I'd get bored.'

'Yes,' said Hild, 'the same for me, I suppose. But the way it's turned out—it's so difficult.'

'Yes,' he said. 'That's the price.'

'Is it possible to make a deal without knowing the price?'

'You can. But, for one thing, it wouldn't be a deal.'

'And for the other?' asked Hild when he hesitated.

'For the other, you'd probably do it anyway. Because you'd reckon that, in some way or other, you'd be able to postpone the payment. You just wouldn't believe that the whole payment would fall due. And before you expected it.'

'You could cheat?'

'Yes, cheat! That's what you bet on.'

Hild sighed. 'If only that were possible, I'd do it gladly.'

'Who wouldn't?' he said.

'Yes,' said Hild. 'Perhaps the world would come to a standstill if we knew the price. Maybe no one would dare let go of their mother's body. If they really knew . . . '

'But maybe they would anyway.'

'Yes, maybe.'

She let go, walked round to face him, and using both hands she stroked his head, neck, shoulders, flanks, placed her hands firmly on his hips. She looked at him with distant, stranger's eyes.

'Tancwoystel,' she said, 'I hereby grant you your freedom. You may take your own name again. In gratitude for your loyalty, I shall give you silver coins—you will be a wealthy man.'

'No,' he said, and took a step backwards. 'No!'

'Yes,' she said, 'that is how it is going to be, because I am going to enter a monastery and I don't want you to come with me.'

'Let me stay,' he begged. 'I'll become a lay brother.'

'No, because you have been my slave, and we would not be able to change. Handmaidens of the Lord don't have slaves.'

Talcuin stared at the floor, blinked and tried to recover his composure. When he looked up, he said: 'Then let me take you there.'

'Yes,' she said. '*That* I shall be happy to accept.'

She stretched out her hand and he took it, pressed it to his lips, put his other arm around her and pulled her close.

She gave a start when she felt his arousal through their clothing, and then her heart thundered in her throat so she could hardly breathe. She pushed him away a little and gazed with incredulity at his eyes and his mouth. She had never seen this face before.

She wanted to ask if he was Talcuin, but couldn't find the words. She closed her eyes and swallowed, took a deep breath, opened her eyes again and looked straight at him.

'Who are you?' she asked with great caution.

He didn't understand her question, thought she was asking where he was, and replied by tightening his embrace.

Then again, she supposed it must be him, because she couldn't work out who else it could be, but the face had changed—as had everything else.

'Come,' she said, and managed to reach the bed before her legs gave way.

He sat on the edge of the bed and stared at her.

'Come, come,' she said, and guided his hand up under her skirt.

He gasped when he felt the warm, wet softness and rubbed across and into it, snatched his hand away as if he had been burnt, gazed at her, his mouth half open.

'Come, come,' she said, and pulled her skirt up over her waist. 'Come now, come.'

He slowly turned his head, saw the fiery glow and was dazzled by the sight. He closed his eyes, but when he opened them it was still there, and her hands were on the small of his back and his belt.

He stood up and moved a few paces away from the bed, arms hanging at his sides, head bowed, trying to fight back the tears—but they won.

He looked at her again, lying there in all her naked loveliness; just as the Lord had created her. He sank down in front of the bed and cautiously brushed his hand over the red splendour. She pulled him up over her, wanted to have him and wanted to give herself to him, clasped him in her arms and thrust her hips upwards.

But he was no longer favoured, and the mercy would not return. He lay across her, she was trembling inside and he was next to dead.

Thus they lay while the fire burnt itself out and the night grew cold—Hild with eyes open, trying to catch an outline, anything, surely she would be able to make out a little faint glimmer of one single thing, but the darkness was impenetrable, not so much as a dim glow filtered through the shutters.

'We're still here, aren't we?'

'Yes,' mumbled Talcuin, 'we are.'

'And it's not the Kingdom of the Dead,' she whispered, 'is it?'

'It's Rendlæsham,' he answered, 'and it's night.'

She lay pondering this for a while, but couldn't understand why there was absolutely nothing to be seen except black darkness.

'We can't be dead until he has fetched us, can we?'

'No,' said Talcuin, 'and we're not in the least dead. Really not. You'll see for yourself when you wake up.'

'Yes, after all, he created us for one another,' she murmured, 'didn't he?'

'Well, so I believe,' said Talcuin. 'Yes, he did. Certainly he did.'

She pressed his head to her shoulder; it was so strangely light and small, so vulnerable and soft.

# '. . . BUT THE WAY OF THE UNGODLY SHALL PERISH.'

*– a red-haired boy by the name of Cædmon –*

They left at dawn. The weather had turned wet and wintry again. Wearing thick woollen travel cloaks, hoods pulled around their faces, they set forth northwards, following the old Roman road that led to Deira through Lindsey. Besides Talcuin, the entourage comprised twelve men.

When they reached Lindcylene, Hild wanted to pray at the church built in Paulinus' day, but it had burnt down—an accident, it was said, when the lamentable news of Oswald's death reached the town.

They continued northwards to the Humbre river, where they had to wait to be ferried across to Burh in Deira—just like the Romans, said Talcuin, as they went ashore. The Romans had built this town too, and the ruins would forever bear witness to the days when buildings were erected to stand for all eternity, in hewn rock, and there they still stood, at the ferry berth, making themselves useful.

They spent the night at Burh; the weather had changed. Hild and Talcuin looked around the large Roman theatre, overgrown with bracken and ivy; ash trees and some elder had also gained a foothold between the blocks of stone.

Hild could picture it: the bard, standing on the crescent-shaped segment at the bottom, holding his listeners on the benches above spellbound with long songs and recitations about the deeds of kings and emperors. Perhaps he had sung about Queen Boudicca and Cartimandua—what would he have to tell about them? That they had been forced to submit to the power of the Romans, of course. Why else would you employ a bard? And Boudicca and Cartimandua had kept their thoughts to themselves; Cartimandua had never told anyone what went through her mind when her ally Caradoc returned from Rome a free man, at the Emperor's command.

This place was little different from the arena Edwin had ordered to be erected at Ad Gefrin, except his arena had been built of wood and was far far smaller. Paulinus had made his great orations there, the elders had held their councils and the annual bardic tournaments had been contested.

'King Edwin had a platform like that,' said Hild. 'It burnt along with everything else.'

'Yes,' said Talcuin, 'old wood burns well.'

'Did you see the remains in Ad Gefrin?'

'I saw it intact too,' he replied. 'I was the one who put a firebrand under it.'

'Well,' she said, 'I didn't know you'd been there at that time.'

'There is much you do not know, my lady. Which is probably for the best.'

'And why would that be? Besides, you are free now, so I can no longer punish you as I might choose.'

'Maybe not, but war is war—and when you're not in the midst of it, well, then it doesn't make any sense whatsoever. That's what grieves me most about my freedom, apart from being separated from you: I'll have to go into battle again.'

'I don't think it will last,' said Hild. 'The day can't be far off when everyone will wake up to the realization that war is simply madness. So few gain any benefit from it.'

'Perhaps it is those few who make the decisions.'

'Even they will eventually, after a period of time, realize that peace comes with greater benefits—their corn can be harvested, their trade isn't disrupted—it's to their advantage.'

'I think that period of time will go on until every single person in the land is dead. If your neighbour owns goods you might covet, then covet them you will, and there will be fighting over those goods.'

'You think badly of your fellow beings.'

'Indeed,' he said, 'which has always been the most prudent tactic.'

'But perhaps not the most correct.'

'It's done the trick so far, and I can't see anything changing—even though I would welcome the day it did.'

'How many slaves worked on your father's estate?' she asked.

'Enough to get the work done. Ten families or so.'

'You could grant some of them their freedom, now that you're going to live a free life.'

'And then who, if I might ask, would do the work?'

'You,' she replied, as if this were the most natural thing in the world, 'and your wife, if you get one.'

'Ha!' said Talcuin. 'Do you really think I'd want a wife who has to run around with the cows and slogs her guts out at harvest time?'

'So you think it's better that the slaves slog their guts out?'

'Yes! And my wife will be busy weaving—for me, and for our sons.'

He was already beaming at the thought.

'I should never have set you free,' she laughed. 'You're not one jot better than all the other masters.'

'And why should I be?' he asked in surprise.

They travelled via Mædeltun and visited Hild's old estate. It had been an age since she had arrived there to live, the newly-married and extremely proud wife of handsome Eadfrid.

She couldn't fathom that she was the same person—maybe she wasn't. She got it into her head that she simply had to see the cave where she had given birth to her twins, so they rode off in the direction of the ford.

Talcuin found the spot without any difficulty, even though the opening was almost totally concealed by bramble runners. The sun glanced off the rowan at the entrance; it had grown into a tall and sturdy tree, the ground was covered with cowslips and lush grass, the trees were in bud. It had been transformed into an entirely different place, and where once the air had been so very quiet, now birdsong was all around.

'Had I killed you,' said Talcuin, helping Hild up into the cave, 'my life would have followed quite another path.'

'And mine would have been over,' she said. 'Regrets?'

'No, and I never have. There's no point crying over spilt milk.'

'Your father would no doubt have liked to see you take over his farm.'

'As he will,' Talcuin smiled, 'from his place up in Paradise.'

'There's something I don't understand,' said Hild, and she started to scrape at the ground. 'How did that lion get in here?'

'Lion?' asked Talcuin. His mistress was not her usual self; perhaps she had started seeing things.

'I found a lion's jawbone when I was trying to block the entrance with soil, to keep the wolves out.'

'Are you sure?'

'I gave it to Cædwalla, he was certain too. It's why he gave me attendants for the journey to Mercia. And you.'

Talcuin glanced around nervously.

'The beast had died a long time ago,' said Hild.

'Oh, right,' he said, and started to help his lady with the digging. It didn't take long before they came across some very large bones—almost too large to be natural—with gnawed ends.

The ravages of time, thought Hild.

Dragons, thought Talcuin, with mounting apprehension. He looked into the darkness where the cave tapered off, and expected to be staring into a fire-spewing orifice at any moment. Chewing such huge bones! And getting through so many!

He stuck his head out of the cave and called two attendants to enter and stand at the back, where it was pitch-dark, spears at the ready; two others helped with the digging.

Hild had found something that looked like the front part of a skull; there were holes, at least, as if for eyes. The nose was lengthened with a thick point of bone tilting upwards. If you didn't know about unicorns, you'd think it was a rhinoceros, but the horn wasn't twisted like the unicorn's; perhaps it had been a very young one, although their horns were usually on the forehead.

'I'm going to take this with me,' she said.

'No!' Talcuin objected. 'They might come to get it back.'

'But they're dead,' she laughed. 'None are left to come and fetch it.'

'Remember what happened to Cædwalla!' Talcuin shouted, suddenly very keen to get out while they had the chance—he could hear something shuffling deep inside.

Hild could also hear a rustling sound. She dropped the bone and rushed out into the light, ran to her horse and was mounted even before the others had come down the slope.

They rode off at a gallop, and it took a while before Hild felt calm enough to think clearly.

'We should just have said the Lord's Prayer,' she suggested.

'Perhaps,' said Talcuin gloomily, 'but does that help against dragons? I'm not sure.'

Hild shuddered.

'Do you really think it's a dragon's den?'

'What else could it be?'

'I don't know,' said Hild, glad they had managed to get well away. 'I didn't ever think of that at the time.'

The memory surged through her: the fragrant scent of her babies, their little sucking noises, Wilbrord's eyes. She had never heard them speak; eleven years old—she would put cowslips on the graves.

They rode eastwards to Hacanos and looked for the burial plot in the forest. The slopes were overflowing with cowslips, but they couldn't find any graves, so they asked the farmer in the valley. He scratched his head, then reluctantly told them the plot had been razed; they'd needed the land and had made a new burial plot by the chapel down here, the one King Oswine had ordered to be built.

'Those children were baptized in the name of the Lord,' Hild cried out wildly. 'And it is most improper to let the cows trample all over them!'

The man wasn't really comfortable with the situation, and he mumbled something about the will of the king, and that he'd objected but in vain. He'd happily ride up with them and point out the spot if she wanted to make a sacrifice.

Hild declined the offer and hurried away; she wasn't going to stand there weeping in front of a wretch like him.

They rode northwards in silence, through wooded uplands, until the low-lying country came into sight, and beyond the lowlands . . . could it be true, was that really the sea out there, or was it just the sky? And then they caught sight of a tiny boat in the distance, looking as if it were floating on air.

Hild insisted on going down to the sea. She simply couldn't pledge her allegiance to the Lord without first touching the watery element that would have carried her to Gaul and onwards, even further out into the world.

'All seas are one,' Paulinus had said. 'All rivers flow into the one big ocean surrounding the world. If you spit into the Humbre river, the core of your being will mingle with water from the farthest North and wash in towards the coast of Africa. Everything returns to the place whence it came.'

Hild wanted to spit in the sea, send a greeting to the elephants bathing in African waters. Maybe they would sense her, very very faintly, when they walked with their calves down to the shore, to cool off in the scorching sun. And she would send a greeting to the Holy Land, where the Lord's cross stood on a hill, and the temple in Jerusalem, which she wouldn't get to see either, and to Gaul. To the apricot trees swaying alongside the wall in Hereswid's monastery. Fluid from her body would form rain, which would fall amongst the apricot trees and, in turn, help to form the beautiful golden-yellow fruit. And two drops would fall, one from each eye, upon her sons' graves—two identical tears—wherever they might be.

'But the Lord knows them, for they are baptized in his name,' she said to herself. 'And he knows where they are.'

Chaffinches and blackbirds were singing with great force, which gave a little comfort as they cautiously worked their way along the winding track down the slope to the low-lying land. But when they reached the bottom, they found that the sea had disappeared. They followed a narrower track leading towards the northeast, where they had seen the coastline; they rode for a long time before finally reaching a hilltop, and the land opened up before them in a vista extending to the sea, far far below.

They rode downhill, the lowlands sloping even further away to the left and ending in a broad bay, a long and steep incline down towards the water.

Hild brought her horse to a halt. Having viewed this strange landscape, she galloped along the track edging the southern ridge of the lowland. From the summit of the hill, she had seen a stone tower rising up from the farthest projection of the coastline—and that tower was her destination.

She leapt from her horse and climbed the tower, Talcuin behind her, taking great care. The sea lay far below and was withdrawing from the land; a section of brown rock had already been exposed at the base of the curved lowland: heavily grooved, semicircle after semicircle, with more seabed coming into view as the water pulled away from the shore. Below them, a falcon hung motionless in the air—a red-backed bird, it dived and vanished behind an outcrop. They couldn't see the coastline below.

'The work of the Romans too?' Hild asked.

'Who else could it be?' said Talcuin.

'But what would they be looking for?'

'Your forefathers, I would think.'

'Of course, yes,' she said, ashamed.

By the power of their swords, her forefathers had seized a country where the people built in stone and spoke Latin. Her ancestors had been brutes who built wooden huts and could neither read nor write anything other than runic letters.

'How strange it must have been!' she exclaimed. 'They couldn't even speak with the inhabitants.'

'Well, that wasn't exactly why they came,' said Talcuin.

'From one day to the next, the lord of the estate became the slave.'

'Some became slaves, some became corpses.'

'It is good those days are gone.'

'But are they?' he asked.

'They are. Apart from times of upheaval, of course. But that won't last.'

'Says you.'

'I do,' she said, and there they stood, staring out to sea.

'It's hard to say goodbye,' she finally whispered, and Talcuin nodded silently. He was thinking about taking his leave of her; she was thinking about saying farewell to the world and preparing herself for the everlasting kingdom.

'Especially when you have only just said hello,' she went on.

He nodded and wondered what she might mean.

Dusk was still a while away. It was hard to believe how high up they were; if those small white dots really were herring gulls, well, then the depth could be measured to many hundred fathoms.

'Just like the farthest North,' she eventually sighed.

'I think rather it looks like the end of the world,' he said.

'I thought I knew Deira,' she said after a while. 'So I simply cannot understand why I haven't been here before.'

'I feel as if I've always been here,' said Talcuin. 'Even though it must definitely be my first visit.'

The air was clear and chilly. A promontory stretched out from the coastline a little way along to the right, behind it another and higher one that looked as if it, too, was topped by a stone tower; far far in the distance a glimpse of something chalk-white.

'Tell me,' said Hild, 'do the scriptures state where Adam and Eve eventually settled in the world?'

Talcuin had a think.

'I've always presumed it was somewhere further south . . . but I don't think the place name has been put into writing.'

'I feel as if I know less and less as time goes by,' said Hild.

'They must have lived somewhere.'

'Yes, and the weather made them feel very cold indeed. It can't have been in Africa, nor in the Holy Land.'

'Well, if it really was here,' said Talcuin, 'what about Noah then?'

'Just think how long they spent in the ark—they could have drifted an awful long way. We only know they came to rest on the mountains of Ararat, not where they set out from.'

'Do you really think so?'

'One other detail makes me believe it could have been here—besides this looking like the place—and that's the huge ox in the cave. Unless it was an elephant, that is. I understand how a lion might have crept up there, but not such a large beast. So, if it wasn't washed in by the Flood, then it must have arrived in some unnatural way.'

'There's nothing unnatural about dragons dragging their prey back to their dens,' said Talcuin. 'And ripping the beast apart first.'

'No, but what about the soil on top? They wouldn't have sprinkled a thick layer of clay over the prey, would they? Or what?'

'We've certainly never heard so,' Talcuin conceded. He stood mulling it over, gazing out to sea, and then abruptly started gesticulating with his arms.

'Well, I understand all that about the Flood, but a lion living in a land like Deira—that's beyond me!'

'No, I don't understand either,' Hild admitted, 'but I've seen the bones with my very own eyes.'

'I think I might prefer just to forget about them,' said Talcuin. 'It's so difficult to take it all in—everything seems to go light-headed.'

Hild laughed.

'Just like the world, when you start thinking about it, or simply look at it. Don't you get light-headed when you look out at this view?'

'Yes, but I'm more used to that kind of light-headedness. The other sort is like trying to count the stars—or thinking about how everything looked before the Lord started his creation.'

'I like feeling light-headed,' she said. 'We don't understand very much. Perhaps that's the closest we can get to the reality.'

'Perhaps,' said Talcuin, 'but I appreciate the warmth of a hall and a good bed.'

'You'll soon have everything for yourself,' said Hild. 'Can you see a track anywhere?'

'I don't think it's possible to climb down there, and we haven't eaten.'

'Of course it's possible to get down,' she said, starting her descent from the tower.

A raven cawed as it flew by; she cursed it. She heard a very faint voice, coming closer, and could make out a tune, a boy's voice, powerful, occasionally breaking into dark tones, the high notes coming through first. The boy was walking northwards on the low-lying land, and now she could also hear bleating, and could just make out a little flock of sheep, light speckles on a barrow between the trees.

She didn't have the patience to wait for Talcuin, so she walked swiftly along the clifftop searching for a place from which she could climb down—it all looked rather unstable.

She found a spot where it was possible to descend a short distance, but she couldn't see how to get any further. Reaching the end of the ledge, she started an easy downward climb, but quickly came to a far steeper cliff. The only option was to start out from the corner, and perhaps just slide some of the way.

She slid further than she had expected, and while slithering down, she started to wonder how she would get up the cliff again. But she soon stopped worrying, even before she came to a halt, deciding it would probably be easier to find a way when looking up from below. She stopped just before the bottom of the slope, and leant forward: below her was air, and much further down was another projection, the last one before the sea—as far as she could tell. It was a long, long way down; she couldn't hear the waves.

Hild looked back up the cliff; there was a furrow where she had slid down—maybe she could crawl back up the same way. There was nothing for it but to try; going downwards would mean certain death. She very cautiously started climbing upwards, but she didn't get very far because the surface crumbled and slid away under her. Fortunately, she knew where the slope ended, and she was able to slow her slide with arms and legs, managing to come to a halt before she reached the edge.

She sat motionless, pouring sweat—when the dripping stopped, she was so cold she started shaking all over. Gulls soared past, but she felt no urge to see where they were flying to; she didn't even dare shout out, fearing the sound would cause the soil and stones to slip away.

She stopped shaking, and called out anyway, at first cautiously, then more vigorously. She soon heard Talcuin shouting from above.

'I'm coming!'

'No!' she bellowed. 'There's no way down. Find a rope.'

She knew they didn't have a long rope with them; and the last farm they had passed had been a long way back.

'Talcuin!' she cried out. 'There's a shepherd boy, singing, maybe he knows . . .'

'Stay where you are!' Talcuin shouted. 'I'll find him.'

Hild wasn't planning to move so much as a muscle, and all she was wondering about was the thickness of the soil where she was sitting, because when she had looked down, there had been nothing but air—right underneath her, too. That picture, at least, was imprinted in her mind.

She started shaking again, but whether from cold or fear she didn't know; she did know, however, that David's psalms were the only means by which to prevent panic getting the upper hand.

> *The ungodly are like the chaff which the wind dispels.*
> *Therefore the ungodly shall not stand in the judgement*
> *nor sinners in the company of the righteous.*
> *For the Lord knows the way of the righteous*
> *but the way of the ungodly shall perish.*

She'd never understood that before; now it made her tremble so much she could feel the rock and soil crumbling and sliding underneath her. She simply had to sit still, completely motionless.

> *Our Father, who is in Heaven,*
> *sacred be your name,*
> *your kingdom come,*
> *your will be done on earth*
> *as in Heaven.*
> *Give us today our daily bread*
> *and forgive us our transgressions*
> *as we too forgive those who transgress against us.*

*Lead us not into temptation*
*but free us from evil*
*for yours is the kingdom and the power and the glory*
*for ever and ever. Amen.*

For the first time ever, she had difficulty uttering the words—especially 'your will be done', because she knew exactly what her 'will' comprised, which made it hard to hand over the final say to the Lord.

Which had the best chance of keeping soil and stones in place—dry weather or rain? She decided on dry weather, like now, so that was good.

The shepherd boy wouldn't be carrying a long rope with him, that was certain, and he was undoubtedly far from home, but he would know where the nearest farm lay. All this was going to take a very long time. Why hadn't she eaten first? And why hadn't she worn more suitable clothing?

David's psalms had dried up and her mouth and mind were overpowered by the one thought: When will the Lord make me perish from the way?

'This is madness!' she eventually exclaimed. 'Today I could have been aboard a vessel sailing to Gaul.'

She raised her face to the heavens and shouted: 'Was I meant to stay just in order to sit here? Was that your plan for me?'

Although she knew it was Aidan's plan, not the Lord's; it had come to Aidan in a dream, hadn't it.

If she died here, she would have atoned for nothing, neither her own sins nor those of her kin, and Hereswid would have to continue her wanderings, and she, Hild, would follow suit. A sight for the gods, but certainly not a good sight for humankind.

'Hereswid,' she said aloud, 'I shall do what I can. But that might not be very much.'

Now she waited calmly. She heard a trickling sound, and wondered if water was flowing out further down the cliff. The sound stopped, then started again, which could only mean the ground below her was giving way.

'Not my will, but your will,' she said, suddenly so very weary.

David's psalms came back to her, and she intoned the words, as was the correct way, while time passed, and she knew the Lord would look upon her with mercy—one way or another. And she knew the shepherd boy would be blessed, such a lovely voice, and he was undoubtedly a handsome lad. He had been singing an old song of thanksgiving the Britons offered to the Lord. She sang it quietly to herself.

By the time Talcuin reached her, it was dark. She saw him in the gleam of the men's flaming torches up above. She recognized the shepherd boy's voice, so gentle and melodious, calling out, telling her not to worry, they'd fastened a rope to the rock and the whole company of men was holding it tight. She had to be very calm and do exactly what he said.

They threw down one end of the rope, but it was too short. They hauled it up again, and then the boy clambered over the edge, his hair shining red in the gleam from the torches. He moved easily and quietly, hardly disturbing the cliff face. A little sand trickled down to her, and the sound of his breathing. Then the cliff gave way and he slithered towards her in a torrent of sand and pebbles.

When she opened her eyes, she was still there and he was hanging, head down, just above her.

'Hold on to me tightly,' he whispered, 'and they'll pull us up.'

She stretched out and reached his fingers—strange how they shone against the cliff face.

'Further, and very carefully,' said the boy, and he managed to hang so close that they could grasp one another's wrists.

'Limp as a rag!' he said, and then shouted: 'Pull!'

By fits and starts, they moved slowly upwards. Hild closed her eyes. His hands felt good and warm, yet her fingers were so stiff she didn't know how long she could hang on. She thought it was taking a very long time. She tilted her head and tried to keep her face away from the cliff so she wouldn't be slashed by grit and stones. He spoke to her, told her she'd done the right thing by sitting so still, and that they'd soon reach the top; told her he'd asked his god to cup a hand under that ledge because it was rather weak; told her he'd just seen the red-backed falcon.

And then they were at the top. She lay on the ground, unable to stand up, wanting to weep and sleep and vanish.

'Thank you,' she murmured to the boy. He was red-haired and slender, red in the face, too, having hung upside down for so long.

'What is your name?' asked Talcuin.

'Cædmon,' he replied, 'son of Brethoc. Allow me to run now, to find the sheep. You can just follow the straight track up from here.'

And without waiting for an answer, he disappeared into the darkness.

Talcuin was pale.

'Then up we'll go,' he said, taking Hild by the arm. Her legs wouldn't stop shaking.

# AT THE ENDS OF THE EARTH

*– Hild and Talcuin in the sea fog –*

Hild woke up, freezing, the tent flapping in the wind; she couldn't see a thing. She wanted to inspect her arms, to check if they were still dotted with livor mortis spots as they had been in her dream. She put her hand to her mouth—it was no longer full of soil.

'Talcuin,' she whispered. She spoke his name louder, but there was no answer. She shouted. The wind was whistling through the canvas, mimicking her cries. She could hear the waves booming against the coast, digging and eating their way in, undermining the cliff, engulfing her, coming closer and closer with every crashing wave; the whole promontory, the tower and everything would soon plunge into the sea.

She leapt up and headed out of the tent, but bumped into a man standing at the entrance. He, too, was icy-cold: Death, on his way in to fetch her. She recoiled, screaming.

'My lady,' the man said in a gentle voice.

It was just Talcuin, he'd gone outside to secure the tents. She clung to him, shaking from top to toe.

'You are cold,' he said.

'Cold, like you,' she mumbled.

'I'm warm underneath,' he said, calmly stroking her hair.

'Lie with me,' she said. He did as he was told, and her teeth gradually stopped chattering.

'The day of fire and blood,' she whispered.

'Just a little breeze,' he said softly, 'you can safely sleep.'

'Lie on top of me,' she instructed, lifting the cover. He did as she asked, and it felt safer.

Talcuin dozed off, but Hild's bones were still frozen through, an icy chill seeping in from below, and from behind where Death stood breathing heavily onto her hair. You had to ignore him; if she turned and looked at him, she would perish.

She focused all her energy on the warmth of the sleeping man lying across her, heavy as a corpse and hardly breathing.

No, not a dead body, and she concentrated on feeling his warmth. He was still alive, breathing faintly; she turned her ear to his mouth, his breath sighed through her. The wind would have to stop at some point, as would the night, like it always had—up until now, at least. The Lord would send his sun up into the sky, he wouldn't suddenly release his grasp on the world and let it plunge into the abyss. Nor would he let his children wander in darkness and cold, even though they might not deserve anything else. She waited, eyes wide open, staring into the darkness.

She so wanted knowledge of the world, to understand its make-up and find her place in it. Like the little red velvet mite crawling around in the sand dunes trying to get an overall picture: all on its own, separated from its kin, washed ashore, stranded in a pile of flotsam, along with bladderwrack, eelgrass, sand, scuds, fossils, sea asters, gull droppings, the gusting wind and the raven's caw. An entire community of bits and pieces all adrift, united by ending up in the same place at the same time.

Hild drank in the aromatic fragrance of Talcuin's neck, pressed her face into his flesh. His blood throbbed below the skin, keeping life in him; if she bit through the artery, it would gush over her, drown her maybe, in warm liquid. Her lips parted slowly, her tongue licking his neck; it tasted salty.

She sank her teeth into his flesh and nipped at him, tears running down her temples. Her fingers traced the outlines of his face, forehead, heavy eyebrows, the bridge of his nose, the sides of his nostrils; traced his lips, the one so narrow, the other plump and soft, cheekbones and the supple skin below, followed the folds of his ear. He muttered in his sleep, and moaned.

A faint trembling radiated from her bones, her skin rippled, a foretaste of the flames of Hell surging through her body; she shuddered and clutched him tight.

He woke up and spoke to her; she couldn't quite hear, the blood was pounding so loudly in her temples, nor could she reply because her quivering lips would only dart back and forth, open and wet, on his neck and throat. Now she was thrusting against him, holding his head firmly, licking his ear, biting his earlobe.

His manhood hardened, thrust forcefully against her groin; he gasped and swiftly drew away. She couldn't see in the darkness, but her hands followed him, moving up his thin linen trousers, pressing the fabric against his manhood. He was sitting back on his knees, quite still, while her fingers squeezed the throbbing organ under his clothing; her other hand slid up his inner thigh and encircled his scrotum in a firm grasp.

He moaned as she got to her knees, rubbed her breasts against him, burning him through her nightdress and his shirt; he raised a hand to push her away, but the hand wouldn't move from her breast, so soft and so warm. The hand insisted on feeling her breast, the other one leapt up and ran through her hair, held her neck and pressed her face to his lips. He gasped when her hands opened his belt buckle, parted his clothes and slipped down around his exposed manhood.

She bent over and the smell of intimacy overwhelmed her, all the life-force seeping away. He made a couple of feeble attempts to hold her off when she held him by the waist and lowered her head. He felt her hair tumbling gently around his groin and her lips encircling the place where their presence really was not befitting.

'No, my lady, no,' he moaned, one hand squeezing her breast, the other her backside.

'Oh yes, yes, yes,' she muttered.

He grasped the hem of her nightdress and pulled it upwards. She felt a hand, gentle as a dove wing, brushing her inner thigh—she started shaking and thrusting her groin forwards to capture it. A finger stroked her wet lower lips, cautiously, entered abruptly, all the way, vibrating against the walls, then it withdrew and his hands clenched her buttocks.

She pushed forwards: he sank back as she mounted him, her thighs spread wide, lowered herself onto his manhood, drawing him in; he stiffened and arched against her, grasping her hips and holding her tight. She moaned, thrusting back and forth, hard, as if riding a horse and her life depended on it, tore at his chest, murmuring his name and jumbled words.

The words had fallen apart, along with everything else, worked loose and flaked off. She was tumbling, piece by piece, and didn't know if the landslide was above or below or inside her, and there was nothing to hold it back: everything was plunging, roaring, downwards, surging, tumbling, until it was swallowed up and slowly settled in the dust.

When she came to herself, she wasn't dead. She was lying in a lukewarm sea, maybe a lake, rocking gently on top of Talcuin. He pulled the cover over her, and she didn't understand why—given that they were drowning anyway.

Next day, Hild sent her men to look for the shepherd boy; she wouldn't leave until he had been found. She wanted to give him a horse and an arm-ring of pale gold. He needed to know who she was, and that he could count on her help to get on in the world.

They still hadn't found him by afternoon, so they had to stay. It wasn't until they had their evening meal that Hild looked at Talcuin—a jolt surged through her, she flared up, burning hot, and looked away. She would have to watch him through her skin, sense his every movement, track him without the help of her eyes, drink in the sound of his voice and tremble at his every word. She had difficulty speaking when he was near, nor could she eat.

As soon as mealtime was over she went to bed, but there was no rest for her; she walked back and forth in the narrow space, sat on the bed, leapt up and resumed her restless pacing. She hadn't dared look at him again.

Hearing his voice outside, she hid her face in her hands and stopped breathing. The time it took him to untie the tent cords, lift the corners of the entrance, step inside and re-tie the cords felt very, very long. She stood, head bowed, her back to him, in the furthest corner, and dared not turn.

He walked across to her, stood behind her and carefully put his arms around her. Her back melted when she felt him so close; she was slowly able to turn and look at his familiar unfamiliar face: the mouth, like that, the eyes, like that, lips, tongue, the lips, her mouth found them. She melted and was nothing but kiss.

She stood like a limp ragdoll while he undressed her, item by item, caressing and kissing the slowly but surely exposed skin. When there was nothing left to remove, he picked her up and carried her to the bed, hands running over her body, from throat to the soles of her feet, across her breasts, around her head.

His eyes were full of calm wonder, his movements slow and lingering. He couldn't get over his astonishment, and all day he'd had to keep his legs in check when they wanted to follow her, and restrain his hands when they wanted to catch hold of her and go where they shouldn't.

Now he separated her knees and stroked his fingers through her pubic hair and down into the wet folds. He lowered his head and caressed her with his lips. When he abruptly pushed his tongue in deeply, she jolted, letting out a little cry of amazement.

She was lying motionless, glowing, when he leapt up and pulled off his clothes. Moving just her head, she watched him in all his wonderful terrifying magnificent nakedness, and caressed him with her eyes.

He knelt between her legs; she spread them further apart, thrusting forwards. He leant over her, holding his manhood and guiding it gently back and forth against her softness. His other hand rubbed her breasts in wide circles, and squeezed her nipples. She moaned and stretched out, seeking him. He continued to rub against her until she was burning and thrusting. She shuddered as he inserted the tip between her lower lips, pressed a little and then withdrew.

He sat looking at her, then lay down and inserted his tongue as far as it could go, flicking hard; she groaned and was saturated. She tensed and tightened, stretched towards him; he rose to his knees and entered her, held her firmly. She felt his resolute thrusts inside her and thought: now I'll die! and that's just the way it has to be.

He laid her down and lowered himself onto her, entered her as far as he could, and having rocked gently against her, he started thrusting as if he wanted to get right inside her, disappear into her body, curl up in her womb and dissolve into her. He roared as he shattered and disintegrated onto her, clutched her tight, could feel her bones, her veins, her flesh, her liver and kidneys through her skin.

She wept and didn't want this to stop, ever. She had one hand between his legs and the other around his neck. She was in a thousand pieces and as whole as never before, light as a feather and heavy as rock, hovering just below the tent canvas, laughing at him down there on the bed. He pulled her back and kissed her eyes.

'Stay with me,' he said. 'Stay with me.'

'I am with you,' she said. 'Feel here.'

She placed his hand where it belonged, sighed and kissed him again; she couldn't get enough of him.

When morning came, they lifted the corners of the tent flap and looked out into a sea fog. White and impenetrable, it had settled across the land. You could just about see your outstretched hand, but nothing else. The world had been engulfed in a dense milky-whiteness that had even stifled all sound.

They could neither travel nor search for the boy. They closed the tent flaps and climbed into the bed.

'Stay with me, Hildeburh,' said Talcuin. 'Come with me to Gwynedd.'

Hild shook her head: she wouldn't go to Gwynedd, nor would she give him up. She nestled her head on his chest and put a hand between his thighs.

'That Cartimandua,' he said, 'the Brigantes' queen—she married her swordbearer!'

'Yes, yes,' said Hild, moving her leg to make room for him. She sighed once he had found what he was seeking; her hand ran across his neck, fingers through his hair, and pulled his mouth to hers. They weren't at the bottom of the sea, they weren't dead and the world hadn't collapsed.

They nonetheless behaved as if they were and it had, submerging themselves with slow movements, re-surfacing incredulous and breathless, and gazing at one another amazed to be meeting in this place—is this happening? Yes, it really is . . .

Laughter and constant embraces—incredible how their bodies wanted to play and slotted together quite perfectly. How strange, they were so very young again and couldn't leave one another alone, just had to touch here and slip in there, almost automatically, without a thought for anything other than stroking, rocking, sucking, grunting, splashing and swaying, the waves around and inside them, the clouds adrift up above, the cliff crumbling away, sand and soil and stones slipping irretrievably downwards.

They had known one another for ever, and it was the first time they had met. They were as they had always been, and yet they met afresh. There were no boundaries between them, and no provisos. They were nothing but eyes, mouths, ears, skin and sex. They talked as they had never previously talked, and Hild was taken aback by Talcuin's knowledge.

'Why haven't you told me this before?' she asked.

'I didn't think you'd want me to,' he replied, and added several times in surprise: 'Anyway, I thought you knew!'

'I ought to be punishing you rather than making you rich,' said Hild. 'Such poor service you have done me!'

Talcuin had just told her for the first time what he had found out about Eadfrid's death on his trip north to search for Hild's sons.

'If I'd told you, you might not have married Penda,' said Talcuin. 'And that would have been foolish.'

'But perhaps more appropriate,' said Hild, 'because now Oswald's blood sticks to me.'

'No more to you than to Penda, or to me and everyone else who thanked the Lord for Oswald's demise.' Talcuin shook his head in disbelief. 'You who are so loyal to the Lord, do you really not know that he took on our guilt when he sacrificed himself for us? I just don't understand why you hang on to your guilt like that—as if Jesus had died in vain!'

'Well, Aidan certainly understands,' she said quietly, frowning. 'My guilt is mine alone, and I alone can atone for it. If the Lord will help me to do so.'

'Aidan is not above worldly matters,' said Talcuin. 'He needs your help.'

Hild stared at him.

'And I think that's a prudent move on Aidan's part,' Talcuin went on quietly. 'If Jesus Christ is to secure a better name for himself in Northumbria, then it's imperative that decent people are seen to be fighting for his cause. Oswald wasn't exactly advantageous in that respect, and his brother was probably of even less use.'

'And I'd be a better example, would I?' exclaimed Hild. 'A woman who has been married to their arch-enemy?'

'Yes, because you've left him; you couldn't live with a heathen.'

'I could, and quite easily too! You know just as well as I do that I didn't leave him of my own free will.'

'I'm talking about how it will be interpreted,' said Talcuin. 'A Christian queen who relinquishes her royal position because she can't live with a husband who makes sacrifices to his forefathers and eats horsemeat! A graphic example of allegiance to the Lord going before all else. That's what Aidan is counting on.'

'You can't be serious!' Hild cried. 'That's sheer nonsense.'

'Of course it is,' said Talcuin, 'but it will certainly be advantageous to the Lord's cause.'

Hild was speechless.

'And when Penda hears that you've entered a monastery up there, well, then he'll undoubtedly stop rampaging through all the other monasteries, and everyone will think our god is good at protecting those who serve him—you get the picture?'

'Yes, absolutely, but it's just ridiculous!'

'I've always thought Aidan was cannier than he let on,' Talcuin continued. 'Do you remember that time he gave away your goose? An astute move, if ever I saw one.'

'He always does that,' said Hild.

'He knew who you were. And that you'd be Penda's wife. He hoped you'd convert Penda. That's why he gave away your gifts—to make an impression on you. He wanted to be your teacher. And maybe the bishop in Mercia.'

'Now that's enough!' cried Hild. 'He couldn't possibly have known how things would turn out. Penda already had a wife. And I was married to Eadfrid.'

'Fine, yes,' said Talcuin. 'Eadfrid wasn't going to last long, everyone could see that. And even though Penda had a wife, he could take a new one—that's not exactly unheard of. It was only because Penda wanted *you* that Eadfrid was allowed to live as long as he did. Penda didn't want to spoil his chances with you.'

'No,' Hild said firmly. 'Penda isn't like that.'

'No, fine,' Talcuin smiled, 'if you say so! But it has never been the custom to keep a captive like him alive—not in Mercia and not with us. It's said to bring misfortune.'

Hild was flabbergasted. Her jaw hung slackly, wordless, and her mind was whirling.

'Don't you think even Aidan can tell the front from the back of a woman?' Talcuin laughed, stroking her front and back. She pushed his hands away and sat up.

'And you a Christian man—thinking so ill of your fellow human beings.'

'I don't in the least think ill of them,' Talcuin smiled. 'I've just always envied Aidan and Penda—that they could get so close to you.' He lay back and pulled her to him. 'Stay with me now, come with me to Dolwyddelan, marry me, be my wife.'

She understood nothing, neither herself nor anything else. She lay down and was his wife; she couldn't let him go, and the everlasting kingdom would have to wait.

The sea fog lasted for three days, a dense woollen blanket covering the land, and for three days they only left the tent to relieve themselves. Everything they needed was brought by Hild's somewhat astonished retinue; they left the requested items in silence—food, water for washing, beer, tea—and they retreated without looking at their mistress and her slave.

'I have to leave,' she said. 'I am not Cartimandua, and you are not my swordbearer. Aidan is expecting me.'

He kissed her ear and caressed her breasts until she was again gasping and panting, desire throbbing under her skin and inside her whole being; he was on top, underneath, inside her and everywhere; she was clutching and hugging him, devouring him, licking and biting, laughing and crying, squeezing the air from his chest, nipping his earlobe and biting his cheek, rocking against him with drawn-out kisses that sent ripples down her spine, plunging downwards, dying and rising again, time after time after time after time.

She closed her eyes and was a falcon, hanging motionless in the air. Cartimandua was standing on the tower below, wafting a piece of parchment in the wind—her agreement with the Romans. Her swordbearer stood behind her, a very short, thickset man, lifting the hem of her long pleated frock. He already had one hand on her naked buttocks, while his other hand was opening his trousers—there was a lot of bustling around inside them, and he was struggling to keep a rhinoceros under control. The rhinoceros kept sticking out its head, blinking its tiny eyes and giving itself a shake. How strange, enough room for such a beast, she thought, and it suddenly leapt into the air and flew away across the sea. It had wings, like a dragon.

She wondered if perhaps her wits were seeping out between her legs, but she wasn't able to hold them back. When she woke up, she strained to recall the order there once had been; she'd known it so very well. She managed to grasp a smidgeon, but it instantly evaporated between her fingers. She snatched at another corner, but that too disintegrated and turned to dust.

If Jesus has taken on our guilt, why do I have to enter a monastery? she wondered. And finding no answer, she repeated the question aloud.

'But you don't have to,' said Talcuin, now awake. 'The Lord has not infused your body with that song for you to close your mouth and ears and sex and eyes and make yourself dead.'

'Who knows what his plans are?' she said. 'And if we carry no guilt as our own guilt, we'll be like the beasts.'

'Well, I don't know about that,' said Talcuin, stroking her back with a gentle and firm hand. 'But I know that you are a woman who should lie with a man and bear children, and that the Lord has said the same: Be fruitful and multiply, spread across the land! he said. He's never said we should lie alone in our beds. On the contrary, he created us without fur, so we can keep one another warm, and you can still bear many children.'

'I lose them anyway,' Hild sighed, nestling into him. 'Fortune has not let me keep so much as one child.'

'You have Wilbrord and Hundfrid and Wulfhere and Ædelræd—four sons. They're just not with you, not at the moment, but you'll get them back, I know you will.'

'Be careful what you say,' she whispered. 'Don't speak like that of the dead.'

'They're not dead!' he said.

She sat up abruptly, spine rigid, staring at him with eyes wide open. He was taken aback, and then a little shamefaced.

'That's how Oswine operates,' he began, and then involved hand gestures to support his explanation. 'He would never have them killed. Cheat and deceive and all sorts of things, yes, he'll do that, and then give Aidan a slice of land and a few silver bowls. But he's far too scared of the Day of Judgement to let anyone go out slaying for the sake of power—and certainly no dead *children.*'

'So do you know something—or is this just your belief?' Hild shouted, beside herself with horror. 'The graves. You've seen their graves with your own eyes.'

Talcuin bitterly regretted that he hadn't simply told her before. He shook his head and put his arms round her.

'Oswine had them dug—they weren't real! I swear to you: no one has ever lain in those graves.'

Hild couldn't breathe: everything was crashing down around her, and there was nothing left to hold onto.

'I think he had them fostered, separately, not in the most comfortable of circumstances. It's easier to buy silence at the bottom of the pile.'

He had to take a deep breath before he could get it out: 'And I thought you knew. I thought that was the reason you wouldn't talk about it.'

'Are they here in Deira?' she asked.

'In Deira or Bernicia,' he said. 'I think they're in Deira. I'm absolutely sure they are.'

The wind got up during the night, and they awoke to a clear and transparent world. Lovely as never before, the dry land stretched out to the sides, pale green, pale green, dark green, bluish-green, yellowish-green, green, green.

Hild was singing as she dressed and then left the tent. She took care not to tread on the harebells, so delicate and fragile, heads swaying in the breeze.

It was good growing weather, the springtime smell of humus in the air, full of promise, dizzying. Air so thick with fragrance and birdsong that you could catch it in your hands; she popped a piece in her mouth and laughed. The air was a touch salty, and peppered with the song of lark and yellowhammer, the screeching seagull, the monotonous bleating of sheep in the distance. A bumblebee buzzed between dandelions; the herald of good fortune, she greeted it as was fitting and gave thanks for its good forecast—the way it was enjoying all that yellowness, there would soon be plenty of butter.

She walked across to the tower and was about to start climbing it when she noticed the large stone slab with carved Latin letters that Cædwalla had also once tried to decipher. The first word could perhaps be *Justus*. She scratched away moss and green algae and could see that it was probably *Justinianus*—a man's name?—and there was quite a lot more underneath the dense green layer. Perhaps the stone announced the name of whoever had built the tower, or ordered his men to build it; he'd placed the slab here so he would be remembered. And now it was unfathomable.

'That's how it goes,' she chuckled to herself, as she climbed up into the tower. The red-backed falcon was flapping around below. The tide was a long way out; there was still a stiff breeze, and the horizon was bright and clear. Looking south, she could just catch sight of a completely white strip of land stretching away far far down along the other side of the brown promontory topped by another rock tower.

Now she was convinced this was where Adam and Eve had lived. But it didn't matter; what *did* matter were the blades of grass eagerly reaching upwards, the open-faced splendour of the dandelions, the skylarks and the boundless vivid sunlight.

She heard a whistling sound, which multiplied into a full warble—the curlew. She saw it drawing a semicircle in the sky above the lowlands to the north, pictured its long downward-curving bill and the strangely long bluish legs stretched out under its tail when in flight. There was no song as lovely as that of the curlew. Was it calling to its mate? Or did it already have chicks down in the grass? Maybe they were stretching their necks, having heard their mother give notice of warmth and a full tummy.

The earth teemed with all manner of lifeforms, and everything pointed to fulfilment. What belonged together would be united—you could sense it from the quivering fecund air.

A flock of geese approached, flying in formation, close to the coast far below her. Northwards—the route went north. The geese passed with a pulsating sound and she watched them until they vanished behind the promontory far in the distance.

She spotted a figure clad in blue, walking along the path that cut its way straight as an arrow through the seabed from the tip of the promontory. The sudden sight of him gave her a jolt; her hands pressed into her stomach, which was turning inside out, bleeding, as if pierced by a sword.

No other man walked like that: long legs, warm and supple, the inner thighs smooth as the finest silk. From up here he looked so tiny, almost indiscernible in the brown rocky depths. He had always been a part of her, not some exterior riddle, and she didn't know if she'd always loved him. But seeing him walking down there, she knew that had it not been for Hundfrid and Wilbrord she would never have given him up. She would have followed him through fire and water, and she would have crushed everything that got in his way. Everything and everybody—yes.

Now so far from her, and yet so close in the memory of hands and skin. All around her—while standing out there, bending down and picking something up. Warm downy skin under his clothing; just below the skin, living flesh; bones below the flesh; the liver, gut, heart, kidneys—all assembled in an almost identical composition to that of a boar. Blood flowing through closed veins; eyes, ears; eyes that saw, hands that grasped and held firmly. Her property—now more so than ever. A free man who belonged to her—but who would soon find himself a wife and have children. A healthy and young wife; he would have many children. And she would get hers back, even if she had to fawn and be sweet as honey to King Oswy in order to track them down. She would find them.

She pressed her hands onto the rough stone and her vision blurred. She smiled and talked to herself and laughed out loud while the tears flowed and she hurried from the one end of the tower to the other. She blinked, and then saw her beloved on his way in; floated down to him and embraced his whole body, all over and all at once, while she pounded her hands against the rocks and laughed.

They would meet again. Yes, they would meet again, that's the way it was. The Lord would permit nothing else, that's the way it had to be. Regardless of whether he married, regardless of whether she served the Lord, and so zealously that she would eventually become an abbess privy to all the details of every life. The Lord would let her meet him again—otherwise he would have created her clad in fur. Yes.

It went without saying: the Lord would not take away the joy of her heart and of her bed for all eternity; no, he wouldn't do that.

Thus she paced back and forth, trying to talk herself into a place of composure. Realising she had gone utterly to pieces and couldn't be put back together, she looked up to the heavens.

'Help me now, my god!' she shouted. Then she climbed down from the tower, legs shaking, and gave the order for departure.

By the time Talcuin returned, the tent had been taken down and everything packed. Hild was already mounted on her horse. Two of her men would accompany him home; her remaining entourage was still sizeable enough.

'You haven't reached your destination yet,' he said, with no hope of changing her mind.

'No,' she said, fiddling with the reins. 'If the weather holds, then . . . '

'Three days, perhaps,' said Talcuin. Adding, after a moment: 'The weather now is good for travelling.'

He cleared his throat and stared at the ground.

'Spring weather, really,' she murmured.

'Or maybe four, actually,' he said.

'If it holds, that is,' she added.

'Many good words are spoken of Abbess Heiu,' he said.

'Indeed they are,' she murmured, gazing intensely at the tip of her horse's ear, capped by a tuft of short fine hairs—delicate, they were, in comparison with its tail, but not in comparison with . . . all the different hairs were joining together.

'Horsehair has many uses,' she said.

When he nodded, she went on: 'And before you've so much as blinked, it's autumn.'

'Yes, you've got a point there,' he mumbled, still staring at the ground.

Then it was impossible to think up anything else.

She held out a hand, but it was hard to tell whether it intended to grasp him or push him away.

He took hold of it and pressed it to his lips, turned it over and placed something in her palm. She looked down, couldn't really see what it was, but thought it might be a stone—or something like that, at least.

'Fare well, Talcuin,' she managed to say. 'The Lord be with you.'

'Fare well, Hildeburh. The Lord be with you.'

She turned her horse and gave the signal for departure, when he suddenly remembered: 'The boy—what about the boy?' he shouted as she rode off.

She stopped, and looked around in confusion.

'Oh, the boy, yes,' she faltered, with trembling lips, re-awakening Talcuin's old spirit.

'Would you like me to take care of it?'

She nodded a couple of times and swallowed hard, then pointed to a horse, which quickly had its load divided between two others; Talcuin found her treasures and passed them up to her so she could choose. She made a rough selection, from which he picked out a gold ring with ribbon interlace, inlaid with nielo—certainly no trifling gift of which she would be embarrassed.

The undertaking had helped Talcuin recover his composure and he was able to look straight at her.

'No matter what,' he said, 'I shall be with you always.'

'And I shall be with you,' she managed to utter, now weeping openly. She couldn't hold herself together any longer, and Talcuin had to give the signal for departure. He could barely stay upright.

He sat on the grass and watched them ride up across the land. When they reached the hill, she turned and raised her arm in greeting.

He got to his feet and waved until they disappeared over the summit.

# In the Service of the Lord

*– the monastery by the giants' settlement –*

Arriving at Heiu's monastery of Heruteu at the mouth of the river Tese, Hild met Aidan and King Oswy, with whom Heiu had made arrangements: Oswy would provide land and, with a small group of women, Hild would establish a monastery at Ediscum on the north bank of the river Wiur, not far from the spot where the giant's way from the west ran into the Deira Way. One hide of land adjacent to an old stone settlement from the days of the giants—that was the plot Oswy said he would grant the Lord.

Hild didn't correct the king's ignorance, but was glad she knew about the Romans—it took the edge off the eeriness oozing from the heaps of collapsed stones everyone avoided.

She was surprised by Oswy's contribution. His brother Oswald had been well-known for his miserliness, except in cases of some spectacular event that would make others pay up.

For the sake of his personal salvation, Oswy had freed seven slaves, on the condition they would serve the new monastery as lay brothers and sisters: three skilled women and four men, who could erect houses and were experienced in tending animals and crops. What was more, Oswy sent them along with building materials, seed corn, a few head of cattle, a herd of pigs and sheep and five horses—which weren't in poor condition at all—plus a little bell that would keep the spirits at bay, and a few other pieces of chased silver for the first building due to be erected: the chapel.

He had recently acquired these items on a campaign of retribution in the west, where the Brittonic monasteries still offered some good pickings. Gold too, for Oswy's goldsmith, to make arm-rings; Oswy would need many a gold ring to pay his people.

He had wanted to give them a holy book, but unfortunately he didn't own a suitable copy, he said, and looked straight at Aidan, who immediately presented them with a beautiful edition of the Gospel according to Saint John, bound in red goatskin. It was Aidan's personal copy.

They set forth for Ediscum. Aidan stood with his cross held aloft and Oswy saluted them from his long-legged Gallic horse as they slowly moved off with the heavy oxcarts.

Once they were a good distance from the sea, Hild could breathe again. The screeching of the gulls had hurt, cutting through her flesh as they cried their loneliness into empty air. She felt safer with forest and farmland all around, the blackbird soothing her pain. She ached all over.

The monastery was to be run by Begu, a nun who had spent five years on Lindisfarena under the guidance of Aidan. Then there was Freawaru, a twenty-eight-year-old nun, who had also lived on the holy isle, for three years. She had brought along her two freed slaves; the couple had married prior to the journey and would serve in secular roles. The woman had a flair for poultry, chickens in particular, and everything to do with milk; with her snakestone in the churn, the butter was never rancid. Her chickens were good layers; she'd brought them with her from her own flock on Lindisfarena—she wouldn't keep chickens she didn't know. She had a talent for bees, too, both the keeping and the rounding-up of new swarms. She had learnt the incantations from her mother; not even her husband knew them. She would be a great asset to the monastery. And then there were four other women, novices like Hild.

They found Ediscum, and it was a dense wilderness. The men got to work clearing the forest so they could start sowing crops. They sited the monastery as far as possible from the settlement ruins; on the other hand, this gave them a view of another set of ruins, no less eerie, on the other side of the river. They could see the remnants of a Roman place of devotion where the goddess Flora and her two sisters had been worshipped, and people had come to be cured at their three springs. A mighty stone statue of Flora still stood on the opposite bank, her face disfigured and nose hacked off in an attempt to purge her from the place; but she looked just as sinister, and it was said she still went about her business at the easterly spring as the sun rose—if, that is, anyone wanted to go over there.

The other ruins were the remains of the Roman fort of Vinovia, where soldiers of the sixth legion had been housed: the engineering troops who had built the Great Wall along the border to keep out the Picts. Their descendants still lived in the area, now slaves for the Angles, but knew little about their ancestors. All they *did* know was the necessity of staying away from their old places if you wanted to be left in peace. This view was robustly reinforced by their masters. When Oswald's persecution of the old gods really took hold, some of the nobles had turned to the giants' settlements as places where they could make their sacrifices without being disturbed. No one else dared visit these colossal blocks of stone, overgrown with ivy, brambles, nettles and a wilderness of thicket and tall trees; a paradise for bears—all those berries and wild bees and overturned sarcophagi where they could spend their winter sleep. When the bears lumbered out again in the springtime, thrushes and tree sparrows moved in and built their nests; a pair of magpies settled on the top of a shattered pillar; the nightingale dwelt near the source of the spring, its piercing song interpreted as the screaming and clamour of the goddess.

Oswy had chosen the location with care. He knew that once the Lord's people took a stand against the spirits, the place would soon be inhabitable for common folk. Then he could give the monastics a new slice of land. Moreover, his spies thought the idolaters had dedicated the old giants' places to Woden, sacrificing beasts and humans alike at solstice. The men he had sent out to investigate had all either disappeared or been found dead, having received a hefty blow to the forehead from a very large bludgeon—possibly Thunor's hammer.

Oswy had a suspicion that the chief farmers in the area were behind the deaths, not Thunor, but he had no urge to make the trip to find out. He was relieved when he spotted this opportunity to get the place purged—he hoped, at least, it would work out, but if it didn't, well, some martyrs would have been won for the Lord's cause, and he could clamp down all the harder on the Lord's enemies.

The locals weren't enthusiastic about the newcomers, and the customary welcome visit was conducted in a profoundly formal manner. The neighbour-gifts comprised a sack of seed corn that proved to contain more chaff than grain, and a scrawny goat that did everything it could to keep you away. The neighbours handed over their gifts sullenly and left—the usual interrogation about the newcomers' family lines and other circumstances was entirely lacking.

'The peace of the Lord be with you,' echoed softly behind them as they departed; they scowled back angrily.

Begu set great store by the good role model. She knew from Aidan that a good deed was the straightest route to the heart of a pagan; medical expertise was effective, too, and her collection of herbs was nearly as extensive as Hild's.

They had soon seeded the cleared land, but the rain failed to fall. While the monastery people, led by Begu, walked up and down blessing their soil with holy water, the neighbours stood at the boundary line to make sure not a drop of the stuff fell on their land: none of that filth on our fields, they said, and their corn was already growing well. After eleven days of relentless wind from the east, the corn had blown away and the monastics had to re-seed their land. By now it was the middle of the month of three milkings, and the rain started to fall, non-stop. At night, the water dripped on them in the temporary huts they had erected—during the day, too. Some days the rain fell steadfastly yet hushed, other days it lashed down. The air turned abnormally cold.

All they could do was pray and walk the fields again—this time to pray for the rain to stop. The neighbours stood in the deluge uttering ungodly jeers in an attempt to drown out the monastics' singing:

> Erce, Erce, mother of the earth,
> the almighty Lord everlasting grant you
> fields that sprout and grow,
> invigorate fertility.

*Hallelujah, amen.*

By the time the rain stopped, most of the corn had rotted away. They would now have to sow the seed they would otherwise have eaten throughout the summer. The corn was re-sown on the first day of the first mild month.

Nor did they have much luck with the livestock. One of the milking cows died suddenly, with no sign of any cause—it was simply lying dead in its shed one morning.

They decided to slaughter the goat, mostly to get away from its evil eyes; having eaten it, they all fell ill. Begu and Hild dragged themselves around handing out medicine to the others. It was a stomach upset, and the chicken-slave, as she was called, also had an abscess under her left buttock—big as a chicken's egg, said Begu, who attended to it, and Hild lost all appetite for eggs.

Aidan visited Ediscum on his summer travels. One by one, they had the opportunity to go to confession and talk with their father in private.

'What is wrong?' he asked Hild.

'It is not fitting to complain,' she replied glumly—the response she had so often received when grumbling to Begu.

'One should speak frankly to one's father confessor,' said Aidan.

Hild wasn't happy: she thought Begu kept too tight a rein on the monastery.

'To live the monastic life is surely to serve,' she said.

'To serve the Lord,' said Aidan, 'not to serve everybody and anybody, and certainly not the novices.'

'Surely it would not hurt an abbess to show a little respect,' Hild pressed on.

'A queen who wants to serve the Lord must learn humility,' Aidan replied. 'If it's respect you crave, then you can return to Mercia.'

Hild bent her head.

'Praise the Lord and thank him for embracing you as his child,' said Aidan, and imposed a minor penance for her recalcitrance.

Hild learnt humility by living in humiliation. When bitterness and fury welled up, she quelled the feelings by reciting a prayer of thanksgiving to the Lord. Every day was full of gratitude.

Begu was officious in some areas, in others strangely negligent. She made sure the former queen learnt the work procedures of a monastery, and not just so she could execute them passably—once she had learnt one job, she was sent to learn the next. All the various jobs, except the most arduous tasks, were taken in turns. Hild wasn't the only one unused to physical work; several of the novices cried themselves to sleep at night, from exhaustion and loneliness. Now they only had the Lord and each other, but bringing the outer world into the new life was not appreciated, so they mostly talked with the Lord. Once they had learnt to give praise, things were easier.

Hild's greatest frustration was the absence of time allocated for study and writing. They only had the one book, and the excerpt from Plinius' *Naturalis historia* sent by Hereswid, but Begu didn't think elephants were any concern of theirs, given how far away they lived.

Hild soon stopped making suggestions; instead, she thought about how she would run things—when her time came.

The harvest yielded much the same as they had sown. Begu had to ask Oswy for help to get through the winter; she didn't think she'd go begging to the neighbours, even though they'd had a very good crop that year.

Five barrels of corn, two barrels of beans and a wagonload of cabbage arrived, with a warning that this would not be repeated; many others had requested winter assistance, people who were perhaps in an even worse situation.

Begu instructed the messenger to thank Oswy for his awareness that their undertaking could only succeed if they were in a position to receive the needy and give them a wholesome meal so they were able to move on.

There were more people in need than ever before. They bemoaned the harsh taxes Oswy had imposed, and claimed this was the reason they had to wander from place to place trying to sell themselves—but, just as often, it was obviously because they had lost everything at the gaming board or on some foolish bet.

'It is not for us to judge,' Begu said sharply when Hild told her the people she had just fed came from a family whose enthusiasm for gaming had driven them to ruin; the man's paternal grandfather had lost his farm, and the grandfather's maternal uncle had even been hanged for stealing cattle during Edwin's day.

'So the children should suffer, should they?' asked Begu, giving Hild such a severe look she was forced to lower her eyes.

'I just thought,' she mumbled, 'it might encourage slovenliness if people know they will always be given food here. And how are we to get through the winter ourselves?'

'Remember, you must be a nun now, not a queen,' said Begu. 'Our duty is to follow in Jesus's footsteps. Do you think he would have turned anyone away? Or enquired about their personal responsibility for the misfortune?'

'I don't know,' Hild prevaricated.

'You know full well,' said Begu. 'He welcomed all manner of sinners.'

Hild chewed her lip: 'But—then how will we manage?'

'That is not our concern,' Begu assured her. 'The Lord will take care of it. Consider the birds of the air and the lilies of the field, he said.'

The neighbours came to complain about the monastery feeding a runaway slave owned by the third neighbour to the west. They could no longer sit by and watch the disintegration of established custom, so now it must stop.

Begu listened benevolently and gave them food and drink. Her own people gazed wistfully at the delicacies disappearing into spacious mouths and slipping down into roomy stomachs.

Begu explained that this was how they served their Lord, and offered them a little more pork. She also advised them to be baptized, so they could avoid the flames of Hell.

The men scowled at one another and rose laboriously from the bench.

'What we can see,' their leader said, 'is you gladly helping honest men lose their property, and gladly ensuring the rightful order of the kingdom is destroyed.'

'We work for the kingdom of Christ,' Begu replied, 'and that is not of this world. But when the Lord returns, then it *will* be—and then you will indeed regret your words!'

'You'll be hearing from us,' their leader said, and they left without another word and without thanking her for the food.

The day after the autumn equinox, a horse's head was found inside the gateway to the monastery. It was Woden's day.

No one had seen or heard anything. Surely there must have been a good loud thump when the large head had landed on this side of the fencing, rolled over in the dust and come to a standing halt as if the neck and body continued down into the ground—which is how it looked to the novice Sæthryd. Pale and shaking, she woke Hild and asked her to come outside. Daybreak was in its muted phase, just at the tipping point between light and darkness, absorbing all colour, the world sketched in rough outline, monotone and virtually lifeless. Sæthryd pointed, made the sign of the cross and turned her face away.

Hild had to walk up close to see what it was; it had been a large creature, black, with a white blaze running from forehead to nose. She nudged it with her foot; it rolled over onto its half-open right eye. As she had thought: its flesh was pale—a sacrificial beast, its blood now stored in some secret place.

She picked up the head with her bare hands, carried it across to the dunghill and dropped it, kicked some muck around the edges, made the sign of the cross, went indoors and washed. A severed horse's head was entitled to no more than a dunghill. The ravens soon found it and set to work, on behalf of their master, needless to say.

The winter arrived, bringing its darkness. Some of the monastery folk were ailing, and Hild told Begu they would not regain their health without better nourishment. Begu could do nothing to help their condition; the destitute needed food, and provisions had to be available for those who made missionary journeys. She didn't want the missionaries to be mistaken for beggars.

At the time of the winter solstice, they saw light on the other side of the river; light that looked like burning torches, coming and going. They immediately held a Mass, beseeching the Lord to drive away the spirits. When they came out of the chapel, there was still light in the giants' settlement, and Hild thought she could hear singing.

They spent the night keeping watch and praying, and immediately after matins they rowed across the river. Begu was the first to go ashore. Holding aloft the silver holy cross from King Oswy, she waited for the others to climb out of the boat and gather behind her. A narrow track snaked through the jumble of stone ruins; they walked along, taking courage from singing the Lord's battle hymns. The knowledge that they were fighting for the mightiest of all helped them keep their heads up and their legs steady, more or less at least, when the track widened and turned into a glade where nine tall sacrificial stakes had been driven into the ground in front of an ancient stone altar.

They were arranged in the old way, in a circle with the tallest in the middle—the one with the head on top—towering above the others. Each stake displayed part of the former man: arms, lower legs, thighs and (so as to add up to nine) the torso in two sections, chopped down the middle, the male parts removed, following time-honoured custom.

No one dared move, and the singing had stopped—until Begu shouted: 'Can't you see? This is the work of Satan!'

One by one they joined in her reciting of Our Father, followed by the confession of faith, and then a hymn of thanksgiving to Christ's victory over death.

During the hymn, Begu walked up to the altar, on which there were two gold bowls. She took one and hurled the contents—the missing parts—into the thicket. She grabbed the other bowl and tipped its contents onto the ground; a clotted lump hit the grass with a squelching sound. Hild thought she might faint, but she didn't; no one fainted, nor did anyone scream. Pale faces regained a little colour once Begu had struck up another battle hymn and they had all filled their lungs with air.

They walked back with as much dignity as possible, singing and still in a straight line behind Begu's holy cross. When they reached the river, two huge cackling ravens took off from the boat, causing the eldest of the novices to scream. Great was their relief when they tied up alongside the other bank, hurried to the chapel and immediately sought the Lord. Their singing resonated at full volume under the thatched roof.

Shortly before the spring equinox, the weather was fine enough to put the pigs out to forest pasture. Their gums had started bleeding, and there was no feed for them. The needy souls also had to make do with cabbage soup, as did the monastery folk.

Hild alone wasn't showing symptoms of hunger. She was in such good condition after her previous life that she only noticed the lack of food as a tugging sensation in her stomach and an almost floating buoyancy. Keeping her thoughts organized could also prove a little difficult; routine work was easiest. All the others were unwell, and now Freawaru couldn't even get out of bed. They had often fasted at Lindisfarena, and Freawaru had been extremely dedicated.

The lay brother who had taken the pigs to the forest had been gone for rather a long time; a search party was sent out to look for him—not a trace could they find.

'One of my slaves has run off, too—it's obviously infectious,' stated a neighbour. 'But we certainly haven't fed him, I can take my oath on that!'

The pigs had also disappeared, which was a considerable loss, and a lay brother didn't come free of charge either. He had been the chicken-slave's husband, and they had to ask Oswy for a replacement. They were given a battle captive from Dalriada; they set him free to be a lay brother. He knew all about animal husbandry too.

When messengers again arrived from Tamoworthig with letters from Hild's sons, they also brought three barrels of corn, a big pitcher of honey and a whole fattened pig in a brine tub.

'The Lord does indeed take care of his children,' said Begu when she saw all the fine produce at the door.

The messengers looked questioningly at Hild, who lowered her eyes; how ashamed she had been of the meal she had offered them last time, and now there was even less to put on the table.

The lay folk gathered around Penda's gifts and gazed mutely at Begu.

'We do not accept gifts from pagans,' she said in an authoritative tone.

'Shall we throw it in the river?' asked the leader of the messengers. 'Because we're not taking it home with us.'

'Do as you please,' said Begu.

'To the needy, perhaps?'

'Throw it where you please,' said Begu. 'But come inside and refresh yourselves while Hildeburh writes her letters.'

'If you throw it on the ground,' said Hild, 'then at least the birds of the sky will reap the benefit.'

They did as she suggested, and Hild settled down to read the letters from Wulfhere and Ædelræd.

'Father has promised I go with him hunting. My red gelding is called Victory. I shall soon go hunting. I will shoot a roe deer for you.' She couldn't imagine her little boy, her Wulfhere, killing any kind of animal, even though he was already ten years old. She had to remember that: he was ten years old, Wulfhere, soon a grown man.

She made a few additions to the letters she had long since written, telling them how well she was thriving in these more modest conditions. And then she put on the happiest face she could manage; her sons were not to be ashamed of their mother's circumstances.

She was relieved to see the messengers sitting each with his mug of beer, and hoped they hadn't noticed that these were the very last drops. They had also been offered porridge, with the last cubes of fat on top. The convent folk gazed wistfully at the hearty food, which the messengers were forcing down from sheer politeness.

That night, Hild crept out to salvage some of Penda's gifts. She pulled back when the moonlight revealed several others acting on the same idea.

Next morning, so little corn was left that it was hard to tell exactly where the three barrels had been emptied. The pork had disappeared too—and the honey pots.

'Woden's birds always know where they can find his gifts,' said Begu.

Hild became increasingly fearful that the pig man had met with an accident. She intimated as much to Begu, but Begu had no intention of pursuing the matter.

'He'll be back,' she said confidently. 'You cannot flee from the Lord.'

She nonetheless imposed a night watch: a nun at one end of the enclosure and a lay brother at the other end—not a popular arrangement, given the very poor physical state of just about everyone at the monastery. When the whisper went around that you could sleep on night watch duty, Begu cancelled the procedure.

A week later, on Woden's night, three fiery arrows bore into the thatched roof of the chapel and a burning torch was thrown over the fencing, but landed in some kitchen waste and put itself out. The fiery arrows, on the other hand, took hold of the straw. Had it not been for a novice and a lay brother who had arranged to refresh their flesh in the only way available, in the shadow of the barn, it would all have ended in utter disaster.

The novice ran from hut to hut raising the alarm while the lay brother put out the flames on the north side of the roof. When the others came outdoors, the fire flared up on the south side, and they quickly formed a line to pass buckets from the well. The chapel, however, was swiftly engulfed in flames and the flying sparks then set fire to the next-door hut.

The wind was far too vigorous; there was nothing for it but to get the animals out and try to rescue whatever else could be rescued. Begu clambered up the bell frame and cut the rope; the bell fell onto the grass with a hollow ring. She shouted that they should hurry, and instructed a lay brother to carry Freawaru as she couldn't walk unaided. The animals were panicking; shooing them past the flames was no easy matter. As they passed through the gate, however, the creatures picked up speed, knocking over the chicken-slave, but she was quick to get back on her feet.

The heat was intense. Hild was running from her hut, carrying an armful of her belongings, when she saw a small hooded figure dash into the chapel, a scarf in front of its face.

The roof hadn't yet burnt all the way through and might collapse at any moment. She screamed at the crazy soul and was just about to run after the figure when a gust of wind blew the fire into high spurts of flame and the heat made her stagger backwards, drop her possessions and cover her face with her hands.

Through the crackling blaze, she heard running footsteps and saw the figure, now looking like a burning torch, fall to the grass. She was on top of the flames in an instant, rolling around on the grass and beating the glowing sparks from red-hot clothing. It was Sæthryd. The spirit had left her, and Aidan's holy book, which she had been clutching tightly to her breast, was lying at her side on the grass.

Hild grabbed her under the arms and dragged her away. A crash and a blast of heat told her the roof had collapsed. She ran back to get the book and threw it forwards, as far as she could. Then she pulled Sæthryd further away, past her own burning hut, where her cloak caught fire, but no more than she could beat it out, and on towards the gate, where a lay brother ran across and carried the lifeless woman out of the enclosure.

Hild dashed back, and in the glare from the flames she was able to find the red leather-bound volume. Tufts of burning straw had settled alongside it; she kicked them away and rushed off, clutching the book to her breast.

They were a shabby band of crusaders, hurrying through the darkness of the night towards the Deira Way. They stayed at a good distance from any farms.

'If only we'd had weapons,' Hild whispered to Begu.

'Those who live by the sword shall die by the sword,' Begu quoted.

'Yes,' said Hild, 'but without the sword perhaps more souls perish—when all the others have swords.'

'Peace has to start somewhere,' said Begu.

They heard a scream from the tail end of their company, and saw a large dark shape, which swiftly vanished again. They speeded up in the knowledge that the Devil had again taken the hindmost.

When they could hardly walk another step, Begu decided they should hide from view in the forest until daybreak. Once they had assembled, they realized the chicken-slave and a red-haired Welshman—the horse-brother, as they called him—were missing. They had also lost the animals.

# Luminous blue eyes

*– Aidan's hymn of thanksgiving –*

A few days later, they arrived at Heruteu; Abbess Heiu received them warmly.

She asked them to show restraint as they threw themselves on the food—the soup would be best for them. Heiu was familiar with the after-effects of food deprivation, and some time passed before they were allowed to eat more than a very small portion of meat. Freawaru was slowly recovering.

Once Begu had regained her strength, and the sun had grown stronger, Heiu sent her and Hild to Lindisfarena in order to report what had taken place.

Aidan listened to their account and then spoke with each separately.

'Does that mean,' he asked Hild, 'you knew the swineherd had been sacrificed, but you said nothing?'

'I believed it to be so, but I did not explicitly voice my concern.'

'When the Lord sends a thought into your head, he does so for you to use it!'

'I am but a novice,' she replied. 'Above all, I must learn obedience, you said.'

'Humility, I said. But now you have learnt enough of that. Heiu has asked to be moved to Kælcacæstir. I have a mind to appoint you her successor in Heruteu.'

Hild flushed hot and cold; she hadn't expected to be made an abbess so soon. She didn't know what to say. It wouldn't be seemly to jump up and down, shouting with joy.

'Thank you,' she said. 'Thank you very much.'

Begu was relieved to get away from the responsibilities involved in the role of abbess. She was very fond of Hild, and was positively happy to be her subordinate. Her radiance vied with that of the midsummer sun as she witnessed Hild's life being dedicated to the Lord in Lindisfarena's thatched church, in the presence of King Oswy and his young wife Eanflæd.

Oswy's first wife had died, most suddenly, shortly after his selection as king in Bernicia. He had soon travelled to Kent in order to woo the daughter of King Edwin and Queen Tata—who had a natural claim to be queen, and in Deira too. And thus Eanflæd returned as queen of the northern part of the realm from which she—with Paulinus' help—had fled at the age of eight.

She was the first person in Northumbria to have received the gift of baptism, and was therefore of the opinion that she had a special obligation to the Lord's cause in the realm; it pleased her to see Hildeburh enter his service. As a child she had admired Breguswid's daughters, feeling honoured and endlessly thrilled when the older girls occasionally let her join in their games.

Now, she was gratified to note, it had all turned upside down. She smiled at Hildeburh, while checking that her deep-blue silk headdress, with its long fluttering ribbons in a slightly lighter shade of blue, was positioned as it should be—it was.

Hild was the happiest of them all. She hadn't passed by a single fifteen-year-old boy without giving him a good looking-over. She had already noticed that people confided in her and asked for advice. It wouldn't be long before she knew everything about everyone in the land—with the Lord's help.

'It's almost like old times,' she said cheerfully to Aidan a few days later as they walked across the damp strip of land connecting Lindisfarena and the mainland. Reflection from the harsh sun dazzled her as they passed the bridge. The eider ducks were rocking gently on the water; further in, oystercatchers were poking the sand for food. Lindisfarena was a blessed place; the air had its very own gentleness, unlike anywhere else she had ever been.

Aidan would accompany Hild down to Heruteu and install her as abbess, so everything would be done properly. He had planned a missionary trip anyway, so going south was just as good as going north.

Hild learnt a lot from listening to him, and even more from his way of associating with people. Aidan had a remarkably good reputation and was welcome wherever he went. When a guest, he ate and drank with great moderation, and he treated slaves and children with the same respect he accorded freemen. This made an impression, on pagans too, and they happily listened to what he had to say.

Begu walked the entire route, as did Aidan, whereas Hild and some of the older people occasionally had a rest on horseback—which was acceptable to Aidan. They also took along packhorses carrying provisions and tents; not that they declined hospitality, but they weren't beggars.

Aidan had heard confession from a woman who had lain with her husband's brother. Penance was set at one mug of milk and four slices of bread daily for thirty days, water as she pleased, one egg on the sun's day, confession of faith and Our Father three times every morning and evening.

'Has Christ not taken the burden of our guilt upon himself?' Hild asked, as they walked on—if she wanted to talk with Aidan, she had to walk as he did.

'Indeed. How can you ask such a question?'

'Because then it's meaningless to do penance—or downright heretical. A rejection of the Lord's gift.'

'The actual penance is obviously of no relevance to the Lord,' he replied. 'But as far as the people are concerned, it is necessary in order to enforce what is right and what is wrong.'

'But guilt is lifted from us in baptism.'

'It is. But there is something people don't understand, and we have to render the gospel in terms they *can* understand. Everyone knows a master punishes disobedience and exacts penance. And if we tell people that our god forgives everything—well, then they'll think he isn't a real master worth serving. If we told them how Jesus really lived, they would only see the drifter and the impoverished infant in a trough in a stable. And there's little exaltation in that.'

'It is perhaps the truth.'

'It is, but the truth is of no use if no one understands it. A king who sits in majesty separating the sheep from the goats—they can understand that. Like the farmer who sits using his power to select which he will buy and which has to go.'

'What if it isn't the kingdom of Christ we are proclaiming?'

'Oh well,' said Aidan, 'at least we're telling the people that they mustn't kill one another! Doesn't that count for something?'

Hild frowned, and Aidan went on: 'That they mustn't put children out; that they must take care of the poor and widows; that they must stop believing their fortunes are all laid out in the guts of animals and all such nonsense; that they are free human beings who must take personal responsibility—even though they have to slave under their masters, the world being what it is, and even if they have no kin, or no master, and no one who likes them; that they don't have to slay hundreds of men in order to win everlasting renown, but that the Lord will always remember them as long as they have been baptized.'

He looked at her, breathless from his hurried speech. 'Does that not make the world a better place?'

'Yes, indeed,' she said. 'But what has that to do with the kingdom of Christ and the life everlasting?'

'Everything,' Aidan replied.

Hild shook her head a couple of times; she still didn't understand, and just had to hope it would all fall into place. Then she got down to her second piece of business; she cleared her throat and straightened her belt.

'When we met for the first time, in Mercia, did you know who I was?'

'I did! And I was glad you came.'

'Why?'

He smiled archly. 'It's always nice with a bond to the queen of the realm.'

She blushed, not knowing whether from anger or shame.

'How could you have known?' she eventually asked.

He shrugged. 'I couldn't really, but it was more than likely!'

Hild felt her face turn scarlet. Everyone had known—except her. How stupid can one person be? she thought, and considered saving her next question, but out it popped of its own accord: 'When you wrote that I should come up here and do penance for Oswald, had it nothing whatsoever to do with my salvation? Was it because you thought Penda's former wife would be an asset for the Lord's cause?'

'Yes!' Aidan replied without blinking. 'Your salvation is a matter for the Lord and, to the best of my knowledge, in that respect you have no influence. We needed you. I thought you would bring good fortune to the realm—and that the work would bring good fortune to you personally. That's how it was.'

Hild was quiet for a while, then she asked: 'Well, couldn't you have written that to me?'

'I was afraid you didn't have the courage. I knew you were adrift, imagining you were a bringer of misfortune. A journey you *could* manage, but you would not have dared take on an assignment.' He shrugged. 'I suppose I might have been mistaken.'

They walked on in silence, and Hild tried to recall how things had been back then.

It was as if she had found herself in a swamp, very close to the Land of the Dead, without the strength and without the willpower to get out of it. With a view of the gates of Hell; she wouldn't have been upset if they had swung open to let her in.

Then Hereswid had sent an extract from Plinius and asked her to find out about Queen Boudicca. Hereswid had enticed her by describing the apricots, so Hild could almost feel the downy fruit in her hand, golden-yellow and warmed by the sun, in a far milder climate than that of East Anglia.

Across the sea, Hereswid had sensed Hild's state of mind and had known how to call her back to the land of the living. She had never forgotten her blood-sister in favour of her new sisters and brothers in the Lord. In her final days, she had fasted and prayed excessively, the abbess had written. Perhaps she had wanted to move the Lord to pull her sister out of the East Anglian swamps, away from the Land of the Dead and back to the grass and succulence of the earth. For Hereswid, blood had been thicker than water. She had staked her life so that her sister would live. And she had lost it. All this became clear to Hild now for the first time.

She took a deep breath and sighed. Hereswid's sacrifice must not be in vain. Her sister's life continued in her. As soon as she had found Hundfrid and Wilbrord, she would visit Hereswid's grave. Afterwards, she would travel to Rome and pray for their family line.

'You undoubtedly did the right thing,' she said to Aidan.

'It is difficult to serve the Lord in Gaul,' Aidan said the following day, as if he knew what Hild was thinking. 'Over there, it's more a case of serving the bishops. Young men would rather be in *their* service than that of the king, because they quickly win riches and status and learn the use of weapons. In my opinion, the bishops lose out, in every sense, when they compete with the king for temporal power and glory. The king procures prosperity for his people, and he protects the weak against the high-handedness and war-mongering of the nobles. To do this he needs soldiers and retainers, and not just from the lowest stock. Without a strong king, the realm turns into a pack of wolves—and therefore we shouldn't vie with him.

'Our task is to preach the gospel, so people learn to live together rather than fight each other. So they realize there is greater nobility in giving a child a bowl of barley porridge than in slaying the king of Mercia. Learn that forgiveness is more honourable than revenge. That all people are each other's brothers and sisters, because we have been created by the same father, and in his image! Thus we should thank him for life and food, and not be naughty children who steal one another's playthings and beat the smallest of the flock. Christ's teachings cannot be spread by might and by sword. Everything we do must point forwards to the kingdom for which we fight.'

'To the kingdom of Christ?' asked Hild.

'Well, the kingdom of Christ, yes,' said Aidan, rocking his head slowly from side to side. 'We can call it that, but we actually know so little. And I believe we must leave that to the Lord. But we do know the poor starve and the rich amass more and more, and send their men to war in order to steal their neighbour's goods. And we know that injustice is avenged with injustice, and blood with blood—all that we know, and we can do something about it! Peace on earth and goodwill among all—that's what the angels sang over Jesus when he was born.'

Aidan's powerful voice broke into a noisy song, booming down the dale and echoing against the rock face. A hymn of thanksgiving for the birth of the Lord and the angels who came to welcome him. The rear party joined in, but Hild was silent in bewilderment, thoughts milling around her mind.

'But—isn't that deceit?' she asked, when the singing eventually stopped.

'Deceit?' he shouted, and stood still, as if this was the most monstrous question he had ever heard. He turned to face her and looked her straight in the eye.

'Love—that is no deceit. It's the only thing we can abide by. Love. That's how it is.'

His eyes were transparent blue, and bottomless.

'There is nothing else,' he added, and as she didn't respond, he went on: 'What would it be?'

She took a deep breath and reeled off what she had learnt from Paulinus and repeated ad nauseam ever since: 'The kingdom of Heaven, the Lord's reward, a place at his table, eternal salvation, the cessation of grief, the happy reunion with loved ones . . . '

'Yes, yes,' he said quietly. 'Which is precisely what love gives us, is it not? So we can forget our own distress—and be one another's loved ones.'

'And afterwards—afterwards, won't we live for all eternity in Heaven?' Hild whispered, afraid he might answer no.

'I don't know,' he said, the same bottomless blue eyes upon her. And she couldn't tell whether it was clarity or despair dwelling within that gaze.

# A SEAMLESS TUNIC

*– Abbess of Heruteu –*

Hild knew how she would lead the monastery. Many monastics were more concerned about the redemption of their souls and their imminent home in Paradise than they were about the state of the here and now—an untenable situation. They would have to engage in the development of the kingdom. They were living, for the time being, in this world; it was their responsibility to take care of those who couldn't take care of themselves. An exemplary life wasn't enough to guide the pagans onto the right path. There was a need for more learning and a more organized approach to missionary journeys. It was absolutely crucial to train more priests. Superstition had to be tackled with knowledge; they needed more bibles so they could go out into the community and *show* the holy scriptures—which had greater impact than simply standing in front of a crowd reciting from memory, as anyone could.

They also needed more resources. No one in their right mind would serve a master who couldn't even provide for his own. Hild therefore asked her people to think about ways in which the monastery could bring in a higher income.

She was rather shocked when it became apparent that her monastics didn't always understand the Latin words they read aloud from the scriptures. Even more effort would have to be put into the teaching. Hild wrote to Bishop Honorius in Cantwaraburh asking him to send teachers of Latin and interpretation of the scriptures. She was sent two well-educated priests, one of whom had taught under Felix.

So numerous were applications to enter the monastery that an extra wing had to be built. Women and men took lessons together in Latin, writing, recitation, arithmetic, interpretation of the scriptures and nature study. When the women went off to weave and embroider, the men went off to the fields and the various workshops.

The monastery had a watermill further upriver, a forge, a pottery and a hut for woodwork, in which monastics worked alongside the lay folk—who continued the task in hand when the Lord's men and women went to lessons. The lodging for the sick and needy also had to be tended, and the guests were put to any work of which they were capable. Everyone went to the Masses.

Freawaru had recovered completely and was developing into a skilled scribe; she also had a talent for numbers. Sæthryd, the oldest of the novices from Ediscum, was becoming particularly proficient in Latin; before long, she could write letters and short interpretations of the bible. Hild and Sæthryd wrote an entire wax tablet to one another for practice, every day.

Their four priests were the most learned of all, and Hild would have liked to keep their days clear for teaching. Often, however, lessons had to be cut short when a priest was called out into the community. He might be away for several days; word travelled quickly, and when there was a priest in the vicinity others would take the opportunity to call upon his services—and they covered a large area.

Hild wrote to Aidan, asking if he couldn't ordain some more priests. For want of suitable men, perhaps he could ordain a couple of women; this was, after all, an emergency, and it was vital to give more people an education.

She knew that quite a few of the nuns on Lindisfarena were qualified. Not that their learning could be compared with that of people from Cantwaraburh or from Felix's school, but they were on an absolute level with the men Aidan ordained—even though he gave women fewer lessons than he gave the men.

But Aidan declined her request, with reference to time-honoured custom.

'What about the holy Brigid of Cill Dara—was she not consecrated to be bishop by Bishop Ibor?' Hild wrote in reply. 'If a woman can be a bishop, then surely she can be a priest too.'

Aidan, himself from Ireland, wrote to inform her that the Lord's cause had been in even poorer standing back then; moreover, he doubted it had actually happened. He would suggest she put more effort into the teaching of potential priest candidates, just like he did.

Sæthryd and Freawaru were disappointed when they had to lose one of their daily Latin lessons to the men—and had to go to the weaving hut instead. Hild explained this was a temporary measure, which would be cancelled as soon as the shortage of priests had been rectified. As things stood, however, it was a necessity and would, in the long run, be of benefit to them.

They found this hard to imagine, and Hild had to give them a lecture: monastic life was primarily a matter of service; pleasure in becoming skilled at Latin must never turn into pride; learning was a means, not an end in itself; the end, the objective, was to convert the realm to the Lord—not the satiety of their thirst for knowledge.

'Yes, yes,' said Freawaru, 'as long as we keep our nature study.'

Hild gladly promised as much; she didn't want to forego nature study either.

Being abbess suited Hild. The role came to her as naturally as had that of queen, even though the work was somewhat different. She was now serving a master who was not of this world; to enhance his power and prestige was, in some respects, like enhancing a king's power, while in other respects it was the complete opposite.

King Jesus valued works of charity higher than gold and cloaks of otter pelt, even though he too enjoyed fine clothing. He had worn a very costly—seamless—tunic; the Roman soldiers who cast lots for it were well aware of its worth and were unwilling to cut it into pieces.

However, these weren't the things that had set him apart; no, his uniqueness was born of his benevolence and his kinship with the loftiest of all masters—his own father—and from his desire to share this special status with anyone who wanted to follow him.

Hild tried to picture Jesus as he walked from place to place in his splendid tunic: a wandering entertainer of sorts, deriding all those who thought themselves better than others. She couldn't really get this image to fit with her other pictures of him. And so she made a magnificent tunic for the priest to wear for Mass: the finest linen, dyed purple, interwoven with thin pale wool in diamond patterns; on the back, a holy cross embroidered with gold thread; tied at the front with red silk ribbon. She scrutinized it during Mass, trying to conjure up a picture of her Lord.

Aidan, however, did not approve of the robe—this was not the way in which to follow the Lord's example, he said. Hild put the tunic away and took out the old plain one for the priest. The superior robe hadn't really helped clarify her notions anyway.

Some of her other ideas met with a better reception, and Aidan put them into practice. She had never reconciled herself to the expectation that the Lord's people should take care of anyone and everyone—and the resulting breakdown of the natural order in the kingdom. It was different when it came to people who were ill and unfit for work and had been abandoned by their families, even though this, too, was a dangerous trend: now everyone could shirk their family responsibilities and just leave them to the monasteries to sort out—and so the tendency was spreading rapidly.

Many people only thought about themselves and disregarded their kin. They forgot to take into account that the days would come of which they would say: *I have no pleasure in them*; when they, weighed down with the frailty of age, would cry out for help from the young ones as fruitlessly as their old folk had once cried out to *them*.

This disregard of the old folk—it was neither natural nor right. The Lord would punish those who stood by and allowed their family to perish. But he required his own people to take care of the frail, and thus Hild never turned anyone away.

However, that didn't mean slaves could have pleasurable days by absconding and seeking refuge in a monastery. She told them that monastic hospitality would only last until the next festival, and until that time they would have to work for their keep. And if any of them thought they could just move from monastery to monastery, then they should be aware that the monasteries were in close and frequent contact with one another.

On festival days, when the Christian freemen came to the monastery anyway, they held slave markets, and in that way many distressed folk found a good home without first having to roam the kingdom. The monastery also set rules for the slaves' forthcoming lodgings and food rations: they were to be treated like human beings, not animals—that was the proviso.

For their part, the slaves had to swear on the holy scripture that they would obey their new masters and not attempt to abscond, unless the master failed to meet his obligations. In such a case, the slave should consult the monastery, and if a wrong had been committed then the master in question would not be permitted to purchase any more slaves there.

The monastery slaves soon became popular. They had gained a little knowledge from their stay at Heruteu; some had even learnt a few letters of the Latin, and a slave like that was of interest—not everyone could boast of having one of those. They were a little more expensive, but you were happy to pay up because they were always in better condition than the ones sold by laymen—who usually had their reasons for wanting to get rid of a slave.

Life in the monastery was frugal, but not one of hardship. They took it in turns to do the practical work, except for the very heavy or highly specialized tasks, as had been the practice in Heiu's day.

Begu took care of the accounts; they were deposited in her mind, and she had the monastery's best memory. Hild had never met anyone who stored away every single detail, important or not, with greater precision than Penda, but Begu even kept a record of the weather conditions throughout her life. If you wanted information about any particular year—when the autumn storm had set in, when the swallows had returned from the south, when the night frost had come to an end—then you asked Begu. She also kept track of kinship relations, annual yield from the soil, the origin and arrival date of every single creature, and everything else they owned.

Hild had begun to wonder if Begu could, in fact, read, so when she requested exemption from writing lessons, on the pretext that the accounts demanded all her attention, Hild asked her straight out and she had to admit her shortcoming—which she didn't personally consider a shortcoming. Begu had never made any attempt to learn how to write, and she couldn't associate the shape of a single letter with the sound it expressed. She had managed to disconnect her mind during reading and writing lessons, and she had done so on the basis of her observation that reading destroyed memory; as soon as you knew something had been written down, you forgot it.

From the very outset of her monastic life, she had decided to commit everything to memory, and she claimed—without naming names—not to be the only one who refused to have her powers of retention ruined. She knew the words of the four Gospels, the Psalms of David, the Book of Ecclesiastes, the Song of Solomon, Genesis and Exodus, Revelation, the Book of Samuel and the Acts of the Apostles. And now she also knew Hereswid's excerpt from Plinius' *Naturalis historia*. Those were the writings she had heard read aloud here and on Lindisfarena, and after one reading she was familiar with the words, after two she was word-perfect.

Hild suspected Begu might be right, because her own memory wasn't what it had been. On the other hand, it *wasn't* right that handmaidens of the Lord couldn't read his words, given that they were written down, so she consulted Aidan.

'In our Lord's house, there are many abodes,' said Aidan, who wasn't a great reader or writer by nature. 'Why destroy a talent that is of such use to you all? You haven't even got enough parchment to record it all!'

Thus it came about that Begu was exempt from lessons in Latin, writing and reading. She still took part in recitation—you had to learn the correct tone of voice and tempo.

Hild was impressed by Freawaru's embroidery. Like Hild, Freawaru had been used to working with silk, gold thread, silver thread, pieces of round and oval silver for ornamentation, threads and yarn in every colour and of the highest quality. Freawaru had embroidered an altar cloth for the chapel, which surpassed everything Hild had ever seen. But Aidan had passed no comment about it.

Now they embroidered Jesus's name in the middle of a wall hanging for the chapel, and surrounded it with a holy cross, forming a circle in the middle and each arm ending in a semi-circle. The hanging was edged with a contrasting colour, and they sewed the evangelists' symbols into the four half-circles. The lion caused them much difficulty, until Freawaru had the idea of shaping it like a male cat, adding a mane, larger paws and a bigger head.

Aidan had no objections, but he preferred the pure patterning of interlace and tablet-woven squares—and so they developed that technique. Sometimes Freawaru had the ideas, sometimes Hild; inspiration came to them at night, during Mass, lessons, at any time.

Hild dreamt about ribbon interlacing and woke up entangled in a huge pattern, her endless arms and legs and neck wound into people she didn't know, but in the edging on the reverse of the woven cloth, Hundfrid and Wilbrord were entangled with Oswy—the one in his legs, the other in his arms. She wanted to wave, but her arms were woven into an old woman's legs and, what was more, they were sewn very tightly into position with almost invisible stitches. She had to make do with just looking across at them, and after a while it didn't really seem necessary to wave, given that she was linked to them through all the others. They could surely feel the connection, just as she so clearly felt their breathing and their tiniest tremble enter through her skin.

She felt an urge to weave a cloth with intertwined human forms all the way around the edging, but had to abandon the project. Faces were too difficult, and so she continued with the coloured ribbon and imagined they were people. A yellow, a green, a dark red, a black length. A yellow, a green, a dark red, a black length. The same ribbon, dyed in various colours, as she had used in Tamoworthig, for Penda and for her sons.

They must still be wearing those cloaks. She had embroidered a wolf on Wulfhere's; quite small, in the very corner, and using almost the same thread as she had used to weave the cloak itself. A secret wolf cub, and under the dense stitching she had sewn a holy cross in gold thread. He was a boy who needed a lot of protection. One of the few things she knew for certain: as long as Wulfhere was wearing that cloak, nothing bad would befall him. She had never worried about Ædelræd; he would have a long life, with or without a holy cross. His birth, for instance—so uncomplicated. It was only so as not to make a difference between them that she had sewn a holy cross on his cloak too—and it couldn't hurt.

She regularly received letters from Ædelræd: he was far better at writing than his older brother. Wulfhere had always found it difficult to sit still.

# THE DEAF EAR

*– visit from Penda –*

Hild had been in charge of the monastery in Heruteu for exactly two years when Penda suddenly appeared, standing in her hut. It wasn't until the man from Mercia—the usual messenger, she thought—threw back his hood that she recognized him.

He laughed at her shock. He'd lost both his upper front teeth; the only teeth he had were on the left side of his upper mouth, as the three lower teeth he'd once had were also missing. His hair had more grey streaks than she remembered; now it was all more grey than flaxen and bushed out at the sides. His forehead had spread upwards, and his eyes looked out from deeper hollows. He had lost some weight, but none of his uprightness or kingly dignity.

She saw all this in a flash as he threw back his hood, and then for a long time all she felt was his familiar embrace, his body pressing against hers, the feel of his manhood through their clothing, the smell of his skin and his hair. The feel of his mouth was slightly different at first because of the missing teeth, but it soon proved to be the familiar beloved mouth that had kissed its way across her body thousands of times.

So dizzy from his touch, she thought she might faint. Only her head, however, had stopped functioning, while the rest of her body took control and reciprocated his embrace with a force that nearly knocked him over.

She pushed him away and watched him closely.

'What are you doing here?' she asked.

'Visiting my wife,' he smiled. 'She left me four years ago, taking all joy with her. But I've just found it again.'

He loosened her headdress—her hair spread across her shoulders; he nibbled her earlobe.

'My dear beloved wife,' he whispered, 'dear beloved wife.'

Her bed wasn't built for two, but that was of no importance. The urge for marital consummation was overwhelming; two bodies had united and become one flesh before they had even removed all their garments.

'You're risking your life,' Hild said afterwards, as they lay close in the narrow space.

'I don't think so,' he replied.

'Have you brought an army?' she asked.

And when he didn't immediately answer, she raised her voice: 'Have you brought war?'

'That depends on Oswy,' he replied, closing his eyes.

'Is there any special reason?' she asked.

'Only the usual—Oswy's people troubling my people in Deira. Oswy thinks he's high king over Oswine. And then there was a minor encounter at the border, so I thought I'd take advantage of the good weather—and the good signs.'

'You and your signs!' she snapped. 'You don't even believe in them yourself.'

'My wife would be lovelier than ever, the pagan priest said.'

'Don't give me that!' she laughed, pulling him closer. It was that kind of masculine cheek she'd always found irresistible in Penda. It had the same effect on her today as it had those sixteen or so years ago when she had been requested to attend his chamber for the first time.

Had he not started on that silliness about the little mouse going up to its little house—across her thighs and breasts—she would have resisted the feeling of being drawn towards him and found another opportunity to exact her revenge. Then his old head would no longer be sitting atop his wrinkled neck; Wulfhere and Ædelræd wouldn't have been born; she would have been executed, and someone else would have been abbess here.

She leapt out of bed, and stood stock still.

'I have forsaken the Lord—and it is to him I belong!'

She hadn't given a thought to the fact that her body was reserved for the divine bridegroom to whom she had dedicated her life.

Penda looked at her lovingly.

'Your Lord, you have always told me, prizes love above all else—you and I belong together, no matter what, or how. Don't you know that?'

'My divine husband probably forgives me,' Hild smiled as she embraced her secular husband. 'I must ask Aidan how I should do penance for this.'

She fetched mead and food, and let it be known that her evening would be spent in her hut writing letters and hearing news of her sons.

They were together and they were just themselves, as straightforward as always. Hild was never so much herself as she was with Penda; he wasn't like anyone else. Their years of happiness and their bad years had all been *their* years. The Lord God had joined them together, and no human being had been able to split them apart.

'I've thought it through,' said Penda, late at night when they were again lying gratified and calm on Hild's narrow bed. 'You can't swindle your way to happiness. And that's why fate took you from me—because I didn't come to you in an honourable fashion.'

'Do you mean that business in Elmet?'

Hild preferred not to think about her first husband, and never mentioned his name.

Penda nodded. 'There are so many other things I never wonder about—even though they were just as dishonourable—but that particular guilt grows heavier year by year.'

'Not that I've had second thoughts,' he added after a moment or two. 'I'd do the same today. But now I know the price.'

Hild lay staring up at the underside of the thatched roof. She stretched, and turned to her husband.

'What if it was actually *me* who came to *you* in a dishonourable fashion?'

He stared at her, not understanding what she was saying.

'Yes, me with my holy cross in need of repair, and all those writing lessons. I indulged you—you know that, don't you?'

'Indulged me?' He sat up. 'You didn't mean what you said about my signature?'

She smiled at him.

'But—did you mean it or did you not?' he persisted.

'I meant it, because I wanted to impress you,' she replied with total frankness.

'So you didn't mean it at all—praising my signature?'

She laughed quietly and looked at him lovingly.

'It's quite possible to mean something because you want to be invited to supper. Just a light Lenten meal, as is proper and fitting. Don't you think?'

Penda was startled—those had been the very words he had used when he had planned to propose marriage to her. But then the pagan priest had read the signs, and Penda had postponed his project. He wrapped himself in the bedcover and acted offended.

'I thought you meant it,' he sighed, and then started laughing loudly as he rolled over to embrace his wife.

Hild was mulling over the past. Penda had fallen asleep; he took up a lot of space. She was trying to remember how it had been back then.

Once she had recovered from what happened in Elmet, she had wandered around in a daze, not aware of much at all. She'd seen Penda as a gross and crude brute, easily flattered and easily fooled. Now she didn't know which one of them had been the fool—both, perhaps.

She got out of bed and opened the door. It was a calm summer's night, the nightingale chirping down on the marsh; in just a few days, after midsummer, it would be finished with its singing. The moon was hanging low above the fencing, almost full; it was never really dark here by the sea at this time of year.

Perhaps they had both been wise enough not to be dazzled by the irrelevant packaging—they had wanted each other, both of them.

She closed the door and nestled into him, arms and legs wrapped around his. Locked in this embrace, her soul grew into his, as always when they lay close together, and time stopped its onward journey. The slow breathing in unison, blood settling, bones gently humming.

Gratitude for this extra night together engulfed her. She fell asleep once the moon had set.

Penda left early next morning; no one had seen him in Hild's hut. He had stationed his army in a dale to the west, also leaving his sons there while he went to the monastery, making do with a very small entourage so as to look like the usual messenger.

Hild rode out with him; she had to see her sons. Four years had passed, and when they stood before her she simply couldn't believe so much had happened in those four years. Wulfhere was no longer a boy: fine pale down now covered his chin, his chest was broader, but his legs were still far too skinny. He was wearing the 'wolf cloak' she had made for him, and a shiny silver helmet.

'Are you eating properly?' she asked, and he was immediately annoyed.

'Are *you*?' he retorted, and it couldn't be denied she had grown thin.

'You're the one who needs to grow,' she said in her defence. 'Eggs and pork are good at your age.'

'Yes, yes,' he said. He had never liked either, and was impatient to get going and ride into battle.

'I've brought down five wild boars, three wolves and nine deer,' he told her, and on the final word his voice cracked and became very deep. 'Now I just hope I'll be the one to fell Oswy,' his unfamiliar man's voice continued.

Hild glanced across at Penda in alarm; he winked at her. At least she knew he wouldn't allow their sons to get involved in hand-to-hand fighting—and certainly not with Oswy's troops.

She took Penda aside.

'Beware their archers. They shoot further than those in Mercia.'

'Of course,' he replied. 'I'll keep them at the very back.'

Ædelræd hadn't lost his little-boy's smile and his happy round eyes; he had more freckles and still looked a touch weedy. He was beaming, as if about to go duck-hunting. He didn't mind being kissed and hugged, and generously returned his mother's embraces. He had only just turned eleven.

As they rode off, it was Ædelræd who kept turning around and waving; Wulfhere was in far too much of a hurry, eager for battle. Penda halted on the hilltop and raised his arm. Hild carried on waving until the entire army had disappeared from sight.

So, she thought, now I just sit back and twiddle my thumbs, and then she wondered why she would think such a thing. She had more than enough to get on with while waiting for the outcome of their fighting.

She'd seen the size of his army—about twice as large as Oswy's usual force—and such numbers were necessary if Penda was to be victorious. Oswy commanded a standing army of carefully chosen men who did nothing but fight and guard their king. He also used freemen; if, that is, they arrived—Hild would surely have heard if they had already been called up.

Penda always had good fortune in battle, for whatever reason that might be: her husband had never yet lost a battle.

This time, however, thanks to Aidan who called upon the Lord to intercede, there was no battle.

Aidan had withdrawn to the Farne Islands, off the coast at Bebbanburh, in order to devote himself to prayer and fasting. He was standing, arms outstretched, offering prayers to the heavens, when the sky above him filled with thick clouds of smoke. At first he thought perhaps this was the second coming of the Lord, but then he saw the smoke was coming from the other side of Bebbanburh and he realized what was happening.

'God!' he cried to the heavens. 'See the actions of evil Penda!'

The wind immediately changed direction; the black smoke, intended to force Oswy's men to abandon the fortress, now forced Penda's men to draw back.

This was the second time it had done so, and Penda was not pleased. He hadn't even pulled down the church; wise from experience, he had made do with the surrounding villages, five in all, and they had burnt very well. Clouds of choking, impenetrable smoke had filled the air, exactly according to plan; until, that is, it turned and blew towards Penda and his men. That's when they got scared, and marched home without plundering anything other than whatever happened to turn up along the way—to the great annoyance of Penda's sons.

Once the freemen had reported for duty, King Oswy set forth southwards to punish Oswine for letting Penda pass through Deira, and without even informing him either. He demanded a sizeable compensation, both to make an example of Oswine and to help fund his own expensive standing army—because he had by now realized that the people of Bernicia not only lacked the will to pay more, but also the ability to do so.

Oswine would have to get by without Penda, who was already down in Mercia by the time Oswy reached Cetreht—but he couldn't. Oswy's claim for compensation was an insult; moreover, it exceeded Oswine's means, and he didn't have enough men.

He sent his troops home and rode westwards, far into the Swalwa dale, then south over the hills and down into the Ure dale—where he took refuge with a distant relative called Hundfrid.

The farm was situated where the traitor queen, Cartimandua, had once lived in her royal settlement, whence she had sent word asking for help from the Romans when her people had rebelled.

Hundfrid and Oswine knew nothing of traitor Cartimandua, nor were they interested, particularly not now, with Oswy on his way.

The past, however, had a way of interfering: nine years earlier, after the death of King Oswald, Hundfrid had been a captive of battle in Mercia; he had Penda's then wife, Queen Hildeburh, to thank for the fact that he hadn't been sold as a slave.

'Hundfrid,' she had said, 'that is what I named my son—and therefore I shall grant you your freedom.'

She had told him about her twins, lying in their graves near Hacanos. He later spoke with the queen's slave, who said that Oswine knew very well where Hildeburh's twins had been hidden away, adding: 'They're no more dead than you and me.'

Hundfrid now spotted his chance to return Hildeburh's kindness. He'd had no idea his plan could go so very wrong; he thought Oswine would simply tell him the twins' secret whereabouts when he asked, but his guest wasn't immediately forthcoming. Oswine, on the other hand, didn't for a moment think Hundfrid would betray his own kin—until it was all too late, and Oswy's soldiers came and dragged Oswine from the pile of straw behind Hundfrid's cattle.

They put him on trial. Oswy had promptly convened a court, made up of his own men, whereupon he departed. They made short work of the proceedings: Oswine was convicted of sedition plus attempted escape, and he was taken to the place of execution in In-Getlingum.

Oswine dismounted his horse and waved the executioner over. He didn't want to die with Hildeburh's twins on his conscience: he told the executioner where he had taken them, and asked him to make sure the information reached Hildeburh, who was now the abbess in Heruteu.

The executioner nodded and got on with his job.

Hundfrid stood at the place of execution and wept. The judges had flatly rejected all his protests; they had also ignored his offer to take Oswine's place. His attempt to bribe the gaoler, a young kinsman at that, had failed. Oswy's men were paid well, and subject to the death penalty for disloyalty.

'Have my head instead!' Hundfrid had shouted to the executioner, who didn't even deign to glance at him, busy as he was pulling the cloth away from the king's neck.

Once Oswine had been split into two pieces, Hundfrid shouted: 'Then take mine too!'

'Do it yourself!' the executioner shouted back; he'd only been paid for the one.

So Hundfrid rode home and hung himself—just like Judas, after he'd betrayed his master.

When Hild heard what had happened, she travelled to In-Getlingum and sought out the executioner; she wanted to know if, in his final moments, Oswine had perhaps confided in the man.

The executioner shook his head, but this stranger wouldn't give up.

'Don't they usually say something?'

'Nothing,' he replied, 'not a word.'

By thus answering her questions, he eventually got rid of her. He didn't think he could start trying to explain the special aspects of his work; other people didn't understand. She might even get him punished for not having paid attention, but he was a professional and never paid attention.

When his 'guests on the hill', as he called them, spotted the axe, they always tried to play for time, in whatever way they could; they simply had to say something or other. In order to get the job done as smoothly as possible, he always lent them an ear and said yes, yes!

But he didn't hear what they were saying; he'd learnt not to from his father. Nine times out of ten, his father had told him, they cursed the executioner, wishing him a taste of the axe, hoping he would end up in the flames of Hell, or they intoned sinister magic spells and the like.

It would be too difficult to explain all that to this fine lady. He was relieved when she finally left.

Aidan had foretold the brevity of Oswine's life. There had been friendship between king and bishop; in Deira, Aidan had a king who was easy to favour. This was not quite the case in Bernicia, because Oswy was belligerent towards everyone and close-fisted towards the Church. He only gave alms when the people crowded round him crying out: 'Long live Oswy! Long live our great King Oswy!' Silver pieces would then fly through the air, while the Church people could wait in vain to receive help for those truly in need.

Aidan never exactly fell out with Oswy, but he avoided him wherever possible. It was different with Oswine, who often invited Aidan and gave him substantial gifts to help the poor. Aidan was grateful, and hoped the good example would gradually teach Oswy a thing or two.

Oswine once presented Aidan with a completely white horse of the best bloodline, a large silver bridle and a harness decorated with scarlet tassels, so his bishop could travel around in a manner befitting his rank, and could more readily visit Deira.

This horse, with all the precious trappings—including its embroidered rug, the edging worked with silver thread—was handed over to the first beggar Aidan came across.

Oswine was furious, because it wasn't the first time Aidan had simply given his gifts away, and what was more, he'd gone to a lot of trouble to find the most suitable horse for his bishop. A beggar could make do with less.

'And what might you mean by that, my lord the king?' Aidan exclaimed. 'Is the child of a mare of greater value to you than one of the Lord's children?'

Oswine stood in front of the fire, staring silently into the flames, wet and cold after an exhausting hunt. He suddenly threw himself at Aidan's feet and asked forgiveness; he would never again question what Aidan did with his gifts.

Aidan gladly forgave him and entreated him to stand up and come to the table so they could eat together. Having received Aidan's forgiveness, Oswine finally sat at the table and became increasingly merry as the evening progressed.

Aidan, on the other hand, stared down at the tabletop and eventually started to weep. His attendant asked him in Irish what he was sad about, and Aidan confided in him: 'I know the king will not live long, for never before have I seen a humble king. I sense he will soon be taken from us, for the realm is not worthy of such a king.'

Given that Aidan's prophecy had now been fulfilled, his attendant broadcast far and wide what he had previously kept to himself. The story soon spread, adding to the ill will against Oswy.

Never had Deira had so good and so Christian a king as Oswine. And never again would they be ruled from Bernicia, by Ædelfred's misfortune-bringing lineage.

# TWELVE WILD GEESE
# MIGRATE SOUTHWARDS

*– Aidan's hunger strike –*

The news of King Oswine's death was passed to Aidan by his own monks—warily, and with many a preparatory clarification—and his only reaction was: 'Where is King Oswy now?'

'On his way to Bebbanburh,' he was told.

It was a good day's walk from Lindisfarena to Bebbanburh, and Aidan set out immediately with a small handpicked entourage. Upon arrival the next day, he didn't go inside, but sat with his back against the wall of the church, staring down the track along which the king would come riding.

When Oswy appeared in the afternoon, worn out after the long journey, he was greeted by Aidan's gaze. He hesitated for a moment, and then rode through the gateway. A little later, a message was delivered: the king requested the presence of the bishop at the evening meal. Aidan did not attend.

'But shouldn't we be moving into the guest quarters?' asked Aidan's attendants. They had always been housed there on the rare occasions they had been invited by the king, or when they had been undertaking a missionary journey in the area. Oswald had built guest huts for people of the Church on all his royal estates, and Oswy had allowed them to keep the buildings.

Aidan shook his head; he stayed where he was, leaning against a buttress supporting the church which Oswald had ordered built and Aidan himself had consecrated. Penda had burnt it down during a siege, but it had been rebuilt exactly as before.

Aidan refused all food and drink. He didn't even deign to look at a boiled fish brought from the king's kitchen the following day—and fish was his favourite dish, blessed as it had been by the Lord Jesus himself. His attendants were frightened, and sent for Finan, the Irishman left in charge of the monastery in Aidan's absence. He arrived with a larger entourage, leaving behind just the minimum number of monks necessary to observe the canonical hours.

Finan cast a quick glance at Aidan and requested an audience with the king. He did what he could to keep a rein on his temper, but when the king didn't instantly drop what he was doing, Finan turned on his heel and left.

King Oswy did, in fact, appear shortly afterwards, followed by an ashen-faced Queen Eanflæd; Oswine had been her second cousin on her father's side, grandson of King Ælle's brother, and she had been very fond of him—more fond than of her husband, with his disconcertingly curt and jarring manner.

Eanflæd was dressed in mourning and walked stiffly. She edged sideways past her husband, who remained seated on his horse, and tottered across to Aidan. She prostrated herself on the ground in front of him, and stayed there until he made the sign of the cross and carefully nudged her into an upright position. Aidan's eyes had not left Oswy throughout the entire episode, and eventually Oswy had to look away.

Oswy's face was wreathed in the horribly ugly smile behind which he hid when he didn't know what to do; a smile that had become a fixed grimace, so distorted and downright embarrassing that his subjects had to avert their eyes. He scratched his neck, flushed with red blotches; large sores had already formed, and he couldn't leave them alone—something he'd had since childhood.

Mounted on his tall horse, Oswy stuck his hand in his pocket and let a few silver coins rain down. He was happy to do so, for the love of Christ and the poor; and the poor lay awake at night, dreaming that the king passed by and threw silver down to them—even though it was more usual, far more usual, to come home from the crowd along the king's route with a flattened nose, black eye, sprained or broken arms and crushed ribs, front teeth in your pocket, and maybe not in a state to walk unaided. Eyes would be shining, however, having seen a silver piece large enough to purchase freedom—or nearly, at least.

Only slaves and vagrants thronged around the king shouting: 'Long live King Oswy!'—even though it wasn't always silver coin that flew through the air. When Oswy was in a hurry, or was in a bad temper, the soldiers' whips cracked down and cleared his path. But not even a lashing could take hope from all those who had heard about the king's silver; they would not give up on their dream of freedom.

The freemen now had to keep a sharp eye on their slaves to prevent them from voicing their usual greeting to Oswy. When her master's eyes fell darkly upon her, a young slave woman had to drop the piece of silver she had caught.

'The silver is for the Church!' he shouted, and anyone with silver in their palm had to hang their heads and place their riches in front of Aidan.

Oswy gestured Finan to approach.

'Tell Aidan we will be expecting him at the dinner table.' Upon which he turned his horse and rode back at a swift trot.

Aidan did not attend the meal. He only moved from the wall of the church once a day, when nature forced him to do so. He then resumed his place, staring at Bebbanburh. The monks observed the canonical hours and erected a canopy over their fasting leader, so he could still see out. He could not be persuaded to consume anything whatsoever. Queen Eanflæd came out during the next few days and knelt before him; for as long as he had the energy, he gave her his blessing.

News of Aidan's hunger strike spread with lightning speed, and reached Hild when she was on her way home from In-Getlingum. She immediately rode northwards, completing the journey in three days.

From a distance, she could see the crowd on the flatland in front of the fortress, and she shuddered—this throng resembled the mental images she had of Cædwalla's notorious paupers' army. The whole plain was thick with people who had set up camp and were waiting to see what King Oswy would do next. It was a mixed assembly, usually only seen at religious festivals, but when she got closer she recognized many of Deira's chief men—the paupers' army hadn't included their kind.

She forced her way through the crush of people around Aidan, all gazing at him with incredulity. All this time, it was said, he hadn't for one single instant closed his eyes, which were steadfastly focused on the royal stronghold.

Hild knelt in front of him. She was going to tell him that the Lord would undoubtedly punish Oswy's deeds, and that Aidan mustn't risk his life on that account. But when she saw the expression in his eyes, she remained silent and bowed her head. She knelt thus for a long time, until she felt the light touch of his hand. Aidan blessed her.

Some of Oswy's men mingled with the crowd, loudly and persistently telling people to stay calm and encouraging them to go home.

How could the kingdom defend itself against Penda if rebellion broke out now? Had they already forgotten it was King Oswy who had recently put Penda to flight? Things would sort themselves out, and the particulars of Oswine's death would soon be brought to light—he wasn't blameless, he had assembled an army against Oswy, he'd just been too gutless to fight once he had realized the slimness of his chances. And were they not aware of the depth of dissatisfaction in Deira? People from Deira had, in actual fact, asked Oswy to release them from Oswine's inept rule, which was far too indulgent with regard to Penda. You'd think they feasted on horsemeat together, Oswine and Penda, yes, that's what you'd think, thick as thieves they were. Deira needed a strong king, and a proper Christian king who didn't gorge on horsemeat with heathens.

Tensions rose, with others from Deira openly accusing them of speaking falsehoods. Swords were drawn, and Oswy's supporters had to flee. The track to the stronghold was cut off, so they ran westwards; one of them stumbled and the crowd pounced, kicking and hitting out. He wasn't a pretty sight once they had finished, and he couldn't be brought back to life. No one listened when Finan furiously called for them to calm down, and the mob threw the body in front of the gateway. Thus passed the fifth day of Aidan's hunger strike.

During the night, the wind got up from the east; by midday it had reached gale force. It was a warm, dry wind blowing off the sea, and it wasn't natural. As people scanned the waves nervously for a sign, the general anxiety intensified when a flock of birds appeared on the horizon, flew in low over Bebbanburh, circled once around the church and Aidan, before continuing westwards. Twelve wild geese, and everyone knew what that meant: the greatest man among them would soon follow.

An emergency Mass was held outdoors. Everyone took part, even those who still adhered to the old ways: they wanted to show they stood shoulder to shoulder with the new god's people, who were now going to lose their spiritual leader.

As the sun was setting, a figure appeared alongside the sentries atop the fortress. The scarlet cloak was unmistakable.

The crowd started chanting: 'Oswy, Oswy, Oswy!'

The figure vanished from sight. Boiled fish, two roast pigs and a whole load of freshly-baked bread were carried out. No one touched any of it. A large cask of beer was placed outside the gateway, tempting a group of slaves. A freeman from Deira hacked a hole in the bottom of the cask; it smelt good, Oswy's beer. But they would make do with the supplies being brought to them by people who supported their protest.

The dry gale dropped, but returned next day with renewed force. Aidan had now been joined by three monks from Lindisfarena, sitting alongside him. Finan assembled the others and gave them a good talking-to: he would not tolerate any more monks following the example of these three men. By the evening, two more monks had joined Aidan.

Heiu arrived from Kælcacæstir, but it was hard to tell if Aidan recognized her. She too sat with the hunger strikers. Finan had no authority over her.

On the seventh day, the chanting started up again: 'Oswy, Oswy, Oswy, come and see your servant Aidan!'

And for a brief moment the scarlet cloak appeared above the palisade. When the fortress gateway was opened, the shouting grew louder, and then silence fell—as silent as the strong wind would allow.

A long file of soldiers marched out, heavily armed, eyes staring straight ahead. There was a break in proceedings while they waited for the king to appear. Queen Eanflæd came through the gateway, deathly pale and supported by her handmaid. She was surrounded by a good forty soldiers as she staggered towards Aidan, terror in her eyes. More soldiers tramped through the gate, pulling two heavily-laden carts; they moved across to the west end of the church, where they started hammering.

'So the king's not short of a piece of silver or two then,' a young man shouted when he saw the number of soldiers.

'No wonder the taxes go up and up,' another man shouted, pointing at the soldiers' equipment—they were all carrying swords.

Oswy's troops were known for their unswerving loyalty to the king. Their allegiance was not purely due to acceptance of bribes being punishable by hanging, but more because they didn't want for anything—the king gave them everything they needed plus a little extra for their families. Only the very best men were taken into his service.

'Not a pretty sight—envy—is it now,' a soldier shouted back. He had recognized the first young man as a lad who had tried to join the army a few months earlier, but had been turned down.

'And he can't protect us from Penda anyway!' cried a woman whose husband had been killed during Penda's last campaign, and their wayside farmhouse burnt to the ground.

'So you think maybe you could!' an older officer shouted back.

'Then why do we pay taxes?' yelled another man as he was shoved aside by the soldiers' onward march.

Eanflæd's frightened eyes latched onto Hild's in the crowd, and wouldn't let her go. Hild recognized the same fear and disorientation as she had seen in the Eanflæd of their childhood, when they played hide-and-seek in the twilight and the little girl had run around calling out in distress. She had been so much smaller than the rest of them, and it had been easy to scare her—you just had to rustle and mumble a sound or two behind the bushes. They might have to bow before King Edwin's young daughter when they were in the hall, but when they played hide-and-seek they terrified her into weeing down her legs.

The memory struck Hild with shame; it was so long ago, and felt like yesterday. She didn't want to, but she couldn't stop herself: she walked across to Eanflæd and supported her by the other arm. She had never seen Eanflæd in such a state, shaking from head to foot.

'Help me,' Eanflæd whispered through lips almost as dry and cracked as Aidan's.

Hild drew herself up and looked firmly at the crowd ahead, which now moved aside without any manhandling by the soldiers. Eanflæd sank to the ground in front of Aidan. He looked like a shadow, haggard, skin of parchment, his eyes still open and directed at Bebbanburh, but unable to focus.

'Forgive my husband,' she whispered, and looked imploringly at Hild who repeated her words loudly and clearly.

'My husband repents his offence against Oswine and against the Lord and against you. He is considering the construction of a monastery at the place where Oswine suffered. He asks you to abandon your fasting and accept ten hides of land for your monastery.'

No reaction from Aidan. A group of soldiers crowded round them.

'Dear Aidan, permit me to move you to the sheltered side, so you do not suffer from the wind,' Eanflæd whispered, and Hild repeated perfunctorily. It seemed as if the hint of a smile crossed Aidan's lips. Eanflæd's handmaid nodded energetically, and Hild automatically drew back while the soldiers lifted the feather-light body. When Eanflæd moved to hold his head, Hild intervened—she couldn't entrust Aidan's beloved head to those trembling hands—and thrusting Eanflæd aside, she carefully placed her palms to support his skull.

The throng withdrew, making way for the renowned abbess who had left her pagan husband Penda and renounced her royal status in order to serve the greatest of all masters.

She was now walking at the front, with Aidan's head between her hands, and no one accosted them. Thus they carried their father around the outside of the church to the tent that Oswy's men had swiftly erected by the west end. And while they walked, Hild's and Eanflæd's eyes became enmeshed, and Eanflæd's eyes said: 'Forgive me! Forgive my deceit!'

And perhaps it was those eyes and perhaps it was the shouting of the crowd, weakly penetrating her ears as the little procession passed the south side of the church, that made Hild comprehend Eanflæd's deceit, and she could see the invisible reins around Eanflæd, which Oswy tightened and slackened from his place in the fortress, but she couldn't let go of Aidan's head, the most cherished, the most precious, and she carried it to the end. But when Aidan's corpse-like body was leaning against the buttress on the wall at the west end of the church, she turned to Eanflæd: 'No, for that I will not forgive you.'

Eanflæd sank to the ground and had to be carried back to the fortress.

This time the people did not draw back; they threw themselves in amongst Eanflæd's entourage, who had to slash their way forwards: nine dead and eighteen wounded were left behind when the gate closed. Two of the dead were Oswy's soldiers; they had brought up the rear and struck down a young woman who had tried to pull off one of their helmets. The crowd had then piled in; the two men had been ripped to pieces and were unrecognizable, to put it mildly. They were thrown to the ground by the gate, so Oswy could deal with his own.

But it was impossible to move Aidan again; his breathing had become irregular and very, very weak.

That was how Oswy, with Hild's help, managed to ward off the evil fate that Aidan's dying eyes would have invoked on Bebbanburh and on Oswy himself.

A good omen, he thought; a sign that he would rule for many years to come, perhaps Deira too. Good fortune would accompany him and his kingdom. He clapped his hands together and rubbed them energetically, as was his habit when something really went his way.

There he stood in the morning sun, high up behind the palisade, looking out to sea, the only sound that of the wind and the screeching gulls. It had been a long time since he had felt so at peace, with his god and with providence. He had yet again received a sign of their goodwill. They had also granted him a night's sleep; he hadn't rested so tranquilly since the days of rocking gently in the soft arms of his nurse. And his digestion had been working fine this morning; he had relieved himself most successfully. He smiled towards the sun, still hanging low in the sky.

He walked across to the other side and looked out over the enormous crowd, pleased they were not in a position to do anything much—except batter and churn up the grass, and that they had well and truly done. People who didn't keep horses were apparently unaware that the beasts actually lived off this pasture, and that it was unacceptable to trample all over other people's grass—least of all the king's!

He summoned the churchmen and the chief freemen, kept them waiting and then eventually granted them audience in the fortress courtyard. Some of them had to stand in the passageway behind the palisade, looking out across the lowland.

'You should have kept your people at home,' Oswy shouted, pulling the covers from the three battered men who had been thrown in front of the gate.

'Look what they have done!'

His men picked up the three corpses and held them aloft, giving the guests a good view of the atrocity. Then he gave a signal and they heard the gate being opened and Oswy's troops marching out.

The soldiers spread out systematically, quickly surrounding the crowd. A shouted order from their commander and they charged into the throng, everything now happening at great speed. Soldiers shoved and slashed on all sides, and anyone trying to escape merely trampled others to the ground and then ended up being struck down from the other side.

The freemen and churchmen were crammed into the passageway behind the palisade; a small section collapsed under the weight. There was nothing they could do except help one another scramble out of the heap of boards. As guests of the king, they had handed in their weapons. Some of the freemen elbowed their way to the gate, intent on helping their people; it was, of course, a hopeless endeavour. Finan was shouting at the top of his voice, and other churchmen dropped to the ground and prayed.

It wasn't the clamorous noise of battle that reached up to the fortress, not the ring of iron against iron and bold battle-cries—no, it was iron against soft flesh, shattering skulls, screams and shouts of outrage from the attacked, muted professional action by the attackers as thudding blows landed and penetrated. A single cry could be heard above all others: 'May you burn in Hell, Oswy!' The cry was repeated, and again, but this time cut off in the middle of 'burn'—the voice of a young woman, and they didn't know who she was.

Hild lay on the ground, praying. She heard the curse, and the words concentrated her prayers: 'My dear god, mighty Lord, take Oswy to you and then cast him down into Hell: let him burn for time without end! Lord, hear your humble handmaiden, pitch Oswy down into Hell and let him be consumed by the flames of Satan; dear Lord, hear your handmaiden's prayer . . . '

The whole attack was over quite quickly. They didn't know if Oswy had been in position throughout, protected by his personal troop, or if he had waited until now to reappear.

'I said you should have looked after your people, didn't I!' he bellowed. 'Pick them up—and go home. Idleness before the king's fortress is not to be tolerated. The peace of the Lord be with you!'

He signalled the gatekeeper to open up, and they slowly started moving off.

The soldiers had finished their job and were now lined up, impatient to get inside and wash themselves, but they had to wait until the distinguished guests had departed.

Are men insane? wondered Hild as she walked between the wounded. The screams were stomach-turning, but the quiet persistent moaning was no better.

What makes them go into battle, time after time? And talk about it as if it were a board game they always win?

'Keep away from combat,' she said to a young man while trying to staunch the bleeding from his belly. She could have saved herself the trouble, because he then breathed his last. She cut the clothing from his body, and took the fabric to use as dressings on the next one.

'The sounds are the worst,' she muttered to herself, binding one of the young man's trouser legs tightly around the stump of an arm. It had been hacked off just below the elbow, but if the girl could manage to stay motionless she ought to recover.

The hoarse screeching of the ravens! She'd never hated Woden's loathsome birds as much as she did now. A very large raven had snatched up the detached forearm and flown off with it. Hild dropped her bandaging and threw a stone at the bird. Woden's feathered friends moved like spectres in the air; that alone was enough to tell you what kind of creatures they were. Fortunately, it looked as if this one dropped its spoils when it flew over the church.

Have they not eyes? Can Penda not see, can no man see or hear—so they just go on and on until it's their turn to lie in the mud? she thought. She had never before seen a battlefield after an encounter, and she realized Penda probably hadn't either—not since he was very young, at least. It wasn't his job to collect weapons and other personal property after a battle, pick the best garments from dead bodies, scavenge rings from arms and fingers with a swift slash of the blade.

He didn't see the wounded until they had been bandaged and had stopped screaming. He saw the dead when they were nicely tidied-up rows on a fern-covered floor in the hall. He wasn't the one who had to walk the battlefield and stab the last sign of life out of anyone who couldn't stand up—or maybe just slice off a body part and appropriate their gold.

'No, not when you've got people to do it for you!' she exclaimed bitterly, and was overcome with mute, incandescent rage at Penda. She had forgotten that this panorama of mutilation was Oswy's work.

She knelt alongside the next body, and her own elation at Oswald's death suddenly flooded through her. There it was, undeniable and burning, her erstwhile passion: pride in possessing his head, calm satisfaction in seeing his pitiful severed limbs.

She bowed her neck, knowing it had been her doing; time after time she had doggedly and unceasingly spurred Penda into battle.

'No limits to your false piety,' she hissed to herself, as she looked down at a very young woman with a nasty wound across her shoulder and chest. Her left breast had been almost sliced off, and Hild had to force the lass's hands away in order to dress the gash.

Suddenly, without warning, splattering across the wound, across everything, a cascade erupted from her mouth.

'I'm sorry,' she mumbled to the young woman, drying her face with the part of her skirt that was still clean. 'I'm sorry.'

She was sweating heavily and had to turn away, but looked straight into a shattered face where large numbers of bluebottles were huddling together, mostly going for the eyes and mouth.

'Lord, have mercy upon us all,' she panted, trying to get her breathing back to normal. She could feel the young woman's hand and hear her voice faintly—'Lie down, lie down!'—but Hild thought there were enough bodies lying down at this place, and instead she looked up towards the heavens. Woden's hideous creatures were on the wing, and then everything vanished.

When she came round, she was so wet and weak that she couldn't stand up. She stayed on the ground, tears streaming. She didn't know why she had started weeping at this very moment, when tears were the last thing they needed, but she couldn't fight it.

Eventually her tears stopped; she sat up and looked across the lowland. The area had mostly been cleared up, the dead placed in straight rows by the church; the end where she was lying was the only section left in disarray.

The woman with the slashed breast whimpered quietly for water. Hild managed to stand up. The sun was high in the sky; many had already departed, others were preparing to leave. Hild went to fetch water, but as she drew close to the well she forgot everything and rushed across to Aidan. He was still alive, if you could call that living: he wasn't dead.

Heiu was no longer sitting at his side. When the massacre started, she had stood up, walked among the soldiers, talked to them. Oddly enough, no one had touched her, nor had they heard her, they had their orders.

Just before the attack, it was said, they had been dosed up with a powerful-smelling drink meant to make them invincible. They had been wilder than usual, their gaze more disengaged.

'A magic potion, I suppose,' said Heiu, and went with Hild to take care of the remaining casualties.

'That breast won't grow back on,' she said to the young woman, who screamed when Heiu, quick as lightning, sliced it right off and dressed the gash.

'You would have died from flying venom in the wound,' she consoled the woman, 'and you can easily suckle with the other one. If your husband won't have you as you are now, you can come to my monastery in Kælcacæstir.'

'I haven't got a husband,' the woman wept quietly, 'and I haven't been baptized.'

'Come if you want,' said Heiu, stroking her hair. They carried the woman to a tent outside the church.

By evensong, nearly everyone had left, taking their injured with them. The dead had been buried in the graveyard by the church. Three of the hunger-striking monks were dead; few were as accustomed to fasting as Aidan.

Hild spent the night prostrate in prayer before Aidan. She prayed for the dead, for Aidan's soul and asked forgiveness for the sin she had committed against him. Because of her intervention, he would now be dying in vain, and many others along with him. She had been a tool in Oswy's hands, and had rendered Aidan's protest meaningless. She could not be granted forgiveness.

All that was left for her was to carry on Aidan's work, as long as her strength would allow. With all her might, she must work to ensure his life and his death would *not* have been in vain.

When the sun appeared, she felt an unfamiliar warmth overflowing within her. She accepted it and let it permeate her stiff body, softening her neck and limbs, and she felt her heart beating calmly again. She stood up, and saw that Aidan had left this world.

'Not my will, but your will,' she murmured to the heavens.

Aidan's life and work was love. Now she understood that the Lord had not wanted to see his servant's final moment sullied by revenge and evil wishes—regardless of how justified they might be. It was the Lord's job to punish Oswy; he would do so, and humans should not intervene.

She sat next to Aidan and was filled with serene calmness. Later, once his people had seen it was over, she helped prepare his body.

Aidan was buried on Lindisfarena. The folk from the monastery carried him home; they wouldn't let him be transported on a cart when during his lifetime he had always walked. All along the route, people flocked to the procession and were allowed to carry their beloved father a short distance. Thus he came home, after a three-day journey.

# YOUNG WILFRID

*– Queen Eanflæd's feast –*

At the end of the holy month, Hild received an invitation from Queen Eanflæd. Her presence was requested at two ceremonies: the anniversary of the death of Bishop Paulinus, the man who had brought the faith to the kingdom, and then, two days later, that of Northumbria's first Christian king, Eanflæd's father Edwin, now dead these eighteen years having fallen against the pagan Penda, whose destructive havoc had yet to be stopped. Paulinus, who had also had to flee Penda, had left this world seven years ago, at a time when he had been bishop of Hrofesceaster in Kent. Furthermore, the queen had an important message to pass on, now, just before the selection of a king in Eoforwik.

This little lecture accompanied an invitation to spend a few days of commemoration at Queen Eanflæd's estate at Cetreht. There was also going to be a big sale of slaves—only quality monastery slaves—and Eanflæd's offer of adding a tenth to the price of the slaves, for the peace of her soul, was hard to resist. The price of slaves had shot up after the events at Bebbanburh, and in Heruteu they were in serious need of funds.

Hild didn't really have time for the trip; she was busy with the many people who had once sought counsel from Aidan and now turned to her. Aidan's successor, Bishop Finan, lacked Hild's level-headed sympathy for the strange ups and downs of existence; he imposed long submersions in cold water, excessive fasting and solitary periods on hilltops, which provided plenty of time for reflection upon one's current status in relation to Heaven.

Hild followed Aidan's system, imposing approximately half as tough a punishment as Finan. Remission of sins could only, of course, be granted by the men who had taken holy orders, but they were guided by their lenient mother; no one was superior to the abbess.

'The Lord does not gauge us by our physical endurance,' she said. But having broken allegiance to your Lord's command, you had to pay—symbolically. The dead could not be brought back to life.

No penance was great enough to compensate for what she had caused by insisting on revenge for Eadfrid's death. Gefmund and Bothelm, Oswald and all those who had died in the battles—how could reparation be made for them, other than by doing good for those still living? She must follow in Aidan's footsteps, work to do away with feuds and fighting, and turn the hearts of men and women to the Lord God. Come the day when everyone served him, there would be nothing left to fight about; everyone would realize that no family is an island, and that in the Lord we are all sisters and brothers, united in one family—humankind—above everything else, above trivialities such as the colour of your hair and your favourite foods.

Hild was looking forward to this very day, and it gave her the strength to get through the difficult period after Aidan's death. Unfortunately, she bore an intense grudge against Queen Eanflæd, and the Lord had yet to hear her supplications about removing this grudge. For Hild to forgive her, Eanflæd would have to give the Lord a large plot of land. But queens, too, needed forgiveness, as Hild knew, and so she accepted Eanflæd's invitation.

She left Begu in charge and reached Cetreht in good time. The weather was dry, and the roads were more passable than usual for the time of year. The sun glimmered on the autumn leaves still clinging to the branches or fluttering through the air to gather in heaps alongside the tracks. The queen had invited all Deira's supporters to the festivities, including those who had taken part in the protest at Bebbanburh, and monastics from both Bernicia and Deira. Many had turned up, and would then ride directly from Cetreht to the selection of the king in Eoforwik.

The Mass for Paulinus' soul was celebrated by Eanflæd's priest Romanus, brought with her from Kent. He had received some of his training from Paulinus, and was therefore qualified to talk about the great man.

Romanus asked them to reflect upon the misfortune into which the realm might well have fallen had his queen's mother—the most deserving and illustrious Queen Tata, in the words of the Pope himself, who had four years since gone to the Lord as abbess of the monastery she had founded in Liminiae—not brought Paulinus to this northern region! And had her renowned father not turned to the true faith! The realm of Northumbria would then have remained in the depths of perdition; and ignorance—yes, he would put it bluntly: the abomination controlling Penda's realm—would still dwell among their people.

Hild shuddered; it was not the first time she had heard these views. And every time she had to stop herself from leaping up and informing them that everything in Mercia might not be as it should, but there was nonetheless better order there than here, where no one looked after their family anymore and where the king, who called himself a Christian, had murdered his own wife's cousin in order to steal his realm.

She stayed put in her place, cheeks burning, well aware that no one would have believed her anyway. Romanus' paean to their Christian kingdom was far easier to swallow. She thought of Freawaru's oft-expressed saying: 'What do you need with the truth, when you can have your back rubbed with a falsehood?'

Romanus ended with a vivid account of how Paulinus had rescued Queen Tata and the then eight-year-old Eanflæd from Cædwalla and brutal King Penda. Nor did he refrain from mentioning that Eanflæd was the first person in Deira to receive the gift of baptism. Thus he made it seem obvious that the natural order of the realm would be re-established if Eanflæd's husband was selected king. Not a word about Oswine.

At the evening meal in the hall, Eanflæd stood up and announced that her husband had decided to give land measuring one hide for a monastery he would have built at In-Getlingum, where prayers would be said for his soul and for that of his illustrious predecessor, Oswine.

Eanflæd remained on her feet longer than necessary and received her applause with a smile. The assembly clapped politely, while sending meaningful looks across the tables. Would the Lord be satisfied with one hide of land from someone who had murdered a king and was now trying to purloin his realm? Not even the surviving relatives of a little freeman would go along with that kind of mollification.

Hild was vexed that she had come at all. If Eanflæd *did* feel remorse, her behaviour was making it hard to tell. The fancy guests were only there to justify her and Oswy's invasion of Deira. Many of the nobles looked as if they were of the same opinion.

'Who is that young man?' Hild eventually asked Eanflæd, at whose left side she had been seated. Hild hadn't been able to take her eyes off him ever since they had gone in to supper. He had been standing in the file of young men called upon to serve at table and, like the others, he had bowed in deference when the guests entered. There was something about him that she recognized: the almost too-upright posture, the light steps on slightly outward-turning feet, the fleeting smile, quick to come and quick to go. She racked her brains; perhaps she had met him in a dream.

'He's Wilfrid, Berhtfrid's son,' Eanflæd replied. 'He has decided to serve the Lord. He wants to go to Rome, for the redemption of his soul.'

Hild called him over.

'How old are you, my son?'

'Sixteen years, mother,' he replied in the most polite fashion. His voice caused her to tremble.

'It is said you will seek redemption at the tombs of the apostles.'

Wilfrid gave a little bow.

'Yes, mother, if the Lord will allow.'

'And can you not find your redemption here?'

'I have served the Lord for two years on Lindisfarena, mother, but the Lord created a world larger than that small tidal island.'

A tentative smile flared up and then instantly vanished.

'The Lord be with you, my son,' said Hild, 'and be quite certain of my assistance.'

Wilfrid was down on his knees and then back on his feet in a flash. All his movements had a grace and swiftness that made him shine in comparison with the other young men. Hundfrid and Wilbrord would have been seventeen years old now; in three days, eighteen years would have passed since they entered the world.

'Is he a legitimate son of Berhtfrid?' asked Hild.

'Legitimate and only son of Berhtfrid and his first wife,' answered Eanflæd. 'And isn't it incredible, the way he resembles my brother Eadfrid?'

Eanflæd didn't wait for an answer, but continued: 'When he came here and asked to enter my service, it was as if my own brother had returned. Yes, your first husband, wasn't he. Even though I was but a child when I last saw him. It was as if my brother came back to me from the dead.'

'I can't see any resemblance at all,' said Hild. 'But he's certainly a fine-looking young man. And if he gets help to travel to Rome, then something good will undoubtedly come of him.'

'I think I'll send him to Kent, so the king can find him a suitable companion. He's not going back to Finan, that's for sure—if you knew the kinds of penance that mad Irishman has imposed on the young people! He will not be allowed to ruin young Wilfrid, I can tell you.'

Eanflæd drew herself up and looked affectionately across at this Wilfrid. She was twenty-six years old now; her husband was approaching forty.

Hild kept her eyes on the young lad. She noticed that he neither ate nor drank, and she felt concern for his health. She called him over again.

'You eat nothing, my son?'

'I am fasting for our crucified Lord, mother,' he replied, his eyes piercing her as if they could count each and every chunk of pork she had devoured; she had helped herself plentifully, both of the one dish and the other.

'Listen,' she said. 'Our Lord has not granted you so pleasing and powerful a body for you to ruin it. A young man like yourself must eat properly, otherwise you won't have many years in which to serve the Lord.'

Wilfrid blushed and looked down. The blue tunic and red trousers suited him.

'Bishop Finan has ordered that I respect a month of fasting: three pieces of bread and a mug of milk each day. And I, of course, adhere to the bishop's order.'

She could now see the hollowness of his cheeks, and she felt truly upset. A fast on that scale was only for full-grown adults who didn't do physical work. Aidan would never have allowed this; but she couldn't sow seeds of doubt about judgements made by a bishop.

'And what might you have done to earn so harsh a penance?'

'I am of the opinion, mother, and it is one to which you might take exception,' and he bowed to her as if to temper the severity of what he was about to say, 'that most people in this country do not celebrate the death and resurrection of our Lord Jesus Christ at the correct time. In this matter, I share our highly esteemed and most gracious queen's opinion, which is also shared by the whole of Christendom, with the exception of the Irish and the Picts and the other Britons who have always been known for their heretical views. In my opinion, dear mother, we should all accede to the proper manner in which to calculate the true time for the Easter festival, so we are in harmony with our brothers and sisters in the whole of Christendom.'

'You speak well for your cause,' said Hild. 'Who has instructed you in the manner of calculating Easter?'

'I have learnt from our great father Aidan,' said Wilfrid, with a sudden change of voice, now sorrowful, 'and while he lived, I did not find it appropriate to propose anything that contradicted so great a man. But now I have listened to a monk from Lindisfarena by the name of Ronan. He has studied in Gaul and prayed at the apostles' tombs, and I have found nothing that could make a case refuting his arguments or his integrity.'

'Is this what compels you to Rome?'

'I wish to learn the true path,' Wilfrid replied.

'Commendable. But once you have learnt what there is to learn in Gaul and Rome, then do not forget to return to this place. For, as you know, our problem here is that far too few people know the word of Jesus and celebrate his resurrection *at all*, never mind on which day they do so. We need young people who can set to work where Aidan left off, and we have a huge task ahead of us.'

'I know,' said Wilfrid, with a slight bow, 'and my only purpose is humbly to serve the Lord and follow the true path. But I will not serve the Devil.'

'Now now,' said Hild, 'surely you are not implying that the Lord's people are servants of the Devil because we follow the manner of calculating Easter that we learnt from our fathers?'

'Of course not,' Wilfrid replied blushing. 'The old folk have acted in good faith and followed the custom of their fathers, as is befitting. But when the Lord sends us a more correct manner of calculation, then we ought to adopt it and join with the rest of Christendom. For division between the people of the Lord is the work of the Devil.'

He now had a gleam in his eye and an added emphasis in his voice, displaying the youthful zeal firing up his enthusiasm for the cause. It was obvious he would go to great lengths to put it into effect. He still needed a broader wealth of experience; a spot of familiarity with the hustle and bustle of life had never hurt a zealous young man.

'But as matters stand in Northumbria today,' said Hild, 'turning the date of Easter into a problem does nothing but stir up discord. The crucial matter is that we all agree on delivering the word of the Lord to the heathens. Is that not true?'

'Of course, mother,' Wilfrid replied, 'provided we are sure it is the true word we deliver. If we say now the one thing and now the other, then we will deliver confusion into frail hearts, and that is why the unity of the Church is so crucial to the dissemination of our word.'

'All right,' said Hild, 'I wish you a safe and successful journey, and I look forward to welcoming you in Heruteu upon your return.'

Wilfrid swiftly knelt and received her blessing.

'Thank you, mother,' he said, and walked back to his table at the far end of the hall.

'A bright young man,' Hild commented to Queen Eanflæd. 'In need of a little experience, but then he'll no doubt prove useful to us.'

'Indeed,' Eanflæd beamed. 'None of the young men I have had in my service have been in possession of such gentle manners and such eloquence. I am really expecting great things of him. Eadfrid would also have gone far, had the Lord decreed differently. Such eyes, he had!'

'He did,' said Hild, suddenly feeling greatly relieved. Those eyes had pursued her all the way to Oswald's death—at which point they had finally disappeared completely.

'The Lord gave, the Lord took away,' she said.

'Praise be the name of the Lord!' exclaimed Eanflæd.

'Praise be the name of the Lord,' said Hild, more sincerely than ever.

Oswy called in at Cetreht. His wife's guests felt a little uneasy about the size of the army he had brought along; no one said anything, but anxiety and anger shimmered in the eyes watching the royal couple during the Mass for King Edwin's soul. The queen was wearing her magnificent silver-interlaced headdress, which no one dared duplicate; the king had chosen to wear the Pope's gift to King Edwin, the wonderfully fine-spun cloak from Ancyra, one of the precious objects saved by Paulinus, and now in possession of the queen.

They were a beautifully turned-out couple. Husband and wife alike had given thanks to the Lord for the accident that had befallen Oswy's first wife shortly after his selection in Bernicia, and which had made this extremely prudent marriage possible: bringing Eanflæd back to the realm she had always considered her property; legalizing Oswy's long-standing ambition to take control of Deira and be just as powerful as his brother Oswald—an obstacle so kindly removed from his path by Penda.

Oswy could have hugged Penda and kissed his feet for getting rid of Oswald—although he didn't, of course, let on. Anyway, gratitude soon gave way to the natural enmity between the two neighbouring kingdoms; over the years, they had enthusiastically accumulated quite a list of issues needing retribution, however often they might have reached a settlement and exchanged hostages.

For the time being, peace had been woven by the engagement of Oswy's daughter to Peada, the eldest of Penda's sons—thanks, he thought, to the interference of meddlesome Abbess Hildeburh. Seven high-ranking hostages had been exchanged, to prevent the kings from regretting this union. The wedding—as she had sorted out after Penda's last campaign— would take place in two years' time. At least two whole years of peace on that front, always supposing nothing came along, which was always a possibility. Should that be the case, well, the enterprising abbess would weave together a new peace; fortunately Penda had many children.

Oswy was so absorbed in weighing up tactics that his queen had to tug at his cloak to make him sit down after the prayer. Then came Romanus' eulogy to King Edwin, which, as expected, concluded in an almost direct appeal to elect Oswy as Deira's king.

This Romanus was more eager to serve King Oswy's lust for power than to serve King Jesus, thought Hild, and had to acknowledge that no one can serve two masters. But she kept her thoughts to herself, also at the meal after Mass; she had long since realized that if her work was to succeed she would have to circumvent Oswy's authority, while outwardly showing him respect. A direct confrontation would leave her without a chance—either to continue Aidan's work or to find her sons.

Next day, Hild made preparations to travel. Her spirits were low, as always on this day, which tore open the wound of sorrow at the loss of her twins, the babies to whom she had given birth eighteen years ago.

Young Wilfrid had offered his services; he proved almost as competent and skilful as he was eloquent. It was a pleasure to hear him speak: well-formed and well-thought-out sentences issued smoothly from his shapely mouth. To play for a little more time, Hild asked him to find a pair of shoes she hadn't brought with her—just to enjoy his presence and see how he would tackle the task.

When he assumed a particular thoughtful air, standing on one leg in the middle of the room, her hearty laughter brought tears to her eyes. He couldn't really see what was funny, but laughed along politely anyway.

'Never mind about the shoes,' Hild said with a smile, 'just forget them.'

Wilfrid bowed courteously and replied that he would never forget either her shoes or her. Whereupon she laughed even louder. He was an utterly enchanting young man, almost too good-looking for the monastic life; but nothing is too good for the Lord, she told herself.

'I expect a detailed report from Gaul and Rome,' she said when they parted. She had accepted his offer to accompany her part of the way. 'In a few years, once the monastery has greater resources and the kingdom is in a better state, I shall travel down there myself. And then I'll need an accomplished companion.'

'I shall always be at your service,' said Wilfrid, and bowed to her, which was an impressive manoeuvre on horseback. 'Should the Lord allow.'

Hild was in a far better mood when she and her entourage rode off; with young people like him at work, the kingdom had bright prospects.

King Oswy offered the guests a retinue of his own men to accompany them to Eoforwik, a gesture they could hardly decline. This would reduce the danger of attack, as Oswy pointed out. Oswy's arrival in the town thus resembled an out-and-out triumphal procession; not only his army, but also the large contingent of freemen totally took the shine off his rival candidate, Ædelwald.

Outrage over the murder of King Oswine might have been forgotten in the face of Oswy's forces—but Aidan's death could not be overlooked. The country had no chance of good fortune under a king who had caused the death of a holy man. No chance whatsoever, was the general—and oft-repeated—opinion.

The choice fell upon Ædelwald, an exceptionally fine-looking young man, just turned fifteen. He was the only son of King Oswald and Queen Cyneburh from the realm of the West Saxons, where he had been raised in the home of his maternal uncle King Cenwalh, with Penda's approval, Penda's wife Cynewise being his maternal aunt.

Ædelwald was on such good terms with Penda that it wouldn't be an exaggeration to call him Penda's man, which was seen as an added advantage. Deira had always had something of a tarnished reputation; they would rather negotiate their path to prosperity than win it in open battle. They were even prepared to live in peace with Penda, as long as they had well-stocked storehouses. They didn't want to be drawn into Oswy's ambitions regarding Mercia, because they didn't think he stood a chance. Heathen or not, Penda's good fortune in war had never failed him so far—wherever he got it from.

After the selection, Oswy's only backup was the army he'd brought along; he cursed himself for not bringing the freemen too. He wouldn't even be able to launch a successful surprise attack, and his spies were telling him that Penda was at the border and, if necessary, would instantly come to Ædelwald's rescue. So Oswy left Eoforwik in greater haste than was actually well-mannered. He bitterly regretted his promise to grant the Lord one hide of land at In-Getlingum—his gesture had been of no benefit whatsoever.

It pained him even more to recall how grossly he had been deceived by his sister-in-law Cyneburh. That last evening in the hall, she'd been behaving oddly, smiling strangely into the air, almost as if she were gloating. And that was when he had decided to strike.

But when the site of the fire had been inspected next day, only Cyneburh, her daughters, and the infant child could be identified with certainty; the boy they found in the ashes had a club foot and was very thin. It was generally accepted that flames had the power to make really quite substantial changes to someone's appearance, and Oswy hadn't suspected anything until his spies in Tamoworthig reported that Cyneburh's son had been welcomed there, along with a troupe of travelling entertainers—and then he saw what a trick his sister-in-law had played on him.

She'd been sly, that Cyneburh, had realized the impossibility of escape and had stayed with the girls so no one had any misgivings. How very ingenious! Not in his wildest dreams had he imagined she would send her son away and stay where she was; he couldn't imagine it because he would never have done so himself, not for any member of his family.

Not even the fire had been of any use, he thought bitterly, and decided he would do penance. Yes, he would talk with Eanflæd's priest; perhaps Romanus would say the hide of land at In-Getlingum was sufficient. Romanus had an understanding for what was in the interest of the kingdom; the same could not be said of Oswy's own Church folk.

# 'AWAKE, AWAKE, VALIANT WARRIORS . . .'

*– weaving peace –*

Hild's efforts for peace were going well, and the future looked brighter than ever. More and more people came to her for mediation when any kind of dialogue had come to a standstill, and in many instances it proved possible to avert bloodshed.

Of her own accord, she negotiated marriage contracts between the kings' children—a son and a daughter each way—with agreements on dowry, morning gift and accompanying hostages.

She also drew up a document demarcating the boundaries between kingdoms, and secured the signatures of Penda and King Oswy, with Bishop Finan and herself as witnesses.

The negotiations required a great deal of tact and subtlety. If she came straight out with her suspicions that Oswy had no interest in peace, the entire endeavour would collapse. It took a long time for everything to fall into place; Oswy was forever coming up with objections, but two years after Aidan's death, the first wedding could at long last take place.

Penda's eldest princely son, Peada, was to marry Oswy's seventeen-year-old daughter, Ahlflæd. The wedding was held in Bernicia on the day after Peada's baptism, and Hild acted as witness at both ceremonies.

Peada's joy at finally serving the true god did her good. She had always had a somewhat unsettling relationship with that boy; he had been born on the same day as her twins, and his rude health and happiness had often caused her to think: why couldn't my sons have a life like this? And then all she could do was to break out in a hymn of thanksgiving, as Aidan had taught her—and which was becoming increasingly effective.

Not long afterwards, Oswy's son from his first marriage, nineteen-year-old Alchfred, was to marry Penda's daughter, Eadburh. The wedding would be held in Mercia, and Hild could make do with sending greetings. Exchange of hostages had also been agreed: Oswy's seven-year-old son Egfred would be raised at the home of Penda and Cynewise, and Eadburh would be escorted to Bernicia by her thirteen-year-old half-brother, Hild's son Ædelræd.

She had worked hard to secure this agreement, because if both kings had a son involved then surely they would be able to behave.

Hild was initially furious when she heard a report of the wedding. This was not the agreement she had negotiated, and she thought Cynewise ought to have prevented such an outcome: instead of Eadburh, it had been Cynewise's daughter Cyneburh, just turned ten years of age, who had been married off to Alchfred.

Eadburh had vanished, and so as not to break the agreement, Penda had taken this way out—which was at least, Hild reasoned, better than war, and she comforted herself with Alchfred's promise to leave the girl alone until her body was ready for a man.

Hild had never worried about her son Ædelræd; he'd always been accompanied by such good fortune that she couldn't imagine anything bad befalling him. Wulfhere was a different matter; she would never entrust him to Oswy, and she had written to him saying: 'Do not marry any of Oswy's daughters. Find a wife in the south. Ask Merewald!'

Merewald had at long last secured his father's permission to be baptized and get married, and he already had two healthy daughters with his wife from Kent. There was nothing wrong with the girls' legs, but Hild had heard that Merewald could no longer walk and now had to be carried around his herb garden in a chair.

Thinking about Merewald warmed Hild's heart. She pictured him bent over the apple blossoms, spotted and striped by shadows from the gnarled branches, totally absorbed in counting filaments. The number of filaments in the apple blossoms varied, as she had checked and corroborated many a time since he had told her about them. Anemones had their problems too; they might have six, seven or eight petals, but she had yet to find out how many seed leaves.

If only all men were like Merewald! she sighed to herself, then all these peace weavings wouldn't have been necessary.

Penda had faced up to the changes afoot and was not unhappy about the peace agreement; nor had he ever had any objections to his former wife's proposals. He simply wished he could have seen her and talked with her and touched her, instead of all these tiresome letters back and forth. Sometimes he got the scribe to add a more personal greeting, but the reply letter would always just be a list of dowry items and such matters.

He would have liked Hildeburh to attend Eadburh's wedding, but had to make do with her message of greetings. He was, at least, happy everything had fallen into place—until the wedding procession with singing and drums and pipes arrived to fetch Eadburh and she wasn't there.

A tearful wetnurse reported that Eadburh and Tibba had fled the previous evening, determined to seek learning in the service of the Lord, as they had been saying all along.

They had undoubtedly already reached the monastery in East Anglia; it would be a very serious matter to get them out again by force.

Penda was ashen-faced. He had thought the learning business was the girls' attempt to imitate Hild, youthful fancies that would pass of their own accord. He had confidently arranged the marriage and closed his ears to their protests.

Oswy wouldn't ignore such dishonour cast upon his son, but Penda really didn't want a war right now so he clutched the nearest straw and didn't think it through until afterwards. He rushed out to find Cyneburh; she was sitting on a rock in the sun, dressing her doll to go to Eadburh's wedding.

He picked a blue cornflower, which he gave to her with a promise that she would have a white horse if she would take Eadburh's place. Cyneburh looked up at him, a smile on her face, and screwed her eyes together in the sun. She'd always wanted a white horse, and she was utterly loyal to her father.

Alchfred, the bridegroom, was asked if he would be willing to accept this change of bride; he looked at the girl and said yes. And so they were wed.

Thus the matter was resolved as agreed, with a slight modification. Penda was relieved when he was able to send a message to Hild telling her everything was now fine.

Alchfred thought Cyneburh looked like his little sister, who had died at the age of six. Her hair, at least, was fairly similar, and her smile, so he didn't mind the substitution. He had been very fond of his sister.

Nor did he mind leaving Cyneburh in her own bed. He had a slave woman back home, so he too saw this marriage as his duty to realm and kin—and to his father, who was simply the mightiest of men. He didn't even dare talk to him, and stumbled over his words when he was asked a question, although that didn't happen very often.

But his father treated him like a man, and had given him his first woman on his fifteenth nameday. When he reached his eighteenth nameday, he was given a new one: a raven-haired beauty with green eyes and skin like mother-of-pearl, of royal lineage, taken during a campaign in the west. His father had broken her in himself, as he put it, back when she was fourteen years old. She was a good one, with her fiery Brittonic blood.

Alchfred had nothing against the Britons—not their women, anyway—and they often proved to be good work slaves; his father said so, too. His woman was devoted to him; she had no family left, and owed him everything.

The messenger from East Anglia brought a letter from Hild's niece Ædelthryd. She was nineteen years old now and was doing well with her morning gift, an extensive area around Elge. She had been married at sixteen, but for some reason—undoubtedly Tondberht's drunkenness, thought Hild—the marriage had never been consummated. Ædelthryd regularly wrote to her mother's sister, for whom she had unconditional admiration—rather too much, actually, in Hild's opinion—but on this point the letters were somewhat hazy. On other points, too, the tone was vague, and she wrote so often about her mother the nun in the kingdom of Heaven that Hild still pictured her as the translucent, wistful child she had once been.

As expected, by giving him Ædelthryd, his foster-daughter, to wed, King Anna had made an ally of Tondberht, chief of the Southern Girvij. The two men had then tried to break free from Penda, withholding payment of their taxes. When they repeated the offence, Penda took action; both Anna and Tondberht had fallen. This had happened a year earlier, a good three years after Aidan's death.

Hild hoped the victory hadn't rekindled Penda's appetite for battle. Neither the loss of Anna nor of Tondberht was, as such, any great misfortune. She didn't share Begu's and Freawaru's view that it was a setback for freedom. Pompous self-importance and war were as bad as one another, and Anna's brother Ædelhere was unquestionably a better king. Hild knew him from the time she had spent down south; he would never try to mislead Penda.

Now Ædelthryd was free, and with that morning gift she could enter into an advantageous marriage, or she could enter the service of the Lord—unless all her devoutness was just a whim, as Hild hoped. She had written to Ædelthryd telling her that the Lord took nothing but delight in the corporeal love between humans, and he had granted them the urge to union in order to give them a foretaste of the heavenly union, and so the lineage should not perish. The Lord commanded us to honour our father and mother, and this was best achieved by continuing the family line.

Hild didn't write that she'd had more than enough trouble with young women wanting to renounce the world for the sake of Christ. What, when it came to it, had they actually renounced? Nothing other than thin air and dreams and vague impressions. How could someone like that help people in need?

The few young women she had taken on as novices were far too absorbed in their own salvation and the huge sacrifices they had made by giving the Lord their maidenhood. They had no know-how whatsoever and couldn't apply themselves to work like the adult women could. They were of no use to the monastery, and she had already turned away three: two because they weren't fit for anything, and one because she attracted spectres to the house.

She didn't write all this to her devoted niece, but she did counsel her to look around for a new husband: not as old as Tondberht, and not such a drunkard. And then when the time came—men often had a short life—she could re-consider the matter, and Hild would be happy to help.

Evenings at Heruteu were spent with needlework and a good story. The women sat in the sewing room and the men in their dining hall, where they whittled wood. Always with a glowing fire in the hearth, and taking it in turns to sit closest. The wind was cold, with so much sea all around.

The stories usually flowed quite naturally, otherwise the company took it in turns. Most had experienced ups and downs in their lives, and their tales were received with the same enthusiasm as the bardic poems and songs and the familiar yarns about werewolves and elves. Ill-starred lovers, lost children and tragic deaths were popular subjects with the women, but they were also happy to hear about witches and all manner of magical beings, will-o'-the-wisps and water sprites, and about the dead who visited their slayers on shuffling feet and with rasping voices. The men mostly liked to tell about conquests and expeditions, especially from olden times under the really powerful kings. The monks' eyes lit up to descriptions of shiny silver helmets and glossy weapons. Those were the days—before they sailed across the sea, before the word of the Lord had reached their ears.

At first, Hild had found it necessary to point out that elves and all manner of sprites had no power whatsoever over those who served the Lord; not so much to spare them from having bad dreams as to ensure they didn't take to incantations and sorcery. The unambiguous light of the Lord had to prevail in the monastery.

She had gradually instilled in her folk an understanding of the sprites' impotence when faced with Christ—all it took was an Our Father and a holy cross. Now she only had to teach this message when new people arrived, and it proved more than necessary. Time and again she was shocked by the tightness of the grip superstition had on otherwise enlightened souls. There are more things in the heavens and the earth, they would say, with an expression meant to justify their actions—usually in explanation of why they insisted on riding across a ford sitting backwards on the horse, with fingers crossed, or some other ploy designed to prevent misfortune striking.

Hild accepted crossed fingers, for that was the sign of the cross and could but bring good fortune, but she wouldn't tolerate old incantations against water sprites. She kept an eye on those who were a little unsteady on their legs, and made it her practice to stop the whole retinue so they could pray an Our Father together before walking past a dangerous spot. This was the best remedy for superstition, and she had already noted from the lip movements of the weak ones that they were now using an Our Father as protection.

'Yes,' she usually said, 'and Jesus is in the heavens and the earth too, keeping an eye on his servants. Don't forget that!'

Our Father, confession of the faith and the sign of the cross: mighty weapons that could keep evil at bay. One novice, however, had been possessed to an excessive extent, and Hild had been obliged to send her away. The spirits were attracted with such force that the woman couldn't be totally blameless, and she had started infecting the others. Once her empty cell had been cleansed with holy water and a whole night of the priest's prayers, the spirits had indeed gone away. No incidents had since been reported.

Consequently, Hild didn't ban stories about magical creatures, because she knew they were of no threat to her people, enlightened as they were. Personally, she preferred the bardic poems and songs: not any particular one, she liked them all.

Now she was sitting by the fire, looking forward to Begu's performance. Begu had an inexhaustible supply of old songs, and she usually gave them a new slant or a little addition. This evening she would sing about the battle at Finn's stronghold: an awe-inspiring story, from the days before they set forth across the sea, about feuds, revenge, fidelity, and deceit, plus the usual unfortunate woman stuck in a tight spot between family and husband.

*Hnæf, replied     the young and powerful king:*
*—You see not the dawn     nor the fire-spewing dragon*
*you see not the gable     of the king's hall in flames.*
*No, here strife begins     black ravens screech*
*grey-coated wolves bark     spears shall ring out*
*shields meet swords     yet the moon shines*
*hidden behind clouds     bitter the pain*
*forsaken by fortune     abandoned to woe . . .*

Begu stopped; the stick she had been using to beat time came to rest on the floor in front of her, and she jiggled the tip back and forth.

'*Awake, awake, valiant warriors,*' Hild whispered the next line. She repeated the words a little louder, but Begu remained deep in her thoughts, jiggling her song-stick.

'Yes, yes,' she eventually replied. '*Awake, awake, valiant warriors* . . . And that's what struck me: if only they would stay slumbering where they are—so we could be spared all this strife.'

She cast the stick aside and sat at the table with her embroidery.

'And then it was suddenly too difficult to sing the words.'

Everyone started talking at once: the merits of the song and its weak points; some preferred a slightly different version, which Begu never used, and there was general dissatisfaction that she had robbed them of the thrilling intoxication so welcome in their not particularly varied daily routine.

Begu looked tired, now divested of the grandeur that took hold of her when performing a song, and which made Hild think about Penda's story of the bard called Taliesin: when in full voice, he grew taller and taller, right up to the ceiling joists of Maelgwn Gwynedd's hall. Begu also filled the whole room when she sang, not that their sewing room was like the hall in Aberffraw, but still.

'Yes!' exclaimed Freawaru, standing up. 'Actually, they're just a fetid throat-fart, those old songs.'

'How can you say that?' hissed Waldburh. Besides loving every single verse, she was yet again offended by Freawaru's coarseness. The same content, as she had often pointed out, could be expressed in a seemly manner; but even though her reprimands had by now become even coarser than Freawaru's remarks, they just bounced off the woman. To stop her tongue running away with her, Waldburh embroidered vigorously onwards, until she pricked herself painfully on the needle.

'In what respect do you think them flawed?' Hild asked.

'War and battle and blood—that's all they're ever about!' said Freawaru. 'And shining helmets and garnet-studded swords and pillaged loot and kiss my arse! We ought to stop singing them.'

Needlework dropped onto laps; everyone looked in silent astonishment at Freawaru, who was staring obliquely up at the straw on the roof, as was her habit when taken by an idea.

'That's what struck me, too,' said Begu. 'They're really pure . . . throat-fart, I think.'

'They're just tales from the old days,' Waldburh protested. 'No more than that—and well told.'

'Won't you please continue?' invited Hild.

'I can't remember the words,' said Begu. 'They've vanished!'

Next evening, Sæthryd told her story.

She was the daughter of a chieftain who had fallen in battle against a neighbouring chieftain. The two families had always been in conflict with one another, often provoked by a dispute about whose pigs should be allowed in the forest between their lands, and every autumn they lost a few slaves up there, which meant exacting a fine or taking revenge. Her father had been slain during a campaign of revenge, and her youngest brother had been taken captive. Through the mediation of a principal elder, an agreement was reached with the aim of a lasting solution: she was to marry the eldest son on the neighbouring farm, and the disputed forest would go to her as dowry and morning gift.

She was fourteen years old, had only ever heard bad things about him, but felt honoured by the role intended for her, and said yes. Six months of preparation; she didn't arrive in her new home empty-handed: chests full of woven fabrics, linen, household utensils, plus silver, three fine horses and five slaves, and clothing more splendid than anything her mother had ever worn. As part of the agreement, her future husband's youngest brother would be sent to work for her mother; and thus no one would feel the urge to fan the flames of conflict between the two families.

Four sons and two daughters she had borne by the time the feud flared up again. She prayed to the Lord while the men fought, but didn't know whose victory she was praying for. Her fourteen-year-old son was slain by her brother, after which her husband could think of nothing but revenge. When he finally rode out to seek vengeance for his son, she felt a deep sense of satisfaction—until they carried her husband back.

She had to move out into a little hut, and her husband's brother and wife moved into the main house. Her children became poorly. When she was told that her dead husband and son had been avenged—her brother-in-law having slain her brother—she started suffering attacks of dizziness and breathlessness. At Eastertime, she rode to the nearest monastery hoping a blessing might perhaps improve the state of her health. When she returned home, the farm buildings had burnt down and all the cattle had been stolen. Her children had died in the fire, along with her brother-in-law and sister-in-law and their workers.

Sæthryd had then ridden back to the monastery and asked to be admitted. Her dowry to the Lord was the forest she had received upon marriage—not much, but enough, the abbess had said.

'And that's why I'm here now,' she ended. 'The Lord is my shepherd, I shall not want.' Which was how they usually concluded their stories.

And then the details could be added. What about this, and what about the other? What did the children look like: eye colour, hair, health, how old, had they really never been ill before? What about the clothes she'd taken into the marriage, what had they been like? Where had the fabrics come from, and how had they made them? And what had it been like, getting married, and what had her intended worn, what about the bridal night and had she really not known what was going to happen? Well, but hadn't her mother told her? And hadn't she ever seen it for herself, with the dogs and horses and so on?

Sæthryd had to admit that although she had been informed about what would happen, she had never dreamt it could be so painful or that he would hold her down like that. She'd never got used to it—being skewered from below. It had eventually stopped being painful, she simply couldn't understand what purpose it served, other than its necessity if you wanted children, and she did. But he was all over her when she was pregnant, too, and that hadn't been at all necessary . . .

Wynflæd shook her head and murmured to herself with a smile.

'Was it like that for you, too?' asked Sæthryd.

Wynflæd laughed out loud, shaking with mirth. When she noticed they were all staring at her, she blushed and held her head in her hands, but she couldn't stop laughing.

'What's wrong with you?' asked Begu.

'Nothing, it's nothing,' Wynflæd replied, her face now scarlet, and she spluttered again with amusement. The others had started to join in, discreetly at first, and then louder and louder. When Wynflæd flapped her hands and made eyes at them, they laughed even more boisterously.

They were eventually exhausted from all that laughter, and Wynflæd took a deep sigh and shook her head.

'All the gold rings in the world—and they are nothing in comparison with . . . '

'No,' Hild sighed, 'you're quite right . . . nothing . . . it's strange . . . '

'I just don't understand you,' Freawaru exclaimed. 'They rob and ransack, they murder and burn down the settlements, they brag about their deeds and go on and on and then you sit there going into raptures about them—it is simply beyond me.'

'Not at all,' Wynflæd cut her short, 'that's not what sends us into raptures, it's . . . '

She smiled at Hild.

' . . . something else entirely, isn't it?'

'Something else entirely, yes,' Hild nodded and could hardly look up, lost as she was in recollection. She sighed deeply several times and stretched a little.

Wynflæd again made signs with her hands and eyes, shuddered and sighed.

'Yes, yes, that was then.'

Freawaru shook her head.

'It is simply beyond me. Not that I have much knowledge of the matter, it's just never interested me, it hasn't . . . But that it can make you utterly suspend your faculty of judgement—I just don't understand.'

Over the next few days, Sæthryd's story was scrutinized and all the details brought to light: what the farm had looked like, the condition of the slaves, number of animals, which crops were grown, and so on and so forth. They also had to clear up what had happened to all her family members.

Sæthryd took them into her confidence, revealing what she hadn't been able to say before: her brother-in-law had broken his loyalty to her. Following her husband's death, they had grown very close; she had trusted him and his desire to settle the feud. He was, after all, baptized. She had felt quite safe telling him about her brother's movements. And thus they had found him, alone in the forest. She was an accessory to her brother's death, and for that she had paid a heavy price.

After three evenings, the only holes left in the story were those that were also holes for Sæthryd. They tried to fill them with various theories as to what might have happened, and together they concocted numerous possible versions. Sæthryd could neither confirm nor disprove them; but they were highly credible, each and every one.

It had been a lovely story, on that they all agreed. Good-looking children; they would have gone far, had the Lord not taken them to join him.

Then it was Freawaru's turn. She also chose to tell them about her life. Her worldly life had been brief; she had always looked forward to being an adult, but had never wanted to marry.

When her father eventually insisted she accept the next suitor, she ran away from home. She had planned it all very carefully, and sought refuge in a monastery, where she came into contact with a woman hermit. She had accompanied this woman for a couple of years, in the forests on the wide-ranging hills south of Ad Gefrin. She had then been admitted to Lindisfarena, where she spent three years before going to Ediscum, and then to here.

It took four days to get through this story, due to interest in the people in the first monastery and on Lindisfarena: she had to provide details about the family lines of everyone at the monasteries, and the reasons they had wanted to enter the service of the Lord. It wasn't the first time they had heard about them, but it was always interesting to hear the stories from a different source, which might provide an extra element or two. They knew the background stories of all the Lord's folk in the kingdom; where Lindisfarena was concerned, they knew all about the laity there too. Having given up their blood family, all the monastery folk were their family; they were united in the Lord and in the work of spreading his glad tidings—which would put an end to strife. They preached this message wherever they went, with great conviction and vigour.

'How many years do you think it will take?' Begu asked Hild.

'That depends on how well we do our work,' Hild replied.

'Three years, perhaps?' asked Begu.

'More like five, I think,' said Hild, having thought for a moment. 'Ten, maybe. But I hope you are right!'

'I go for three,' said Begu. 'They'll surely get the message by then!'

# SACRIFICED FOR PEACE

*– the battle of Wynwæd –*

Four years after Penda's visit, Hild saw him again. It was dusk, a wet and windy day towards the end of the winter full moon phase, and there he was, standing before her, dressed as the messenger from Tamoworthig.

'Go away!' she shouted, when he pulled the hood from his face.

His hair was all grey now, and not a tooth left, but his bearing was regal, dignified as ever. He had once been the best-looking man in Mercia.

She had recognized him the moment he dismounted—his upright posture and his physique—and had thus been able to compose herself before they came face-to-face in private.

'It's just me,' he smiled, reaching out for her. She rebuffed his outstretched hands and stepped backwards.

'I no longer wish to see you,' she said in a firm voice. 'Leave this place.'

Penda stayed where he was, unsettled.

'What's happened?'

'What has happened is that I don't want any more strife and fighting. And if you don't leave, I'll send for Oswy.'

Penda shook his head.

'Oswy?'

'Oswy, yes, and he has a troop of men stationed nearby for this very purpose.'

'Because I visit you?'

'Because you come with swords drawn, and don't you even try to tell me you've come alone.'

'I haven't come with an army,' he said. 'Just the men you've seen.'

'So where *is* the army, then?' she snapped.

Penda looked down; he couldn't lie to her, but nor could he disclose the whereabouts of his troops.

'Not here,' he chose to say.

'I'm not blind,' she hissed. 'Where is it?'

'Oh Hild, I simply can't tell you.'

'No, but you can attack blameless people and strip them of their belongings. That's how honourable you are!'

Penda sighed. He'd heard her ideas about peace so many times before, but never expressed as militantly as this.

'Whetted your appetite when you defeated King Anna, did it?' she shouted.

'Hildeburh,' he entreated, 'I've come to visit you, not to argue over a subject about which we'll never agree. I've received a sign . . . I had to see you.'

'You with your signs and auguries. I serve the Lord God, haven't you realized that yet? And he punishes those who cannot live peacefully with one another.'

'Well, here and now, you're the combative one,' he mumbled.

'I don't use the sword,' she retorted. 'But I'll stop you from using it, and therefore I would rather see *you* killed than see you kill hundreds of blameless people. If you don't get out of here immediately, I'll send word.'

'Did you hear me, Hildeburh,' he pleaded, 'I had to see you . . . '

Hild had heard enough; she opened the door and shouted for Begu, who came running from the neighbouring hut.

'This here is King Penda of Mercia,' Hild announced, pointing at the old man in undyed flax linen. 'You will ride out immediately and tell Oswy's men.'

Begu nodded and left. Without delay, a couple of horses were heard galloping through the gateway at full pelt—and Penda realized her threat had been genuine.

He sat down, shaking his head.

'No one escapes his fate,' he said, and looked up at her. 'But that's not the kind of death foretold by the sign.'

Hild became uneasy, and stepped towards him.

'Yes, yes,' he said, 'your lord punishes disloyalty too, I suppose. I'll go now, so you don't have to betray the one to serve the other.'

He stood up, but had difficulty taking his leave.

'Fare well, Hildeburh! May your lord reward you for your faithfulness.'

He gazed at her with the caressing eyes that had always made her melt, and which now again pierced her most sensitive spot—but there was more sorrow than smile in them, more sorrow than she had ever seen. She felt an aching tenderness for the man, and she wanted to say something but didn't know what.

He had already reached the door, his back to her, but he stopped.

'Perhaps you're right,' he said into the doorway, 'about putting an end to all this fighting. But this time it's too late.'

He had just opened the door when she leapt across and grabbed him by the arm.

'Penda,' she implored, 'spare my sons!'

He had a strange expression on his face, as if he was laughing but was also on the verge of tears.

'They are my sons, too, Hildeburh. My princes.'

'Yes,' she smiled, struggling to hold back her own tears. 'Fare well, Penda. May good fortune be with you.'

He turned and flung his arms around her in a brief and intense embrace, and just as abruptly he had released her and vanished into the darkness.

A few moments later, she heard them galloping away, and to the closed door she whispered: 'Fare well, my love, my husband until death do us part.'

Defeating King Anna had not whetted Penda's appetite, and he could well have done without that particular campaign. But he needed the support of the East Angles in order to hold his own against King Oswy. Besides, the revolt might spread and he couldn't manage without Lindsey. There was no way round it.

He'd had bad dreams all through his stay in that swampy place. By threatening his freemen with the removal of their privileges if they pursued the enemy, he'd been able to defuse the old tactic of luring the opposition out into the bog.

But it wasn't the anxieties of campaigning that had been tormenting him. Rather, it was the water sprites, sticking their heads up all over the place and buzzing around him at night. He knew there was a natural explanation, as there was for everything, so when they arrived at Rendlæsham he rode out to make an offering at Sigebert's grave. Even from a distance, the cause of the problem was obvious. The old burial place was overrun with brambles, the barrows riddled with rabbit holes and he could see where wild boars had rummaged and trampled. It was an absolute disgrace.

Had it been the enemy, then he would have understood; but to allow the memory of one's own kin to be obliterated like this! Such arrogance was the speciality of the new god's followers, thinking they could simply flout what people had always held dear. As if the old folk had been fools and only the new generation endowed with any intelligence—which led to the egg trying to teach the hen. Such unnaturalness did not go unpunished.

Here was the very proof, and now he was actually glad he had slain King Anna. The message about what was right and proper would get through to Anna's brother and successor, King Ædelhere, in no uncertain terms.

Before Penda left East Anglia, the burial place was tidied up, the rabbits and boars were driven away and the whole area was fenced in.

On the way back, the water sprites left him in peace. Now there was just the one mare riding him at night, but he knew it well. It whispered in his ear about Trumhere, and kept on asking *how* exactly she had become a widow, the woman he coveted.

He would wake to the sound of his own voice echoing the name of the all-too-loyal servant. And remember in glaring detail; the pain, powerlessness, craving, drunkenness, and cleaving through it all: Trumhere's eyes when he received his lord's clear, unequivocal command. And worse still: his expression when the command was repeated. Trumhere had not misheard.

The painful conversation under a frosty sky outside the hall, the arrow in his throat and, afterwards, so pale.

Yes, he had got Trumhere off his hands, and instead he had the nightmare, grim and heavy across his heart. That was the price, but he didn't consider it too high; he had always known everything has its price.

Mercia's greatness had a price, too. Like this campaign of retribution, which had frankly disgusted him. Perhaps all Hildeburh's chatter about peace was beginning to chip away at his fighting spirit and his love of gold. Perhaps it was age. When the swords sang, and elated battle-cries rang out across the field, he had to repeat over and over to himself: this has to be done, otherwise we'll lose Lindsey, then Mercia will be laid waste. Better to have this little battle to keep things evenly weighted than to let the balance shift and cause real war, and devastation, and the deaths of innocent people, women, slaves, children. Yes, children too, even little babies. A battle like this—between grown men who knew what they were dealing with—was, despite everything, far preferable.

He nonetheless felt the nausea rising. He had tried to keep his eyes off the wounded, but leaving the battlefield was not an option. The memory of Bothelm and Gefmund, his fallen king's sons, suddenly threatened to overwhelm him—that was the very worst.

The peace negotiations of the past few years must have affected him. He had children up in Bernicia now: Ædelræd, and little Cyneburh—he could never think about her without smiling. She hadn't been a son, no, but he'd had five princes at the time, and Merewald. Cyneburh with her blonde curls, his darling jewel, a little ray of sunshine.

And it had undoubtedly been on account of her name that fate had sent her to Bebbanburh as queen. Just like her mother's sister Cyneburh, but hopefully to a better husband than Oswald. Penda was also tormented by the fate of this Cyneburh, the dowager queen, burnt to death with her little girls. He had never really given it much thought until now, but twenty-two years was a short life. Should his little darling be widowed, he would fetch her home immediately, with or without children. She would not be left a prisoner of Ædelfred's family.

Penda sensed the dawning of a new age and he bid it welcome. After all, much progress had been made in many areas. Perhaps there really would be peace one day, just like Hildeburh had always said—but the first time she had spoken about it, he hadn't known what she meant.

Now he knew: after his death the realm would convert to the new god. Personally, he wouldn't have had anything against it, and it would certainly have eased the transition, but he had no say in the matter. He didn't repent the most serious ill deeds; he would have done just the same again, even today.

In the late summer of the following year, Penda received a message that sent him reeling.

'Leave it,' said his wife, Cynewise, once she had recovered her composure. 'She's one person, and you can't let hundreds of people pay with their lives for just the one. And anyway, she's not dead, so leave it.'

But Penda couldn't just leave it. He marshalled all his allies—kings of the Britons in the west, East Anglia, Lindsey, the West Saxons—and set forth to wage battle against Bernicia. That was when he had taken the opportunity, left his army where it was and ridden north to see Hild.

The message had come from his daughter Cyneburh's wetnurse, along with a letter from Oswy promising it would not be repeated—from now on there would always be a sentry watching over Cyneburh, plus the nurse, who could always run for help if anything happened. He didn't think anything would happen; with the assistance of the Lord, everything would undoubtedly be fine. She was certainly attended by the best doctors, and prayers were said for her on Lindisfarena. None were more unhappy than Alchfred—and Oswy himself, who sent his sincerest greetings.

Oswy was worried about his son; this was the third incident. At least the girl had survived this time, unless the wound became infected with flying venom. It was all just one big wound, from what they said; he'd been at it here, there and everywhere—just like he had with his sister that time. But his sister had been too small, and it had gone horribly wrong. It was hard to say whether it had been the lesions or the beating that had done it, but—whatever—the Lord had taken her to be with him.

He had thus given his son a woman who knew about such matters, and all had gone well for a while. Personally, he was convinced that time spent well is time well spent—and, yes, it had actually gone fine for a while, and it wasn't what she had died from anyway. She was fully-grown and could withstand a lot, Oswy knew: he'd had her himself. No, it was the beating, not the stabbing, because by the time he started on that, she was already dead, those who knew about such things said, because there was hardly any blood from the stab wounds, even though they were deep. No, it was the beating: belly, chest and head. That's what they'd said, anyway.

Oswy had been something of a wild one himself, so he knew that most children's afflictions disappear of their own accord. He waited until the boy was eighteen years old and then gave him a girl he'd had the pleasure of himself. She wasn't the type to complain; easily trained and obedient.

It had gone well, and nothing had given Oswy pause for thought before letting him marry one of Penda's daughters. She was a girl who knew her own mind, he'd heard. She'd undoubtedly retaliate if needs be.

Then he'd got the wrong daughter, and so the damage was done.

Oswy found all this upsetting, both for Alchfred and the kingdom as a whole, because Penda might not take it calmly. So he summoned the army and headed south to Deira. When reports about the hugeness of Penda's army reached him, he took a quick decision and raided Eoforwik; it had been a long time since the town had been looted, and he sent a message to Penda with detailed descriptions of what he could offer for the sake of peace. Peace would be honourable, now that they were fathers-in-law to each other's children.

Penda's reply dripped with scorn: not only was he going to wipe out Oswy and his son and all his kinfolk, he would also utterly annihilate Bernicia, high and low, without respect of persons.

Oswy increased his offer with a whole range of his personal treasures.

'Send me your youngest daughter,' Penda replied. 'And I'll take her as my wife, in just the same way your son took my daughter as *his* wife!'

Oswy felt sick. Ælfflæd was barely one year old, and for some reason he couldn't explain, his love for this child was limitless. He had waited a long time for her; his wife had been slow, and even though he had done what he could, even when he didn't feel the least inclined, four years had passed before his son Egfred arrived. Two stillborn infants had followed, and then this little one had come along. Healthy and vigorous from her very first day, his beautiful little doll. That's what he called her: his little doll. His wife couldn't understand what had happened, so devoted was he to that daughter. But that's just how it was: he loved her, that's all there was to it. And he was perfectly happy to say it out loud: he simply loved her.

He went into his tent and wept, his hands covering his face, until a scout informed him that Penda was getting closer; his army was probably about ten times bigger than theirs. Oswy was overwhelmed by an impotent rage and threw the scout out. His allegiance to the Lord had in truth been poorly rewarded! Twice as big, he could have managed, but not ten times as big.

And then—his anger obviously having made some kind of impression—the Lord sent him an idea. Oswy despatched a secret message to his brother's son, King Ædelwald of Deira, who was a Penda ally. He shared his concerns about the Lord's cause, for which Ædelwald's father Oswald had so heroically shed his blood. For his own part, Oswy's greatest desire now was to enter entirely into the service of the Lord, but this battle against Penda, his brother's murderer, was something he still owed the Lord and his brother. Afterwards, he would go to Lindisfarena and fight the heavenly fight. Given that his sons did not have the necessary skills, he had informed his retainers that he wanted Oswald's son Ædelwald to be his successor—a decision they approved—because he was a strong king, a worthy heir to his father. Was he familiar with the valley around the Wynwæd brook in Elmet?—an excellent location for a battle. And Penda had such trust in Ædelwald, well, he'd most likely follow his advice—it was, after all, taking place in his kingdom! In the name of the Lord, he concluded, if victory be ours then, in the name of Christ, I implore you to embrace the legacy of your father, as king of a forever united Northumbria!

Oswy felt calmer once the messenger had ridden off. The Lord had given him a good idea, but it was going to take more: only a miracle could save him. He summoned Romanus. He intended to offer the service of his beautiful little doll, his Ælfflæd, to the Lord, plus six plots of land, of six hides each.

Romanus frowned. 'Twelve plots, I'd say, twelve like the twelve disciples. And if each measured ten hides, then they'd honour the memory of Paulinus, he who went to the Lord on the tenth day of the month of sacrifice.'

Oswy would have suggested seven hides of land, in order to end up on eight, but was overcome by the thought of his little doll. He accepted the proposal, even though it was too much.

Romanus quickly wrote everything down and secured the king's signature. Oswy hardly knew what he was signing, his eyes wouldn't stop watering. Just think: Penda believed he would sacrifice his own daughter! That was the kind of thing pagans would do! He sent Romanus away, and then he wept and wept. How could anyone think like Penda.

King Ædelwald was profoundly moved by the letter from his uncle—after all these years.

He was nineteen years old and utterly indebted to Penda, both for his life and his throne. Penda had treated him like a son when he had arrived at Tamoworthig with the troupe of entertainers, to be told that his mother and his sisters had died in the flames at Bebbanburh. Penda trusted him unreservedly.

Now Penda had turned to Ædelwald for advice about the terrain. Penda was an expert at using the lie of the land, but he wasn't familiar with the area. Ædelwald suggested the valley of the Wynwæd, which Penda thought sounded like a reasonable plan.

When the battle commenced, Ædelwald kept his men up on a hillside. He followed the course of the fighting as it raged back and forth, but couldn't break his allegiance to Penda; nor could he bring himself to go against his own uncle, who had now shown confidence in him and exhibited paternal love. Every time Penda and his enormous army fell back, Ædelwald prayed for Penda; and every time Oswy fell back, he prayed for Oswy. He was fond of them both, and he sided with them both too. He just hoped the battle would continue, because whatever the outcome he had already forsaken both of them, and it would now be impossible to look either in the eye.

Ædelwald wasn't familiar with the ways of the high water at this part of the river. He knew there had just been a new moon, but not that this would often be followed by what was called a spring tide, a great gushing torrent leaping forth. And as he had positioned himself on the west-facing slope, he didn't really notice the easterly gale whipping up the tidal current and giving it even greater force; his helmet was lined with otter pelt, earflaps tied under his chin.

Nature resolved the problem for him: a surging spring tide, the wave taller than a man, flooded the valley in an instant and engulfed the bulk of Penda's army. When the waters swept away the middle section, the frontline spear-throwers were left standing on their own, and when the rear troops saw them being cut down, with no chance of coming to their rescue, they fled.

The episode was later compared with the passage of the Jews through, and the disappearance of the Egyptians in, the Red Sea. This marvel of nature in the Wynwæd river, which turned into a disaster because many hundreds of people were at the very spot at the very time, was in Romanus' interpretation a sign from the Lord—even though nearly all Penda's allies were Christian: King Cadafael of Gwynedd, Ædelhere of East Anglia, Peada his eldest prince, and several of his own nobles.

But Penda had not been baptized, so the outcome was construed as a sign that the Lord had accepted Oswy's offer. Northumbria was the Lord's favourite, and now they knew: they were the strongest realm in the land.

When she was told about the battle, Hild refused to believe what she was hearing. Penda, the most vibrantly alive being she had ever met—she was simply unable to imagine him dead.

There were no reports about Wulfhere. She'd always known: Wulfhere would be killed, good fortune did not accompany him. It was a bitter grief, one she had anticipated ever since he was a little boy. His stubbornness; he'd never changed.

But not Penda. She hung on to the possibility that he had been spared by escaping at the last moment; that he was living in the forests of Gwynedd, perhaps in exile with King Cadafael, who really *had* fled. Cadafael wouldn't have escaped without his ally; he was a man of honour. Like Cædwalla, he was a descendant of Ambrosius Aurelianus, and he owed Penda a great deal.

At the same time, she knew Penda would never flee; even though all lay slain around him and he was offered a fresh horse and the track was clear. Penda would never flee the battlefield.

How could she grieve over a man whose dead body she hadn't seen, whose death had not been proven, but who was suddenly absent from where he should be? A man whose fate would remain a mystery because any witnesses perished with him? How could she grieve for him?

Penda was an army commander, above all he was an army commander. And thus his death had to be on the battlefield, killed by sword or spear. Picturing him drowned in mud and washed away by some random act of nature, through the clayey-yellow water of the Humbre and out into the ocean, food for mackerel—that simply wasn't possible.

She had always known that one day he would be carried home, and she knew how she would have him buried—if she had any say in the matter. He would be shown every honour, as befitting a king of the olden times.

She scanned the hills every day. At some point he would ride over the crest, undoubtedly in disguise.

A good month later, it was rumoured that Penda's body had been found in the still waters of the bay behind the strip of land at the mouth of the Humbre. Not long afterwards, it was reported that his head adorned the Eoforwik town gates, giving the folk of Deira an opportunity to think the matter over. The body could be viewed on a gable at Bebbanburh, the limbs at the royal estate of Ad Gefrin.

Hild had to check. She recognized him from his hair. A man was standing in the gateway trying to keep birds away by wielding a long stick; the ravens were no longer bothered by flames and rattles. The face was swollen and had virtually disintegrated; it could have been anyone. But not the hair.

Nor the clothing, which they readily showed her; no one else had clothes like Penda's. They were his, no one else's. She had woven and sewn the tunic herself, the last piece she had made in Tamoworthig. There was no blood, no sign of slashing or stabbing.

She asked to take him with her, but they said no. She would settle for the head, if need be, but she wasn't allowed anything, so she went home.

# GOD SEEKS THAT WHICH IS PAST

*- Abbess of Streonæshalch -*

So—work. Work and prayer and work. Hild allowed herself no rest. Nor did she grant her subordinates much respite.

Her son Ædelræd and his half-brother Peada had survived: Ædelræd because, being Oswy's hostage, he had stood on the northern hillcrest; Peada because his father had positioned him far back.

Peada had already been king of the Middle Angles for some years. Oswy now gave him the kingdom of the Southern Mercians, the land south of the river Treante, comprising five thousand hides of land. Oswy didn't want to see his daughter Ahlflæd, who had married Peada two years earlier, living in lowly circumstances. He also spared Ædelræd. Given that his own son Egfred was held hostage by Queen Cynewise in Tamoworthig, and even though Ædelræd wasn't of her flesh and blood, she might decide to take revenge. Oswy knew the family, and had nothing good to say about any of them—the way Cynewise's daughter had driven his son to the end of his tether.

In an effort to restore Alchfred's good name, Oswy installed him as sub-king of Deira. King Ædelwald had disappeared shortly after the battle and, as matters stood, selection wasn't required. In Northern Mercia, Oswy personally took over the responsibilities of king, and Cynewise fled to the realm of the West Saxons where her brother Cenwalch was again king, after his involuntary period spent with the East Angles.

Cynewise was therefore not present when her twelve-year-old daughter became queen of Deira. Cyneburh was still unable to sit on a horse, so the young royal couple entered Eoforwik in a beautifully carved and painted cart bedecked with gold-brocaded woven coverings. She sat as straight-backed as she could on the thick down pillow the nurse had placed on the seat. When the ceremony was over, her father's head was removed from the town gateway; she was glad, he didn't look himself.

At the time of the Easter festival, Peada was murdered. A horrible and dishonourable death, hard to understand: the man who had brought along four priests after his baptism and his wedding in Bernicia, Mercia's first Christian king, also popular for many other reasons, was discovered in a pool of blood alongside the waste-pit wall, his throat slashed, slain while sitting on the plank of wood with a hole in it, unable to defend himself. His wife Ahlflæd was accused of being responsible for the murder, and she was beheaded as soon as the Easter peace was over.

Oswy couldn't ignore this deed. He set himself up as king of all Mercia, avenged his daughter by hanging twelve freemen, and introduced a merciless regime. The people were given a choice: baptism or banishment. Many fled to the West Saxons.

Hild visited Ædelræd at Bebbanburh. He was fifteen years old now, a handsome lad. He confided in his mother that Wulfhere was alive, hidden away with one of Penda's retainers.

She slapped his face, and was immediately sorry, but she just wouldn't listen to such talk. She knew her son was dead; she also knew he might still be alive if his mother hadn't acted so stupidly with all her endeavours to devise peace.

The conclusion she had reached in East Anglia had been perfectly true: fortune didn't smile on her. Everything she touched had turned to ash. If she tried to devise new peace weavings, there would be war.

Two years passed before Oswy finally fulfilled his promise to the Lord. He ended up giving six plots of land in Deira and six in Bernicia, each of ten hides—hardly excessive, considering the needs of a monastery.

A number of the plots were sited on the old coastal early-warning stations, and came with a stipulation that the monastery would take over the job of signalling. This also applied to Streonæshalch, the small town at the mouth of the Esca river, through which Cædwalla had once passed on his way to Hræfenclif with the hermit.

Hild was asked to move to Streonæshalch and establish a new monastery; she would be happy to do so. Following Penda's death, she was having difficulty finding composure anywhere: she was forever hearing hoofbeats, but no one came; sometimes he was standing in the doorway or sitting on her bed. She was only fooled for the first few months, then she realized it was his ghost returning. He always disappeared the instant she turned to face him.

But every time was like a laceration to her flesh. The wound wouldn't heal, the scab was ripped off nearly every day; she threw herself into work, but next day the wound opened again. She often talked with him, at night or other times when she was on her own. She did most of the talking; he would sigh or just sit with his head in his hands. She told him Ædelræd was alive, never mentioned Wulfhere and thanked him for having positioned Peada so far back. Nothing helped.

She knew she would find peace if his mortal remains were respectably buried, and she sent a petition to King Oswy. The reply: sorry, but those who had buried King Penda were already dead.

So, when riding around the realm, she never knew if she was at that very moment passing by her husband's bones. She heard the soil whispering about generations gone by who didn't want to be forgotten, who wanted to be remembered and honoured. Some seemed to have carried heavy burdens, of which death had not relieved them. She could feel it so clearly: the earth held knowledge it was trying to share with the people walking on it, if they would just stop and listen. One day, when accompanying a priest northwards, the earth was speaking to her so vigorously that she asked the entourage to halt. While the others rested, she searched the ground until she found the spot; after a little digging, she immediately unearthed some old horse bones.

She became increasingly attuned to the hazy speech of the earth, and she never had to search at length before finding an item that had been hidden from the world, maybe briefly or perhaps for a long time. She didn't always know what it was and what it might mean, but she took the objects home and kept them in a box under her bed. Large and small pieces of metal, bird skeletons, strange stones, animal teeth; remains of lives that had once been lived, by beings she didn't know. They had left these traces behind for her, all were signs. Day and night she puzzled over what the objects were trying to tell her, and then she was interrupted by the tasks involved in moving home. There was no end to her responsibilities.

Streonæshalch was to be the stronghold from which the Lord's cause would be fought, and their weapons would be those of learning. She selected the nuns and monks who were best at Latin and writing, and who had an understanding of the long-term goal. Farming and work with the needy had to have firmer guidelines. Begu was indispensable, Sæthryd and Freawaru too; of the men, Bosa and Oftfor. With a small hand-picked company at her side, she set forth for Streonæshalch.

First they built down in the sheltered area by the brook flowing into the Esca river. Later, when Oswy complained they had missed the sighting of a ship, and threatened to repossess the land, they moved up to the east cliff, still on the southern banks of the river mouth. They would just have to put up with the stiff wind, and it was always going to be very much colder up here than down by the river. A chilly spot summer and winter, but with a view across the sea, and to the west across the high range of hills.

Hild felt more comfortable once they had moved up to the wind-swept early-warning station. From the monastery she could count six hillcrests, the one vanishing behind the other. The last ridge was often enclosed in a bluish mist; in the springtime they sent the goats up to its poor scrub-covered soil. A Roman road wound through the barren landscape. She called it Cartimandua's road, and the section down by the town was more than the worse for wear.

The view to the north was also breached six times, but they were vertical rifts—to the west they were horizontal. The vertical lines appeared where land met sea; when the sea cut in, the land would jut out again a little further away. She couldn't decide whether the land was trying to push its way into the sea, or the water was eating its way into the land. The two elements were battling it out, and the outcome seemed uncertain. The wind, element of the air, was an ally of the water; when the one really got going, you could quite clearly see the other gnawing away at the coastline. So in Hild's assessment, the fourth element—fire—must be an ally of the land, and it was, of course, the natural enemy of water. When the easterly gale was at its height, she had a bonfire lit on the top of the cliff; it seemed to keep the sea's appetite a little in check. Yes, she liked the sea, and more so as each day passed, but she wouldn't give up even one tiny corner of her ten hides of land—she could easily have used more.

These six horizons were a sign. She had returned to the place whence she came: Ad Gefrin, with six horizons visible from the top of the Hill of the Goats. Your eyes had to let go of the land six times so as to meet it again further away, and so she and Hereswid had chosen six as their secret number. Just childish nonsense, of course, but nonetheless—six was still her number. Penda had fathered six children, in the good years before Cynewise arrived on the scene. Hild had borne six children: the twins, two stillborn infants and two healthy sons. The Lord had worked for six days creating the earth and everything in it, and then he had rested. She would work until her number six had run out, and then she would rest. If the Lord would accept her, if he would show her mercy, she would rest in his arms.

From the Hill of the Goats you'd been able to count twenty-seven hilltops. You could do the same here: if you looked very carefully, you reached twenty-seven, no more nor less. She counted them every morning as soon as there was enough light. Twenty-seven summits.

And now she understood the words in Ecclesiastes about her god seeking out that which is past. She had thought she'd put the years behind her, but they were still there, right alongside her.

Sometimes she was in the one time, sometimes in the other. Years weren't behind her, they were all around, calling her back and forth as they chose. Her entire life was happening at this moment, at every place, and there was no time. In the gloaming, her father came and sang to her, from down in the thicket by the brook. And when the sea fret surrounded them, she could feel Talcuin with her: his soft, soft mouth, so warm, so startling. When she rode out with the priest, she thought she saw the twins, but then she remembered they were twenty-five years old now and had probably fathered many children themselves. Sometimes Paulinus lectured her, she was standing outside with the birds, weaving for Wulfhere, and her mother was muttering about how everything returns to the place whence it came. She frequently spoke with Aidan, but most often with Penda—her beloved husband.

Her life-blood, her own flesh, now disintegrating at some unknown place and whispering to her. He was whispering about betrayal. And she had told him, a hundred times at least, that it had been prearranged with Begu: Oswy hadn't had any men there, and she would never have betrayed him to Oswy. Never—not even if her life had depended on it. But Penda couldn't hear her; drifting in his misty land, she couldn't reach him.

She went down to the beach. At ebb tide you could walk along the bottom of the cliff, as long as you remembered to come up before high tide.

'Cartimandua!' she cried out to sea. 'Cartimandua!'

The gulls screeched back, and she didn't know if they were answering her. She tried one way, then the other, with all the tricks she knew, but nothing worked; she simply didn't understand what they were crying out to her.

She sat up in bed, and it was obvious: if she could find Cartimandua's grave and offer a sacrifice, then maybe the stain would disappear. The traitor queen, they had called her. And she'd done it; she'd handed him over—not her husband, but nonetheless—her ally, who had sought sanctuary with her. Penda had only come visiting, after all; he'd wanted to tell her something, but she wouldn't listen.

She clutched her head and screamed. She screamed for Penda and for Cartimandua. They didn't come. After a while, Begu came and applied a cold compress to her brow, gave her warm beer and spoke gently. It was good; it was good to have Begu. She fetched the priest, to hear Hild's confession. She received a mild penance; she hadn't betrayed him, had she, just made it seem as if she had—for the sake of peace.

Now the strife had come to her, had entered and made its abode within her. That was the price, and she would have to live with it. Without sacrifice, peace could not be won.

Even though the sacrifice had been in vain, and she had sacrificed her husband and her most beloved son—but not herself.

She implored the Lord that the new time might treat its people more gently, not tempt them to forsake their own flesh in the name of peace, or in the name of any cause. He couldn't let it go on like this.

# What the Lord joins together

*– Penda's soul –*

The women in Streonæshalch, with the exception of Begu, compensated for the reduced number of Latin lessons by writing to one another, as Hild and Sæthryd had always done. Every day they would exchange two or three closely-written wax tablets: draft letters, short paragraphs about the weather, the loving-kindness of the Lord, the mission of peace or problems with the crops. If they couldn't agree about case and declension, they would present the dilemma at their next Latin lesson. Their standard was still completely equal to that of the men.

One evening, contrary to her usual practice, Hild rushed into the hut Sæthryd shared with Freawaru, carrying two wax tablets covered with Latin verse. She came to a halt, and couldn't believe her own eyes.

Sæthryd and Freawaru, both blushing, leapt apart, straightened their clothing and tried to look perfectly natural—an endeavour at which they both failed, and the abnormal, yes, downright unnatural was written all over their red faces.

Hild clenched her mouth shut, and then managed to speak.

'Report to me, when you can in decency leave the hut,' she snapped, and turned on her heel.

'We'll be there straight away,' Sæthryd's voice followed her out.

Hild chewed her lip and wished she could have asked Aidan for advice. What would he have done in a case such as this? Had he ever experienced the like? Or did the Devil only stick out his ugly visage in *her* monastery?

She didn't have to wait long. They were still a little flushed, but more because of what they had been up to rather than any awareness of its aberrance.

'Adultery has no place among the handmaidens of the Lord,' Hild informed them.

'We know,' said Freawaru, 'and we are not committing adultery.'

Hild had to take a deep breath.

'Freawaru and I love one another,' said Sæthryd, without the least hint of shame. 'We have sworn fidelity to one another, and that has nothing to do with adultery.'

'Adultery is adultery!' shouted Hild furiously. 'And the lusts of the flesh will not be indulged in my monastery! In this place we serve the Lord, not Satan!'

Sæthryd and Freawaru looked at one another; Freawaru pursed her lips into a narrow line.

'Talk about Satan!' she said, stressing every syllable. 'Is Sæthryd closer to Satan than was Mercia's pagan king?'

Her glowing eyes looked straight through Hild, who took a step backwards.

'And what might you mean by that?'

'King Penda is what I mean—the idolater who ravaged the land right up until the moment of his death—is he more acceptable to the Lord than Sæthryd here?'

'What has he to do with this?' Hild sighed, now seated, playing for time until she could regain her composure. 'Penda is dead, isn't he,' she murmured.

'He was very much alive when he was here!' Freawaru continued in the same tone.

Hild's eyes flickered from the one to the other. They both knew, had obviously known all along.

'He was,' she said quietly. 'As alive as alive can be. He was. He was very much alive, yes.'

She looked down at the hands in her lap: they had held him, had caressed him, embraced him tightly, stroked his back, stroked his thighs. Her hands—and if he came here, she would do so again.

'Penda was my husband,' she said to no one in particular. 'And we two *should* be of one flesh.'

She had to breathe deeply to get enough air. Her ears were buzzing, and outside sounds converged in an indistinct murmuring. That's how it felt when the dead were talking about you. That's how it felt, and Penda, she and Penda, her husband, and his head, it was his but unrecognizable, they'd taken it down now, his head, and she'd not seen the body, she knew that body so well, his body—always warm it was, and her place was right next to it—the man's parts possibly cut off, like Oswald's, maybe thrown to the dogs, her parts, and why not, because without the spirit of life then the flesh is just flesh, is just there, isn't a person, isn't a being, is just matter in decay, in disintegration, but Penda, her flesh, he was still there, his spirit, his what? His soul, his what? His heathen soul, perished, gone, dissolved, decayed, putrefied? Would the Lord reconstruct him, the man who had refused to receive baptism, who didn't repent of his sins, who time and again ravaged Northumbria? And would Woden receive this warrior king, swept away in the river, drowned in mud, dead without the stroke of a sword—would Woden bid him welcome? Would anyone other than the worms take pleasure in him?

'But the name he earned for himself,' she mumbled, 'that can't, surely, no, it can't, can it ...?'

Speaking loudly, into the air, she said: 'They cannot take his name from him. If fairly earned, fame will not die. And it was fairly earned. It will not die from the passage of time, regardless of the smears spread by Oswald and all the others; he won it himself, he did, Penda, on the battlefield.'

She looked up. Sæthryd and Freawaru were standing in front of her, and she didn't know why.

'You two didn't know him,' she said sadly. 'There's no way you can appreciate the man he was, his hands, and when we lay together, you can't know anything about that.'

She fell into reverie—it wasn't only the hands, it was just as much the voice, but it probably wasn't that either, the eyes played a part too, and then the mouth. The mouth, yes, there had been a mouth, and the arms. And then something about his upright bearing, or was it the gait, his way of placing his feet? Those feet, she'd always had a soft spot for them. She'd been fond of taking them by the arch and pressing the foot upwards—then it felt as if she were holding his entire body. Upwards, she pressed, as if he were an infant child. Then he became very small, as if she could hold him all over, all at once.

'No, you see, you two didn't know him, so you can't know anything about that,' she directed at Sæthryd, who simply stared back at her.

'Yes, stare all you will!' she went on. 'But had you known my husband as I have known him, then you wouldn't just be standing there, you'd be ripping your clothes to shreds and rubbing ash in your hair, and perhaps you would be digging your way down into the earth so you could lie in the same element as he—those are my thoughts. But they are forbidden by the Lord: he has lent us life, and thus he wants to repossess it himself, and therefore my husband is lying all alone in the earth, and the grass is growing above him, and no one knows where he is ...'

'I didn't know him,' said Sæthryd, 'but had I known him, I wouldn't have thought about him in the way you do—because I have never felt like that for any man.'

'And the neck,' Hild continued, 'the skin is so smooth, just there, below the hair ... almost like the inner side of the thigh ... not quite as soft, but almost, don't you think?'

'Freawaru is the only person I have loved in that way,' said Sæthryd.

Hild looked intently at her and leapt up from the stool. Before she had stopped that mouth, she realized why they were standing there; she sat down again.

'Hild,' said Sæthryd, 'you just haven't been yourself since Penda died. And we don't know what we can do to get you back.'

Hild knew she ought to stand up and scold them, but she was too tired to bother. She felt the urge to weep, but refused to give in to it.

'Now I don't know what to do,' she said bluntly.

'Nothing,' said Freawaru with authority. 'You can't do anything other than take care of your monastery and give thanks to the Lord.'

'Easy words,' said Hild. 'You don't know what you're talking about.'

'One thing I do know—no one has power over fate,' Freawaru replied with the same authoritative composure.

'And I don't even know where he is,' Hild muttered. 'Oswy won't say.'

'We will pray for him,' said Freawaru. 'We will both pray for his soul—and for you to meet him again.'

'Yes,' Hild sighed, 'I also beseech the Lord but, you know, he wouldn't, he was so loyal . . . '

'Yes, yes,' said Freawaru. 'You just thank the Lord that he has granted you a love you would not want to lose. If you recover yourself and work for the cause of the Lord, then surely you will benefit Penda's soul more than by grieving for him like this. We miss you in our daily lives. You are no longer present among us.'

'You're down on us all the time,' Sæthryd added. 'Everything's wrong, and you're never satisfied with anything.'

'You used to make everything blossom,' said Freawaru, 'but now you're all over us with an officiousness that isn't befitting for the Lord's people; between us, peace and love ought to reign.'

'Yes, yes,' said Hild, suddenly overcome by unbearable fatigue. Fortunately she was sitting down, and in a moment she would stretch out and rest. She wished someone would dig a deep dark hole she could crawl into, so she could finally be left in peace and find a little coolness. First, however, she had to sort out this business. What was it she was meant to say? Something about their vow to the Lord. That they mustn't betray him, the one to whom they had sworn allegiance.

'I let him down,' she said, having trouble raising her eyes to them. 'Last time he came, I wouldn't listen to him.'

The words had slipped out and couldn't be called back. Now she was weeping freely.

'I said I would summon Oswy's men. I didn't want any more fighting, I said. And that's why he was slain.'

She hid her face in her hands and rocked back and forth, weeping.

'I'll never forgive myself. And I believe the Lord cast us apart because we had never received his blessing.'

'The Lord joins together, with or without blessing,' said Freawaru firmly. 'When he sends love between two people, he isn't concerned about whether a priest has blessed them or not.'

'That's what you've told us,' Sæthryd cut in. 'You've always taught us that love takes precedence over everything because the Lord has sent it to us.'

'But when he married Cynewise, he did it in the right way,' Hild went on. 'And therefore the Lord cast us apart—he hadn't joined us together *properly*.'

'But he *did* join you together properly,' Freawaru corrected, 'in the very act of sending you the love from which you are now suffering so greatly. Penda loved you! Didn't he?'

'Yes, indeed,' Hild nodded pensively, 'and there was nothing to be done. And I loved him, that's all there was to it. I didn't want to know he'd disposed of my first husband. But I knew it all along. I might well have done the same to get Penda.'

Now she looked straight at them, prepared to receive their condemnation.

'The ways of the Lord are past understanding,' said Sæthryd, 'particularly the way he handles love. Love one another!—that's what Jesus said.'

'I don't think he meant it quite like that,' said Hild.

'Maybe not,' Sæthryd conceded.

'I think he did,' said Freawaru. 'Love is the Lord's greatest gift to us. But we're so covetous that we clutch at it and think we own it. So when the gift is taken away again, we get angry at the Lord and at fate. But it's not our property at all, and it never will be. When we grieve for those we loved, we should rather thank the Lord for giving us some love in the first place! Well, that's what I think, anyhow.'

Hild frowned. 'So there's nothing at all called adultery?'

'Well, probably,' said Freawaru, 'but I don't really know much about that.'

'Now I find myself at a loss for words,' said Hild.

'You know,' said Sæthryd, 'to all those people who desire someone of the opposite sex, you can say: Not here, you can't, you'll have to go forth and lead a worldly life together like other people! But for people like us, who can't marry one another, there's no other way in which we can live together than here at the monastery. And we want to serve the Lord. But the Lord has sent love between us, and I can't believe he wants it to finish us off.'

'How do you know it isn't Satan who has sent you this desire?' asked Hild.

Sæthryd looked at Freawaru, her face shining as if encircled by a halo. Hild had to look away. Such gentleness did not come from the old enemy, no, that it didn't.

'Yes, yes,' she said, 'well, it's obvious. And, personally, I have always known what is what in that respect.' She wrinkled her brow in thought, and added: 'Nonetheless, there must be guidelines.'

'Indeed, yes, there must,' Freawaru nodded.

'Make sure no one finds out,' said Hild, standing up.

She walked across and opened the door, but closed it again. She scrutinized them carefully, first the one and then the other; they looked just as they had always looked. She couldn't imagine how they could do what she had always believed to be the prerogative of woman and man; nor could she stop herself picturing it. There was no mention of the act in the scriptures; not as far as she knew, anyway. She let go of the door catch.

'How do you actually do it?' she asked, immediately blushing; but she had to know.

'Well, much the same as everyone else!' Sæthryd laughed. 'Don't we?' she added to Freawaru.

'Something along those lines,' Freawaru said with a smile. 'It just comes naturally.'

'When the spirit moves you, well, you don't really think about it that much . . . there's nothing mysterious about it . . . ' Sæthryd stopped, her face glowing.

'Oh, like that,' said Hild, not understanding anything except that the ways of the Lord are past understanding—and today more so than ever. She opened the door again, but when they were half-way through, she called them back and closed the door.

'Can't you put a catch on your door?'

'Yes, we've talked about that,' said Freawaru, 'and we should wait until after last Mass.'

'We usually do,' Sæthryd demurred. 'It was just this evening, we . . . ' And she sparkled again.

'I would appreciate it. And now, good night.'

'Good night,' the voices spoke in unison as Hild finally let them leave, and then she dropped to her bed.

# MAIDEN AND MOTHER

*– what Wilfrid and Baducing brought home from the outside world –*

Three years after Penda's death, and the year after Hild had moved to Streonæshalch, a message arrived from Wulfhere.

At first Hild didn't dare believe the news, but the messenger confirmed the content of the letter: Wulfhere had ousted Oswy's men and was now king of Mercia. Since the battle at Wynwæd, he had been in hiding with three retainers who had followed Penda's orders: if they saw the battle was lost, they were to throw Wulfhere to the ground and take him home with them. This had been impressed on them before each battle; Penda had also given instructions that his son should be kept in hiding for three years—the passage of time would do much of the work for him.

The letter was brief and authoritative, and concluded: 'Stay where you are for the time being, mother.' He had obviously used a scribe who knew how to put sentences together; but he had signed it himself, his signature very similar to Penda's back when he hardly knew how to hold a pen.

'My dearest little hatchling,' she murmured, clasping the letter tight. Her beloved son, he was alive and had become king. The wolf cub, her own cub. He would know how to honour his father's name.

She hurried across to the writing hut and came back with a letter before the messenger had finished eating; he had to take the rest of his meal with him. Once he'd left, Hild couldn't remember what she'd written, so she wrote a new letter in which she called upon her son to seek peace with King Oswy; she, personally, wouldn't get involved. She asked him to come to her as soon as he could, or to send word when circumstances allowed a journey to Mercia.

Before long, it was rumoured that the young Wilfrid had returned after five years away. His companion Baducing, who was one of Hild's young friends, had long since returned; he had been obliged to leave Wilfrid in Lugdunum, where the bishop had asked him to stay and be his son.

It was said that Wilfrid had also been offered the bishop's niece—his brother's daughter—and a large plot of land, but had stuck to his promise to the Lord, also about visiting the apostles' tombs. And now he had returned home, equipped with the Pope's blessing and eight horses loaded with bones of the saints, books, altar furnishings, Mass vestments with gold filigree, and an entourage worthy of a king, both in splendour and weaponry.

The latter was anathema to Hild, for the Lord's folk did not bear arms. The more she learned, however, the more eager she was to hear his account of Rome and all he had seen in the big world outside. But Wilfrid went to Kent first, then to King Cenwalch, and on his recommendation he was received with great reverence by King Alchfred of Deira—the latter eventually inviting the monastic folk of the kingdom to meet the young traveller.

Hild was astounded when she saw Wilfrid's horses in front of the royal settlement. The hair on their foreheads, flanks and back thighs had been singed off in the shape of holy crosses. And Wilfrid was surrounded by what could only be called a personal troop, sword-bearing men, worthy of a king. She caught a glimpse of him as he entered the hall; she called out, but he didn't notice her.

When the door was finally opened, she was hot with excited tension. Alchfred and Wilfrid were seated at the far end of the hall, the Lord's people parading past one by one to greet them. Hild noted that Wilfrid only stood up for the few men who had shaved their hair according to the practice in Rome—as had he. Others were given a handshake, some just a little nod. That tonsure really didn't suit him at all; even the most handsome of men looked rather foolish with a rounder than round head, and he'd been such a striking beauty, manly too.

When she stepped in front of him, he merely nodded; not even the hint of a little smile disclosed any pleasure in their re-acquaintance. Anger got the better of her.

'You perhaps do not remember accompanying me part of the way from the queen's estate at Cetreht?'

'I remember very well,' he replied politely.

'What has brought about such a change in you?' she blurted. 'I, for one, am the same as back then.'

'With all respect,' Wilfrid replied, in the same polite manner and with a slight inclination of his upper body. 'My conviction does not allow me to rise for any women other than those who, like the mother of Jesus, preserve their maidenhood for the Lord.'

'Meaning that if your mother had lived, you would not have got to your feet for her?'

'Meaning exactly that,' Wilfrid nodded.

Alchfred looked at him in wonder, clearly impressed by such firmness of principle.

'Which means,' Hild went on, 'that you have forgotten the fourth commandment, telling you to respect and love your father and your mother?'

'Which does not mean that,' Wilfrid replied calmly. 'But it does mean that I obey the new law, rather than the old law. And as far as I recall, Jesus said that every person who has forsaken his father and mother shall receive a hundredfold and shall inherit everlasting life.'

Blood rushed to her face. 'Then perhaps you also remember Jesus's words, that the one who lives by the sword will die by the sword?'

Wilfrid was just about to rise from his seat; he looked across at Alchfred, who immediately came to the rescue.

'Wilfrid has seen a thing or two in Gaul,' Alchfred explained, 'and I have given permission for his men to bear arms, here also. In my realm, he will never fear the fate that befell his patron when he shed his blood for the sake of Christ.'

Hild now merely sought an opportunity to withdraw.

'I give thanks to the Lord that he protected you on your journey,' she said with a curt bow. 'And, of course, I would be happy to receive you in Streonæshalch. The peace of the Lord be with you.'

And thus she extracted herself from this uncomfortable encounter.


Wilfrid didn't visit her. According to rumour, he was strongly against double monasteries, claiming they didn't exist in the outside world because they would always be a cradle of adultery. Up until now, this hadn't been a point of discussion: men and women lived separately, and were only together for some aspects of the teaching and at Mass.

Nor was it befitting, Wilfrid was cited as having said, that priests and bishops were governed by an abbess—and absolutely not if she had lived a worldly life. If she had preserved her maidenhood for the Lord, she might take charge of a convent. An abbess who had abandoned herself to carnal life could in no way be considered clean.

Hild asked Baducing, the young man who had accompanied Wilfrid as far as Lugdunum, to call on her. Some time ago, she had been of help to him, and he now showed his gratitude by answering all her questions about that outside world with which she so desperately wished to be acquainted. He spoke about it in quite everyday terms, but she'd never even heard of some of the fruits he mentioned. He claimed the Romans were no bigger in stature than the Angles, not much at any rate. He then had difficulty explaining how they could build with such huge stones. He thought perhaps the Romans had been larger in olden times, but they'd come down in the world, just like their empire. Anyway, he'd seen some very strong and very big men in Rome, certainly one-and-a-half times the bulk of a good-sized Angle—it just wasn't the norm.

Baducing had been in Oswy's service, but after the massacre at Bebbanburh he'd wanted to leave and seek redemption for his soul. Hild had counselled him to wait and see, mostly because she thought him too young to enter the service of the Lord. Baducing's father had been of the same opinion. First you had to get used to the ins and outs of the job, and as you got older you could make more of your own decisions. Baducing had been second in command, and didn't feel he had any say in anything—apart from getting them to spare Heiu, the mad abbess, when she got in their way during the operation. Oswy had rewarded him with a plot of land, where he could have spent his days quite happily, but that wasn't a life for him. After one more battle, now against Penda, he had decided to turn away from this world, and he was then selected as Wilfrid's travel companion.

'My sister lived in a double monastery in Gaul,' said Hild. 'I never heard about any problems.'

'That doesn't mean there weren't problems,' Baducing replied.

'The neighbouring monastery was also both for men and women, and governed by an abbess,' Hild went on, 'so it can't be such a rarity.'

'Well, yes, in the northwest of Gaul there are a couple, but the really well-reputed monasteries are ones just for monks. They outstrip anything we have here in terms of learning.'

'Not so strange,' said Hild. 'They have known the word of the Lord for far longer and, if the whole realm is Christian, then they must have greater resources available.'

'Well, most of all, they have a better system. Not like here, where every little monastery is the dominion of its own abbess. Over there, they're all under the bishop, who's under the archbishop, and the only one above him is the Pope.'

'And if the Pope makes a mistake, then all the others have to make a mistake too?'

'The Pope is Peter's successor!' said Baducing with emphasis.

'What I mean is: here the main missionary work is conducted by people from Lindisfarena and Iona, following the practice of their spiritual fathers, which stems from knowledge of how things work in *this* country. The Pope in Rome knows nothing about any of that, so how can he take charge of work here? Just imagine if people like Paulinus and Romanus had single-handedly preached the word of the Lord on these islands! Then the only people who heard it would have been kings and the topmost retainers. I never once saw Paulinus speak to a slave, and when it came to teaching us children, well, that certainly wasn't his preferred activity, I can tell you. Nor do Romanus and his people ever go anywhere other than a turn around the royal estate.'

'It was necessary to start there,' said Baducing, 'and after all, Romanus is the queen's personal priest.'

'Those people are always just the king's or the queen's personal something or other. It's been useful, yes, but I simply have to say: the basic missionary work has been done by people from up north, and it's never occurred to them to ask the Pope about anything. Otherwise they'd never have achieved as much as they have.'

'It's not the trifling issues, it's the overarching substance and matters of principle, such as when we observe Easter and how the Lord's folk manifest their allegiance.'

'Nonsense!' said Hild. 'The crucial point, surely, is that we celebrate Easter at all, not on which day we celebrate it! And as to how you cut your hair, well, I think you could find passages by Paulus rendering external manifestations a matter of secondary importance. Outer appearance is not a matter of principle!'

'Then let me put it differently: as things stand, every abbess governs her monastery in her own way.'

'Yes, and that's how she does it best!'

'And thus there is a great disparity between the priests who are ordained,' Baducing went on, 'and some areas continue to be underprovided. The abbesses won't relinquish their best people and aren't thinking of what's best for the realm.'

Hild shook her head.

'I have done everything possible to train priests and send them on missionary assignments. And I have never heard tell of an abbess who doesn't do exactly that.'

'You might not have heard about such cases,' Baducing pressed on, 'but the option of only thinking about your own good is always present.'

'Not if you serve the cause of the Lord! Here, the women have accepted that they receive less tuition than the men. They understand that the foremost task, at the moment, is to train priests.'

'You could also turn it around and say: they *still* receive tuition!' Baducing smiled. 'And you could ask: is teaching women Latin worth the effort? I know it's been valuable for you personally, but, on the whole—do they need it? For most of them it's just a private amusement; so you have to ask yourself if maybe the Church of Rome is right in concentrating fully on the men's education and leaving the women to work on what they're good at—it's not an inferior assignment, is it, just look at Maria! It's also a more efficient usage of resources. Later, when we don't have a shortage of priests, then maybe . . . but as things stand, still letting women learn Latin strikes me as something of an extravagance. They're not going anywhere with it.'

'Nor will many of the men!' Hild replied sharply. 'Not every man is suitable priest material.'

'Then why not concentrate every effort on those who are?' asked Baducing earnestly. He had a most polite manner.

'Because you can never tell completely,' Hild explained. 'Some get it straight away, others take longer—the ways of the Lord are past understanding, even when it comes to scholarship.'

'Maria was satisfied with her native language. She never asked to learn Latin.'

'What makes you say that all of a sudden?'

'Because she is—or should be—the great example to handmaidens of the Lord.'

Hild was startled; she'd never heard that before.

'Serving the Lord—is that not to follow in Christ's footsteps?'

'According to some. Whereas we are of the opinion that—for natural reasons—it is not possible for women to do so, and thus they should rather seek their great example in the virgin Maria, God's mother.'

'Oh really!'

Hild had clapped her hands and nearly laughed out loud, merriment compelling her to her feet. But Baducing was a serious young man who took everything very literally. She settled for circling the room, sitting down again and then asking with a meek and compliant expression on her face: 'Then tell me, Baducing, is it her motherhood or her maidenhood that we should take as our model? The combination can be challenging, you know.'

'Don't be so silly,' Baducing sighed. 'It shouldn't, of course, be taken literally. To imitate Maria is to imitate her heart. She gave herself up to the will of the Lord—not what *she* wanted, but what *he* wanted, even though she didn't understand any of it. The Lord chose her and she gave thanks and obeyed. Imitation of Christ has its obvious reasons for men, imitation of Maria its same reasons for women. And Maria never endeavoured to learn Latin!'

'That may well be the case,' Hild smiled to her young friend, 'but do you really believe she thought she had anything to talk about with the Romans anyway?'

Baducing was startled by her poor argument, and was overcome by an acute attack of boredom. He suddenly longed to be back in Rome, where he had mixed exclusively with learned men, not once encountering a poor argument; there he had been among equals, in good company, people who knew what they were talking about, who had studied every single book in the libraries of the monasteries and could compare the various versions of the Gospels— at a high level, always at the highest level. There were no trivialities in Rome. On these little islands in the sea, however, it was hard to spot anything else—and they had scarcely a book between them.

He suppressed a yawn and stood up.

Aidan had been dead for ten years when his successor, Finan, sensed his hour approaching.

He had nothing against leaving a world that had become too chaotic for his liking; that he personally carried part of the blame only made matters worse. Now he would do what he could to ensure that, at least among the people of the Lord, peace prevailed.

He sent for Abbess Hildeburh; he would tell her what he had wanted to tell her since Queen Eanflæd's feast in Cetreht. He had been extremely concerned by Hildeburh's interest in the young Wilfrid, and thought he should warn her—but courage had failed him time and again.

At one point, Finan had thought he was the only person who took secret pleasure in the good-looking young man appointed by the queen to serve one of her retainers who, after a stroke, had been sent to spend his final days on Lindisfarena. It was quite a task looking after the ailing old man: his broth trickled from the left corner of his mouth, he never knew when he'd wetted himself, or worse, and he might suddenly start blubbering like some woman.

Finan had admired Wilfrid for his efforts; until, that is, he noticed just how many assistants the young man called upon. Talking with the helpers in private, and dispensing promises of forgiveness and threats of dire punishment, Finan got to the truth of the matter.

Wilfrid had quickly worked out which monks were receptive to the special and almost imperceptible wiggle of his cute little backside—and if they just once stretched a hesitant arm towards him, well, then he could get all the help he wanted, with the rough and nasty work too.

He had flattered the slightly older women, courteously and persistently, until after a while, and finding themselves in a secluded corner, they might well be overcome by maternal feelings and give this sweet young man a tight hug. One novice tearfully admitted to having run her hand through his shining curls.

Finan had summoned Wilfrid and imposed a one-month penance. He had also advised him to seek a future in the secular sphere, for which he seemed better suited.

Wilfrid had wept and kissed his abbot on the feet and elsewhere and promised his actions would never be repeated. His only wish was to serve his abbot, none other.

For the sake of this irresistible young man's salvation, however, Finan had thought it wise to send him away, packing him off to the queen with the best possible testimonial—and hoping never to see him again. Wilfrid had then plunged into the argument about how to calculate the right time for the Easter festival. Many hadn't dared disagree with him, and were just as relieved as Finan when they heard he had travelled out into the world. They hoped with all their hearts that he would fall among thieves.

Finan hadn't told anyone, fearful that by so doing he might damage the reputation of the monastery and lose the king's favour. Now he realized he was duty-bound to speak up about the way in which Wilfrid had sown discord. Hildeburh would know what should be done; personally, he couldn't think further than his own shame.

He would also tell her what Wilfrid's father, Berhtfrid from Eoforwik, had confided to him. He had travelled all the way up to Lindisfarena to talk with the bishop about his son.

Something had happened to the lad when his mother died and the new mother started bearing children. He took to wandering around down by the banks of the Use, where the ships from overseas berthed. Berhtfrid had followed him, and saw how he would lure a ship's dog with titbits he had stolen at home, hide the dog for a day or two, then be welcomed aboard the ship as the dog's saviour. He only went home to pick up supplies, and he was an even bigger thief than a magpie. When receiving a beating, he would mumble in the foreign languages he learnt on the ships.

His father had thought the boy should be a sailor, but now he could tell he'd always aimed far higher.

'And is it not true, Bishop,' he had asked Finan, 'that if you are not of royal descent, and yet nonetheless wish to stand above all others, then you must enter the service of the Lord?'

Berhtfrid had spent half his money on equipping his son, so the queen would give him a good reception, and was relieved when she did exactly as he had hoped. He'd had so much trouble with that boy, and had often reproached himself for not following his master Oswine's order to put the two little boys out.

It had been his then wife who desperately wanted a child; she had claimed to be pregnant so many times that no one believed her anymore. But given her stoutness, it was impossible to see what was actually making her belly swell. So Berhtfrid had solved the problem, or so he had thought back then, by keeping the one infant. They had behaved as if the boy was their own, but he didn't make his first public appearance until after his baptism—by which time he could already walk. Advanced for his age, it was said.

He had taken the other child to Hacanos, and used a gold ring to persuade the farmer to place him with a slave family; the child had ended up somewhere near Hræfenclif.

Berhtfrid wouldn't have dared meet the holy Peter with the blood of a child on his hands, but he had since wondered if he'd actually done the right thing. There must have been good reason for Oswine wanting those twin lads put out. He didn't know about the second one, but as far as his own son was concerned, well, he would put it quite bluntly: he feared the man was bewitched. He had done what he could to knock the evil out of that boy, with apparently little effect as it seemed to have become entrenched.

He was nonetheless happy to see the lad in the service of the Lord: prayer and fasting and Christian charity were probably the only hope of turning him into a decent human being. He certainly hadn't managed to do so.

And then Berhtfrid had wept.

Finan had assured him that he had taken the correct action—putting children out was a major sin, be they bewitched or not—which had been of some comfort to Berhtfrid.

All of this, Finan would tell Abbess Hildeburh. When she stood by his bed, however, courage failed him again. And then, before it had a chance to return, the Lord called him home.

Hild grieved over Finan's death. He had been a support to her, and she needed encouragement now.

Rumours of immoral behaviour made her vigilant. She noticed one of the novices was rather taken with a lay brother, and gave her a ticking-off.

'Either—or,' she said. 'You haven't promised yourself to the Lord yet, so if that stable boy is more to your liking, then off you go.'

This gave the young widow food for thought, and from then on she gave no more trouble.

Everything, however, was turned inside out and criticized: above all, the manner of establishing the date for Easter. The holy Columba, who had founded the monastery on Iona, had brought the tradition with him from Ireland: Easter should be celebrated between the fourteenth and twentieth moon after the first full moon after the spring equinox. Wilfrid maintained it should be between the fifteenth and twenty-first moon.

The next point of criticism was the manner of manifesting affiliation to the Lord. Aidan and his men had shaved the hair from the forehead, but let the hair on the back of the head grow normally. Women did the same, even though it wasn't really visible under their headwear. Wilfrid and his men shaved their heads nearly bald, leaving a rim of short hair meant to resemble the crown of thorns Christ wore at his crucifixion; this, in their opinion, was the correct way to follow in Christ's footsteps. Women, they said, should shave their heads completely bald, given that lust often accumulated in the hair, and Maria had ripped every hair from her head when her son was crucified. And then there was the matter of strong leadership and greater unification.

Wilfrid told Alchfred about the best way in which to serve the Lord: deriving from the founder of Monte Cassino monastery, the holy Benedict of Nursia, it comprised a timetable with equal parts of spiritual and physical work. Monks living on these isles only undertook hard physical labour when necessary for the sowing or harvest of crops; apart from the canonical hours there was no fixed daily routine. Their thoughts, therefore, flew off in many directions, necessitating strict penance. And what else could you expect, given that temptation was right there alongside them, on the consecrated ground itself? How could the soul thus rise from its mortal frame?

Benedict of Nursia also required monks to serve their abbot as loyally as personal guards served their king. There were too many opinions on Lindisfarena, in Wilfrid's view; it hadn't been a problem in Aidan's day, but now it was. Everyone was trying to be saved, each in his way, and they didn't always observe the canonical hours. Such behaviour should be called laziness, not service of the Lord.

Alchfred thought Wilfrid's ideas were interesting, and granted him the recently founded monastery in Hrypum, so he could see how the ideas worked in practice. The nuns would have to find somewhere else, and the monks were given the choice between following Wilfrid or leaving. Most opted to return to Magilros and Iona, where they could be true to the practices of their fathers.

Hild welcomed the expelled nuns, even though she thought they could have been sent along with a patch or so of land—after all, she only had ten hides, and eight at Heruteu. She sought out Romanus, to ask him what it was really all about, but she couldn't get a straight answer. On the one hand, he conceded that no one else could have done the work undertaken by the—according to Wilfrid—heretical monks and nuns. On the other hand, he wouldn't dismiss the thought that there could be some substance to the criticism. His queen was very fond of young Wilfrid.

A year was now approaching when adherents of the Church in Rome would celebrate Easter a week later than Church people on these isles. They simply had to reach an agreement before the heathens started pointing fingers of scorn. And all the various issues had to be sorted out at one go. The main Easter problem would arise in the year of the Lord 665; King Oswy thus convened a meeting to be held the year before, at which the problems would be presented and, on that basis, he would make a decision as to when and how the festival would be observed. The meeting would be held in Hild's monastery—he came there frequently, anyway, to visit his little doll.

Hild had tried long and hard to make Oswy keep his daughter.

'You've already given her to the Lord,' she said, 'by having her baptized.'

But Oswy wouldn't be dissuaded, and eventually Hild could no longer turn him down. Shortly after Wulfhere had been made king, the now four-year-old child arrived at Streonæshalch. Her presence involved frequent visits by both the king and the queen, a disruption Hild could happily have done without. What was more, entertaining them came at a cost: they didn't come alone, and Hild knew what was fitting for such guests.

On the other hand, they kept her up to date with what was going on in the realm. Oswy was easily flattered, and would then blurt out every detail. She held back the best mead and the finest beor for his visits, and she always succeeded in extracting the information she was interested in hearing. Nor had she ever forgotten Aidan's directive on the advisability of supporting the seat of royal power—regardless of how hard that might be with a man like Oswy.

She also endeavoured to maintain a good relationship with Oswy for Wulfhere's sake. She had asked him to ban use of the battle-cry 'Raise swords against pagan Mercia!' And please would they stop referring to Mercia as 'Satan's realm'—because Wulfhere had been baptized, persuaded by the Kentish princess Ermengyld, his chosen bride, and many had followed his example.

This was how they could best be loyal to King Penda: by supporting his son. Everyone had realized that by now, even those who had murdered Peada. When the young King Peada, enthusiastically following his new Lord, had pardoned a traitor—merely because the man repented—seven of Penda's most loyal retainers entered into a conspiracy. They simply couldn't serve a king who let people get away with treason; it had never been King Penda's intention that the new god should dishonour and undermine the natural order of the realm.

And so they took action, and they were well pleased when Oswy's daughter got the blame. The seven men were outspoken opponents of this modern peace-making with Northumbria; they all had dead kin who needed avenging up there in the north. As they understood the situation, peace with Northumbria would only have to last until Wulfhere had consolidated his position to the south, and so they decided to follow him under the new god.

# LIGHT OF THE WORLD

*– visiting the double monasteries –*

After the Easter festival, Hild decided to visit Ebba in her monastery at Coludesburh in the north of Bernicia. Hild's husband had killed Ebba's brother Oswald, but that was in the past, twenty-two years ago, and now the double monasteries and Aidan's successors had to stick together.

She took along a copy of Saint John's Gospel, which Wynflæd, the best scribe, had recently finished copying in her neat and very small handwriting. Freawaru had bound the sheets of parchment in red goatskin, and then decorated the back and front each with its holy cross: she had pressed the still-wet goatskin onto a wooden cross stuck to the thin wooden cover board. The idea came from the cover of the red book of Gospels that Aidan had given them when they moved to Ediscum; it was still their most precious treasure.

This was the second time Wynflæd and Freawaru had made such a book; they kept their first one for themselves in Streonæshalch, where they now had a total of sixteen books, some in two copies. They had been given permission to makes copies of two of the books Baducing had brought home from his travels: *Moralia, sive Expositio in Job*, in which Pope Gregorius the Great interpreted the Book of Job, and the Church Father Saint Hieronymus' commentary on the Book of Ecclesiastes.

Baducing had more books, but Hild hadn't been allowed to see the rest yet, and now he'd set off again to the scholarly world. King Alchfred would have liked to go too, but his father couldn't do without him, he said. There would be plenty to copy when Baducing came home; they'd prepared several hundred sheets of parchment, which was of course expensive. A single calfskin rarely gave more than four good parchment sheets; the rest was used for shoes and cord, bits and pieces.

Only the kings knew for sure what Wilfrid had brought home with him, but it was rumoured he was also in possession of a book in which all four Gospels had been put together, written in gold on scarlet parchment and kept in a silver chest studded with precious stones.

Hild took Wynflæd and Freawaru along on the trip, also four monks and five lay brethren: twelve in all, a good number. They rode westwards until they met the giant's road stretching from Eoforwik all the way up to the mouth of the Tuidi river—a more easterly route than the Deira Way, which led past Magilros.

She hadn't been in the north since taking Oswald's mortal remains up to Aidan twenty-two years ago. It was a pleasant reunion: the huge curves of the landscape, the broad views, always several horizons, often six when you counted carefully. Everything was bigger up here, only the people were small; making their living had always been an exceptionally hard graft. The livestock had to roam far and wide to find enough food to survive the winter; not all succeeded.

'Wolves and ravens,' Hild said to Freawaru, 'they're the ones who come off best up here.'

'It was tougher out to the west, where I come from,' said Freawaru. 'King Edwin gave my father some land over there in return for his service. But the Britons hadn't been driven out as we were told. They ambushed us in the forest, and even on the road too. That's how I learnt to use weapons.'

'Did you ever *really* use them?' asked Hild. 'I mean, have you killed anyone?'

'Three or four,' said Freawaru, 'but I wounded quite a few, so they cleared off. Britons. But we never rode out alone. When they were hungry, they'd gather in packs and lie in wait. In wintertime they came right up to the farms. And there was a limit to how many slaves we needed to buy.'

'So did you give them food?' asked Hild.

'Well, we weren't some kind of monastery, and we worked hard for our living. We put porridge out for them at yuletide, so they wouldn't curse us during the holy festival. Otherwise, we threw stones; but once they'd got hold of weapons for themselves, we used spears. If that didn't make them pull back, we had to go for them with swords. Not that I liked it, especially when the women just stood holding out their children. But if you wanted to live there, you had to fight for it—a plot of settler land like ours came with four swords and thirty spears. Just think: four swords—we were twelve families in that area. But the farmhouses weren't very far apart, so we could ring for help—every farm came with a bell. King Edwin had taken them from the monasteries.'

'Have you visited any of the monasteries?'

'They'd been burnt down. And the monastery folk had been killed.'

'Not by King Edwin!' Hild exclaimed indignantly. 'Others—others must have done it.'

'Who?' Freawaru smiled. 'Did they kill themselves?'

'But, well, did you see it with your own eyes?'

Freawaru nodded. 'They hadn't even buried them, they just lay around like wolf food.'

'King Edwin's objective was a righteous realm and a Christian realm.' Hild shook her head. 'I think someone must have been going behind his back.'

'Conquest is conquest,' said Freawaru. 'People are reluctant to relinquish their land, so there's only one way to get hold of it.'

'They never called it conquest,' said Hild half-heartedly. 'They set out to convert the unbelievers to Christianity—that's what they said.'

Freawaru laughed out loud. 'Well, that's one way of putting it—when you're sending people to Paradise. But you didn't believe them, did you?'

'I perhaps didn't think too much about it. I've always believed what the adults said. Well, sort of.'

'But your slaves—Britons—weren't they Christians long before you were?'

'I'm not sure I thought about it like that in the circumstances.'

Freawaru was amazed. 'Incredible what you can make people believe! Just as long as you say it loud enough and you've got the wherewithal.'

'Well, your family must have thought there was a nice vacant plot for them, too, didn't they?' asked Hild.

'My father had been out west with them,' Freawaru responded, with a slightly wry smile. 'A good Briton is a dead Briton, he used to say. He hated the Christians, so when Edwin got himself baptized, my father and a couple of other big landowners planned to kill him. But then he gave them land over there for themselves, so they settled for killing Britons instead.'

Hild hailed a young man walking along with a heifer in tow. She asked him about the road, the route, where he came from, his family, this and that.

'Don't you know the way?' asked Freawaru in surprise.

'Always good to check,' said Hild evasively.

'Upon my word, I do believe you are just like our queen when it comes to the young men!' Freawaru laughed.

Hild blushed, but she'd rather have that kind of reputation than let word get around about the real reason she was looking at young men. If her twins were still alive, and if Oswy got wind of them, then it was all over. Her only option was to get them sent down to Kent, and from there to Gaul. That was her plan.

Reaching the Tina river, they made a detour to the Tinanmude monastery on the estuary coast.

The abbess was frightened by the rumours, and she didn't understand what was going on. Her name was Frigyd, which was enough to make Hild feel a bond. She had been trained on Lindisfarena, had spent two years in Magilros, and then taken over the monastery here, among people who had very little interest in receiving the word of the gospel.

Hild and Freawaru told her about their life in Ediscum; this was the first time they had been able to laugh about it all.

A horse's head thrown over the fencing—they'd had three of those here in Tinanmude, they didn't bother about them anymore. And things had improved; especially after they'd started dispensing medicines. Frigyd laughed while she told them about her 'miracles': perfectly ordinary illnesses she had cured with perfectly ordinary and much-used remedies from *Medicina Plinii*. She'd done nothing mysterious, but had always ended with a prayer—and then they believed it was the prayer that had cured them.

'And that has far greater effect in getting people off to baptism than the words we preach,' in her opinion.

'As long as they get baptized,' said Wynflæd. 'Have you got your own copy of that book by Plinius?'

Frigyd nodded and, blushing, Wynflæd glanced across at Hild. It was agreed that the Tinanmude scribes would make copies of the Plinius books in their library; in return, they would receive the passage about elephants that Hereswid had sent Hild, along with Saint Hieronymus' commentary on the Book of Ecclesiastes, *Etymologiae* by Isidorus of Seville and then two more books when Baducing returned and let them see his treasures. Then they would be more or less all square.

They stayed for two days, during which they studied the books and agreed on the exchanges. The abbess accepted Hild's invitation to the meeting with King Oswy. If they popped in on the return journey, she'd give them a couple of hens that laid eggs every other day; they were a new breed, which she had been given by her mother's sister in Kent—the hens came from Gaul.

Next destination was Lindisfarena, where Colman was now bishop and abbot following Finan's death. He was pleased to have the opportunity to vent his rage, and immediately offered them mead.

'I will simply refuse. I'll step down if need be,' he shouted, waving his arms around.

'Do you think that will bother them?' Hild asked with a smile.

'They will regret that they ever started all this nonsense!' he shouted. 'Just think if Aidan had witnessed such absurdity! And Columba! Think about him!'

'Times change,' said Hild.

'And not for the better! But whatever might happen, no fiend in human clothing is going to make me forsake Aidan and Columba! The gospel and the true path—that doesn't change, no matter how many of the queen's young men have been to Rome, or wherever else they run around playing the fool!'

'What do you say to the adultery issue?' asked Hild.

'Stuff and nonsense, I say. Not a matter worth wasting our time on.'

'No,' Hild agreed. 'And what do you say to the tonsure issue?'

'I have received my tonsure from Aidan's hand. And that is all I have to say.'

'Isn't it just a matter of outward appearance?' Hild suggested. 'Aidan received my vows, too, but I couldn't actually care about shaving off my hair. I have no use for it anyway.'

'Maybe not, but why?' grumbled Colman. 'What is the point of all this nonsense? They're just making it up so we'll look as silly as they do with their absurd heads. My hair grows how my hair grows, and that's all there is to it!'

'And what do you say to the lack of overall regulation?'

'Regulation and regulation,' he said. Once his rage had been aired, he was more subdued. He refilled their drinking vessels.

'We harbour many opinions. The work of abbot and bishop would perhaps be more straightforward if there was a greater degree of compliance, but on the other hand: there are many assignments, and of different kinds, and I think these are best resolved by different people trying each in their own way. The crucial point is that we turn men and women to the way of the Lord. People aren't identical, and the more the merrier, I would say. If everyone took my approach, there is much that would never get done.'

'Have you ever refused to assign a priest?'

'If anyone wants one of our priests, I consider it a great honour.'

'Have you heard of anyone who has refused?'

'Never! And it would be utterly foolish.'

They agreed that Colman, being Northumbria's bishop, should plead their case at the meeting, and that he should rein in his fiery temperament for the sake of the cause.

They also stayed for two days on Lindisfarena; the mead was exceptionally good and they had two new books by Isidorus of Seville in their library: *De ortu et obitu patrum* and *Synonyma*. The scribes immediately set to work on a copy of the first, in return for a copy of Saint Hieronymus, which they could pick up on their way home.

Wynflæd had spent the entire visit in the writing room and asked permission to stay, but Hild didn't want to leave her there. In just two days, Wynflæd had already learnt how to concentrate pigments without the ink becoming viscous, and how to make it fluid and smooth without blotting—and how to make a new yellow mixture. Here on Lindisfarena, they used two main colours; the first letters were red—a brilliant scarlet made from the large sea snail found in such abundance at Streonæshalch—and the rest were black. Within the text, Jesus's name was coloured with red. Wynflæd was itching to get started; she could hardly drag herself from the writing room when it was time for Mass. On the other hand, she could teach them a thing or two about quills. Thanks to the poor ink she had worked with at home, she had been obliged to experiment, paying the locals to bring her all sorts of birds and then trying out various ways of cutting the feathers. As Lindisfarena's wading birds were not suitable for fine points, she promised to send a selection of the best quills if they would also make a copy of Isidorus' other book. The visit to Lindisfarena turned out to be profitable in every respect.

On the fifteenth day, they arrived at Coludesburh—a rougher and harsher place than they had imagined. The monastery was situated on the top of a hill, pulled back from the cliff; rocks and stones, even the earth, were a reddish brown. The landscape was a riot of intense colour: the crisp-green grass, the red rocks and the blue sea, today with white foam crests matching the white of the clouds. There had also been a fortified settlement on the promontory here, but Ebba wasn't that scrupulous about surveillance.

'Oswald gave me this place, not Oswy,' she laughed.

The huts were built of mud, as they were in Streonæshalch and on Lindisfarena; a pair of lay brethren were busy plugging holes left by the storm. The buildings had been erected very close to one another and right up to the fencing, to provide shelter from the wind. Hild felt closed-in.

'You obviously don't worry about fire, that's for certain!' she exclaimed.

'Well, the Lord surely protects his own,' said Ebba, showing them into the church, which was draped with the loveliest wall hangings and felt almost warm, despite the stiff wind.

Ebba was pleased to receive a visit from her relative. To Hild's surprise, Ebba didn't see her as the former wife of her brother's slayer, nor as the daughter of the son of the brother of her father Ædelfred's slayer. She saw her as daughter of the son of the brother of her mother Acha, and thus they came from the same family line: Acha's brother Eadfrid was the father of Hild's father Hereric—well, at least, he'd been married to Hereric's mother.

'We have a surprise for you,' she smiled to Hild before they entered the women's room.

A richly-dressed young woman leapt up and ran to meet them. She fell to her knees in front of Hild, head bowed, the white skin of her neck taut against the bright pale-green fabric. Her skin was almost transparent, her very fair hair gleaming in competition with the silk cord of her hairnet.

Hild raised the young woman's head.

'Ædelthryd!' she cried. 'Oh, but do stand up!'

'Not until you have blessed me, mother,' said Ædelthryd's crisp and very emphatic voice. Hild blessed her; Ædelthryd leapt to her feet and embraced her mother's sister.

Hild couldn't get enough of the sight of her niece; her beauty illuminated the room like a blazing torch, and just looking at her lightened the heart.

'It seems as if you are thriving up here,' she laughed. 'I think being married suits you well. And with such a young man!'

She winked at Ebba, who sent a worried look back and quickly invited them to sit at the dining table.

'Yes,' Ædelthryd replied, once they had taken their places, 'my husband Egfred has just turned eighteen. But my true husband is extremely old! For he is the Lord God.'

The smile she sent to Hild could have melted a stone. 'Didn't you know, mother? That I have long since promised the Lord my maidenhood?'

'Indeed,' said Hild, somewhat hesitantly, 'so much can be promised. And matrimony is greatly pleasing to the Lord.'

'Well, yes,' smiled Ædelthryd, 'when you have no other option, as Wilfrid says!'

'But I thought . . . ' Hild went on, now confused, 'given that you nonetheless entered into matrimony . . . '

'Wilfrid made me understand the true way,' Ædelthryd said excitedly. 'Marriage is pleasing to the Lord, he says, and fleshly love, well, that's for the masses, and it's necessary to keep your worldly possessions in the family. But the highest form of love is love given to the Lord, and if you are true to that, well, then you possess a treasure that will never perish.'

She looked straight ahead, transfigured, and broke into a radiant smile.

'Wilfrid also made Egfred understand that there is greater honour in having a wife who is true to the greatest of all masters than just having an ordinary wife. And that the Lord will reward him, too, for this. He says Egfred must build a monastery where I can worship the Lord, and his effort will be repaid hundreds of times over.'

'Weren't you given Hagustaldesea as your morning gift?' asked Hild.

'Oh yes,' Ædelthryd beamed, 'but Wilfrid thinks it would be better for my husband to build a monastery. To show the Lord that he agrees, he says.'

'Well,' Hild muttered, 'nothing wrong in building a monastery, I suppose.'

'Absolutely not,' Ebba nodded, and offered them more beer.

Ædelthryd didn't want any beer, she ate and drank very little, but Hild and her people were happy to accept.

After evening Mass, Ædelthryd asked for Ebba's permission to spend the night in front of the altar, for the salvation of her soul. Ebba and Hild walked across to Ebba's hut.

'What could a young girl like her possibly have done to require penance?' asked Ebba.

Hild shook her head. 'I thought it would pass when she married again.'

'Why is that Wilfrid mixed up in it?' asked Ebba.

'It's Queen Eanflæd—she wants her son to be king after Oswy, and not Alchfred, Oswy's son from his first marriage. So she sent Wilfrid down to Elge to persuade Ædelthryd.'

'I don't really keep up with what's going on,' said Ebba, 'but how does Egfred benefit from one of King Anna's daughters?'

'Didn't you know that Ædelthryd is my sister Hereswid's child? Anna accepted her as his own daughter when Hereswid entered the service of the Lord.'

Ebba beamed with delight. She had wondered why Ædelthryd called her 'my own family', but had thought she meant the family of the Lord. She stood up and wandered around humming, smiling, pleased to learn that the devout young woman who had married the king's son was of her own lineage. She brought out a pitcher of beor and two elmwood beakers.

'Well, that was certainly a surprise,' she laughed, raising her beaker to Hild. 'Then it's not such a bad thing if he wants Deira too—in that case, she's an excellent match, so everything will be all right.'

'Except it can never all be right!' said Hild.

'Oh, of course, no, it can't.'

'Until he's got Deira, perhaps.'

'Yes,' said Ebba, 'one day . . . ' She thought for a moment, and then burst out: 'Just imagine—this morning she asked, in utter seriousness, if I thought she should hand over her morning gift to Wilfrid!'

'What did you say to that?' asked Hild, appalled.

'Well, I asked her how much the young man has, and do you know the answer? Forty hides of land at Hrypum! And do you know how much I have? Oswald gave me eight hides, and now we're up to fifteen, everything included.'

'I have ten hides in Streonæshalch and eight at Heruteu,' said Hild. 'If we had more land, then we could increase the numbers who attend lessons. We aim to train more priests, and that comes at a price—just the amount we spend on parchment! But we simply have to acquire all the learning we can.'

'Indeed,' said Ebba absent-mindedly, and filled their beakers. 'Did you see those sheep in the north enclosure? They bred them in Magilros, and they haven't lost a single one in recent winters. I thought you might take a couple of lambs with you, so you can mate them with your own.'

'Thank you, how very kind,' said Hild. 'We lost eight the year before last, and twelve lambs. Has Oswy invited you to the meeting at my monastery?'

'What meeting would that be?'

'At which he will decide upon the date of the Easter festival, the correct form of tonsure and if the Lord's people must be more co-ordinated.'

'Co-ordinated? How?' asked Ebba in surprise.

'Well, by putting all the monasteries and all the priests under the authority of the bishop, as Wilfrid wants.'

'But why?' asked Ebba indignantly.

'They say adultery takes place in the double monasteries, and that the abbesses disregard the best interests of the kingdom. That we should act together.'

Ebba was astonished.

'What actions should we take together? Except praise the Lord at the appointed hours?'

'I don't know—perhaps we could exchange books . . . '

'I can't really say I'm particularly interested in all that scholarship these days,' said Ebba, 'but don't you already exchange books?'

Hild nodded, but then she couldn't think up any more good arguments, and so she presented Ebba with the bad argument, as she saw it: the wish to turn the people of the Church into a force, led by a bishop, comparable in power and glory with that of the king, as was the case in Gaul and many of the Christian kingdoms.

Ebba clapped her hands together.

'Oh, but dearest Hild, this cannot be true. Because Jesus has told us: *My kingdom is not of this world*, he said. I can't believe any of the Lord's people would want it otherwise.'

'Aidan said it was like that in Gaul, and he was much opposed. He wanted a poor and humble Church, adhering to the words of Jesus and speaking out resolutely against injustice. And a strong king, who punishes injustice with the sword.'

'Of course,' said Ebba. 'There can't be two kings in one realm, as everyone knows. Don't you think you're worrying too much, dearest Hild? Because it's all utterly impossible and contrary to the Lord's own words.'

'Well, you'll have the opportunity to hear for yourself what they've got to say,' Hild sighed.

'Yes, and people do so like the sound of their own voices,' said Ebba, patting Hild's hand. 'We mustn't concern ourselves with that—we must go about our work and serve the Lord, and then he'll indeed reward us as he sees fit.'

She smiled encouragingly at the fretful daughter of her brother's son, and refilled their beakers with her rosehip beor, a wonderfully smooth and strong drink, which gradually dispersed Hild's worries.

Ædelthryd had experienced a vision during the night: a light had appeared above the altar and then vanished abruptly. Ebba nodded—she had dreamt something similar. They decided to spend the day in gentle pursuits.

During the morning, Hild and Freawaru were shown the sewing room and the weaving room. They had heard a great deal about the textiles from Coludesburh, but had never seen any—and they weren't disappointed. With goods like these to sell, you could easily get by with the poor soil. They memorized a few patterns and Freawaru made a deal: a Gospel for a rug she simply couldn't leave behind. She would replicate the weave; it would earn them a good profit.

Wynflæd and the monks Bosa and Oftfor went to the writing room. Wynflæd taught them to cut quills from the feathers of small birds, and Oftfor found some deviations in their version of Saint Matthew's Gospel, which they discussed until midday.

'You should have a little rest,' said Hild to Ædelthryd as they finished the midday meal. 'Afterwards you can come out with us and see the sheep.'

Ædelthryd looked unwell; her transparent skin had turned a greyish hue.

'I'll watch and pray until then.'

By the time they left, she had a slightly better colour in her cheeks, but Hild didn't want to ask if she'd slept. Her concern for her niece grew; Ædelthryd ate next to nothing. Hild reproached herself for not taking more care of this young woman who was so very worried about the salvation of her soul. Wilfrid this and Wilfrid that—it was just like hearing Hereswid going on about Sigebert, she thought with a sigh.

'Remember, the Lord does not gauge us by our physical endurance,' she said. 'At your age, you have to eat and sleep properly.'

'Wilfrid says that if you take care of your prayers and fasting for the Lord, then he will take care of the rest,' Ædelthryd replied firmly.

The sheep had very long and curly fleeces. No one had lost any of their sheep this winter, the weather being exceptionally mild for the season. They hadn't needed to use as much firewood as other years, but it wasn't natural; and the warmth continued. The trees had sprung into leaf three weeks too early. At first, the weather had been called a blessing, but now they needed rain; the seed grain lay scattered on the fields, unable to grow into seedlings.

Having picked out the lambs Hild would take home with her, they had just started walking back when they saw a shadow far away in the distance, blowing across the land. They looked up at the sky, but it was still completely cloudless—all the way round. They looked at one another and tried to keep their composure as the shadow swept in over them. More than a shadow: dusk was falling, the day was ending.

Ædelthryd screamed loudly and pointed up towards the sun, then threw herself to the ground and cowered, sobbing, her arms wrapped around her head.

'The Lord be with you, dearest Hild,' said Ebba, hugging her gently. She then lay on the ground and started to pray.

Hild looked up again, but there could be no mistake. It had happened and she knew it wasn't a dream: the light of the sun had been extinguished. The vast hand of the Lord had seized the sun and would cast it into the darkness. So, it was over. The end of days had come.

The birds had stopped singing and were preparing themselves for the end. And they had eggs, thought Hild, nests full of eggs, maybe already a brood. Her arms fell limply to her sides. It was all too late, and she had nothing to say in her defence. Judgement would fall, and she would be cast out into the darkness.

She held her breath and waited, as silently as the birds. Scanning the horizon, the firmament, she spun slowly round, her face turned upwards, to catch a glimpse of the Lord when he came galloping down from on high, surrounded by his divine army. What a magnificent sight that would be; she didn't want to miss it.

Ebba lay prostrate on the ground; the psalms of David had come to her and she was reciting them with her usual calm confidence.

. . . *The waters saw you, O God; the waters saw you, they were afraid: the depths trembled also. The clouds poured out water; the skies resounded: your arrows flew far and wide. Your roaring thunder was in the whirlwind, lightning lit up the world, the earth trembled and shook. Your way went straight through the sea, your path through great waters, but your footsteps were not known. You led your people like a flock, by the hand of Moses and Aaron . . .*

The Lord was a long time coming, and the silence of death prevailed across the earth. Not even the waves could be heard, just Ebba's rapid murmuring. Hild waited with bated breath.

'If you could show mercy,' she said, looking up to the heavens, 'then let me see my sons before you cast me out, just the once. And look with mercy upon my husband, King Penda, and upon my father and my mother; look with mercy upon my people in Streonæshalch and in Heruteu, and upon Talcuin—Tancwoystel from Dolwyddelan. Look in mercy upon my son King Wulfhere and my son Ædelræd, and upon my sister and Sigebert, both gone before us; look with mercy upon your little handmaiden Frigyd, and upon Penda's children, look in mercy upon this Ædelthryd and this Ebba, and upon King Oswald whose blood clings to my hands. Send my greetings to Aidan who rests in your bosom, and take into account, O Lord, whatever has come to pass, my sons are your sons! They are baptized in your name, Hundfrid and Wilbrord they are called, and, if they live, they are now thirty-one years of age, both of them, but before you let me go, then grant me one glimpse of them, grant me leave to wave to them before you take them to yourself; they have done nothing wicked and you must take them to you as your own, lift them to your lap and dry the tears from their cheeks—they left me too early, so I could not . . . Hundfrid and Wilbrord I call them, remember. And look in mercy upon King Edwin and Queen Tata, and upon King Anna's children, and upon little Frigyd, and do not forget King Wulfhere of Mercia, who is my son, and your servant Baducing, who let me see his books . . . two daughters I have carried, you took them to yourself before they saw light, greet them in Paradise, and look in mercy upon my husband's little daughter, who was married to that abominable man, let her not spend eternity together with him; my husband Penda burnt many of your houses, but he was loyal to his family, and we were one flesh, even though we never received your blessing . . . '

She stopped, because she couldn't decide if she should pray for Cynewise. Could she do that from a pure heart?

She heard her father; his greeting sent a warm current flowing through her and caused the tears to surge. He would never abandon her.

The blackbird piped up, and a chaffinch joined in. She was standing with her arms outstretched to the sides, and something started itching on her left hand: a cabbage-white butterfly, with no thought for the salvation of its soul, happily sitting there in the sun. The gulls screeched out at sea, she heard the curlew and now she saw it swinging in across the land, heard its long summoning warbles.

Her arms flopped down and the butterfly fluttered away; she watched its shadow flapping across the grass. She looked at her hands, moved them back and forth—the shadow followed. She looked up, and it was true: the sun had returned.

'He'll come some other time, I'm sure,' said Ebba confidently, brushing grass from her clothing. She looked out across her lands and smiled at the sight. She had actually resigned herself to the likelihood that it wouldn't happen in her lifetime, and then it had anyway—well, nearly. To give the pagans time to turn, no doubt about that: he was merciful, her Lord, he had given the lost souls another chance. Magnanimity, generosity, patience, such was his nature. She was filled with joy, and her old lungs pumped with all their might as she burst into a loud hymn of thanksgiving.

Hild walked quietly by her side. It had happened in a flash: she had realized that light was life itself. Now, in her thoughts, she was trying to explain this in greater detail, but she was falling short. She knew it to be true, nonetheless, but in a manner hidden from the world, and for the time being also hidden from her. She would go through all the books again; she couldn't recall anything about it, but there must be something. Otherwise, she would have to write to Baducing and ask him to make enquiries in the learned world. She was in no doubt: something must have been written about it.

They had to support Ædelthryd, one at each arm: she was shaking so much she could hardly walk.

'He's always said it wouldn't be in our day,' she wept.

Ebba had run out of breath for her hymn of thanksgiving, and heard what the young girl said.

'Who?' she wheezed.

'Wilfrid!' Ædelthryd wept. 'He promised it wouldn't be now. There was time to mend one's ways, he said.'

'Well, that seems to be true,' said Ebba, 'so there's nothing to be unhappy about, is there.'

'When they beheaded his bishop,' Ædelthryd sobbed, 'they would have done it to Wilfrid too. Like this!' she shouted, making a gesture across her neck. And then she collapsed.

'There there,' Ebba comforted her, 'but they didn't do it, did they.'

'No, but still,' Ædelthryd snuffled. 'A man like him! And right up onto the scaffold. That's where he had his revelation.'

'There is much that ought to be different,' said Ebba.

She used this phrase to soothe people when they complained, but she didn't personally want anything to be different. She had reconciled herself completely to the world as it was. She hummed her tune all the way back to the monastery. It had been a lovely day.

The light filtering down through the trees. The new beech leaves all a-shimmer. A forest burgeoning with hundreds of shades of green: blue-green, yellow-green, pale green, in the sun more yellowish, in the shade almost bluish. Still a few anemones on the forest floor, brown around the edges, most with their fruit sticking out to all sides. The cowslip petals, already coming to an end when they travelled north, now just the long curved leaves left. But the beech leaves: did a leaf like that cast shadow?

Hild dismounted from her horse to check—yes, it cast shadow. The light shone through the leaf, but lingered on its underside. Not like the animal bladders and skins they stretched across the window openings, allowing the light to pass into the room. You couldn't make a window of beech leaves.

It seemed as if the birds were only now aware of the luxuriant world in which they could build—and all those little flying insects! They were visible to the human eye in the streaks of light, but the birds caught them in the shade, too.

Much is invisible to us, thought Hild, because the light has not reached us. Jesus is the light of the world, which is the fact of the matter. Light is the Lord's gift to humankind. When his words reach us, we will understand the deep bond—the interconnectedness of all things.

Oftfor called out; he was impatient to get home, murmuring Latin declensions into the air as they rode onwards.

'If the rain doesn't come, we'll have a poor harvest,' said Freawaru.

Hild didn't respond. She looked up at the leaves and the speckles of light and just let her horse follow along with the others.

When the poplar comes into leaf, it sparkles like molten copper, she thought, but gradually it turns into its normal green. Perhaps the poplar is the same as the birds Merewald talked about: once they have become accustomed to the light and plenty, they think life's nothing but sunshine and cabbage-whites, and then they forget to say thank you.

'Thank you, Lord!' she said resolutely to the heavens. 'Thank you for your light.'

# HEADS WITHOUT HAIR

*– the meeting at Streonæshalch –*

The meeting was scheduled for the middle of the holy month, and Hild had kept back the best of everything; the harvest had failed. Even the honey wasn't right, so dry it was almost impossible to get it out of the combs. The brewing had started, so the beer would be at its best when the guests arrived; the bread was being prepared, dough needed to rest for a couple of days.

Begu had selected the pigs for slaughter. The guests would not be making do with the porridge mush usually eaten at the monastery, twice a week, with the addition of a little smoked mutton or salted pork. Hild nodded to Begu: yes, they would have to put up with these scrawny pigs. Had they been in Tamoworthig, she smiled to herself, she would never have offered guests a couple of scraggy bones—they'd had sows so fat they could hardly stand up. That kind of luxury was a thing of the past.

The only queenly practice she did enforce was a degree of cleanliness, which caused much shaking of heads. Bedlinen, wall hangings, clothing, even the altar cloth, all were carried outdoors on the first day of every month and given a thorough beating; bedlinen and clothes were then washed. She also insisted that anyone who had slept elsewhere should have their clothes washed when they returned. They couldn't let monastery fleas mix with those of strangers, because there had been many instances where coupling with strangers had resulted in larger offspring. You just had to look at the remote settlements where the animals only ever mated with one another, always ending up as weaklings. Mixing things together produced something better and stronger. Therefore, thought Hild, if they could keep their fleas for themselves, they would gradually be reduced to tiny little pinpricks.

Rubbing away at the cloth with water had a price, of course, and it also meant they had to have duplicates of many items, but Hild didn't want the Lord's people to be mistaken for vagrants and spurned as a consequence of their appearance. People would rather listen to a well-dressed and washed preacher, without head-lice, someone who didn't keep stopping to have a good scratch. And the message about purity of the heart was more likely to sound convincing if the messenger was nice and clean.

Everything was ready when the guests arrived. Agilbert, former bishop of the West Saxons, now Bishop of Paris, was accompanied by Wilfrid and King Alchfred. Oswy and Queen Eanflæd came with Bishop Colman and the people from Magilros.

Hild received the guests in her magnificent red frock and was a bountiful hostess; she wasn't going to let them think she was struggling with her mere ten hides of land. After Mass, they were served fresh pork and lamb, followed by honey-preserved blackberries with beor.

Ebba had sent word to Bishop Colman and obviously felt he would represent her interests. Fortunately, Abbess Frigyd from Tinanmude had come, and brought with her a new story: some of her people had been crossing the river when a sudden wind grabbed the raft and carried them downstream; they had cried out to the farmers and fisherfolk standing on the banks, asking for their help. 'You're getting your just reward, you lot are!' came a shouted reply, and not one person had made any attempt to assist them.

Hild was shocked; Frigyd wasn't particularly surprised.

'Just think how the new teachings have turned everything upside down,' she said. 'People don't know what to believe. They say we've taken everything away from them, but not given them anything in return. They're no longer allowed to make sacrifices, and they don't understand the other option. It will take at least two generations for Christianity to take root—at least! But the people who stood there scratching themselves, they'll be baptized before yuletide. Because just before the raft was blown out to sea, the wind changed direction and guided my people to shore, all in one piece, and the onlookers saw it with their own eyes—and now they're receiving preparation for baptism.'

'Praise the Lord for turning the wind,' said Hild. 'Both for the sake of your people and for the sake of others.'

'Miracles and medicine,' said Frigyd, 'that's what works!'

Hild took her across to the writing room and showed her the books Bishop Agilbert had brought from the abbess in Hereswid's monastery. They agreed to have a copy made, and in return Hild would receive all Frigyd's formulas for remedies—the Magilros formulas that had passed from mother to daughter for generations.

While they were talking, Hild suddenly felt a burning sensation all over her body. She had to sit down, sweat pouring from her, infuriated that now she would have to miss the meeting. And then the sweating stopped, and she was fresh as a morning daisy.

'How odd,' she said. 'Do I look normal now?'

'You have all along,' Frigyd replied.

Next morning they visited the herb garden, and Hild gave Frigyd the seeds from some useful plants. She had cultivated a perfectly good herb garden down by the beck—not like the one in Tamoworthig, of course.

Hild wasn't apprehensive about the verdict Oswy would deliver. He was baptized and trained on Iona, and often visited Lindisfarena. He was perfectly satisfied with the basic food served, and he never demanded royal trappings. On the other hand, he didn't give anything to the monasteries—they would just give it away, anyway—and a poor and humble Church suited him well.

If his ruling fell in favour of Wilfrid and his supporters, then not only would he be forsaking the doctrine in which he had been trained, he would also be saddling himself with a rival. At the moment, the Church people only represented a moral force, which could indeed be persuasive, but when the stakes were really high he could simply ignore them—as he had clearly demonstrated, and more than once.

During his reign, two of Deira's kings had met a violent death: first Oswine, and then, shortly after the battle at Wynwæd, King Ædelwald had vanished. A herdsman had found Ædelwald in the forest half a year later, his pigs in the process of devouring the king's remains. He had obviously been buried in haste, as the pigs had no problem snuffling out his shallow grave. He was identified by the new silver spurs on his boots, a gift from his wife; so it hadn't been a robbery. His remains were reburied in Læstingaeu, as had been his wish.

Nothing could be proven, though. But when something like that happened, everyone's first thought was: Oswy again. No one felt they had to say it out loud—done was done—and anyway, there was a general understanding of the situation: kings lasted as long as they lasted, and then another one came along, rarely a better one.

If Oswy backed Wilfrid, then he would also be acknowledging Alchfred, who was so vociferous a champion of Wilfrid's cause. For that reason alone, Oswy would stick with things as they were. Such was Hild's reasoning.

Oswy had other ideas. While mulling over the dilemma, he had given a great deal of thought to the sign he had received from the Lord: in the middle of the afternoon, awe-inspiring, even the gulls had fallen silent and sat motionless.

He still hadn't worked out what it meant, but he was certain it bore relevance to his ruling in this matter. He had asked Romanus, Bishop Colman, Abbess Hildeburh and his sister Ebba for advice, but their answers had by no means been of one mind. He would have to make his own decision.

His son Alchfred spent more than enough on zealous young men of the Church like Wilfrid and Baducing, but that was how things were nowadays. Hildeburh's son King Wulfhere was doing the same in Mercia. News of their exploits thus spread far and wide, and prayers were said energetically for their souls. He had long been thinking over the positive potential of this investment. In any event, he didn't like being outshone, and certainly not by his son. If he was to retain his position as the highest authority in all matters, he would have to keep abreast of developments, not dig in his heels. Otherwise, he risked a situation in which Wilfrid played the kings off against one another and only deferred to Alchfred—as far as the outside world could tell, of course, because in reality Alchfred was at Wilfrid's beck and call.

Oswy wanted to avoid conflict with his son, however foolish that son might be. He already dreaded what the holy Peter would have to say about Deira's two former kings; he couldn't add yet another sin to his account, and certainly not one committed against his own son. He simply had to prevent insubordination, and thus he would have to concur with Wilfrid—even though that would be inviting a cuckoo into the nest.

At least twenty times now he'd heard the account of how Queen Baldhild, widow and ruler after Clovis the Second, king of the Franks, had ordered nine bishops to be beheaded, including Wilfrid's patron, Bishop Annemundus of Lugdunum. He understood her action so very well, and if they'd included Wilfrid, well, many a problem could have been avoided. Those bishops weren't like Aidan or Colman; over there, they had extensive areas of landed property, reigned in both a worldly and spiritual sense, and within their sphere had far more power than the king—who, at the moment, was a queen.

The battle would come, but decapitating one bishop after another wasn't the route to victory. The Church would always be left with the ultimate power. Jesus and his word remained steadfast, while kings would come and go. Kings were necessary to rule the realm, but Jesus was the light of the world.

That was the difference, as Oswy well knew: in this battle, the king would be the underdog—but he wasn't about to let that happen in his lifetime.

Accordingly, Oswy made his decision: Easter would be celebrated between the fifteenth and twenty-first day of the moon—and if anyone insisted on sticking to the sun day between the fourteenth and the twentieth, they wouldn't be doing so in his kingdom. In addition, monks would manifest their affiliation to the Lord by wearing the tonsure favoured by the Church in Rome, nuns by shaving all the hair from their heads. Unity and the spirit of community were to prevail amongst the Lord's folk.

Oswy had asked Agilbert—he being the eldest—to speak on behalf of the Roman observance: given that Wilfrid's eloquence and familiarity with the historical details were famed, Agilbert asked the king to let Wilfrid speak instead, also noting that he had not himself mastered the language of the Angles.

And how Wilfrid shone! His studies at the centres of scholarship in the outside world had not been in vain. Rich in words, fluently and without the slightest hesitation, he trounced Bishop Colman; some thought he did so with extreme elegance, others that he was unduly rude and defamatory. He calmly explained that the customs of their fathers were heretical and contrary to the word of the Lord. Colman's references to the apostle John, to their reverend father Columba and to the holy Anatolius were countered with such perspicacity that many became aware of Colman's inadequate learning and intellect. All Colman's arguments were eventually undermined, and his insular obstinacy was laid bare.

Once the king had delivered his judgement, Colman went in search of Hild, but she had again been struck down with the fever; by the time she returned, Colman had called his men together and announced his departure.

Hild and the king saw him out, and his parting words were less than gracious. He did, however, have the presence of mind to ask King Oswy to let Abbot Eata from Magilros take his place at Lindisfarena. Eata had been one of the twelve boys Aidan had selected from among the Angles to receive instruction in Christ; Oswy was happy to show his respect for Aidan. He also gave Colman permission to take some of Aidan's bones, to aid their ministry in the new setting. Thirty of the Angles who had been trained on Lindisfarena, and nearly all the Irish and other Britons, went with Colman.

The monastic leaders now gathered their remaining people and took them to task: unity among the people of the Church, they insisted, and much more. Tempers did indeed calm down—until they were told to kneel in front of Wilfrid and Agilbert, who sheared hair and shaved heads, leaving the men with just the circular wreath that made them look utterly foolish. The women looked like eggs and hurried to cover their skulls. The men, however, had no possibility of hiding the indignity.

The shame led a few of them to sneak out of the assembly and gallop off in pursuit of Colman. For some of the older brethren, having to line up was enough humiliation to cause their departure. They had been reminded of the mass baptisms of terrified Britons, arms tied behind their backs, at which they had officiated. Many had probably been baptized before, and re-baptism was a grave sin. But the king had ordered wholesale baptism once an area inhabited by Britons had been conquered, and he had impressed upon his clerics that remonstrations should not be taken seriously, since they were due to the Britons' obstinate paganism—which might have been true in some instances, but not in others: you could never quite tell with the natives.

Hild was struck by another feverish flare-up while standing in the queue. She felt like a cow on its way to slaughter and grabbed hold of Frigyd, who was standing in front.

'It's come again,' she whispered.

'Sit down for a moment,' said Frigyd, but Hild refused; if she left the queue now, the whole line would break up and all would be chaos.

'I'm boiling all over,' she murmured. 'Hold onto me if I faint.'

'You look perfectly normal,' said Frigyd.

And then Hild's inner eruption was over.

'I don't know what it can be,' she whispered. 'I've never felt like this before.'

'How old are you?' Frigyd whispered back. 'Do you still have your bleedings?'

'Hardly ever,' said Hild. 'Do you think that's what it is? I'm fifty years old now. Well, yes, then it must be that.'

'Most likely,' said Frigyd. 'But those hot flushes will stop eventually.'

'So that's all it is,' said Hild, relieved, and then it was Frigyd's turn to kneel before Wilfrid.

Hild focused all her attention on a cobweb stuck to the rafter above Wilfrid's head. If it was a poisonous spider, and if she could make it slide down . . . and then she too had to kneel.

'I'll never forgive you for this,' she told him soundlessly, in her mind, as the young upstart sliced off her long red hair. There were a few grey ones now, not many, and her mane still shone like newly-burnished copper—even when piled on the floor along with short and long locks of every colour and texture. She recognized Begu's thick white hair, and Sæthryd's, very short and pitch-black, with Wynflæd's abundant fair curls, all heaped together. What was the point? Before any further speculation was possible, she was told to stand up. She pulled up her headdress and wished they would all just leave, ride away that very instant.

At King Alchfred's request, Agilbert had ordained Wilfrid in the abbey church at Hrypum. Wilfrid had just reached the right age.

Oswy had selected Northumbria's new bishop: a learned and respected monk educated in the south of Ireland, his training according to the precepts of Rome, and he was one of the few who would be able to unite the divided Church people. But he died before his ordination, of a plague that had already claimed the lives of many.

King Alchfred suggested Wilfrid, but Oswy wouldn't countenance the idea of a thirty-year-old bishop—the elders had suffered enough humiliation. Wounds must now be allowed to heal so work could be resumed, and that would require a mature man, a resolute and humble man who concentrated on the word of the Lord and was devoid of personal vanity.

'We can look at Wilfrid in fifteen to twenty years,' he said, and proposed Chad, a man who satisfied all his criteria.

Chad and his brothers—Cedd, Cælin and Cynebil—had numbered among Aidan's boys, and they had all become priests. Cælin had been King Ædelwald's personal priest, and Chad had recently followed his brother Bishop Cedd as abbot in Læstingaeu, which King Ædelwald had originally given to Cedd so that his king's soul would be prayed for and his body would have a worthy burial ground. Cedd was one of the four priests Peada had taken along to Mercia when he had been baptized and become Oswy's son-in-law. His missionary work had taken him far and wide, even to the East Saxons when their king had agreed to be baptized after pressure from King Oswy. Later on, when reports of Bishop Cedd's plague death in Læstingaeu reached his monastery in the realm of the East Saxons, thirty monks had journeyed up there to be with their father—be it under ground, alongside him, or above ground praying for his soul. It was under the ground; in Læstingaeu, the plague had spared just one boy.

At the meeting in Streonæshalch, Cedd had been Agilbert's translator, and he and his brothers had accepted Oswy's decision without hesitation. They were also the first to present themselves before Wilfrid to have their heads shaved—even though Cedd was already ill at the time. He died shortly afterwards.

They were an outstanding family, and Oswy simply couldn't imagine any better bishop than Chad.

Alchfred turned up his nose at the thought of a bishop who consistently refused to ride a horse and justified his rejection of the beast by saying his father Aidan had also refused! He couldn't stomach that outdated loyalty displayed by 'the old ones'; nor could Wilfrid. Alchfred shook his head and, stumbling over his words, tried to explain to his father that times had changed. But his father never understood, and while speaking the words even Alchfred could hear how unconvincing they sounded. He sighed at the thought of Wilfrid's eloquence, and inwardly prayed to the Lord asking him to send just one tenth of that skill. It didn't arrive, and his father travelled home with a shake of his head.

The thought of having to put up with another outdated bishop, tottering around like any old beggar, wearing undyed flax linen, and accompanied by an entourage of equally wretched folk, made Alchfred wince. At one point during the meeting at Streonæshalch, he had been standing right next to Bishop Cedd, and the stench was enough to make Alchfred's stomach turn at the idea of being in the company of this man's brother. They all stank, all 'the old ones', undoubtedly because of the crude basic fare in which they prided themselves. His father had no awareness of such niceties.

Alchfred would have to take independent action, and swiftly. He couldn't count on co-operation from the local bishops, no matter how much he gave them for their church. And so he sent, in secret, one hundred well-armed men to Kent with orders to buy a ship and make it ready. He himself rode to Hrypum and, on his knees, implored Wilfrid to become his and Deira's bishop. He would be consecrated by Bishop Agilbert, in the proper canonical manner—not by the heretical Britons in this country. All he had to do was hurry to Kent.

He gave Wilfrid letters to Agilbert and to the king of Neustria and his bishops, along with some very precious gifts. Plus a large handful of silver coin: enough to travel to the Holy Land with the entire entourage he had sent, he thought proudly. Great would be their wonder in Gaul when they saw the bishop chosen by King Alchfred of Deira, the accompanying entourage and the gifts he brought from his king! They thought the isle of the Angles was the back of beyond, populated by brutal Britons, and they called it the 'remotest island of the ocean', as Wilfrid said. Now they'd see a very different picture.

Wilfrid had no hesitation in hazarding his life for the cause. Here he risked dying from the plague; there was a chance he could get on board before King Oswy intervened.

Oswy's men arrived in Kent two days too late, and they had no means of stopping the ship.

'You only have yourself to blame,' said Hild, filling Oswy's glass when he sat with her using words that were not seemly for a Christian king. 'You have relinquished your power over Church affairs, didn't you know?'

Another stream of abusive words poured from his lips. When they were all used up, he sat quietly for a moment and then straightened his back.

'On the contrary, I was attempting to keep it—so my own son wouldn't rise up against me.' He sat in silence.

'That's what I had wanted to avoid,' he said eventually.

Hild refilled his glass. He was doing greater justice to the drink than usual.

'Children don't always act as their parents think they should,' she said.

'Yours certainly don't,' he snapped.

'They don't, no,' she replied. 'I should never have left them.'

'Nonsense,' he said. 'They've just been fed too much heathen horsemeat.'

'Possibly, but I don't really think that does as much damage as is said. According to Paulus, anyway. I've just received a book written by him.'

Oswy drank heavily, draining his glass almost as swiftly as she poured. So she drank next to nothing; one of them had to keep a clear head.

'What's the punishment?' he asked, gazing at her with his watery-blue—and now somewhat bleary—eyes.

'For what?'

'You know quite well,' he said, maintaining his watery-blue gaze.

'Perdition!' she replied.

'Are you sure?'

'All eternity in Hell, cast back and forth between freezing iciness and red-hot flames. Your name obliterated and forgotten. A curse upon your kin.'

She refilled his drink; this time he didn't take it immediately.

'Who knows?' he whispered, staring into the red glass.

'You do.'

'Yes,' he eventually murmured, and emptied his glass. 'It's probably just as you say, all of it.'

He had to be helped to bed, and early next morning he left on horseback.

# PLAGUE

*– Queen Eanflæd's sacrifice –*

Hild could have warned Alchfred, but she didn't. She'd never really warmed to this awkward prince, and when she heard about his conduct in the place of love, she was filled with an unadulterated loathing of the man.

She wouldn't risk the lives of any of her people for his life. Every journey involved risk, given how the plague was on the rampage. She had forbidden all travel other than visiting a deathbed. Alchfred might have died from the pestilence long before her people got there, and before Oswy's people got there, too—you couldn't flee from his rage anyway.

Besides, they had enough to do praying for the end of the plague plus looking after its victims. She had imposed continuous prayer in the chapel, to be undertaken by three people at the same time; after each Mass, three others took over.

When King Alchfred vanished, no one thought they would ever see his bishop again either. After waiting for half a year, King Oswy sent Chad to Cantwaraburh to be consecrated bishop of Northumbria by Archbishop Deusdedit. When Chad arrived, however, the plague had long since taken Deusdedit; the king of Kent and half of Cantwaraburh's monks were also dead. Chad travelled on to the West Saxons, where Bishop Wine consecrated him, helped by two bishops from Cornwalum. Two Angles had now been made bishops in the realm, and they were much in demand.

Oswy and Kent's new king jointly selected a monk from Cantwaraburh to be the new archbishop. Roman practices had always been followed in Cantwaraburh; to ward off any criticism, they sent the man to Rome first. A letter arrived a year later: their envoy was dead, and the Pope would select a suitable replacement. It was a long letter, bristling with excerpts from the scriptures and praise of King Oswy, who had guided the unenlightened home to Christ and the successors of the holy apostle Peter, and had driven the heretical Britons from his realm.

Oswy was the first of Ædelfred's family ever to have received a letter from the Pope. Utterly stunned by the event, he ignored the plague and rode to Lindisfarena, then down to Streonæshalch to show the document to Abbess Hildeburh and his little doll. And he was only the second king in Northumbria to receive a papal despatch; but from what Oswy had heard, the letter to Edwin hadn't been quite as long and nowhere near as appreciative. Hildeburh would know. The accompanying gifts had certainly been of poorer quality. Edwin had received a tunic and a cloak, both absolutely splendid—Oswy wore them himself, didn't he—but the Pope had sent Oswy a collection of bones, relics of the blessed apostles Peter and Paulus, and of the holy martyrs Laurentius, Johannes, Pancras and Paul. Also of Pope Gregorius the Great who had initiated this mission to the Angles—a mission that King Oswy, with his wise decision, was truly putting into effect, as the Pope wrote.

Each relic was kept in its own costly box with a name plate; he didn't dare take them with him. He would ask Hildeburh's opinion as to how their power could best be used.

For his wife Eanflæd, there was a holy cross made of iron from the chain that had weighed heavy on the holy Peter before his martyrdom, with a key of pale gold. What had Queen Tata received—but a mirror and a comb!

Hild didn't mention Alchfred's disappearance. When Oswy asked if she had any information that might shed light on the matter, she gave him a surprised look. She hadn't heard anything, nor did she think it necessary, she said, and suggested he build monasteries to house the powerful relics—she also had suggestions as to where—which would be highly advisable now that the Lord was punishing the realm so harshly. Yes, a hefty penance was highly advisable.

'But what have I done wrong?' Oswy exclaimed. Her proposal would cost him dear.

She simply stared at him.

It wasn't until he was on his way home that Oswy realized what she had been thinking; he immediately turned his horse. He had to clear up the misunderstanding and find out how far it had spread, but then he realized he would merely reinforce suspicions, so he turned round again.

There was nothing for it: he would have to build new monasteries. Maybe that would head off the Lord's wrath, maybe it wouldn't, but it would certainly remedy the wrath of the Church folk. It was his only option; the more said about that matter, the worse it would be for him, whatever the facts of the case. He could do with more prayers for his soul—that much was certain.

She had suggested Hacanos—so he'd build one there—plus, for some reason, the ford at the spot where the road from Piceringas crossed the Welburn. Maybe it was an old sacrificial site like Læstingaeu, so that was also fine; land was cheap out there in the wilderness. Ediscum, too, where they hadn't had fortune on their side, would still be worth giving another go, perhaps even in the actual giants' settlement on the opposite side of the river.

Hildeburh had said they should build in stone. He'd have to think about that—Aidan had always been satisfied with oak.

By now entire villages were empty, and the Lord wasn't sparing his own either. Hild knew something radical had to be done, so she assembled her people. They had to choose: prayer inside the monastery, looking after the sick in the guest hut, or working outdoors. Until the plague had passed, the three groups would be kept apart. Those who chose the guest hut would have to hold Mass there; those who carried on riding out and about would have to pitch tents and stay outside at all times.

The priests would have to stay outdoors, except for three who would hold Mass in the monastery and with the sick. This arrangement meant they wouldn't have to interrupt their intercession as had been the case in Læstingaeu. Everything now depended on their prayers.

Hild wanted to be in charge of work among the sick, but she was persuaded that the intercessory prayers of the abbess were more important; Mass and unbroken prayer would, after all, have the greatest impact.

Gyda would thus be in charge of work in the guest hut. She had initially learnt her medical skills in Magilros, where she had been a novice along with Frigyd from Tinanmude, and then she had taken part in establishing Hrypum, but had moved on to Streonæshalch when Wilfrid wanted to show Alchfred his all-male Benedictine order. Gyda was a force to be reckoned with.

The priest Bosa would stay in the monastery; John, who was good with the sick, and two other monks would go to the guest hut. The food was allocated, providing most for those indoors; those on the outside could still fish and forage. The monastery had four cats, which caught rats, and a dog; the cats were distributed between locations, the dog went with the priests.

Oftfor was in charge of the outside work; there were many deathbeds to be visited. Fortunately, as the end approached, quite a few people agreed to baptism—almost as many as those who lapsed. As they rode from one place to another, the priests noticed growing numbers of sacrificial stakes set up at the farms, even at the ones where they had baptized all the occupants. They couldn't ignore them and just ride past: they burnt the stakes and lectured the people about what awaited them. This they did so as not to replicate the fate of the East Saxons, where the king had lapsed and rebuilt the old shrines. Reports of their sacrifices caused horror among the Church people; at least Northumbria made do with horses.

The East Saxons had been struck by double misfortune: they hadn't had rain for three years. Stories were told of whole families and whole villages of starved people who decided to depart this life together rather than wait to die in their beds. They took one another by the hand—men, children, women, some with infants at their breast—and threw themselves off the cliff. This they did after they had sacrificed all their animals, eaten all their seed corn and scrabbled through every handful of soil looking for roots. By then there had been nothing left. Further north, the crop failure had only lasted one year—then again, they had served the Lord for longer.

Ædelthryd arrived on horseback, wan, trembling, and somewhat swollen just below her jawbone. She had come to speak with Hild, but wasn't allowed to pass through. She said she had promised the Lord to enter his service.

The swellings increased and the boils needed lancing. This was how one variety started, but it wasn't the nastiest. The most dreadful version started with coughing and breathlessness, and then just got worse. Faces gradually turned a blue-black colour; there wasn't much you could do about that kind. The one with swellings and pus had brighter prospects—unless it settled on the lungs.

Ædelthryd wept and wept, and reproached herself loudly for the vanity to which she had succumbed ever since childhood: she had always worn a necklace, and therefore the Lord was now sending her boils—on her neck!

Freawaru and Gyda glanced at one another, but didn't comment. Ædelthryd obviously couldn't see that all the sick had boils on their necks—and many also on legs and in the groin—even though they had never owned a necklace. The boils had to be lanced and emptied, some every other day, others less frequently.

Once Gyda felt she understood the ways of the plague, she decided to segregate those with afflicted lungs. The people who only had boils would be moved into a former stable. At first Ædelthryd refused, but after Gyda had a little chat with her, she complied and even started to help out—for the salvation of her soul. Gyda and Wynflæd stayed with those who had sick lungs, along with a priest and four layfolk.

The plague lasted for over a year, but Hild never lost heart. She slept less than ever and spent the rest of her time prostrate before the altar, in prayer, beseeching the Lord to forgive the king and spare his realm. When her energy ran out, she could feel Aidan's presence, and his strength kept her going.

When Bosa fell so ill he couldn't preside over Mass, she gathered her people in the chapel and had him carried up to the altar. He could barely sit upright in the chair, but he channelled all his energy into his voice and managed to repeat her words in a ritual conferring the role of priest on Hild and two of the monks. Afterwards, they prayed together, asking the Lord to accept this makeshift solution. They all knew the correct procedure: he should have been a bishop and she should have been a man.

The two new priests went to the guest hut by the beck, while Hild stayed in the chapel; during the final months, she only left her place in front of the altar when the call of nature forced her to do so.

Streonæshalch lost two-thirds of its priests and everyone who had been looking after the people with afflicted lungs. Half of those who had moved across to the stable survived. Of those indoors, they only lost a lay brother. Bosa and two nuns still had boils. But many other monasteries and settlements had been laid waste.

Once they no longer had to be kept apart, nothing was as before. Everyone bore the marks of undernourishment and lack of sleep, and many were disfigured by scars. But the Lord had heard their prayers and shown mercy. They embraced one another and wept with joy. When they assembled for a service of thanksgiving, the hymns of praise resonated louder and stronger than ever before. Half of their community had been spared; looking around, they were now filled with gratitude.

Hild had been weakened physically, but her spirit had been fortified. Aidan's strength stayed with her and also spread to the others. Now they would rebuild what the plague had destroyed.

They journeyed methodically throughout the land, preached, baptized and healed people, burnt sacrificial stakes and erected crosses in the villages. But given the numbers of priests they had lost, they simply couldn't reduce the number of hours spent on teaching.

Hild asked Bishop Chad to ordain some of her nuns, but he thought they should wait until the promised archbishop arrived from Rome. Chad was extremely busy and Hild rarely had a chance to ask his advice. So she did what she thought was right, taking guidance from the Lord.

It helped that she could administer the sacraments. She journeyed far and wide, leaving the real priests to concentrate on teaching. She was never shocked by what people confessed, and to her own surprise she was no longer annoyed when they were confounded by trifles. She could make people laugh if they were weeping over a broken leg or a mishap with their animals. She spoke calmly and with authority, quoted uplifting passages from the scriptures, and frequently broke out in robust laughter which made people see things in a new light. The faces saying goodbye when she left a farm were often smiling and full of fun, even when she had initially been greeted by sombre expressions. Having put words to adversity and aired your problems with someone else, you could put those dilemmas behind you. There were greater misfortunes at large than a burnt crop.

Hild was, however, shocked the once: Queen Eanflæd confessed that she had offered a sacrifice so her son Egfred would be made king after Oswy, and not *his* son Alchfred; she had risked her salvation.

'For that, you must do penance,' Hild said, once she had collected her thoughts. 'You will have to build a monastery.'

'I daren't confess it to Romanus,' Eanflæd confided. 'He'll just say I'm damned. You know he was friends with Alchfred.'

'Then you can hear it from my mouth,' said Hild decisively. 'To the best of my knowledge, if you don't do penance you will be damned. Your atonement will not just be for Alchfred, but also for all those of your subjects struck down by the Lord's punishment.'

Eanflæd thought it had more to do with Oswy; after all, the plague had started before Alchfred's disappearance, and if the Lord's wrath really *was* directed at her, then why had he spared her? She hadn't had a single boil, whereas her husband had developed nine.

'How long did you think about having him slain?' asked Hild.

And when Eanflæd lowered her eyes, she continued: 'Perhaps the Lord will give you an opportunity to repair your wrongdoing.'

The term offended Eanflæd; she didn't think it could be called wrongdoing, given Alchfred's temperament. Moreover, she had only done it to help her son, which meant she had even risked her salvation. If anything, surely it should be termed a self-sacrifice?

'Call it what you will,' said Hild, 'and pay with a monastery, twenty hides of land and built in stone.'

Eanflæd would think it over; maybe then she wouldn't have to listen to all the terrible things Romanus would undoubtedly say.

# THE KINGDOM, THE POWER
# AND THE GLORY

*– the new ecclesiastical rules –*

Five years after the meeting at Streonæshalch, and four years after the kings' candidate for archbishop had been sent to Rome, the Pope's man arrived: Theodor of Tarsus.

It had taken him a year to get there, and he had spent time with the Parisians' bishop, Agilbert, who had brought him up-to-date with the situation in these rather—in terms of Church matters—backward isles.

Theodor had been trained in the Orthodox tradition and was therefore accompanied by a learned abbot named Hadrian, who could instruct him in the true canonical faith. They had been obliged to wait for four months while Theodor's hair grew, so he could have the correct tonsure before ordination. As he was about to board the Kentish royal ship he collapsed, and everyone thought he was now going to leave them: he was sixty-six years old. But after a while he recovered and set sail, with the befitting entourage sent by the king of Kent to meet him in Gaul.

Baducing had accompanied Theodor all the way from Rome. He had been away for a long time, spending two years in a monastery where he had taken his monastic vow and the name Benedict, after Benedict of Nursia. Baducing had thought about staying abroad; he couldn't live without scholarship. He had eventually decided to take scholarship home with him: an entire library, seventy-six books to add to the thirty-two he already owned.

One hundred books plus eight more were now in the possession of Baducing, known to the Lord as Benedict.

The long wait had also been caused by the first men on the Pope's list declining his offer. The Angles lived so very far away, they were still an uncivilized people; just the thought of the lengthy journey! Hadrian, who was abbot at the monastery where Paulinus and his siblings had spent their childhood, wasn't alarmed by the thought of the journey, but when he realized the assignment was to knock the unruly and more or less heretical Britons into shape, he suggested sending Theodor of Tarsus and offered to accompany him. Given that Theodor had dropped his Orthodox ideas, the Pope agreed.

On top of that, Hadrian had been detained in Neustria. He had previously undertaken various papal missions around Gaul, and there was a strong suspicion that he was on his way to the Angles to promote the cause of the Holy See and work against Frankish interests. He was eventually released when the king of Kent sent his men across the waters to fetch him.

'An old man!' Hild whispered to Freawaru when they saw the white-haired figure disembark. He was eleven years Hild's senior, and she certainly didn't feel young any longer.

'They probably haven't got any younger ones,' Freawaru whispered back. 'Gyda always said they were a lot of old men down there in Rome!'

'All honour to her memory,' said Hild, and offered a quick prayer for her soul. Gyda had been one of her best; she would have made an excellent priest.

Wilfrid had also come to pay his respects to the archbishop. Once the plague had passed, he had returned from Gaul, two years after his king and patron had disappeared. Wilfrid had protested vehemently against the appointment of Chad, and refused to acknowledge him. An ordination with the assistance of heretical Britons wasn't valid; furthermore, he had been ordained to Wilfrid's bishopric, and therefore Wilfrid had to regard him as a thief.

Oswy totally ignored the protests, so Wilfrid complained to Bishop Agilbert, who advised him to wait for the outcome in the monastery at Hrypum. Agilbert would acquaint the new man with details of how things stood.

It was reported that twelve bishops had attended Wilfrid's ordination at the royal estate in Compendium. Eight bishops had carried him into the oratory, seated on a gilded throne, it was said.

Archbishop Theodor was initially a great disappointment. He had misgivings about double monasteries and about the influence of abbesses. He reinstated Wilfrid as Northumbria's bishop and reprimanded Chad, who had allowed himself to be ordained by Britons and to another man's bishopric.

Chad repented his blunder and said he had never thought himself worthy of the office anyway. Theodor then ordained him in the proper Catholic manner, and later made him Bishop of Liccidfeld near Tamoworthig—and lifted him onto horseback with his own hands, commanding him to forsake the old-fashioned ways of following the fathers: now he should ride wherever he needed to journey. This Chad accepted too; he was a most humble man.

Theodor examined the emergency measures implemented while the plague raged and disallowed all ordinations of women. On the other hand, he agreed to ordain quite a few men, so work didn't grind to a halt. His advice was to put more effort into training priests.

It didn't take long before they could feel the effects of a new kind of bishop. Wilfrid imposed taxes on the monasteries, expected regal board and lodging for his entourage, and meddled in their every undertaking. He ordered Hild to stop lessons for the women in anything other than reading and writing, and he was also going to decide the subjects to be studied by the men. That's how it was in Gaul, he maintained, when she rejected his every demand. She ended up having to ask him to leave her monastery; once he was gone, she discovered that the altar cloth and three costly wall hangings he had asked for, but not been given, were missing.

Some monasteries capitulated to Wilfrid when they were unable to bear any more of the misfortunes befalling them—sudden fires, unaccountable loss of animals. The smaller communities couldn't afford disobedience, and the archbishop had recently enjoined them to obey the bishop. Following a visit from Wilfrid, the Abbot of Magilros decided to expel the women, who were then taken in at Hild's two monasteries and by Frigyd in Tinanmude.

Hild and Frigyd kept one another informed about what was going on. They avoided fires and other disasters by posting guards at night. They didn't believe the explanations circulating that the Devil had called in and taken their animals—unless the Devil was actually a man from Hrypum.

They were determined to fight for their rights. They would occasionally discuss moving to Ireland, where the old practices still held good, but the conclusion was always the same as the one they had reached after the fateful meeting: they would stay and fight. Gyda had been right; she'd always insisted they had to work towards women being able to become priests. It was the only way they could ensure that women weren't excluded from the blessings of scholarship, she had said. At the time, however, the others had thought it was enough just to present their case.

'When you've never learnt anything, you haven't got a case!' Gyda had replied. 'You don't know things can be different until you've learnt something and thought things through, had ideas.'

Now they could see how right she'd been: women's access to learning would be threatened for as long as they weren't considered fit for every assignment. They knew they faced a lengthy struggle. Gyda had also said it wouldn't happen in their lifetime, and they should have pushed their cause through before those old men in Rome gained too much influence over here. It *hadn't* happened in Gyda's lifetime, and perhaps it wouldn't come to pass in their lifetime either. Never mind, they expected the struggle to be long and hard. It was their only option.

Archbishop Theodor examined everything in great detail, and a few years later he convened a meeting at which he presented ten points with which everyone must comply. Wilfrid alone sent representatives rather than attending in person; afterwards, he would be able to say he hadn't endorsed the decisions. Many a complaint was made about his interference, by other bishops too, but *he* had sent even more complaints about disobedience.

Theodor called upon everyone to exercise flexibility to ensure the new canonical statutes could be successful. They would have to respect the division into dioceses and obey their bishop. Bishops, in turn, must not interfere with the affairs of other dioceses or forcibly remove any goods, and they must be satisfied with the hospitality offered.

He also stressed the duty of obedience to the abbot or abbess. The Lord's folk must no longer move from place to place, and should be turned away unless they were in possession of letters of permission from their superiors. The punishment for breaching these articles would be excommunication.

Theodor hoped this strategy would rid him of the Brittonic monks who still wandered around with no other master than the one in Heaven and, to Theodor's mind, brought the Lord into disrepute. This was not a practice he had met before.

Hild and Frigyd protested vigorously against this point.

'Surely it is the Lord and not the leader of the monastery who is to be served,' Frigyd reasoned. They had received many of Wilfrid's people who didn't feel able to serve the Lord in this new way.

But Theodor remained firm. A vow was a vow. He wanted everything organized and under control. He also promised to think about partitioning the bishopric of Northumbria, which was too extensive for just one man.

Shortly after the meeting, Theodor dismissed Bishop Wynfrid from Mercia for offering sanctuary to a fugitive who had escaped, flogged to a bloody pulp, from one of Wilfrid's many monasteries. Theodor had to demonstrate that his words would be backed up by action.

In other respects, Hild appreciated Theodor. He and Hadrian taught her that the bible should be read as a book with historical information. There was nothing mystical and secret in it, they said. The Song of Solomon was a love song, no more, no less; and a lovely love song, they said, and laughed. She could just have a look and see what it said: not a word about the Church and Jesus! Desire and fleshly love, that's what it was all about!

Each conversation with the two men was a revelation. Hild felt as though she was being given new eyes to see with, and she took in everything. But when they said the psalms of David hadn't been written by David, she made her excuses and went outside. Their straightforwardness had diminished the songs that had helped her get through and carry on. Once they had explained everything in terms of commonplaces, there was so little left of all that had been her fixed ground, the steady support under her feet. Not even now, when she was old, was the world a firm and steadfast place.

'There's nothing to be upset about,' said Hadrian in surprise when she came back indoors. 'The psalms are just as lovely as they have always been, are they not?'

Hild nodded politely. She couldn't even explain to herself what she felt she had lost.

When Oswy had ruled Bernicia for twenty-eight years and Deira for nineteen, he fell ill. He promised the Lord that he would travel to Rome if he would spare him, and he asked Wilfrid to accompany him. Not long after Wilfrid had demanded a hefty payment to his monasteries in recompense for undertaking such a journey, Oswy was brought down by a stroke.

Hild visited him and tried in every way she could to understand what he was endeavouring to say. He struggled for sixteen days to get the words out, eyes constantly flicking back and forth, not even resting at night. Then he released his spirit in the middle of a sudden storm.

He was succeeded by his son Egfred, married to Ædelthryd; his mother Eanflæd could now finally withdraw from this world. She moved to Streonæshalch for the salvation of her soul and to be with her daughter Ælfflæd. Fortunately, she came with ten hides of land, of which they were in great need as Lindisfarena had followed Bishop Wilfrid's call to disallow the admission of women.

The queen dowager was much concerned about the salvation of her soul, and frequently told Hild tales of her good deeds: as when she had made her husband do penance for Oswine—she had threatened divorce unless he built a monastery.

'You know how mean he was. But without King Edwin's daughter, he wouldn't have been elected in Deira—and then he wouldn't have got anything out of slaying Oswine.'

Hild muttered a response, and they carried on with their embroidery in silence.

'I couldn't bear to think the gates of the heavenly kingdom would be closed to my husband,' said Eanflæd, rummaging around for a yellow thread.

Hild looked up.

'I didn't know you cared for him so much.'

'No, no, it wasn't that,' Eanflæd assured her, holding a length of thread up to the light. Some moments later she added absent-mindedly: 'Well, as far as I was concerned, he could burn in Hell.'

She held out her needle for a novice to thread, and sighed: 'But the thought of spending all eternity as a widow! Just like my mother when we came to Kent!'

The novice returned the needle, and Eanflæd continued filling in a line of holy crosses.

Hild cleared her throat and found a green thread for the wing tip of a bird she had almost finished.

'Have you not read in the scriptures—there's no marriage in the realm of the Lord.'

'Well, yes, but you see I was married.'

'And the poor will be rich and the rich will be poor.'

Eanflæd was startled: 'Does it really say that?'

'And the married will be widows, and maidens will rejoice in a man! And queens will be slaves, and slaves will be queens. And huts will be replaced with castles, and royal estates with caves.'

Eanflæd dropped her embroidery.

'And the sick will be sound, and the sprightly will be lame, and the deaf will hear the strains of Heaven, and singers will be struck with muteness . . .'

Hild could have gone on and on, but the words had already had their effect. Eanflæd had turned a pasty colour, beads of perspiration shining on her temples. She fumbled to loosen the cloth at her neck and signalled the novice to help. They had to lay her down on the bench.

'Well, yes,' said Hild, once the colour had returned to Eanflæd's cheeks, 'the threads of our fate are in the hands of the Lord, and his will is done!'

She made the sign of the cross and finished off her wing tip, humming as she worked. She had already forgiven herself for the petty revenge she had been planning ever since Eanflæd made her help move Aidan. She would pray, asking the Lord for forgiveness, because now she would probably be able to treat Eanflæd as was befitting for the queen dowager of the realm and the daughter of King Edwin.

It was also a relief that Eanflæd had come to live at the monastery. Hild could now be absolved of all responsibility for the impossible child she had never really liked, however hard she tried. Ælfflæd had her head well and truly in the clouds, even when you took her age into consideration. She was fifteen years old now. Hild had never managed to get that girl into shape. She still couldn't read, but she was an expert when it came to making eyes at the men. When Wilfrid visited, Hild had to send Ælfflæd out of the room. She couldn't bear his subtle way of putting ideas into the young girl's head, but unfortunately banishment from his presence merely compounded Ælfflæd's idolization of him. She idolized every man. Now her mother would have to deal with her.

Hild had enough worries with her own offspring. Wulfhere's aggression was a source of regret; he couldn't stop waging war. His royal estate was full of plunder from every single neighbouring realm. Cynewise wrote that she had given up trying to make him listen to reason. His mind was set on shining gold.

He had inherited that side of his character from his father—Eadwacer, the watcher of wealth. Greedy for gold. But Penda had been more than Eadwacer; she hoped his son was too. But she didn't know, because she'd only seen him once after he had become king—a very short visit, at that. And he never invited her; at rare intervals he might reply to her letters, always briefly. He didn't understand why she behaved as she did towards Wilfrid, he had written. She hoped the Lord had given him more of his father than just Eadwacer.

She wrote to Cynewise, asking her to continue trying to influence Wulfhere; he was more inclined to listen to her than to his mother. Hild had accompanied Cynewise's daughter, twenty-one-year-old Queen Cyneburh, to Mercia when her husband Alchfred had disappeared. She had also helped in the selling of her morning gift, and Cyneburh had now established a monastery where she served the Lord along with her sister Cyneswid and half-sister Tibba. Eadburh had gone to join the Lord not long after she had fled from her planned marriage. Cynewise was very grateful to Hild, and there was no bad blood between them.

Oswy's son Egfred had been king for two years and married to Ædelthryd for twelve when he wished to consummate the marriage. Ædelthryd resolutely refused, and was supported unconditionally by Bishop Wilfrid. Egfred gave Wilfrid a largish plot of land and explained the necessity of heirs. Wilfrid expressed his thanks, but didn't change his view on the matter.

The dowager queen supported her son and moaned to Hild about his contrary wife.

'It was you who wanted him married to her,' said Hild. 'And she had already promised her maidenhood to the Lord.'

'Well, yes, but still,' said Eanflæd, 'now that he's king . . . she could make an effort.'

Hild said no more and didn't get involved in the issue, which otherwise occupied the entire realm, particularly the Lord's people. Ædelthryd had given her morning gift of Hagustaldesea to Wilfrid, and he had started building a monastery and a mighty church of stone. Her husband had been enraged; he complained to the archbishop about Wilfrid's attempt to purloin royal property and also about the difficulty in finding good young men—they would rather serve Wilfrid.

But when Ædelthryd sought counsel from her mother's sister, Hild said what she thought: Ædelthryd would have to choose between marriage and maidenhood; to expect both was unseemly, in her opinion.

'For Ælfflæd's sake, I won't say it aloud,' she said, 'because all that talk about maidenhood perhaps assuages the fate to which her father sold her in order to triumph over Mercia. But if, of your own free will, you keep your legs crossed—and, what is more, take pride in doing so—well, it's an insult to the creator. Union of the flesh is a part of love, and it is the greatest gift he has given us. Everything else pales in comparison—take my word for it!'

'That's not what Wilfrid says,' muttered Ædelthryd.

'Wilfrid's only mission is to get worldly possessions out of you and your husband, Ædelthryd. He knows nothing of the other business. My mother always said: Gold is gladly given for a husband's loving embrace.'

'Your mother wasn't baptized!'

'No, but she knew what she was talking about. And your mother would have said the same.'

Ædelthryd wept. She still had boils on her neck and was extremely apprehensive about the day of judgement. She would think it over, she said, and departed for home.

Not long afterwards, she fled her husband. He pursued her all the way up to Coludesburh, where Ebba refused to let him in. When he tried to force entry, he was repelled by Wilfrid's men, who were in no way inferior to the king's. He besieged the monastery, but under cover of darkness Ædelthryd was taken down to a boat and sailed away. Wilfrid had, in all haste, married her to the Lord.

Ædelthryd returned home to Elge, her morning gift in East Anglia, as a bride of Christ. Here, she founded a double monastery and gave thanks to the Lord. She surpassed all in humility, wearing coarse wool and only washing in cold water.

# Eostre's lilies

*– a new son in the Lord –*

On a day in the yuletide month, a perfectly ordinary overcast day with sleet falling, Hild was suddenly struck by the certainty that she had lost Hundfrid and Wilbrord.

The thought hadn't been provoked by any specific occurrence, but suddenly there it was, as incontrovertible as frost or fire: she would never find them.

She had dropped her quill and had to sit down; she felt winded and everything went fuzzy. When she tried to stand up, she couldn't, and had to ask Begu to help her to bed.

As she lay there, warmth returning to her limbs, tears overwhelmed her, by turns soft and loudly plaintive. She was quiet for a while, thinking: what has happened? And then the tears returned, she couldn't hold them back. Nothing had happened, as far as she was aware; but she just *knew* her boys were gone and she would never see them again. At the same time, she was surprised she was making such a fuss.

Her gigantic strength, seemingly inexhaustible, had vanished, and there was next to nothing of her left. She wept about that, and when she woke up she wept again. Dreaming, she had been holding them in her arms; they were at her breast, sucking noisily and grunting like little newborn lambs, and when she woke again, they were gone and her breasts were old and haggard.

Begu was standing alongside the bed; she handed Hild a mug of beer.

'You have a fever,' she said. 'You must rest.'

Hild wept quietly, and lay back in the bed; the tears had washed away all her strength.

'You must look after the monastery,' she said to Begu—the woman nodded silently.

'Any news?'

'Nothing,' said Begu. She wasn't going to tell Hild what she had just heard: in East Anglia, Wulfhere had gathered a very large army from all the southern realms, and it was on its way up through Lindsey, and—as was usually the case with Wulfhere—not even monasteries were being spared.

King Egfred had called up his men, but they were numerically inferior. There was nothing they could do, except ask the Lord for advice—as he saw fit.

The news reached Hild's ears anyway, and over the next few days it was hard to see if she was worked up by anxiety or fever.

The fever vanished when the message arrived that her son had been beaten. His army had been vanquished; he was wounded but alive. She got up and ate; she would ride out immediately, to take care of him, but then a message arrived from his wife—King Wulfhere did not want visitors. Flying venom had entered the wound, but he had the best doctors.

Hild's fever returned at regular intervals, intense and enervating; once a bout was over, she was completely alert, but as soon as she tried to get back into her usual routine it knocked her off her feet again.

The pattern was so regular she could plan meetings and short trips around the outbreaks. But when Benedict Baducing wrote that now they could travel to Rome, she was obliged to reply that he would have to set forth alone.

So she wouldn't see Rome—a journey she had long planned to make, but perhaps it had never been among the Lord's plans.

When Hadrian visited her some time later, he consoled her by saying the world outside wasn't so very different; on the surface it was, of course, but not once you got to know it. She could be well satisfied with staying in Deira, where she belonged.

'That's easily said by someone who was born in the land of Africa and has seen Vesuvius and elephants and Rome and everything,' she exclaimed angrily.

'Yes,' he said, and paced the room. 'But if the Lord let me choose, I would rather revisit the place I come from than anywhere else. My entire mortal family perished when the Arabs conquered the town. I can never return, and now the Arabs have pushed even further onwards. When I was a child, all the lands around the Mediterranean were Christian. Christendom is now beleaguered.'

Hild sat up.

'Was that why Pope Gregorius sent the mission up here?'

'At that time, it was the Persians who were advancing,' said Hadrian, 'and maybe that was the reason. There's always someone pushing onwards.'

'Just like here,' said Hild. 'But the Britons were Christian long before we were.'

'If you can call them Christian,' said Hadrian.

'You can,' Hild said decisively.

'Whatever the case, Gregorius made a wise decision in sending that mission. His writings are just nonsense, but on that point he showed great foresight.'

He abruptly stopped pacing and turned around.

'You new people, you weren't Christian, were you?'

'Only the queen in Kent,' said Hild. 'She came from Gaul.'

Hadrian looked a lot calmer.

'I was suddenly nervous that everything we had learnt back at home was falsehood. We were told you sacrificed human beings, that kind of thing. I didn't think it would be possible to talk with any of you, like we're doing now. Actually, you're just like us.'

'But we aren't,' she said.

She knew she should be flattered, but Hadrian and Theodor were very foreign to her. They were pleasant enough to talk to, but very different. They seemed so light and supple, almost airy, even though they were actually quite robust. No one here was like them.

'Hadrian,' she said, 'my husband's son Merewald made a discovery, and now it might not be possible for me to pursue the matter.'

Hadrian pricked up his ears; he was an extremely learned man with an extremely inquisitive mind.

'You know, some plants come up from the soil with one seed-leaf, some with two. Merewald discovered that those with one seed-leaf, well, their petals and filaments and everything are either three or something to do with three—six or nine or twelve—when they unfurl. And they are the plants that sacrifice themselves for us, by letting people eat them!'

Hadrian frowned; he didn't know what a seed-leaf was.

'In Merewald's opinion, by observing nature we can see the Holy Trinity: first, the Lord as the seed-leaf, then the Son and the Holy Spirit, in the number three—the plants we live off, and which our animals feed on. Merewald tried to get his father to understand that the Lord has revealed his will in creation itself, so it is also visible to those people who might never receive a visit from missionaries but are able to keep their eyes open. But Isidorus of Seville doesn't write anything about all that, so I was wondering if perhaps you had any information?'

Hadrian regretted the words he had just spoken. From the outside, they seemed reasonable enough, the people up here; but once you went just a tiny little way below the surface, their mentality was incredibly primitive. He hadn't expected such lack of sophistication from the most prudent abbess in the land, however weakened and fevered she might be. She clearly didn't have much time left, and perhaps the fever had entered her brain. She just kept gazing at him, her face full of expectancy, full of confidence that he would pursue this insane matter.

'An interesting observation,' he said. 'I look forward to examining it more closely, and I'll certainly keep you informed.'

'I would like to have spent my life investigating the earthly creation,' she said, 'for the Lord must have had an intention with it all. But there has always been something else I had to see to—and we haven't had many books.'

'No,' he said, 'it's probably all been for the best.'

He knew all her seed-leaf talk was sheer nonsense, because neither Plinius nor Isidorus had written on the subject. So it was fortunate she had applied her skills to practical matters, for which she was well suited.

Hild soon came to terms with her condition, and unless a bout of fever had just started, she always attended Mass.

She found a new source of delight when a man with the grace of song was brought to her. Having been introduced, he stood for a long time, smiling shyly. Eventually, he said: 'Cædmon is my name, mother.'

'Indeed,' she said. 'I am Abbess Hildeburh.'

'Many have slipped down that cliff,' he continued. 'The Lord put his hand around you.'

'What do you mean?' she asked.

'Or under you,' he smiled, and showed his pale-gold arm-ring. 'It was many years ago.'

And then she remembered. The red-haired boy with the lovely voice, the boy who had slithered down to save her.

'Forgive me, my son,' she murmured, blushing, 'everything except your name I remember.'

Cædmon was a slave working for the descendants of the sheep-breeder from Hacanos who had held the only speech of his life at the meeting with King Edwin and Paulinus. He had spent his entire life together with the sheep around Hræfenclif, and he had no objection to being bought free and then serving the monastery as a lay brother, as long as he was still allowed to be with the animals.

'He's like Wilfrid,' Ælfflæd exclaimed after he had left.

'Nonsense,' said Hild.

'She's got a point,' said the dowager queen, who always backed her daughter. 'A milder version, both the voice and all the rest. Can't you see it?'

'Absolutely not,' said Hild. Cædmon was a good-looking man, which was not a word you could apply to Bishop Wilfrid—even though everyone did. Fortunately, he had left for Rome, to complain to the Pope about Archbishop Theodor splitting Northumbria into three bishoprics. He, who owned monasteries all across the realm and thought he was superior to every other bishop. Hild hoped they would keep him down there.

Cædmon had never learnt anything other than how to look after sheep, and trying to teach him to read proved impossible. So they read passages from the scriptures to him, and a day or two later he had turned them into a song—of the kind they needed: descriptions of King David's victories and of the time Christ heroically mounted the cross would soon replace the old battle songs.

'May I write them down?' asked Sæthryd.

'I think we can remember them,' said Hild.

They needed all the parchment they had in stock for copies of Benedict Baducing's new books. King Egfred had given him seventy hides of land—Wiuræmuda, at the mouth of the Wiur river—for a wonderful work of cosmology, and also because the king wanted to keep him in his realm. Benedict Baducing had established a stone monastery, with the help of Gallic craftsmen. The windows were made of glass, it was said, so the light shone through in every colour. Hild had only heard about it, the journey being too long in her infirm condition. But she received fresh descriptions every time her scribe came home with books they had been given permission to copy. She could almost picture it in her mind, and she had recently started thinking that perhaps Oswy had actually made the right decision: the increased links to the outside world were proving to be of great benefit. Streonæshalch now had sixty-two books, Heruteu not quite so many. Their new monasteries—to Maria at Hacanos and to the holy Gregorius by the ford over the Welburn—still only had the Gospels and the Psalms of David; they needed more books and writing materials.

Hild took pleasure in time spent with Cædmon. He found it all quite simple: life and light were the Lord's gift to human beings, and they mustn't take the gift from one another—it was no more complicated than that. Hild recalled all her speculations over the years about what the Lord might have intended; they hadn't actually brought her any closer to an answer, she thought, and couldn't help but laugh. Perhaps it was all just as simple as Cædmon said.

One morning in Eostre's month, she saw him standing in the herb garden, arms outstretched and face turned upwards to the sharp sun. He paid no attention to her and didn't know she had already seen him standing out there before Mass. She had noticed his absence and had to reprimand him; no one stayed away from Mass without a compelling reason.

'I lost track of time, mother,' he tried.

'You remember what you want to remember.'

'Yes,' he said. 'I decided to stay here, gathering the sun.'

'Nonsense,' she said. 'You can't gather sun. It's there when it's there, and when it's gone it's gone.'

'I'm gathering it anyway,' said Cædmon, nudging a winter leek with his foot.

'That's enough of all those excuses,' Hild snapped. 'I can't keep covering up for your remissness.'

Having vented her feelings, her shoulders sank and she could feel the warmth of the sun penetrating her thick cloak. She had been in bed for three days; it was overwhelmingly wonderful to see the sun again.

'Did you mean that, or was it just something you made up on the spur of the moment?'

'Of course I mean it,' he said. 'Just look at this leek. There it stands gathering light, which makes it grow stout and tall. Everything gets stouter in the springtime, when it sucks up light. We also grow most in the spring—have you noticed?'

Hild shook her head. 'Plants live from water and earth. If they lived from light, then they'd be at their stoutest for the summer solstice and grow lean at yuletide—which they don't. This tree,' she said, patting the trunk of a young apple tree, 'I've known since it was quite small, and it gains weight year by year. It hasn't grown leaner during any single winter.'

'Well, it has actually,' Cædmon pressed on, with his usual doggedness. 'Because it sheds its leaves, and that makes it smaller.'

'Well, yes,' said Hild, 'but those two things don't have anything to do with one another. And light isn't something you can suck up.'

She continued in the rather chanting tone she used with the novices: 'When the plants appear in the springtime, it is because the Lord recreates the world, year by year, because in his love for humankind the Lord has been reconciled with us in Jesus Christ.'

Cædmon couldn't contradict her words, but a devil leapt up in him at her lecturing tone; it was as if she were no longer herself, and that irritated him, along with all the rigid regularity of the whole place. He longed to wander off and follow the sheep and just let the ideas the Lord sent him develop gently in his mind. Out there he wouldn't have to turn up for the one thing and the other because the pointer on the sundial had moved to the next line. It seemed so unnecessary; he'd always known what time of day it was and had never before felt as if time was dragging like he did during Mass here. Nor did he understand why the Mass couldn't be held in the language of the Angles or the Britons. The words they had to use sounded lovely, and he had quickly learnt them by heart, but he'd like to know what they meant too. He wanted to provoke her.

'Yes, yes, mother, but what about Eostre's lilies?' he asked, pointing at a large cluster of lilies.

Hild felt light-headed and weak-legged. The yellow buds were close to bursting and releasing their big bell-shaped, sweetly-scented, shining yellow-golden crowns into the light.

She was overcome by the ache to see at least one of them unfurl. Her body was like a limp bean plant and was in fierce need of springtime. For many winters now she had thought: might the Lord grant me one more bite of a light-green beech leaf? And he had granted her just that. Every spring was a revelation. Earlier in her life it had been a pleasure, a delight, when she was a child too; but now she knew that springtime was more than that—it was a revelation of the grace of the Lord.

Cædmon had also been pondering the matter. He had finally spotted a chance to get the better of her; he was going to ask: 'Surely Eostre's lilies aren't filled with joy by the Lord's death?' But he immediately realized she would reply: 'No, they are filled with joy by his resurrection.'

He wiped his brow, dizzy at the thought something could mean both the one thing and its opposite—depending on your vantage point. So he kept his counsel, and by way of ending the discussion he just mumbled: 'The ways of the Lord are indeed past understanding.' He shuddered slightly in an attempt to shake off the difficult questions, and the possibility of the abbess's anger.

Perhaps Hild had similar thoughts; she muttered distractedly and yet composed, as if from another world: 'Verily, yes.'

Upon which she walked resolutely across to the lilies, picked six of the most swollen buds, and went indoors.

When the fever took hold again, she lay staring at the lilies, their buds now open.

I still don't understand a thing, she thought to herself, but perhaps it's all like Cædmon says, and the Lord's loving-kindness lasts from eternity to eternity.

With great exertion, she turned onto her other side.

Otherwise he wouldn't have made those lilies over there, she thought as she finally fell asleep. She dreamt of Cædmon's little red-haired son with the dancing eyes. He was racing across a green meadow with her own sons; their eagerness softened the hearts of the adults. His little boy's laughter made them feel their age. She could have been his grandmother.

Waking up, she was reminded that she was both old and sick; she had difficulty getting out of bed, and everything took an age. Perhaps she wouldn't live until the little boy was seven years old, and if Ælfflæd succeeded her as abbess, he shouldn't be raised here. She must remember to tell Cædmon that if she didn't survive until then, he should take Beda up to Benedict Baducing. He would know how to make sure the boy received an education. And if Beda's mother still wouldn't marry Cædmon—which she probably wouldn't—then she could be a lay sister in the new monastery to the holy Gregorius. Ælfflæd wouldn't look graciously upon a young widow she would consider the weaver of her own misfortune.

# CÆDMON AND THE LIGHT

*– the Song of Hild –*

When Hild rose from her bed after the bout of fever, she again found Cædmon standing in the herb garden. She told him what she had planned for his son, and was just about to reprimand him when he forestalled her.

'So what is light?' he asked. 'It's not plant, not animal, not a matter like earth and water—so what is it?'

'Dear Cædmon,' she said in her most irritating finger-wagging voice, the one she used when trying to convince someone of something she wasn't actually sure about. 'Earth and water are not matter, they are elements, just like fire and air. The four elements—that's what they're called. They worked it out in olden times when they were pondering many circumstances and wrote it all down for the generations to come. So remember, the four elements: earth, air, water, fire. Matter arises when the elements mix together. Light: made from fire meeting air. Wind: comes from air meeting earth. Rain: water meeting earth, and you can just go on and on. You must pay more attention!'

'So what's heat?'

'Heat comes from fire . . . and air, of course.'

'You just said that air and fire make light!'

'And so they do, but when it's very strong it turns into heat. Heat and light are the same thing—it's just that the one is very condensed.'

'Are you saying that light is diluted heat?'

'Something along those lines, yes, that's how it is.'

'There's not much light in a cauldron of boiling water,' Cædmon objected.

'Thrust your hand into it and it feels like putting your hand in the fire—even if you do it at pitch-dark night!'

Cædmon scratched behind his ear.

'But Oftfor said that wind occurs when air gets caught in caves. I think it was Plinnus who wrote about it . . . '

'Pli-ni-us!' she corrected him, and then had to think this over. 'No, your memory fails you, and not just about his name. In that instance, Plinius was referring to earthquakes. They occur when too much water enters caves in the mountains, and then . . . '

Now she wasn't quite so sure about her facts; her memory wasn't what it had been. All that writing and all that reading—Begu was right: you ended up with a slack brain. Hild used to be able to remember every word she had read in Plinius' writings. Had he been writing about volcano eruptions? Yes, now she could remember the place in the book too, and the little vignettes in the margin—they were painted with red—so she could happily raise her voice again: 'Plinius writes that large quantities of water flowing into a mountain will cause a volcanic eruption. It happened in his day when fire spurted out of Vesuvius—the big mountain near Neapolis, where Hadrian was abbot—with ash and molten rock, and it all rained down across the towns, and people died.'

Cædmon shifted uneasily.

'What about the caves in the mountains around here? Isn't there water in some of them too?'

'There is—there's often water in caves, but the difference is that here the water flows *out*. At Vesuvius, the water flowed *in*. And that's when they spurt it all out—when they can't contain any more—that's understandable.'

'So you don't think we have to worry about volcanoes here?'

'Not while the water continues to flow outwards, of that you can be certain.'

'Yes. Because there's a cave near the new monastery to the holy Gregorius, isn't there?'

'Indeed—and a very strange cave, at that,' she said, and wandered in her own thoughts before abruptly brightening up: 'You can ride with me and see it—I'm going there tomorrow.'

'I would like that, very much,' said Cædmon, bowing to her. 'And thank you.'

'You just have to ask, if there's some issue you need clarifying,' she said, and went indoors.

Talking with Cædmon was lovely; he asked all the elementary questions she too had once asked. It did her brain good to brush up her learning. She would have to take another look at the writings—she wasn't quite sure about what she had told him.

There was a heap of parchment at the bottom of the bookcase, half-covered by a length of cloth. Hild bent over with difficulty, fretting about the disarray. She folded the fabric and placed it on a bench, laboriously dragged out the pile of parchment and lifted it up onto the table.

She was usually quite untidy herself, and she was still only visited once a month by the clear-up urge—then she would attack the writing room, her own hut, the kitchen and storeroom while scolding right and left. They would soon hear about this expensive parchment, left in a messy heap where it didn't belong.

She glanced at the sheet on top; the word 'Wulf' caught her eye, a word that cut to the quick. Wulfhere, her precious, her grief. Four years had passed since he died of his wounds. She read the words and sat down; read again and started to burn up. It was as if the fever had taken hold of her, but she couldn't stop—she read every sheet in the pile.

All Cædmon's songs were written here—and many others. Some took their material from the lives recounted alongside the fire in the sewing room. Sæthryd's story, Freawaru's, Gyda's, Begu's. She had never read the like. She took the first sheet again and read aloud:

> *Folk see him as prey     an outsider to hunt*
> *rip him to shreds     if he comes with men*
> *Much divides us*
>
> *Wulf is in one realm     I in another*
> *that realm is protected     surrounded by fens*
> *formidable foes     rule that realm*
> *rip him to shreds     if he comes with men*
> *Much divides us*
>
> *Eager expectation     of my young Wulf*
> *rain pouring down     sorrowfully I sat*
> *warrior arms     wrapped me tight*
> *filled with joy     likewise filled with disgust*
>
> *Wulf, my Wulf     loss of you*
> *laid me low with longing     sickened with sorrow*
> *by such seldom visits     not by my fasting*
>
> *Do you hear, Eadwacer?     The wolf is dragging*
> *our wretched cub to the forest*
>
> *What is never rightfully joined     is easily riven*
> *our song together*

She felt a strange redemption saying the words out loud—her guts and muscles softened and started falling into place, having long been painful and out of tune. She recited it once again, in a more forceful voice.

She hadn't been able to say these things; and she didn't know how they got here.

Having read it all through, she sent for Sæthryd—it could only be her, no one else.

'How could you know it was like that?' she asked, holding aloft the song sheet she had just read.

Sæthryd bowed her head and blushed.

'I don't know, I just thought . . . '

'But, well, it's completely accurate—that's how it was. But how could you know?'

'I tried to imagine it,' Sæthryd said after a moment. 'All of me vanished, I entered your body and looked out through your eyes. And that's how it looked, seen from inside you.'

'Did you make them all?'

'Freawaru helped on some of them. And Waldburh.'

'Why didn't you ask Cædmon for help?'

'He finds it hard to hold his tongue,' Sæthryd whispered. 'We've really tried to save parchment, we've written on both sides, and in tiny letters.'

'Yes, I can see.'

'It can be re-used,' Sæthryd explained. 'And I have never used parchment for the drafts—only for the final finished versions.'

'Why have you kept it secret?'

'We've got to cut down expenses,' said Sæthryd, her face turned away.

'Yes, indeed,' said Hild. 'For this . . . you have my gratitude.'

The song didn't change anything. Wulfhere's death was still heartbreaking and meaningless. Everything was as it had always been—the song had no impact in that respect.

But words had been chosen and they had been written down; there they were, clear and elegantly crafted, ink on parchment. The pain and the anxiety had been given form, a body that lived and would live on—when she could no longer live on, too, which would be soon. Some of her life would still be here, even though all her children had been dead. A moment in time had been pinned down: an independent existence in the world, now without her, but there it was and it would live on and speak to others.

So perhaps something survives our sufferings, after all, she thought, lifting the pile of parchment carefully in her hands. Something that remains once the grass has grown over us.

Her grief about Wulfhere had been purged. The mire of self-pity had vanished; left was the pure anxiety for his life, her mixed passions for Penda, and the incurable sorrow of loss.

The moment was now before her—purged—on the parchment, still quivering with anxiety, bitter and blended emotions. But the mixed feelings were now clearly defined; she could see what was what. That's how it had been: delight and disgust. She had always known. Penda was no man of peace, and they had become one over the corpse of her husband. Yes, she had always known. The disgust applied to herself, and to the desire, which happily forgot just how she had become a widow. And the delight had blended with the disgust; both had always been present. That intense desire, that craving for his otherness. The insurmountable distance between them.

She had never found her way into him, had never been able to imagine him from the inside. He had been alongside her, and his otherness had filled her with such a thrill, such an urge to overstep the boundary. She had always thought the distance between them was caused by their marriage not having been blessed by the Church—whatever she might have preached to others—and that was why the Lord hadn't let them keep one another. Such vast delight had made her greedy to possess happiness.

It was probably as Freawaru had once said: the Lord joins together, with or without blessing. Much had he given her—and taken away again.

'*Blessed be the name of the Lord!*' she said aloud into the air.


Before the fever again took her strength, she had settled matters. Sæthryd should have all the parchment she needed, and the songs would be kept in a proper manner. Copies would be sent to their new monasteries; the songs must not perish.

She also decided to give Ælfflæd permission to decorate their manuscripts. Ælfflæd had long dreamt about imitating Freawaru's weavings, but on parchment: a whole coloured page before each Gospel, she had said. True, they couldn't afford it, and they never would be able to afford it—but if it had to be done, they would nonetheless have to do it.

It *had* to be done; joy in colour and flowing forms was the only gift Ælfflæd had been given. She should be allowed to decorate the manuscripts to her heart's content. Pages woven in paint, the words full of colours and patterns—how lovely that would be. Nothing was too good for the Lord. Even if they had to economize with everything else—their books had to be the very best.


Hild died in her monastery of Streonæshalch, after a year of almost constant fever, sixty-six years of age.

On her deathbed she gave her gold holy cross to Ælfflæd, her successor, and Ælfflæd promised she would not hand it over to Wilfrid. Hild then blessed all her people, gave thanks to her Lord and died with a peaceful expression on her face. They thought she almost looked as if she was smiling. And when they approached her one by one and kissed the body from which her soul had departed, they noticed a quite clear scent of lavender.

Twelve of her people immediately set off to visit her other monasteries and inform them of their mother's death.


That night, Begu woke in Hacanos to the sound of the monastery bell ringing out across the valley. She saw a glow of light in the heavens and recalled the dream she had just had: she had seen Hild carried up to Heaven by a host of strong angels, all wearing radiant silk tunics with gold embroidered holy crosses on the chest.

Begu ran to the prioress and, weeping, told her their mother had left them and was on her way up to the eternal life.

The prioress was Frigyd, who had joined forces with Hild after Coludesburh had burnt down. She had decided she could no longer protect her monastery from the misfortunes continually befalling them. The day after a disaster, someone usually turned up and asked if she would bequeath her monastery to the exiled Bishop Wilfrid. She wouldn't, and therefore she and her people had moved down to Hild's new monasteries, where they were greater in number and thus better able to protect themselves.

Frigyd immediately woke everyone and assembled them for Mass. They realized their bell had vanished and the new barn was engulfed in flames. It couldn't be saved, but only the barn would be lost, so they didn't worry about that now.

They quickly posted new guards and hurried in to Mass. They lay down and together prayed to the Lord to receive with mercy their beloved mother, now ascending to his kingdom. They then stood and sang with all their might, as richly and loudly as they could, so the song would reach all the way up to Heaven.

Had you on that night come through the forest at Hackness, on the seventeenth of November in the year 680, you would certainly have drawn to a halt at the sound of high echoing women's voices mixing with the men's deep richness. Occasionally a single clear voice cut through the others, at times several voices responded, one to the other in the style they had recently learnt, and at times all the voices came together in a vigorously compelling refrain that carried out into the darkness and could have lit up the whole valley.

*A full list of people and places
mentioned in this book
can be found at*

# www.SONGofHILD.com

# Illustrations

The vignettes at the head of each chapter have been drawn by Eva Wilson. The motifs are derived from more-or-less contemporaneous manuscripts, utility articles and jewellery:

Printed in November 2022
by Rotomail Italia S.p.A., Vignate (MI) - Italy